"Tough as a night in jail."

The Kansas City Star

"Masterful."

*The Chattanooga Times*

"An American classic."

Greil Marcus

"Terrific."

*The Washington Post*

"Sets a new standard."

*The Los Angeles Times*

"Compelling."

*The Seattle Post-Intelligencer*

"Audacious."

*The Dallas Morning News*

"Muscular and incendiary."

*The Philadelphia Inquirer*

"Excellent."

*The Library Journal*

"A testament to the power of Tosches' writing."

*The Arizona Republic*

"A *feat*."

*Esquire*

"Tough, tender, knowing, and tense."

*The San Francisco Chronicle*

"Tosches's book is a work of art."

*The Boston Globe*

"Definitive."

*Time Magazine*

"The story-teller of hell."

*L'Officiel Homme*

"Riveting."

*New York Newsday*

"The ultimate epic bard of Little Italy."

*L'Express*

"Wonderful."

*Loaded*

"Nick Tosches stands out as the kind of writer other writers only dream of becoming—amazing at fiction, unparalleled in journalism and biography, and possessed of a stature and genius his lessers can but crouch beneath, gazing up in wonder, awe, and more than a little terror at what this man, in a single, unfinished life, has been able to accomplish on the page."

Jerry Stahl

"A new vision."

*Options*

"Plunges to the heart of the forces of evil."

*Le Monde Livres*

"Nick Tosches's pen is a knife that can whittle anything well!"

Alexander Theroux

"Terrific . . . beautiful . . . one hell of a poet."

Hubert Selby, Jr.

"Darker than the dark."

*Libération*

the
# NICK TOSCHES
reader

the
# NICK TOSCHES
reader

by Nick Tosches

DA CAPO PRESS

Many of the designations used by manufacturers and sellers to distinguish their products are claimed as trademarks. Where those designations appear in this book and Da Capo Press was aware of a trademark claim, the designations have been printed in initial capital letters.

A CIP catalog record for this book is available from the Library of Congress.

ISBN: 0-306-80969-9

Da Capo Press is a member of the Perseus Books Group

Text design by Jeff Williams
Set in 10-point Legacy Serif by the Perseus Books Group

1 2 3 4 5 6 7 8 9 10—03 02 01 00 99
First printing, February 2000

Da Capo Press books are available at special discounts for bulk purchases in the U.S. by corporations, institutions, and other organizations. For more information, please contact the Special Markets Department at HarperCollins Publishers, 10 East 53rd Street, New York, NY 10022, or call 1-212-207-7528.

Find us on the World Wide Web at http://www.dacapopress.com

*To those who did not run.*
*To those who broke and entered with me*
*Into the cathedral of the heart.*
*To those who took my back,*
*In right and in wrong.*
*Vobis.*

# Contents

Introduction                                                          xiii

1. Still /Life                                                          1

2. Review of *Paranoid*                                                3

3. Review of *Good Taste Is Timeless*                                  6

4. Review of *Joseph and the Amazing Technicolor Dreamcoat*            9

5. Absolutely Dead!                                                   12

6. Leuk                                                               14

7. The Heartbeats Never Did Benefits                                 20

8. God-Crazed Hippies Reap Boffo B.O.                                24

9. Be Bop A Lula                                                      29

10. The Box                                                           31

11. The 24-Hr Sound of Country Gospel and the Dark                   33

12. Beyond Euclid: Pool!                                              38

13. The Real Avant-Garde                                              40

14. Review of *Gately's Cafe*                                        44

15. Muddy Waters Rarely Eats Fish                                    46

16. Eye: Disease                                                     49

17. Review of *The Mollusks of Tartura*                              50

18. Sex and Booze                                                    53

19. Valerie                                                          59

20. Screamin' Jay Hawkins and the Monster                           61

21. Patti Smith                                                      67

22. Country                                                          80

23. Excerpt from *Country* 84

24. When Literary Lights Turn on the TV 86

25. Letter 91

26. Patti Smith: Straight, No Chaser 92

27. God Created Dean Martin in His Own Image,
    Then Stood Back 97

28. Jim Morrison: The Late Late Show 99

29. Blondie Plucks Her Legs 102

30. Review of *Always Know* 106

31. The Gospel According to Jerry Lee 108

32. Journal Entry 114

33. A Christmas Carol 115

34. The Sea's Endless, Awful Rhythm & Me Without
    Even a Dirty Picture 124

35. The Sweet Thighs of Mother Mary 131

36. Pizza Man 133

37. Lust Among the Adverbs 134

38. Letter 146

39. Purity 147

40. Pizza Man 159

41. The Butt and I 166

42. Pleasant Brits and 180-Degree Spins 170

43. Excerpt from *Hellfire* 172

44. Felicity Opens Wide 175

45. Journal Entries 185

46. Good Book Made Better 189

47. Lust in the Balcony 192

48. Review of *A Child's Adventure* 197

49. Review of *The Maximus Poems* 199

50. Elvis in Death ... 203

51. Maybe It Was My Big Mouth—Carly Simon: Free, White, and Pushing Forty ... 211

52. Review of *A Choice of Enemies* ... 215

53. Review of *The Garden of Priapus* ... 218

54. Review of *A House in the Country* ... 220

55. Review of *Renaissance and Reform* ... 222

56. Excerpt from *Unsung Heroes of Rock 'n' Roll* ... 224

57. God Is My Cosponsor ... 232

58. *Frankie: Part 1* ... 234

59. Hillary Brooke's Legs ... 247

60. Elmer Batters ... 250

61. Review of *Canned Meat* ... 252

62. How to Pick Up Girls in Albania ... 254

63. Excerpt from *Power on Earth* ... 256

64. Excerpt from *Frankie: Part 2* ... 268

65. Pentecostals in Heat ... 276

66. The Short-Shorts of Satan ... 286

67. Excerpt from *Cut Numbers* ... 294

68. Exile on Twenty-first Street ... 308

69. Review of *Killer: The Mercury Years* ... 310

70. Miles Davis: The Hat Makes the Man ... 313

71. James Douglas Morrison, 1943–1971 ... 317

72. The Singer Madonna Arraigned by the Ghost of Pope Alexander VI ... 321

73. Lester ... 323

74. Excerpt from *Dino* ... 329

75. Oedipus Tex ... 335

76. J. Edgar Hoover: The Burroughsian Nightmare ... 345

77.   Memories of Joe                                         349

78.   My Kind of Loving                                       352

79.   George Jones: The Grand Tour                            353

80.   My Overcoat, My Brains, and Me                          385

81.   Notebook entry                                          392

82.   *Nightmare Alley*                                       393

83.   Excerpt from *Trinities*                                396

84.   Letter                                                  409

85.   The Holy City                                           410

86.   Ophis Ovum Opium Olé                                    414

87.   There's a Woman Here, Baby                              416

88.   Who Holds in Her Belly the Power of Life                417

89.   A Slab of Grease, a Bottle of Carbona, and Thou         418

90.   Excerpt from "Entering the Barrens"                     428

91.   Requiescat Dino                                         431

92.   De Niro                                                 434

93.   The Unfuckable                                          442

94.   The Coin                                                447

95.   Why I Am Great                                          449

96.   Sea of Love                                             452

97.   Faraglione 9/16/96                                      453

98.   If I Were Robert Stack                                  454

99.   Letter                                                  458

100.  Letter                                                  460

101.  Letter                                                  461

102.  Letter                                                  463

103.  Letter                                                  465

104.  *Spud Crazy*                                            466

105.   The Things I Got                                    488

106.   Ash Wednesday                                       491

107.   The Devil and Sidney Korshak                        493

108.   Excerpt from *Where Dead Voices Gather*             526

109.   Night Train                                         529

110.   Dear Privileged Intimate                            557

111.   Hymn for Charlie                                    558

112.   E-mail                                              559

113.   Please Be Quiet—Please                              560

114.   From *Chaldea*                                      562

       Hymn to Paean, Physician of the Gods
       All of Gust and Sigh
       Old Nick's Song of Songs
       May the Gods without Names Redeem Me
       Ptolemy II
       Dante in Ravenna
       Contrapasso
       From the Dream-book of Artemidorus
       Invocation
       What the Coptic Guy Said

115.   Excerpt from *Scratch*                              567

116.   Excerpt from *In the Hand of Dante*                 584

       Bibliographical Appendix                            586

*"Now, Mr. Faulkner," she said, "what were you thinking of when you wrote that?"*

*"Money," he replied.*

# Introduction

I write these words on a hot and humid morning toward the end of a dying century, some years after I myself was written off and left as dead. As they said, I was not expected to make it through the night. But they did not know that the night was mine.

I remember the first time, thirty years before that night: cold-cocked unconscious by that bottle of rotgut across my skull, dumped into that city-park lake, and left for dead. I walked out of that dirty water, made it back to the poolroom; thirty years later, walked out of that dirty hospital, made it back to the bar. It was all one night.

Somewhere, early on, in the course of that river of dark night, I became a writer. It seemed an unlikely thing. In my neighborhood, books were not read. There were few books, many bookies. I was discouraged from reading, on the grounds that it would "put ideas in your head." There was, of course, a certain wisdom in that. Ideas and thought are wretched folly from which few escape. But, then again, one can only go beyond them by going through them. They are the passage that separates the wise guys from the men of wisdom. Sometimes they seemed so close, the wise guys and the men of wisdom. "I don't do thoughts," said Eddie D. from the projects. "The Great Tao," said Ch'an Buddhist Master Niu-t'ou Fa-Yung thirteen centuries earlier, "is free from thought." So close and yet so far.

I wrote terrible things. One of my first pinches as a teenager was for stealing books. The sonnets of Shakespeare were in that batch, and it was to be a long time until I finally got to read them; and longer still until I came to perceive at its heart the one line that said it all: "O learn to read what silent love hath writ." The greatest poetry is wordless. The greatest poets are those blest and humbled by this truth. "I have tried to write Paradise," Ezra Pound would say near the end of his life's work: "Let the wind speak/that is paradise." To learn to read what silent love hath writ, to bow to the power of the breezes. To embrace these things is to live, and to know that what one can write is as nothing before that silence and that power is to begin to write. Fa-Yung again: "How can we obtain truth through words?"

These were things I came to understand only after the long night yielded to light.

But, anyway, there I was boosting books. I couldn't tell the bad from the good. I kept trying to read and to like *Moby Dick,* but I never succeeded and felt that it was my failing. How could I become a writer if I didn't "appreciate" the great American novel? If it was, as they used to say, over my head? So I pretended that I read and liked it, and, over the years, I may have even conned myself into believing it. In the end, I simply embraced the sad truth that it wasn't much of a book at all. In 1829, aboard the whaling ship *Susan,* Frederick Myrick of Nantucket, the first scrimshander to sign and date his work, had etched into the tooth of a sperm whale all to which Melville had so beautifully aspired: "Death to the living," reads the scrimshaw, "long life to the killers." And that is that. Melville never escaped from the passway of thoughts and ideas; Myrick may never have entered it. As much as I admire Melville and his vision and what he wanted and tried to do, it is Myrick's scrimshaw that speaks to the ages. And whence did Myrick steal those words? The true originators are lost to us. How many centuries, how many millennia, before Sappho did someone behold the dawn and see it "rosy-fingered"? As Qoheleth/Ecclesiastes had it: "The thing that hath been, it is that which shall be; and that which is done is that which shall be done: and there is no new thing under the sun." And who knows whence he stole that one from, and whence who before him.

Immature writers plagiarize, mature writers steal. Looking through the pieces that the volume at hand comprises—and, believe me, that is all I can bear to do: look, and not read, through them—it strikes me that, while the former, I did the latter. Above all, I stole from myself. Words and phrases that enamored me, whether I had come upon them or they had come to me from within, were endlessly repeated, recycled, ridden like horses until they were dead. In periodicals published months apart, this modus operandi was not so obvious. Here, with early theft following early theft as page follows page, it is.

So, as I had been a thief in boyhood, I became, while learning to write, a fool of a thief who stole from himself. I wrote five books on a stolen typewriter.

Why did I want to become a writer? It was only a few years ago that the true answer, or what I believe to be the true answer, came to me. I thought of myself as a tough guy. That is to say, I pretended to be a tough guy. Writing, in this regard, seemed a respectable racket. Hemingway and others like him had rendered it so: a manly art. Only after I became a writer, did I come to see this lie for what it was.

I came to writing through cowardice and fear. Deep inside me, I needed to communicate my feelings, and there was no one to whom I could. In the old neighborhood, honest expression was, if not quite the equivalent of a death rap, a sure means to ostracism. Besides, it wasn't in me. To look someone in the eyes and speak from the heart was beyond me. Writing was a way of communicating without looking anyone in the eyes. It was not a manly art. It was a cowardly art. Then again, maybe the two are the same.

But Hemingway, for all his ridiculous fraud, made money: a lot of it. One of the consummate bend-for-bucks boys, he followed *The Old Man and the Sea* with a series of similarly written advertisements for Ballantine ale ("I would rather have a bottle of Ballantine Ale than any other drink after fighting a really big fish . . ."). And that was something that I wanted to do. I'm not talking about writing ad copy or fighting really big fish; I'm talking about making money. I wanted to make money. It was something I needed to do. As I look at—not even through—the periodical pieces at hand, that need is as clear as my thievery. (It was even more clear in looking through the boxes of old tearsheets and yellowed photocopies from which these pieces were culled.) Perhaps the two, the thievery and the need to eat and drink and pay my rent, were entwined. This is said not as an excuse for the wretched writing that may, indeed *will* by all but the most pitiable, be discerned in the pages of this book. It is said rather as an excuse— granted, pitiable—for my persistence in it.

So there you have it: cowardice, theft, hard times. A true love for the sounds and colors of words, the rhythms and meters of lines, the evocation through them of the ultimately inexpressible, came later. With it came the true love and awareness of that silence and that wind and the gods and demons they enlaced.

Strangely the presence of the demons seems to increase through this collection as the will to write transmutes into writing, as fear becomes exorcism, as darkness becomes light.

I have chosen to arrange the pieces of this book as time has arranged them, divided not by type—reviews, fiction, essays, poetry, and so on—but left to flow in their natural and telling chronology. Good, bad, poetry, prose, the lot of it, as it came out of me through the last thirty years. Sometimes the chronology is approximate, as I may know the publication date of a piece but have no precise idea of when the piece was written. Nothing has been fixed, nothing rewritten, but, where it has been desirable and possible, titles imposed on pieces by magazine editors have been replaced by the original, unpublished titles. I have decided, not without trepidation, to present an accurate picture of this writer's journey, through the slum alleys as well as through the high places. I have annotated some pieces, when they brought memories or explications that I felt would illuminate that journey.

I was nineteen years old when I was first paid for writing. Before that, my friend Phil Verso was the only one with whom I shared all of what I wrote. We had known one another since the eighth grade, before the publication of the book that would deliver to me what *Moby Dick* had failed to do, the book that woke me and freed me and inspired me: *Last Exit to Brooklyn*, by Hubert Selby, Jr. I was fifteen then; and Selby, who is now a dear friend, continues these many years later to wake me and free me and inspire me in ways that have little or nothing to do with writing. Of the three living writers whom I consider to be great—Peter Matthiessen and Philip Roth are the others—it is Selby whose art and whose soul reach the highest, and it is he whom I most respect, as a writer and as a man.

But before there was Selby, there was Verso. Phil and I ran together, robbed together, got shot at together, drank and took dope together, laughed together. The laughter is what I remember and miss, for everything else seemed for us in those days to end in laughter. All of what I wrote in those days is long vanished except as tantalizing shards of half-buried memory; but the laughter of those wicked days still echoes clearly, and, though the echo is forlorn, it is more tantalizing than the shards.

The heart and holy place of our world was Hubert's Museum on West Forty-second Street. At street level, Hubert's was a faded pinball arcade and shooting gallery; downstairs there was a freak show. Outside, in front of the joint, a man, or a boy, could connect with anything. Many of the twisted and surreal little things I wrote were inspired by the twisted and surreal spirit of that place. Phil loved them. I can still see his face, hear his open evil laughter as he read them. He was my conspirator and my first, and therefore most important, supporter. He remained so through the years. Even prison could not kill his laughter, and in later years the words and tales I stole from him were many. When he read my first novel, he recognized himself and exulted that he had "made it as a character in Nick's book." His kid brother told me this at Phil's funeral, a month before what would have been Phil's fortieth birthday, a few days after Phil went down in "one of those things," as he used to say, on a hot summer night in Coney Island. I dedicate this book, for what it is worth, foremost to the memory of him.

And here I am, alive, talking of heat and humidity: cut loose from the noose and bitching about the weather. I could go on here and bitch about the nature of the beast of publishing, a rather drab, unimaginative, and unsuccessful form of corporate salesmanship that grows every day more devastating in its mediocrity. But that is like forgetting the noose and dwelling on the weather, for I've been more fortunate than most as far as this racket, and life itself, are concerned.

The weather here is always better than it is six feet down. And while I can bitch and moan, the pay is, too.

This project commenced under Yuval Taylor when he was with Da Capo, and was carried forth by his successor, Michael Dorr. In the end, the publication of this book found its greatest ally in Marco Pavia, gentleman, laborer-sage, and projects editor for Perseus Books.

In the task of assembling, copying, and placing in order the pieces of this book, Carrie Knoblock, the most masterful of master librarians, was invaluable. My friend and cohort Richard Meltzer supplied things I had written that were long lost to me. While there are few people I call friend, to describe Richard simply as such is wrong. What Phil had been to me as a writer in the years before I was published, Richard was to me in the years that followed, and I cherish our friendship to this day.

Would that the countless others, the remembered and the forgotten, the living and the dead, who were a part of this journey could here be named and thanked, or damned, as well. Some of those who have meant much to me come readily to mind—my mother and my father and my Uncle Giovanni and the rest of them whose blood ran into mine; Jimmy Ivory, Mike McGovern, Frank Fortunato, Bob Hofler, Roberta Brandstrader, Michael Pietsch, Tommy Donovan, Dominick Rondinone, Bobby Tedesco, Dario Cella, Vincent Pardodi, Fred Tamburri, Nicky Fiori, Vera Dunkle, Noni Watters, Jerry Stahl, Lisa Nicoll, and more. But to summon all of them to mind would involve a labor greater than the depth of either my gratitude or my rancor. Some of the remembered will be found in the annotations throughout these pages. One who can and should here be especially implicated is my agent of twenty years and more, Russell Galen of the Scovil-Chichak-Galen Literary Agency. In the final battle for the integrity of this collection's form, and in the ongoing struggles of its stages of production, it was Russell Galen and my right-arm girl, Sarah Fabbricatore, who were the godsent forces in my corner. It is here that I should also thank, for their care in the postbellum stages of production, the editorial understanding of Marco Pavia and the generous and expert help of Catherine McRae.

I've spoken of the silence and the wind. But life does not always afford us the luxury of nobility, and there is another lesson that I should like to leave you with. It was taught me by Don Siegel, the movie director, who said that he himself had learned it early in life. If you're going to be a whore, Siegel told me, be a high-priced whore. For money buys freedom from whoredom, as in ancient Rome it bought freedom from slavery. And without freedom, there is no doing what a writer should do, which is to share and give to others, through what poetry he or she can make, of whatever God has given of the gift of entering the wisdom and the power of that silence and that wind.

I remember, at the age of twenty-one or twenty-two, strung out on speed and booze, silently asking a God I didn't believe in to please let me live at least until thirty. And here I am, writing an introduction to thirty years of writing. That said, I've said enough. Let the thirty years' squalor and splendor speak for themselves.

*Nick Tosches*

the
**NICK TOSCHES**
reader

# 1

I was eighteen or nineteen years old, working days at the Lovable Underwear Company, when I came to know the poet Ed Sanders. Ed, who twenty years later would win an American Book Award for his poetry, was then the ringleader of the notorious band The Fugs, and he also ran the Peace Eye bookstore, which at that time was on Avenue A.

Ed had a degree in classical languages, and could read fluently in their own Greek and Latin those ancient poets that I could only understand through the gauze of translation. I had tried to teach myself Greek from the two volumes of *A Reading Course in Homeric Greek* that I had robbed from a divinity student a few years before, and I had taken Latin in high school; but it was beyond me to truly delve the beauties and powers of the poetry of those tongues, as Ed could. He had even studied Egyptian hieroglyphics.

We shared, he in his erudite way and I in my unlettered fashion, a love for those ancient fragments that were the wisps of the source, the wisps of origin, the wisps of the first and truest expression of all that since had been said. And we both had dirty minds, given as much to the gutter as to the gods.

The Lower East Side was a different place back then. It was still a neighborhood. East Thirteenth Street was still known as the Street of Silence, a name I would bestow on another Mafia stronghold, Sullivan Street, in my novel *Cut Numbers*. The joints were still joints. We drank a lot in those joints.

Ed was a great guy. He was about ten years older than I, and was the first real poet to whom I showed my poetry. "Hell, man," he told me, "you're a fucking poet." As I doubt he ever realized he was my first mentor, so I doubt he ever realized what a shove forward, what a turning point, this was for me.

That poem, which bore the title "Still/Life," and which I later invoked in my novel *Trinities,* is long gone. Fragments of it follow.

# Still/Life

A blunt shock to find your life in episodes on a Mochican vase
[ . . . ]
& the cool white tile
[ . . . ]
emergency room, 3 AM
[ . . . ]

# 2

The first published thing for which I was paid was an interview with Ed Sanders that I sold for two figures to *Fusion*. That was in 1969, shortly before I turned twenty. In the summer of 1970, *Fusion* published my first substantial piece, "The Punk Muse."

Based in Boston and edited by Robert Soma, *Fusion*, which sold for two bits in 1969, was one of several rock-'n'-roll magazines for which one could make a few bucks writing pretty much whatever one wanted, as long as it was under the pretext of writing about rock 'n' roll. I don't think a kid coming up today has the same opportunity, as there is very little ground between those publications that pay nothing and those that are big, slick, well-paying, and hard to break into. And, back then, there was something not unlike freedom of speech. Advertisers in the so-called alternative press did not yet dictate editorial policies, and the vile and hypocritical concept of a "politically correct" culture, and the censorship inherent in it, was unimaginable except as the futuristic scenario of a science-fiction tale.

My first appearance in *Rolling Stone*, in early 1971, was a review of an album that didn't exist. My buddy Lenny Kaye was working at a record store on Bleecker Street, and he told me that kids were coming in to buy the record. Jon Landau, a *Fusion* alumnus who later went on to manage Bruce Springsteen, was the record-reviews editor of *Rolling Stone*. He called and said he needed somebody to review the big-money acts, and he wanted me to do it. As far as I was concerned, it didn't matter who or what I was writing about. The words under my byline usually had little to do with the act or album named above it, as in this 1971 review of a Black Sabbath record.

# Review of *Paranoid*

A young girl's voice. She is dressed in a nun's habit. The boy turns and faces her. She proffers a chalice of cervical exudate and he drinks from it. She gets down on her knees and elbows, *como peros,* and tosses the nun's hem above her posterior. On each naked buttock is the scrawled sign of Ashirikas; "Fuck me, Rolf." The boy whips out a 10" personal vibrator, adorned in waterproof acrylics with the image of the Nazarene. He intones the words *"nuk Khensu tenten nebu"* and approaches her intendant fundament . . . impletion . . . across the room the fresh corpse of an illegitimate hippie baby is dis-impaled from the ceremonial sword of Baphomet. The myrrh is extinguished with the collected saliva of priests listening to tales of carnal abuse in warm, dark confessionals. The Shadaic numinae are chalked over with the mirrored sign of Ariael, the eleven rubies returned to the vessel of Dione. A dark, handsome youth with the physique of a Dionysos—eyes, though, glazed and cold—grasps the two-foot stem of an imported El-Douhab hookah by its hilt and shoves its tip, sans mouthpiece, into the dry, collapsed rectum of the dead hippie baby, pushes until thin rivulets of blood ooze from the nostrils and lips of the infant. The hookah's stem-tip surfaces and the suck-piece is restored. Those in the room gather about. One youth wears a mosaic-inlaid Aztec skull mask, ornamented with the symbols of Gnostic adoration. He fills the hookah bowl with black opium tars and a dash of Asthmador powders . . . in the corner of the room, clutching a smuggled police photo of Sharon Tate with her hacked-off tit crammed up her snatch, a lone boy masturbates slowly, moaning *"tempora mutantur et nos mutamur in illis."*

No "flower children" they, the sinister emanation of a generation who only yesterday, it seems, were set on changing a world in the shadow of nuclear holocaust and overpopulation into a utopia of peace and love. They drop the knee of fealty before the Antichrist. They shoot "M" and they engage in group sex. No act is too depraved, no thought too bizarre as they plunge deeper and deeper into the realm of perversion, into the ultimate "trip" of their own self-fashioned Hell. Orgies, incest, drugs, homosexuality, necrophilia, public nosepicking, Satanism, even living sacrifice.

And this is their music. Although you may not enjoy its "message," although you may not enjoy a lead singer (Kip Treavor), who sounds like Keith

Relf whining about the tampons stuck up his nostrils, you owe it to yourself as a person concerned with contemporary society or merely with the artistic underground of the youth movement in general to be aware of the "heavy" sounds of bubble-gum Satanism and if you see them live sometimes they undress a hippie girl.

# 3

Sometimes, when I was writing about people I liked, I not only listened to the record but also wrote somewhat of the music itself, as in this review of The Holy Modal Rounders, also from 1971.

Peter Stampfel, who, with Steve Weber, was, and remains, half of the driving force behind the Rounders, later paid off a debt he owed me by giving me fiddle lessons. Or trying to give me fiddle lessons, as we discovered I had a tin ear and couldn't learn a goddamned thing.

# Review of *Good*

mastophilia "Boobs Alor" (w
to the shitkicker melanch
ous insane raunch of "
to be confused with
ready, Hezey?

Peter Stampfel used to play with a lo[t]
Old Timey Wool Thumpers ("wool th[
when the boy sticks his thing in the
Telegraph Avenue Freedom Fighters String Band (which changed its collective name to The Merrie Order of St. Brigit String Band—which appellation was derived from an eighteenth century whipfreaks—after Stampfel was sick of explaining that the band was *against* "freedom bullshit"—"we weren't doing any 'If I Had a Hammer shit'"), the Strict Temperance String Band of Lower Delancey Street, et cetera.

Steve Weber, who holds the all-time record of walking barefoot in New York City without pedal injury (seven months), poet and creator of such masterpieces of contemporary sculpture as "Chinese Sailor Eaten by Octopus," met up with Stampfel in 1964, whereupon the two men metamorphosed toot sweet into the Holy Modal Rounders, produced two nifty efforts for Prestige Records, joined the Fugs for public appearances and the first Fugs LP on Broadside Records, left the Fugs in a dubious state of mental stability (said state being preserved for posterity on the ESP Rounders album, *Indian War Whoop*, the first LP to establish amplified amphetaminism as a valid genre of American folk music), subsequently met up with: (a) a drummer; (b) a renegade church organist; (c) a minister's son who was once Cowboy Bob on a Syracuse, NY, TV kiddie show who played bass; and, lastly, (d) an ex-masseur with a complexly weird autobiography who played fiddle, mandolin, guitar, clarinet, and miscellaneous.

Together they created (with the exception of (d), who came later) an album for Elektra, The Moray Eels Eat the Holy Modal Rounders (subsequently brushed aside by Stampfel), got involved with doing the score to Sam Shepard's *Operation Sidewinder,* split from Elektra, drank a lot, almost signed with Atlantic, and finally signed with the newly-founded Metromedia. Which brings us to *Good Taste Is Timeless.*

There's not really all that much to say about the new Rounders LP except that it's great. They've finally produced an album of what they're best able to do—create beautiful flowing, stomping waves of wort-ripped, futomaniac honk. With two exceptions, Jimmy Newman's "Alligator Man" and Virginia Joe Maphis' "Melinda," it's all original stuff, from the wonderful reel of bathroom

...nich is lots better than the original Fugs version), ...olia of J. Michael McCarthy's "Once a Year" to the joy- ...Happy Scrapple Daddy Polka" and "Black Bottom" (not ...the Fats Waller wax of yore). Which is why they say: Are you

# 4

Then, two weeks later, I was back to my usual course.

# Review of *Joseph and the Amazing Technicolor Dreamcoat*

I really don't want to make myself sound corny, but if that's the risk involved in my communicating this album's effect on me, it's a risk I unconditionally accept.

I'm no religious fanatic; God knows but I've had my share of the pot, the pills, the "new Morality." I'd gotten involved in the hippy trip a number of years ago, long after I'd forgotten the warm feelings I'd experienced during early youth, those warm feelings that overwhelmed me with their comforting radiance and purity as I strode forth from church after being cleansed of my sins of lying, stealing, and self-abuse through the sacrament of confession or while genuflecting before the likeness of the crucified Nazarene, without Whose sacrifice I and all others would be destined to an Heavenless eternity, or, upon doing a good turn or conquering a temptation, sensing the loving approval from the Great White Throne. Well, I strayed. And for a goodly number of years, too, I might add. I spent my days, my months, my years in getting high, hanging out and spilling my procreative seed within the lubric flasks of a series of LSD-trepanned Jezebels. Many of you, I'm sure, know the feeling.

And then two years ago next July 17th, He returned to slay the succubus of Satan that had commandeered my soul upon loss of innocence. For months previous I had been plagued by impotence (which I now realize was only His way of telling me to "cool it" with the sin scene) and recurrent nightmares of the Madonna unveiling her genitals much to my arousement, only to further reveal, on closer inspection, a vaginal conduit constructed as the multitoothed throat of a conger eel. I thought I was losing my mind. In desperation I consulted a priest. If I hadn't, God knows where I'd be today. I've since returned to a normal state, both physically and mentally. I've even organized a telephone counseling service. (If you ever feel yourself straying, call us at 201-332-3609.) Well, I guess *I've* been straying again—from the subject at hand, that is!

This record, like *Jesus Christ Superstar,* is an informal recounting of a part of the Bible. It is the story of Joseph from Canaan, his sale into slavery by his brothers, his subsequent rise to princely stature due to his aid (through soothsaying, and management) to the Pharoah, and his re-union, on better terms, with his long-lost brothers. All in all, it covers a good nine chapters of the Book of Genesis and proffers a highly moving—much of which, I must admit, is due to the groovy score the operetta sports—testimony of one man's unswerving fidelity to God.

Although at times the music does seem a bit irreverent to what's being recounted, the LP's "now sound" is often quite effective, as in the rocking accompaniment to Joseph's pronouncement to Potiphar's daughter: "Joseph wanted to resist her/till one day she proved too eager/Joseph cried in vain/'Please stop, I don't believe in free love!'" Talk about your strong stuff.

Well, it's time to head for my Monday Novena. Where are *you* heading?

Praise the Lord and blessed be His Name.

# 5

The following poem, published in *Fusion,* was written upon the death of Jim Morrison in the summer of 1971.

During the heyday of the Doors, I had sniffed a lot of glue and snorted a lot of lighter fluid, drunk a lot of booze, and took whatever dope I could get my hands on. I preferred fluid, which was a rather unique electrical high—you could almost see and hear the atoms dart and hum—to glue, which was a death-row blowjob of a down. About eight or ten years ago, drunk and suddenly of a mood to recreate that time, I got out a handkerchief and a can of Ronsonol, put on a CD of the Doors, and got down to it. It wasn't quite the same, and I've never done fluid since. Later, in a detox joint, I was told that inhalants, such as the toluene in glue and the naptha in lighter fluid, were the most brain-destroying of drugs. Maybe the audio-visual electrical aspect of the fluid high was in reality the neuroelectric experience of synapses short-circuiting and neurons exploding. Who knows. Maybe I coulda been a contender.

Anyway, I often felt that Morrison could have been the next Sinatra. With him gone, Iggy Pop was the only hope.

# Absolutely Dead!

*"Do you know how pale & wanton thrillful . . . "*
Abas unto Gaea 7/3/71
& drank using
the same grotesque chords
over & over "*Death* playing Swinburne
*makes angels of us all*
    *& gives us wings"* vanity press poesies 1970
his limp scotch-numbed dick
    peeping out mommy, mommy
to Dade County Rear Admiral
    date nite gym class locker room
    penis size anxious holding hands
    face
in a bathtub like anybody else
    probably watching his fart-bubbles
    in Gay Paree
frozen in juillet *Paris Match* velox

# 6

# Leuk

*Tony Bennett. Roy Clark. The Mike Curb Congregation. Johnny Mathis. Andy Williams. The Ray Conniff Singers. Anthony Newley. Vikki Carr. Eddie Holman. Astrud Gilberto. Percy Faith. Shirley Bassey. Charlie Williams. Chucho Avellanet. Frank Pourcel. Billy Vaughn. Peter Nero. Herb Newman. Ferrante & Teicher. The Living Strings + Two Pianos. Lenny Dee. Hubert Laws. The Exotic Guitars. Al DeLory. Mantovani. Henry Mancini. Roger Williams. Andre Kostelanetz. Santos Colon. Liberace. Francis Lai. Chet Atkins. Vincent Lopez. The 101 Strings Orchestra. Ronnie Aldrich & Two Pianos. Sammy Kaye. Georgie Barnes & Bucky Pizzarelli. Eugene Ormandy & The Philadelphia Orchestra. Paul Mauriat. George Feyer. Kings Road. The Melochrino Strings. The Music City Orchestra. The Vincent Lopez Piano Trio. Hugo Winterhalter. Boots Randolph. Rondella de Saltillo.*

## Eros & The Lilies of Leukemia

*Love Story* is the tender tale of an idyllic albeit ill-fated love affair between a well-to-do Harvard student and his individualistic Radcliffe paramour. Author Erich Segal displays both a rare empathy for the love generation's lifestyles and a fine ear for its playful and energetic argot throughout his first-person narrative, from the two youths' original star-struck meeting ("'Listen, you snotty Radcliffe bitch, Friday night is the Dartmouth hockey game'") to their earliest sexual liaisons ("'Jenny, for Christ's sake, how can I read John Stuart Mill when every single second I'm dying to make love to you?' She screwed up her brow and frowned. 'Oh, Oliver, wouldja please?'") to Jenny's burgeoning interest in Oliver's hockey escapades ("'I wish I coulda seen it. Maybe you'll beat up somebody in the Yale game, huh?'") to their first connubial fallings-out ("'Stop!' She cut off my apology, then said very quietly, 'Love means never having to say you're sorry'") to the final days preceding Jenny's leukemia-begat death ("'I had finally persuaded her to allow me to clean up, though she gave me heat about it not being 'man's work'").

Segal has, in *Love Story*, combined the daring contemporaneity of *The Catcher in the Rye* with the tragic ultranaturalism of *A Stone for Danny Fisher*, thus creating a true modern romance of an even more searing, powerful calibre than such generical *comarades de lit* as *West Side Story* and *Requiem for a Schoolgirl*. *Love Story* has the strength to move us to laughter, tender remembrance, sympathy, and, yes, tears with its peripatetic simplicity. It's been over a month now since I've read the book or last seen the motion picture, and yet I still am totally overtaken by the most wistful of smiles when recollecting any of the various playfully risque lovebirds' baitings ("'Hey, listen, you bitch,' I said. 'What, you bastard?' she replied") that only a true prude could find offensive. And who could claim to be untouched by Segal's poignant limning of desolation in the tough, grimy city streets: "I just stood there, lost on that island in the dark of Harvard Square, not knowing where to go or what to do next. A colored guy approached me and inquired if I was in need of a fix. I kind of absently replied, 'No, thank you, sir.'" It may not be pretty, but it does make its point.

## Talent Justly Rewarded?

*Love Story* the book (which succeeded *Love Story* the screenplay) enjoyed a phenomenal nine-month stay on the *New York Times*' Bestseller List. *Love Story* the film has the highest total gross to date (far in excess of $17,000,000) of any currently-shown film according to *Variety*'s 50 Top-Grossing Films register and, grossing upwards of $105,000 per week, is being hailed as "the biggest picture of the decade. During the month of July alone, *Love Story* was shown in more than 2200 theaters around the country and was seen by millions.

Famous Music, the people who publish "The Theme from *Love Story*," have made more than $1,000,000 on the song's property rights so far. Their entire catalogue of single sheet music goes at a rate of about 400,000 per year. The single sheet music for "The Theme from *Love Story*," going at a rate of 200,000 per month, has already sold well over 1,000,000 copies. They have licensed over 200 versions of the "Theme" thus far.

According to *Billboard*, the song, in its various incarnations, is faring quite well on the charts in such varied places as Great Britain, Italy, Malaysia, Spain, Mexico, Singapore, and Japan. Three albums bearing the title *Love Story* are currently listed in Billboard's Top LP's roster.

Though *Love Story* is most assuredly an opus of considerable merit, is not, one may find himself asking, its profit somewhat out of proportion to its aesthetic capital?

## Of Fatalism & Leukemia Queers

Surely today we, as a country, as a people, recognize that we are in the midst of great turmoil. This talk of ecological disaster, this heated controversy over freedom of speech, the Middle East crisis, the Cold War, militant civil rights leaders threatening to dance with their guns and black panthers up our very driveways.

Yes, in the back of most, if not all, of our minds, I think we are wont to side with the protesters and placard-wavers who forecast our doom. We have become "fatalists," i.e., worn and weary souls whose only answer to the murkier side of fate is a hardened "C'est la vie."

Thus it does not seem surprising to this writer that we have embraced a work of art in which all that is good, all that is life itself, is crushed underfoot by the callous tootsie of that cold destiny, La Muerte. In head-shrinker's lingo, we have become "compulsive masochists" in lieu of facing up to our responsibilities of active effort. (Which, if you've read your Toynbee, you'll recognize as a not too hopeful indication of our manifest destiny!) We, like the narrator of Poe's "The Raven," get some kind of sick kicks out of torturing ourselves with fantasies of ill-fated love.

We have bowed the knee of fealty to the passive aspects of our personae. What do you think all this "unisex" stuff is really about? Why do you think there are more sissies today than ever before? I'll tell you one thing, Mr. Age of Aquarius, it's not from any nitrates in the soil or any phosphates in the water, that's for sure!

Just look at the Japanese. The Lord knows but they've had their share of grim fate. Hiroshima. Nagasaki. Entire populations reduced to radiation mutants ambling about in A-bomb rubble. Shit, man, no wonder they are more than glad to shell out a few yen to see a love affair get snuffed by leukemia. That's why "The Theme from *Love Story*" is doing so phenomenally well in Japan. The No. 3 song this week is "Love Story" sung by Andy Williams; the No. 4 song is "Love Story" sung by Andy Williams in Japanese (he recorded the song in English, Japanese, French, Spanish, and Italian): the No. 10 song is "Love Story" by Francis Lai (the Original Soundtrack version).

But, socioanthropologically-speaking is *Love Story*'s prodigious success completely explained, sans residuum, by this factor of fatalism?

The phenomenon of *pathovoyeurism* has long been known and studied among clinical circles since Stekel's pioneering monograph "Das Guckloch von Tod und Neurose" (*Zentralblatt fur Psychoanalyse*, I, 1911). Though you or I, as laymen, might not comprehend all the clinician camarilla's patter, we've all heard stories about terminal cancer wards rigged with one-way whorehouse mirrors, state witnesses coming off in their pants at electrocutions and gassings, women with long histories of frigidity suddenly shaken by violent series of multiple orgasms while inadvertantly catching a late-night performance of "Look at Us, We're Walking" on some muscular distrophy telethon, otherwise impotent men overtaken by tumescence upon entering hospital foyers, those Dr. Kildare 8-pagers, et cetera.

Probably all of us are doubtless acquainted with the maxim, "The only thing worse than a child molester is a leukemia queer." Now most people in the biz knew long before The National Insider spilled the beans a couple of months ago that Ali MacGraw, the charming leading lady of *Love Story,* actually had, still does have leukemia, not unlike the feminine protagonist of the novel! Which makes *Love Story,* to your average leukemia queer, the brass ring, the black rose, the stele of Thoth. (One Times Square theater, in a no-holds-barred attempt to cater exclusively to the leuko clientele, marqueed: "She's Cute! She's Sexy! She's Got Leukemia! See It On The Inside!") Yes, it's an old cliche that it's an old cliche but there're two sides to every story. And that includes *Love Story.*

## Nenia D'Amour:
## Ray Conniff Among The Phagocytes

*Where do I begin*
*To tell the story of how*
*Great a love can be?*
*The sweet love story that*
*Is older than the sea*

And so begins "Where Do I Begin," the theme from *Love Story.* And where indeed does one begin to convey in mere syntax-fettered words the wondrous alchemy of artists: the frail abandonment of Andy Williams' "Theme from *Love Story*"; the Stoical bravado of Tony Bennett's singular version; the wistful Mediterranean melancholia wrought by Ray Conniff; Roy Clark's down-homey intimacy; the manly elegance of Johnny Mathis' stately lection; the *etouffe* flowingness of Andre Kosclanetz' maestoso expressionism; Henry Mancini's madrigal-like empiricism; the surging corona-chesque epiphany of Roger Williams' neoclassical rendition; the eldritch power of George Barnes' & Bucky Pizzarelli's pristine lamentation; the cool understatement of Boots Randolph's jazzed-up interpretation; the sheer emotional force of Paul Mauriat's idyllic passacaglia?

Once the bogus ploys at capitalizing upon *Love Story's* auspicious name have been cleared away—and I'm speaking here primarily of a Jethro Tull ditty, "Love Story," and a Carla Thomas tune entitled "Love Means You Never Have To Say You're Sorry" (Mrs. Thomas has even gone so far as to audaciously call her latest Stax LP *Love Means . . .* ), both of which songs have nigh nil relation to *Love Story* per se—one is left with a great plenitude of "Where Do I Begin" incarnations.

Over 200 of them to be exact. And the query which I feel Philly Dogging in my cerebral cortex, gyring with shin-pokes of conscience and public interest the assured equilibrium of this expository periphrasis that would sluice from my noggin like spunk from the nookie of Gaeia were I of less high-minded stature, is how much of this plenitude is, in fact, not plenitude but *plethora!*

What I'm saying is that—and damn those whose critical faculties are swayed by their emotions—there is not one iota of difference between The Living Strings plus Two Pianos' version of "Where Do I Begin" and that of Ronnie Aldrich & Two Pianos! Nor between those of Ferrante & Teicher and Liberace.

The roster grows: Sammy Kaye and George Feyer; Frank Pourcel and Peter Nero; Astrud Gilberto and The Exotic Guitars.

And who among those who have, as I, followed Shirley Bassey's career since the first snowy days of 1965 and *Goldfinger* could fail to recognize her shallow G.T.M. performance here? It may not be a nice fact to fondle but for every Tony Bennett and Andre Kostelanetz driven by the fires of Euterpe to add themselves to the *Love Story* register there are two Hugo Winterhalters trying to return to the lucrative "Canadian Sunset" of 15 years ago. One will recall the advice of Matthew 7:15 in perusing these seedy Lotharios of the muse's dowry.

Traipsing back into the domain of true art, one of the ironies resultant in the veritable Mesopotamia of creativity fostered by *Love Story* is that what is perhaps the finest version of the theme has garnered little recognition. Lost in the multitude and all that. I'm referring to Santos Colon's Spanish language rendition. Though there are two other cuts of "Where Do I Begin" in the *lengua de amor*— those of Rondella de Saltillo and Andy Williams (whose English version is the biggest seller of all, surpassing even the Original Soundtrack wax)—Colon's poignant rendition in the Spanish idiom of bicho/chocho soap opera mesmerizes the listener into a chingo-chingo melancholia where the folly of life tongue-bathes one's midbrain like the waves of the Atlantic lapping the white sands of the Candada right in back of the Holiday Inn. It's available on Santos' new LP, *Tu Calle*, which is also the only album to include a version of "The Theme from *Love Story*" that's not entitled *Love Story*.

## Love Story Generation

It is a common precept among the love generation that the tribal *agape* that culminated a few years ago, giving birth to Woodstock Nation, was anticlimatically dashed apart months later at Altamont, consequently giving birth to the decadent Altamont Nation. This precept has been canonized to the station of theorem by counterculture journalism here and abroad.

A couple of months ago, Mick Jagger, lead singer of the Rolling Stones rock group and the individual most associated with Altamont Nation, was wed to Bianca Perez Morena de Macias at St. Tropez, France. And during that solemn rite of the sacrament of marriage, the somber strains of "The Theme from *Love Story*" played on an harmonium wafted aethereally through the chapel's solacious aisles.

If we as a people can embrace the *logos* of *Love Story*, if we are able to embrace it for the life-direction and love it conveys, and not for the fatalistic and pathovoyeuristic leanings it caters to, if we could reach out during these times of great stress and pain to our fellow human beings, not in rhetoric but in reality, we would indeed be much closer to the peace, the love, the *ahimsa* which we once sought to bring about through a self-fulfilling prophecy that was co-opted *in-foeto* years ago. That there would be a community of loving spirits, transcend-

ing geography and nationalistic concepts, that there would be a true nation
built upon concepts unguided by time, climate or economics, that there would
be a true Love Story Nation.

*Not knowing why, I repeated what I had long ago learned from the beautiful girl now dead.*

*"Love means not ever having to say you're sorry." And then I did what I had never done in his presence, much less in his arms. I cried.*

# 7

# The Heartbeats
# Never Did Benefits

I honestly don't know all too much about this Bangla Desh business. I see them on the subway sometimes. Walking around. Talking funny. Looking like the Good Lord left them in His rotisserie a little too long. And the ladies with those shiney doohickies on their foreheads, or *frons*. I don't go in for their food because all that curry and stuff doesn't get along too famously with my hemorrhoids. A little chicken biriani and I shit blood for a week. Hemorrhoids are actually disgustingly painful tumors or tubercules made up of enlargements of the mucous membrane in one's asshole. Sometimes hemorrhoids are really cancer of the rectum, in which case *the sleep that knows no dawn* could be just around the corner. Anyway, you might as well forget about getting ass-fucked, or *pedicated* (not even a pinky finger) for at least a week after you first notice blood spiralling from your stools, or *faeces*. Even farting hurts after awhile. Many psychiatrists, or "headshrinkers," believe that hemorrhoids are merely God's way of punishing people for liking the smell of their own number two.

In Bangla Desh, most of the people being murdered by "the pigs" are Hindus. The Hindus call their god the "Three-In-One." Hinduism is *the only religion in the world teaching the belief in the division of people into castes*. Many persons believe that that is really why Jesus is now punishing them.

Anyhow, there are lots of East Pakistani refugees in India living in abject squalor. They're dying from disease. They're dying from starvation. They're dying from all sorts of things. And Jesus isn't going to help them. And Jehovah isn't going to help them. And those esoteric gook gods aren't going to help them. That leaves it up to da people.

So last August 1st there were two gala Bangla Desh benefits, one in the afternoon and one in the evening, at Madison Square Garden in New York. They were Ravi Shankar's idea but I seriously doubt if there were any people there that had come to hear him. (I guess he's got about another two years before he goes the way of Don Ho and Kyu Sakamoto before him.) Da people were there to see George Harrison and Leon Russell and Ringo Starr and Eric Clapton. Dylan performed too.

Harrison did some of his Beatles stuff and some of his theological puppy-love shtick. Dylan leaned heavily on his early folknik catalogue. Some people say Dylan did the stuff he did because that's what Leon Russell wanted him to do. Others, like A. J. Weberman, feel that Dylan's performance that Sunday signalled a return on his part to the purer shores of righteousness. Well, it was crummy stuff in 1963 and it's crummy stuff now. As for Harrison, he seems like a swell guy with swell intentions and all, but, still, what does somebody like him have to do with 1971? Fie!

In any case, the concerts were a complete success, financial-wise. The tickets went like hotcakes quicker than you could shake a stick at them. The night of the concert there was some idiot outside offering a few hundred dollars for a ticket. I don't know what the current rate of exchange is on the philanthropy market, but I bet you could save an awful lot of gook kids with a couple of hundred dollars. Which is why we say . . .

Da people didn't give a fuck about Bangla Desh. It could have been a Polish wrestler from Philadelphia who had just been done foul by Bulldog Brauer or something. Everybody was there to see Leon Russell's nifty hair. I know it's bad to make generalizations, but it's my typewriter.

On teevee they showed what the ticket-line area looked like after da people had, after waiting hours, gotten their tickets. It was just a whole big, dense trail of garbage. Soda cans, beer cans, newspapers, food wrappers, liquor bottles, wine bottles, paper bags. All sorts of ugly shit. And it just seems like plain old logic that people who don't give a shit about so totally contaminating their immediate environment couldn't possibly give two garboons about a few Pakistanis getting snuffed out of the carbon cycle scene thousands of miles away. What's all this "Blowin' In the Wind" shit? How come no songs about litterbugs? A person incapable of holding on to an empty wine bottle until he gets to a garbage receptacle is incapable of empathizing with Hollis Brown. And "My Sweet Lord" is the same scam. What did the "sweet Lord" ever do for anybody? How about some songs like "My Sweet Ralph Nader" or "My Sweet Betty Friedan" or "My Sweet Garbage Man" or "My Sweet Jack Daniel" or "My Sweet Adelle Davis"? I mean, people are dying and getting bricked out and the whole world is contaminated and this guy gets up there and sings "My sweet Lord/Hmmm my Lord/Hmm my Lord." The total tepidity and quasi-philosophic non-relevance of such macrokitsch is on a par with Schopenhauer's literary luncheon suicide spiels and Bertrand Russell's "war crime tribunals." Think of it as a two-track stereo tape and out of one channel you've got all these groans and screams and tuberculosis vomits and death noises and sobs and out of the other channel there's this saccharine voice crooning nice Lord, sweet Lord, kiss kiss, here comes the sun, nice Lord, kiss kiss, sugar sugar, kiss kiss, glitter glitter.

Four little old ladies, infatuated with their detective neighbor, light on a scheme to attract his attention.

A telethon would have been far, far better. They could've gotten NET to donate thirty-two hours. Think of all the money they could've gotten *that* way, what with Leon Russell and Ringo Starr and The Cast of *Hair* (they seem to show up everywhere, don't they?) taking pledges over the phones. Besides, on telethons if you give a super amount of money they bring you up on stage (remember? ". . . and Lou Marciano's brought in a check from Local 411 in the Bronx for $801. The dollar is from his little daughter Audrey—it's her milk 'n' cookie money for the week . . . "). Could you imagine stuff like ". . . and Howard Stein of the Capitol Theatre in Portchester . . . whose ushers have been canvassing all morning with their Bangla Desh cans . . ." Or George Harrison loosening his collar and doing a ". . . and now let's take a look at the big board. . . ." thing. Sure, muscular dystrophy is more interesting because if the big board reaches $80,000 they herd a bunch of stricken kids out and do that "Look at Us, We're Walking" act. Maybe they could've had a little starving East Pakistani kid on stage and every $20,000 or so they could've given him some lamb curry ("courtesy of Nathan's . . . ") or something. It's about time they had a few telethons for some hip charities.

But *is* all the iodine in the ocean? I mean, does rock 'n' roll have anything to do with anything? Once it adopts pretensions of meaningfulness outside of that of a self-contained expression, matrical and flashing, doesn't it become art or pop/kitsch? If not, how come all the psychedelic dreck of the last five years, in retrospect, can't hold a candle, in terms of cosmic epiphany or plain old life-energy, to Little Richard of The Heartbeats? Little Richard, *via* his pure white-energy raunch and total over-simplification, had the power to make people say "fuck it" and turn their backs on their own control conditioning and just go out and debauch and cop a glimpse of the violent, drunken, loving, dancing Universe. The Heartbeats sprayed more *ahimsa* and luv-eye-flow from their beans than three Woodstocks ever could. The Harptones never played any benefits for anybody. But they *benefited* more people than George Harrison ever will. I mean, *really* benefited people, not in a monetary or philosophical sense, but in an immediate, gut-level, *affective* sense.

And you have to remember that we're not here talking about an ethos or a mores, not about the paradigm of the performer-audience/donor benefit concept, or wrist-slapping a too-rare occurrence of beneficence, but, rather, questioning the validity, the healthiness, the truthfulness of ensconcing a phenomenon, here rock 'n' roll, in the pretensions of lofty ideals and noble purposes. Because, as the entire psychohistory of the human race attests, *once the illusion of fulfillment is allowed to co-opt the fulfillment, or the honest striving toward that fulfillment, boy, you are fucked!* In other words, the *easier* possibility of a self-conning neurotic or pre-psychotic pattern or overview is never to be chosen over the real McCoy which that (mass) neurotic construct purports to be. Racka racka.

I guess it sounds ugly, but I really don't think that rock 'n' roll, or any other form of aesthetically-oriented form of communication, has anything to do with the concrete reality of a bunch of babus kicking off from cholera in Karimpur. Surely the concrete reality in point is of far greater importance than rock 'n' roll. Death doesn't have shit to do with metaphysics. On the other hand, however, it is impossible to separate the metaphysics from the metaphysicality of rock 'n' roll. If you do, it's The Dave Clark Five. Very bad. Helping Bangla Desh might mean a lot *re* the successful emergence of a Third World schema, but the pretension of construing rock 'n' roll as an integral intermediate in that cause and effect is not only meaningless in terms of the effect but also detrimental to the spiritual status quo of the music and its aura. Once the *terminus ad quem* of a folk aesthetic is changed from a self-contained, simultaneous alpha-omega to a more totalitarian concept of "function" or "virtue," the aesthetic energy becomes moribund and vestigial. It's the old "every time you use the word 'revolution,' you delay it by fifteen seconds" thing. Nope. The Harptones never did any songs about helping mankind.

The very fact that an OK (albeit star-studded) concert (and subsequent record album) can confusedly be taken as some kind of *ipso facto* agape of sancrosanct proportions seems to signify a lack of spontaneity and involved emotional response somewhere along the lines. A deterioration of energy and involvement is inevitable in any phenomenon which transposes its kinesis/logos from an *inherently* spiritual to a *seemingly* spiritual, or easier and more superficial, whatchimicallit. What I mean is that people like Jerry Lee Lewis or The Cleftones or Commander Cody & His Lost Planet Airmen or Archie Shepp have very definitely changed more heads around for the far better than a truckload of George Harrisons asking people to kiss it up to God and make it all better ever could. Just one of those honking one-note saxophone solos off *Here's Little Richard* has more spiritual energy, vision and Tau-fuck than five *All Things Must Pass* could shake a tube of Mani-Magic Cuticle Remover at.

So send your loot to the East Pakistani Relief Fund c/o The United Nations, but remember that you can't be a litterbug and save mankind at the same time. But who says you should care about saving mankind in the first place? A-womp bop a-lu bomp a-womp bam boom. *Cuentaselo a tu abuela.*

Later.

# 8

# God Crazed Hippies
# Reap Boffo B.O.

### *Henny Youngman Smashes Highest Energy Force in Universe*

August 3rd. Henny Youngman up there on teevee rat-tat-tatting the David Frost studio audience with old stand-up comic Thompson's *Motif-Index of Folk-Literature* re-hashes. Rat-tat-tat the robber who went into the Chinese restaurant and said "give me all your money" and the little Chinese fella behind the counter says "to take out?" rat-tat-tat. Then there were the six rough-trade hippys who motorcycled up to a diner and went inside and started taunting this truckdriver so the truck-driver gets up and leaves and one of the hippys says to the counterman "he isn't much of a man, is he?" and the counterman says "he's not much of a truck-driver either, he just backed up over six motorcycles." And the ever-present violin, old slick-haired vaudeville Jew and that sere obsidian get-the-money string of one-liners and toppers 1902 *ff.* Massachusetts, introduced by Frost in Copacabana voice of limousines and satin Times Square older than teevee.

Commercial. Piano player. Mike Metelica and Ronnie I forget his last name from the Brotherhood of the Spirit commune in Warwick, Massachusetts, introduced by Frost in some vague allusion to the pianist preceding them. Frost asks about the commune. Well, there are two hundred some odd people presently in the commune trying to grow with one another and to maintain contact with the forces of Creative Energy and to attune their lives to those forces.

Henny Youngman keeps interrupting with "How do you pay the rent? Where do you get your money from?"

Metelica won't give Youngman a straight answer, starts talking about "auras" and helping neighboring farmers. Reincarnation.

"Yeah, but how do you pay the rent?" Everybody in the audience is cracking up by now.

Station break cuts in on fading laughter and Metelica explaining that he'd like to talk more about reincarnation. After the station break, Frost assures him. After the station break. Frost introduces William B. Williams, who shares the rest of the air-time with Henny Youngman.

## "Hey, Man, What's All This 'Spirit' Shit?"

The previous July 2nd, the day of the Frost Show taping, most of the Brotherhood of the Spirit commune had ventured down to New York City for a march up Fifth and Sixth Avenues that was to culminate at 1700 Broadway, where the Metromedia Records (Spirit In Flesh's label) offices are located. Everybody meets in Washington Square Park early that morning. There's a big pile of Spirit In Flesh placards. The Spirit In Flesh mob are milling about. There're Spirit In Flesh balloons. (Practically the entire Spirit In Flesh publicity campaign has been completely the product of the Brotherhood of the Spirit commune. Months previous to the album's release, silk-screened posters with Metelica's dashing mug and the hand-lettered words "SPIRIT IN FLESH" had appeared miraculously glued to an unbelievable number of walls and street-lights around the metropolitan area. The commune had begun to flood radio stations with phone calls about Spirit In Flesh. They'd also taken to flooding Metromedia's switchboard with inquiries as to why the album wasn't being released yet, hunh? More of this matter anon.) David Peel is there hanging around. A few of the St. Marks Place alkies are there. Beautiful brown-haired woman slugging on the old Calvert's in the fantastic sunshine and an old black wino stumbling along. "What's all this 'spirit' shit?" Short, squat starry-eyes comes over and says "Hi," which I have since learned is the most commonly uttered expletive of the commune. "Hi." "Dija hear the Spirit In Flesh album?" Yup. Blah blah blah. Everyone in the commune has absolute undifferentiated faith that the Spirit In Flesh album will change the world. But what if it doesn't? I ask. "Oh, but it *will*." Yeah, but, you know, what if, by some gnarl in the stemma of manifest destiny, it doesn't? She looks at me in patronizing bewilderment. "It has to." This is the commune party line. No buts about it, Spirit In Flesh is gonna change the world.

## Itinerary

Aug. 16—The Warehouse; New Orleans, La.
Aug. 25—The Factory; St. Louis, Missouri
Aug. 27—Civic Center; Oklahoma City, Oklahoma
Sept. 22—Carnegie Hall; New York, NY

## "Talk To Me"

They've got this super beezarro cripple in the commune who they wheel around in a wheelchair. He's all palsied and scuzzy-looking with this antenna pointing out from his forehead. It's held on by some kind of headband. There's a re-converted ouija board hooked up over his lap—it's got the alphabet, "yes" and "no" squares and the inscription "Talk To Me." He "talks" by hitting his antenna-tip to various portions of the alphabet board. Say "rubber baby buggy bumper" five times fast. Hey, Carmine, c'mere and take a look at this. Abklingen.

The march up Fifth Avenue was pretty neat. No incidents, though. A bunch of "Hi"s. They consume a lot of garbage, though; for people in touch with the highest energy force in the universe, I mean. Lemon ices. Orange "drinks." Sodas. If they really ever *do* make the big time, athletes might be in jeopardy of their soft-drink advertising monopoly. ". . . Hi, I'm in touch with the Highest Energy Force In The Universe. This? It's the Un-Cola . . . " (and then they could have that beezarro cripple spell out "7-Up" on his character grid) . . .

Upon reaching the main entrance to 1700 Broadway, they all converged in this big circle and began chatting a medley of Spirit In Flesh stuff. When I whipped out my cassette machine a series of pimply pusses assaulted, osculi agape, its meagre microphone apparatus with rasping monosyllabic spiels of perpetual high and cosmic one-ness.

Upstairs, a little while later, I'm in a room with Michael Metelica and Ronnie Whatsizname, fresh from their David Frost taping. The trusty old tape-recorder's on the desk in someone's unoccupied office. I'm nervous, Michael's wary. I start off by asking him about the consciousness level he refers to so often, can he describe it? (*Aside:* Back in the 1960s, as the ISB would say, when I was a mere college drop-out, I was, to say the least, quite big on energy-levels and chromosome damage and transcendence and stuff. Although I have since forsaken these more esoteric preoccupations for a life of, as my dear mum once put it, "just fooling around and hiding behind a bottle," I have retained the patois of the *ars arcuni* for retaliative use among the intimidating spiritual hoi polloi of the outer Sephir.) OK. Well, first let me say that Michael Metelica is one of *the* most mesmerizing, magnetic people I've ever come up against. Put him in a room and he'll beam openness and love into every brain-eye there. An amazing, amazing person. Now, I'm not being *qualitative* here, because, as far as I'm concerned, Michael may be just a unique psychotic. I'll bet my pretty blond locks, though, that he's absolutely sincere and beneficent in all his words and intentions. He just sort of pinned me with those eldritch fantastic baby-blues of his and told me that when he was very young, in a grade school classroom, he was on his way from his seat to sharpen his pencil at the pencil sharpener at the front of the room and Zomp! it hit him—fabulous eerie visions of lives past, future manifestations, and total lovely flowingness of universal life/death continuum. Scared the shit out of me, he did. He told me things that he asked me not to reveal in print. They were about past life-form manifestations that he said might be construed as some kind of hype. He agreed that there were other auro-gangs emitting high levels of life-energy. They, though, themselves weren't in touch with the outermost sphere of consciousness as were Spirit In Flesh. In my own no-pushee no-shovee way, I'm trying to get him to acquiesce to Little Richard and Archie Shepp and their holy stature of godfuck and flow. Nothing doing. Spirit In Flesh is *the* centrifugal force of the contemporary eth-noastronomical universe in flux (they don't talk that neat, but I try to condense it and make it sound better). I ask the question for the umpteenth time that day. But what if Spirit In Flesh don't catch the human race by the mid-brain? But it *will.* The old Socratic full-pitcher analogy. But it *will.* Echoes of 1966 peace/love time-loop Maharishi Mahesh Yogi trying to muzzle in on Mia Farrow's nookie and heroin *Medicine Ball* (". . . lots of naked girls . . . ") *Caravan* radio commercials. But it *will.* Hence the amount of thryoxin produced may remain the same.

### "Hi! Are You a Disc Jockey?"

On Saturday morning, July 31st, Metromedia bus'd a bunch of people out to the Brotherhood of the Spirit commune in Warwick. Splendidly hungover from an all-nite debauch in the bowels of the lower West Side, the Air Raid Kid and myself boarded the rented bus parked in front of 1700 Broadway. Jon Tiven wore a green jumpsuit. Toby Mamis grinned. A few women from the commune served as hostesses. The long journey into the nether regions of Massachusetts was lightened by Mamis' spirited readings from *The Quotations of Chairman Mao* and the rendering of Tiven, the 16 year-old editor of The *New Haven Rock Press* (send 25¢ for a copy to: NHRP, 528 Lambert Road, Orange, Conn. 06477), into a state of public drunkeness, one of my favorite pastimes.

We dis-embarked the autobus to resounding cries of "Hi!" There were signs up on the trees. "No Drugs." "No Booze." And, yes, "promiscuity" was a no-no, too. I was taken on a tour of the communal house (built by the commune them-selves—nice job, too!), had my decadence expounded upon. I had "a lot of poten-tial," though.

Everybody asked, "Are you a disc jockey?" No one was asked less than say, sev-enteen times, "Hi! Are you a disc jockey?" People started hiding behind shacks and shit to escape conversation. Within an hour, "Hi! Are you a disc jockey?" had developed into a running joke among the potato salad-scarfing, conversa-tion-refugees who chanced to meet in the more clandestine reaches of the com-mune grounds.

We didn't get to hear Spirit In Flesh perform that afternoon because we were supposed to go see the Dead in New Haven. Should have stayed. Anyway, upon leaving, I/we were accosted by the same woman who had acknowledged my "po-tential" earlier. "But you seemed to have so much *potenial,* Nick." Yeah, I know, but I gotta go, my friends are leaving. "Well, then, go ahead, but you'll be sorry; you *owe* it to yourself to hear Spirit In Flesh." Don't make me feel guilty. "I can't make you feel guilty, only you can make you feel guilty." The car pulls away. Zomp! It's one of them at the wheel, and an hour-and-a-half ride ahead of us. Beautiful long red flowing hair. Glad I'm not in the front seat. We get to fall out, rain pitter-patter on the windows in the back seat, Tiven up front talking to Mr. Energy.

## "Riverside Song"

The Spirit In Flesh lp, *Spirit In Flesh* (Metromedia MD 1041) doesn't get much airplay on the radio, I don't think. Alex Bennett of WPLJ-FM in New York seems to have set the reactionary (technical sense, buddy) tone to their "publicity campaign" (flooding the station's switchboards and all that) by downmouthing them as "punks," with an aside to the effect that Metromedia Records (who'd almost gotten sued by the city for the commune's poster-posting orgy) shouldn't be held in responsibility for the group's punkness. (A motion that I wholeheartedly endorse; Barry Shaw of Metromedia is responsible for bringing The Holy Modal Rounders into the public eye, big-time-wise, a move which will bring more loving raunch energy to the Universe than a thousand energy-level punks.)

I like "Riverside Song," which I think is one super-fine aw-reet cut. The whole scam, though, is that Spirit In Flesh doesn't grid re musick, but, rather, in terms of literally turning around the course of civilization. Well, it's just Heraclitus and *panta rei* and if Heraclitus couldn't bend the carbon cycle scene in three thousand years, these guys sure aren't going to do it overnight.

I mean, it seems like a whole lot of naivete for a bunch of kids who put restrictions on people (remember those signs I was telling you about?) and who don't even eat non-honko food to expect to change the monster divine Universe, *literally,* when there are true red line shifts the likes of Jerry Lee Lewis, who's had one hand on a shot glass and the other hand on some Einsteinian dimensional warp for fifteen years, and Archie Shepp, who could play thirty-two racks of 9-ball with Ra and come out on the money side every time, stalking this planet in overall unacknowledgement.

Last line: What we've got here is a cross between Jesus Christ and Florence Foster Jenkins and everybody knows Jesus sucks.

# 9

Gene Vincent, age thirty-six, died of booze and bleeding ulcers on October 12, 1971. Another death, another poem.

# Be Bop A Lula

Rockin' Robin Barfing Blood Lost
Weekend Wife Took The Kiddies
Bye Bye Gene. Ulcer. Death.

# 10

This, from *Creem* in the first, cold days of 1972, must have been the idea of Lester Bangs: to have different writers address different physical components of this pretentious boxed set by a band that sucked and made a lot of money. I took, or got, the box.

By this time, I had quit my job at the underwear company, and, soon finding myself homeless, had split for Florida with an old buddy, Bill, who was living and working in Tampa. I ran into him one night in a bar when he made a brief trip home to bury his mother, and left with him for Tampa either the next day or a few days later.

The bar where I ran into him was the bar of the old Broadway Central Hotel, which had degenerated into a welfare hovel. The cavernous bar itself had come to be called St. Adrian's. It was also where, some time before this, I had met my future wife. In fact, for many years, every woman in my life entered it through one barroom or another.

# The Box

Why is this box different from all other boxes?

The answer is nine-fold; irony abounds.

Its spine is predolated. A hint of verdrian lake at the upper right-hand spinal corner. Spinal imprinting is off-center. Intentional so as to affect casualness? Unintentional, the fault of paste-up man or production assemblist? Conjecture reigns. Mainly on the plains.

Acoustics: a pen placed in the hollow of the box takes on an obsidian and macabre aire of silence. When shaken in a regularized forward-backward pattern, one is reminded of the somnorific chuga-chuga-chuga of a trans-continental express train. A lighted cigarette in the box and shaken alternates mammalian thud with hushed anguish, ember 'gainst cardboard.

Imprinting: front and back, "Chicago" as sole dominant hieratic, empiricized, stately lection, the last remaining leave of autumn.

Timeliness: as perishable and auto-obsolescent as all get out. Will dissipate into a laughable-looking piece of spineless crap within a decade. This could have been prevented by re-inforced binding.

The rectangular opening of the box veritably reeks of the ricorsic saga of Man. If only it could speak! What wonders it might unfurl for the curious and callow ears of young and young at heart alike. Nor Byron with his lecher limp, nor Poe with starry stare, nor Villon, that petty thief and pimp, but the sere testament of muted existence. Once a sapling, now pulp.

It may be used as a large, rather unorthodox dice-shaking cup if one is actually quite stupid. This and Linear B have perplexed scientists for years, simply years.

For a total of five exterior planar surfaces involved in the whole kit 'n' kaboodle, the angular vectors are only slightly less than unique.

It cannot house a runaway child.

The implications are myriad, the teeth shiney and white. Dental floss. Vitamin D. Nibbling the coronal regions, lips parted softly wet. All while it quietly snowed outside.

What we have here is a historical process.

# 11

While driving to Tampa, we broke down on the outskirts of Savannah, which turned into something of an odyssey. Little did I know that what lay in store for me in Florida was to be even more of a misadventure. The following piece, previously unpublished, came out of those days.

# The 24-Hr Sound of
# Country Gospel and the Dark

Savannah.

She looks up her eyes are sin ancient fear as in delirious T4 virus age 11 jerking-off in cold sweat dead relatives & dog hit by car 1960 looking down from heaven hurt as the watery treacle leaves the reddened fish mouth cock wets the dry-heave guilt hallucination sheets long ago & slips the dick into the mouth. The synapses are still shattered after all these hours, feel the brain growing too large like on the old *War of the Worlds* bubblegum cards, the dick peeking down from gasket of tongue & palate into alimentary canal. Comb the fingers thru the matted fake blond hair, toying with the lacquer very dark a fear of blindness eyes strain for ebbing hints of texture I come in her mouth.

Next day 12 miles out of Savannah sucking on a pint of Richard's Georgia Peach Wine the brakes give out while we're doing 65 on 17 South. Six hours later we're cruising thru Savannah 4 a.m. in Luther's ridiculous extinct Ford sipping his piss warm Miller. The 24 Hour Sound of Country Gospel sputtering thru now & then at various Herz levels.

"Yeahup, the best way t' fuck sheep is ya git their hind legs 'n shove'm down yr boot fronts lak so so's 'at way they can't get away nor kick ya either." Pensive alchemist pause eyes lost for a breath in the Georgia swamps insects in the hi-beams as we clank around a bend, ostracons of Tom T. Hall & the Story Tellers singalonging "Me & Jesus" Bill snoring. Sounds in the floorboards.

"Now chickens is a differnt can o' shit." Can't even make out the features on his ratty face. "Best way t' fuck chickens is ya do 'em up agains' the wahll so's their feet kin touch the wahll. An' when yew start fuckinum thay'll kick lak all hell agains' that wahll 'n' let me tell you it's lak nuthin' yew evuh felt in yo' lahf. Yeahup, chickens are funny lak that." Hint of tender loving in the whites of the eyes.

Roadside. Cricket noises the three of us pissing numero una numero dos numero tres into the dirt half asleep.

"Ah tell what let's us do. We drink mah beer 'n' then we drink yo' wahn 'n' then we go get some coffee 'n' then when the store opens up Ah'll get us some vahs-grip pliers 'n' a new brake linin' 'n' we kin fix yo' car."

20 minutes later there's a sign over a bar on a side street no lite coming thru the windows

HOG'S
Very Cheap
Will Butcher
& Dress
Joe Kline

Luther buying us glasses of beer sets of nervous red eyes shots of Carstairs the *Today Show* in ghosts on the TV headache Luther's wife comes storming in in his old fatigue jacket & cork wedgies old fat hysterectomy 18 year old retarded son slapping self in face saliva from mouth at home knocks the glass of beer out of his hand & slaps him hard across the face You dirty son of a fucking bitch stay out all nite & think you're gonna get away with it you stinking son of a bitch & slaps him again he twists her wrists the bartender throws them both out into the sunshine little Norman Rockwell pickanannies going to school.

Sunset under the car bleeding the brakes in Enco station See Our Beautiful Tropical Fish Aquarium murky concrete pond grotesque bloated goldfish. Sad lonely feelings looking from the sign to the goldfish as when very young seeing clowns with holes in their costumes or alcoholic dirty men selling cheap tin battery-operated toy cars my mother pointing them out to me. See Our Beautiful Tropical Fish Aquarium murky concrete pond grotesque bloated goldfish the cars farting by on 17 looking down from the pedestrian bridge in Bayside 1967 watching the cars. I feel like shit should be back there 1967 Peggy dryhumping in the park summertime & Bill fishes out the last few dollars & we're in a bar in downtown Savannah. Mary Grave asks for a quarter for the juke box drawing a line down my drunken spine with her Fabulous Fake'd index finger Ten High bourbon breath tongue in my ear old washed-up honky tonk blow-for-dough routine as old as the hills two more drinks & we're broke Bill looking up from the bar We're never gonna get out of Savannah, Nick. It's just like last year I couldn't get out of Ogalala, Nebraska, for eleven fucking days I did everything but I couldn't get out.

Getting cold late at nite we broke into a Volkswagon bus in a used car lot & slept drunk on the rusty metal floor. I awake an hour later & no Bill. I head out on the deserted streets I feel compelled to sit down on this extracted car seat on the corner of Winston Avenue & Tenth Street and jerk-off. So I pull my cock out & start stroking it getting it hard strange asexual libido frustrated apes in the Central Park Zoo yanking their dicks in the corner of the cage & then I realize what I'm doing visions of myself thrown before the judge & his fatass clerk Yeah, we found him abusing himself on a public street at 8 a.m. No money & no identification. God, it was disgusting, yr honor. So I amble off into the deserted streets & after awhile lifts the hammer out from under the seat of the car:

"This hammer kills rednecks" no Woody Guthrie doing his drugstore macho This Machine Kills Fascists act & the shitkicker quits tailgating as he sees the hammer displayed in the Tampa noon & make a right on MacDill, right by the MacDonald's Over 9 Billion Sold thinking of that shitass hamburger place on 72nd Street calling itself Mike Donald's selling Big Mikes—chachalacas scream & we spin around on our heels in the dirt alley, it's been a long time.

"Why Ah jest wanna tawk to yew, pussyass, Ah jest wanna tawk" shadows 2 of them oozing out worms from the dark sponge nite behind him. We run out onto El Prado the nicotine filmed lungs making wheezing sounds running past the bars until the inevitable cry shoots thru the ears/chest & the calm observant eyes turn malevolent & arms reach out to grab at arms touch concrete unreal skin skidding the pretty skin skidding touching concrete kidney-punt the chachalacas screaming that split second pure clear as day behind my eyes I am sitting there watching *A Man For All Seasons* w/ a hardon 1968 I think it was raining in the summer all there for a split second & then I wake up 4 miles from El Prado sore checking for my money the first impulse is to clear the nostrils I pick the nose sore . . . "Two-foot-high woodpeckers shatter the days with their unearthly shrieks." He smiles like he should be whittling pinewood & be a patriarch figure. Fucking wino Indian. Fucking drunk doesn't remember shit.

Next morning Bill wakes me up hands me his grey herringbone pants & blue shirt It's 20 after 11. Ten minutes later I'm at a table in the Chatterbox on South Howard air-conditioned cool softly clinking the ice in my glass of Jack's. Mr Sleazo from Rapid Falls to my right & moneybags across from me.

"We're going to make it the biggest thing in the Bay area. We've got the money. We've got the know-how. We've got the right people—and once you've got the money it's not the distribution that matters—it's the right people, the *right* people. I've got signed agreements from 27 hotels & motels in the Bay area, all agreeing to place it in each & every one of their hotel or motel rooms every week. We're giving it to them. We're giving it to them gratis. We're putting a sales price of 10% on each issue & we're not asking for a penny in return from them. We are going to make *all* of our money from advertising. We will have the perfect vehicle for advertising—a motel-hotel, public entertainment guide. I have never failed. Would you care for another drink?"

18 hrs later we slouch out of Sleazo's Olds at 3 in the afternoon & squinteye into the Crazy Horse up in Orlando. Put 25¢ in the jukebox & short mumbo incest girl takes her top off & gets on stage her titties chuga chuga Creedence Clearwater on the jukebox she slowly tilts the head-neck-spine backwards in beautiful Hatha Yoga solar plexus thrust the legs spread wide slow counterclockwise circular grinding faster & faster a dick lathe on that stage when acneface comes sauntering in, claps a quarter down on the cushion of the pooltable takes his cue stick out of his case "Why that bwoy's either a hustler or he got one mighty skinny suitcase" start counting the bills in my pocket by touch.

I am very drunk & being blown off outside the Salvation Army in Orlando,

> BED & 2 FREE MEALS
> OR
> 1 FREE MEAL EVERY 30 DAYS
> NO DRUNKS

"Full House" penciled in 2.30 a.m. in Orlando she has pretty hair soft brown her name is June.

# 12

These kids that Meltzer and I knew were putting out a mimeographed and stapled magazine called *Teenage Wasteland Gazzete*. The ringleaders were Andy Shernoff, who in print went by the name of Adny Shernoff, and Richie Blum, who later became Handsome Dick Manitoba of The Dictators, a band that Shernoff led and that Meltzer helped to mastermind.

This may have been the first of the few pieces that I wrote for *TWG*. More than a quarter of a century later, Shernoff and Manitoba are still my buddies and still grinning.

# Beyond Euclid: Pool!

They call it pool on account of the shape of the table. The shape of the table is rectangular.

Many people play 3-D pool but only faggots.

Jon Tiven plays 3-D pool.

Pool was invented in Mexico in 1821. It was called "poule" which also means "chicken" in ze French tongue but only if you pronounce it right (retards take note).

Fans of "deejay" patois will be interested to note that the term "cueing-up" is also used by poolplayers in the argot of the "pocketjack" (subculture jargon meaning "poolplayer") it means chalking up your cue stick with a cube of blue chalk. Cues are also long lines, the things on chinamen's heads and a magazine and softdrink.

See ya at the White Rose!

# 13

Without a doubt the greatest publication of its day was *Candid Press,* which came out of Chicago and was the secretly pseudonymous creation of a crew that put out one of the prestigious literary quarterlies of the time. Meltzer and I knew of only one newsstand in New York, on East Eighth Street, where it could be bought, and we were there bright and early every week to get our copies.

I wrote this when I was living in Tampa. By the time it was published, I had returned to New York, where I moved from a flophouse on Fourteenth Street to the apartment of my soon-to-be wife on Fifteenth Street, where there arrived a letter from *Candid Press,* to whom I had sent a copy of the piece along with a brief note, which, I was informed had been "selected AT RANDOM from the thousands we receive each day as the LUCKY LETTER of the week." With this distinction came a check for twenty-five dollars and a Hot Pink One necktie, which, that September, along with the only suit jacket I owned, a second- or third-hand red polyester doubleknit monstrosity, I wore when I got married down at City Hall. Meltzer, my best man, wore a Hot Pink One as well, and our wedding picture, taken outside City Hall by our bridesmaid, Meltzer's girlfriend Roni Hoffman, was published in the *Candid Press* of November 12, 1972, above the words "They got married in Hot Pink One Ties!"

# The Real Avant-Garde

If you still think that existentialism is anything more than getting laid in Paris and acting twenty years older than you are or that the concepts of literary syntax/exposition have the least thing to do with the human brain red-shift/man-on-moon 1972 Universe or that happenings or destruction art differ greatly from a mah-jong gathering, watch out because here comes a little piece of god-fuck barrelling down the road.

Or, rather, two little pieces. Two examples of future-now, two noble instances of literature keeping up with technology and shitting on the grave of James Joyce in one valiant, sweeping gesture of your favorite abstract noun. Yes, two beautiful entities that neither mourn the deaths of beatnik poets nor know nor care whom the Nobel Prize was named after. Pants down, people, because here come *The Candid Press*, and *The Teenage Wasteland Gazzete*, the only extant magazine that unintentionally misspells its own name.

*The Candid Press* has been around for a few years, usually sold at newsstands in the same rack as *The National Enquirer*, *The Insider*, *Midnight*, etc. Nothing could be more misleading.

A typical issue of *CP* includes the headline, "HAND JOBS TILL YOU PUKE!!! JOHNNY REB BANGS A SOUL CHICK, P. 11! PLUS: NAKED SHAME FOTOS & TALES OF ENEMAS, SPANKING, FETISHES, NEGRO SEX, QUEERS!!!" And, boy, do they deliver. Their unbelievably poor quality of photo reproduction is a marvel to behold. The main gist of each issue is anal-repressive oriented, with regular columns by Ben Dover ("Enema Hot Line"), Herb Cann ("Toilet Talk") and Walter Whiz a.k.a. The Keelow Eel. There are usually features on amputee fetishism written in a hee-hee tone, sex question-and-answer panels that fortify the reader's most deep-rooted neurotic sexual fears and anxieties, and an advice to the love-lorn column, "Dear Scabby," which runs along the lines of:

DEAR SCABBY:

The thought of sex with a man scares the s—t out of me, but I love to let Mike, my pet mouse, crawl in and out of my vagina. Is that OK?

*CHEESE CLIT*

DEAR CHEE:

Why do you perverts always ask me if what you do is OK? Anything you fools do is OK with me 'cepting showing up at my apartment! As to you lady, why not find a guy with a "bald-headed mouse" between his legs?

—*Scabby*

The infantilism of Scabby's column comes off as a discussion of Oxford theologians when compared to Herb Cann's recent campaign against cripples being allowed to go out in public. "Those f-cking gimpsters!"

When one of their columnists recently died, *CP* reported that the burial site stank of alcohol and "s—t."

Walter Whiz and his "Let's Whiz Off! With Walt" column invariably begins with, "Hi, guys, how the hell are you?" From there he goes on to waste two columns each issue with the likes of:

DO YOU REALIZE HOW MANY SHEETS OF STAMPS ARE USED EVERY DAY IN THIS COUNTRY?

I thought not.
In Xanadu did Kubla Khan
A stately pleasure-dome decree:
Where Alph, the sacred river ran
You think the stuff you read in THIS column is tripe? Huh!
So that's it, faithful readers. The cook he made some coffee, it tasted mighty fine.
They took it to the dispens'ry, used it for iodine. Bye, guys.

Isn't that alot better than anything you've ever read in *Paris Review.* You bet!

So, if you can't find it on your newsstand, a subscription (20 issues) is $5 (cheaper than this magazine) from CP, 2715 North Pulaski Road, Chicago, Ill. 60639

*The Teenage Wasteland Gazzete* is only a few issues old. The most recent issue had for its cover a photograph of a guy eating a woman's cunt, her moaning, "I want to pop my cork! I've got to! But he isn't letting me yet! What a stud!!!" and he's thinking to himself, "Ah! Now that's what I call a good Gamahooch!" Man, it's the best fucking magazine in the world!

Ostensibly a rock magazine, there's always stuff by R. Meltzer, Sandy Pearlman and yours truly in it.

Here's a recent editorial:

The New Haven Rock Press really sucks my noodle. Those faggots really think they're writers (no such thing). If I see another sucky record review by Jon Tiven in

Phono, Record or Fusion I will take action. As a matter of fact I'm going to take action right now. I challenge Tiven to any form of competition he wants. I want to fight but I think he's going to want to play golf (they have a lot of country clubs in N. Haven). Well, when he's not looking I'm going to knock his fuckin head in with a five-iron. Eat lead, faggot.

There's always a bit of unorthodox vocalizing ("The jiggaboos and the queers get too much"), fantastic typos, and record reviews like this:

On side two piano is doubletracked with Moog Synthesizer by Pepe who distinguishes himself as the leader of the band especially on John Entwistle's Heaven and Hell where his moog sounds just like a harmonica. I for one agree with Al Aronowitz who says that this album is the sound of things to come in music.

Last issue had an article about Judy Fogel's pimples and coverage of the palsy telethon complete with a glossary of "palsy slang."

A subscription costs $1.50 per year: 59 Chestnut Street, New Paltz, N.Y. 12561.

Shit on the search for meaning and read some good stuff.

# 14

Richard Meltzer and I used to drink at this old dive on Seventh Avenue called Gately's, which was around the corner from where I lived on Fifteenth Street. When there arrived in the mail a promotional copy of an album featuring on its cover Gately's dilapidated neon sign, I had to review it.

# Review of *Gately's Cafe*

Gately's Cafe is one of the finest bars in New York City. It's located at Seventh Avenue between 14th Street and 15th Street. It's not as economical as the Blarney Stones or the White Roses, but for an atmosphere of absolute, undifferentiated drunkeness it can't be beat west of the Bowery. The beer is only 25 cents a glass, which is actually only 5 cents more expensive than the Blarney Stone (and word has it that *their* prices are going to go up also sometime after the February Liquor Tax Increase). They have special shot glasses available at Gately's that hold *2.5 shots* in them. It's Gately's way of giving you more when you order a double. So you can get 2½ ounces of whiskey or gin or whatever plus a beer and pay only $1.50. A quite attractive concept indeed. The clientele is mainly washed-out widows and violence queens and a few nefarious-type homos thrown in for good measure. Plus of course your usual quota of obsidian-livered facelesses. They have a pinball machine and a juke box specializing in the sounds of Polish weddings. The bartender's name is Hank. Quite a personable fellow. At last check the pinball machine was broken. It's still a swell place to go though. The pinball machine might even be fixed by now, come to think of it. Why not give Hank a call and find out? (212) 243-9531.

So next time you're having more than one, why not make it Gately's? You might even meet this guy there named Michael Gately. He's a cousin of the guy that runs the place. Who knows, maybe he'd be able to get you a free drink or two? Or at least play you a song on the juke box from his new album (produced by fellow boozer Al Kooper). What a treat! Yessir, it's *the* place to go for those in the know.

# 15

Based, he said, mainly on my review of the Chicago box in *Creem,* the editor of *Playboy*'s new magazine, *Oui,* asked me to be a contributing editor. (At our appointed meeting at the Oyster Bar of the Plaza, I wore the same red polyester doubleknit jacket in which I had recently got married.) This contributing editorship was a godsend, bringing me a monthly three-figure paycheck and giving me the opportunity to steer work and money to my friends, among them Meltzer, Patti Smith, and even the *Teenage Wasteland Gazzete* guys, who, along with Meltzer, were in with me on this Muddy Waters interview.

# Muddy Waters
# Rarely Eats Fish

Three of *Oui*'s finest encountered Muddy Waters in his hotel room one recent afternoon, and an interview took place. Here it is:

**OUI:** Do you use drugs?
**Mud:** Never. I drink champagne.
**OUI:** What's your favorite champagne?
**Mud:** Piper Heidsieck.
**OUI:** Are you married?
**Mud:** Indeed. With four grandbabies.
**OUI:** I ask because I've heard rumors concerning you and Mia Farrow.
**Mud:** What? Them's just rumors. Not true.
**OUI:** Has Mahalia Jackson's death affected you?
**Mud:** She was a real close friend of mine. Mahalia was my favorite girl. And my favorite preacher is Reverend C. L. Franklin, Aretha's father.
**OUI:** Are you religious?
**Mud:** Oh, definitely.
**OUI:** Then do you go to church every Sunday?
**Mud:** I can't. There's no way.
**OUI:** How did you feel playing for Truman Capote and Andy Warhol and Bob Dylan at Mick Jagger's birthday party at the St. Regis?
**Mud:** I always feels the same no matter where or for who I play. I just get up there and do my thing.
**OUI:** I heard there was a stripper at the party; did she have big tits?
**Mud:** They looked nice-sized to me.
**OUI:** What do you think of women's lib?
**Mud:** Women's limbs?
**OUI:** Lib, lib. Women's liberation. A lot of women believe that they should have the same rights and opportunities that men have, that they shouldn't be forced to just cook and stay at home with the kids.
**Mud:** I think they should stay home and raise the kids. I don't think a woman should do much work. Men should take care of the girls. I've been taking care of mine for 35 years.

**OUI:** In New York there's a group of radical lesbians who go around the city cutting off men's cocks and putting them on their walls.

**Mud:** Well, uhm . . .

**OUI:** Do you like getting drunk?

**Mud:** Never get drunk, never. I used to.

**OUI:** How has throwing up affected your music?

**Mud:** I don't like to throw up. Uh, no; I don't like throwing up.

**OUI:** Do you like to watch TV?

**Mud:** Yessir, that's my hobby, watching the TV.

**OUI:** How do you feel about Chess Records giving Howlin' Wolf the Stones and Humble Pie and all to record with, while they gave you Rory Galagher?

**Mud:** Well, what's wrong with him?

**OUI:** Do you think the Rolling Stones gave you enough credit?

**Mud:** Yeah, they gave me enough credit. Without them nobody would've known me.

**OUI:** What's your own favorite record?

**Mud:** By myself? Well, I've got a few. Most of those songs way back there on the *Best of Muddy Waters* album.

**OUI:** Do you eat fish?

**Mud:** Once every blue moon.

**OUI:** Do you think you've made as much money as you should have?

**Mud:** No. Definitely not.

**OUI:** Is there still a market for black music among black people?

**Mud:** My type of music? It's not quite as popular as it was when I started.

**OUI:** Are you registered to vote?

**Mud:** Sure.

**OUI:** Do you know who you're going to vote for in the Presidential election?

**Mud:** Nope. I may not even vote. I may be away from Chicago at the time, I don't know.

**OUI:** Well, they've got absentee ballots.

**Mud:** I don't wanna talk about politics. Let's talk about the music.

**OUI:** Do you listen to any jazz?

**Mud:** Yes, I sure do. I like a lot of Dixieland. I like Count Basie. I like Miles Davis, Horace Silver.

**OUI:** Do you have a favorite rock group?

**Mud:** The Rolling Stones.

**OUI:** Who were your biggest influences?

**Mud:** Son House. Robert Johnson. I knew Son.

**OUI:** When you play down South, are your audiences mostly white?

**Mud:** Yeah, more whites than colored.

**OUI:** Do you believe in petting on the first date?

# 16

# Eye: Disease

She touches it & dreams of Olmec eye
the lips parted slightly wet
nylon stockings & ectomorph leg
an angel w/ gin
while the stick people in
the myasthenia gravis commercial
wheeze in the background & IAO
hunches somewhere off Route 17

She touches it & dreams of Olmec eye
the lips parted slightly wet

# 17

A review of an album that never existed, from the 1973 April Fool's issue of *Rock* magazine.

Sandy Pearlman was the manager of The Blue Öyster Cult and The Dictators.

# Review of
# *The Mollusks of Tartura*

It is indeed quite difficult to approach this album with the pedestrian sensibilities that suffice for most musical creations. Sandy "Sam" Pearlman, long-time manager, songwriter and *Meister-Schwung* to the renowned and notorious Blue Öyster Cult, you see, is a man of very, how you say, *singular* proclivities.

On *The Mollusks of Tartura*, Pearlman, utilizing most of the Blue Öyster Cult, slide guitarist extraordinaire Dave Roter and, on three of the cuts, the Viennese Children's Choir, tears through a string (or *"Kindertotenleider,"* as he puts it) of eleven original compositions that run from the merely arcane to the leeringly heinous.

The title cut, "Mollusks of Tartura," is a soft, lilting ballad about the "wondrous, molluscan ebb-forms/a-courting in the depths of the mighty Styx." Compared to the remaining content of the album, "Mollusks" is perhaps the most accessible song on the lp.

"Bakehouses of Silesia," Pearlman's own favorite cut, is a rousing and yet weirdly tender tale of that most well known concentration camp of the Upper Silesian region.

No less opinionated is the raunchy "Guilt of the Eskies"-*"The sin of the Eskimo/The dark and gnarling stench that oozes from his measly/Flat-faced blubbery soul/ . . . /The sin of the Esky is."*

There are also the credo songs. "Despicio Ergo Sum" is a pedimentally-structed round canon proving, in the manner of Socratic irony, that "despicio ergo sum"—"I hate therefore I am." Sandy plays the clarino on "Despicio," as he also does on "Ophis, My Love," a hymn of devotion to the great and cold Ur-Snake of the primordial slime.

On the lighter, though no less arcane, side, there's "Soft Leather Sphinctres" ("O, leather-lady/Thy sphinctres encircling my dizz/O, leather-lady/Let thy uterus accept my jizz"), "Sashimi Amistran," a song of *l'haute cannibalisme*, and another food song, "A Feast In Slant-Town":

> *Zipper-eyed homunculi at my call*
> *Bringing me dry shredded beef*
> *Camphor duck and some mustard ball*
> *Lay that sweet and sour capon at my feet*
> *You exist, little gook, that I may eat*

Of the remaining songs, "Thalatta, Thalatta" is perhaps the least satisfying. Just something about the tale of a dalmation obsessed with the "saline mother out there beyond the buoys" that rings a bit too odd, I guess.

"Hamadryad," however, could very well be called the album's crowning achievement:

> I am Hamadryad—eat me
> I am Hamadryad—beat me
> I am Hamadryad—the pulse within the tree
> I am Hamadryad—I kill the soft ones of the lea
> I am Hamadryad—the ancient catkins call my name
> I am Hamadryad—I make insects die in the heavy rain

All in all, *The Mollusks of Tartura* is quite unlike any disc to hit the aural scene in recent months. Buy it and mewl.

# 18

I find it hard now to believe that I wrote this while I was married, that I used real names, and that it was published, albeit in an obscure little Boston fanzine. But such were the times. And such are the times today that all names have here had to be censored.

# Sex & Booze

*While recently scanning the "Sex, Love, & Yonic Weirdness" chart, one in a series of categorical "time grids", that I had assembled for no apparent reason one reefer-trepanned night about a year ago, I was hit with the realization that upward of $^3/_4$ of all my fuck/suck activities since the age of 18 had been inseparably connected with drinking and hanging out in bars.*

*That booze was, and is, perhaps the only true universal aphrodisiac (universal in the sense that it veritably decimates the discriminatory factors of sexual attraction in the libido's drive to satiate itself, whereas other substances possessing "aphrodisiac" properties such as grass, acid, psilocybin, etc., can only accentuate a sexual attraction that is already there, and still other substances, those, like methyl salicylate, cassia, and cantharides, purported to be true chemical aphrodisiacs, are just so much bullshit [it should be ceded, though, in all fairness, that pharmaceutical methedrine, dexedrine, and LSD are capable of producing orgasms befitting to conceive a Horus, and that cocaine, in proper quantities, can do wondrous things to the nerve-endings in a young lady's puss lips]), a truism upheld by several thousands of years of literature, mythology, and history, from the absolute wino culture of Periclean Greece manifesting itself in the form of a democracy of pig-shtupping, belching paederast poetasters and barfly philosophers to 18th-century England's inundation of cheapo "gin houses" bringing about a deluge of whoredom, veedee, and fetishism unequalled anywhere else during the Industrial Revolution to the forces of puritanism which brought about the Eighteenth Amendment, the Volstead Act and still-lingering phenomenon of the "dry county", was not a realization that led me to hanging out in bars to get laid, but vice versa.*

I was 18, just like Alice Cooper, and just floating around taking dope and writing crummy poetry after a 2-year stretch of domestication that ended in my being ditched after too many moons of unconvincing procrastinations of (a) getting a job, and (b) making it legal. Thrown like a mewling cat into the fierce winds of whatchimicallit, I got a job doing paste-ups at the Lovable Underwear Company ("No Bag! No Sag!") and started hanging out in Louie's, a bar on Bleeker Street in New York, which has since been metamorphosed into the Now Bar in a disastrous change of ownership. Every night after work I'd walk down to Louie's and drink beer until I got drowsy and then I'd go home and go to sleep. Everybody there on weeknights—Bobby, Tommy, Jr., Robert, Wesley, and the rest whose names I forget—did the same thing, except they all lived, except for Bobby, right accross the street in the Hotel Greenwich, a fleatrap of the first rank. There were 2 lesbian barmaids, Joey and Chopsy. Joey was the young pretty one; she still works there and the last time I dropped in, all the old regulars were gone and she pretended she didn't know me. Anyway, nobody ever picked-up anyone in Louie's, they just drank. Once Tommy, an Indian longshoreman from New England, turned to a zoftig female human who was sitting next to him and asked slurredly, "Could I eat your pussy?" But he literally fell off his stool in an unconscious mass of drunken midden and the pert young miss just kept on drinking, so that was the end of that.

Then one brisk autumn Friday night, a few days before my 19th birthday, I got picked up in Louie's. She was some washed-up fashion model then working as an interior decorator. She was drunk. Her name was VS (that spelling might be incorrect). She began babbling to me about this son of hers whom she seemed to think was some kind of gift to humankind's manifest destiny. He seemed like a little shit to me, the way she described him. She showed me a photo of him and I said, "Yeah, he looks like a wonderful kid. I bet he really loves you." She liked that. Heh-heh. About the third time she excused herself to piss, it dawned on me that I should check out her body structure as she walked toward the john. She looked pretty good, so I started buying her drinks. After a few we were holding hands and rubbing each other's thighs beneath the bar. Soon I was fairly sloshed and I asked her if she wanted to split somewhere. Just then, 2 friends whom I hadn't seen in months, Greg and Jim, came sauntering in, waffled-out on some orange acid. We all decided to go to Slugs to see Pharoah Sanders. Then, all of a sudden, this unbelievably drunken 6'2" girlfriend of ex-fashion-model-with-the-son-with-the-universe-in-his-eyes is babbling to her about how she shouldn't *dare* go with those three. Why, *look* at them! They take *drugs!* You can tell! You'll be sorry, Valerie, I'm telling you, don't you *dare* go with them! So I buy her another drink and she decides to go, becoming totally freaked when my friends start ingesting more drugs in the car. We get to Slugs' and Pharoah Sanders turns out to be Yusef Lateef, so we split and I talk Jim into giving Valerie and I a ride way up to her place in Riverdale. He renumerated himself, I later found out, by lifting $100 and change from Valerie's purse—which is no mean feat to perform when you're driving up the West Side Highway stoned on acid at the same time.

To say that she lived in opulence would be only to scratch the proverbial surface. Bearskin rugs. Marble tabletops. Picture windows. And all over the place, pictures of No. 1 Son.

I didn't like the way her snatch tasted, sached as it was with Rose Scent Cupid's Quiver, but I kept eating away at it and then she sucked my cock and then we fucked and she cried and cried she loved me and I felt really weird and then she just slept and I lay there smoking Kools, my first truly Heraclitean epiphany ever, that it *does* all flow and you never know where on the river's shores the tides of honky tonk seraphim and shot glasses will puke you up. It was then that I realized that John Barleycorn would, through thick and thin, remain a friend for life.

But then I started to sober up and I did not want to see her face in the day light (years later, when I heard Rod Stewart's "Maggie May", I was sure that he also had seen the wallet-size likeness of No. 1 Son) and it was getting close on 5 a.m. so I woke her and told her I had to split somewhere and talked her into giving me a lift downtown in her car. When Jim had robbed her, however, he had also taken her ID's and driver's license by mistake it seems, so I had to to do some extra babbling to get her to drive her car (she was under the impression that she had misplaced the wallet in the apartment somewhere). She decides to bring her poodle with her.

The elevator down to the garage was well-lighted and she looked older and more burnt-out now, with that ridiculous little white poodle in her arms and that nervous eyeball action checking me out in the silence.

When she dropped me off she reminded me once more that her phone number was in the book, but she didn't seem to like me so much anymore.

That was the first time I ever picked anyone up in a bar.

I never picked-up anyone else in Louie's during the next 2 or so months that I continued to hang out there. I did however get some suicide case from Pennsylvania who started to have a nervous breakdown when I began to streetfuck her against a building on Thompson Street. She said she wanted to jump off the Brooklyn Bridge, but since she didn't know how to get to the Brooklyn Bridge and didn't have enough money for a cab, I decided she was safe, as was the case obviously because I received a note from her c/o: Louie's a few days later telling me to come up to Chester, Pennsylvania, and live with her. Wunnerful.

After Louie's, I started going to new bars, most notably St. Adrian's, a then newly open bar (and now closed down) on Broadway near 3rd. Street.

King Street Smith and I used to go there to fuck Jewish girls from Queens. Every weekend night the 2 of us would get roaring drunk (by this time I had graduated to gin and bourbon) and start babble-pawing forms in the dimly lighted crowd. I would get miraculously drunk (one night Joel, one of the bartenders, kept count and it turned out that I had knocked-off 14 Jack Daniel's on the rocks and 7 bottles of Budweiser) that I didn't care who I fucked. Once I even tried to pick-up a *dwarf* at 4 a.m. closing time—and I got rejected too!

One night as I was walking to St. Adrian's a girl approached me and asked me if I had any speed. She was nuts. I told her to come to the bar with me and get drunk. She said she didn't drink but she agreed to come anyway. She told me her life story. After a few hours of sip-sip she was pretty drunk. I was really loaded myself. She was really pretty cute and I asked her if I could sleep with her. A lot of times, if I felt someone would react adversely to being asked if they wanted to fuck, I'd just tell them that I only wanted to hold them all night in my arms, which usually worked. One time, though, someone came home with me and *really* didn't want to get laid. I think I was drunk and tripping at the same time and I had to struggle with her to get it in. I don't remember that night too well. Anyway, this particular nutso (her name was C. T. S.) said OK, sure, let's go to bed. We were so fucked-up that we just went right next door to the Broadway Central Hotel, a run-down welfare dump that averaged one fire and one murder per year. We registered under the name of Mr. & Mrs. Drunke. It turned out that she was waiting for the results of her syphilis test, but I was loaded, I just, oh, well, what the fuck. We fucked 4 times that night and in the morning I jerked-off as she kissed my body. Then I remembered that now I'd have to go for a blood test too but I postponed it for a couple of days because it was St. Patty's Day and King Street Smith and I were going to march in the parade down Fifth Avenue. I felt really wretched that day, but the same afternoon Jonathan Eisen and I drove up to Vassar to make tape recordings of bad jokes (we were doing a book called *Margaret Rutherford in Siam,* a book which we subsequently never sold) and we met a bunch of sophistoid females and I talked them into robbing some booze from this little hick liquor store. We went back to their dorms and one of the girls (I think her name was J. O.) and I got wasted on Old Grand Dad's 101. I knew there was a chance that I might have syphilis, but I fucked her anyways, figuring that I'd drop her a line if the blood test was positive. Jon Eisen didn't get drunk (he doesn't drink) so he didn't get laid. The next morning I had a really bad hangover and this dorm lady came around and threw Eisen and I out.

I also met S. K. at St. Adrian's. Now we're married and living happily ever after. One night she was real sick, with something like a 102° temperature and we fucked and it was the hottest, steamingest vagina I've ever slipped Percy into. It was sort of like a thermos of hot oysters.

Once I ran into one of S.'s friends in a bar and brought her home and tried to fuck her (L.) but I was too drunk and I fell asleep while I was trying to get her to take my pants off. I woke up at 2 o'clock the next morning and she was gone and the television was still on. The only other times I fell asleep while fucking were once when I was fucking M. F. in September of '71 and the first time I fucked E. B. in January of '72. Drunk on both accounts.

Once in San Juan there was this really beautiful lesbian who hated to fuck guys but we got so drunk that she let me fuck her. We were drinking gin and tonics at El Batey, a Puerto Rican bar that stays open all night. (The only cities in the States where the bars stay open all night are Key West, New Orleans, and Las Vegas.)

I met the notorious Hound while drinking. King Street Smith and I were drinking away and we picked up the Hound and her friend Swifty, both older women. We drank until the bars closed and then went back to the Hound's place and fucked them during "Modern Farmer" at 6 a.m. I fucked her a few times after that and the Air-Raid Kid and Richard Meltzer both tried to fuck her, too. One night when Jon Tiven was in town we set him up with her, but she wasn't home when we came calling.

Then there was Wildebeaste, a seventeen-year-old nymphomaniac from Jersey City (her real name is C.) who used to buy me whiskey because she knew I'd only fuck her if I was drunk. Now she's married.

And then of course, there's the world's worst fuck, whom I also met at St. Adrian's. Her name is S. T. and she is the worst fuck on the sets, so remember the name. Her father was some kind of famous painter or something but I never heard of him. I saw her three times; the first time I didn't fuck her because she had some kind of cunt disease and I wasn't drunk enough to brush it aside (I'd only been drinking beer). The second time I saw her I wanted to suck her pussy, but she said she was menstruating and she didn't want me to, so I just fucked her and it was like necrophilia without any of the sensationalism. And after I got my cookies off, she asked me with contrived openness, "Well, how am I as a fuck?" Mumble, mumble. And then I saw her again and I was tripping on red acid and drinking whiskey too and it was snowing out and I got wiped-out and decided to bring her home, but when she got in bed, all she did was talk about how talented she was. Great actress, great poetess, great this, great that. So I left her there and went downtown to see L. G., but she didn't even let me touch her and she said my breath stank (she was always against drinking) and I got mad and delivered one of my famous "Part of the Universe" speeches and split and went to a bar and then back home to Miss Talent. In the morning she borrowed $5 from me and she still hasn't paid me back. So she's not only a bad fuck, but she doesn't pay her debts either.

His slurred voice comes out over the tape, addressing some imaginary audience: *"We are here tonight, ladies and gentlemen, laying down some fine sounds that you haven't heard and probably will never hear on the radio, simply because Decca is a stupid-ass record company and refuses to . . . "*

He laughs. "I didn't mean for you to hear that." He hits the Fast Forward switch until he finds "Game of Love."

It's not the old Wayne Fontana song, it's a Screamin' Jay original, a slow, ballad-type thing about some guy caught between his wife and fresh cunt and how he has to choose between one and the other. As the song progresses, Jay's wife grows ostensibly more and more pissed-off. I'm beginning to feel like I'm in a movie.

"All right, Jinny, you win," he spits out as the song fades off.

"Did you listen closely to that song? Did you?" Jinny flares back at him in her Filipino accent.

"Will you come *on*," Jay moans, "the lyrics keep repeating over and over and over and over and over that the wife finally won, so what's the problem? What's the argument? The tune is dedicated to the *wife*. You understand?"

"Yeah," shouts the wife, things getting progressively more unreal, "but at the end it says 'I'm gonna love you forever.' Now *what* does that imply, huh?"

"Just what it says! 'I'm gonna love you forever!' I'm talkin' to the *wife!*"

"Don't give me that! What you're saying is that the wife won but at the same time you're gonna love this other woman forever."

"Oh, for Godsakes, you misinterpret it!"

"No, no. Not me. Maybe *you* do!"

"Me? Come *on*, Jinny, who recorded the goddam thing?!"

"You! And the song says you're in love with this other . . . "

"Oh, come on, that's enough! I'm *finished*, I don't got no more to say."

"Well, then, you shouldn't have brought it up."

"God*dam!* Nick wanted to hear the tune! Blame Nick!"

"Well, you know, then, you, you don't have to . . . "

"Oh, man, come on, let's not have an argument, it's only a goddam *song*."

t the age of 43, it's been over 15 years since Screamin' Jay Hawkins recorded "I ut a Spell on You."

"I originally wrote the song 'cause at that time I was going out with some girl o decided that she was gonna put me down. I decided that I didn't want her put me down, so I wrote a song to her. And the song was called 'I Put a Spell You.'

I had messed around with about three different companies prior to going to umbia. 'I Put a Spell on You' was actually released prior to Okeh, which was bsidiary of Columbia. It was released on the Grand label in Philadelphia. It the same song, but it was a sweet ballad. No gimmicks. No groans. No ms. No moans. Just a ballad. And then I got picked up by Columbia.

## 19

I'd say you might call this "found art," if art it be: four lines taken directly from the spread-copy of a dirty magazine.

# Valerie

Valerie's torrid flesh
sings with the lyrics of
passion and singes with the
heat of burning desire

# 20

# Screamin' Jay Hawkins and the Monster

A year, two years ago, he stayed perpetually oiled. Black & White Scotch. Pre-served in alcohol, he used to say. Drunk. Once, in the early '60's, traveling from Jamaica to Boston, he wound up in Buffalo after boarding the wrong plane at what was then, in those days before the donkey's demise, Idlewild Airport in New York. Blearily thinking himself to be in Bean Town, he hopped a taxi and asked to be taken to a certain hotel where he had a reservation. The hackie to him there was no such address, no such hotel. Jay got pissed, jumped out of cab and found a couple of Buffalo's finest. They told him the same thing wasn't until later that evening, whilst sobering up in the clink, that he real he was in the wrong city. Which is pretty drunk.

He's on the wagon these days, though. One of those cyclical drying-out ods. Coffee, lots of coffee. Orange juice. Not even a beer. And cigarett smokes Luckies. Sometimes he rolls his own Buglers, but right now it's L

He's living in some seedy hotel room nine floors above mid-town Br in Manhattan with his wife Jinny and an obnoxious four-month-old cat named Cookie. There's a *Jet* calendar on the wall. Hats of various d weirdness on nails over the bed. The TV's on, but no volume. He's sittin bed in a wool knit hat, Hawaiian sport shirt and horn-rimmed glasses Frank Sinatra album off his record player. There's a little ceramic fc ashtray next to him where he snuffs his Luckies. He hasn't been sha and he's not overly enthused about having his picture taken.

There are a slew of reel-to-reel tapes lying around, stuff he recor years for sundry record companies that never got off the shelf. The a label that says "Game of Love" on it. Thinking that it was a cut Jay doing the Wayne Fontana & The Mindbenders song, I ask hin He looked at me as if I had just said something I wasn't suppo turned to his wife and said, "Did you hear which song he want gives him a dirty look. He makes with the little noises of resigna the tape up.

Arnold Makson was the head of Columbia at the time, and he felt we had to do something different in regards to the song. So he brought in a case of Italian Swiss Colony Muscatel and we all got our heads bent. Me, Panama Francis, Al Lukas, Big Al Sears, LeRoy Kirkland, Sam "The Man" Taylor, Mickey "Guitar" Baker. We all got blind drunk. Ten days later, the record came out on the Okeh label. I listened to it and I heard all those drunken screams and groans and yells. And that's how I became Screamin' Jay Hawkins."

When the Okeh version of "I Put a Spell on You" hit the transistor scene in 1956, it became, to put things mildly, a sensation. The collective pubes of the breathing universe were brashly tweaked by this human known as Screamin' Jay, a gent who not only puked forth one of the first truly rock 'n' roll retch-forms to sully the cultural doilies of America, but who also seemed to fuck, shit, piss, fart, and do the Dallas Two-Step with his larynx.

The record sold a quarter of a million copies. Puritans and mores-punks across the nation felt that the song's closing segment was an aural portrait of unimaginably heinous goings-on. Screamin' Jay's vocal hallucinations were accused of being invocative of everything from cannibalism to fucking your baby sister in the heinie. A concession was made: the groan-coda was censored from the song. Not enough, screamed American mom-hood, driven sleepless by spectral visions of their 12-year-old daughters being forced to suck this nefarious cannibal's 14" dong under the threat of a curare-dipped blow-dart. The song was completely banned from radio. But the sticky teenage mid-brains would not be so easily allayed. The record went on to sell another quarter-million copies by word of mouth.

Jalacy Hawkins went on the road. Jalacy Hawkins encountered certain problems, problems both of the soul and of the meat.

"I didn't know what I had done. This record comes out and I've created a monster. Man, it was *weird*. I was forced to live the life of a monster. I'd go to do my act at Rockland Palace and there'd be all these goddam mothers walking the street with picket signs: WE DON'T WANT OUR DAUGHTERS TO LOOK AT SCREAMIN' JAY HAWKINS! I mean, I'm some kinda bogeyman. I come outa coffins. Skulls, snakes, crawlin' hands, fire and all that mess."

He had troubles with the caskets he used in his act also. He first used one in 1956 at an Alan Freed Show at the Paramount in New York. For his first few shows he used rented coffins, which usually set him back about $50 a throw. Then, the National Coffin Association got on to him and accused him of "making fun of the dead." They sent word around to all the funeral parlors not to rent any more coffins to one Mr. Jalacy Hawkins. He finally bought his own for $850.

Jay remembers some unpleasant run-ins with certain notable good guys of the early rock scenario.

"Somewhere around 1956 or so, there was this guy by the name of Bob Horn who did *American Bandstand* from the Philadelphia Arena, which was located at

46th and Market, in West Philadelphia. He got busted for a certain reason which isn't necessary to discuss at the present time, and that's when Dick Clark took over *Bandstand*. And when he did, he started off at the Steel Pier in Atlantic City, New Jersey. He called me to open his first show for him. He was so pleased with the opening that he asked me to stay over and do the show the second day also. His parting words to me were, 'If I can ever do anything for you, don't hesitate to call me.' And then when I made 'Shattered' and a few other records for Decca, I sent word to Dick Clark, asking him if he would please play my records on his show. The reply which I got back was: 'Who's Screamin' Jay Hawkins?' So I said, To hell with you too, Jack. Man, there's some assholes in this business, some real *ass*holes. People forget. Quickly."

And then there's Jay's First meeting with Paul Anka, formerly of "Diana"— "Lonely Boy"—"Puppy Love" fame, who's currently occupied with Bunetta-Anka Management and hosting cerebral palsy telethons:

"In 1957, I was on a show with the Cadillacs, Billy Williams, Billy & Lillie Ford, and Fats Domino. A young kid by the name of Paul Anka was on the show. He had just had a hit tune out called 'Diana.' I'm already tired, I just come off the road. Fats Domino was slated to close the show, but Fats cancelled out for some reason which we don't have to go into here. My manager asked me to go on in Fats Domino's spot. So I insisted on the closing spot on the show, and I was politely told that Paul Anka was going to close the show. I said, 'To hell with Paul Anka.' So Paul Anka walks over to me and he says, 'I'll come to your funeral.' What a goddam punk."

After a few years, Jay got sick of things. He felt, and still feels, that there was some vaguely organized conspiracy that kept his records from getting airplay after "I Put a Spell on You." His Epic albums went nowhere.

"I guess I've rubbed a lot of people the wrong way, but when you work your heart out for somebody and they pay you half your money in cash and the other half by check and that check bounces, or they stop payment on it, or you spend your bread travellin' to a gig and work hard and then some cat stands there with five or six musclemen and tells you that he ain't gonna pay you 'cause he didn't make his money, you get to the point where you start questioning things. . . .

"I used to go with a girl in Philadelphia. Some disc-jockey hit her. I punched his face. He never played any of my records again. . . ."

"In those days, a nigger wasn't supposed to talk back, wasn't supposed to open his goddam mouth. Wasn't even supposed to say the word 'nigger.' Now things have changed cause they found out that some of those niggers will kill ya. It's as simple as that: in those days nobody fought back . . . I can't be concerned with other people, cause I'm a nigger and I speak from a nigger's viewpoint. . . .

"I got fed up. I went to Honolulu for ten years 'cause I figured the world wasn't ready for me. In the meantime, all these people are recording my goddam stuff. Nina Simone. Alan Price. The Animals. Creedence Clearwater Revival. The

# 19

I'd say you might call this "found art," if art it be: four lines taken directly from the spread-copy of a dirty magazine.

# Valerie

Valerie's torrid flesh
sings with the lyrics of
passion and singes with the
heat of burning desire

# 20

# Screamin' Jay Hawkins and the Monster

A year, two years ago, he stayed perpetually oiled. Black & White Scotch. Preserved in alcohol, he used to say. Drunk. Once, in the early '60's, traveling from Jamaica to Boston, he wound up in Buffalo after boarding the wrong plane at what was then, in those days before the donkey's demise, Idlewild Airport in New York. Blearily thinking himself to be in Bean Town, he hopped a taxi and asked to be taken to a certain hotel where he had a reservation. The hackie told him there was no such address, no such hotel. Jay got pissed, jumped out of the cab and found a couple of Buffalo's finest. They told him the same thing. It wasn't until later that evening, whilst sobering up in the clink, that he realized he was in the wrong city. Which is pretty drunk.

He's on the wagon these days, though. One of those cyclical drying-out periods. Coffee, lots of coffee. Orange juice. Not even a beer. And cigarettes. He smokes Luckies. Sometimes he rolls his own Buglers, but right now it's Luckies.

He's living in some seedy hotel room nine floors above mid-town Broadway in Manhattan with his wife Jinny and an obnoxious four-month-old Siamese cat named Cookie. There's a *Jet* calendar on the wall. Hats of various degrees of weirdness on nails over the bed. The TV's on, but no volume. He's sitting on the bed in a wool knit hat, Hawaiian sport shirt and horn-rimmed glasses, taping a Frank Sinatra album off his record player. There's a little ceramic foot-shaped ashtray next to him where he snuffs his Luckies. He hasn't been shaving lately and he's not overly enthused about having his picture taken.

There are a slew of reel-to-reel tapes lying around, stuff he recorded over the years for sundry record companies that never got off the shelf. There's one with a label that says "Game of Love" on it. Thinking that it was a cut of Screamin' Jay doing the Wayne Fontana & The Mindbenders song, I ask him to put it on. He looked at me as if I had just said something I wasn't supposed to say. He turned to his wife and said, "Did you hear which song he wants to hear?" She gives him a dirty look. He makes with the little noises of resignation and hooks the tape up.

His slurred voice comes out over the tape, addressing some imaginary audience: *"We are here tonight, ladies and gentlemen, laying down some fine sounds that you haven't heard and probably will never hear on the radio, simply because Decca is a stupid-ass record company and refuses to . . . "*

He laughs. "I didn't mean for you to hear that." He hits the Fast Forward switch until he finds "Game of Love."

It's not the old Wayne Fontana song, it's a Screamin' Jay original, a slow, ballad-type thing about some guy caught between his wife and fresh cunt and how he has to choose between one and the other. As the song progresses, Jay's wife grows ostensibly more and more pissed-off. I'm beginning to feel like I'm in a movie.

"All right, Jinny, you win," he spits out as the song fades off.

"Did you listen closely to that song? Did you?" Jinny flares back at him in her Filipino accent.

"Will you come *on*," Jay moans, "the lyrics keep repeating over and over and over and over and over that the wife finally won, so what's the problem? What's the argument? The tune is dedicated to the *wife*. You understand?"

"Yeah," shouts the wife, things getting progressively more unreal, "but at the end it says 'I'm gonna love you forever.' Now *what* does that imply, huh?"

"Just what it says! 'I'm gonna love you forever!' I'm talkin' to the *wife!*"

"Don't give me that! What you're saying is that the wife won but at the same time you're gonna love this other woman forever."

"Oh, for Godsakes, you misinterpret it!"

"No, no. Not me. Maybe *you* do!"

"Me? Come *on*, Jinny, who recorded the goddam thing?!"

"You! And the song says you're in love with this other . . . "

"Oh, come on, that's enough! I'm *finished*, I don't got no more to say."

"Well, then, you shouldn't have brought it up."

"God*dam!* Nick wanted to hear the tune! Blame Nick!"

"Well, you know, then, you, you don't have to . . . "

"Oh, man, come on, let's not have an argument, it's only a goddam *song*."

At the age of 43, it's been over 15 years since Screamin' Jay Hawkins recorded "I Put a Spell on You."

"I originally wrote the song 'cause at that time I was going out with some girl who decided that she was gonna put me down. I decided that I didn't want her to put me down, so I wrote a song to her. And the song was called 'I Put a Spell on You.'

"I had messed around with about three different companies prior to going to Columbia. 'I Put a Spell on You' was actually released prior to Okeh, which was a subsidiary of Columbia. It was released on the Grand label in Philadelphia. It was the same song, but it was a sweet ballad. No gimmicks. No groans. No screams. No moans. Just a ballad. And then I got picked up by Columbia.

Arnold Makson was the head of Columbia at the time, and he felt we had to do something different in regards to the song. So he brought in a case of Italian Swiss Colony Muscatel and we all got our heads bent. Me, Panama Francis, Al Lukas, Big Al Sears, LeRoy Kirkland, Sam "The Man" Taylor, Mickey "Guitar" Baker. We all got blind drunk. Ten days later, the record came out on the Okeh label. I listened to it and I heard all those drunken screams and groans and yells. And that's how I became Screamin' Jay Hawkins."

When the Okeh version of "I Put a Spell on You" hit the transistor scene in 1956, it became, to put things mildly, a sensation. The collective pubes of the breathing universe were brashly tweaked by this human known as Screamin' Jay, a gent who not only puked forth one of the first truly rock 'n' roll retch-forms to sully the cultural doilies of America, but who also seemed to fuck, shit, piss, fart, and do the Dallas Two-Step with his larynx.

The record sold a quarter of a million copies. Puritans and mores-punks across the nation felt that the song's closing segment was an aural portrait of unimaginably heinous goings-on. Screamin' Jay's vocal hallucinations were accused of being invocative of everything from cannibalism to fucking your baby sister in the heinie. A concession was made: the groan-coda was censored from the song. Not enough, screamed American mom-hood, driven sleepless by spectral visions of their 12-year-old daughters being forced to suck this nefarious cannibal's 14" dong under the threat of a curare-dipped blow-dart. The song was completely banned from radio. But the sticky teenage mid-brains would not be so easily allayed. The record went on to sell another quarter-million copies by word of mouth.

Jalacy Hawkins went on the road. Jalacy Hawkins encountered certain problems, problems both of the soul and of the meat.

"I didn't know what I had done. This record comes out and I've created a monster. Man, it was *weird*. I was forced to live the life of a monster. I'd go to do my act at Rockland Palace and there'd be all these goddam mothers walking the street with picket signs: WE DON'T WANT OUR DAUGHTERS TO LOOK AT SCREAMIN' JAY HAWKINS! I mean, I'm some kinda hogeyman. I come outa coffins. Skulls, snakes, crawlin' hands, fire and all that mess."

He had troubles with the caskets he used in his act also. He first used one in 1956 at an Alan Freed Show at the Paramount in New York. For his first few shows he used rented coffins, which usually set him back about $50 a throw. Then, the National Coffin Association got on to him and accused him of "making fun of the dead." They sent word around to all the funeral parlors not to rent any more coffins to one Mr. Jalacy Hawkins. He finally bought his own for $850.

Jay remembers some unpleasant run-ins with certain notable good guys of the early rock scenario.

"Somewhere around 1956 or so, there was this guy by the name of Bob Horn who did *American Bandstand* from the Philadelphia Arena, which was located at

46th and Market, in West Philadelphia. He got busted for a certain reason which isn't necessary to discuss at the present time, and that's when Dick Clark took over *Bandstand*. And when he did, he started off at the Steel Pier in Atlantic City, New Jersey. He called me to open his first show for him. He was so pleased with the opening that he asked me to stay over and do the show the second day also. His parting words to me were, 'If I can ever do anything for you, don't hesitate to call me.' And then when I made 'Shattered' and a few other records for Decca, I sent word to Dick Clark, asking him if he would please play my records on his show. The reply which I got back was: 'Who's Screamin' Jay Hawkins?' So I said, To hell with you too, Jack. Man, there's some assholes in this business, some real *ass*holes. People forget. Quickly."

And then there's Jay's First meeting with Paul Anka, formerly of "Diana"— "Lonely Boy"—"Puppy Love" fame, who's currently occupied with Bunetta-Anka Management and hosting cerebral palsy telethons:

"In 1957, I was on a show with the Cadillacs, Billy Williams, Billy & Lillie Ford, and Fats Domino. A young kid by the name of Paul Anka was on the show. He had just had a hit tune out called 'Diana.' I'm already tired, I just come off the road. Fats Domino was slated to close the show, but Fats cancelled out for some reason which we don't have to go into here. My manager asked me to go on in Fats Domino's spot. So I insisted on the closing spot on the show, and I was politely told that Paul Anka was going to close the show. I said, 'To hell with Paul Anka.' So Paul Anka walks over to me and he says, 'I'll come to your funeral.' What a goddam punk."

After a few years, Jay got sick of things. He felt, and still feels, that there was some vaguely organized conspiracy that kept his records from getting airplay after "I Put a Spell on You." His Epic albums went nowhere.

"I guess I've rubbed a lot of people the wrong way, but when you work your heart out for somebody and they pay you half your money in cash and the other half by check and that check bounces, or they stop payment on it, or you spend your bread travellin' to a gig and work hard and then some cat stands there with five or six musclemen and tells you that he ain't gonna pay you 'cause he didn't make his money, you get to the point where you start questioning things. . . .

"I used to go with a girl in Philadelphia. Some disc-jockey hit her. I punched his face. He never played any of my records again. . . ."

"In those days, a nigger wasn't supposed to talk back, wasn't supposed to open his goddam mouth. Wasn't even supposed to say the word 'nigger.' Now things have changed cause they found out that some of those niggers will kill ya. It's as simple as that: in those days nobody fought back . . . I can't be concerned with other people, cause I'm a nigger and I speak from a nigger's viewpoint. . . .

"I got fed up. I went to Honolulu for ten years 'cause I figured the world wasn't ready for me. In the meantime, all these people are recording my goddam stuff. Nina Simone. Alan Price. The Animals. Creedence Clearwater Revival. The

Who. The Trackers. Them. Manfred Mann. The Seekers. Audience. Arthur Brown. Melvin Van Peebles copied my whole act and put it on Broadway . . .

"I mean, I've had some piss luck. All those people 'cept me having hits with my songs. I started Chuck Willis wearin' turbans. I started Little Richard wearin' capes. Lord Sutch. Arthur Brown. Look at *Shaft*. Look at *Blacula*. They're all usin' coffins. Everybody at one time or another has taken a little something from me and I get this impression that everybody's going places with what I was doing fifteen goddam years ago. Everybody but me. . . .

"Decca promised me the *world* if I'd only record for them. So what happened? Nothing. The record doesn't even get *played* on the radio *once*. . . .

"Jesus, I recorded a country & western song for Phillips ('Too Many Teardrops'). I mean, that song was *something*. The steel guitar player was from the California Symphony Orchestra and the rest of the band were jazz musicians. So what does the record company do. They only release the record in *Hawaii!* Did you ever in your life hear of anything like that?

"I recorded 'Itty Bitty Pretty One' recently, and what happens? A week later the Jackson Five record it and have a hit with it and meanwhile the company I cut it for (Hot Line) goes bankrupt and the record never gets distributed. It doesn't make sense to me. . . ."

Hawkins' proclivity toward continually receiving the faecal end of the stick in his native country is fortunately somewhat offset by the appreciation, though minimal, he has accrued Over There.

His bimonthly royalty statements always include passably nice-sized residuals from England, Germany, Istanbul, Australia, Austria, Japan, Mexico, Portugal, Spain, Finland, and other such places.

Jay's "Constipation Blues" (*"It was the first time I'd ever been constipated so I decided to put it on wax. To this day I don't know what brought it on. I thought it was pretty unusual, y'know? I was in the hospital at the time and I said to myself, a subject like this must be put to music"*) was a smash hit in Japan, and only Japan, in 1968. (*"I guess the pains of not bein' able to get it out were understood by the Japanese."*)

These days, Screamin' Jay is a bit more sedate. He's getting ready for an extended concert tour of France. He recently recorded Paul McCartney's "Monkberry Moon Delight" (which McCartney once said was inspired by Jay in the first place) on the Queen Bee label. And he seems to be more shit-tired of the old Screamin' Jay Hawkins phantasm-image than ever.

"If it were up to me I wouldn't be Screamin' Jay Hawkins. My screamin' was always just my way of being happy on stage. James Brown, he does an awful lot of screamin' himself, but he didn't become Screamin' James Brown.

"I mean, I've got a voice. Why can't people just take me as a regular singer without makin' a bogeyman out of me? My musical background is people like Roy Milton, Wynonie Harris, Roy Brown, Eddie 'Cleanhead' Vinson, Jay McShann, Louis Jordan, Varetta Dillard, Big Maybelle, Roy Hamilton, people like that. I come along and get a little weird and all of a sudden I'm a monster or something, people won't listen to me as a singer. I'm some kind of monster. I don't wanna be a black Vincent Price *(Jay was offered the title role in* Blacula *by Jack Hammer, which he turned down)*. I'm sick of it! I hate it! I wanna do goddam opera! I wanna *sing!* I wanna do *Figaro!* I wanna do *Le Sacre du Printemps!* 'Ave Maria'! 'The Lord's Prayer'! I wanna do real *singing.* I'm sick of being a monster."

# 21

The Church of St. Mark's in-the-Bowerie still had pews in it when Meltzer and I went there to see our friends Patti Smith and Lenny Kaye perform together for the first time. It was the only time I ever sniffed lighter fluid in a church.

After being dumped by the foundering *Oui,* my next decent-paying work came a year later through *Penthouse,* which is where this interview with Patti appeared in the spring of 1976.

# Patti Smith

Patricia Lee Smith hit the linen on December 30, 1946, in Chicago, and was raised, the eldest of four children, in Deptford Township, New Jersey. She had been slapped about by tuberculosis; she was a frail-seeming punkling, skinny and daydreamy. She attended Glassboro State College, briefly, and tried doing piecework at a toy factory. Both made her carsick. In 1967 she came to New York. From there she went to Paris with her sister Linda. She wanted to be an artist, but her drawings became poems. She returned to New Jersey, then to New York, where she slowly but steadily became arch moll of rhythm'd word.

Patti coauthored a book with playwright Sam Shepard, *Mad Dog Blues & Other Plays.* She appeared in a film, *Robert Mapplethorpe Gets His Nipple Pierced.* Late in 1971, Telegraph Books published her first volume of poems, *Seventh Heaven,* which she dedicated to Mickey Spillane and Anita Pallenberg. She began to publish prose-poem essays about rock 'n' roll in such magazines as *Rolling Stone* and *Creem.* A second book of poems, *Kodak,* appeared in 1972. By the time Gotham Book Mart published her *Witt* in 1973, Patti had become a legend on the New York poetry circuit. She was feared, revered, and her public readings elicited the sort of gut response that had been alien to poetry for more than a few decades. Word spread, and people who avoided poetry as the stuff of four-eyed pedants found themselves oohing and howling at what came out of Patti's mouth. Established poets feared for their credence. Many well-known poets refused to go on after Patti at a reading, she was that awesome.

The music, too. It had started with just Lenny Kaye on guitar. Intuitively the two reinvented melic poetry. The band grew: piano, another guitar, then later drums. Finally, after all those years, rock 'n' roll had a poet.

In early spring of 1974, financed by her friend, artist Robert Mapplethorpe, Patti issued two thousand copies of a record, "Piss Factory" coupled with "Hey, Joe," on the Mer label. The rhythmics were coarse and truculent, the images were alternately raw and aflash with hallucination. In "Hey, Joe" she transmuted a sixties rock classic into an *Iliad* of subliminal violence that culminated with a fantasy image of Patty Hearst worshipping black revolutionaries in a world ruled by phantom guitars and confused girl-things.

Poetry readings became concerts, audiences grew. Patti spewed forth a mix of sheer rock 'n' roll power and delicately wrought poetry. She sang a Marvelettes song. "The Hunter Gets Captured by the Game," or sometimes Van

Morrison's "Gloria," and then, somehow, she was in some ineffable dream-closet:

> *yum yum the stars are out. I'll never forget how you smelled*
> *that night. like cheddar cheese melting under flourescent light.*
> *like a day old rainbow fish. what a dish. gotta lick my lips. gotta*
> *dream I daydream. thorazine brain cloud. rain rain comes*
> *coming down.*

The music ebbed to feedback sounds and low piano:

> *I'm gonna peep in bo's bodice. lay down darling don't be*
> *modest let me slip my hand in. ohhh thats soft thats nice that's*
> *not used up. ohh don't cry. wet whats wet? oh that. heh heh.*
> *thats just the rain lambie pie. now don't squirm. let me put my*
> *rubber on. . . .*[1]

The record companies came to sniff and hedge. Finally, she signed with Arista, and her debut album, *Horses,* was released late in 1975. Everyone from *Rolling Stone* to the *New York Times* showered it with petals. Still, some said, Patti was too weird to sweep the masses. The ever underestimated masses, however, proved otherwise, and Patti and her album rose to the top of the national charts.

This interview was conducted in New York City. It begins with the one question with which all interviews should begin.

**Penthouse:** Were you a horny teenager, Patti?

**Smith:** Yeah, I was horny, but I was innocent 'cause I was a real late bloomer and not particularly attractive. In fact, homely. See, nobody told me that girls got horny. It was tragic 'cause I had all these feelings inside me. I was like one of those boys in school who flap their legs frantically under the desk. I always had this weird feeling between my legs and I had no idea what it was. I didn't know girls masturbated. I never touched myself or anything . . . I did it all in my mind. I was so horny in school it felt like my body was filled with electricity. I felt like I had neon bones or something. All my report cards said. "Patti Lee daydreams too much." I didn't know what it was but I couldn't wait to get home each day. And when I got home I'd just lay down and let my mind spill out, y'know?

Remember when Anne Frank was real big and *Life* was doing all that stuff on Nazi atrocities? Well, I'd read that stuff and I'd get really cracklin' down there. Anytime I'd read about a dog getting beaten or any weird thing, it would trig-

---

[1] From "Rape": copyright © 1973 by Patti Smith.

ger me off, and the only way I could relieve myself was by laying in bed and putting a flashlight on inside my brain. There'd be this flood of light and then these movies would start up in my mind. Nothing specifically dirty or anything, just a lot of abstract action. It was like being horny in a really vague way.

My one regret in life is that I didn't know about masturbating. To me that's really sad. Think of all that fun I could've had!

*Penthouse:* Were you a juicy date?

**Smith:** I never had any dates. I never really had any boyfriends. I was the girl who did the guys' homework. I was really crazy about guys but I was always like one of the boys. The guys I always fell in love with were completely inaccessible. I didn't want any middle-of-the road creep. I always wanted the toughest guy in school, the guy from south Philly who wore tight black pants. Y'know, the guy who carried the umbrella and wore white shirts with real thin black ties. I was really nuts over this guy named Butchie Magic 'cause he let me carry his switchblade. But I couldn't make it with guys.

I was always trying to pick guys up. I'd ask guys out and stuff like that. I had no pride. I was the biggest lurch at dances, waiting for the ladies' choice. I'd lunge at my prey like a baby wolf. I was really skinny, and guys would tell me I wasn't their type. But I was ready, y'know? I got along better with the niggers, but they didn't wanna fuck me either. They kept saying, "You gotta stay a virgin 'cause if we find the right rich colored guy he'll pay five hundred bucks for a virgin white girl." I believed in love, so it never worked out.

Y'know what it was? I was really stupid. I mean, on one hand I was totally aware, totally in tune with cosmic stuff. But when it came to basics, like the fact that I was a girl, I just never noticed it. I was so involved in my boy-rhythms that I never came to grips with the fact that I was a girl. I was twelve years old when my mother took me inside and said, "You can't be outside wrestling without a T-shirt on." It was a trauma. In fact, I got so fucked up over it when my mother gave me the big word that I was absolutely a girl and there was no changing it, that I walked out dazed on a highway with my dog Bambi and let her get hit by a fire engine.

And then that whole thing about masturbating. Most girls, I guess nobody has to tell them, they just figure it out, right? I had to be told. Some girl actually had to show me a hairbrush and demonstrate exactly what to do. I just never figured that stuff out naturally.

I'm still pretty dumb about girl stuff. For a while I said, "Ah, girls are stupid." But after seeing all these Jeanne Moreau movies, I think being a girl is where it's at. Like when I'm about thirty-five I'm gonna start wearing black cocktail dresses and become a real cunt.

*Penthouse:* Do you get a kick out of being sexy?

**Smith:** I guess I like it. Actually, the only time I ever tried to cultivate being sexy was when I read *Peyton Place*. I was about sixteen and I read that this guy's watching this woman walk and he can tell she's a good fuck by the way she walks. It's a whole passage. He's telling Allison McKenzie. "I know you're a virgin." And she says, "Well, how?" And he says, "I can tell by the way you walk." And I thought, *Uh-oh, everybody knows!* I was ashamed to be a virgin, so I tried to cultivate a fucked walk. I tried to figure out what it looked like. I figured I'd watch any hot woman I could. I mean, look at Jeanne Moreau. You watch her walk across the street on the screen and you know she's had at least a hundred men.

**Penthouse:** In a lot of your material, such as your version of "Hey, Joe" and your poems "Rape" and "Sally," there's a preoccupation with violent sex.

**Smith:** Yeah, that's a complex thing. It's ironic how God made women, how women are real intellectual in bed. I mean, it's really hard for a woman to get out of her mind, y'know? I think guys are more emotional. Men are supposed to be the strong ones, they have pressure on them to be strong, but when it comes to sex men are much more emotional than women. I really don't like how women are in that respect. The only way I can lose my mind in bed is to destroy myself in a fantasy.

I wrote a poem where this guy comes in this girl's window and she's sitting there and she has this real dense mind, so he simply takes a pistol and shoves it in her mouth and shoots it. That's what I think of sperm—it's the shell that bursts brains, y'know? I mean, women need their brains burst out.

**Penthouse:** Do you feel that girls want to get slapped around?

**Smith:** Yeah. It's not masochistic or nothing. I just think that women need help in getting their minds out of bed. It's the plight of women. It took me years to get over that, to be totally, physically involved. When I was younger and couldn't come, I figured there was something wrong with me. I went to all these doctors and shit, and I kept saying. "There's something wrong with me." Most broads don't come, but nobody told *me* that. I used to beg girls in the bathroom at school. "Please tell me, is something wrong with me?" It was like, "Would you look at my pussy and see if it's made right? I'll look at yours." And all of a sudden they'd think I was a queer, y'know?

**Penthouse:** What did doctors tell you when you told them you couldn't come?

**Smith:** They'd say, "Oh-ho-ho. You're a normal young girl." They'd say stuff like, "Tell your partner to engage in more petting." Petting. Let me be your dog.

**Penthouse:** Do you jerk off a lot?

**Smith:** Only when I'm working. It's such an intense procedure for me. It's like a ritual, 'cause I take it real seriously. I try to eat some hashish and then I read a little. It doesn't have to be dirty, just so long as it's well written.

I think masturbation is a really important function in art. People don't like to hear that kind of stuff, but it's true. That's what Genet did to create. I can always tell when somebody's been jerking off. All the great writers, Alexander Trochi, William Burroughs, and Arthur Rimbaud. To me, fucking and masturbation and art is all the same because all it is is total concentration. And that's what performing is, too. When I'm doing a long piece, a ten-minute "Gloria" or a really long "Land of a Thousand Dances," I have to concentrate just like I'm trying to come with a guy or just like when I'm masturbating. A good artist's always got his hand in his zipper.

*Penthouse:* Do you feel any ties with the current flock of female writers?

**Smith:** Well, the only parts I like out of any of those women books is the dirty parts. But I don't think their dirty parts are any good, really.

Most women writers don't interest me because they're hung up with being a woman, they're hung up with being Jewish, they're hung up with being something or other. Rather than just going, just spurting, just creating. These women get so caught up with their heritage that they can never really spiral out. I mean, to me Erica Jong ain't a woman; she's just some spoiled Jewish girl who'd rather whine than go out of her brain.

They don't do anything to me, those broads. I don't care whether they're men or women, that's bullshit. A good writer can get into any gender, can get into any mouth. When I write I may be a Brando creep, or a girl laying on the floor, or a Japanese tourist, or a slob like Richard Speck. You have to be a chameleon when you're writing, and to get caught up with being a Jewish girl or a black girl or a divorced girl or a girl period, to me that's a big bore and a lot of silly bullshit.

I've never felt grounded because of my ancestry or my gender. I think until women get away from that they're not going to be great writers. Now, I can tell you about some women writers who truly are fantastic. One is Anna Kavan. She writes stories like I approach "Land of a Thousand Dances": she's caught in a haze and then a light, a little teeny light, comes through. It could be a leopard, that light, or it could be a spot of blood, it could be anything. But she hooks onto that and spirals out. And she does it within the accessible rhythms of plot, and that's really exciting. She's not hung up with being a woman, she just keeps extending herself, keeps telescoping language and plot.

Another great woman writer is Iris Sarazan, who wrote *The Runaway*. She considered herself a mare, a wild runaway. She was a really intelligent girl stuck in all these convents with a hungry mind. I identify with her 'cause of her hunger to go beyond herself. She wound up in prison, but she escaped and wrote some great books before kicking off. Her books aren't page after page of her beating her breast about how shitty she's been treated, they're books about her exciting, telescoping plans of escape. Rhythm, great wild rhythm. What Erica Jong and people like that lack is rhythm, rhythm and strength. They write only boredom, pages and pages of fidgety self-examination.

The French poet, Rimbaud, predicted that the next great crop of writers would be women. He was the first guy who ever made a big women's liberation statement, saying that when women release themselves from the long servitude of men they're really gonna gush. New rhythms, new poetries, new horrors, new beauties. And I believe in that completely. But hung-up women can't produce anything but mediocre art, and there ain't no room for mediocre art.

***Penthouse:*** Has the women's movement had anything to do with your growth as a poet?

**Smith:** No. I remember getting totally pissed off the first time I got a letter that started off with "Dear Ms. Smith." A word like Ms. is really bullshit. Vowels are the most illuminated letters in the alphabet. Vowels are the colors and souls of poetry and speech. And these assholes take the only fuckin' vowel out of the word *Miss.* So what do they have left? *Ms.* It sounds like a sick bumblebee, it sounds frigid. I mean, who the hell would ever want to stick his hand up the dress of somebody who goes around calling herself something like Ms? It's all so stupid.

I don't like answering to other people's philosophies. I don't have any philosophy. I just believe in stuff. Either I believe in something or I don't. Like, I believe in the Rolling Stones but not in the Dave Clark Five. There's nothing philosophic about it. Whenever I'm linked with a movement, it pisses me off. I like who I am. I always liked who I was and I always loved men. The only time I ever feel fucked around by men is when I fight with a guy or when a guy ditches me. And that's got nothing to do with women's lib. That has to do with being ditched.

I don't feel exploited by pictures of naked broads. I like that stuff. If it's a bad photograph or the girl's ugly, then that pisses me off. Shit, I think bodies are great.

Every time I say the word *pussy* at a poetry reading, some idiot broad rises and has a fit. "What's your definition of *pussy,* sister?" I dunno, it's a slang term. If I wanna say *pussy.* I'll say *pussy.* If I wanna say *nigger,* I'll say *nigger.* If somebody wants to call me a cracker bitch, that's cool. It's all part of being American. But all these tight-assed movements are fucking up our slang, and that eats it.

***Penthouse:*** Do you have many encounters with groupies?

**Smith:** Yeah, but they're almost always girls. They're usually pretty young, too. They try to act heavy and come on like leather. I always act as if they're real cool. I never go anyplace with them. They bring me drugs and poetry and black leather gloves and stuff like that. It's pretty funny. I don't really know what they want. I mean, I think they're actually straight girls.

The guys that I get, they're always such great losers. Really pimply faced fuck-ups with thick glasses, but a lot of heart, y'know? My heart really goes out for those kids 'cause I can still taste what it feels like to be sixteen and totally fucked up. I remember everything. And I figure if I came out of it okay, then these kids are going to be okay, too. They just need to be told that they're going to be okay, that's all.

*Penthouse:* Is there a lot of New Jersey in your stuff?

**Smith:** Yeah, south Jersey. There was a lot of railways there. All this bullshit about me being a street poet—did you ever read that shit they write about me? I had nothing to do with the streets. It's all railroad tracks, hanging out by the tracks.

I danced a lot. I'd put on a stack of records, all the Marvelettes' stuff. Most of them are in the key of A, and that's my key. I'd stand in front of the mirror and sing and dance. I guess it all goes back to that.

Most of the cool people I knew in south Jersey are dead now, or in jail, or disappeared. A couple are pimps in Philly. I haven't seen them in about twelve years, but a week doesn't go by that I don't think of 'em. The coolest things I have, the coolest rhythms, all come from my life in south Jersey and Philly. All my dance steps, all my sensibilities. I think about that old stuff a lot when I'm onstage. Those people, they haunt me in a real sweet way.

Me and my family are still real tight though. I've always been the black sheep of the family, always getting in trouble or fucking up the family name—of *Smith!* But I'm finding that in my old age I'm affecting my mother's gestures. She's all cigarettes and coffee. I told her to sing harmony on my record, but she said, "No, doll, I got a cigarette tenor." Someday I'm gonna do a jazz album called *Cigarette Tenor.*

*Penthouse:* Did you start writing when you were a kid?

**Smith:** Yeah, I decided I wanted to be a writer when I read *Little Women.* Jo was so great. I really related to her. She was a tomboy, yet guys liked her and she had a lot of boyfriends. She was a real big influence on me, as much an influence as Bob Dylan was later. She was so strong and yet she was feminine. She loved guys, she wasn't a bull or nothing. So I wanted to write. I had always been a daydreamer. I mean, I had a gang and stuff, I'd beat up Irish kids and things like that, but basically I was a daydreamer.

I was a terrible writer back then. I read a lot of Spanish poetry by Lorca and I wrote these long, stupid romances about men in love with their dead wives.

Very Spanish. Orange trees and glowing moons and incestuous brothers and sisters and fathers kneeling in the dirt trying to get their dead wives to show them warmth. Or killing their wives. It was always the same long story. Archaic language. Terrible, terrible stuff. "Ach! You are as cold in death as you were in life!" That was my big line. I thought it was really great. Then I realized I was a lousy writer so I started to paint.

*Penthouse:* What brought you back to being a writer?

**Smith:** I was living in Paris, painting and messing around. And I started to notice that my paintings were becoming more and more like cartoons, and that the words in these cartoonlike things were becoming more important to me than the paintings. I had gone to Paris to immerse myself in painting and I came back wholly involved in words and rhythms. I returned to New York and concentrated on poetry. That was in 1970, 1971.

*Penthouse:* You got a lot of heat from publishers at first, didn't you? Was it your style or your content that most editors found hard to swallow?

**Smith:** They objected to both. They said I had sick attitudes for a woman. I'd get letters, "We find your thinking and ideas and your morals very immature. Write back when you mature." I was twenty-six for Chrissake! They were looking for the usual jive-ass poetry, I guess. But now they're all knocking at my door with bags of money. Fuck 'em.

*Penthouse:* When did it first occur to you to blend rock 'n' roll with poetry?

**Smith:** I had that idea all along. I always wrote the rock 'n' roll as poetry. And I always listened to rock 'n' roll as poetry. I'm not talking about that dippy singer-songwriter stuff. I'm talking about "I Sold My Heart to the other Man," shit like that.

At first it was just me and Lenny Kaye on electric guitar farting around at poetry readings. Then it started to gather force. We advertised for a piano player. We were really just bluffing, y'know? And all these guys would come in and say, "Hey wanna boogie?" Me and Lenny were stoned, trying to talk all this cosmic bullshit to them, like, "Well, what we want to do is go over the edge." And finally Richard Sohl came in wearing a sailor suit, and he was totally stoned and totally pompous. We said, "This guy's fucked up." Lenny gave him the big cosmic spiel and Sohl said. "Look, buddy, just play." We felt like we were the ones getting auditioned. So Sohl said, "Whadaya want? Ya want some classical?" He played a bunch of Mozart. "Ya want some blues?" He played a bunch of blues. I mean, the fuckin' guy could play anything! So we started talkin' and it turned out that he'd been raised as a Jehovah's Witness, which I had been too. We'd both rebelled against the same shit, and that helped. So we just brought him in.

And then we started looking for another guitarist. We had days and days of guitar players, all sorts of maniac baby geniuses from Long island, kids with $900 guitars who couldn't play anything. Mother had sent them—in a cab! We'd make them do forty minutes of "Gloria." I'd go off on this long poem about a blue T-bird smashing into a wall of sound or some shit like that and Lenny would keep the same three chords going, louder and louder. And we'd see who dropped out first. If the guy auditioning dropped out first that meant he wasn't any good. These kids couldn't believe it, they thought we were nuts. So finally Ivan Kral came in. This little Czechoslovakian would-be rock star. He said, "I am here to be in your band." He was so cute. And we said, "Oh, yeah?" So we did "Land of a Thousand Dances" and it went on so long I thought I was gonna puke. But Ivan was so nervous he wouldn't stop and we figured that was really cool. He ain't no genius, but he's got a lotta heart. Ivan does.

Then we picked up a drummer, it was natural, we had to have a drummer for Ivan. We didn't really need a drummer, but Ivan wanted to be a rock star. He'd keep saying, "Oh, we must have a drum!" So we figured, Oh, fuck, okay, let's get Ivan a drummer. That's where Jay Dee Daugherty came in. The reason I like Jay Dee so much is that he's really young and wants to be part of something that's really cookin'. He was the most recent addition to the band, so we had to give him a crash course in everything. We'd tell him about the Aracs and six-teenth-century Japan and flying saucers. The poor kid had to carry all these books and records home every night.

Now it's at the point where I really love the group. I did a solo reading the other week in Philadelphia. It went great, but I was so lonely, I read "Land Without Music," and right away I'm thinking, Here's the part where Lenny always fucks up. Here's where I'd look at Sohl and tell him to stop sleeping on the keyboard. I missed them so much that I didn't want to ever again perform without them. They give me tremendous energy. I get like a little kid, and it's beautiful.

*Penthouse:* Do you prefer live performance to recording?

**Smith:** Oh, yeah. I like energy. I like to feel it cracklin', I like sexual energy in a room, and I like tension. I get mad when some asshole goes *"Shh-h-h"* when I'm doing a poem. People can talk. I don't give a fuck. I don't demand nothing from my audience. They're the ones who are payin', I hate to be told anything by a performer. Don't you hate it when some guy up on stage tells you to be quiet? I mean, fuck him, y'know?

*Penthouse:* Some people say they hate to play in bars because people drink and make noise.

**Smith:** Shit, I like that stuff. I love playing bars. Hearing that pool cue really inspires me. When we used to play on the Bowery, I would almost burst into tears 'cause of all the stuff that was happening. I'd look out at that long line of neon beer signs over the bar and that dog running around shitting while I'm in the middle of a beautiful ballad. There'd be a bunch of niggers beating the shit out of each other over by the pool table and all these drunks throwing back shots. It was the greatest atmosphere to perform in, it was conspiratorial. It was real physical, and that's what rock 'n' roll's all about: sexual tension and being drunk and disorderly!

**Penthouse:** What about those who try to place rock 'n' roll in the context of conscious intellectualism?

**Smith:** I don't like people interpreting or psychologizing pure energy. They should go read tea leaves or something, 'cause they're fuckin' up rock 'n' roll with their jive.

Another thing that's fuckin' up the music is television. I think that Helen Reddy hosting "Midnight Special" is bullshit. That broad never had a place in rock 'n' roll. That "I Am Woman" song is a piece of shit! All that stuff has warped kids' minds. Kids see that schlock on TV, then they go out and buy it.

It's like when they censored radio. You'd hear "Dance with Me, Henry," but you wouldn't hear "Work with Me, Annie." You'd hear Pat Boone doing "Tutti Frutti," but not Little Richard. That's what it's like all over again. It's the fifties.

But we're past the midpoint of a decade now, and I think a lot of people are ready to take a leap. I think we've had enough mediocrity. There is no way that singers like Elton John or Helen Reddy can ever transport people the way that Jim Morrison or Jimi Hendrix did. There's just no way. They just ain't there, y'-know? I don't feel that people will allow this shit to go on much longer. They won't really let rock 'n' roll die or peter out or turn into Hollywood: 'cause when you clear away the tons and tons of bullshit, the heart of rock 'n' roll is integrity.

**Penthouse:** Now that you've begun performing for bigger audiences, do you think you're in danger of losing anything, or of having to alter your music and poetry?

**Smith:** Nah! I just think I'll be talking less onstage. I have a lot of confidence in what we do, and I ain't changing nothin'. As long as something's perfect, as long as something's effective, it doesn't really matter.

I'll never do a number in which I don't have to put myself on the line. By that I mean that I'll always enjoy putting myself on the spot, always enjoy playing with fire. That's what "Land of a Thousand Dances" is for; that's the one where I always hallucinate a long story at the end. And sometimes it's really frightening. It's like boxing: go crazy or go down.

*Penthouse:* You've been getting a lot of press lately. Is it the kind of press you like?

**Smith:** I really don't want somebody writing something positive about me if they don't believe in it. I'd rather somebody write something real mean, y'-know? I like reading bad stuff, it gets me excited. In fact, the only reviews I keep are the bad ones 'cause I think they're the cool ones. I like when some guy in *Variety* gets outraged about my stuff. Or some school teacher writing for the *Villager.*

I'm pretty moral about what I do. If I didn't think I was worthy of doing something, I wouldn't do it. I ain't gonna waste a bunch of people's time. So good press don't really mean anything to me, 'cause I think I deserve it. I'd be full of shit if I said I didn't think so. Good press, bad press, whatever, only means a lot to me if it's writ by somebody I respect, by somebody I like.

*Penthouse:* A lot of people are very interested about what goes on between you and Bob Dylan. What do you talk to him about?

**Smith:** Nothin'.

*Penthouse:* Absolutely nothin'?

**Smith:** Nah. Well, like he came backstage to see me, and he's a totally physical guy. There was a period in my life when I thought about Dylan constantly. It was as if he had been my boyfriend. But when he walked into the room he was just a guy, a really cool guy. He ceased being Bob Dylan to me.

I enjoyed hearing him say my name. It was like high school. It was real embarrassing teenage stuff. He didn't have nothing to say to me. I didn't have nothing to say to him. We kept walking around, like dogs in a pit. He said, "What do you read Rimbaud in?" I said, "English." He said, "I read him in French." Totally teenage nonsense. But I thought he was a really cool guy, y'-know? And that's all he is to me now, a cool guy. I don't like being around him too much 'cause we're two very restless people, and that creates a lot of nervousness. Plus I'm shy around really cool guys until I get to know them. Like, when I met Hendrix we just talked about the weather. When I met Jim Morrison we sat around looking at girls' legs and discussing who had the best ass.

Dylan asked me about a poem I had written, the one about his dog. I felt like I'd been caught writing about a boy in my diary. I said. "Ah, c'mon, don't get mad at me." Really stupid. I told him it was just a dream I had. He said, "Oh, I like dreams. I ain't mad. I really like what you're doing." He didn't make any heavy statements.

He gave me a fantastic singing lesson. He really lives by singing. We were in a room with a few people who are gettin' drunk and singing, taking turns singing all this soft, folky shit, and when it was Dylan's turn to sing he started singing like he's at Madison Square Garden. It was pure heart, and I don't think anyone's ever captured that successfully on record.

Like I said, he ain't Bob Dylan to me anymore, he's a guy. I wasn't that cool around him, but let me tell ya, he wasn't no cooler. It was touching to see such great verbalizers acting like non-verbal jerkoffs.

*Penthouse:* If it came down to it, would you rather make books or records?

**Smith:** I like making records right now 'cause I can express myself that way in a very immediate, physical sense. You can always write a book, but you can't always do a rock 'n' roll record that's gonna work. When I'm forty I don't wanna try to do a rock 'n' roll record like Gene Vincent tried to do right before he popped off. It would have been much better if he'd written a book, y'know? Just a book about piss and shit and watching baseball and getting drunk and beating up broads. I mean that's nobler than dying an old rock 'n' roll failure.

*Penthouse:* You sometimes mention that there's a housewife side to you. Can you envision indulging that side?

**Smith:** Well, actually that's just a romance of mine. I'm a total failure at housewifery. I always have been, 'cause I daydream too much. If I start doing the dishes at one in the afternoon, I'll still be there at six in the evening. Besides, housework makes me nauseous. Repetition makes me carsick. I used to get carsick when I did piecework at the factory in south Jersey. I'd have to inspect baby buggy bumper beepers—no shit— y'know, beep, beep, beep: and I'd wind up puking in the bathroom. I'd have to take those little yellow pills

*Penthouse:* That's what the song "Piss Factory"'s about isn't it?

**Smith:** Yeah, right I inspected beepers, steel sheets. It depended, it changed every week. I cut leather straps for baby carriages, made big cardboard boxes for baby mattresses. Toys, strollers, all that stuff.

Some people told me that "Piss Factory" was immoral, that I was base. It's not immoral, it's total truth. To me that little "Piss Factory" thing is the most truthful thing I ever writ. It's autobiography. In fact, the truth was stronger than the poem. The stuff those women did to me at that factory was more horrible than I let on in the song. They did shit like gang up on me and stick my head in a toilet full of piss. People like beauty and purity. They pretend that's what it's all about. I don't like that. *That's* immoral.

# 22

Richard Meltzer had moved to Los Angeles in 1975, and a year later I moved to Nashville, where somebody had offered me a job doing nothing. As Richard later said, if we'd both stayed in New York together we would've ended up dead.

I had been listening to country music for some years, and had started to write about it because writing about rock 'n' roll no longer offered the freedom it once had: as rock 'n' roll became more a part of mainstream culture, so the rock-'n'-roll magazines became a respectable, predictable, stultifying adjunct of the record companies whose advertising supported them, and in many ways as mediocre and conservative as the press of the mainstream culture. The whole racket was turning into journalism. Country music at this time was still sneered upon, still without respect or acceptance by the cultural establishment and its press. It was, as a premise for writing, all that rock 'n' roll had been.

In late 1973 or early 1974, I had signed a deal with Bantam to do a book on the poetry of country music, tying it to Greek lyric poetry. That book never came to be. In the spring of 1975, I signed another deal, with Stein & Day, to do another, but wholly different, book about country music; and it was in Nashville that I finished that book.

While living in Nashville, I continued writing for whatever rags would have me. This sample of a monthly column of country-music reviews I did for something called *Gig* is not unrepresentative.

# Country

### Kinky Friedman:

*Lasso from El Paso (Epic)*

If I were Kinky Friedman, I'd be embarrassed, cuz judging by this album I'd be (A) a mediocre Jewish comedian, (B) a leftover from 1968, and (C) stupid.

What happened, Kink? I mean, most of these songs are so dumb I'd lock my five-year-old kid up in the cellar if he wrote them. And why would anyone not suffering with cerebral lesions write and record a serious, sensitive song about Abbie Hoffman? Besides, the whole thing sounds, well, yecch. Nice cover, though.

Let's just kick this one under the sink, OK, Kinky? Forget Dylan, start hanging around with Henny Youngman.

### Jim Ed Brown & Helen Cornelius:

*I Don't Want To Have To Marry You (RCA)*

The title here is a hot one, a bold defense of premarital whupa-whupa. It gets me all sweaty and makes me wanna paint my nails and strangle kittens. Seriously, it's wonderful how much one can learn about life simply by listening to records. There's more smut here: "I've Rode with the Best" is about riding . . . broads! God, gimme a kitten quick. There's a Paul Anka song too, but I ain't even gonna tell about that one, cuz I don't like Paul Anka's face. Really, it's as simple as that.

### Red Steagall:

*Texas Red (ABC—Dot)*

Howdy, pardners, and welcome to overkill country. Take y'self a nice swig of Lone Star, practice up on your best I-ain't-no-CPA's-son drawl, and put on your favorite ten-gallon persona.

You too can be a genuine Lone Star schmuck. Just fit the words San Antone, honky-tonk, Bob Wills, and Lone Star into one three-minute song, using a I-IV-

V chord progression. After a little practice, you'll be able to puke out the likes of "Texas Red," "San Antonio Champagne," "Take Me Back to Texas," "There's Still a Lot of Love in San Antonio," and "Lone Star Love." But don't use those exact titles, cuz good old Red Steagall's used 'em in his new long-playing record, *Texas Red*.

When the Texas fad stiffs out, we can all turn to Idaho. Just think! "Bring Me Back to Boise" and "Gimme a Spud and a Can of Three-Point-Two," and rich kids faking flat midwestern accents. But for now, just remember: there ain't no Mexicans in Tennessee. Yahoo indeed.

## Roy Head:

*A Head of His Time (ABC—Dot)*

Real nice title, guys. This is a very good record. How about this for a title: "Baby Please Don't Stone Me Anymore." Or better yet: "Angel with a Broken Wing." Like I said, this is a very good record. Believe me. Without me, you're nowhere.

## Chet Atkins:

*The Best of Chet Atkins & Friends (RCA)*

Chet Atkins has been with RCA since 1947, when he cut "Canned Heat" (Chet not only picked but sang in that first record). In the last 30 years he has been RCA's busiest executive: recording as a solo and as a session man, and producing more records, from Elvis to Perry Como, than anyone in Nashville.

Since 1964, when he and Hank Snow joined for their *Reminiscing* album, Chet has recorded several duets with men such as Arthur Fiedler (the white-haired geezer on educational TV), Les Paul, Jerry Reed, and Merle Travis. Some of the best duets are included here, and some new ones recorded for the occasion.

Much of *The Best of Chet Atkins & Friends* is MOR, the sort of music Atkins has never claimed to dislike, but much is great stuff: "Sweet Georgia Brown" (with Nashville guitarist Lenny Breau), "Do I Ever Cross Your Mind" (with a very giddy Dolly Parton), "Fiddlin' Around" (with Johnny Gimble), and "I'll See You in My Dreams" (with Chet's mentor, Merle Travis).

## Merle Haggard:

*The Roots of My Raising (Capitol)*

A nostalgic album by Ken Nelson and Fuzzy Owen. It's basically a straight country plunge into ten songs—only one of them written by Haggard, an excellent writer (but quite a short fellow). Mellower than much previous Haggard product, this contains potent versions of such ballads as "What Have You Got Planned Tonight Diana" and "Make Mine Vindaloo." A few uptempo numbers balance the majority of slower songs like "Colorado" where voices, strings, and Haggard's voice merge for a highlight (nice sentence, bub). Interesting assortment of material includes two songs by Jimmie Rodgers—one of Haggard's favorite composers. Display prominently.

# Ronnie Milsap:

## *Live (RCA)*

I never much liked Ronnie Milsap's records. "Pure Love" and "Please Don't Tell Me How the Story Ends" were dull and mushy, and I was glad to hear that Billy Sherrill filed suit on "(I'm a) Stand by My Woman Man." But, unlike most country performers, Milsap's live shows are better than his records. True, I've seen Milsap concerts so dreary that the only excitement was when he almost tottered off the edge of the stage (Felt Forum, New York City, 1975), but I've also seen Milsap concerts that yelled with energy and good music.

This set, recorded at the Grand Ole Opry House in 1976, is Milsap at his best: urbane, raunchy, and free of pomposity. There are a couple of dull moments: the "Country Cookin'" routine is a stale breeze from 1966, and where, oh where, is that symphony orchestra coming from in "I Can Almost See Houston from Here"? But when Milsap lets loose, as in Hank Williams's "Kaw-Liga" and the Stones' "Honky Tonk Women," there is some of the best junk music you're going to hear all year.

# Michael Murphey:

## *Flowing Free Forever (Epic)*

This is one of them cosmic cowboy records. On the back of the album cover, right up there in the upper left corner, is a quote from T'ao Chi'en, something about wind and flesh and blood. I can't read it too well, cuz CBS has embossed upon it in gold "DEMONSTRATION: Not For Sale." Well, hell, who cares. Ernest Tubb never quoted no dead Chinaman.

Got the words to all the songs printed on the record sleeve, so us literary types don't even have to listen to the sucker. First cut looks like a goodun': "Even now the Holy Man is singing/May Wakan-Tanka spare his life." Makes you feel good all over, doesn't it? Yeah, sort of, well, glad to be alive. I know a creep down the street who once made me eat a sesame-seed cookie. I am gonna give him this album. Wakan-Tanka would've wanted it that way. Not to mention T'ao Chi'en.

# 23

From my first published book, *Country,* which came out in the fall of 1977, right around the time my marriage ended.

# Excerpt from *Country*

Emmett Miller sits on a bed. He wears light trousers, light vest, white shirt, and dark bow tie. He is leaning forward slightly, toward the camera. His left hand rests on his knee. There are a diamond ring and a long, lighted cigar. Close to his right stands a woman, young and thin and pale. Her hair is bobbed. She smiles, but there is a drunken, puffy reluctance in her face. Emmett Miller's arm surrounds the girl's thighs, lifting her skirt almost to her hips. Where his hand holds the inside of her leg, there is another diamond. The girl's thin, silvery garters show above her knees, and her legs are pretty and dully incandescent in her fine silk stockings. Near the girl is a small, low table, on which are three glasses, variously full, and a bottle of Crawford's Five Star. The wallpaper is of a thousand trellised roses.

Emmett Miller has no face. There is a hole in the photograph where it was burned away by a cigarette, a hole of precise and perfect wrath. A piece of chin, a sliver of ear pressed to a girl's hip, one temple and its dark receding hairline— this is all. By the line of the chin and the tightness at the ear and temple, it seems Emmett Miller is smiling.

On the back of the photograph, in crisp, faded blue: "Me and Emmett— Union Square Hotel, New York City—8/10/28—Sitting on Top of the World!"

I found the photograph, brittle and tawny with its age and its travel, sticking from between pages of *Countries of the World, Vol. II*, in a junk store in Southport, North Carolina, a small ocean place near the bottom of the state. I asked the owner of the store where he had got the book, but he didn't recall. I bought the photo for a nickel.

That was in 1972. A year later it was blown out a ninth-floor window in Manhattan, off the kitchen table of someone I disliked. I watched after it, trying to follow it as it fell, but I didn't see it touch the ground.

# 24

Regarding the curse and contagion of journalism, I must admit that during this time I was not wholly immune. A low point came when I wrote for the *New York Times*.

The piece, published on Christmas Day of 1977, was inspired by a quotation from William Faulkner in Joseph Blotner's two-volume *Faulkner: A Biography*: "Television is for niggers." This was, of course, a quotation that the *Times* quickly and automatically excised. I don't remember what I originally called the piece, and so have let stand the trite title imposed upon it by the *Times*.

In the fall of 1976, I had gone to Los Angeles to interview the movie director Don Siegel for *Playboy*. Siegel, much to my pleasure, turned out to be a knock-around old-timer from whom the superficial mien of Hollywood fell and vanished at the slightest incitement, as it did from his protégé Clint Eastwood, who spoke with me at length and leisure during my days with Siegel. My experience with Siegel was as misleading as it was gratifying and illuminating: misleading in that it led me to believe that real human souls could be found even in Hollywood. But guys such as Siegel were a dying breed, and in my later dealings with the movie business I discovered that the hollow men and women who ran it were mackerels rather than the sharks they saw themselves to be, and that Hollywood itself, whose commerce in dreams and mediocrity was vaster, more ruinous, and more despicable than any global trade in drugs, was a citadel of fraud meant only to be robbed.

I no longer have either the tapes or the transcripts of my long talks with Siegel, which were never published. But I never forgot what Siegel told me: "If you're going to be a whore, be a high-priced whore." And, in the end, though most working stiffs and creative assholes alike are loath to accept it, the truth is that anyone who performs for pay is a whore.

As the first decade of my writing career, such as it was, neared its end, I became more aware of the Moloch of mediocrity whose maw was the common end of most writing. I knew good writers who, after lingering too long in the comforting poppy field of journalism, wholly lost their ability to write as well as their ability to feel or express themselves honestly (or perhaps I should say "perversely," as I did not yet know what true honesty was, and I myself was capable of it only in its most demonic forms). If one worked too long within the hypocritical and ill-written strictures of the *New York Times,* indeed for any of the disposable pulp Torah scrolls of mediocrity, one became ultimately not only a deadened whore but an ill-writing one, not only a creature of mediocrity but a creation of it as well. (Looking back, it occurs to me that my little piece for the *Times,* about writers' favorite television shows, obliquely addressed, or was obliquely inspired by my growing awareness of, the precarious precipice that separated creativity from all-consuming mediocrity.)

I did not know then if there was any way out, nor did I know much then of the silence and the wind, having not yet found that lost and hidden light within me. But my darkness served me well, and I believed that, armed with booze, my wicked wits, and my stolen Greek primer, I could and would become a high-priced whore whose income subsidized what was then still an inchoate impulse to write that silence and that wind. Liquor helped me to believe this. It and the darkness served me well; for I simply did not give a fuck.

# When Literary Lights
# Turn On the TV

In the early 1960's, William Faulkner refused to allow a radio or television set in his home; yet, he would arrive punctually at a neighbor's house every Sunday night to watch the NBC series *Car 54, Where Are You?* He made no social engagements for Sunday evenings that might keep him from his rendezvous with Tooty and Muldoon. When his daughter happened to mention to him Henry James's *The Turn of the Screw*, Faulkner smiled and said, "That would make a great plot for *Car 54, Where Are You?*"

Intrigued by these revelations in Joseph Blotner's *Faulkner: A Biography*, I recently drafted inquiries to a number of literary figures asking them what their favorite TV programs were. Herewith their responses.

John Cheever, whose latest novel is *Falconer*, replied: "I bought my first TV set about a week ago. So far, I've seen a *Nova* program about Mars—it was magnificent—and *Monday Night Football*. Both great. I got the set because I'm writing a TV show. I figured I should take a look at it, case it out."

Joan Didion's latest novel is *A Book of Common Prayer;* her reply was: "I don't watch anything regularly, although I did watch *Upstairs, Downstairs* when it was on. Once in a while, I'll watch *Hawaii Five-O*—mostly for the stock shots of the waves and there's always a shot of the Iolani Palace."

Annie Dillard, author of *Pilgrim at Tinker Creek* and *Holy the Firm*, answered: "The last thing, and the best thing, I've ever seen on television was the broadcast of the Winter Olympics in Sapporo, Japan. I was crazy about those Olympics, wild with excitement, slaloming about my daily rounds."

Robert Penn Warren, the novelist and poet, said: "I like football on TV and am enthralled by the ads, not to mention politics. Particularly ads at 7 A.M. in motels; often with one shoe on and one off I sit for an hour watching ads. But in general my life is a book or outdoor life. Also children: After seeing many children lie on their bellies all afternoon watching, I hardened my heart and in the summers took mine to the deep country woods where they could make their own lives. They have never once asked for TV, though they happily enough look at it when visiting friends.

"My own defects cannot be blamed on TV, however—to end on a cheerful note, I was born in 1905 and I never saw a TV until after the damage had been done.

"I make no generalizations. Each to his own taste in a free country. Besides, my days are too full now."

George V. Higgins, whose novels include *The Friends of Eddie Coyle, The Digger's Game* and *Cogan's Trade,* answered: "I haven't had a favorite television series since *Maverick* went off the air. Unless you count the Red Sox telecasts, which I watch whenever I can. That, I want to add, is not a boast but a confession. Friends whose judgment I respect have repeatedly admonished me to watch some series they have found absolutely riveting, and I have just as regularly ignored their advice in order to see my kids, do my work, catch a plane, or spend a rare free evening at a dinner party, in conversation with my betters. I like *Saturday Night Live* but I say that on the basis of perhaps six viewings. I like *Today* because it goes well with my coffee and cigarettes."

James Leo Herlihy, who wrote *Midnight Cowboy* and is now working on a study of prostitution in what we call the "New Age," replied: "I watch nothing regularly, but I probably average two or three hours a week in front of the set. *Mary Hartman* was a great favorite, especially in its first year. I liked [Norman] Lear's series *All in the Family* and *Maude* but have by now seen enough of them. What I really like best are interview shows. Tom Snyder's *Tomorrow,* Berwick's *At One With;* sometimes Merv Griffin comes through.

"I see television as a consciousness-raising machine, invented in the nick of time as a survival tool. If we don't get to know one another, we perish. TV is saving us. (I can argue this point by the hour, and it's a favorite subject with me.) TV is definitely doing its job—violence, vulgarity and commercials notwithstanding."

Louis Auchincloss, whose many novels include *The Rector of Justin* and *The Dark Lady,* said: "The two series that I have enjoyed most on TV have been *Upstairs, Downstairs* and *The Forsyte Saga.* Both of these caught my interest and held it to the end. Operas on TV, although rare, have been a high spot: the *La Boheme,* live from the Met last year. Opera fans hate one for saying it, but it seems obvious to me that if grand opera is to survive in the future, it will be in live performances on TV.

"For thrillers, I think there has been nothing as good as the best plays in *The Twilight Zone.* I was sad to see this series disappear from the air. Some of them had the chilliest twists that I have ever seen on the screen.

"I think there is a place for an occasional police drama in the life of every busy man and woman who is tired by 9 o'clock. I have watched most of them and have found that *Hawaii Five-O* has the most consistently interesting and exciting plots."

Hubert Selby Jr., whose novels include *Last Exit to Brooklyn, The Room* and *The Demon,* replied: "I have owned a few sets through the years and have the honor of having killed three of them. The first one was inadvertent. It was bugging me and I kicked it and it exploded, and fire and glass went zipping past my abdomen and I almost got torn apart. I just happened to be standing in exactly the right place or would have been seriously injured if not killed. The other two I did deliberately with absolute and complete malice aforethought. I stood to the side and killed them with a hammer. On the last one I did such a beautiful job that we have moved the defunct set to the middle of the living room and everyone thought it was a piece of modern sculpture, a hymn to technology.

"A couple of years ago a network was going to do a series of the Ten Commandmants, and I wrote one of the two-hour segments, the Third Commandmant: Remember the Sabbath Day and keep it holy. The entire project was ultimately cancelled, probably because I was too radical. But the thing that really amused me was the fact that the network only took five of the Commandmants with an option on the other five. That, my friend, is television."

It was not the fact that she had never read Pindar that set her apart, but rather a more visible fact: she had brought an electric-guitarist with her, and he was standing there, plugged-in. Her and Lenny Kaye, two skinnies from New Jersey, out to recast poetry with the nighttime slut-gait of rock 'n' roll. The other poets, being mostly wimps whom rhythm never knew, didn't like this at all. You might say they feared it, for none of them, once they had seen Lenny's amp sitting there like a dark Homeric vowel, wished to follow Patti's performance, and she was asked to close the show. So we sat there, Richard Meltzer and I and two girls who didn't seem to enjoy our company, sniffing lighter-fluid (the audience sat in pews, so there was privacy enough for one to douse one's hanky with the juices of the blue-and-yellow can) and waiting. Waiting while poet after poet bared his soul, which invariably turned out to be a dead mackerel. Then, as we sat knee-deep in the detritus of bared souls, Patti and Lenny came on, and Lenny struck the first notes of the Midnighters' "Sexy Ways," and Patti opened her mouth and loosed the ratted-hair rhythms of her poem "Sally."

> you been messing around sally
> and you ain't been messing with me
> torn pants
> torn pants
> and juice all down your dress
> you been ripping it up with someone
> I think you better confess

When she started to do "Rape," many of the gathered poets packed up their souls and departed.

> I'm gonna peep in bo's bodice. lay
> down darling don't be modest let me
> slip my hand in. ohhh that's soft that's
> nice that's not used up. ohhh don't cry.
> wet what's wet? oh that. heh heh, thats
> just the rain lambie pie. now don't
> squirm. let me put my rubber on. I'm a
> wolf in a lamb skin trojan. ohh yeah
> that's hard that's good. now don't
> tighten up. open up be-bop. lift that
> little butt up. ummm open wider
> be-bop. come on.

As I said, this was 1972. CBGB's, which would soon exist a few blocks farther down the Bowery, did not yet exist. (The new owner, Hilly, had bought the place

---

# 25

8 March 1978

Dear Richard

Here's a twist of King B. Knock yourself out on St. Paddy's Day with it.

Seems definite that I'm movin back to NYC. Got this joint on Commerce Street lined up, and I'm supposed to be set up there by April 15. I'll keep you posted.

Went down to pay for my D-I-V-O-R-C-E yesterday. Gonna have to show up in court in 60–90 days to make it final. Meanwhile, I'm bein real friendly and nice to Sunny, tryin to make the thing easy on her, cuz these days I sorta feel that bein nice is OK. (But sometimes I feel that bein a mean sonofabitch is OK too. Aint life funny.) Anyway, freedom is startin to look real pretty. Some nights I get the feelin that I never wanna be obligated to share a fuckin bed with somebody again, likin too much to lay there by myself and read, shit like that. Shit, man, startin to feel outright fuckin good.

Say a hep hi to Sculatti and the rest.

Recycle Yr Broads,

*NICK*

# 26

# Patti Smith:
# Straight, No Chaser

I moved back to New York, alone, in early 1978, sleeping, or, more precisely, passed out, for some nights with a sneaker under my head as a pillow on the floor of the otherwise empty apartment where I would remain for more than twenty years.

*Creem* wanted me to do a story about Patti Smith. I gave Patti a call, and she said, in so many words, "Hell, Nick, you know me. Just make it up." And that is what I did.

We are sitting in the Tropical, the darkest bar in New York. Outside on Eig[ ]Avenue it's late afternoon. In here it's midnight on the outskirts of Mayag[ ]There is a day-glo Madonna next to the cash register. Above her head is a s[ ]Absolutely No Credit This Means You. Patti orders tequila and I order gin. S[ ]we are speaking English and are not drunk, we are the object of many cry[ ]Hispanic stares. The barmaid pulls at the hem of her brassiere through he[ ]shirt, then pours herself a shot.

*"No importa nada más que toma icor,"* she says, and the bar stirs with rheu[ ]laughter.

Patti lifts a quarter from our change and goes to the jukebox. A moment la[ ]Tom Jones is singing "The Young New Mexican Puppeteer." Several custom[ ]begin to sing along in phonetic approximation.

"I heard you got divorced," Patti says.

"Yeah," I say.

"The Virgin Mary's face is chartreuse," she says, gesturing with a toss of h[ ]chin toward the icon that guards the till. "They should have the Holy Ghost [ ]the other side of the register, where that cerebral palsy can is."

"Color-coordinated, of course," I say.

"Yeah. Black and red. Black for sin. Red for defloration. The colors of salva[ ]tion. They were my high school colors, too. I used to dream about getting[ ]fucked by the Holy Ghost when I was a kid. Black and red. Christ, what a shitty[ ]football team we had."

"You could always fuck Jerry Lee. I guess that's about as close to the Holy[ ]Ghost as a girl can get these days," I counsel.

"It ain't the same," Patti says. "We need a new cosmology. New gods. New sacraments. Another drink. I wanna go to Alexandria, to the grave of Ibn al-Farid." We settle for Corby's Bar, on Sixth Avenue.

I first saw Patti Smith perform in 1972, at a poetry reading in St. Mark's Church on the Bowery. A few months earlier, Telegraph Books of Philadelphia had published her first, slender volume of poems, *Seventh Heaven*. But Patti wasn't like the other creatures of slender volumes who were there that night.

the year before, but didn't yet know what he was doing with it. Before he ruined it, it was one of the last great skid-row bars. Ed Sanders had wanted to buy it and leave it in its original state. Hilly's first alteration was to paste a sign in the window declaring that the joint no longer wished the patronage of bums.) The Bowery was still for bums and poets, not for people who knew the words to "Stupid Girl."

Soon there was another book, *Witt*. The band began to grow: piano, another guitar, then later drums. In the spring of 1974, Patti's friend, the photographer Robert Mapplethorpe, financed her first record, a version of "Hey, Joe" coupled with "Piss Factory," a wrathful song about her days at the Dennis Mitchell Toys factory in south Jersey. Patti named her record label Mer, which is both an Indogermanic root meaning "to die" and an Old English word for the sea.

Less than a year later, Patti signed with Arista, and her first album, *Horses*, was released late in 1975 and received massive attention from the eyes and ears of the media. *Radio Ethiopia* came the following year, and it did not receive massive attention. There was no Patti Smith album in 1977, and toward the end of the year there were rumors that Arista had dropped her. But in the spring of 1978 there came *Easter*, one of the most successful albums of the year, and the single "Because The Night," Patti's first hit.

In Corby's Bar there is, for a reason known only to God and Corby (neither of which are here to explain), a faded map of the solar system taped to the mirror behind the bar. A man of indeterminable age, whose physical appearance lends much credence to the medieval theory that all life is born in a dismal swamp, sticks his face in mine and shouts, "Hey, wise guy, where's Pluto? I'll tell ya where it is, wise guy. It's in the upper left-hand corner." Then he turns and informs the rest of the bar in a loud voice, "Fuckin' guy don't even know where Pluto is." The clientele, which seems to have been there so long that its faces are the color of the floor's once-white linoleum tiles, waves him away and groans the groan of Job.

"This place is even worse than I remember," Patti says.

"At least they know where Pluto is," I say.

"And now we do, too," Patti says.

"Some people say you have a messiah complex," I say.

"Aw, fuck them. Goddam psychiatric doubletalk. Why can't they just say they hate my guts or something? People who need reasons to hate somebody are fulla shit. Buncha creeps. Who said that, anyway?—Hey, look, that guy was wrong. It ain't in the left-hand corner, it's in the *right*-hand corner! This whole goddam joint is *nuts*."

A few hours later, we are in the Bells of Hell, a couple of blocks from Corby's, on Thirteenth Street. I go take a leak. When I come back to the bar, I find Patti in dialogue with Al Fields, the Bells piano-player whose legend extends in rays for many blocks, if not as far as the cold planet Pluto.

"Hey, nigger," Al, who is himself the only patron of color in the establishment, calls to the bartender, "this girl don't believe I was raised by nuns. You tell her, am I right or am I wrong. I'm Al Fields, girl, I don't lie. Shit! Is a pork chop greasy?!"

Patti goes to the jukebox. "Hey, they got my record. No 'New Mexican Puppeteer,' though." She plays two Rolling Stones records.

"Hey, you ain't related to her, are you?" Al Fields asks me in his typhoon whisper. "What is it, she got somethin' against nuns? Shit, I'm Al Fields, the Village Legend. You know what I'm talkin' about. Am I right, am I wrong? No, really, she's a very nice girl. She come to hear me play?" He excuses himself and heads towards the men's room. "I gotta go pay my water bill."

"What was it like opening for the Stones in Atlanta?" I ask Patti, recalling the poets who had feared to follow her onstage a few years ago.

"It was great. When I used to open for all these acts, most of 'em usually made me carsick. I used to think how great it'd be to open for the Stones. One of my dreams. Now all I wanna do is open for Rimbaud."

"He doesn't play the States too much, though, does he?" I say.

"There hasn't been the right promoter," she says.

"What do you figure will happen now that you're Top Twenty? Are you gonna clean up your act for the bigger crowds?"

"Nah. Bein' top-of-the-pops just makes crowds more docile. Look at Jim Morrison. He just kept gettin' weirder and weirder. King's new clothes, y'know?"

"When are you gonna start makin' movies?"

"I don't know. There ain't that much I'd really be interested in. A Muslim *Star Wars*, maybe. *The Paul Verlaine Story*. I'd like to do one about an international plot to assassinate MOR singers. Get all these Debby Boone-types and wimpy country singers to play themselves. Bang, bang, eat lead, dog of mediocrity."

"What's the next record gonna be like?"

"Very Plutonic. Liner notes by the Holy Ghost. They'll love it in Corby's."

# 27

# God Created Dean Martin in His Own Image, Then Stood Back

Since 1972 life has been amiss, and there has been emptiness. Bare, unbudding, the saplings of stark need knew no spring. Candles were lit, letters were writ; prayers said, tears shed. But greyness begat naught but bleak greyness, and the new Dean Martin album never came.

Some of us, such as Elvis, who had declared Dino his idol, could not bear the agony of forebearance. Others, such as myself, endured by listening to the original, mono version of "That's Amore" and reminding ourselves that it had taken Michelangelo eight years to fresco the altar wall of the Sistine chapel—and Michelangelo didn't even drink!

Now we faithful can rejoice. Let there be the pouring of liquors and the raising of skirts. The man has returned, and life as we knew it may resume.

It is no secret that Dean Martin has influenced more singers than any man alive. He taught Elvis the dramaturgy of sincerity, Jerry Lee the powers of diplopic decrescendo. Jim Morrison the nuances of erotic detachment, and Randy Newman how to comb his hair. *Once In A While*, Dino's first album in more than six years, proves that *il padrone* (as Jim Morrison called him) is still the master.

The love song has been the center of Dino's art from the beginning. (He first hit the charts, in 1950, vowing "I'll Always Love You.") Here the gurglings and gropings of love are celebrated in all their glory. "Without a Word of Warning" and "The Day You Came Along" tell of answered dreams of the moist kind. "It's Magic" and "Only Forever," two beauties from the '40s, bow the knee of fealty to She-Whose-Face-Launches-Ships-and-Smiles-Salaciously-After-the-Fourth-Drink. "If I Had You" and "Once in a While" wallow sweetly in the lappings of unrequited love. "I Cried for You" is a savoring of vengeance. In "Love Thy Neighbor," Dino advises us to bless the skin of errant wives in no uncertain terms.

Two of the album's most impressive performances are found in "Twilight on the Trail" and a version of the World War I killer "That Old Gang of Mine." The first, remindful of Dino's "Houston," is an homage to irresponsibility and the joys of immediate gratification. "That Old Gang Of Mine" shows that while Dino is always singing about broads, his old buddies are still where his heart is. What a guy.

*Felice ritorno,* Dino! Let's make it a regular thing again, okay?

# 28

# Jim Morrison:
# The Late Late Show

What Jim Morrison wanted more than anything—more than fame, more than wealth, more than the women's wet submission that fame brought with it—was to be taken seriously as a poet. But he was too immature. Too unfinished to sense how little he knew about the job of turning a vision into meaningful words and rhythms.

The Doors' most ambitious work was often their worst. Trying to make of rock & roll something it could never, should never, be, Morrison seemed a pompous fool rather than the intrepid seer he fancied himself. With dark, messianic urgency, he delivered images and ideas that were embarrassing in their unoriginality. In the small book of poetry from which this record takes its title, Jim Morrison asked, affectedly forsaking any question mark, "Do you know we are ruled by T.V." We might be surprised by the dullness of those words, or by their arrogance, but we aren't surprised that a vanity press published them.

The failings of his boyish poetry don't efface the fact that Morrison was one of the great rockers. He and the Doors, in their four fast years in the public eye, made a music unlike any other, and that music was more often brilliant than not. *An American Prayer*, like every Doors disc, offers further testimony. Though the new album concentrates on spoken poetry rather than songs, it contains a live version of "Roadhouse Blues," cut in Detroit during the 1969/1970 *Absolutely Live!* tour, that, by itself, is a solid enough plinth for rock & roll immortality to rest upon.

*An American Prayer* also strongly suggests that Jim Morrison might've eventually gotten what he wanted, and deserved it, had he not died at twenty-seven— the same age at which, in 1913, Ezra Pound (who'd also been a vanity-press poet) remarked: "Most important poetry has been written by men over thirty."

Jim Morrison's obsessions were sex and death, and while he wore the uraeus of those obsessions well and always, he looked upon them as impenetrable enemies lying within. When love and the funeral pyre were sung about in the same breath in the summer of 1967, it seemed a pretty conceit. It seemed less pretty when, in the months and years after "Light My Fire," it became obvious that Morrison, his figure ever darker and more estranged, wasn't only writing and singing rock & roll songs but was also trying to vanquish his demons and curses by invoking new demons and curses. "I am the Lizard King. I can do anything," he had the strange, young nerve to say and believe. It was mythopoeic, but it was also classic paranoia.

Most of *An American Prayer* was recorded on Morrison's last birthday, December 8th, 1970. By then, his libido and his death wish were becoming one, entwined and inseparable, and that perverse oneness seemed to enthrall him. As Ray Manzarek's funereal organ weaves a lewd threnody, Morrison declares, in "Lament," that "Death and my cock are the world." In the same piece, he says, with a sweet voice: "I pressed her thigh and death smiled."

His most impressive poetic efforts are his thoughts about death. In "An American Prayer," he sees death as "pale & wanton thrillful . . . like a scaring over friendly guest you've brought to bed." Toward the end of the poem, with an almost Miltonic metrical precision, he writes: "Death makes angels of us all/& gives us wings."

Suggestions of sexual impotence slither through the record. "I'm surprised you could get it up," a woman ("Vaguely Mexican or Puerto Rican") taunts him in "Stoned Immaculate." The essence of "Lament" is one of ritual mortification: "All join now and lament for the death of my cock/. . . I sacrifice my cock on the altar of silence." Morrison's reflection upon this impotence is oblique, resigned but maybe more perceptive than he himself knew: "Boys get crazy in the head and suffer." Lizard psychiatry.

As death was in his mind, so was murder. Jim Morrison's fantasies encroached on his rock-star reality. At dusk one day, he went into a phone booth outside the Alta-Cienega Motel in Los Angeles, close to both the Doors' office and Elektra Records, and called poet Michael McClure in San Francisco. In his wasted voice, he told McClure that he'd just killed somebody out in the desert: "I don't know how to tell ya, but, ah, I killed somebody. No. . . . It's no big deal, y'know." Morrison's friend, Frank Lisciandro, who'd worked on the singer's film, *Hwy,* taped the call, and it's one of *An American Prayer's* eeriest moments.

It all comes together, or falls apart, in "Stoned Immaculate," the LP's most striking passage. Drunk in a dirty room, with a strange woman and his obsessions, he utters, slowly and simply, all it seems he'd ever really wanted to say:

> *Come 'ere.*
> *I love you.*
> *Peace on earth.*
> *Will you die for me?*
> *Eat me.*
> *This way.*
> *The end.*

Looking for once toward life, Jim Morrison says with quiet resolution in "Lament": "Words got me the wound and will get me well." But a few months later, he died. It's a loss. *An American Prayer* is shot through with youthful, flawed aspirations, yet whenever it touches its tongue to brilliance (which it does for long, sensuous moments on end), it illuminates the meaning of that loss and what might have been.

# 29

# Blondie Plucks Her Legs

Deborah Harry, formerly of Hawthorne, New Jersey, sits there. Deborah Harry, who arrived at the Seventies from the Sixties in a Camaro, eats tuna salad from a little cardboard container with a little plastic fork, Deborah Harry scratches her knee and speaks.

"Sorry I'm late," she says. She gestures toward the tuna salad in vague defense. The tuna is silent.

"How old are you?" I ask.

"I'm not telling." She laughs. The tuna doesn't. "Come on. I won't snitch," I have made three different bets around town that I could get her to reveal her age—I'll bet on anything. Even broads.

"No, I'm not telling." She doesn't laugh this time.

"Why not? You can't be *that* old. You still menstruate, don't you?"

It's a Mexican stand-off. Thirty bucks down the drain. Maybe I can win it back at three-card monte. Life's like that. I pour grape juice into a coffee mug. I add club soda. I take a sip and light a Camel. Next question.

"Do you plan to still be rocking when you're 40?"

"I don't know. If I still have legs, I guess."

"Your legs. They're great. Do you shave them, or do you wax them?"

"Ugh! I pluck them. One hair at a time. I like the pain. I like the slow approach."

"Do you start from the ankle or the thigh?" Now we're talking.

"I work from the bottom up. It takes about a week for each leg."

"The ancient Romans were big on plucking. There's that great phrase from Persius, *'voisas loevia'*—plucked smooth."

We speak for many minutes of legs and their lore. Each of us learns a great deal from the other. A mutual respect is born. In an atmosphere of great (albeit tuna-scented) ease, we pursue lesser matters.

"In a lot of stuff, like 'Rip Her to Shreds' and 'Just Go Away,' you come off pretty nasty. Do you think of yourself as a mean bitch?"

"No. I'm very nice to people. I mean, I have my bitchy side, but I don't think I'm really nasty. I think that a lot of other people probably think that I am. Fuck them."

"Do you get a lot of groupies?" I'm fast today.

"Um. Yeah, well, I have a lot of fans. I don't have sex with them, though. I live with Chris, and we're working together constantly, so I don't fool around. So far, nobody's been overly aggressive."

"What sort of fans does Blondie attract? I saw a bunch of beatniks at one of your shows."

"We get everybody. Our favorite audiences are those that applaud or dance. I like noisy crowds. I like them to yell. Whatever age. I don't care."

"Do you like foreigners?"

"Oh, yeah. It's really great over there. The English are really traditional rockers, really wild. At least they are for this. They get up and go crazy. A constant shouting and leaping and swaying. The audiences here are generally tamer. We always get encores in the States. That's not the problem. It's the general attitude, the general response. Appreciation is expressed differently here.

"Nobody in America is a 40-year-old rocker. Except for Jerry Lee. There are middle-aged rockers in England. Forty-year-old guys with kids.

"Things take longer to catch on here. Everything is really spread-out and regional. I think the American people suffer from a lack of press. European press is very important. Here, television is what's important. Press makes more of an organized statement. The printed word is where it's at. Not some creep sitting on TV saying, 'Hi, there. Blah, blah, blah. Bye, there.' American culture has no definition because TV has no awareness. I think that the future hope of TV lies in video cassettes."

"How come you don't have your own TV series? Blondes always do great on TV. Look at Suzanne Somers, or Hillary Brooke. Or how about movies? You could be in movies."

"I know. Yeah. A lot of our titles are stolen from movies. 'Kung Fu Girls,' 'Pretty Baby,' 'Heart of Glass.' 'The Attack of the Giant Ants' sounds like a movie title, but it isn't. *Them* was the movie with the giant ants.

"Our original title for 'Heart of Glass' was 'The Disco Song,' which was kind of stupid. Mike Chapman, the producer, suggested we use 'Heart of Glass.' It's the title of a German movie. I've never seen it."

"There's no such movie."

"Why would he lie to us?"

"The human mind has its mysteries. Why did Richard Speck kill eight nurses?"

We sit in silence and ponder the meaning of it all. The tuna salad is gone. Someday we, too, shall be gone. Our minds reel with revelation, and our lips curl slowly in wisdomful smiles. We know. Yes, no matter how fleeting our time, we know. Our souls are seeds in the wind of a vast and loamless dark. And I have to go to the bathroom.

"Tell me about your new album," I ask, with piss on my fingers.

"On one side, we're gonna do a thirty minute disco extravaganza. And I met Gene Simmons the other day. He's gonna write us a scenario for the other side."

"No country songs?"

"Nah. I'll leave that to the Ramones. Besides, there are already too many female country singers. There's no room for me in country music."

"Do you have housewife instincts?"

"I wouldn't mind being a mom. I already am a housewife, I guess. I vacuum once in a while."

"Don't wanna take pills and watch TV all day?"

"Oh, god, no. I think the top of my head might hit the ceiling."

"Do you like drugs?"

"Sometimes. I know it sounds crazy coming from somebody like me, but the most satisfying feeling I have is when I'm completely straight and accomplishing something. The feeling of accomplishment is what I really like, what I really get off on. I think that love is better when you're straight, no matter what anybody says. Everything is better when you're straight, except fucking up.

"Lately, whenever I take anything, I regret it. But there have been times in my life when I really enjoyed taking dope. Right now I don't. I like what I do a lot. Dope is for when you're not satisfied with what you're doing. Drugs subtract. I'm talking about booze, too."

"What kind of birth control do you use?"

"Let's get back to music."

"For you, anything. In a lot of your stuff, especially early cuts like 'X Offender,' I hear the influence of classic girl groups, like the Crystals. Is that really there?"

"That was definitely there. That was Richard Gottehrer, the producer. He put that on there. He felt that it would really make 'X Offender' work better. We didn't write that intro, he did."

"Do you feel any ties to music of that era?"

"Oh, yeah, sure. I don't really wanna wallow in nostalgia, but I can't help but acknowledge the fact that Ronnie Spector's voice and Fontella Bass's voice were great inspirations to me. I love them. That style of music isn't really what I wanna do now. I don't even know if I could do it well, really."

"Do you see yourself as an extension of those girls?"

"No, because, despite what a lot of people think, I wasn't *that* old to be thoroughly living that existence. Music back then didn't mean all that much to me. In the mid-Sixties and late-Sixties, music had much more impact on me. Hendrix, Cream, the Beatles, the Stones, Janis. All that stuff."

"How come everybody calls Blondie a new wave group?"

"Um, well, I don't know. We're a pop group. We feel that we're part of the new wave, but when it comes down to musical definitions, we're definitely a pop group. We always tried to be a pop group."

"Did you start writing when you were a kid?"

"I seriously started to write in '64, '65. Poems. They weren't very good. I used to write little stories. Creative writing classes."

"Where'd you go to school?"

"Hawthorne. I guess some people have fun in school, but I thought it was dull."

"Hawthorne is near Paterson, right?"

"Yeah. Both my grandmothers lived in Paterson."

"A lot of people don't believe that there is such a place. In the *London Times,* in 1965, there was a piece about William Carlos Williams's poem *Paterson.* They said that, 'Paterson is an imaginary town in New Jersey which Williams created as his symbol of America.' Thirteen miles outside Newark, and those limey intellectuals thought it was a myth."

"Paterson's a great fuckin' place. They're renovating a lot of the old buildings there. They're turning all those factories near the waterfall into SoHo-type lofts. Compared to Miami, where I was born, Paterson is a vision of paradise."

"Next time you pass through Newark, drop by my old man's bar."

"What's the name of it?"

"Nick's. Tell him you're a friend of mine. He'll give you a free glass of water."

"I'll do it."

"Deborah?"

"Yes. Rick."

"Nick."

"Nick."

"Say something deep."

"Deep. Let's see."

Deborah Harry reveals that she is intrigued by the subliminal effects that music has on people; that she thinks people should try to understand the psychic phenomena that exists within themselves; and that she is looking forward to taking space shuttles. In layman's terms, no less.

Far away, in the cold Atlantic, a spear pierces the lung of a tuna. Evening is upon us. We part.

# 30

# Review of *Always Know*

What I've always liked about Thelonious Monk is exactly what I've usually found wanting in most jazzmakers since the Charlie Parker era: a disdain for intellectual sobriety.

Listening to John Coltrane, Marion Brown, and others play *Ascension* in the Sixties was a lot of fun, but the fun diminished once you realized how unnecessarily serious and straight-mouthed many of these musicians were while playing. It's as if they adhered—or, in some perverse way, *wanted* to adhere—to the awful precept that the deed of art is as somber and headachy as being forced to conjugate Greek verbs. Now we have Anthony Braxton, whose song titles are complex, mostly meaningless mathematical symbols. (And he's not trying to be funny either. If that were the case, we might have to accuse him of stealing from Abbott and Costello's old "carry the seven" routine, to which his titles bear more than a casual resemblance.)

Through all this, Thelonious Monk has remained Thelonious Monk—pure, unmysticized, unharmed by dogma or theory. The fact that he's so rarely heard is his own doing. He never liked studios much, and years ago decided he wanted the remainder of his recording done in clubs—a decision no record company has been willing to abide by.

*Always Know* is a collection of tracks spanning the years 1962 to 1968. Ten of the thirteen songs have never been released before, and the finest of these come from concerts: "Criss Cross" from the 1963 Newport Jazz Festival, "Light Blue" from New York City's Lincoln Center that same year, and "Honeysuckle Rose" from San Francisco's Jazz Workshop in 1964.

This version of "Criss Cross" was cut soon after Monk recorded the tune for his second Columbia album. It's almost twice as long as the studio original, and much of the additional length is given over to tenor saxophonist Charlie Rouse, who, during his years with Monk, proved to be a perfect musical complement to the pianist's jagged melodic lines and fast-switching meters.

In "Honeysuckle Rose," Monk does what he does best: takes an old song and loves it to death, until what remains is an essence cruelly and beautifully bared. (Anyone who's heard his version of "Dinah," on the monumental *Solo Monk,* knows that it's possible to smile with joy and feel a certain subtle horror at the same time.)

It'd be nice if Monk were making records again, but he's not. He's still in semihiding from the record companies, and until one of them is willing to give him a contract that meets his demands (in which case, he shouldn't be too hard to find: he's the only Thelonious Monk listed in the Manhattan telephone book), there's surely no reason to complain about LPs like *Always Know*. But I'm still waiting for Monk and Jerry Lee Lewis to get together for the disc that could make all these years of listening truly worthwhile.

# 31

# The Gospel
# According to Jerry Lee

Dressed like a side-street gambler from the days when chrome was chrome, Jerry Lee Lewis sits in the dressing-room of the Palomino Club, holding loosely in his lap a half-drained quart of Seagram's like the unglowing scepter of an ancient fading kingship.

He looks mean. But not as mean as last night, when he straightened out that chump in the audience with one fast, cruel line; when he threw that swaggering record-company lifer from his dressing-room; when, at night's end, he dared any man present to lift a hand against him. I tried to talk to him last night, but he was in too dark a mood. "What's the weather gonna be like tomorrow in China?" he asked me. I told him I didn't know, didn't care; and he snarled his disgust. "Where do you wanna be buried?" he asked me. "By the ocean," I answered. That was better. He nodded his indulgent approval. And so it went last night. Toward the end, he would talk of nothing but the Bible. At the end, he would talk of nothing at all.

But, yes, tonight the Killer is in a better mood. He hasn't thrown anyone out of his dressing-room, nor threatened anyone's life, nor cussed anyone too badly. Not yet, anyway. He looks at the tape-recorder which I have set before him the way a man might look at a snake, trying to decide if it's venomous. He takes one of my cigarettes and starts smoking it. I say something:

**NT:** *Yesterday we were talking about the Bible, and you said that your favorite book was Revelation.*

**JLL:** That isn't what I said. I said from Genesis to Revelation. Take it as a whole. It'd be hard to choose a favorite book in the Bible. Lord, there's so many great books. I studied it, studied it all my life. Greatest history book in the world, if you take it word for word, from Genesis to Revelation. All the way. Don't leave nothin behind. Don't skip over here and skip back over there, take what you want, leave what you want. That ain't the way God intended it to be read.

*NT: Haven't you ever run across anything in the Bible that you can't understand?*

**JLL:** You know why you don't understand it? Cuz you're lookin' for an easy way out. Now, if you can show me somethin' in there that'll show me how to get outa this thing without burnin' my ass off in hell, I wanna know where it's at.

   You and me, we're gonna burn in hell. We're in trouble. We're sinners, goin' to hell.

*NT: I ain't so sure about that. You really think we're goin' to hell?*

**JLL:** Straight as a gourd. I think we've been extended long enough. We've been smiled upon quite a bit. The time is near.

*NT: How near, Killer?*

**JLL:** Well, nearer than you think. We don't have the promise of the next breath. We're goin' to hell. Fire and brimstone. The fire never dies, the burnin' never dies, the fire never quenches for the weeping, wailing, gnashing of teeth. Yessir, goin' to hell. The Bible tells us so.

*NT: Ain't nobody going to heaven?*

**JLL:** Very few, very few. It's a hard place to get to, son. Can't get there through the Palomino Club, that's for sure. Church can't get you to heaven. Religion can't get you to heaven. Ain't no such thing as religion anyway. The Bible never speaks of religion; it speaks of salvation.

*NT: Next week, Jackson Browne and a bunch of other singers are going to perform at an anti-nuclear rally, nearby in San Luis Obispo. How do you feel about people who combine music and politics?*

**JLL:** Bunch of damn idiots.

*NT: So you don't figure on playing at any anti-nuke shows in the near future.*

**JLL:** To hell with 'em all! Blow 'em all up! Blow everybody clear to hell! Get it over quick!

   Just don't kill no alligators in Louisiana. Leave them alone. I married a few of 'em.

*NT: Did you keep the hides?*

**JLL:** They damn near got my hide.

*NT: Have you ever thought of producing your own records?*

JLL: Every record I ever done, I produced. All them cats ever did was follow me around in the studio, try to keep up with me.

Who would you vote for, me or Linda Ronstadt?

*NT: I never voted in my life. Never will.*

JLL: Well, son, what if you had to vote?

*NT: I wouldn't vote for either of you fools, that's for sure. What could force me to vote?*

JLL: Cat with a hide-whip standin' over ya, whuppin' ya on the butt with it.

*NT: Hell, I'd vote for him.*

JLL: That's sharp. You'd vote for me then.

*NT: Anything you say, Killer. Somebody was telling me the other day about your pushing a piano into the ocean.*

JLL: You're damn right I did. That was in Charleston, South Carolina, a while back. I pushed it outa the auditorium. I pushed it down the street. I pushed it down the pier. Pushed it right into the ocean.

Don't rightly recall why I did it. The piano musta been no good. I just started pushin' it and it built up steam. Conway Twitty was standin' there starin'. I don't think they ever redeemed that piano. I think Jaws got a hold of it.

*NT: You've been married five times now—*

JLL: That's my goddam business.

*NT: Do you know any more about women now than you did the first time you got married?*

JLL: A skirt's a skirt.

*NT: Is that knowledge gonna lead to a sixth marriage?*

JLL: I don't know, son. Maybe God intends for me to live out my life alone.

*NT: Have you ever thought of getting into real acting?*

**JLL:** I don't want no part of it. I hate it. Actors work hard at their job, like I do. But I never did care about actin'. That's somethin' I just never did wanna get into. There's been some great actors, though. Humphrey Bogart, Charles Laughton, Robert Mitchum. I like watchin' them old movies. I'd hate to take that part of my life away. I like to sit back and watch them suckers, enjoy 'em, knowin' I don't have to be in 'em.

Take them guys, Abbott and Costello. They were sharp, very sharp. Singin', dancin', duckin' under water, talkin', or what; it made no difference. They had it, boy, they truly did.

*NT: Do you think you might have missed out on much if you had remained down in Ferriday, Louisiana?*

**JLL:** I really don't know. I never thought about it, Killer. Hand me back my whiskey. Buncha damn drunkards around here.

Y'know, one of them things *(points to the recorder)* can get a man buried. Could get a man killed. A man be sayin' somethin' drinkin', somebody take that tape and use it against him. Get 'im killed. *(Sings:)* I'll be here, son, when you're gone. . . .

Know what I think's your problem? You want your cake and eat it, too.

*NT: Sure, why not?*

**JLL:** Damn! You just pissin' against the wind. You gonna live, you gonna die. You got a soul, you ain't no animal. And that soul's goin' to heaven or it's goin' to hell. There's just two places to go. On Judgment Day, you and I are gonna have to give account for the deeds that we've done, the sins that we've—

*NT: Why are you so obsessed with dyin' and goin' to hell, Jerry?*

**JLL:** I'm a sinner, I know it. Soon you and me are gonna have to reckon with the chilling hands of death.

*NT: Why the hell are we going to hell?*

**JLL:** Because Satan has power next to God. We ain't loyal to God, we must be loyal to Satan. Got to be loyal twenty-four hours a day, brother. There ain't no in-between. Temptation is the lowest of sins. Jesus was tempted, but he overcome it. That's why we're sittin' here now.

You are what you are. You shall serve whoever you served on earth. You can't serve two gods. You love one and hate the other. The Bible says you cannot serve God and Mammon. Can't serve two gods. You'll love one and hate the other.

**NT:** *Do you figure Elvis went to heaven or to hell?*

**JLL:** You're not draggin' me into that one. I'll tell ya, it sure is a shame. Elvis had plenty of time to prepare hisself. I talked to him quite a bit about his soul. *(Starts singing Tumbling Tumbleweeds.)*

Y'know, son, there's only been four of us: Al Jolson, Jimmie Rodgers, Hank Williams, and Jerry Lee Lewis. That's your only goddam four stylists that ever lived. We could write, sing, yodel, dance, make love, or what. Makes no damn difference. The rest of these idiots is either ridin' a damn horse, pickin' a guitar, or shootin' somebody in some stupid damn movie.

**NT:** *What other piano players do you like?*

**JLL:** Chuck Berry. Hell, I can't think of any piano players. I don't know none but myself. *(Sings:)* "Down the road, down the road, down the road apiece. . . ."

I remember that one, the piano player who did that one. That was in 1947. Then in '48 he came out with *(Sings:)* "Have fryers, broilers, and good old barbecue beef . . . you never seen such a sight, down at the house, the house, the house of blue lights." That's one of my favorites, man, I swear. People don't realize that I have been doin' these songs ever since they were number-ones, 1947, 1948. Since I was a little child, man, growin' up. *(Sings:)* "Down in New Orleans where everything's fine, all them cats are drinkin' that wine."

I got the original record of that, *Drinkin' Wine, Spo-Dee-O-Dee.* My cousin gave it to me many years ago. I played that sucker and played it and played it till I wore the damn thing out. It had it. But it didn't have it like my version had it. A song can be good, but it can't be great till I cut it.

**NT:** *Do you ever get sick of singing* Great Balls of Fire *night after night?*

**JLL:** I gotta do it. Them folks would yell for their money back if I didn't. I mean, hell, we sold like thirty-eight, thirty-nine million records on it.

*Whole Lotta Shakin'* done sold over a hundred million records, if y'can believe that. The guy that wrote it, he's been dead. They got in a big squabble over who wrote it. They don't rightly know who wrote it. The publishin' was all tied up. It went back into court again. Big Mama Thornton did it. She didn't do it like I did it, though. Hell, they oughta give me credit for writin' the damn thing. I rewrote the whole song.

It's funny that me and Elvis should have two big hit records by Big Mama Thornton. That's strange. She's been dead now for many years.

**NT:** *No, she's still alive.*

**JLL:** Hell, no, she's been dead for at least twenty years now, son, that's a fact.

**NT:** *Is it true, Jerry, that your ancestors used to own Monroe, Louisiana?*

**JLL:** That's a fact. Before it was Monroe. The Lewis Plantation. My great-great-grandfather owned it. He could take his fist, hit a horse, knock that horse to his knees. A hell of a man, Old Man Lewis. Then they turned his slaves loose.

Hell, they got a big history, the Lewises. Wild drinkers. Wild gamblers. Sinners, all of 'em.

I tell you, son. I'm a mean, mean man.

**NT:** *It would seem like that at times.*

**JLL:** Man, I could take that there tape-recorder and shove it up your—

**NT:** *Why in hell would you wanna try to do something like that?*

**JLL:** Just to prove I can.

**NT:** *Do you really think you're that mean, Jerry?*

**JLL:** Hell, I don't know. I wouldn't think so. They say I am. They've always called me the Killer. I often wondered why. I think they meant it musically-speakin' not like I'd go around killin' people. Hell, the only thing I ever killed was a Louisiana mosquito. The Killer. Lord, I hate that damn name.

# 32

# Wednesday:
# Nov. 14, 1979

| | |
|---|---|
| cigs | $ .65 |
| lunch (Szechuan House) | $4.00 |
| falafel sandwich | $1.00 |
| | $5.65 |

# 33

# A Christmas Carol

## I. Marley's Ghost

Marley was dead, to begin with. There is no doubt whatever about that. This must be distinctly understood, or nothing wonderful can come of the story I am going to relate.

Scrooge knew Marley was dead. How could it be otherwise? Scrooge and he were partners for I don't know how many years. Scrooge was his sole executor, his sole administrator, his sole assignee, his sole residuary legatee, his sole friend and sole mourner. And even Scrooge was not so dreadfully cut up by the sad event that he was not an excellent man of business on the very day of the funeral and solemnized it by signing the most lucrative government contract of his long career.

Scrooge never had old Marley's name removed from the wall directory in the lobby of their East Forty-second Street offices. There it stood, years afterward. Scrooge & Marley, Inc.

The two men had made their fortune in the manufacture of tubular products. The unlikely decision to take a crack at the nuclear-power racket had been Marley's. Oh, the unsmiling pride both men felt as they signed their first contract with the Duke Power Company of South Carolina! Three days after Tacolee Unit One commenced operation, old Marley died. His last words to Scrooge, uttered hoarsely from the starched-muslin bed of his finality, were "Always bid low, then kill the cocksuckers with escalation clauses."

Scrooge did not forget Marley's advice. How proud the deceased partner would have been of Scrooge! After Tacolee Unit One, there was Tacolee Unit Two, then Three! The Rancho Seco Station! Arkansas Unit One! Three Mile Island Units One and Two! True, Metropolitan Edison and—I quote from one of Scrooge's memos—"all those Save-the-Whale ninnies" bitched when LNI-2 went on the fritz last spring, but the PR boys down in New Orleans did their job, and not a single one of the 17 orders for reactors on hand was canceled because of the fuss. Yes! Old Marley would have been proud.

But, oh, he was a tightfisted hand at the grindstone, Scrooge! A squeezing, wrenching, grasping, scraping, clutching, covetous old sinner! Hard and sharp as flint, from which no steel had ever struck out generous fire, secret and contained, and solitary as an oyster. The cold within him froze his old features, nipped his pointed nose, shriveled his cheeks, stiffened his gait, made his eyes red and his lips blue, and hissed out shrewdly in his grating voice. No wind that blew was bitterer than he, no pelting rain less open to entreaty.

Nobody ever approached Scrooge in the street. No winos implored him to bestow a trifle toward the purchase of their midmorning Night Train; no Moonies accosted him with their proselytizing grins; no hookers sought to snap a Trojan on his gnarled, icy pecker. Such was the picture of Scrooge.

Now, once upon a time—of all the good days in the year, on Christmas Eve—Scrooge sat busy in his office. The door to his office was open so that he might keep his eye upon his clerk, Bob Cratchit, who in a dismal little room beyond, a sort of cell, was toiling at the ledgers that were the diary of Scrooge's greed. The clock struck five, and the clerk rose to leave.

"Good night, Mr. Scrooge, and Merry Christmas," said Bob Cratchit, in his small, weary voice.

"Bah!" said Scrooge. "Scumbag!" Then, under his loathsome, mint-sucking breath, as Cratchit turned away: "Eighteen-five a year, a dump full of brats to feed, a wife who's twice left him for a Roto-Rooter man, and talking about a goddamn Merry Christmas. What a fucking work of art."

Scrooge took his melancholy veal in his usual melancholy restaurant, left his usual melancholy 10 percent gratuity, went home, and, having read the day's issue of *American Metal Market* and beguiled the rest of the evening with his thoughts upon the rising price of bauxite, went to bed. Scrooge liked to sleep, for sleep is cheap.

He had no sooner broadcast his first tentative snore than the slamming sound of his front door caused his eyes to snap open and his head to snap up. This was succeeded by a clanking noise and slow, heavy footsteps, as if some person were dragging imponderable chains across the hardwood floor of the Exchange. The footsteps came straight toward his bedroom. Then he saw it.

The same face, the very same. Marley in his Brooks Brothers suit. The chain he drew was clasped about his middle. It was long and wound about him like a serpent. From it hung ledgers, petty-cash boxes, Touch-Tone phones, calculators, wire-bound bundles of rotted *Business Weeks,* deeds, Dictaphones, and a kite-tail of credit cards. His body was transparent. Scrooge had heard it said often that Marley had no balls, but he had never believed it until now.

"In life I was Jacob Marley, your partner," said the Ghost. "I wear the chain I forged in that life. I know no peace, no rest, but the incessant torture of remorse."

Scrooge stammered and sputtered and then finally demanded, "What is the main thrust of your business here tonight?"

"Business!" cried the Ghost, wringing its manicured hands. "Mankind was my business. Charity, forbearance, and benevolence were my business. The petty dealings of my greedy trade were but a drop of Perrier in the ocean of my business!"

"But," yelled Scrooge, "those thing you mention simply aren't viable. Nonoperational, the lot of 'em!"

"Hear me!" implored the Ghost. "You will be visited by Three Spirits. For the sake of your soul, heed them".

The Ghost receded from him, moaning, over and over, in a low, ghastly, and pained voice. "Let's have lunch . . . let's have lunch . . . let's have lunch . . . "

Scrooge lay alone, alarmed. He tried to say "Scumbag!" but stopped at the first syllable.

## II. The First of The Three Spirits

Scrooge awoke near midnight with a strange feeling in his dead, wizened cock. Damned if there wasn't a hand on it! This, trust me, was more bizarre than the visit by Marley's ghost, for it had been too many years to count since any hand but Scrooge's own had touched that cock, and then only to aim it toward some cold porcelain receptacle.

The Spirit to whom this hand belonged wore a tunic of the purest white, from which one lovely breast peeked with disarming innocence. She puckered her lips and made a kissing sound to the unbelieving Scrooge.

"Who and what are you?" Scrooge demanded.

"I am the Ghost of Christmas Past." The Spirit threw back the sheets, baring the cock that protruded from the faded fly of Scrooge's pajamas. She bent and caressed it with her tongue.

"Rise! Walk with me!" said the Spirit.

In a manner that was no more plausible to Scrooge himself than it would be to you were I to describe it, the Ghost of Christmas Past bore Old Scrooge through a mist of time, to places of long ago. Scrooge saw himself as a rueful young boy, sitting alone in his room at Mammona Prep. All the lads' parents had claimed them home for the Christmas holiday—all except little Ebenezer Scrooge's, whose hearts were as cold as the ice that hung from the bare oak limb outside their faraway son's window.

Scrooge saw himself again. He was older, a man in the prime of his life. His face had not the harsh lines of later years, but it had begun to wear the signs of avarice. He was in bed with his wife. Belle. In the adjacent living room the vinyl needles of a factitious fir glowed with tiny, twinkling lights. These lights cast a soft, faint patina on the ass of Belle Scrooge, who wore nothing but a pair of alligator pumps.

"Watch me play with myself," she whispered salaciously to her husband. "Bite my nipples as I play with myself."

Young Ebenezer Scrooge rolled toward her with a compromising grunt. She took his cock in her hand and massaged it until it stiffened finally.

"Eat me, Ebenezer. Spread my lips and blow on it; kiss it. Ebenezer."

He complied listlessly, staring blankly over the soft lea and vale of Belle's torso, staring at her head, which tossed and turned and moaned. "Oh, Ebenezer!" she cried. "Come inside me!" Again, he complied listlessly. "Fuck me!" Belle said into his ear. "Fuck me hard, Eb! Oh! Fuck me!" She wrapped her legs around his waist, and his balls banged against her buttocks. "Oh, Ebenezer!" she wailed at last. "Make me come; make your little Belle come." She uttered something, a sound that was like the last, vanquished petal of summer being borne by the first, chill wind of winter. Ebenezer rolled over and made a great display of sleeping.

"Spirit!" said Scrooge. "Show me no more! Conduct me to my home. Why do you delight in torturing me?"

"One shadow more!" exclaimed the Ghost, placing her hand again upon Scrooge's cock.

"No more!" cried Scrooge. "Show me no more!"

But the relentless Ghost forced him to observe what happened next.

They were in another scene and place. A man whom he did not recognize lay on a couch: naked, eyes closed. Scrooge turned to the Spirit, seeking an explanation. Then he saw *her*, slightly older now but still beautiful, saw *her* enter the room in a midnight-blue peignoir, crotchless panty hose, and—oh, cruelty!—the alligator pumps. The naked man took his flaccid cock in one hand and grabbed *her* with the other.

"Suck it, Belle," the naked man said, in a voice of cool Prussian sternness. She complied, the sounds of her sucking not unlike soft wavelets lapping against the pilings of a deserted pier.

"Suck it harder, Belle," the naked man said. She purred with delight, and the wavelets became waves. And when she had finished, Belle hugged the naked man and pronounced her undying love for him.

"Oh, the slut!" cried Scrooge. "Show me no more of this. No more, I tell you!" The Ghost saw that there were tears in Scrooge's eyes, and she removed him from that place.

Scrooge was conscious of being exhausted and overcome by an irresistible drowsiness and, further, of being in his own bedroom. He had barely time to reel to bed before he sank into a heavy sleep.

## III. The Second of The Three Spirits

Scrooge was not conscious of how long he had slept or if, indeed, he had slept, when a singular sound took command of his attention. It came from the living room, a sort of unholy purring. He rose and tiptoed toward it. The moment he crossed the doorway, a strange, girlish voice called him by his name and bade him enter. He flicked on the ceiling light and saw her, reclined in a state of easy pornography upon his couch.

She wore a full-length coat of Kojah fur, lined with black satin. Beneath this, and fashioned of the same black satin, she wore a brassiere and panties. There was a ruby in her navel. She was tall and made taller by four-inch spike heels. She tossed her blonde hair and spread her legs.

"I am the Ghost of Christmas Present," she said. "Come here, chump. Give me your hand." The Spirit placed Scrooge's hand, which was very cold, upon her satin crotch, which was very hot. His cock stirred and rose like a waking lizard within his pajamas—something it had not done in the presence of the Ghost of Christmas Past, had not, in fact, done since the night of Marley's funeral, when Scrooge and the widow Marley had performed *coitus interruptus* in the basement of the Frank E. Campbell Funeral Chapel.

"Insert two fingers!" commanded the Spirit, lowering her panties with a hooked thumb. Scrooge did as he was told. All vanished instantly. They stood in the city streets on Christmas morning. The Spirit led him straight to Bob Cratchit's home, on West Twenty-second Street. They entered, invisible.

Mrs. Cratchit's belly was pressed to the control knobs of a stove. Squeezing her, nibbling her neck and rubbing her hips, was a little fellow in an olive green uniform. His cap bore the proud insignia of the Roto-Rooter corps.

"No more," whined Mrs. Cratchit. "Enough. You'll have to leave. Bob and the kids'll be here in ten minutes."

"Aw, c'mon, sweet thing. Just lemme stick it in, then jerk off on your ass." He brought shame to his uniform.

"Oh, *men!*" cried Mrs Cratchit, suddenly pulling down her drawers and hiking up her dress with practiced expertise.

"The slut!" exclaimed Scrooge, feeling kindly toward his clerk for the first time in his life. "Judge not, chump," said the Ghost of Christmas Present. "The Lord works in strange ways."

The Roto-Rooter man stuck it to Mrs. Cratchit from behind and proceeded to rotate his swarthy root within her. "Oh! You fuck so good, Gomez!" she moaned, her eyes on the kitchen clock. He withdrew from her suddenly, shaking his head violently from side to side, like an apoplectic orangutan, and flailing his thing against Mrs. Cratchit's quivering ass. "Come, Gomez! Come, Gomez!" Mrs. Cratchit chanted. The Roto-Rooter cap shook loose from his ignoble noggin, and he came. Mrs. Cratchit reached above the sink for a handful of Bounty paper towels and then wiped the seed of Gomez from her buttocks. "Now leave, Gomez!" Gomez zippered himself, retrieved his cap, begrudgingly wished her a Merry Christmas, and slunk from the apartment—just in the nick of time, for within a matter of minutes, Bob Cratchit and all the little Cratchits were heard at the door, stamping the snow from their boots.

Bob Cratchit looked as worn and weary as ever, and yet, Scrooge thought (with something not unlike warmth), he looked happy. The children ran to the kitchen to cavort with Mrs. Cratchit. Martha was the oldest, a creature of rife virginal flesh. Belinda, the younger daughter, seemed less rife and less virginal, too. She cockled her nose: "Ick! What's that smell?" she asked her mother. "Blah! Smells like the sewer!" Mrs. Cratchit cast her a stern glance. A droplet of Gomez's seed, which she had failed to wipe away, trickled down her leg. She squeezed her thighs together and pronounced in vain the names of both Gomez and the Lord.

And, oh! Here came Tiny Tim, poor little Tiny Tim. In 1973, when Scrooge & Marley. Inc., was constructing the first Three Mile Island reactor, Scrooge had insistently requested that the Cratchits take their annual two-week vacation in Hershey, Pa., so that Cratchit would be nearby should he be needed. The Cratchits saw all there was to see of beautiful Hershey: the streetlamps shaped like Candy Kisses, the avenues dyed brown, and so forth. When Mrs. Cratchit gave birth to Tiny Tim the following year, the Three Mile Island vacation proved to have been a serious mistake. Some claimed the faint ultramarine glow that Tiny Tim cast at times to be an aura, the blessed sign of his profound purity of soul. Others, however, spoke of radiation poisoning and refused to be in the same room with the frail little lad. It must be said that he did now luminesce distinctly as he entered the kitchen at the side of his father.

Mrs. Cratchit tore into her husband immediately. She began with the shopping list and then went for his balls. It was a familiar routine, and humble Bob persevered admirably.

"I sincerely hope that you enjoy this turkey, Robert, because you may as well know it cost twenty-three dollars. And did you know that Stove Top Stuffing has hit the dollar mark? No, I don't suppose you've even noticed. And these Royal Prince Fancy Yams don't grow on trees, either. Four bucks. Robert. Yes, that's right. And, of course, you can't go without your dessert; we couldn't have that." She paused affectedly. "Betty Crocker Snackin' Cake, *a buck eighteen!* The cranberries, I won't even talk about.

"We're being eaten alive, Robert. That's what the man on 'Phil Donahue' said this morning. His exact words: *eaten alive!* We are the *casualties of inflation*, Robert. You should be taking home twice as much. That cheap bastard has you *scared*, Robert. You ask him for a raise, he threatens to replace you with some Harvard Business School graduate, and *you back down*. Call his bluff, Robert! What's the worst that can happen? We end up begging in the street for our daily Snackin' Cake? Robert, it's almost come to that already! Jesus, you give that bastard your life's blood for a shitty eighteen-five a year. Robert, you know there are *Roto-Rooter men* out there clearing twenty and change—"

As usual, she had gone too far, and Bob Cratchit left the room. He glanced at *TV Guide* and then, with a resigned sigh, turned on the WPIX Yule Log, which blazed brilliantly. Tiny Tim, who held his own against the glowing Yule Log, curled up at Bob's side.

Soon Mrs. Cratchit came into the living room, kissed her husband on the head, and apologized. Tiny Tim smiled. The two daughters rubbed their tender loins against pieces of furniture. Bob Cratchit rose to carve the turkey.

"God bless us every one!" said Tiny Tim, spraying out the words and causing the room to fill briefly with the faint, noxious odor of ozone.

"Spirit," said Scrooge, with an interest and a guilt he had never felt before, "tell me if Tiny Tim will live."

"I see a vacant seat by the TV," replied the Ghost. "If these shadows remain unaltered by the Future, the child will die."

"No, no," said Scrooge. "Oh, no, kind Spirit! Say he will be spared. They all seem so pitiful and yet, somehow, so happy, so *viable*."

"Better believe it, chump. That's as good as it gets."

"But I must know! Tiny Tim—"

"Eat me, chump."

Falling to his knees, as the Cratchits ate their Christmas dinner, Scrooge filled his mouth with the wet cunt of the Ghost of Christmas Present. And he liked it.

## IV. The Last of The Spirits

Having returned miraculously to his bedroom upon the very moment of the Ghost's orgasm, Scrooge, for the first time this night, felt no exhaustion, no drowsiness, naught but eagerness for the arrival of the last of the three Spirits that Marley's Ghost had promised him. He sat there, Old Scrooge did, like a little boy, bouncing and twitching and smacking his lips—lips anointed by the nectar of the cunt of a wondrous Spirit, he reminded himself, with an elderly giggle—yes, bouncing and twitching and smacking in great expectations.

Then he saw it, and he became still.

The Phantom slowly, gravely, silently, solemnly approached. When it came near him, Scrooge bent down upon his knee, for the very air through which this Spirit moved seemed to scatter gloom and mystery and despair.

The Spirit was not so much dressed as shrouded, in a deep black garment, which concealed its head, its face, its form, and left nothing of it visible save one outstretched hand.

"Are you a boy or a girl?" inquired Scrooge. The fact was, he had experienced quite a sexual rejuvenation during the course of the night's events and was, by this time, nursing a singularly awesome erection.

The Spirit answered not.

"But," said Scrooge, "you are the Ghost of Christmas yet to Come?"

Again, the Spirit answered not but pointed onward, with its outstretched hand.

"You are about to show me things that will occur in the time before us," Scrooge pursued. "Is that so, Spirit?"

The Phantom kicked Scrooge swiftly in his ass, and off they went, into blackness, uncertain horror, and the shadows of things to be.

They came to the Cratchit apartment. Much had changed. As the mighty WPIX Yule Log flickered, it illuminated lines of premature aging in the face of Mrs. Cratchit. And, oh! What was this? Bob Cratchit's beloved E-Z recliner was occupied by the loathsome Gomez! Tiny Tim was not to be seen, but an empty pall was to be felt. The two Cratchit girls stared blankly at the Yule Log. When they rose and went to the kitchen, Gomez spoke.

"C'mere. sweet thing, feel this, heh-heh." he said.

"You're a beast, Gomez. Tiny Tim's not three days in the ground, and you won't quit hounding me for a goddamn handjob," hissed Mrs. Cratchit.

"Hey, you don't have to remind *me* that Tiny Tim's dead. Who paid for the funeral, after all? Not that wimp of an ex-husband of yours; that's for sure. A lead casket, no less. Couldn't be aluminum, like everybody else's."

"Gomez, stop it! I've explained to you. There were health regulations!" she fairly yelled. The Yule Log burnt a sorrowful blue.

"Spirit!" Scrooge cried. "Say it is not so! What, what has become of poor Bob Cratchit?"

Scrooge was then swiftly led across town on this gloomy future Christmas, led to a funeral parlor on Lexington Avenue, where, in a small, lavender room, Bob Cratchit, who was looking none too well in either heel or soul, sat silently, grayly, by a coffin.

Scrooge at first thought the coffin to be Tiny Tim's. But, no, that could not be. Mrs. Cratchit had said poor Tim had been laid to rest three days past; besides, this coffin was much too large for little Tim's body. The unspeaking Phantom brought him closer, and he gazed down into the coffin. He saw himself, and he wailed and he wailed. The Phantom moved not.

Soon another man entered the room. Scrooge recognized the man, barely, from the Accounting Department. Cratchit and this man spoke, and, slowly, piece by piece, Scrooge learned the details of his own death.

"If only he would've been satisfied with what he already had," said the accountant. "If only he hadn't gotten involved in that reactor-vendor scheme down in Brazil—"

"He'd still be alive," said Cratchit.

"Hell, fuck him," said the accountant. "There'd still be a Scrooge & Marley Corporation. We'd still have jobs."

"What an awful way to go, nonetheless. They say the blast wiped out a third of the population of São Paulo."

Scrooge suddenly collapsed in a sobbing heap at the feet of the Phantom. He awoke that way: sobbing and clutching his sheets.

## V. The End of It

He was dressed and out the door this Christmas morning in a matter of minutes. To the grocer's he went, buying with glee a king's ransom of delicacies, including several packages of the cherished Snackin' Cake. Then to Bob Cratchit's home!

Scrooge and the Cratchits ate Christmas dinner together. Scrooge promised to raise Bob's salary and disclosed to Bob his plans for getting out of the nuclear-energy racket and into something more honorable.

Scrooge was better than his word. He did it all and infinitely more, and to Tiny Tim, who did *not* die, but became, rather, a solvent cult figure, Scrooge was a second father. And to Mrs. Cratchit, who appreciated Bob's new salary as much as Bob did, Scrooge became a second Gomez. And so, as Tiny Tim observed, God bless us, every one! And that includes you, Gomez.

# 34

I always felt that my friend Richard Meltzer was the only true philosopher with rock-'n'-roll sensibilities, a man whose brilliance allowed him to perceive the pre-Socratic elements at the heart of rock 'n' roll. If there ever was a great rock-'n'-roll writer, it was Richard, who *wrote* rock 'n' roll as purely and as wildly as Jerry Lee and Sam the Sham made it. And, while Richard and he don't see eye to eye, I've always felt that Greil Marcus was perhaps the most perceptive, and certainly as a writer the best and most gifted, of those who wrote about rock 'n' roll in a manner more traditional than Richard's.

The piece that follows appeared as the prologue in the book *Stranded,* which was edited by Greil, and which Knopf published in December of 1979. (The true first edition has Greil's name spelled wrong on the spine.) The story of how this piece caused the book to be abandoned by Oxford, the publisher that had contracted it, amid an uproar over a single line that was viewed by some Oxford workers as a communiqué direct from the Antichrist of all that was politically correct—a line that I drew from life—is fully recounted in the introduction that Greil wrote to the later edition of *Stranded* that Da Capo published in 1996.

# The Sea's Endless,
# Awful Rhythm & Me Without
# Even a Dirty Picture

Call me Gilligan. As I confront in earnest the problems of divine retribution, way-out sex, and the value of the Folk Mass, so I confront the desert-island question.

I must say that the idea of being marooned somewhere with neither whiskey nor Jewish girls troubles me greatly, and I believe, as the nightmared child believes in morning and its peace, that the God of the New Testament shall see to it that I am accompanied upon the rough-hewn raft of my solitude by at least a case of Tullamore Dew and La Louise in Diorissimo ultrasheer, off-black panty-hose. But, Lord, I am a humble man, and would settle for Carstairs and my first wife.

And what book should I take with me from the lending library of poetic justice? Perturbed by the fate of the Russian ivory-hunter in *Heart of Darkness*, who was stranded with naught to read but *An Inquiry into Some Points of Seamanship*, I have given the matter much thought, and have chosen Richmond Lattimore's translation of Pindar's *Odes* (Chicago, 1947), with issue number twenty-six of *Leg Art* (San Pedro, 1976) concealed between its pages. And Mr. Kurtz be damned.

But the phonograph record. Ah, the record. Presuming that some dolt and colleague, less dignified with the meter and metaphor than myself, has elsewhere in these pages brought something not wholly unlike wit to bear upon the Las Vegas odds against encountering electric circuitry on an uninhabited island, I shall ignore the opportunity for runny-nosed humor—reminding all who would not of Goethe's remark to Chancellor von Müller, "The possible will be attempted only because we have postulated the impossible"—and instead, sacrificing at the altars of charm and hyperbole as little honesty as possible, speak from the heart. Together, in my bathroom, like this.

The record I would take is *Sticky Fingers*, by the Rolling Stones. There is something about the dullness of my choice that bothers me; but *Sticky Fingers* it is. The Tullamore Dew, La Louise, the *Odes, Leg Art*—of these things I am sure beyond doubt. But *Sticky Fingers* is a choice as mysterious and as difficult to explain to myself as to anyone else.

At first, I thought of bringing a Jerry Lee Lewis album. The Killer has been a constant inspiration to me, and I've always believed that he's the last man to have been touched by the Holy Ghost of Gnosis. The powers of his music—that loud, unspeakable philosophy of his Horus-Snopes soul; the search through mania and excess for that unknown, unknowable sin without which there can be no redemption or damnation more thrilling than any redemption or damnation known to the gelt rest; the pitting within of good against evil without knowing, maybe even caring to know, or refusing to know, one from the other—are more than rock 'n' roll, or whatever you want to call it. They are powers of light and dark, wickedness and strength, and they are powers that can cure and heal and cause miracles. The trouble is that Jerry Lee has never made a great album, largely because of Jerry Kennedy, the member of the Nashville mediocrity conspiracy who produced his work from 1968 to 1978. For these sins, as sure as the Venerable Bede deals three-card monte in the hereafter, Jerry Kennedy will pay. And I will disembark upon my desert island without the music of Jerry Lee Lewis.

Then I thought of the Chieftains, and how I love to play *Bonaparte's Retreat* in the middle of the night, and how I could listen to it forever. But there is something too eerie, too wraithful in the Chieftains' wedding of pagan joy and Gaelic mourning. To be left alone with such music, especially after the whiskey ran out, could be quite dangerous to my spiritual well-being, the stability of which has not commonly been likened to a large rock. Besides, it is rare for me to hear the Chieftains without thinking of (*a*) La Margaret, the prodigious mucus of whose lust I was anointed with while "An Chéad Mháirt den Fhomhar" filled the Nashville night and the first chill hours of 1978 with the caws of estrangement, and (*b*) the Bells of Hell, that New York bar where I sat, leaning toward 4 a.m., hugged by perniciousness, listening to the Chieftains' sullen juke-box magic, night after wasted night. No, it simply wouldn't do.

I turned to the Doors, to their reduction of all to sex, death, and rhythm. Before I decided which Doors album I would bring, I realized that, in solitude, I wouldn't want to be with the voice of someone so newly dead. I wanted a *memento vivere*, not a *memento mori*. For the same reason, I resolved not to bring Lynyrd Skynyrd's *Gimme Back My Bullets*, an album I listen to far more often than *Sticky Fingers*.

I listen to Randy Newman more than I listen to anyone else, but while Randy Newman's songs give me more pleasure, and impress me more, than anyone else's, I don't think one of his records could much assuage my solitude, for his are songs of people and people's delicate mysteries (of which I would not care to be reminded on my unpeopled isle), and little of his work reaches, with word or rhythm, into the greater, indelicate mystery—Tá MUothrion DeLuxe—which makes and vanquishes the lesser mysteries. And here even I cease to understand what I'm saying; so let's move on.

The Rolling Stones supplied the soundtrack for much of my grown-up life. When I first heard "(I Can't Get No) Satisfaction," I was fifteen years old, and had never gotten laid. I remember sitting with my *citrulli* friends on the concrete steps of a store, where one could either play the numbers or buy dog food, beer, cigarettes, and the full line of fine Contadina products, on the corner of Clendenny and Miller in Jersey City, smoking two-cent loosies, and hearing that new Rolling Stones song blare from a transistor radio. It was unlike anything else to be heard that summer of 1965. Lurid, loud, and concupiscent, it was at once a yell of impotence and of indomitability. Its conspiratorial complaints sanctified our frustrations, and its vicious force promised deliverance. It gave us power over girl-creatures, and made of our insignificant, wastrel cocks spigots of wordless insolence—which, of course, we had always wanted them to be. I was arrested for the first time that summer, for D&D.

When I first heard "Have You Seen Your Mother, Baby, Standing in the Shadow," I had taken five blood-orange capsules of Dexedrine and was riding with friends through the streets of Hoboken, looking for girls who would let us share the miracle of physical love with them. It was the first really cold night of the fall, 1966. The apocalyptic dissonance of the record struck me first, and then the surly notion of throwing at the face of the neurotic, castaway girlfriend the image of her mother, and sneering, in afterbreath, at the girl's pregnancy. Swathed and speeding, we prowled with the windows shut against the black coldness, looking for feminine throats in the shadows, where there were none, listening to that, smiling terribly, and feeling, with something like orgasm, our existences contract beatifically into that terrible smiling.

In the late summer of 1969, I wasn't thinking of music. I had then terminated two years of bliss, or its reasonable facsimile, with La Dominique, the lovely daughter of Perpignan and of the sea, upon the small of whose lithe back I had painted a perfect Day-Glo Ronsonol can, its spouter cocked, like the slender finger of Botticelli's *Calumny*, toward the dimple of her dextral shoulder, and within the penetralia of whose softness I had, for seven-times-seventy nights, studied the craft of prostatial eloquence. I was employed as a paste-up man for Lovable Underwear in New York, devoting my creativity to tasks such as the production of cordate stickers for pantyhose packages which bore the legend, "No bag! No sag!" I knew contentment. One night I went into Ojay's Bar on Ninth Street near Avenue A, right around the corner from Ed Sanders's Peace Eye Book Store. I stood at the bar between a moist short man with dried blood on the front of his shirt, at whom the bartender frequently glared, and a young couple who hissed at one another in clipped cadences of wrath—there was a journey to Pennsylvania, to visit someone's relatives, involved; also a matter of stingy behavior regarding the sharing of egg rolls. And from the jukebox came the lewd, commanding sound of Charlie Watts's cowbell, making with a stick and a piece of copper a truer, greater rhythm than most can make with a wealth of electric equipment. I realize now that "Honky Tonk Women" was welcome detumescence for the sixties, and a surly, languid waking from the restless sleep of ideology. It strutted its indolence, as one who nods off while fucking. As "Satisfaction" had been innocent in its discontent, "Honky Tonk Women" was wise in its slavering contentment. It washed my mind—indeed, washed Ojay's and the slow river of dark night that ran without—in a perverse peace; and before the evening was over, it had become my favorite song.

And I will tell you of crab music, and of much else besides. In the spring of 1972, my friend Charlie and I were living in Tampa, and were without money. Charlie had been working for Budweiser and wanted to get fired so that he could lay back for a while drawing unemployment. With that end in mind, he had sat down with a crisply sharpened Budweiser pencil, a Budweiser Clydesdale calendar, and a small pad of Budweiser stationery. To be eligible for unemployment benefits, he needed a minimum of twenty work-weeks under his belt. After checking, double-checking, and triple-checking, he had circled upon his Budweiser Clydesdale calendar the date that would mark his hundredth day of loading Budweiser beer into Budweiser trucks. The hundred-and-first day was to have been M-day. There was only one sure way to be canned at his job. On his first day at work, his supervisor (a man who, it is said, listed "Gum" as his hobby on a job application) had informed Charlie that anyone stupid enough to crack open a ceiling sprinkler valve while operating a forklift would immediately receive his walking papers. Such was the Budweiser *lex non scripta*. Two in the past had been careless enough to transgress, and they had both been fired before—and here came the phrase the supervisor savored—the first drop of water hit the floor. Thrilled by the notion of whiling away the summer drinking Georgia peach wine in the Clearwater sand, Charlie had arrived at work on M-day, mounted a forklift, scooped up eight feet of clanking Budweiser cases, looked to be sure his supervisor was nearby, elevated the lift to its maximum height, drawn a bead, and proceeded to smash into a sprinkler valve. The next afternoon, while sitting in the downtown unemployment office, certain errors in his computations had come to light. Pencil, pad, and calendar notwithstanding, Charlie had somehow fallen short of the hundred-day mark by eleven days. His reply to the lady at the unemployment office included strange allusions to the miracle of the loaves and feverish indictments of those who would manufacture defective calendars.

As for myself, I had been fired from my job as editor of *TV Weekly* ("The Bay Area's Only TV Magazine"), for a number of devious deeds, such as fabricating an exclusive interview with Joan Blondell, in which La Blondell confessed that she had cooked and eaten her three-year-old daughter. ("'It tasted like *blanquette de veau,* which I love,' said the former star of ABC's *Here Come the Brides,* indicating with coy fingers the bloated, sixty-year-old flesh of her midsection, which mutely testified to the love she professed.") The publisher, who was also a local disk jockey, told me, upon delivering my final paycheck, that I was deranged. I told him, in response, that I planned to blow his bowels asunder with my AMP .44.

Charlie and I sat and thought. Between us, we had ninety dollars in folding money and a pint jar of pennies and dimes. We owed ninety-eight dollars for the rent and fourteen for the electric. It was then that we conceived Grab-a-Crab.

Our closet contained thirty cases of beer, conservative estimate, which Charlie had stolen from Budweiser over the months. We decided that we could load the trunk of our car each morning with beer and boiled crabs (which we were to harvest from Tampa Bay), and drive to the Courtney Campbell Causeway, where, parked on the side of the road, we would sell our goods to the beach traffic. For a dollar, you'd get a crab and a beer. Perhaps we would include a few saltines to fancy things up. Since paper plates and napkins were to represent our only overhead, profits would be considerable. Soon, Grab-a-Crab franchises would proliferate along the Gulf. We would acquire great wealth, wed lovely girls with hyphenated names and masochistic streaks, sire children with strange, Nordic noses. Money would lose its value, but greed would not. I would sit, high above Newark, gazing into the night and pondering the meaning of it all: Charlie dead by his own hand; the woman of my life's summer locked in a home for the sweepingly insane. I sip the fine Armagnac, watching passion pull at the face of La Contessa. She grasps my arm. I look into her eyes and see something I would never dare betray unto words. She speaks, and the sound of her voice makes me think of the Aegean and that night in Kálimnos, how many years ago?

"Fuck me," La Contessa says. "Fuck me till blood runs down my leg."

To celebrate the birth of the Grab-a-Crab empire, Charlie and I ate many micrograms of psilocybin and lay by the sea. A crab—the Magna Mater of all crabs—marched from her saline source and danced at our feet. She reared up and snapped her claws, commanding silence throughout the garden of God. In the distance, the voice of a he-child whined, "I don't want no hamburger. I want a crab, mommy! I want a crab!" As the child's voice faded, the crab spun around and marched back into the sea. And from somewhere came, quite loudly, the Rolling Stones' "Sympathy for the Devil," a record perfectly suited, we realized at once and forever, to the hermétic dance of crabs. The song's demonic owlings whistled through us as day became night, and we felt fate to be a faithful wife at our feet, and we felt blessed.

But we discovered that it took nearly two hours to pluck a lone crab from the gazpacho of pollutants that is Tampa Bay. We knew pain and emptiness, and eventually we knew eviction. I soon found myself, thick newspapers wrapped around my legs with wire, hunting snakes in the Everglades. Doctor Haast of the Miami Serpentarium, the nation's largest dealer of antivenin, paid two dollars per foot for live rattlesnakes and cottonmouths; more for coral snakes, America's only neurotoxic reptile. And there was a standing reward of a thousand dollars for anyone who could bring in a rattlesnake over six feet long. One morning, hung over unto the point of apoplexy, I was bit on the shin, right through the realestate section of the Sunday *Herald*. Next to me in the emergency ward was a boy who held a Maxwell House coffee can to his neck, to catch the blood that dribbled from a cut in his throat. In his lap was a cassette recorder playing the new Stones album, *Exile on Main Street*.

And from there things got worse. But I was young. I got over it.

[Here occurs a pause, the gravity of which mere indentation could only hint at, but which additional leading would render too melodramatic.]

The Rolling Stones have always been looking over my shoulder, and I feel comfortable with them. I probably would not play *Sticky Fingers* too often on my desert island, but I know it would, like Pindar, like *Leg Art*, fulfill a need finely. Whenever I felt as if I were missing something back home, I could play "Bitch" or "Dead Flowers" to inspire cynical estrangement. "Moonlight Mile" would be perfect for staring out into the white-capped nothingness. For a spiritual anthem, I'd have "You Gotta Move," that song of sacred fatalism written by my father, Fred McDowell, and the Holy Ghost, and done best by the Rolling Stones. And should the days of solitude run into years, I might even figure out the lyrics of "Sway."

And when that devious-cruising *Rachel,* in her retracing search after her missing children, finds me, I will tell all about it. You can kill Grab-a-Crab, but you can't kill the dream. No, never.

# 35

I don't really recall when these lyrics were written, but my inclination is to put them here, at the end of the seventies or the start of the eighties.

Over the years, several musicians and singers tried, or wanted to try, to set these words to music; but it was not until 1998, when I began working with the legendary Homer Henderson of Dallas, that these and other of my lyrics became songs. "The Sweet Thighs of Mother Mary" was the first of them that Homer recorded, with Lulie Scott as the voice of the Virgin Mary.

# The Sweet Thighs of Mother Mary

I dreamt last night of a bosom divine,
a bosom so pristine, so pure,
and from it bubbled whiskey like milk;
I sucked till my poor jowls were sore.

I raised my head to cop a look
at the face of this nocturnal queen;
I reeled back, my loins shrank in fear
at the wonder that I seen:

Above her head hovered a band of gold,
a halo of unearthly light,
and when she spoke, a voice so pure
did shatter the silence of night:

"I am Mary, mother of God;
please try to understand:
I ain't had no rough stuff since way back B.C.;
won't you be my lover man?"

O sweet thighs of Mother Mary!
Please hear the prayer of my heart:
rock me and roll me and bear me away.
O what a swell Mom thou art!

# 36

# Pizza Man

I'm a pizza man.
Got a pizza-man apron,
Got a pizza-man pan;
Sometime it gets real hot,
I turn on the pizza-man fan.

Been a pizza man most all my life.
Every Tuesday night, I bring some home to the wife.
Got anchovies, pepperoni, sazeech too;
Just tell me what you want, I'll make it up for you.

One night a colored boy come in,
Stuck a gun to my head,
Said, "Hand it over, pizza man,
Or you're gonna be dead."
Took that gun right outa his hand;
Teach the colored boy to fuck with the pizza man.

I'm a pizza man,
Wouldn't trade places with no man in town.
The economy, she goes up,
The economy, she goes down,
But the pizza man, baby, will always be around.

# 37

# Lust Among the Adverbs

Literary obscena, the secret smut of famous authors, is an area of literature seldom spoken of. Goethe is celebrated for *Faust,* but far less dull are the dirty letters, written at the time of *Faust,* in which he begged his wife, Christiane, to "Please send me your last pair of shoes, already worn out in dancing," so that the pensive poet might perform unclean deeds with them. Joyce's *Ulysses* is taught in schools, but not so those less pretentious letters, penned in 1909, in which he tells his wife, Nora, that "the two parts of your body which do dirty things are the loveliest to me. I prefer your arse, darling, to your bubbies because it does such a dirty thing. I love your cunt not so much because it is the part I block but because it does another dirty thing. . . . I wish I could hear your lips spluttering those heavenly exciting filthy words, see your mouth making dirty sounds and noises, feel your body wriggling under me, hear and smell the dirty fat girlish farts going pop pop pop out of your pretty bare girlish bum and *fuck fuck fuck fuck* my naughty little hot fuckbird's cunt for ever."

Unlike the dirty letters of James Joyce, which were published in 1975, in *Selected Letters of James Joyce,* the dirty letters of most other famous authors have not seen the light of day. Joseph Blotner, the editor of *Selected Letters of William Faulkner,* declared that some of Faulkner's correspondence, "of the sort to be found in the published letters of James Joyce," had been omitted, with the wish that "the reader will not begrudge the artist this shred of privacy." And so it goes, more or less, with the editors of other literary letters when confronted with the hot stuff.

Privacy is not as important as a good laugh; we herewith present a packet of dirty love letters which might have been written by some of America's most important authors, who shall remain anonymous. These letters are fake, of course; but, then again, so is the greater part of literature.

June 7, 1961
Ketchum, Idaho

Maria,

Do you remember? Do you remember the time I came to your bed the night before the attack at Pozoblanco and I placed my hand upon your breast? My hand was rough and hard. Your breast was smooth and soft.

"I am afraid," you said.

"No. Do not be afraid, *mujer.*"

"I am ashamed," you said.

"No. Do not be ashamed."

"I am ashamed and frightened," you said.

"No. Do not be ashamed and do not be frightened, *mujer.*"

"We can not go on speaking like this," you said.

"Here," I said. I placed your hand which was smooth and soft upon the buttons of my fly. *"Que salga el toro,"* I said.

You took my *carabine* in your hand, which was smooth and soft.

"It is the color of burnt gold," you said.

"Watch it, *puta*. There is room for only one *escritor* in this bed."

"I am afraid," you said.

"Speak not. Speak not."

I lay upon you and within you. My body was rough and hard. Your body was smooth and soft.

"Your chin scratches my shoulder," you said as you felt the earth move beneath you.

"I have no tools to shave," I said as my *carabine* discharged.

You shuddered as the earth halted beneath you.

"Speak not. Speak not," I said. "Your eyes tell me that you are happy and that once you wanted to die but now you are happy that you did not die. You are so happy that you did not die. Truly happy. And you love me, *mujer*. And you will never do with any other *hombre* what you have done with me. And I am Oak Park, Illinois's greatest living Spanish-speaking writer."

I was tired from speaking such a long paragraph, and I slept. You held my *cojones,* and you wept. A woman who has felt the earth move weeps much.

That was long ago, Maria. My Spanish is better now. But my *carabine* is old and rusted. I must know, Maria. Was I the only one?

Have you felt the earth move with other men? Was my Spanish really that bad? On second thought, speak not.

Another long paragraph. I must rest. Yes. My *carabine* and I, we must rest.

*Adios from Idaho,*
*Papa*


May 12, 1968
New York, N.Y.


Dearest Joe,

I can no longer suffer in silence. My heart is burning with desire. The warm, sopping lips of my womanhood sing a blue song.

I can't stand it. Every night the same dream. You stand over me as I lie naked in my bed. You remove your shirt, then your pants. I stare at the huge, angry penis standing erect against your stomach. It's so red. All those veins. It looks like it would burst.

"Kiss it, baby." You push it toward my face and fill my mouth with your base, throbbing manhood. My lips tremble as my tongue goes mad.

You lie on top of me. You mouth my breasts. Suddenly you stab that cruel pulsing thing between my legs. Pushing, pushing. I feel your fingers everywhere. On my breasts. In my rear. The repeated thrust of your penis is ripping me apart. O God, you're killing me, Joe! I bite my lips to keep from screaming and dig my Revlon Fabu-Nails into your manly back.

"Great, eh, baby? Fuck me. Fuck me!" I hear you mutter as a blinding pain tears through me. Suddenly you wrench your penis from me and mount my face. I feel your hot goo shoot onto my forehead and drip down my nose. My darling poodle, Josephine, hops onto the bed and licks your juices from my skin with her little pink tongue.

Then you lie next to me and say vile, nasty things as I masturbate. Faster and faster, my taut fingers strum between my legs. You hiss foul words about my nipples and my rear. You threaten to make me eat my panty hose. You call me a bitch and a floozie and a cheap one-night stand.

"I'll fuck you till the cows come home, you dirty little nympho." That is what I hear you say as I explode with orgasm.

You hold me in your arms and softly sing "I've Got a Lovely Bunch of Coconuts." Sleep overtakes me, and I drift off smiling.

Make my dream come true. You must, Joe. Come to me, you hunk. We'll cohost an evening on your talk-show that neither of us will ever forget. I promise.

*Long, deep kisses,*
*Jackie*


November 9, 1952
Oxford, Miss.


Dear Miss Joan:

Last night I had the strangest dream. You and I were walking, walking down creekside in the mist, in the drenched myriad waking life of grasses, at that moment after the false dawn, that interval's second between it and the moment which birds and animals know: when the night at last succumbs to day; and we began to hurry, trot, not to get anywhere quicker, for we knew not where we were going, but because we must get there, somewhere, wherever it was, soon, without fear, calmly, in the growing visibility, the subtle gradation from gray through primrose to the morning's ultimate and indomitably bright gold.

We came to a run-down one-room shack and entered it, not so much from curiosity, for now the merged and mingled breath of our being had been overtaken by a greater, darker, and more unvarying breath, a breath beyond things such as curiosity and fear and strength and the countless other lesser and greater things that cause men to do what they do, but rather in spite of curiosity. The shack was dark. Across a missing pane of its only window a sheet of rusted tin was nailed. There was a quilt-and-straw bed in the center of the shack. When I saw that bed, I knew, knew not so much from intellect or from experience but rather from that same preternatural reflex of knowing which causes the parched soil to know that rain is impending and the hog to know that the barbecue is near, what I must do.

"Lay down," I said to you. "Lay down; hit won't hurt you none. All you got to do is lay down."

"That's what that nigger said and that Jew lawyer from Memphis. 'Lay down; hit won't hurt you none.' I bled for days," you said.

"But this is differ'nt, you see. I ain't like them. I ain't. I'm William Faulkner, I am. I got me a *No*-bel Prize. These old boys over there, they taken me to dinner and give it to me, let me keep it they did."

"Sho. You tellin' me you got a prize for—" you looked at the bed in bemused disbelief.

"Don't you worry none what I got it for; just you lay down," I said.

"Hell fire," you said. "Why should I?"

"Because," I said. "Because you must flee from something of suffering, surrender the burden of lust and desire and pride, even that of functional independence, to become as an embryo for a time yet retaining still a little of the old incorrigible earthy corruption—the light sleeping at all hours, the boredom, the wakeful and fretful ringing of little bells between the hours of midnight and the dead, slowing dawn—yes; this for a while, then to be born again, to emerge renewed, to bear the world's weight for another while. And because my britches is about to burst with this hyar boner."

"Sho," you said.

I touched you then, got you all nekked and fiddled with you, saw your green eyes go cloudy like hothouse grapes and your mouth fall open in a kind of sullen wonder. You laid down there on that quilt-and-straw bed, and you closed your eyes, and I stared at you, stared at all that rife young female meat. I grasped your flanks and sank my laureate head into your loins.

There was a string there. The Old Colonel had told me of many things in my youth. He had prepared me for much, but not for this. *Hell fire.* I thought, *that Jew lawyer from Memphis never truly took her price tag off.* I gave it a yank with my teeth and out it came, attached to a piece of your inner workings. *Hell fire,* I thought, as the blood trickled down my chin, *I busted her, tore a piece of her galmeat plumb out.* Then I realized what it was: some new variation upon the device of menstrual bandage. I spat it upon the ground and silently prayed that the Old Colonel bore me no witness from above.

"Do it to me, Mr. Bill," you said. "Do it to me. Like them hogs in Sutpen's front yard. Penetrate me, Mr. Bill. Penetrate me and make sounds like them hogs."

I stuck it to you then, planted my flesh within the sorghum fastness of your loins, began to jerk and whinny as your flanks rippled with the thick, lightninglike celerity of badgers or coons. But jerk and whinny as I might, my flesh would not unleash its seed. I cursed the nine tumblers of Jack Daniel's I had had for breakfast, and I withdrew my flesh from the clenching sorghum source of its frustration.

"Put it in your mouth," I said. "Hit won't hurt you none. All you got to do is draw on it a while."

"I never seen Sutpen's hogs do no such thing," you said.

"Sutpen's hogs never got no damn *No*-bel Prize, neither," I said.

You took it into your mouth, tasted your own gal-juice. I moved against your face and told you all about the last ding-dong of doom and the last worthless rock hanging tideless in the last red and dying evening and the indomitability of man. As usual, that did the trick: my flesh expectorated its seed into your gullet. I thought of grandmother's funeral and the way the sun refused to come out from behind that one dark cloud. Then I reeled in my cock and headed for the door.

"Wait, Mr. Bill," you said. "What about me?" You spread the sorghum lips of your galhood in adjuration.

"Women, shit," I said. "I got me business to attend to, *No*-bel business." And I left you there, left you lying prone and vanquished in the early-morning embrace of the season of rain and death.

I am aware, Miss Joan, that there is 30 years of difference in our ages, that nothing like what happened in the dream, no matter how beautiful such a notion might seem, is likely to happen between us. But maybe you might could send me one of those things with the strings anyhow, just so maybe I could fiddle with it a while out back.

*Indomitably,*
*Mr. Bill*

May 7, 1873
Rome

Mother Dearest:

Your devoted son Henry has come to be possessed of a most delicate and disconcerting perplexity. It is this perplexity that compels me, once again, Mother, to seek to lay my head in your softly enclosing lap; to gain the counsel of your patient wisdom and the solace of your exquisite maternity.

There is a young lady, Mother, whom I have encountered here amid the grandeur and gloom of the Eternal City. I hasten to assure you, Mother, lest you succumb to the wages of an hasty interpretation of the foregoing disclosure, that this young lady is not a *native* of the place, but, rather, like myself, a civilized—or, so I thought—person abroad. Her name is Elena Lowe, and she is the daughter of the eminent Bostonian Francis Lowe.

I met her at Assisi, where I had journeyed to celebrate the eve of my thirtieth birthday—oh! how your little Henry has grown, Mother!—by absorbing myself in the frescoes of Giotto that adorn the Basilica Superiore of St. Francis. As I encountered her, she was regarding, with a most particular species of bemusement, a likeness of Gregory IX. She was extraordinarily white, and her every element and item was pretty: her eyes, her ears, her hair, her hands, her feet—to which her relaxed attitude as she leaned against an arch gave a great publicity—and the numerous ribbons and trinkets with which she was bedecked.

"Pardon me, Miss," I said, daring the impropriety of a casual introduction. "I suspect that we are compatriots. My name is Henry James. Risking both backache and gastric fever, I have ventured abroad to compose a novel."

She smiled as I tugged at the bell rope of my brain for a feeble tinkle of conversation. Her smile mesmerised me. It was beautiful, mysterious, melancholy, inscrutable. In no way, however, did it prepare me for what she was about to say.

"Don't you find this place to be filled with a great erotic electricity?" she asked insouciantly.

My heart struck a single mighty beat, and I fairly felt that the sacred walls of St. Francis would tumble down upon us. I stammered the most anxious of adieux and improvised an escape. Returning hurriedly to my rooms at the Hôtel de Rome, I bolted the door and repaired to my bed. I wept and trembled until, mercifully, sleep overtook me.

Imagine, dear Mother, my horror upon discovering in the morn that Miss Lowe was also occupying rooms at the Hôtel. She bade me to take breakfast with her, and, like the most unwitting fool in the most shabbily written penny dreadful, I complied. She apologised for frightening me the previous day, and she asked me to tell her something of my writing. Inexplicably, I soon became quite relaxed and began to converse with great ease. This relaxation and ease cast a balmy haze over my remembrance of the past day, and I found myself, at breakfast's *finale*, inviting her to ride with me that afternoon in the campagna, to traverse the flower-carpeted slopes and hills of the Tiber, to watch the play of sapphire and umber as the sirocco whispered through the Sabine mountains.

"I know a better way to spend our afternoon," Miss Lowe suggested. She smiled her beautiful, mysterious, melancholy, inscrutable smile, and maneuvered her tongue to extend in subtle dalliance between her lips.

"Better than watching the play of sapphire and—?" I began.

"Much better, Mr. James," she spoke in a tone that fairly pierced the starch and patent leather of my being, a tone that fairly stirred within me a new and splendid chord.

Moments later, I found myself in Miss Lowe's bedchamber. She explained to me—or, rather, I now suspect, feigned to explain—that when a young man and a young lady of breeding are alone in the quarters of the latter, certain precautions must be taken so as to insure that there will be no violations of decorum.

"Quite," I said, hesitantly, as she began to bind my wrists and ankles to the teak curvatures of an armchair. She excused herself. Several minutes later, she returned—*wearing naught!* I shut my eyes and struggled to suppress my tears.

Then—and here you must excuse me, Mother, for I must lapse into a plain and direct prose—she unbuttoned my trousers and withdrew my urinary organ. Her mouth commenced to perform a deed which was at great variance with the pacific pastoral pleasures of the campagna which she claimed we might this afternoon surpass.

"Haven't you ever been with a woman before?" Miss Lowe inquired, in an almost cruel manner.

"Not in any *vulgar* way," I stammered, tasting the salt of my tears.

"Do you prefer making love to men, then?" she asked, in a more than almost cruel manner.

"Oh, no! I should imagine that to be even more dreadful!"

As the ferocity of her ministrations increased, my urinary organ seemed to ossify—perhaps Brother William, with his medical training, might shed some light upon this for us—and I grew decidedly faint. Of a sudden, she raised her rump upon my lap and let fall her weight, so that my urinary organ was swallowed by that dark and purpling item that resided at her groin. Mercifully, I lost all consciousness of any further proceedings.

Upon awakening, I found that I had been untied. Miss Lowe, in a flowery robe, reclined on her bed, regarding me with cold eyes. I buttoned myself and fled. Within a matter of hours, I had relocated at a smaller hostelry farther from the centre of the Corso.

These past weeks, I have been abed, fretting, in a condition of great anxiety. I dare not walk the streets of Rome, for fear of encountering Miss Lowe. This most unspeakably horrible situation must be remedied. I await your advice, Mother. Please don't speak a word of this to Father. He would simply defecate.

*Junior*

September 18, 1971
New York, N.Y.

Listen, Bitch:

I know that the purpose of your little game is to bust my Balls. It won't work. Go ahead, run around town whispering and giggling with your gangrenous slit of a mouth about how I can't get it up. No one will believe you, Bitch. The truth, as all can see, is that I've sired more offspring than you've had orgasms.

Let me tell you something else, my stretch-marked Irish whore, about the night upon which you base your cheap lies. It was not a matter of the author being unable to get it up. It was a matter of *you* being unable to get the author up.

When next we meet, Bitch, the author will show you exactly what can happen when he gets it up. And believe me, you will suffer, as other Bitches have, the avenging wrath of it.

You will feel the author's open hand across your face, then both of the author's hands at your throat. You'll stink like antiseptic fear, like a bank during a holdup, and *crack!* the author will choke you harder, and *crack!* the author will choke you again, and *crack!* the author will give you payment—never halt now, brave bucko— and *crack!* your impotent silent terror will send life to the charnel house of the author's Balls.

The author will throw you down and force you to suck his root while your fingers work like a team of maggots at the open sore of your heat. Compassion, the trapped bird of compassion, will struggle to fly from the author's chest to his throat, but *crack!* the author will force it down, and your tears, the thin, colorless blood of your dead vampire soul, will run down the ponderous length of the author's White Negro root.

The author will force his root into the canny hard-packed evil of your butt and bugger you as you listen to the sour rot of clotting blood in the pits of the wind. The author's thrusts will reverberate through your frail, creamy Catholic body like a thundering herd of lust's poisoned hoofs. In due time, the dank, evil sewer of your butt will give back no life. Then, and only then, will the author force his root into the deserted warehouse, the empty tomb of your cunt, and drain the cold, dead Ovarial gasses of existential despair from your stinking womb. The author's Balls will puke their vengeance into you, flood you with his unfailing and angry Scum. And then, just for the hell of it, the author might stab you in the tit with his Bic Banana.

Bitches like you cheapen sex, make it dirty with your frigid giggles and coy lies. The author will cure you of your nasty habits. He will cure you but good.

*Shut up, Bitch,*
*The Author*

February 4, 1931
New York, N.Y.

Darling Zelda,

Your letter worries me. Dr. Forel is a very respected psychiatrist, and Les Rives de Prangins is the finest sanitarium in Europe. I seriously doubt that the former is your Uncle Reid disguised "in one of those utterly outré gag noses," or that the staff of the latter is selling your "tinkly-water to an utterly revolting colony of Lesbian dwarves that dwell in nearby Geneva." You must learn to relax, darling.

You ask me to write you a letter that you might "rub against the utterly eensy pink eraser-tip" in your bloomers. Well, prepare yourself, darling: the master of romantic realism is about to indent.

I can feel your lips half open like a flower as we lie in the Saturday-night darkness on the first tee of the golf course and see the country-club windows as a yellow expanse—make that: a glimmering tiara—over a very black and wavy ocean. Our hips press together and sway to the plaintive African rhythm of Dyer's Dance Orchestra.

"Jeepers-creepers, let's play around," I whisper. I reach beneath your white, billowing dress—make that: lovely dress, soft and gentle in cut, but in color a hard, bright, metallic powder blue; no, better yet: pink crepe-de-chine dress sprinkled with soft, blue blossoms that are the color of your eyes.

"Oh—" you whimper. You unbutton my impeccable trousers and caress my geegaw. It responds to your touch as a gin-dizzied flapper responds to *le jazz hot*. You draw my throbbing two inches into your mouth, and your thick, warm tongue licks it in a manner your staid parents would find quite alarming.

I press my face between your thighs. "Holy cow," I whisper, "it's as big as the Ritz. I wish I could crawl into it and be safe forever." You are wet, so very wet, my darling Zelda. The softly shining porcelain cheeks of your tushy glisten in the moonlight.

"Yowza-yowza," you pant.

I mount you as an aeroplane passes overhead. Perhaps the passengers are watching us: the golden beauty of the South and the

brilliant success of the North. It is the mating of the age. My dapper white-on-white sperm slowly bubbles into you like a champagne fizz—no, make that: like a Bix Beiderbecke solo—and then we
hold each other close, knowing that even though we search
through all of eternity we could never again recapture these fleeting moments on the first tee.

There. Now, darling Zelda, do try to relax. Just keep telling yourself: everything's going to be hunky-dory.

*Your loving and brilliant hubby,*
*Scott*

December 18, 1977
New York, N.Y.

Young Sir:

When I found you, you were nothing, *la merde,* a creepy little rich
boy with a creepy little personality ("Oh! It's such a thrill!") and a
creepy little dick. I autographed your copy of my first novel (you
didn't even have the class to hand me a first edition) and let you
kiss me with your creepy little mouth.

I took you, re-created you, taught you to use the Tuc and the Buf-
Puf, and to cockle your delicate nose in distaste whenever someone
mentioned war or cancer; to order pastries by pointing and to keep
your nice ass pink and pretty with Jhirmack.

"I am afraid of New York," you cried that first night. I comforted
you. "Some cities," I said, "like wrapped boxes under Christmas
trees, conceal unexpected gifts, secret delights. This is your Christmas Eve." Then I fixed you a drink and some Seconals, and I taught
you to fuck properly.

Now I find you slinking about Studio 54 (where you wouldn't
even be allowed to peek inside the door if I hadn't brought you
there, introduced you around, to begin with), telling everyone, but
*everyone,* what a shame it is that I've become such a recondite (*I*
taught you that word!) old bitch and isn't it simply *the* most perfect
shame because deep down he is the most *dear* little old man.

I will use your prepuce for Ko-Rec-Type! I will put Drano in your
Pazo! I will change the dedication in my next great novel!

Maybe I am over 40. Maybe I have been getting *un peu* bit testy. At
least I can still write. (I finished an entire sentence and the rough
outline for another book just last week.) And I can still fuck. (Just
ask any of your so-called friends, dearie.)

Now you're crying the blues again. You say that you want to come back to me. Well, my tender young sir, you can just suck on a purple donut for all I care. My only advice to you is simply to steer clear of me. Studio 54 isn't big enough for both of us.

*In cold jizz,*
*Your Ex*

# 38

1 November 1980

Dear Dicko,

Sorry for the long delay. Autumn, usually my favorite time of the year, has for the second twelvemonth in a row brought me shit: mainly those ignoble and dreaded crab-lice of the crotch and psyche which we refer to as Broad Problems; also some drastic Dental Problems. As might be expected, my solution to all these problems has been to Drink Too Much. While the problems have not yet subsided, the drinking has, and I'm back to the grindstone here (although feeling like the meanest monk the Middle Ages ever knew).

The Frankie stuff is great. Your summary of the chapters to come made me and the one or two characters I showed it to howl like coloreds in heaven. I'm eager, real eager, to churn out a few masterful F-installments; and I will, soon as I clean up my current commitments, which I've been putting off like there was no fucking tomorrow. Did you send the stuff to Lish like you said? I plan on broaching the tender subject with my agent the next time I'm around him while he's drunk.

Lester called from Texas the other week. Said he was pulled in for Public Intoxication and spent two nights in jail there. Said he was never coming back to New York, was gonna stay in Austin to work at a magazine called Contempo Culture. Sent me a copy. Looks like New Haven Rock Press. Called back a few days later. Said he couldn't wait to get out of Texas.

Blum dropped by unannounced. Went into my bathroom and came back out totally fucked up on duji, babbling about Jodie and how she broke his heart, and how he's not really a junkie because he just uses it to relax ... Meanwhile, the Air Raid Kid is now completely grey-haired. Even the old men he hangs out with call him Old Timer ... And that's about it on this Saturday morning at this end of our one-horse universe ... Take care and keep pumpin ...

*Love,*
*Nick*

# 39

# Purity

Salvation Weaver had seen it all. That was what men said. "Now, take Sal Weaver," they said. "There's a man that's seen it all." Because Sal Weaver had seen it all, men listened to him when he spoke, as these three were doing right now as he sat enunciating, moving his fat pinkie listlessly through the familiar maze that adorned the paper place mat that lay before him on the linoleum tabletop in this particular booth, which every Nu Diner employee knew was Salvation Weaver's and Salvation Weaver's alone, to be kept available for him at all times. This was done gladly by the staff of the Nu Diner, for it was well known that Salvation Weaver always left paper money beneath his saucer when he walked.

As his pinkie arrived at the end of the maze, at that fanciful destination where pilgrims found their reward in the smiling countenance of Cap'n Fishsticks, Salvation Weaver rapped thrice upon the table and closed his eyes, which had seen it all.

"Gen'lemen," he said, "we are fucked."

And so they were, each to the extent that his particular fate had rendered him, and they sighed.

Harry Cudd sighed. The $7,000 that he had invested had been money he rightfully owed to the Ulysses S. Grant Memorial Nursing Home. This meant that Mama Cudd would soon again be residing with him, sucking her teeth and endlessly demanding that he play euchre with her for owesies. His wife, Iona, who loved Mama Cudd less than he, had been led to believe that the nursing-home bill was paid.

Junior Riley sighed. The $5,000 that he had invested had not even been his to begin with. He had borrowed it, at ten percent compounded monthly, from his nephew Hezekiah, who sold drugs to college students in Champaign.

Prof. Parker Leach sighed. He—who, it should be explained, was not a professor but merely a high-school teacher of biology and the only veterinarian in Alexander County who had his license revoked by the VMA Board on grounds of gross malpractice—had invested no money, but he had given a full six months of his life to the undertaking. Night after night he had sat at his typewriter, working and reworking, tightening and strengthening the prose that eventually became *Jesus on Wall Street: Playing the Market to Win—the New Testament Way!* Now the fruit of his labor would not even see the light of publication.

When the three men had done with their sighing, Salvation Weaver sighed. No sigh was graver than the sigh of a man who had seen it all. "It just wasn't meant to be, or else it woulda been," he said. The three men nodded in sullen agreement. They knew that Salvation had invested more than any of them, and that he bore the greatest shame.

Like all the other mail-order schemes that these four men, who composed the legally chartered Mammonco Corporation, had been involved in over the past seven years, *Jesus on Wall Street* had been Salvation Weaver's idea. Twenty thousand dollars' worth of advertising in *TV Guide* and the *National Enquirer,* he had figured, would sell at least 50,000 copies of the book. At the price of $9.95 each, this would bring in $497,500. One hundred thousand dollars of this money would then be spent in printing the book; another $15,000 would be spent on packing and postage. This would leave them, the Mammonco Corporation, with a net profit of $362,500.

But this scheme, like the two that had preceded it—Obsceno-Guard, a telephone attachment that could be made to emit a painful shrillness into the ears of obscene callers, and Skeeter-Kwell, the miraculous insect-repellent of the ancient Thebans—had failed and failed miserably. Harry, Junior, and the Professor had agreed with Salvation that a get-rich-quick book based on Scriptural teachings was sure to succeed. But fewer than 3,000 people had responded, and now those people's checks would have to be returned, along with little Xeroxed notes explaining that the book had been sold out.

"It was a good book, Professor," Salvation said consolingly. "I guess I just didn't see, didn't wanna see, that folks had turned their backs on Jesus. It's a hard thing to accept, but I think the bottom line is that these days the Lord couldn't sell a two-dollar whore to a drunken sailor."

The men sipped their coffees, which had become cold, and pondered their futures, which had become bleak. After minutes of silence, Salvation spoke again.

"I been thinkin'," he said, "and I tell you, boys, this mail-order business has just about had it. Stick with it another day and we're just pissin' in the wind, no *if*'s, *and*'s, or *but*'s. We got to change with the times"—he snapped his fingers—"we got to move. We're goin' broke, and we can't afford to crap out again.

"I know what you boys are goin' through. It hurts me to see it. Every time I hear your wife yell at you, Harry, I feel responsible. Whenever I see Junior here drivin' that Pinto, I'd like to cry, rememberin' how he looked behind the wheel of that big, red Eldorado. And you, Professor, cuttin' up frogs for a buncha snot-nosed kids over at Cairo High. It hurts me, it really does, and it's got to end, all this nickel-and-dimin'. It's just got to. I made us rich once, and I'm goin' to make us rich again. So help me, God, I will!"

Then Salvation Weaver told them how he had been driving past the Sonic Drive-In on Sycamore the other night and how he had been struck by an idea and how it was the best idea that he had ever had in his life, and then he told them what the idea was.

At first they thought he had lost his mind, and they even raised their voices against him in angry consternation. Little by little they became quiet. They began to grin and to nod their heads, and soon they were discussing this new idea with a growing excitement, an excitement that seemed to obliterate the despair that had hung over them.

"But maybe we shouldn't do it here," Junior Riley said. "Maybe we should do it across the state line, in Paducah, someplace like that."

"Why?" Harry Cudd said. "Ain't no bagel-snappers here in Cairo."

"We got colored," Junior Riley retorted.

"That ain't the same," Harry Cudd said.

"The hell it ain't," the Professor exclaimed.

"All of you, be quiet now," said Salvation Weaver. "We aren't goin' to rile nobody with this thing. It's all goin to be done in good taste."

"I hear you," Junior declared. "Sorta like that, uh—now, what the hell was the name of that thing?"

"'Hogan's Heroes,'" the Professor said.

"Yes, yes, that's the idea!" proclaimed Salvation Weaver.

"We can get that fellow from the show to do radio spots for us," suggested Junior.

"No, he's dead," the Professor said. "He was a homosexual. Him and Sal Mineo, they both got it right around the same time."

"No, not him," said Junior. "The other one. That fat old boy, that—"

"Sergeant Schultz," said the Professor. "He's dead, too."

"He wasn't no queer."

"I know he wasn't. But he's dead all the same," said the Professor, in a tone he usually reserved for his students.

"Well, there's always that bald guy," offered Harry.

"Gen'lemen!" declared Salvation Weaver, calling an end to his companions' digression. "Gen'lemen! Are we agreed, then?"

They were agreed, and each of them swore to raise $15,000 by the end of the month. Salvation Weaver placed two crisp singles beneath his saucer, and the Mammonco Corporation rose and left the Nu Diner. They stood for a moment on Washington Avenue in the cool, late-fall breeze that swept in from the Mississippi. Then they departed into the dusk, each of them feeling once again that fortune was a faithful bride at his feet.

Salvation Weaver knew that his wife, Louise, had something shaking on the side, but he could not for the life of him figure out who the sonofabitch was. Now, sitting in his living room, glancing through last week's *Barrons* and sipping a bourbon-and-Coke, he wondered where Louise had gone, and he pictured her lying beneath that unknown sonofabitch, and he cursed. A little before nine, she came through the door and smiled at him.

"Where the hell you been?"

"Madine's Magic Touch," she said, displaying the curls that she had not had earlier in the day.

"Sheeit," he muttered, pretending to return his attention to the newspaper in his hands. Louise began to undress in front of him, and he peered at her. He firmly believed that all evil women were eventually betrayed by their own underwear, and that diligent scrutiny of his wife's lingerie would in time result in the disclosure of her adultery. So far, his efforts had been in vain. Once, he had noticed that her panties were being worn over her panty hose, while he distinctly remembered that he had seen her put on her panties before hitching up her panty hose. He had questioned her about the matter, but she only laughed and told him that he was crazy. On several occasions he had seen that the gusset of her panties bore the stains of intense excitement, when she supposedly had been occupied with nothing more exciting than shopping or having her hair done. "How come these britches are all gunked up?" he would say, confronting her with the panties in question. But she would always foil him with talk of discharges and spotting and other such baffling unpleasantries.

He watched Louise remove her bra and touch her fingers to her breasts. He loved those breasts. He had married those breasts. They were as beautiful as her mind was plain (and perhaps "plain" was not even the right word; for Louise, now 29 years old, still had trouble with the crossword puzzles in TV Guide). For five long years he had provided for those breasts, and he had been faithful to them. He could not bear the thought of another man's hands caressing those breasts or the thought that his hands alone could not satisfy them.

He pulled her to him, and he put his mouth to her. His penis stirred in his britches like a waking lizard. Louise descended to her knees and withdrew the fat, familiar inches from his fly. She opened her mouth to them, and Salvation grasped her curls and listened to the sound of her benign slurping, which affected him like that of distant breakers. The unknown sonofabitch vanished from his mind.

Louise leaned back, reclining on the pile carpet. She spread her legs as wide as she could, and she told Salvation that she wanted him to come inside her. He crouched over her, kissing her breasts as he pushed into her, feeling her become wetter and warmer. He watched her face wax febrile beneath him, and he moved harder and harder within her. Suddenly he withdrew, and she moaned in vague confusion. He pressed himself to that lower, more occluded cranny, and he entered it fully and with violence. Louise uttered a deep and wild sound, and saliva trickled from both corners of her mouth. She came apart in blissful ravishment beneath him, and he, in his way, within her.

They lay, softly entwined, and he told her that he was going to be rich again, and that this time next year Cairo would be her oyster and the world her back-yard, just so long as she played her cards right. Then he put his face close to hers, and he summoned from somewhere within him the courage to ask the plain and simple question that had for so long been cowering beneath his other-wise fluent tongue.

"Have you been whorin' around on me, Louise?"

"Oh, Sally," she sighed, sounding almost insulted and almost flattered. "There ain't nobody but you, and there never will be."

Salvation smiled and said nothing. He lighted a cigarette and recommenced wondering just who in the hell that sonofabitch was.

Meanwhile, across town, Junior Riley was beseeching his nephew Hezekiah for a second loan.

"Fifteen thousand dollars is a lot of money," Hezekiah said.

"I'll cut you in," pleaded Junior.

"I don't wanna be cut into any pie you and that Weaver fool might be bakin'."

"You listen to me, boy, and show a little respect. This could be your uncle's last chance to recoup."

"Hell, you're only five years older than me, and I ain't but twenty-six."

"I'm still your damn uncle, and you gotta trust me."

They went on like this, back and forth, for many minutes, until finally Hezekiah told his uncle, "Look. I don't have the cash. But you help me get it, and I'll let you hold onto it for a while, at ten percent."

Four days later Junior Riley headed north on Highway 57, destined for Canada. Within the backseat upholstery of his Pinto were 75,000 capsules of Preludin, some sort of drug that he had never even heard of. As he drove, he tried to envision the hopheads with whom he was to rendezvous in Toronto, and all of a sudden it hit him—*free sex*—and he commenced to sing. "*Just a gigolo, and ever'where I go, people they stop and stare . . .*"

Iona Cudd was sitting by the window when the Ulysses S. Grant Memorial Nursing Home van pulled up. Her jaw dropped as she saw the two white-uni-formed Negroes slide open the door of the van and haul out a wheelchair con-taining her mother-in-law.

"Harry!" Iona screamed. "They canceled yo' mama for nonpayment! Oh, my God, Harry, you lied, you lied! I refuse to live for one second under the same roof as that wretched creature!"

Iona was packed and gone within the hour, informing Harry that he would hear from her lawyer. In a way, Harry was relieved, for now he would not have to explain that he was mortgaging the house. He watched her drive off in the sta-tion wagon, hearing behind him the voice of Mama Cudd calling from another room: "The cards, Harry! Get the cards!" As he sorted out the 32 highest cards from the deck, he told himself that everything was definitely going to be all right.

When the professor stopped off at the Rex Package Store, he parked his pickup truck a good distance away, in the obscuring nighttime shadows of an ancient chinquapin tree. After he returned to the pickup, he took a long drink from the pint of Heaven Hill that he had just bought and then drove toward the river, saying not a word to the sweet young thing who sat apprehensively beside him.

"What do you reckon on doing when you finish high school?" the Professor asked, long minutes after halting the pick-up at the river's edge.

"Well, Mr. Leach, I been thinkin', and what I really wanna do is become an anchorperson."

"That's a mighty fine ambition, Lucille. Mighty fine. You sure got the looks for it. That's for sure."

Then they said nothing but gazed through the windshield, watching the moonlight play upon the rippling, rising Mississippi. The Professor drank, and his student drew on a filtered cigarette.

"Why do you think I brought you here, Lucille?"

"To fornicate, of course."

The Professor touched his hand to her knee and then slowly raised her skirt, baring her rife pink flank. Her panties were embroidered with the name of a weekday, and he touched them. He inserted two fingers into her and then lifted those fingers to her mouth. He pulled her legs up, toward him, and he hunched over her, unzipping himself.

"Put it in, dear. Put it in," the Professor said.

She took hold of him with both hands and led him to the wet warmth that was the center of her being, and he pierced it and began to pound his hips upon her. She was so girlishly tight that he fancied he might cleave her in twain with his mighty sword.

"What sort of birth control do you use?" he panted.

She did not immediately respond but instead raised her face to his heaving breast and darted her tongue against his nipples; then, as he loosed himself within her ruby youth, she answered, "Prayer."

He looked down at her in dismay, and he saw that her eyes were as wide and coldly insensate as a viper's. He turned the ignition key and shifted into reverse, muttering. He dropped off the child two blocks from her parents' house on Poplar; then he headed toward the Kentucky line, to do what had to be done.

Iona Cudd lay abed naked, watching the sudden rain cascade against the window of her room at the Cairo Motel. She barely felt the fingers that dallied warmly upon the lea of her abdomen.

"I've left him for good," she said.

Her thighs parted, and the fingers entered her. She closed her eyes, and her breathing became pronounced as the fingers within her massaged the rugae of her cunt and then, withdrawing, fondled perfectly the tender tumescence that pulsed faintly beneath the cowl of her vulva.

"Let's go away," Iona pleaded. "Chicago, New York—as far away from Cairo as we can."

But the tyranny of those fingers silenced her, made her belly rise and her legs become as taut as murderous moments, and everything within her shuddered.

"But, Iona, I'm just not ready to leave Salvation, I'm just not," said Louise Weaver, kissing the forehead of her lover and rubbing wetly against her trembling hip.

It was one in the morning when the Professor reached Sedalia. Nearing the farm of Ezra Bruton, the most renowned trainer of pit-dogs in Kentucky, perhaps in the entire South, he shut his headlights and rolled slowly down the winding dirt road that led to the wooded clearing where Bruton's most vicious and unconquerable bull terriers were sequestered in a long, low cinder-block kennel.

Breaking the padlock shackle with bar shears, he entered the kennel, carrying with one hand a Ray-O-Vac lantern and clutching with the other a Palmer $CO_2$ pistol, the same kind that Marlin Perkins used.

The pit-dogs, a dozen of them, snarled murderously at the intruder, snarled in that low, ghastly way that is more terrifying than the most ferocious bark of their fetching and flea-collared kin. Stepping from one cage to the next, the Professor methodically fired a mixture of Ketamine and Xylazine into each of the beasts. After the final injection had been discharged with a gaseous whoosh into the neck of the final terrier, the Professor closed his eyes, inhaled deeply, and silently waited for the tranquilizer to fell the dogs.

By two o'clock he had delivered the unconscious pit-dogs to Mound City, to the man with the money. On his way back to Cairo, he finished the Heaven Hill, hearing the sound of that word reverberate over and over again within his mind: "Prayer."

On the first morning of December, as the Hecate wind howled coldly through the streets of downtown Cairo, Salvation Weaver and his cohorts, each of them bearing the sum of $15,000, and the tale of how he had acquired it, met at the Nu Diner. Thence they strode down Washington Avenue to the First National Bank and Trust Company, where the $60,000 was duly deposited in the account of the Mammonco Corporation. Using this $60,000 for credence and Salvation Weaver's house for collateral, the Mammonco Corporation succeeded in borrowing another $60,000 from the bank. The corporation then adjourned to the Atomic Club, where they all drank with great abandon and cursed with lurid vigor the soul of all women save for fair Fortune.

Construction began in late January. Winter passed, and spring broke. Then, at dawn on the day after Easter, the four men stood on Poplar Avenue, looking across the clean, black expanse of a freshly tarred parking lot—*their* parking lot—and beholding in proud exultation the gleaming edifice that was the glory of their dreams and the justification of their hopes.

The structure, with its cream-colored stucco brick facing, arched plate-glass windows, and pitched aluminum-shingled eaves, resembled the Berghof, the

Führer's quaint Bavarian retreat, a picture of which Salvation Weaver had found and torn from a book in the Cairo Public Library. Across the top of the facade, large Gothic letters of red plastic spelled the word SCHICKLGRUBER'S. Perched atop the G was a magnificent imperial eagle, also wrought in plastic, clutching a hamburger in its talons.

The decor of the restaurant was that of a rustic German inn. (Unfortunately, no book in the Cairo library offered a glimpse of the Berghof's interior.) The wood-paneled walls were adorned with prints of the Führer's Viennese watercolors, strategic air maps of Europe, and World War II propaganda posters of every sort. Above the plastic menu board was a large portrait, executed in oil by a local cartoonist, of Maria Anna Schicklgruber, the Führer's paternal grandmother. The menu that her stern, maternal visage oversaw featured the usual fast-food items but under a variety of novel alliterative names: Blitz-Burgers, Waffen-Wieners, Fokker-Fries, Schickl-Shakes, and so on. Background music was supplied by a cassette tape-loop that included selections ranging from Wagner's "Liebestod" to Jerry Fielding's "Theme from 'Hogan's Heroes.'"

The help arrived at the appointed hour of nine. The cooks were dispatched to the stainless-steel grills and fryers. The counter girls were instructed to change into their uniforms of black jodhpurs, jackboots, and epauletted blouses. Each girl wore an armband bearing the emblem of a hamburger pierced by a bolt of lightning. Schicklgruber's filled with sounds of industry and the scents of frying, and the doors opened wide at eleven o'clock sharp.

The citizens of Cairo came forth in curiosity and in hunger. A few—very few— of these citizens expressed their distaste and quickly departed Schicklgruber's without spending a cent. Another few, composed of elderly Bundists and their offspring, seemed to be overcome with nostalgic delight. But most of Cairo's citizens accepted Schicklgruber's as they would a new television series or a new brand of designer jeans: with plain and purblind enthusiasm.

"I think we've done it, gen'lemen," grinned Salvation Weaver toward the close of that fine April day. "Yessir, I really think we've done it."

That night Harry Cudd, who had neither seen nor heard from his wife in several months, called his lawyer, explaining that his divorce settlement should be finalized as soon as possible so that his alimony payments would not be based on that year's income. The Professor, who had taken a leave of absence from his job at Cairo High, typed a letter of formal resignation to the principal. And Junior Riley, who had already priced the new Eldorados, stopped off at the Cadillac dealership in Patierdale and put in an order.

When the men arrived at the restaurant the next morning, they were met by a camera crew from the nearest television station, WSIL in Harrisburg. A woman with a microphone and a colorless accent began to ask questions.

"We wanted somethin' differ'nt, somethin' with a little pizzazz," Salvation told her. "We decided to go with the Nazi motif." He pronounced the word *Nazi* so that it rhymed with *snazzy.*

"What has the community reaction been like?" the woman asked.

"Oh, the folks love it, especially the kids. I don't think there's any doubt about it: what we've got here is the biggest thing since *Star Wars.*"

Salvation was sitting home alone that night, examining his wife's inner britches for evidence and wondering where in the hell she was, when he heard the colorless voice of the woman with the microphone. He turned and saw himself on television, and he smiled. But after only a few seconds it became obvious that the television people had cut up what he had said, and that they were making a fool out of him. When he heard that lady's voice say that Schicklgruber's was a bad thing, he slapped the television shut and began to drink. He was still drinking four hours later when Louise finally came home.

"I'm in love with Iona Cudd," she said.

Salvation said nothing but continued to drink.

"Iona says that me and her are married in the eyes of God, and that if I let you stick yourself in me, I'm committin' adultery."

He said nothing.

"She wants me to move to the country with her and grow Chinese food. We'll eat what we need, sell the rest."

Salvation still said nothing.

"And that's what I'm gonna do. Try to understand, Sally. It don't mean I don't love you."

Without putting on his shoes, Salvation Weaver walked out the door and drove to Harry Cudd's house. The two men sat together, barely speaking, listening to Mama Cudd suck air in her sleep.

"I thought I seen it all," Salvation muttered as dawn broke. "I really thought I seen it all."

He borrowed a pair of shoes from Harry, and the two men repaired, bleary-eyed, to Schicklgruber's, where they found that someone had spray-painted a six-pointed star on the front door. Junior Riley was out front with a bucket and a scrub brush, trying to wash the paint from the door, when the two chartered buses from Chicago pulled into the parking lot. He hurried into the kitchen to find Salvation.

"There's a buncha kids with, uh—now, what the hell d'ya call them things?" Junior mumbled, pointing to the summit of his head.

The Jewish Defense League students positioned themselves before the entrance to the restaurant, and then they began to distribute handbills to passers-by. Salvation suddenly snatched one of these printed sheets from a student's hand and then glanced at it:

CLOSE THESE OVENS!
TODAY A FEW CHEESEBURGERS,
TOMORROW 6 MILLION JEWS!

Salvation went to the pay phone to call the police, but he distractedly hung up the receiver in mid-dial as several pickup trucks bearing Indiana plates screeched to a halt a few yards from the JDL protesters. From these pickups there poured forth men in white sheets, one of whom, introducing himself as the exalted King Kleagle, explained to Salvation that he and his brothers in imperial knighthood were eager to help in whatever way they could. As Salvation recommenced dialing, the King Kleagle instructed his muslin myrmidons to form a line of protection between the students and the restaurant. The police arrived, shifting their stomachs and belt buckles with magisterial gravity.

"Where'd all these Joosh kids come from?" a young cop asked one of the men in white sheets.

"Yonder," replied the man in the white sheet, gesturing neither east nor west nor north nor south.

By mid-afternoon the television minicam crew had arrived. But this crew, the Mammonco Corporation observed, was not from any piss-ant station in Harrisburg but from WMAQ in Chicago. Once again, the woman with the microphone spoke without any accent that might betray the fact that she had actually come from somewhere, but, Salvation noticed, her breasts were greater by far than those of the lady from the piss-ant station.

"I just don't understand what's goin' on here," Salvation told the lady. "Ever-'thing's gettin' all outa hand."

"Didn't you foresee any of this when you decided to align yourself with the image of Adolf Hitler?"

"Hell, woman!" Salvation hollered. "Adolf Hitler, Ronald McDonald—*what the hell's the damn differ'nce?*"

As he was yelling, new figures arrived on the scene. One of these was Rev. Sumter Cutberth, pastor of the Christ Holy Temple Church of God Anchored in the Holy Ghost, which was located down the road apiece.

"You fools!" the reverend shouted, casting his arm in a violent arc, as if to encompass all around him, those in white sheets and skull caps and blue uniforms and earphones alike. "*You egg-suckin' fools!* To call down upon Cairo like this the wrath of *Gawd Almighty!* I warn you he shall not suffer this to be! Build you an ark, all of you! G'wan, *git!*"

To the left of the reverend were three intense-looking young men. One of these men carried a placard stating DER FÜHRER WAS A VEGETARIAN and led his two companions in chanting, "No more lies! No more lies!" A priest from St. Patrick's walked across the parking lot, raising his arms in a call for peace. One of the chanters hailed him in the name of Pope Pius XII, the blessed and infallible pontiff who had asked God to bestow his blessing on the Third Reich. The priest lowered his arms, retreated across the lot, and drove away in a silver Buick.

The most singular aspect of this most singular day was that the sound and the fury of this multifarious siege upon Schicklgruber's did not detract in the least from the day's business. If anything, business was better on this day than it had been.

Harry and the Professor were standing together, wondering at this very fact, when the Professor heard a piercing, girlish voice. "That's him!" she screamed. "That's the teacher that fornicated me!"

The Professor ran through the kitchen and out the back door, never to be seen again in Alexander County but maintaining his ties with the Mammonco Corporation by means of a series of missives bearing an assortment of southerly addresses, the eventual last of which was that of the Shelby County Regional Facility of the Tennessee Department of Correction.

This day, like all others, finally ended. Salvation Weaver leaned against the portion-control scale and wearily beheld the buttocks, resplendent in black jodhpurs, of Henrietta Moline. In the breadth of 24 hours, he had lost his wife and his most trusted partner. He had been beset by the Jewish Defense League, the Ku Klux Klan, neo-Nazis, Pentecostal preachers, and television newsmen. But all that was behind him now, and he was alone with these buttocks in the silent, shadowed kitchen of this monument to his own ingenuity. He raised his eyes and looked upon Henrietta's face. Of all his employees, she was the most alluring. The curl of her lip, by which she expressed disdain for any man who addressed her, was as irresistible as it was affected. Her 19-year-old body was like that of a goddess.

"Play your cards right, Henrietta, and Cairo will be your oyster," Salvation whispered, placing his hand upon the rondure of those buttocks, "and the world your backyard."

Henrietta did not say a word but merely descended to the kitchen floor, resting her head upon a sack of defrosting Ore-Ida Shoestrings. Salvation stood over her. He unclasped the promotional Billy Beer belt buckle that had been given to him personally by the former First Brother himself, and he stepped from his britches, hunkering down between Henrietta's long, lithe legs, and pulled her jodhpurs from her. Dipping his hand into a nearby gallon of Frymax liquid frying fat, he greased her rife young loins and then entered her slowly and sublimely, whispering to her again of the oyster and the backyard and of franchise expansion untold. They slept together on the kitchen floor that night, beneath the protective gaze of Maria Anna Schicklgruber. French fries were their pillow, and vast were their dreams.

On the following morning, the "Today" show broadcast the report that had been aired the night before by WMAQ, the NBC affiliate in Chicago. Schicklgruber's became a national sensation, receiving coverage not only on television but also in such publications as *People* (where Salvation Weaver's face shared a page with those of Erik Estrada and Gilda Radner), the *New York Post* ("Heil, Hamburgers!"), and *Restaurant Business* ("Novel Concept Provides 'Final Solution' to Businessmen's Woes").

Amid the uproar, Schicklgruber's continued to make money at a disarming pace. Salvation no longer discouraged the protesting *Untermenschen* who gathered daily before the doors of his restaurant, but rather, believing them to be good for business, encouraged them. At the end of May, the *Wall Street Journal*, in an article titled "Fast-Food Führers to Franchise," announced that Salvation and his partners were about to expand operations. Two types of franchises were offered to prospective investors: The DeLuxe Berghof model, patterned after the Cairo original and carrying a fee of $70,000, and the smaller, more austere Polish Pillbox model, which carried a fee of $35,000. Interest was great, and within a month the Mammonco Corporation had sold 12 franchises for $595,000. The push toward the East had begun. By summer's end Schicklgruber's was an inexorable part of the landscape of America.

"I've done it," Salvation Weaver exclaimed, sitting at home at his desk one autumn evening, feeling the hands of Henrietta Moline upon his neck and upon his shoulders. "I've really done it," he exclaimed, looking up. "I'm a millionaire on paper, Henrietta. I'm a millionaire."

He had no sooner finished his sentence when the telephone rang. The lawyer, calling from Los Angeles, introduced himself, explaining that he had been retained by Mmes. Weaver and Cudd, who jointly and presently sought to be awarded their estranged and soon-to-be divorced husbands' interests in the Mammonco Corporation. Salvation began to say something very vulgar to the lawyer, who interrupted him, asking him if he was aware of the penalties for mail fraud; then he bid Salvation good-bye, promising to call again soon.

It was spring again in Cairo. Harry Cudd and Salvation Weaver drove down Poplar Avenue in the warming sunshine, both of them staring straight ahead as they passed Schicklgruber's.

"Health-food emporiums," Harry Cudd spat. "Ever' damn one of them damn franchises: *health-food emporiums.*"

"Lezzie food," growled Salvation Weaver.

"They'll never make it. They'll go under, sure as I'm born."

When they walked into the Nu Diner, they did not say good morning to Junior Riley or to his bride, Henrietta. But looking straight ahead, they strode silently and solemnly to that particular booth that every Nu Diner employee knew was Salvation Weaver's and Salvation Weaver's alone, to be kept available for him at all times. This was gladly done by the staff of the Nu Diner, for it was well known that Salvation Weaver always left paper money when he walked.

# 40

I don't know which came first, this story written in the spring of 1981 or the lyrics I wrote bearing the same title.

# Pizza Man

My mind goes back to the spring of 1953, when I cut my first slice. I can still feel Papa's hand wrapped around mine, enclosing it in his own, guiding it, as the circular blade rolled slowly across the diameter of the pie. The four cuts made, the anchovy-and-pepperoni special divided into eight. Papa let loose my hand.

"There," Papa said to a man on the other side of the counter. "See how nice my boy does it? A regular little pizza man, my boy. Nine years old. And smart? Like Doctor I.Q." Then Papa turned to me: "Tell him, Angelo. Tell him what's a pumpkin." Then back to the man: "What's a pumpkin—a fruit or a vegetable? Eh?" The man sipped at his bottle of Knickerbocker beer and shrugged. "Neither—she's a berry!"

Things were still nice then on Forty-second Street. Nice shops, nice places to eat. Nice people went to the movies. Papa was so proud of his stand. "There she is, Angelo," he used to say, pointing toward Times Square, "the crossroads of the world."

Back then, the pizza man got treated with respect.

Now look. These lunatics. Sometimes I thank God Papa's not here to see it.

I should've been out of here three years ago. All that noise about cleaning up Times Square. There were speculators—fools—with money, big money, making offers. But then came Luisa, and look at me now.

She seemed like such a nice girl. Eighteen years old, face like in a soap commercial.

"Excuse me, sir," she said. *Sir!* That's a word you don't hear too much on Forty-second Street. "Excuse me, sir. Could you tell me how to get to the Port Authority bus depot?" *Depot,* mind you.

I told her, and she thanked me. More *sirs*. She turned to leave, then she stopped.

"You can go almost anywhere from there, can't you? That's what someone told me, that at Port Authority you can get a bus to anywhere."

"That depends," I said. "Where do you wanna go?"

"Oh, that doesn't really matter." She smiled, but she was nervous. "I just want to get away." She smiled again, and she was more nervous.

"You want a slice or something?"

I was sort of concerned for the girl. Hell, to be honest, I had pussy on the mind. The truth is—I can tell you this because I know it won't go any further than you—I hadn't had any in almost two years. Angelina, she had hurt me. Hurt me bad. My, uh, manhood—pfft!—like a wet noodle.

But it wasn't just that. No, really. I was concerned. This girl struck some sort of—something nice in me, I guess. Anyway, I give her the slice. I don't take her money. Papa—he must've spun around twice up there in Woodlawn cemetery.

I blame it all on that free slice. Without that fucking slice, none of this would've happened.

But, like I said, it was obvious—or so I thought—that the kid was in trouble. I took her downtown to my place, on Cornelia Street; made a pot of coffee.

She's looking around the apartment—you've been there; you know what it's like—and I figure she must think I'm weird. All those Madonnas and Saint Ritas, and the little Jesus with the eyes that follow you around the room. I explained to her about Mama, how Mama's last words to me were "Be good to all my little saints."

"What's *that*?" Luisa said.

"That's Papa's pizza-man apron. What's left of it. Mama had it framed after Papa passed on. She tried to get the priest at Our Lady of Pompeii to bless it, but he wouldn't. She managed to sneak a squirt of holy water on it, though, when the priest wasn't looking."

We drank the coffee. I told her about the nice house I used to have in Bay Ridge; all the nice furniture. I told her how Angelina took it all when we got divorced.

All the time while we're talking, I'm looking her over. God, she was beautiful. I wanted to grab her and shove her face in my lap, fuck her where she breathes. It was scary; I never felt like that before. I could see the headline: PIZZA MAN RAPES NICE GIRL.

But then I notice she's got her fingers on my neck, and there's this strange look in her eyes.

"You're a very lonely man," she says.

Now her fingers are all over me, like spiders. "Relax," she tells me, "relax." Then that face like in a soap commercial is right near mine. Her mouth opens, real slow, and she makes this sound that you could barely hear. It's like she's whispering a little chant. Then I make it out: "Fuck me, fuck me, fuck me." She unbuttons her blouse. She's got one of those bras that unhook up front—*pop*—and I'm staring at a pair of *capezzoli* like you never saw. "Lick 'em," she says. I lick 'em. She starts making those little purring sounds again.

"Angie," she says, "do what I say."

To make a long story short: five minutes later, she's on the rug—the one Mama brought over from the other side—blindfolded, with her ankles tied together; and I'm sitting on her tits, like King Farouk, with my tool in her yap. This is the first boner I got in almost two years, right? I'm happy as a pig in shit. I came like you wouldn't believe. All over her face, like forty days and forty nights. Twelve years of marriage, and Angelina never let me do that.

But this Luisa, she wants more. Up the ass, up the box; this way, that way. *Bangity-bangity-bangity-bang*—all the saints are shaking on the walls; the little Jesus with the eyes is wobbling like he's on the high seas; Papa's apron comes crashing down. I'm not lying.

Right then and there, that night, I forgot all about Angelina. I was a new man. What I didn't know was that I was also fucked.

I let Luisa stay with me. Hey, you would've, too. Every night, I cooked for her; we'd talk, then *bangity-bangity-bang*. I felt good. I figured, for once in my life, I deserved to feel good.

But little by little, I began to smell something fishy. I mean, this girl was no innocent like I first made her out to be—*fuck me in the ass, do this, do that, the broomstick, bobby pins on the nips*—what, I'm made with a finger? I'm stupid? But that wasn't it. She was up to something. All these little phone calls, all this secrecy. So one night after I come home from the stand, I take a stab.

"Look," I tell her. I'm acting mad. "I ran into somebody who knew you today. We got to talking, and now I know everything, bitch." It's always good to throw in a *bitch* when you're trying to catch them up. Papa taught me that.

"Who?"

"Who do you think?"

"*Who?*"

"Listen, bitch. Never play the pizza man for a fool. Never. I just wanna hear *you* tell it. *You* tell me about all this so-called trouble you're in, about all this running away."

"Let's make love first."

"Nah, nah, nah. Start talking."

And she did. And I almost shit. I'm telling you, until then I'd thought I'd heard and seen it all.

Eighty bucks an hour. Eighty fucking dollars an hour she was making. For what? These guys, they paid her to do all sorts of sick shit to them. One guy wants her to dress him up like a baseball player—except he's got a diaper underneath the knickers, right?—and he beats his meat while she yells at him about how he'll never make the majors. Another guy wants to piss in his pants and get slapped for it. One character wants her to tie him up with clothesline—he's been lugging it around with him since God knows when; it's from his mother's backyard, before the war—and rap him on the ass with a rolled-up *Daily Mirror*—a certain issue, no less—that he lugs around with him. Eighty bucks an hour these idiots paid. You'd think that anybody who could afford eighty bucks an hour shouldn't have to worry about making the majors. And broads, too! She had broads paying her to do stuff.

Of the eighty bucks a pop, she was supposed to be kicking over thirty to the head bitch. That's where all the trouble and running came in. See, she had a blackjack habit. She was in over her head down at the after-hours joint. You can't beat them down there; push goes to the house, all that crap. Anyway, the head bitch found out and came after her looking for a five-grand palm-greasing, so Luisa took off. And of all the fucking pizza men in all the fucking pizza stands in all New York, I give her a fucking free slice. I should have my head examined.

But, God, I was crazy for her. Blinders like a horse I had on, I was that crazy for her. When she first hit me with the idea, I told her to go sit in the shower. But, little by little, it began to sound good, especially the money angle. Who couldn't use an extra grand or two a week? Love and money, that's the sickest perfecta in the world.

We started in the last week of June. I remember, because that was when the big Mastro pizza oven went on the blink. Me, Luisa, and this twenty-three-year-old blond broad from Jersey named—get this—Squaldrina; the three of us, we started that June. Those two must've known what they were doing, because by the Fourth of July that telephone was ringing off the hook day in and day out.

"I'd like one Squaldrina Special, please," the guy might say, and then give me his address.

"And what time would you like it delivered?"

"At two o'clock," he might say.

Between the two of those cunt "pizzas," I was making money hand over fist. I was bringing in more over the telephone than over the counter. I bought a car, paid cash. I thought I was King Shit. The one thing that bothered me was that I was still crazy for Luisa, and I couldn't get used to her fucking with these others, sucking them off, telling them they'd never make the majors, whatever. But, what the fuck, it's like they say: Money buys a lot of Band-Aids.

On Christmas Eve—get this—Luisa tells me she's got a present for me when I get home from the stand. So I go home, walk in the door. There's the two of them, Luisa and the other one, Squaldrina, on the bed with ribbons around their hips. One's got a green ribbon, the other's got a red one. "Merry Christmas," they say. They want me to plug them both.

I drop my pizza whites and start pumping away on Luisa. Squaldrina's got my balls in her yap. They're both making these chain-gang noises.

"Come, pizza man, come," they're moaning.

My dick could've been in Perth Amboy for all the good it was doing me. I was fucked out. This thing is getting out of hand, I told myself. Faithfully married—no shit—faithfully married twelve years to a broad who won't let me stick it in on Monday nights because that's novena night: won't let me stick it in on Thursday nights because that's the night of the week her father the drunken horseplayer died—then I go the two years with the limp noodle—and now here I was, running a goddam call-girl operation for sick fucks in baseball suits out of my pizza stand, banging away in the sack with two lunatic broads in Christmas wrapping. Christ Almighty, but ain't life funny, know what I mean?

Finally I come. My dick is sore, feels like it's ready to fall off. I roll over on my back, listen to my heart try to run out through my ears.

"Me, too, pizza man, me, too."

Right then the phone rings. Saved by the bell. Except it's my ex-wife. This is the first time she's called me in a year, and she's telling me she wants to get back together with me. Amazing. Sixty miles away, and they can still smell it when you get pussy on your dick. I hang up on her, hitch up my whites, kiss the two broads good night—they're rolling around bumping pussies, giggling—and run downstairs to the fag bar across the street. Running away from two beautiful broads and hiding in a fag joint. Right? Now I know I'm going crazy.

But, wait. It gets worse. A few weeks later. I'm at the stand. It's closing time. Nobody's ordering pizza anymore anyway; everybody's ordering pussy. Papa's up there in Woodlawn doing his cartwheels. The phone rings.

"Hello there, pizza man," the woman on the other end says. I recognize her voice. She's one of the two broads who call up every once in a while for the Luisa Special.

"The one and only. So, what is it today, darling?"

"I want you," she says. "I've been wanting you for a long, long time."

"Yeah, huh?"

"Yeah." She's jerking off over the phone. "What's your price, pizza man?"

"For you, darling, two yards."

"You know the address." She's serious. "Oh, one more thing. Bring that pizza paddle. That big, wooden paddle. You know the one I mean."

In for a penny, in for a pound, I figure, right? I close the stand, catch a cab, lug the damn paddle down to this broad's joint. Nice place, East Thirty-something. She opens the door. She's wearing one of those . . . you know, like Lloyd Bridges in *Sea Hunt*—wet suits. But this one's different. It's got zippers up here, a zipper down below. Sort of spooky.

"I'm glad you could make it, pizza man," she says to me.

"The money," I tell her, "the money." She hands me the two hundred, and I shove it in my pocket.

I figure she wants me to slap her ass with the paddle, some sick shit like that. No; she wants to fuck on it. On my pizza paddle, she wants to fuck—on the pizza paddle that *Papa* gave me. I tell her no, that's going too far.

"Just let me lick it, then." I let her lick the paddle. She unzips the zipper down below and bends over the arm of the couch. She sounds like one of those whoopee cushions when she moves.

"Fuck me, pizza man. Fuck me good and hard, pizza man."

So, there I am, staring at this rubber thing with the cunt hanging out of the zipper, and I know I couldn't get a hardon to save my mother's soul. I'm back where I started from: the wet noodle.

I split, leave Mrs. Lloyd Bridges draped over the arm of her couch, and walk downtown in the freezing cold. About halfway home, I decided that I'd had enough, that I was through with the whole thing. No more Squaldrina Specials, no more guys with clotheslines in their briefcases, no more nothing. I would change the phone number at the stand and tell Luisa to shape up or ship out. It was either me or the ballplayer in the Pampers. I felt clean. When I got home and those little Jesus eyes started following me around the room, I was able to look right back into them.

They busted me the very next day. Plainclothesmen. You can always tell a plainclothesman: He never takes oregano on his pie. They hit me with the whole shebang. Procuring, unlawful use of a business, tax evasion, corrupting the morals of a minor—yeah: Luisa; it turns out she's sixteen, not eighteen—this, that, the other thing. They had me fucked nine ways from Sunday—and they weren't about to be bought off by no free slice. I was facing seven years max. Papa should only know.

But they were reasonable men, and their friends were also reasonable men, and *their* friends were reasonable men. Everybody was very reasonable. Altogether, it cost me twenty-two thousand dollars' worth of reasonable. Papa's finger's sticking out of the dirt up there, pointing at me: Fool! Fool!

And Luisa, goddam her eyes. She skipped out, ran off with a souvlaki guy over on Eighth Avenue.

Here, have another slice.

You know, all I used to see when I looked at one of those things was a bunch of mozzarella and tomato sauce. But now—ah, fuck it.

# 41

# The Butt and I

Neptune, New Jersey. It is the summertime, maybe 1959, maybe 1960. My father and I are sitting on lawn-chairs outside our room at the Howard Johnson Motor Lodge, near the Exit 102 turn-off of the Garden State Parkway. There is no lawn. Cars speed by, heading toward Asbury Park, city of dreams. We come here every summer, south from Newark in a two-tone Buick 6.

"This is the life," my old man says, and I agree.

He is wearing black Italian-stitched shoes, no laces, no socks; crimson swimming trunks, a white-on-white dress shirt with a high-roll collar, and a stained and faded gray fedora which he claims was worn by Dutch Schultz the day he was gunned down in the men's room of the Palace Chop House in Newark. (I am not yet twelve years old, and I believe anything.) There is a Parodi, or what is left of a Parodi, in his mouth, and in his hand a plastic tumbler containing maybe a quarter pint of Cutty Sark.

A girl, maybe fifteen years old, walks past us, toward the swimming-pool. She is wearing a bikini, muttering ouch-sounds as the hot concrete burns the soles of her feet. I stare at her. My old man stares at her.

"That broad moves her ass like she's been around," he says. It's his way of telling me about the birds and the bees.

Summers pass, as in a dream, and I am eighteen years old, living on Bergen Avenue in Jersey City with a girl who moves her ass like she's been around. In the daytime I work across the river in Manhattan. I am a paste-up man for the Lovable Underwear Company. I do things such as design little heart-shaped stickers for pantyhose packages. These stickers bear the legend "No Bag! No Sag!" I am fulfilled in my career.

In the nighttime the girl who moves her ass like she's been around and I hang out. In the chambers above us dwell a husband and wife named Jude and Cookie. They own a battery-operated phonograph and one record, "Cloud Nine" by the Temptations, which they play over and over.

"This is the life," I say, but the girl who moves her ass like she's been around does not agree. She wants to get married. She thinks I'm cracking Cookie. There's nothing on TV except reruns. "Eh," I say.

She's the prettiest girl that I've ever seen outside of a dirty magazine. One night I tell her I'll marry her, and she lets me do anything I want. The next morning she calls me up at the underwear company and says she's not going to let me do that ever again. That's all right, I don't want to get married anyway.

A few more summers pass, as in a dream, and I am more mature. I get drunk one night in a bar on Broadway and Third Street, and I wake up the next night in Tampa, Florida. I look at the help-wanted ads in the Tampa *Tribune*. I get a job as the editor and art director of *TV Weekly*. I make a hundred and fifty big ones a week, and I spend most of it at the Crazy Horse, a topless bar in Orlando. There's a dancing girl there named Louise, and I'm in love with her ass. Louise tells me that she's married.

"But he stutters," she says.

*TV Weekly*'s circulation begins, or rather continues, to fall. It's a give-away, but the people in the Seven-Eleven checkout lines aren't biting, and the advertisers are bitching, especially Sambo's Pancake House, our biggest account. To improve the situation, I decide to create a little excitement. I publish an exclusive interview with Joan Blondell, in which she confesses that she cooked and ate her three-year-old daughter. ("'It tasted like *blanquette de veau*, which I love,' said the former star of ABC's *Here Come The Brides*, indicating with coy fingers the bloated, sixty-year-old flesh of her midsection, which mutely testified to the love she professed.")

I'm fired. I go to the Crazy Horse and tell Louise that I'm in love with her ass and that I want to take her away from all this.

"But my husband," she says.

"But he stutters," I say. I put my hand on her backside and my fingers find fulfillment.

She goes home and discusses the situation with her husband. They have an open relationship, respect each other's space, talk things out like adults.

"F-f-f-follow your heart," he tells her.

We move south, to Marathon Key. Louise gets a job at a diner owned by Doris Day. I'm still in love with her ass. This could be the real thing, I tell myself.

She's in love with her ass, too. She tells me to tie a ribbon around the top of each of her thighs—"tighter," she says—and walks around the house all day like that. I wax artistic and take Polaroid shots of her beribboned tush. She pastes the pictures into an album. On Christmas Eve, we take out the album and reminisce.

"This is the life," I say. She purrs and primps her thigh-bows.

This goes on for maybe six or seven months. One night she's watching *Adam's Rib* with Katherine Hepburn on TV. She decides she wants to be a lawyer. It's not long before the lessons start arriving from the DuLac Extension School of the Mail in Tallahassee. She studies all the time. The ribbons disappear.

I follow my heart and go back to New York, to the same bar I got drunk at the year before. I meet a girl with blonde hair. She tells me everybody thinks she looks like Joanne Woodward. We get married for five years. But I can't talk about that.

For two years I watch the butts go by. I am unfulfilled. One night in a bar on Thirteenth Street, I meet somebody named Slick. We talk. One thing leads to another.

"Do you—?" he whispers in my ear.

"Yeah," I say.

"Not me," he says. "Too close to their brains."

I think it over.

"How about—?" His hand gropes in the vague area under his beer belly.

"Yeah," I say.

"Me too," he says. "But first I gotta—you know (he gestures)—set the mood, sort of."

The guy makes sense, sort of. Like snake-hunting.

Then, a month later, there's a girl from the Salvation Army. I go to her place for iced tea in the middle of the afternoon.

"All I want is a new nice man," she keeps telling me.

"Uh huh," I say. I start undressing her.

"A woman has a little thing—," she says.

"Uh huh," I say. I've got her panties off. As she explains to me about that little thing, I read the underwear label.

"It's an itsy-bitsy little thing," she says.

"Uh huh." Size 5 RN 1496 100% Combed Cotton Exclusive of Decoration— *Where's the decoration? I can't find the decoration*—Machine Wash Warm Wash Darks Separately Gentle Cycle—

"—and when it peeks out from under its little pink babushka—"

"Uh huh." No Bleach Cool Iron Made in U.S.A.

"—but it's very, very shy—"

"Uh huh." The things I do for love.

"—and it needs to be punished—"

"Uh huh."

"—and—"

She collapses in a heap of guilt and lust. All those jingling tambourines. Blood and fire.

"No," she says, "not there—quick, then."

"Does it feel good?" Mr. Original here.

"It feels . . . it feels like . . . like Sunday in Bayonne," she moans. Then it's over. I look at her clock. Four-thirty, time for *Gilligan's Island.* I split. Walking homeward I reflect upon the melancholy fact that without Ginger, no man can know satiety.

These are just a few of the butts in my life.

# 42

# Pleasant Brits and
# 180-Degree Spins

I remember buying the first issue of *Country Music Magazine* at a New York City newsstand nine years ago. I had moved back to town that summer from Florida and was making a reasonable facsimile of a living writing about this and that for various monthlies and weeklies. (I was also a contributing editor of Hugh Hefner's new *Oui* magazine, but this was a position that sounded much better than it paid.) I liked country music very much and wanted to write about it, but the magazines simply weren't interested. It was, in their precious eyes, an undeserving subject, and they were prejudiced against it. The sole C&W periodical I read—and not with unwavering allegiance—was *Country Song Roundup,* a magazine whose lack of substance was equaled only by its lack of literacy: a magazine that seemed to confirm those other magazines' low opinion of country music.

So I bought *Country Music* and I was impressed. Here at last, I thought, was a well-made magazine that knew who Ernest Tubb was. I wrote a letter to the editor, who at that early time was Peter McCabe, a pleasant little Brit who had written a book called *Apple to the Core,* perhaps the best book that we have about the darker side of rock 'n' roll big business. I offered Peter some ideas, and a week or so later he took me to lunch at a Japanese joint near the old *Country Music* offices on Fifth Avenue.

The first story I wrote for *Country Music* was about moonshine and moonshine songs. This appeared in the magazine a few months after the Japanese lunch. It was the beginning of a happy five-year relationship between me and the magazine.

Working for *Country Music* was fun—at least that part of working which occurred away from the typewriter. I remember going to a series of Jerry Lee Lewis recording sessions in Memphis that was like a cross between *Nightmare Alley* and *Ma and Pa Kettle Go to Town.* I remember spending a weekend with Hank Thompson at a Nashville hotel where every other guest was a conventioneering black Baptist preacher. I remember hunting for women with Johnny Rodriguez in the sleepy little Rio Grande town of Harlingen, Texas—hunting for women and waking up the next morning with nothing but hangovers. I remember playing all-night poker with Tom T. Hall as his bus barreled through a seemingly endless thunderstorm in seemingly endless rural Michigan. (I think we were both cheating.) I remember Doug Kershaw's wedding at the Astrodome in Houston, an occasion for which half of Louisiana's Cajun population seemed to have come west. (At least three gentlemen introduced themselves as the undisputed Boudin King.) I remember being asked by George Jones's manager to hide the pistols in preparation for driving George to perform at a benefit concert at the Nashville penitentiary. I remember creeping through Macon, Georgia, in a taxi at five in the morning with Delbert McClinton's piano player, Lewis, looking for a bootlegger. (We didn't find one. To vent our frustration, we picked the lock on Delbert's motel-room door and covered his snoring body with shaving cream.) I remember a 180-degree spin on ice in Tompall Glaser's Cadillac at a Nashville intersection at rush hour. I remember Waylon Jennings when he was modest. I remember other things that are better left unprinted.

By 1977 I was living in Nashville, editing the record review section of the magazine. By then the attitude of the establishment press toward country music had spun round almost as drastically as Tompall's Cadillac. Country music was now the darling of the media, and *Country Music Magazine* had helped to bring about the change. I had just written a book called *Country: The Biggest Music in America.* Five years earlier, it perhaps would have been impossible to sell this book to my New York publisher.

My friend Patrick Carr, another Brit who had long since taken over from Peter McCabe as editor of the magazine, was eventually replaced by someone new—someone with whom I did not get along. We argued, and I was fired, swearing never again to write for the magazine. Then, a year or so ago (the editor had long since gone), as I was working on *Hellfire,* a book about Jerry Lee Lewis, I published an interview with the Killer in *Country Music.* And now here I am again, if only to say happy birthday to us all.

# 43

Russell Galen had come to work at the Scott Meredith Literary Agency in June of 1977, while I was living in Nashville. The Meredith agency, whose big gun was Norman Mailer, had represented me since 1974. But it was with Russell, after my return to New York, that I entered into the most important conspiracy of my career.

The first deal of substance that Russell and I made was for *Hellfire*. The deal, dated June 19, 1979, was with Delacorte Press. It was to be the first book edited by Morgan Entrekin, who had worked under Chris Kuppig of Dell when Dell published the paperback edition of *Country,* eight weeks or so before the *Hellfire* deal. Though I never drank when I wrote, I drank more than I wrote; and it was not until early 1982 that *Hellfire* finally saw the light of day. Morgan, who went on to own and run Grove/Atlantic, republished *Hellfire* under the Grove Press imprint sixteen years later.

It was with *Hellfire* that I truly began to write. These are the opening pages of that book.

# Excerpt from *Hellfire*

*There is laid in the very nature of carnal men, a foundation for the torments of hell. There are those corrupt principles, in reigning power in them, and in full possession of them, that are seeds of hell fire.*
—Jonathan Edwards,
*Sinners in the Hands of an Angry God*

*I'm draggin' the audience to hell with me.*

– Jerry Lee Lewis

It was three o'clock in the morning, and the master bedroom of Graceland was still. Elvis Presley lay in his blue cotton pajamas, dreaming. A small bubble of saliva burst softly at the corner of his lips, and, breathing heavily, he turned. It was the same old dream.

He walked through Tupelo in the late afternoon on a summer's day toward the home of the virgin Evangeline. He was smiling as he turned a corner and entered a street where lush hackberry trees swallowed the sun. There was the house of her father, where she waited, wrapped in that magic, unholy thing from her mama's bottom drawer.

He felt a chill. He was naked. Pleasance became dread, and he flushed with panic. He would retreat across town, where his mother was not dead, and there fetch his clothes. If he hurried, there was time. He took a shortcut through a backyard that he recognized, but he was soon lost, running scared in a strange, unfriendly place until he came to a meadow like none he had ever seen, and afternoon became night and the meadow became endless and he screamed.

The telephone at his bedside was ringing. It was one of the boys downstairs, calling to tell the boss that there was trouble.

Robert Loyd, a Graceland security guard, had watched nervously as the 1976 Lincoln Continental sped up the gravel driveway and struck the gate.

"I want to see Elvis," the driver had shouted, with a voice as harsh as the clangor of chrome and wrought iron that preceded it. "You just tell him the Killer's here."

The guard recognized him and told him that Elvis did not want to be disturbed. This displeased the Killer. He pulled out a .38 derringer, and his eyes, which were already partly closed, tightened with a further wrath.

"Git on that damn house phone and call him! Who the hell does that sono-fabitch think he is? Doesn't wanna be disturbed! He ain't no damn better'n any-body else."

Elvis motherfucking Presley—his heart hastened—setting up there in that goddamn mansion pretending he's God, and all he is is some fat old dope ad-dict who dyes his hair like a goddamn woman. As the words of Job admonished: "They spend their days in wealth, and in a moment go down to the grave." To the grave, to the grave, to the grave. He almost laughed, but instead spat in dis-gust, then commenced howling anew. He did not relent, and the guard went to the phone.

"Elvis says to call the cops," the boy at the house told him. The Killer howled and waved his pistol toward the manor.

The guard did as he was told, and a patrol car arrived in less than a minute. Officer B. J. Kirkpatrick peered into the Lincoln and saw that the Killer had the derringer pressed against the door panel with his left knee. He pulled the door open, and the gun fell. He picked it up and found that it was loaded.

"I'll have your fuckin' job, boy," the Killer hissed.

Kirkpatrick drew him from the car, spread him, frisked him, and locked his wrists. More patrol cars came, and the Killer was taken away.

Riding slowly, against his will, the prisoner glared into the slow river of dark night, wondering what had gone wrong. The thought must have come to him, and just as quickly fled, that there were no Breathalyzers in Old Testament days. This must mean something. He must have thought about singing a song, the old one about meeting in the morning; but he didn't. Then at last he grinned and shook his head, for he knew that the cold, brilliant handcuffs would not long contain him.

# 44

# Felicity Opens Wide

The story begins with a girl named Shirley Sweeney, without whom there would be no story; Shirley Sweeney, who, in a younger and more innocent day, had knelt, candle in hand, staring at the black Cordovan shoes of the bishop who stood before her reading aloud from a little gilt-leaf book.

"'My beloved spake, and said unto me, Rise up, my love, my fair one, and come away.'"

Upon hearing those words, she had taken the veil and the bridal ring, and, thus consecrated, Shirley Sweeney of Bayonne, New Jersey, had become Sister Felicia of the Kingdom of God, for which no exit exists on the Garden State Parkway. Her mother, weeping with joy, had risen from her seat in the front pew of Our Lady of Famine and pressed the shutter release of her Kodak camera, feeling secure that the life of her problematic and withdrawn and beautiful daughter now rested securely in the hands of a loving Father.

She had good tits. This was the first thing that Bobby Dempsey noticed when he met her eight years later in a bar on West Side Avenue in Jersey City, barely a week after she had thrown in the veil. At first he did not believe a word of what she said. He had been raised by nuns, but he had never encountered one who wore a silk crepe-de-chine blouse and drank shots of Green Chartreuse. Then she showed him the Kodak picture. It was eight years old and somewhat faded, but the face, pale and striking, was unmistakably that of the woman who now sat beside him. Bobby Dempsey, who had been confused since birth, presently grew more so.

"How can you drink that stuff?" He gestured with his chin toward the syrupy, virid dregs in the pony glass round which his companion's slender fingers were enwrapped.

"I've never really drunk before," she said. "This looked the prettiest."

God, they were good tits. He couldn't keep his eyes from them. He had been laid off at Union Carbide six weeks before, and he had been spending his days at this bar ever since. Aside from the morning when the old fellow down the end burst into tears when "Botch-A-Me" by Rosemary Clooney had come over the radio, the sudden presence of these tits was the first break in the boredom of those six weeks.

The liquor he drank was now nectar, and he beheld those wondrous breasts as their possessor spoke of many things—of young years misspent in repentance for sins imagined but undone; of mornings reigned by prayer and evenings by desire; of a maiden's vision of hell that no killer's mind could conjure; of reclining seats in movie theatres. . . .

"I don't get it," Dempsey said, redirecting from her bosom toward her eyes his own.

"You know, those reclining seats. When you lean back in them, they sort of slide forward?"

"Yeah."

"My father invented them."

"Yeah?"

"That's why I'm rich."

Dempsey cockled and uncockled his eyebrows in a mixture of feigned interest and sincere perplexity, then returned his eyes to her breasts.

"Last year, when Mother died and I inherited everything," he barely heard her say, "my first thought was to give it all—most of it, anyway—to the Church. Even after I'd gotten the sign and decided to leave the order, I was still going to give it to the Church. But then, well . . . "

Dempsey turned away from her breasts to seek reassurance from the aproned wretch behind the bar. The wretch glanced at the breasts, then grimaced and shrugged to Dempsey in vague and solemn disgust, muttering the word "broads" as he veered labored toward the ice machine.

"Whaddaya mean, *sign?* I don't get it," Dempsey said.

"A sign," she said. "I received a sign." They drank in silence for many moments, and it was not until Dempsey's eyes once again rested their work upon her bosom that she resumed her explanation. "I knocked a crucifix down."

"Yeah, so?"

"I knocked it down without touching it."

"I don't get it."

"What you've been staring at for the last hour, that's what did it. That's what knocked it down."

Dempsey drank mightily and looked straight ahead.

"I'd been troubled for a long time. Saint Augustine called it *epithymia*. The little man in the boat had ants in his pants. That's what my Aunt Catherine from Passaic kept saying before she got into trouble: 'The little man in the boat has ants in his pants. Whatever shall I do? How shall I cope? The little man is driving me gaga.' That's how I was beginning to feel. Day after day, it was getting worse and worse. Every little thing set me trembling. The smell of myrrh, which had always seemed to me the most funereal of scents, was like an aphrodisiac. Devotional candles cast shadows of unreal lovers on every wall and floor. I dreamt the Flying Nun embraced me, and I woke crying because she wasn't really there. It was awful."

*This broad is nuts,* bethought Dempsey to his drink. The old man who had cried at "Botch-A-Me" walked in, nodding in occult resignation to the wretch behind the bar. There was a loud peal of thunder. "De angels are bowlin'," announced the wretch; then all was silent again as rain began to fall without.

"I was a nervous wreck," Sweeney continued after renewed sipping. "I took a leave of absence and made a pilgrimage to the Holy Land, but even there I couldn't find peace. I knelt in the Church of the Sepulchre, and all I could think of were the words of St. John Chrysostom: 'Where there is death, there too is sexual coupling.' The little man in the boat had me by the neck.

"I came back to Our Lady and tried to resume teaching." She inhaled melodramatically, almost hiccupping in the process. "All those eyes, those tiny eyes, looking to me for knowledge—and I had none. That had always troubled me. But now it was worse. All those tiny eyes seemed to be staring at my breasts—like you're doing right now. I had never been self-conscious of my breasts before, but now it seemed that every eye was on them. Even the other sisters were staring.

"Late one afternoon I locked the door and drew the shades in my room. I took off my wimple and undid my habit and sat before the mirror in my bra, looking at myself. They're just run-of-the-mill breasts, I kept telling myself. I unhooked my bra and let it drop, and I kept looking at myself in the mirror. Slowly my nipples began to harden. As I watched them harden, I could see the reflection in the mirror of the crucifix over my bed. I touched one finger to my nipple, and the crucifix fell. It was His way of telling me to take a hike."

Dempsey listened to the rain fall against the pane for many moments. "How did you end up here?" he asked, rapping a crooked index finger upon the bar.

"I walked."

It was still raining two hours later when Bobby Dempsey unlocked the door to his apartment six blocks away, on Commingway. He offered Shirley Sweeney a beer, but she declined.

"Well, here we are," she said, almost giggling. "You and I and the little man in the boat. And my breasts, my sinful, magic breasts. We mustn't forget my breasts."

Dempsey placed his hand upon her head and grabbed at her thick, curling blondeness, still short from the penitential shears' cropping and wet with rain.

"You're beautiful," he said, losing his balance.

"Get it over quick," she said, her eyes scanning the walls for crosses.

Kind thunder concealed the sounds of unzipping and stumbling. They were both naked, Dempsey and Sweeney, and were not ashamed.

Shirley Sweeney's eyes saw what they had never seen. She touched it, tentatively at first, then as if forever; and she drew it to her prayer-weary lips.

*She's gonna bite it off, I know it,* Dempsey thought.

But her mouth was like an angel's, and her tongue was like no tongue Bobby Dempsey had ever known—not even that of Louie the Rat's wife. He closed his eyes, and she did what she had dreamt of doing since she had been old enough to dream.

Then he was upon her, wild, pitting his boozy tumescence against the knot of her intact virginity, going where neither man nor tampon had gone before. There was the gnashing of teeth, and all seemed hopeless; but he got it in. She shrieked, and Dempsey almost withered in fear as the next day's *Jersey Journal* headline passed behind his eyes—UNION CARBIDE WASHOUT RAPES NUN—but the shriek became a teary moan of joy, and then an utterly vulgar sound, with which Dempsey was more familiar, and he reveled onward, mad-headed with pleasure. For many, many weeks, his love-life had been restricted to furtive liaisons among the pages of an old issue of *Horny Housewives,* but now, thanks to the strange creature who writhed beneath him, his manhood was redeemed, and as he loosed the ounces of his love within the glory that was the source of all sorrow, he could almost hear the gods proclaim of him, *What a guy!*

Dempsey rose to take a leak, and he noticed then the rose-red blood like dew upon his mighty sword. Wiping it away, he felt as he had never felt before, for he had finally, after all his years at play in the fields of Eros, plucked a maidenhead—and it had only cost him the price of two shots of Chartreuse. He returned to Sweeney, who lay in soft shadows, unclenched and becalmed, and he lay beside her.

"Kiss him," she whispered. "The little man in the boat."

He lowered his noble face to the wet hollow of her softness, and he parted the dainty folds of her flesh with his tongue. She exhaled loudly through her teeth, whewing as if suddenly relieved of the heaviest of burdens, as the little boatman was drawn, Jonah-like, into the mouth of the great Dempsey. Then, abruptly, Dempsey recalled the love he had so recently deposited, and also the rose-red blood like dew, and he recoiled in Hibernian horror.

"What is it?" Sweeney panted.

"Nothin'," Dempsey faltered. "I just remembered, I was supposed to go down to Unemployment today, that's all."

"Come here," she said. She placed his hand upon her mysterious bosom. He felt her nipple rise hard against his life-line, and he took it between his fingers. Her own fingers embraced his, tightening their grip on the purpling pinkness of her icon-felling tit. She closed her eyes and, softly, dreamily, told him of Saint Felicity, whose name she had taken in sisterhood; Saint Felicity, who had entered the arena forth-shining and serene, smiling to the devouring beasts of her martyrdom.

"Of all the female saints, she was one of the very, very few who did not abstain from sex. I dreamt of her often when I was a child. I saw her striding with her master, Perpetua, into the Carthage amphitheater. The sky was overcast. But it was odd. In my dreams, Felicity always devoured the wild animals, then just walked off, still smiling, wiping the blood from her lips." She shrugged softly, hugging Dempsey and kissing him on the forehead; then, sighing, spoke again, "'Let her breasts satisfy thee at all times; and be thou ravished always with her love.' Know where that's from?"

"That thing that was on Channel Nine the other night? *Planet of Prehistoric Women?*" He felt her ribs and belly shake, as with subdued, silent laughter. This gave Dempsey the willies, for he had always associated unprovoked mirth with insanity.

"Let's go to Japan," Sweeney said. "I've always wanted to go there."

"Sure," Dempsey said. "Whatever you say."

Sweeney fell asleep, breathing warmly and serenely on Dempsey's hale arm. But, try as he might, Dempsey achieved no similar repose. He rose from the bed and walked into the other room, feeling the familiar mantle of confusion descend upon his shoulders like a Robert Hall special. He sat by the window and lighted a cigarette. It had stopped raining, and the street lamp across the way was encircled by a hazy rainbow glow.

*Hell,* thought Dempsey, whose saintly mother, he now reminded himself, had raised no fools, *that wasn't virgin blood. Just her monthly run-off, that's all it was.*

But these unuttered snarlings rang empty within him, and brought him no comfort. The truth of the matter was that Bobby Dempsey felt himself falling in love. His mind drifted back to an afternoon two years before, when he had come home from work early and discovered his beautiful Betty sitting naked in the hand of a Weehawken pizza man. On that cruel afternoon, he had sworn to love no more. But what hope had the oaths of man against the will of God?

He found Sweeney's purse on the floor by the couch, and he began to rifle through it. Among the wadded Kleenex, lipstick, powder, and paint, he found a wallet containing photographs of people in various stages of mourning. Visa and American Express cards, and seventy dollars. He took two tens, shoved them under a cushion, and replaced the wallet. He also found an Ovral palette with seven of its pellets missing and a piece of paper bearing words which Dempsey recognized as Latin but could not understand: *"Tu spes hominum, quos conscia mordet Men sceleris, quae per Veneris contagia sordet."* Then he found the little blue New Jersey Trust Company savings-account book. He opened it and squinted. Her latest withdrawal, dated the previous day, left her with a balance of $623,845. There was also a checkbook, but he didn't bother looking at it. He put the purse down and lighted another cigarette. He could hear the garbage trucks in the distance, and he knew that dawn, the vanquisher of dark confusion, would soon come.

Bobby Dempsey had never traveled in an airplane before. Indeed, he had never before been farther from Hudson County than Monmouth Raceway, where, betting every possible combination of a long-shot trifecta that could not lose, he had lost two weeks pay and with it his taste for any further traveling. That had been two years ago, before the cursed pizza man had ruined his life.

But this was a new day, and the losing trifecta and the fornicating pizza man were as barely remembered shades from an ended dream—a dream less palpable than the heavenly fleece of clouds which he now looked down upon from the window of the JAL 747, sailing westward through the Pacific sky. He held Shirley Sweeney's hand, and he kissed her. Her lips tasted to him like hope.

He wondered at her: not only at the angelic beauty of her flesh, but also at the boldness of her spirit. He had watched incredulously as she, on that morning after he had taken her virginity and two tens, shelled out almost seven thousand dollars for the two round-trip tickets to Tokyo. He had followed her incredulously to the United States Passport Office, where, incredulously, he had stood in line bearing the certificate of his birth and listening, incredulously, as Sweeney told him how the bombing of Nagasaki had wiped out the oldest Christian community in Japan, and how in childhood she had so feared that Bayonne might be the target of a similar holocaust should the Lord decide to obliterate from the face of His creation that place that, according to Sweeney's Aunt Catherine, was the most evil and wicked on earth, namely, Chester's Bar & Grill on East Twenty-first Street. He had returned with her, weary from incredulity, to the split-level Bayonne manor of her inheritance, where they became naked as children, and she bade him to do as he should. At night's end, he had sat, Sweeney in one hand, a can of Schlitz in the other, watching a rerun of *"The Name of the Game"*—the two-parter with Sammy Davis, Jr. For the first time in his life, he had felt superior to television.

Anxious incredulity had become blissful wonderment, and Dempsey came to trust Sweeney as a child trusts its mother. She had, he felt, made a new man of him. Little more than a week ago, even the *Horny Housewives* had seemed to sneer at him, and he had spent his days watching a Budweiser clock erase the every unfurling moment of his life. Now he had a woman lovelier and wealthier than any he had imagined might ever lie beside him, and he was flying with her across a sea he had never seen, to a place he had never been, and he was not perplexed; and it was all her doing.

Twilight became night, the cabin lights dimmed, and all was still but for the hushed griffin-roar of the engines. Drawing the woolen airline blanket over himself and the angel of his salvation, Bobby Dempsey closed his eyes, counted his blessings, and joined Shirley Sweeney in dreamland.

Abed in the Imperial Hotel, Dempsey knelt behind her and pressed himself to that tight-dimpling cranny which he had never known. He held her hips in his hands, looked down upon her back's luscious sloping, and—"Now," she said—plunged. Sweeney gasped, and Dempsey gasped, as quick as that.

"I'm yours," he thought he heard her softly say.

For many days, they lived in a revery. Dempsey, who still had most of the two hundred dollars with which he had left America, watched with child-like awe as Sweeney picked up the tab for a seven-hundred-dollar steak dinner at l'Osier, then paid for round after round in one Roppongi nightclub after another. His every wish, it seemed, was her command; and the effusion of her love left no desire untended. He ravaged her against a pillar in the Meiji-Jingu-mae subway station, stood over her in ecstasy beneath a leafy eave in the Inner Garden, luxuriated in her wondrous breasts in the dressing-room of a Ginza silk-shop. They stood beneath the *torii* of the hallowed Meiji Shrine and swore undying love, while a white-robed Shinto priest plucked red and yellow flowers from the garden of the earth; and when the old priest turned and walked away, Sweeney raised her skirt, and Dempsey cloyed her from behind.

As the days of their dream passed, Dempsey began to grow proud, and in his pride he fancied himself to be more than a laid-off die-cutter, indeed, to be more than a man. *After all,* he felt, *could any mere man have cuckolded the Lord?* Further, he began to think of Sweeney not so much as his saving angel, but as his privileged courtesan.

One night he went out by himself and got drunk at a place called Nishino-ki. He returned to the hotel, where Sweeney was in bed reading a little auburn book, and he took off his pants and belched magisterially.

"*Ching,*" he said. "Know what that means? Guy in a bar told me. It's Jap for . . ."

But Sweeney did not respond, or even look up, but only turned a page and continued to read.

"What's that you're readin'?" Dempsey asked, nonplused by her manner.

"Origen," Sweeney said, still not looking up.

"What's that?"

"Origen," she said, as if she were talking to an annoying child, "was the greatest of the Church Fathers."

"Was he from Bayonne, too?"

Sweeney arched her eyebrows. "He died in Alexandria in the third century."

"Huh," Dempsey said; then, uncertainly, "C'mere, baby."

"Not now. I want to read."

He stroked her breast, her magic breast.

"*Noli me tangere.* Know what that means?" she said, mimicking his voice in an unkind manner. "That's Latin for *don't touch me.*"

"Oh, yeah?" said Dempsey, defensively. "Well, what am I supposed to do with this?"

"Why don't you do what Origen did with his?"

"What's that?" Dempsey snarled.

"Cut it off."

His gift to womankind wilted in his trembling hand, and he stammered with an anger that barely cloaked his pained confusion.

Dempsey did not sleep well that night, nor did the rising sun bring him peace. He pretended that the preceding evening had not taken place; but to no avail. Whenever he tried to touch her, Sweeney pulled away. He was more confused than he had ever been, and he no longer felt like more than a man, but rather like some trifling thing, lifted for a moment and regarded as wondrous, then dashed, broken against a rock, as worthless. What Sweeney had given, she was now taking away, and Dempsey could not bear it.

"What's wrong?" he implored.

"You defiled me," she said, and there was neither rancor nor irony in her voice.

Dempsey almost apologized, and he almost reminded her that it took two to tango, but in the end he said nothing.

"It could have been pure," she said. "I came to you. I was serene and ready. But you just didn't have it in you. It was my mistake, and it's my loss."

"I don't get it."

"You're weak." She placed her hand beneath her breast, then pressed her chin downward, flicking her tongue to her nipple, and she closed her eyes. Dempsey went mad with the lust that only sadness with its wild black cawings could inspire; but when he reached to caress her, she drew away.

"Why me?" Dempsey despaired.

"I don't know. Why don't you ask him?" Sweeney tossed aside the sheet and spread her flesh with her fingers. "Go on," she whispered, "ask him."

Bobby Dempsey gazed down at that lovely heartbreaking thing, and he almost spoke to it. That was when he knew that it was time for a good stiff drink.

When he returned to the hotel two hours later, Sweeney was gone. There was a little piece of paper on the bed, on which was written the word *Kakemeguro*, followed by three X's and the name of Felicia.

The red petals and the yellow petals scudded in the wind, and Bobby Dempsey, head hung low, took the saddest leak of his life.

He glanced at the Budweiser clock, then ordered another shot.

"Hey," he said to the aproned wretch behind the bar. "Remember that broad I was in here with a few weeks ago?"

"Yeah. The one with the tits."

"She took me to Japan. Paid for everything."

"Ah, quit pullin' your prick, buddy."

"I'm serious."

"You're nuts, buddy."

Dempsey waved the wretch away in nervous disgust, but the truth of the matter was that he himself had begun to worry over his sanity. Upon returning home, he had taken the Boulevard bus to Bayonne. There was a For Sale sign on the lawn of the Sweeney manor. He called the realtor's office, but was told that Miss Sweeney was no longer the titular owner of the house and that there was no record of her current whereabouts. (Hearing the word *titular*, Dempsey immediately perceived that the realtor was part of the cabal. For days afterward, his mind tictocked, *TIT-ular, TIT-ular, TIT-ular*, in syncopation with the Budweiser clock that commanded the moments of his life.) He had called the convent of Our Lady of the Famine, but no one there had heard from Sister Felicia since the week before Dempsey had met her. Now, in his anxiety and confusion, he sometimes wondered if indeed he ever had met her.

Not one waking minute passed without Dempsey's heart crying out for her. He thought he saw her distant figure on every avenue; thought he heard her voice in every passing conversation. His obsession weltered his memory—had she really said that? had she really done that?—and as the reality of his memory of her ebbed, so did that of his everyday existence. He began to converse silently with the *Hungry Housewives,* explaining to them that he wasn't such a bad sort, asking them whether or not they enjoyed Chinese food, and so on. He reminded himself frequently that no one in fear of going insane was in true danger of insanity, that all roads led to Rome, and that one should never draw to an inside straight.

Having great difficulty sleeping, being plagued by horrid nightmares in which the Pizza Man that was all men, entered his beloved Sweeney slowly and endlessly and doomfully as she lavished beneath him, loudly loving it, Dempsey began to rise well before daybreak. Every morning at four-thirty, he watched reruns of *"The Abbott and Costello Show"* on Channel Eleven. He was convinced that Lou Costello, the preternatural man whom death could not contain, was trying to help him. From five o'clock to six, when the bar opened, he sat and tried to figure out exactly what Lou was trying to tell him. Then he would breathe deeply and descend to the bar.

He took to sitting beside the "Botch-A-Me" man, who, like Lou Costello, seemed to understand his suffering. Every day they drank and conversed for more hours than not.

"How do you figure broads?" Dempsey asked him late one night, when they and the aproned wretch were the only reasonable facsimile of life in the joint.

"Yeah," his elder answered, "I know what you mean. That Rosemary Clooney, boy . . . "

"I think Lou Costello had the right idea."

"I know what you mean."

"Ah, what's the use."

"A broad took me to Japan. Here, look." Dempsey withdrew the scrap of paper that Sweeney had left on the bed that fateful morning in Tokyo, the scrap of paper with the strange word that Dempsey had asked the bellman to translate for him. "That's all she wrote. Know what it means? Huh? It means World of Dreams."

"I went to Europe in '44. They got nothin' over there."

"Japan. An ex-nun, no less."

"I bet that Rosemary Clooney sold a lot of records over there in her day."

"The only woman I ever loved."

"Oh, botch-a-me . . . "

The wretch behind the bar saw them first. The three who came in the front door looked like Cubans. The kid who came in the side door was blond. He put the clip into the semi-automatic, then released the safety. He held it at gut-level, aimed at the bar, while the other three produced linoleum-cutters and cleaned out the cash-register, the aproned wretch, Dempsey, and the "Botch-A-Me" man. Dempsey only had three dollars to last him till his next unemployment check, and they took it. After breaking bottles on the floor, the three Cubans joined the gunman at the side door. Laughing, they began to leave.

Dempsey heard the awful, sundering noise of the firing, and he fell, swearing that if ever he got out of this mess alive, he would straighten himself out and forget all about Shirley Sweeney, goddamn her crazy eyes.

In that hairbreadth of supernatural time between the wild flashing and the 5.56mm thunder, Dempsey's bleary, frightened eyes met those, clear and serene, of the fair-locked gunman and he realized—not so much saw as sensed who the gunman was. He had fucked married women before, known the maddened jealousy of trespassed husbands before. But this—then there lay Dempsey on the barroom floor, dead as Kelsey's nuts.

Such is the story of a man named Bobby Dempsey, who lost his mind, his life, and three dollars in folding money, all for the sake of love. But remember this, as its moral you try to discern: It wasn't Shirley Sweeney who killed Bobby Dempsey. It was the guy with the machine-gun.

# 45

Entries from a scattershot journal from early 1982. The ellipses do not indicate omission: in those sporadic seasons when I kept journals, I was a most elliptical diarist. The names of certain individuals, however, have here been reduced to initial prenominal capitals in the quaint manner of yore. (There were two different J——'s, here undifferentiated: soon after these entries end, there would be three. This was, as I would later write in *Scratch*, "the time of all those J's.")

### Jan. 20

C came to town . . . drank w/her at Tippin & Dodge's . . . then back here & shot some scum into her . . .

### Jan. 21

More of C & scotch.

### Jan. 22

Ditto . . . borrowed Bobby T.'s Cordova & drove to J.C. w/C
186 to pick up her check . . . back to Dodge's, then Tippin . . . J
showed up & we three came back here, ordered pizza—but C
got pissed when I told her I was fucking J. that night—so split—to bed w/J
after the *Honeymooners* ("poloponies" episode . . . came five times: once in her figa;
once in her yap; & thrice on her skin . . . bad, sickly sleep . . .

### Jan. 23

Shaky, sick day . . . woke early & sat here till after noon, when J
& I went to Tippin, then she off for work on 57th Street . . . sat w/Coady all day,
sickly sipping beer . . . then here for further recuperation . . . J brought me ribs
from work round midnight . . .

### Feb. 2

Woke around ten . . . la Parisienne for coffee . . . interviewed by Mark & Jeannie of
KLBJ "Talk of Austin" (". . . and next so-and-so who will be talking about women
who are allergic to sex") . . . Tippin: Vito, Tedesco, Dutchie, Giuseppe, &c . . . back
here at 12:30 . . . looks and feels like rain . . . to work . . . Interviewed by Don & Sh-
eryl, WWJ-Detroit . . . glass of water at Tippin at 3 o'clock . . . S

Louise dropped by, 3:30–5:00 . . . roast beef sandwich from la Parisienne . . . brief
nap . . . dismal depression . . . reached page-five of piece . . . took a bath . . . ate
lamb chops . . . finished piece . . . R called; came by, soft & weepy & confused,
round midnight . . . tea, then bed: fucked her like crazy, came between her tits, on
her ass, & her crotch . . . then sweet, rainy sleep . . .

### Feb. 3

Woke round eleven, to Hofler's call . . . showered . . . to corner w/R; uptown to
lunch w/Bob [Hofler, of *Penthouse*] at Manhattan Market (paté, penne w/seafood,
chocolate cake). Gave him "The Lord Thy Windbag," contracts; he gave me six
March *Penthouse*s. We discussed "Getting Rid of Friends and Lovers" and other
VFT's ("Picking Up Girls in Albania") . . . downtown in the gray rain . . . Tippin
. . . here to change at three . . . Pendleton at Dell called . . . F left message for me
at Tippin: Domenico, Giuseppe, Donovan, &c . . . la Parisienne, then here; talked
with Nancy Naglin, who had nothing much to say . . . napped, ate salad. Interview w/Les Hughes at WTWN-Grand Rapids (8:30–9); fundamentalist guy called
in . . . la Parisienne . . . to bed after *Honeymooners* . . . R called "to say thank-you"
. . . stayed up some more . . . to sleep around two; dreams of murder &
Uncle John.

### Feb. 5 [one week—no booze]

Woke abt. 10:30. Showered, shaved. Tippin for coffee . . . Aqueduct closed again
Friday . . . letter from Richard, w/clipping of *Hellfire* review in L.A. *Herald-Examiner*
. . . J came by w/friend Roberto . . . met Soozie at Tippin; came back here at 4;
peanut-butter sandwich & T.V. dinner . . . talked w/K. Moline: we have tentative
dinner date for next Tues. . . . Mary the photographer called; we have a tentative
shooting for next Wed. . . . Cooley called; said the book is in all the Nashville stores
. . . cleared out *Hellfire* files . . . Morthland called, sd. Boston guy is interested in
buying out my collection . . . Old Reliable J didn't show for laundry duty . . . cut
birthmark on my hand; worried abt. cancer . . . J called, finally, round ten; came by
at midnight w/white stockings on . . . J split; to bed at three . . . J returned at six,
came to bed w/hose on, & I came inside her . . .

## Feb. 17

It turned cold again today . . . Urge to drink, but still no $$—down to my last $10 again—fuck . . . to the Tippin & John Dewar . . . drunk, drunk, drunk . . . ended up at R's . . .

## Feb. 18

More of same . . . borrowed $50 from Tommy D . . . Pendelton called, re: N.P.R. interview next Friday . . . conked out by eleven . . .

## Feb. 19

Up by nine . showered, shaved . . . la Parisienne . . . wet, dismal day . . . L.A. *Times* review of *Hellfire* from Sculatti . . . Got copy of Lester Bowie's "The Great Pretender" . . . bought bracciola at Ottomanelli . . . Gary Cuomo came by . . . R came by . . . dinner and melancholy . . . Pat from *Daily Nebraskan* interviewed me. sadness . . . sweet sex with R tied & untied . . . deep sleep round 2:30 . . .

## Feb. 23

Coffee at Tippin w/Bobby Lonergan, who ran down his A.A. broad rap—remarkably like that of John the Actor . . . Nice clear, cool day . . . Saw Phil Di Biasi in Jimmy Day's . . . Fenoula called, just as I was thinking of ashes . . . Michael O'Shea in Minneapolis interviewed me at five o'clock . . . Gristede's for dinner grub . . . went crazy, head & got drunk . . . Tippin, Dodge's, Chumley's, Head; back here; got R & drunk-cabbed over there . . . dismal-fucked her brains out—felt like the last time . . .

## Feb. 24

Ash Wednesday. Split R's—directly to Dodge's . . . Tippin . . . drunk, drunk, drunk . . .

## Feb. 25

Drunk all day, Tippin & Dodge's . . .

## April 2

Drunk all day in Dodge's . . . Dom, &c . . . lunch there . . . met Carol's daughter Loretta—sixteen-yr-old knockout blonde . . . J came by after I called her, while roaming evilly w/Bobby G . . . came back here. I fucked J, her on top, me numb & all but sexless; sleep.

*April 30*

Up at eight. Showered. Bought can of coffee & cigs at Gristede's; Xeroxed *Forum*
piece; back here by nine . . . beautiful spring day . . . S D
came by round 10:30, had tea; we left together . . . I took "E" to *Forum,* met Frankie
there. Michael Bulger—a kid, but a nice one—took us to lunch at Dustin's on 2nd
Ave—calamari, salad, stuffed shrimp, choc. cake—eh food, but free . . . Frankie & I
fast-walked over to Times Square at 2:30 to meet Krauss & see "Amin: the Rise &
Fall," which gave me a few laughs . . . We walked down to the Village. I left them at
the Riv, came home & took a bath & changed . . . lonely for love & for her, lost &
smiling . . . J came by—she's off to Palace banquet . . . ate leftover lamb; napped
8-10 . . . "The One & Only" on Channel 7 . . . Morthland called, shaken, around
10:30—Lester is dead———————

# 46

# Good Book Made Better

*Reader's Digest*, the magazine for people who love to read if it doesn't take too long, has announced the forthcoming publication of a condensed version of the Bible.

According to executive editor Herbert Lieberman, "The essential fabric of the text, and its familiar sound, has not been altered in any way, and the full spiritual message has not been at all diminished. It is our hope that the many people who may have been hindered from reading the Bible because of its length and complexity will find the *Reader's Digest* condensation a warm invitation to become intimately acquainted with the greatest book mankind possesses." (He obviously has never read *I Married a Lesbian Slut*.) Getting down to brass tacks, Mr. Lieberman explains that "the overall percentage of reduction is about 40 percent."

I, for one, eagerly await the new, streamlined Bible. Granted, it's not all that bad a book as it stands; but I, like those many whom Mr. Lieberman refers to, have always been a bit repelled by its length, and have found it lacking that certain, shall I say, *pizzazz* that we have come to expect from our more modern sacred works, such as *Raiders of the Lost Ark* and the Revelations of Phil Donahue.

Don't get me wrong. Jehovah was one heck of a God. When it came to dividing light from darkness, splitting oceans down the middle, or wiping out the firstborn of an entire Middle Eastern nation, He was in a league by Himself. But, let's face it, He was no editor.

His writers were often given too free a rein, where they would have benefited inestimably from stricter editorial control. ("Two thousand words by Friday on the founding of the temple, Ezra"—that sort of thing.) Nor were the prophets themselves the sort of characters that the *Post* would try to lure away from the *News*. The plot of the Old Testament is rather simple: God meets chosen people, God loses chosen people, God gets chosen people. Yet we are asked to shuffle along, theeing and thouing, through more than half a million words before the story ends. (Bear in mind that the most complex *Love Boat* script rarely exceeds ten thousand words.)

Though it is less lengthy and less overwritten, the New Testament could also use some tightening up. It is astounding that, given the quality and quantity of His miracles, Christ comes across in the Gospels as a very one-dimensional figure. The excision of the Gospels' slower passages would give us a Christ more suitable to modern times. I should not go so far as to say that we should outfit the Lord in jogging gear; but it is only right that we be given a Christ who would not seem so utterly out of place on *That's Incredible!* (And, oh, wouldn't it be a sight to see Him raise John Davidson from the dead!)

I admit that my advice has not been solicited by the esteemed and learned team in charge of shrinking the Bible down to nearly half its size. Nonetheless, I herewith offer gratis, but while remaining unopposed to appreciative tokens, some basic suggestions.

First, make the Word of God clearer and more accessible. Take, for an example, the First Commandment: "I am the Lord thy God, which have brought thee out of the land of Egypt, out of the house of bondage. Thou shalt have no other gods before me. Thou shalt not make unto thee any graven image, or any likeness of any thing that is in heaven above, or that is in the earth beneath, or that is in the water under the earth: Thou shalt not bow down thyself to them, nor serve them: for I the Lord thy God am a jealous God, visiting the iniquity of the fathers upon the children unto the third and fourth generation of them that hate me." Wringing the purple from this tirade, we are left with a much more reasonable commandment, which today's readers would have less difficulty relating to: "After all I've done for you, if you so much as look at another god, you'll be sorry. I have a problem with jealousy that I've never been able to work out; but if you respect My space, we can make this relationship work."

Second, lighten up on the broads. Sure, Jezebel was a floozy. But is it really necessary to have her devoured by dogs, a scene that has doubtless cost the book countless female readers? Why not give her a nervous breakdown, or a career crisis, after which she is allowed to find herself? This has worked well in many recent books, and I see no reason why it wouldn't work here.

Third, tell us more about Jesus—hobbies, pet peeves, favorite color, that sort of thing. Finally, leave the Book of Revelation exactly as it is. This is a hot property, potentially another *Star Wars,* and there should be no trouble in getting a movie deal.

I am sure that there are those conservatives among us—those same who scoffed at new, improved Tide—who will frown upon the compact, streamlined Bible. Most of us, however, will likely tell our grandchildren with pride that we were around when the Good Book became the Better Book.

Once the Bible has been given its proper short shrift, I propose that attention be directed toward some other of our so-called classics—bloated offenders all.

Is there any reason why *The Iliad,* a tale whose action takes place in a mere four days' time, should ramble so interminably on? Once we begin to see Achilles as Henry Fonda, Agamemnon as George Brent, and Helen of Troy as Bette Davis, we begin to see just how much air might be let out of the Homeric windbag. The same goes for *The Odyssey,* which might be condensed and rewritten along the lines of the 1955 film *Ulysses,* a much livelier work, starring Kirk Douglas instead of a lot of dumb words. I mean, an epic is an epic, but do they have to be so *long?* Where is it written in stone that we have to hurt our eyes and get headaches and miss *Hart to Hart* just to get culture? And, come to think of it, if this stuff is so great to begin with, how come kids go to college to become journalists and not epic poets? Answer me that, Mr. Dactylic Hexameter.

And what of *The Divine Comedy?* Sure, the part in Hell is all right, almost as good as Stephen King, but all that sappy, ethereal stuff that follows has simply got to go. Beatrice this, Beatrice that. You would think Dante was the only guy who had ever gotten laid. If he had had a regular job, he would have been far better off. More than anything else, his *Divine Comedy* stands as a monumental example of just what can happen when one has too much time on his hands.

I might here also discuss Chaucer's *Canterbury Tales,* Cervantes's *Don Quixote,* and Dickens's *Bleak House.* But since these works have been read by only eighteen living persons, all of them pale, nervous creatures who believe that the world is on the level, I shall not.

Ah, but *Moby Dick!* Now, there's a fat, old blowhard that could use a little cutting down to size. After being nearly forgotten, *Moby Dick* has, within the last fifty years, risen to the status of the Great American Novel. Yet has anyone considered the fact that Melville would have an extremely hard time finding a publisher today? Just envision it: "Mr. Lazar, there's a gentleman here with a book about a large white whale." Would Moby Dick have even a fighting chance in the literary-sales arena against Miss Piggy? I doubt it. But in a less obese state, perhaps the book would find new readers. There is in *Moby Dick*—pardon this next phrase, but I, too, am of human flesh—much blubber that might well be hacked away. I mean, a three-thousand-word chapter on "The Whiteness of the Whale" ("Bethink thee of an albatross . . . ")—give us a break already, Herman! Call me insensitive, but if a big white shark can kill Robert Shaw in two hours, I don't see why it should take more than two hundred pages for a big white whale to kill Ahab.

Let us hope we will eventually be able to reduce the *Encyclopaedia Britannica* to a single, pocket-sized volume, discarding all those pieces of reputed information that are not directly applicable to the completion of an average *TV Guide* crossword puzzle.

Maybe then those men of literary length who still walk archaically among us (hello there, Thomas Pynchon) shall get the message: the last thing that any nation that consumes vast quantities of diet cola wants or needs is a fat book. Bethink thee of *I Married a Lesbian Slut.* Bethink thee that, and learn.

# 47

# Lust in the Balcony

In my glorious and ill-spent youth, I went to the movies with the hope of picking up girls. The Loews, the Stanley, the State—these were the temples of unclean desire in Jersey City's Journal Square, where my sleazy friend Phil and I sought each weekend to rid ourselves of the irksome curse of virginity.

Looking back, I am sure that, in the course of our carnal search, Phil and I saw every film released between the years 1961 and 1965. I remember little of those films vividly—Victor Buono pushing Joan Crawford in a wheelchair; Sean Connery clutching Ursula Andress; a black gentleman being catapulted from an exploding yacht, screaming the scream of overdubbed horror. What I remember best is endlessly changing our seats and lurking behind girls.

Movies and sex had been bound together in my mind since before puberty. I was only seven years old in the autumn of 1956, when I stood with the rest of Our Lady of Victory's congregation and repeated a vow that we would not, under threat of eternal damnation and being barred from bingo, allow our eyes to be assaulted by the movie *Baby Doll*, which had just that week come to Jersey City. Silently I thanked the priest for bringing to my attention something sinful of which I had not been aware. (Were it not for the warnings of adults, children would be doomed to spend their childhoods in innocence.) Immediately, I wheedled my seventeen-year-old cousin Louise into taking me to *Baby Doll*. Our neighbors in the theater audience seemed to regard us as an odd couple, and I didn't really comprehend much of what I was seeing. But still, I was thrilled to be there.

Though it would be another three years before tumescence stirred the sharkskin of my adolescence, I knew that I was already on the right track, and that given a choice between redemption and Carroll Baker's mouth, I would choose the latter.

By 1961, when Phil and I, callow apprentices in the guild of degeneracy, visited the dark balconies of Journal Square in our pursuit of the miracle of love, or at least a quick hand-job, Hollywood seemed to have sunk to its nadir. Movies were generally foolish, tawdry, depthless and possessed of certain childish prurience—qualities which, in a less polished state, defined our own scummy little minds.

Saturday after Saturday, we skulked from balcony seat to balcony seat, rutting like moonstruck wolves beneath the flickering, magic motes of the projectionist's beam. As our frustration grew greater, we were drawn more and more into the seductive images that overshadowed our fruitless quest. By 1965, when we finally stumbled upon what we had sought, the moving pictures had taught us much about life, love and sex. Luckily, we have since forgotten most of it.

What first struck us was that the girls in the movies bore little resemblance to the girls of Jersey City—or of anywhere else, we eventually discovered. (The kind darkness of the theaters, however, did much to enhance the beauty of our pubescent prey. Not that this was really necessary; at this stage of the game we would have been willing to mount a snake had it been dipped perfunctorily in Shalimar.) What next struck us was that womankind, as portrayed on the screen, was divided neatly and clearly into three categories: seductive virgins, sluts and beautiful creatures who slept only with Agent 007.

Nowhere were the seductive virgins so plentiful or so salaciously pure as in the movies of Elvis Presley. In the thirteen Elvis pictures released in the years 1961 to 1965, Presley sang, danced, and (to choose a merciful word) acted his way through an endless gauntlet of young, wet female flesh—without ever once getting laid. This perplexed us truly, but what confused us more was that the possibility of getting laid was never even intimated. It was as if there were no such thing as fucking, as if all lust were slaked by a kiss. This did not seem to bother Elvis, but it certainly bothered Phil and me. We tried to understand when he chose not to deflower Joan Blackman in *Blue Hawaii*, but when, in *Girls! Girls! Girls!*, he turned away from Stella Stevens in order that he might sing "Song of the Shrimp," we knew that we would never buy another Elvis Presley record as long as we lived. Had we realized that, in real life, Elvis was masturbating in a ringside seat as white-undied damsels wrestled before him, we might have thought differently. But, alas, we did not know.

Even more otherworldly in its chastity was the series of films directed by William Asher and starring the Romeo and Juliet of all-American asexuality, Frankie Avalon and Annette Funicello: *Beach Party, Bikini Beach, Muscle Beach Party,* and *Beach Blanket Bingo*. There was something vaguely frightening about these spayed and gelded California beach creatures, so unlike the habitués of our own Jersey shore—something that seemed to imply that brutal desires, like beer bellies and unfiltered cigarettes, had no place in the land of happiness. The Clovers and Jerry Lee Lewis had both been supplanted by the Beach Boys and the Singing Nun. Now sex, like rock 'n' roll, had also gone soft—or so it seemed in our view from the balcony—and we feared ourselves to be doomed throwbacks, forlorn and obsolete as lambskin Fourexes at one of Annette's beach parties.

Were it not for occasional glimmers of old-fashioned lewdness, we might have lost all hope. I vividly recall Rita Moreno hitching up her black nylons in *West Side Story* (a film we found quite as ludicrous as *Beach Blanket Bingo,* insofar as our minds, try as they might to suspend disbelief, simply could not accept the idea of a pirouetting hard guy); Shirley MacLaine hitching up her green nylons in *Irma La Douce,* then baring her garters again the following year, in *What a Way to Go!* Also recalled, albeit less vividly, are Natalie Wood, Joanne Woodward, and Virna Lisi disrobing quite lewdly in, respectively, *Gypsy, The Stripper* and *How to Murder Your Wife.* But these glimpses, however inspirational, really offered nothing more than we had already found in the pages of *Gent* and *Dude,* and served only to deepen our respect for, and appreciation of, that most glorious and praiseworthy aspect of womankind, namely, smutty underwear.

Hollywood disallowed any middle ground. No woman with any interest whatsoever in the one organ that she did not possess was portrayed as anything other than a slut, a whore or a nymphomaniac. There was Claire Bloom drooling her way through *The Chapman Report,* Jane Fonda sucking for sawbucks in *Walk on the Wild Side,* Melina Mercouri collapsing in a heap of unclean hunger in *Topkapi,* Carroll Baker (and, oh, how she had grown since *Baby Doll*) trying to drag her stepson into bed in *The Carpetbaggers,* Kim Novak staining every sheet in eighteenth-century England in *The Amorous Adventures of Moll Flanders,* Raquel Welch bending for bucks in *A House Is Not a Home,* Suzanne Pleshette dragging herself around by the clitoris in *A Rage to Live.* And let us not forget Barbara Stanwyck as the hideous dyke madam of *Walk on the Wild Side,* which left one with the impression that lesbianism was an only slightly more forgivable atrocity than the Holocaust.

Aside from Hollywood's uncanny ability to depict these sleazy characters and lurid goings-on in a manner no more graphic than that of *Son of Flubber,* what most impressed us about these purportedly worldly and mature movies ("This Picture Is for Adults Only" warned the posters; we had to sneak into most of them) was the striking similarity between the view of human sexuality they presented and that view of sexuality with which the nuns and priests of our childhood Sundays had made us all too familiar over the years.

We wondered why the Lord's field reps denounced rather than approved these films, since we would not think of a more effective means of scaring girls away from their own desires, or of advancing the notion that degradation and ruin (not to mention being tyrannized by Barbara Stanwyck) were all that an itchy vulva could ever lead to. These pictures, we knew, impeded our cause just as much as those of Elvis and of Annette.

There were a few movies which we looked forward to with a special relish, and thus usually came away from with a special disappointment. *Lolita* was one film that we expected to be truly wicked. How could the story of a middle-aged man's love affair with a twelve-year-old schoolgirl be anything but wicked? But, alas, the poster photo of Sue Lyon sucking on a heart-shaped lollipop was more lascivious than the movie itself. (Looking back, I realize that *Lolita* was one of the very few good pictures we saw during those years of balcony rutting. Perhaps it was the picture's quality, rendered undigestible by our cinematic diet, that disagreed with us.)

Then there was *The Skull,* the tale of dark, evil powers set free by the unearthing of the Marquis de Sade's cranium. We had that very year, 1965, stolen a copy of the Grove Press edition of *Justine,* and we knew what to expect—or thought we did. We realized that we were wrong as soon as the usher handed out the cardboard 3-D eyepieces. The biggest ruse we fell for, however, was *Sex and the Single Girl.* Little did we know that the two nouns in that provocative title were twain that would never meet. (The film's star, Natalie Wood, had failed us the previous year as well, in another film whose title promised much but delivered nothing, *Love with the Proper Stranger.*)

Most rewarding, we felt, were those pictures that, though not directly about sex, offered sage counsel regarding the procurement and proper maintenance of women. In this respect, the James Bond series was in a class by itself. Ursula Andress in *Dr. No,* Daniela Bianchi in *From Russia with Love,* Honor Blackman in *Goldfinger,* Claudine Auger in *Thunderball:* These were women who could let the air out of Frankie Avalon's beach ball simply by running the tips of their tongues along their lower lips—and Sean Connery, no singing surfer celibate he, did the horizontal hully-gully with them all.

We were quite impressed by Paul Newman's manner and success with the target sex in *Hud,* but after some serious thought we came to the conclusion that becoming Jewish cowboys was out of the question. Vampires also seemed to exercise a wondrous power over women. But vampirism, too, struck us as a rather outlandish tack—though I must admit that *Vampire in a Girls' Dormitory* did make us think twice. In the end we owed more to Mickey Spillane in *The Girl Hunters* than to anyone else. It could have been worse: at least we didn't take to the beach.

But slithering among the balcony seats of the Stanley Theatre one afternoon in 1965, undaunted by the worst movie that ever was—*I'll Take Sweden,* starring Bob Hope and (him again!) Frankie Avalon—whatever god resides over the relentlessly horny finally took mercy on us and sent us two angels from heaven.

Actually, they were a couple of fallen schoolgirls from Bayonne; but I doubt that even Pussy Galore brought greater happiness to James Bond than they to us. Mine was called Peaches, and Phil's was called Maria. Bob Hope's voice faded as in a dream, as the four of us filled the balcony with our muffled unh-slobbering. Sitting there, entwined in the pitch darkness amid the flickering hues, the mysterious softnesses, wetnesses and tumescences of sex were even more mysterious. In the slow-moving moments, in the dimness, it was not hard to lose all sense of precisely which anatomical part one was caressing. Awkwardness was lent a new and awesome dimension. In the end, however, we were sure that Mike Hammer, if not Agent 007 himself, would have been proud of us.

That was seventeen years ago. I don't even go to the movies much anymore. But you can believe one thing: I'd still trade it all in for that mouth I saw back in '56.

# 48

I had been in and out of the bar business since adolescence, when I was a porter at my father's joint in downtown Newark; and I was still working sporadically as a bartender after *Hellfire* came out.

There was a joint called The Tippin Inn on Bedford Street in the Village. It was one of the last of the old neighborhood joints, along with Dodge's down the street, where I also worked, and outside of which my friend Bobby T. and I once handcuffed a cop to the street post, left him there, and drove his squad car to the after-hours joint. The Tippin Inn was owned by a guy named Biaggio Urgola, who went by the name of Benny because he thought it was a more manly name. Benny, who deserves a book unto himself, often consulted in business and personal matters with his dead brother, Sal. I drank around the clock when I drank, often for months at a time, pausing only when I fell into unconsciousness, and during these periods I neither wrote nor tended bar. Benny, and I assume Sal, proved quite understanding and accepting of this pattern, and in that respect Benny was the ideal boss.

Meanwhile, uptown, the magazine *Vanity Fair*, which Condé Nast had purchased in 1913 and folded into *Vogue* in 1936, was revived in 1982, at which time I was asked to write for them. I did one long piece and this review of a Marianne Faithfull album. Then, in the spring of 1983, the magazine sent me to China. When I returned, I went to the magazine's office on Madison Avenue, and everybody there had been replaced by somebody else. I came to miss the magazine's fine multicolored checks, and while I can't remember the amounts on those checks, I do believe they were at least as big, or maybe bigger, that what *Penthouse* paid me. Although *Penthouse* actually allowed me to write with greater freedom and independence, writing for *Vanity Fair* brought with it an air of prestige, which is not without its market value on the road to high-priced whoredom.

My relationship with *Vanity Fair* would be renewed a decade later, through the editor George Hodgman, under the aegis and régime of Graydon Carter.

# Review of *A Child's Adventure*

In mid-'60s England, Marianne Faithfull was the sad girl of rock 'n' roll, the tomboy with the propitiatory candy bar, lost at the party. Amid the callow revelry, bravado, and peacockery of the time, hers was the singular soft voice of melancholy.

It has been nearly twenty years since "As Tears Go By" was released, in 1964. Its singer is still sad, but not in the privileged, romantic fashion of her candy bar days. Of the eight songs on *A Child's Adventure,* only two are not of a decidedly dark-vapored mood; and those two—a bored-chic disco caprice called "The Blue Millionaire" and "Ireland," a piece of Hibernian twaddle connected so utterly of clichés that one almost expects Paddy to come gamboling through the aural clover with a whittled cake of Irish Spring and a cry of "Aye, and manly too!"— seem to have been fashioned with an eye toward the till. The remaining six songs, the dark blue ones, are more striking and well made than anything on her last album, *Dangerous Acquaintances,* or on her 1979 *Broken English,* where even the good material was ruined by too much synthesizer silliness.

Much of what Marianne Faithfull is singing about here has to do with her own entwined weaknesses, fear, and booze. When her songs lapse into dreaminess or, more often, into nightmarishness, she is running or falling, or both, as in "Falling from Grace," the song that is most evocative, lyrically and musically, of the scary, through-the-looking-glass enchantment of the album's title. "Times Square" and "She's Got a Problem" are grim ponderings on alcoholic dissolution, distinctly suicidal about the edges, but unmarred by self-pity, and seductively lovely to hear.

The opening song on the second side, "Ashes in My Hand," is the album's most despairing; the only hopeful moment, "Morning Come," is also the truest. Although she perceives herself as weak, it is her strength, immanent in the somber grace and force of the songs and of the voice that sings them, that gives Marianne Faithfull's gloom its heroic quality. Some beasts prevail in the dark, and she is one of them.

# 49

I was introduced to the poetry of Charles Olson by Ed Sanders, back when Olson was still alive. For Olson, epic meter and continental drift seemed but the immense mingled breath of an all-mysterious, all-powerful eternal rhythm shared by the finite human heart and the infinite universe; and, even in his failures—inevitable when one sets out to make the impossible—the big granite and delicate flowers and tidal storms and kingfishers of his poetry were an inspiration that was ever new and ever growing.

This review, from *The Village Voice,* of the first complete edition of *The Maximus Poems,* came at a time, in 1983, when Olson's posthumous reputation was low: that is to say, at a time when the modishness of the desiccated, the louche, and the affected in poetry were high. *The New York Times,* as I recall, received the same volume with tepid dismissal.

# Review of *The Maximus Poems*

Charles Olson's was a voice of power and splendor, one of the greatest our century has heard. It's good to see that his repute, which grew steadily during the last part of his life, has continued to grow in the years since his death. The publication of this big, well-made, first complete edition of *The Maximus Poems,* obscured though it may be by partisan aerobics, tushie tales of ancient Egypt, and the analects of Garfield the Cat, is one of the notable literary occurrences of this year.

Olson began writing these poems—over 300 of them, varying in length from a single line to more than 10 pages—in the spring of 1950, when he was 39. For the rest of his life, they were his main work. The breadth and depth of his knowledge was immense. He seemed to have absorbed, and to have at his command, the whole of history, mythology, and language. From his years working in government—as an associate chief of the Office of War Information, as a director of the Democratic National Committee, as an agent at the United Nations Security Council—he understood how the racket of politics worked and how it affected America. He put all of what he knew into these poems, which were to form an epic telling of three concentric, simultaneously presented histories.

The first history was local, the story of Olson's hometown, Gloucester, Massachusetts. The second, larger history was of America, its rise and decline. The third and largest was that of Western civilization. He saw the immense forces that shaped history in terms of myth; and that was the glue that held *The Maximus Poems* together.

He made it work. He was quite different from those poets with whom he has often been associated—stern, lofty Pound, his early mentor; the San Francisco butterflies of the '60s. He was a big man with a sense of humor, and his poetry reflected it. He could grab a vast historical principle by the shirt-front, draw it to him, and address it one moment, then, turning round laughing, quote Jimmy Durante the next (as he did in his 1953 essay "Post-West"). Olson's sense of poetry was very nearly Homeric. He didn't write the sort of *étrangé* stuff we so often see lying alongside advertisements for crystal frogs. He was, by nature and spirit, a part of that long exhalation of the heroic tradition.

A great fuss has been made about Olson's "projective verse," about his belief in "breath lines," lines arranged according to natural tendencies of breathing and speech, rather than ordered metrical schemes. But Olson was a classically skilled worker—"He who controls rhythm/controls" was the precept he put forth in "Against Wisdom As Such"—and there is remarkable metrical order beneath the seeming chaos of *The Maximus Poems*.

> We drink
> or break open
> our veins solely
> to know. A drunkard
> showing himself in public
> is punished
> by death

These lines from "Maximus, from Dogtown" have an inherently classical rhythm. "We drink/or break/open/our veins/solely/to know" is trimeter—an iamb, a pyrrhic, a spondee; an iamb, a pyrrhic, a spondee—broken up by Olson according to the way it might naturally be said. The real brilliance of these lines lies in his sudden shift in tone and rhythm, to the stark old-law statement about a public drunkard being punished by death.

But the true glory of *The Maximus Poems* lies closer to the heart than to the brain. Olson does not, for instance, just retell the story of Aphrodite's birth; he brings it to life, as Hesiod brought it to life 2000 years ago:

> Down came
> his parts
> upon the sea. Out of the foam the form
> of love
> arose. Was ferried over
> by the waves
> to the shore.

He summons gods to attend the deathward sundering of a barroom drunk—

> The four hundred gods
> of drink alone
> sat with him
> as he died
> in pieces

—because that drunk is no less a part of Olson's threefold human universe, and no more to be pitied, than the governor of Massachusetts who imagined

> that men
> cared

for what kind of world
they chose to
live in

Olson stated his beliefs bluntly. "I believe in God/as fully physical," he said; "I believe in religion not magic or science." He saw humanity as "a species/acquiring/distaste/for itself." In the end, he felt that

Gloucester too
is out of her mind and
is now indistinguishable from
the USA.

But he continued to love that small fishing town; a few pages later he thanks God that he came to live there. "I'm going to hate to leave this Earthly Paradise," he wrote in 1968. Late the following year, he found out that he would soon die, of cancer of the liver. He spoke of "Lady Liver," and on November 23, he finished *The Maximus Poems*.

A few weeks later, on January 10, 1970, he was gone. He had spent 20 years, a third of his life, on *The Maximus Poems*. He had discovered that "the color/of the god of war"—Enyalion—"is beauty." The last, isolated line of *The Maximus Poems* seems to convey the realization that it is not so much the color of the god of war that matters, but rather

my color and myself

George Butterick has edited this massive work carefully and with devotion; and there is every reason to think that his will become the standard edition of Olson's masterwork. Though published at a time when anything of heroic dimensions is regarded askance, as somehow uncool, *The Maximus Poems,* unflattened tummy and all, resplends.

# 50

I didn't like the Beatles, and except for one or two songs on their white album, I couldn't stomach the music they made.

Nor had I ever much cared for Elvis. But for a small few of his early RCA-Victor recordings, he seemed to me a mediocrity who was not so much the embodiment of rock 'n' roll as he was the manifestation of the death of rock 'n' roll's golden age.

# Elvis in Death

On Tuesday, August 16, 1977, I was sitting at home, which at the time was in Nashville, lost, as was my wont, in lazy midday broodings of dirty lucre and dirtier deeds. The telephone rang, and I picked it up. It was my buddy Al Bianculli, a song-plugger at Combine, the publishing company owned by Bob Beckham and Kris Kristofferson. Al was, and is, one of the greatest admirers of Elvis Presley's whom I have ever known, and there was actual distress in his voice as he spoke to me that day.

"Hey," he said, "you're not going to believe this. Elvis is dead. He O.D.'d."

He told me that Beckham's son-in-law Chip Young, who played guitar on some of Elvis's recordings, had been set to leave for Memphis that morning for a session that Elvis had scheduled at Graceland. A mysterious call had informed Chip that the session had been canceled. Then, at noon, a second call had informed him that Elvis had been canceled.

Less than twenty minutes after I hung up the phone, the news was being tolled forth with morbid excitement by every radio and television station in America. Elvis Aron Presley was dead, at the age of forty-two. I shall never forget the thundering storm clouds that darkened the Tennessee sky that afternoon, as if the Four Last Things, descending to Memphis, had rented the day in brandishment of their sovereignty.

So that was his end. I was nonplussed. I had not known Elvis Presley as a man. I had never even met him. I started then to realize that, on some level of faint illogic, I had never truly thought of him as a creature of flesh and blood but rather as an absurd effulgence of hoi polloi mythology, an all-American demigod who dwelt, enthroned between Superman and the Lone Ranger, in the blue heaven of the popular imagination. He had been so distant from reality—even the pope was more visible, more likely to grant an interview—that he seemed unreal, thus immortal. But now, less than two hundred miles from where I sat, a pathologist prepared to make a large Y-shaped incision in Elvis Presley's thorax and eviscerate the quite mortal organs from his cold remains.

Five days later, traveling east, I saw a sign outside a Baptist church on Highway 178 in Orangeburg, South Carolina. All That Hip Shaking Killed Elvis, it gloatingly declared. Snazzy dressers, too, those Baptists, I reflected.

By then, of course, the world knew that hip shaking had nothing to do with it. Traces of thirteen different drugs were found in Elvis's system—grim corroboration of the sensational allegations that had been published less than a month before in an ill-written paperback called *Elvis: What Happened?* But that stupid, malicious sign, posted as it was in the shadow of the great wooden cross that stood before the church, set me to thinking about the matter of Elvis's fame and the nature of his death.

It was an immense fame. In his own lifetime, his name was as immediately recognizable and as legendary as the names of Jesus, Caesar, Charlemagne, Shakespeare, Napoléon, and Einstein. And like those other names, his will live on. Yet what was his achievement, the source of his fame's enduring power? He won no wars, created no masterpieces (I hope that none among us will argue the depths of "Heartbreak Hotel" against those of *Coriolanus*; those days are over), made no great discoveries.

Elvis was, simply and supremely, a singer. Although he was, in the early days, popularly given credit for having invented rock 'n' roll, this was, of course, not remotely true. Rock 'n' roll was not invented. It evolved in the years immediately following World War II. While Elvis was still a blossoming schoolboy, rock 'n' roll, as fine as any that would ever be heard, was being made by Wynonie Harris, Amos Milburn, Fats Domino, and other less-known black recording artists. It cannot even be said in truth that Elvis was the first white rock 'n' roll star. Bill Haley's "Crazy, Man, Crazy" was on the pop charts when Elvis, paying four dollars to cut an acetate souvenir disc, made the first visit to Sam Phillips's Memphis Recording Service, on a Saturday afternoon in 1953.

No, Elvis did not invent rock 'n' roll. But he was its avatar, the embodiment of its spirit and might. He was more than a star. He possessed the souls of his followers. Virgins burned for him, and boys strove to recast themselves in his image. He had charisma, in the true and Greek New Testament sense of that word, meaning, divine grace. It was that grace, that mysterious, innocent power, that raised Elvis, the singer with no song of his own, the praiser of abject mediocrity (proclaiming at the height of his fame, in 1957, that Pat Boone had "undoubtedly the finest voice out now"), from the merely mundane to the profoundly ineffable. He could have started a religion. In a way, he did.

The years 1956 to 1960 were the golden lustrum of his reign, when he was the god of teenage America. By the mid-sixties, when he descended to the likes of "Bossa Nova Baby" and "Do the Clam," he had become an embarrassment of sorts, a gaudy anachronism in a day of more momentous and sensitive pretensions. Though he regained respect at the end of that decade—and that new respect grew in direct proportion to the increasing abandonment of the "new age" meatball mentality of the 1960s—he never again regained the magnificent success that had been his. His records in the seventies rose to the tops of the C&W and Easy Listening charts, but there were no more Top Ten pop hits for the king of rock 'n' roll, who had begun to recede into dark solitude and deathward ways, the curse at blessing's end. But through all those years, though his following waxed and dwindled, the cult never died.

This cult was almost of a religious sort. In the extreme, there were fanatics—mostly adult, middle-class males—who forsook their own identities and were born again in Elvis. These men, a few of whom I had the quite singular pleasure of meeting, lived vicariously through their idol, surrounding themselves with icons and sacred Presleyana, immersing themselves in the facts of his life, listening endlessly to the sound of his voice, until that life and that voice became more meaningful than their own. They presented him with gifts, expensive guitars and such, and with vows of undying fealty, that his acceptance of these things might bring them, the adorer and the adored, closer and more intimately together. This odd religiosity was evident, in lesser degrees of fervency, throughout the saner majority of Presleyans. Like pilgrims to the Holy Land, they arrived in endless numbers at the two-leaved gate of Graceland, cherishing ever after the handfuls of gravel they picked up from his driveway. Small pieces of his clothing, such as those RCA packaged in a 1971 record album, were also treasured, not unlike *brandea,* the pieces of cloth, blessed by the remains of Saint Peter, that were sold to Christians in the early Middle Ages. This was more than the frivolous devotion of fans to their idol. It was worship. And there falls the shadow of that Baptist cross.

The Crucifixion is the heart of Christianity, the center of its mystery and power, without which Christianity most probably would have died out along with Mithraism and the other cults of the late Roman Empire. It is also the heart of another, related mystery, the mystery of popular idolatry.

When one man idolizes another, the hate and envy in his heart are as great as the love and respect of his outward homage. The idol, whom the idolator would, but never can, be, is both the object of his adoration and the cause of his effacement and insignificance. So overwhelmed is the being of the idolator by that of the idol that only the latter's supreme sacrifice, martyrdom, can justify and sanctify their relationship. Popular culture especially thrives on the self-killed. Fanatical fantasizers love to feel that Jean Harlow, James Dean, Marilyn Monroe, Jim Morrison died for them, Christ-like, on the cross of reciprocal love. (We have now even entered an age when idolators take a more active part in the process of martyrdom and canonization. Thus, John Lennon being blown away by a "fan.") As it has been said, the biggest mistake Bob Dylan made in his career was not to die in that motorcycle crash.

And so Elvis, who had fallen from grace, who had not had a Top Forty album in nearly five years, was redeemed. His old records sold as fast as RCA, with pressing plants running overtime, could ship them. "It don't mean a damned thing," Colonel Parker was rumored to have remarked about Elvis's death. "It's just like when he was away in the Army." As sales rose on the third day, the excitement—and it was excitement, of a decidedly perverse and hysterical sort, to be sure—waxed more and more ecstatic. Mourners lost their lives, crushed in the frenzied funerary convergence on Memphis. The cemetery tomb, to which the dead king had been delivered by a Cadillac hearse the color of the Resurrection raiment, was defiled by thieves in search of grisly spoils; and the body was reinterred within the hallowed, guarded walls of Graceland.

Like the fourth-century impresario who hauled Saint Stephen's coffin through Christendom, a holy huckster toured the South in Elvis's limousine, allowing believers to sit in it for a fee and to have their pictures taken in it for an additional charge. (When I encountered him that fall at the Tennessee State Fair Grounds, he was also doing a brisk business selling photocopies of Elvis's autopsy report and death certificate.)

Morbid "tribute records" (ah, euphemy!) flooded forth in waves of formaldehyde and glucose. One of these was Billy Joe Burnette's "Welcome Home, Elvis." Sung as if by his twin brother, Jesse Garon, who died at birth, the song warmly welcomed Elvis to the hereafter, where mama was "waitin' for ya, Elvis. Yeah, she's right over there. And soon our daddy will take our hand, and we'll be a happy family once again." Eventually, there was a record called "The Shroud of Memphis," celebrating the miraculous retention of Elvis's divine image à la the Turin winding sheet.

Sleazy weekly tabloids like the *Midnight Globe* and the *National Examiner* promulgated Elvitic apocrypha. Among other things, there was foretold the coming of Baby Elvis, who was to be born to a Midwestern virgin who claimed that she had been supernaturally impregnated by the spirit of the king. There were stories that Elvis was not really dead, that he had faked his own death. (These stories bore a striking likeness to the Crucifixion theory put forth in Hugh Schonfield's 1966 bestseller, *The Passover Plot,* and, more recently, in *Holy Blood, Holy Grail.* The ill-wishing cynicism of our time seems to be equaled by its gullibility.)

The Nashville entrepreneur Shelby Singleton cashed in on the fantastic notion that Elvis had not truly departed. He released an album, *Reborn,* by a masked Elvis imitator called Orion. Publicized as the risen Elvis, Orion was reputed to be a prophet who could make the blind see and the lame walk. Unfortunate cripples attended his concerts in the hope of being cured, and fanatics bought his records—there were in time six Orion albums—as if they were buying Elvis's own.

The ultimate Elvitic text came in the form of Ilona Panta's *Elvis Presley: King of Kings.* The insinuation that Elvis was none other than the Son of God was also made in *The Truth About Elvis,* written by Jess Stearn with Larry Geller. The equivalent of *The Day Christ Died* arrived in Neal and Janice Gregory's obsessive chronicle *When Elvis Died.* Members of the Presley family also turned to the typewriter. There were books by Elvis's uncle Vester and by his stepmother, Dee.

Then came the carrion birds, those in whom hate and envy are more than just the mere and natural concomitants of love and respect. Though such creatures hate omnivorously, their cowardice prevents them from preying on the living. For them, Elvis's corpse was the feast of the aeon. The popular press, its eulogizing done, cawed forth scandalous tales of drug abuse, violence, madness, and perversion. It is distressing that of the many books about Elvis published since his death, the most successful has been *Elvis* by Albert Goldman. To behold Goldman, a miserable little wad of failed manhood, gnawing in abject rancor at the crotch of a dead hero is to be reminded of the depths of moral penury to which a man can be driven by self-loathing and greed. The fact that his ghoulish grovelings have made him rich does not speak well for the rest of us.

Veneration had become desecration. When there was no more blood left to drink and no flesh left to eat, the feast was done.

Now it is 1984. Seven years have passed since that hot summer day when the storm clouds passed over Tennessee. The long, mad spectacle of Elvis Presley's death is ended; but the Elvis cult is as strong as ever it was.

The cult's principal shrine is Graceland, the Memphis mansion where Elvis lived since 1957 and where, on that August morning twenty years later, he died. There, in the Meditation Garden, beneath a stone cross and a stone Christ, Elvis lies near his mother, Gladys, who alone of all her sex was loved by the king.

No other tomb in America is the object of so many pilgrimages as Graceland. Even the grave of her most beloved martyr, John F. Kennedy, is ill attended in comparison. Day in and day out, they stream through the gates, their eyes wide, their cameras strung round their necks: middle-aged women in print dresses, their lizard-skinned husbands in tow; children too young to know for sure why they are there, led by parents who were his disciples, drifting now between lust and menopause, youth and their own, less noticed, place in the ground; skeptics and zealots; lunatics and the dull, ordinary grist of democracy. They come from everywhere to gawk in fascination at the grave of the American dream, to walk where Elvis walked, to touch what he touched, and to send postcards of death to their loved ones back home.

The faithful bring flowers and tokens of their undying love. Housewives stand transfixed and dolorous before the tomb, like the women who kneel lost in prayer for hours at the sarcophagus of Pope Paul VI beneath the Vatican Basilica. Like those prayerful women, they seem to be petitioning for divine intercession. Elvis was the supreme son, sacrificed on the altar cloth of maternal love and laid to rest by his mother's side. He was their son, the son of all motherhood. He died for them, they seem to feel.

Younger women lavish the grave with less motherly affection. Some of them place love letters on the tomb, or floral displays bearing romantic sentiments. They knew him only in their fantasies while he lived. What mattered death to a love that had never been real? He died for them, too, of course. He died for everyone and everything, but for the drugs that had killed him.

Teenage boys enamored of death in their innocence, children of a later rock 'n' roll culture, approach the grave with delectation. Like Jim Morrison's numbered stone in Paris, it is for them a symbol of self-destruction, one of the sacred monuments of the rock 'n' roll church of death.

Some of the older males regard the grave as if it holds a kindred spirit, a good old boy like themselves, but one who got lucky and who paid for that luck with his life, just as they would doubtless have ended up paying if they had been lucky, for such are the ways of the Holy Spirit that wields the sword that moves them.

Other men seem merely to be satisfying themselves with the fact that lies in the dirt at their feet—the fact that they are alive and Elvis is dead, his fame and wealth and wet young girls gone with the breeze that is yet theirs to savor.

"How many towns in every kingdom hath superstition enriched!" exclaimed Robert Burton on the subject of holy shrines. Like much else in his *Anatomy of Melancholy,* this remark is no less trenchant today than it was in the early part of the seventeenth century. Burton surely would have been stirred by the instance of Graceland.

The Graceland mansion was built in 1939 on 500 acres belonging to the Moore family. Though it was popularly believed in later years that Elvis gave Graceland its name, the estate had been christened by its original owner, Dr. Moore, in honor of his aunt Grace. By the time that Elvis purchased Graceland, in early 1957, the estate had been whittled down to its present size of thirteen and a half acres.

Graceland is now owned and operated by Elvis Presley Enterprises, Inc., a division of the Elvis Presley Residuary Trust, all the assets of which will soon belong to Elvis's daughter and sole heir, Lisa Marie Presley.

Officially opened on June 7, 1982, Graceland attracted more than 520,000 people in its first year of business. (The prices of admission are $6 for adults and $4 for children.) Designated as a historical landmark by the Tennessee State Historical Society, Graceland has grown into one of the major tourist attractions in America. It has transformed the city of Memphis into a vacationers' mecca, enriching the municipal treasury and local economy with a steady flow of millions of tourist dollars. In death Elvis is worth far more to his hometown than he was in life.

Crass commercialism has always flourished around the major religious shrines of the world. Thriving souvenir shops surround Saint Peter's Square in Rome, and similar commerce constitutes the only big business in the remote Pyrenean town of Lourdes. As far back as the eighth century, when the decomposing bodies of the early Christian saints and martyrs were torn apart to satisfy the international demand for holy relics, such merchandizing was an immense and very lucrative industry. (In his book *Western Society and the Church in the Middle Ages,* Richard W. Southern states, "If we were able to draw up statistics of imports into England in the tenth century, relics would certainly come high on the list.") It is by means of such items that common men have always sought to bring themselves closer to the supernatural. Today as in antiquity, relics, icons, religious medals, and the like are superstitiously used to ensure good fortune and ward off bad luck. The medieval farmer who believed that his possession of a blessed relic would result in better crops and the modern automobile driver who feels that a Saint Christopher medal will help to protect him from accidents are in essence subscribing to the same magic.

No marketplace of necrolatry can compare with that which has burgeoned on Elvis Presley Boulevard, directly across from Graceland. (Ironically, this shopping center is situated on eleven acres of land purchased by Elvis in the 1960s. This property and the Graceland estate were his only landholdings at the time of his death.) Here, in a number of jerry-built stores, one may purchase all manner of Elvis Presley mementos, souvenirs, and bric-à-brac. Vendors offer everything from T-shirts and license plates to crucifixlike pendants and plaster-of-paris devotional statues. There is no telling just how much money is spent at this vast and tawdry bazaar of kitsch. One store alone, the Graceland Souvenir Shop, did more than $1,000,000 in business in 1983. Much of the merchandise sold in the great mall of death is developed and designed by Elvis Presley Enterprises, Inc., which profits directly from its sale. I was told by one of the administrators that more than a million postcards are sold at Graceland each year and that graven images of the king are in general the most popular merchandise.

Though a court ruling has now disentitled him to share in the large profits of Elvis Presley Enterprises, Inc., Colonel Parker's original appraisal has proved to be accurate: "It don't mean a damned thing. It's just like when he was away in the Army." Death has not hampered the marketing of Elvis. If anything, it has enhanced it. Elvis is more salable in death than he ever was in life. The Graceland shrine is more than just a monument to him. It is a monument to the majesty of the almighty American dollar. It is a temple of eternal revenue, a place where the thronging populace of the middle classes can dream the dream of kings and taste the miraculous glory of he who died for them—providing, of course, that they have the price of admission. There are no free dreams.

However we choose to look at Elvis Presley—as a saint, a savior, or a monstrosity; as the apotheosis of America's fatal and garish yearning; or as the final god in the pantheon of the West—we can be sure that the likes of him will not soon pass this way again. America heeds the call from his grave, where Jesus, Gladys, and Elvis form a new Trinity—the Lord, the mother, and the sacrificial son of the dream. It heeds that call as it heeds no other.

One thing is certain. In an age bereft of magic, Elvis was the last great mystery, the secret of which lay unrevealed even to himself. That he failed, fatally, to comprehend that mystery gives the rest of us little hope of ever doing so. After all, the greatest and truest mysteries are those without explanations.

# 51

# Maybe It Was My Big Mouth

### *Carly Simon: Free, White, and Pushing 40*

On the Monday morning on which I was to visit Carly Simon, I picked up the New York *Post* to see what number had come out. It was 071, which meant nothing to me. Browsing backward from the Belmont charts through the rest of the paper, I saw Carly's face beaming forth from the *Post*'s gossipy "Page Six." Beneath her picture was the following item: "Hotter than hot. That's what insiders are saying about Carly Simon's sexy new video, 'You Know What To Do,' from her about-to-be-released Warners album, *Hello, Big Man*. Slotted to debut on MTV a week from tomorrow, the video shows Carly, clad in a slinky white-and-black maillot, splashing around in the surf near her Martha's Vineyard retreat. Advance viewers of the 'sizzling' display say the sultry songstress is a natural on film."

An hour later, in not-so-sultry dishabille, she opened the door of the lavish Central Park West apartment where she lives with her children, Ben and Sally, and a sorrel-haired poodle named Johnny. The kids were at school, but the dog was there. Carly's colored housekeeper, Irma, was occupied in the kitchen.

"Did you see yourself in the *Post* this morning?" I asked her.

"No," she smiled. "What did it say?"

"'Hot . . . sexy . . . sizzling.'"

"Really?" Her grin widened.

"Yeah, made you sound like a real slut."

We went into the master bedroom, where her video machine was hooked up. On a night-stand by the unmade bed was a hardcover copy of Judith Rossner's *August*. A suitcase radio stood nearby on the floor. On a shelf there was a small, expensive tape deck, and on it a cassette of *Synchronicity* by the Police. Leaning behind the television was a broken blackboard on which a child's hand had lettered "MOMMY LOVES BEN." A wicker basket was filled with fashion magazines.

"This is the unedited version," Carly said, inserting a tape into the video machine. "It makes it look like I enjoy being raped," she laughed.

"Do you?"

"Uh, no comment."

The tape, which had been directed by Dominic Orlando, and which had taken two days and $40,000 to make, showed Carly diving into and emerging from the swimming pool behind her home on Martha's Vineyard, observed by a peeping Tom.

"Who's the guy?"

"My mystery man," she smiled.

As the song went on, the mystery man pursued her into a wooded copse, attacked her, and won her love.

"See what I mean?" she said.

"Yeah."

We adjourned to the living room. A grand piano was set imposingly near the large easterly windows, which overlooked the treetops of Central Park. On the coffee table lay a copy of her brother Peter's reggae book and a volume of Picasso reproductions. There were no ashtrays.

"Were you really ugly when you were young?" I asked.

"I wouldn't say *ugly*. I was just a homely, gawky kind of teenager. But even then, when I was very young, people used to say that I was sexy."

"Uhm."

"I remember always being called sexy. People said that I had a kind of raw sexuality." The poodle hopped into her lap, and she stroked it. I noticed then that her toenails were painted red but her fingernails were not. "Maybe it was my big mouth, or maybe it was my long legs."

"Did you feel sexy?"

"Did I feel a violent sex urge? Yes. I've always felt a very strong sexuality."

"It comes and goes, or what?" *No ashtrays.*

"What, you mean my strong sexuality? It's fairly even. I've always been in touch with it. I think a lot of people aren't in touch with their sexuality. They don't want to accept it, or they sublimate it, or they hide it. There are various ways that people can avoid meeting it face to face."

On the wall of the hallway that led from the bedroom to the living room, I had seen framed photographs of Carly's family and friends. One of the pictures showed her father, Richard Simon, a founder of Simon & Schuster, shaking hands with Robert Ripley to celebrate the publication of *Believe It Or Not!* in 1928. Richard Simon had died in the summer of 1960, little more than a month after Carly's 15th birthday. I recalled reading, in a 1981 *Rolling Stone* cover story by Timothy White, that Carly's failure to get close to her father had left a profound impression on her. I asked her about it.

"I don't think that you can get away from the influence of your parents," she said. "I think that your taste in either men or women is dictated by how you felt about your father or mother. Usually a girl will either go for someone who is like her father or will react against her father and go for someone who is the opposite of her father. It's always dictated by an original perception, whether it's pre-Oedipal or post-Oedipal."

"Uhm."

"I was always trying to win my father's love. Since then I've gone for men whose love is hard to come by. I've always had to reach. I like the reach, because it's what I was used to."

"And what happens when you get what you reach for?" I was in the wrong racket. If only I had gone to college . . . Dr. Tosches . . . Neuroses Fixed While-U-Wait . . . Rich Broads a Specialty . . .

"Ah! A lot of different things happen. I'm fortunately not so neurotic that once I get someone's love I want to throw it away and pursue something else that I don't have."

"Is it true that you've been going to psychiatrists since you were 11?"

"Not continuously. But, yes, on and off through the years. I prefer to be in treatment. I find that it's really good for my work. It's a way of understanding myself—my motives, why I do certain things that I do. It keeps me on course. I don't think I've become overly dependent on my analyst. I don't see him that much."

"Does he give you drugs?"

"No. I don't take any hard drugs. I've only done cocaine once, and I was so scared by it that I've never wanted to do it again. I don't like my heart to go above about 80. Whiskey makes my heart beat fast also. I've been trying to figure out which alcohol you can drink that doesn't make your heart go so fast. How about vodka? But I don't really like alcohol for more than five minutes on the way up. I must have a very weak liver, or a very pure liver."

I asked her about her album *Hello, Big Man,* which was just being released. (The "Big Man" of the title song is her father.)

"I've allowed myself to be simpler. At first I was so excited by irony that I wanted everything to have an ironic twist. Everything I wrote had to have an O. Henry ending. Now I allow myself to write about moods.

"Sometimes I wish I could write like Marvin Gaye, who writes very explicitly about his sexual feelings. I don't really ever write directly about sex. Actually, the new single, 'You Know What To Do,' is the closest to that I've ever come."

As Carly spoke, I looked around. It really was a beautiful joint. Get those pictures of the old man off the wall, send the kids off to one of those academies in the back of the Sunday *Times* magazine, slip the maid a few bucks to lose the poodle in the park. "Do you think about getting married again?"

"I would be just as happy to stay single. I feel as if I had a wonderful marriage. I look back on it, and I feel very, very glad that I was married to James. I enjoyed being married. More than that, I was very much in love. I don't feel the necessity of being married again. I can see it happening, but I can just as easily see it not happening. It's not a goal. I don't necessarily want to have any more children."

"Are you a strict mother?" Ah, well. At least I got ashtrays downtown.

"No, I'm not particularly strict. I should be a little bit stricter."

"Do your kids like your music?"

"They say I'm their second favorite singer."

"Who's their first?"

"Their father."

# 52

# Review of *A Choice of Enemies*

Years ago, after reading George V. Higgins's first three books (*The Friends of Eddie Coyle*, *The Digger's Game*, and *Cogan's Trade*), I sent him a letter. I asked him, basically, where he got his style from. His response, typed impeccably beneath the letterhead of his law firm ("Cable Address: Eddiecoyle, Boston"), arrived quickly. "I invented my style; I am a fucking genius," he wrote. At the end of his letter, he said, "This is a long way of saying that I have no better idea about the origin of what I do than you do. Perhaps I simply have a dirty mind and the good fortune to live in a generation that talks and does dirty."

That was in early 1975, not long before his fourth book, *A City on a Hill*, was published. In that novel, Higgins broke away from writing about small-time criminal society, and attempted instead to render the more urbane and deodorized, but no less maleficent, world of state and local politics. Like the politics that the book dealt with, *A City on a Hill* was as boring as it was grim. As I saw it, Higgins had failed on the job.

In *A Choice of Enemies*, his tenth novel, Higgins has returned his attention to the political machinations of that city on a hill. This time, however, he delivers the goods.

The hero of Higgins's tale is Speaker Bernie Morgan, a character inspired by, if not quite based on, John "The Iron Duke" Thompson, the Speaker of the Massachusetts State House who died in 1964 of alcohol poisoning while awaiting trial for racketeering. Morgan, unruly and unkempt (his own chief counsellor likens his appearance to that of "an out-of-work faro dealer"), is an old warhorse whose ways have grown intolerably repugnant to the new, squash-playing, made-for-TV breed of political crooks. *A Choice of Enemies* is about Morgan's downfall, and about the men who bring it about.

During his final summer as the Speaker, Morgan is persecuted by a special, and most likely unconstitutional, commission controlled by a senile Yankee plutocrat named Otis Ames; harassed by his lawyer and right-hand man, the slippery and expedient-minded Francis X. Costello; vexed by an apostate bribe-giver; distressed by the knowledge that his mistress, Maggie, is dying; pursued by a Hispanic mugger whom he battered for scratching the maroon finish on his Cadillac Seville; and surrounded by aspiring young wolves in Dorset suits. The course of action that Morgan decides upon is a simple one: drink more.

As usual, Higgins draws his characters and tells his story primarily through dialogue. (The importance that he bestows on dialogue, and his concern for its perfection of effect, are remindful in a perverse way of Henry James, another fucking genius who went from Boston law to literature.) Thoughts are never directly revealed. It is only what is said—lies, small talk, confessions, gossip, tirades—that matters. Hemming, hawing, tortuous circumlocutions, and the endless maundering excursuses of quotidian conversation are the devices that Higgins expertly uses to build suspense and tension. At times his characters' utterances can make the flesh crawl with loathing. More often they can evoke loud laughter. Sometimes they can do both. Higgins is the master of what he does, and *A Choice of Enemies* contains some of the most brilliant and outrageous passages that he has ever brought forth.

At one point, Francis X. Costello makes plain the reasons why he is backing the incumbent governor: "Because he *looks* good, because he *is* good, and most of all because he's probably the biggest asshole that God ever made to look just like a movie hero. I know gentlemen in other states who'd *die* to get a guy like Tierney in as governor. The guy is absolutely *perfect*. There isn't a spot on him, he can rattle off that social justice shit like he was Bing Crosby rolling into 'White Christmas,' and he hasn't got the foggiest idea of how on earth to do it."

Vinnie Mahoney, a building contractor who learns the hard way that sweetheart contracts are not always so sweet, expresses himself on the subject of affirmative-action quota systems: "Goddamned commissions. You know what it is, don't you? I know what it is. They're countin', they're down here countin' niggers again. . . . That's what they're doin'. They love to do that, count niggers. They must think there's only a certain number of darkies and we all got together in the business and just go shiftin' 'em around from job to job. Soon's they're counted here, ship 'em over to the next place. Keep 'em one step ahead the commissioners, comin' 'round to count them. Hope to God none of them damned commissioners get to recognize any of them, realize all they're doin's countin' the same niggers all the time."

In one of the book's strongest moments, Bernie Morgan, nearing the end of his days, explains the difference between the fact and fancy of politics: "These professors from the universities, the young reporters that ain't been around us and our jobs and seen the way we do them long enough to understand things? They come in here, all they know about the State House is John Kennedy came up here right before he became president, and he made this real crowd-pleaser of a speech so there wasn't one dry eye in the whole House when he got through. About how everybody that's in politics, especially in Massachusetts, is some kind of angel of the Lord, or ought to be, at least. And they've all seen the movies of him doing that, slinging all that bullshit and looking like he should've been a knight done up in silver armor, and they come up here looking for him. Who never gave a shit about state government. And what do they see when they come into this place? Guys who do give a shit about the Commonwealth. Me, and a lot of other ordinary guys that eat too much and drink too much and never had all the advantages when we were growing up so heavy hitters in the Mafia would want to share their girlfriends with us and Marilyn Monroe would sing us 'Happy Birthday.'. . . They've all got theories. They went to Boston Latin School or one of them prep places and they read Plato's *Republic* or some other goddamned thing, and they think that's the way the government is run. They think that Plato knew the score, and when all the presidents and senators and guys like Alexander Hamilton made speeches, it was all for real."

Reading this book made me think back to the years of my misspent youth in Jersey City, and to Thomas S. Gangemi, one of the various implausible characters who occupied the mayor's office of that city. He was called "The Watermelon King," and was known for his apocryphal campaign slogan, "Remember, Is-a No Voting Booth at the Bottom of the River." In 1963, more than two years into his term, it was discovered that Mayor Gangemi was not a citizen of the United States. *A Choice of Enemies* does not redeem men like Gangemi, nor does it mean to; but it does affirm that there are indeed no voting booths at the bottom of the river. And it leaves one hoping that the dirty mind of George V. Higgins sullies ever onward.

# 53

# Review of
# *The Garden of Priapus*

Not since the publication, more than a century ago, of Friedrich Forberg's *De Figuris Veneris* has so much golden filth been gathered together in a single volume. Amy Richlin has culled the most salacious morsels of those great Roman grouches whose souls wavered between the gods and the gutter—Lucilius, Catullus, Horace, Ovid, Persius, Petronius, Martial, Juvenal, and the other big guns—along with some of the sexiest stuff from the Greek *Palatine Anthology,* and even a few obscene graffiti from the walls of Pompeii. And she does not flinch where other translators have. In fact, she approaches her chores with delectation. Catullus's immortal reply to his critics, *Pedicabo ego vos et irrumabo,* is given a literal rendering: "I will bugger you and I will fuck your mouths." *Cunni vermiculos scaturrientes,* one of the grisliest images in the anonymous *Priapea,* is plainly translated as "the swarming worms of your cunt." Compared to the standard bilingual texts, such as those of the Loeb Classical Library, Richlin's Englishing is refreshingly straightforward.

But *The Garden of Priapus* is a very silly book in that it contains a deadening abundance of academic drivel. The poems and fragments are never allowed to stand on their own, which they surely can; they are deluged at every caesura by waves of analytical jabbering. Pedantry is something that has come to be expected of modern scholarship, and it is inevitable that a book of this kind should impose pedagogical torture on its readers as penance for whatever mundane enjoyment they might derive from it. But when we are told with a straight face that a graffito which translates as "lick my prick" is "paradigmatic of the relationship between the graffitist and the viewer," we have left the realm of pedantry for that of the absurd. Taking a vague eight-line epigram by Dioscordies in which the most explicit phrase is "straddling the middle of me with her extraordinary feet," Richlin, peering with lowered lashes through the attar-scented millennia, says: "I would suggest that the scene describes anal intercourse (or vaginal intercourse from the rear) with the woman prone, her legs"—talk dirty to me, Amy—"hooked over her lover's, her head turned to one side (so that her eyes are visible)." She speaks of Horace "pitting the phallus against the threat of sterility, death, and the chthonic forces." She outdoes herself when she observes that, "whereas the male originators of Roman sexual humor had anuses . . . none of them had vaginas."

There are occasional fits of populist flippancy, too. Burt Reynolds is "a Priapic Figure," but "Chaplin and Woody Allen are the opposite." Julius Caesar is compared to Mick Jagger. The primary Latin obscenities are said to "correspond roughly to the list of words that caused WBAI such trouble with the Federal Communications Commission in 1973." This flippancy sometimes affects her translations. Subura and Summoenium, seedy districts of Rome mentioned in the poems of Martial and others, are given as "42nd Street." When Horace refers to *Falernum,* the wine known as Falernian in English, Richlin changes it to "champagne." While she seems to think her readers might not be acquainted with Falernian wine, she is quick to implore them not to sweep Horace's poems "under a carpet of *Quellenforschung,*" and she uses, as if it were English, the word "raphanidosis," her own Anglicizing of an obscure Aristophanic term denoting anal rape with a horseradish. When translating Latin passages that contain Greek quotes, the Greek is rendered, *s'il vous plait,* into French.

As devoted a classical smut-hound as Richlin appears to be, her pornolinguistic knowledge leaves a bit to be desired. Discussing a poem by the first century Greek poet Nicarchus, she interprets the verb φοινικίζειν as "apparently signifying 'perform cunnilingus.'" Though the Liddell-Scott Lexicon says nothing more explicit than that it described an "unnatural vice," the word is closely related to other Greek words meaning "red" and "bloody," and it had a very precise meaning in the ancient world. Richard Burton defined it in the 1885 Termical Essay of his *Arabian Nights* as "cunnilingere in tempore menstruum." Burton, however, is not to be found among Freud, Huizinga, and Kate Millett in the book's bibliography. Richlin also says that "there is not even a word for 'dildo' in Latin." Martial and Petronius both used the term *penis scorteus* ("leather penis"), and Juvenal simply used the word *phallus.*

It really is a shame—and paradigmatic of some chthonic force or other, I'm sure—that this great and wicked poetry is not presented in the spirit in which it was written. Maybe Richlin has, with *The Garden of Priapus,* exorcised her scholastic demons. If so, we can look forward with interest to her future work, which presumably will be more concerned with classical literature than with whether Woody Allen has a vagina. For now, Amy Richlin is fortunate that Catullus is not around to reply.

# 54

# Review of *A House in the Country*

I almost shut this book soon after I opened it. First, barely more than a page into it, there was the nine year old who asked, "Didn't you think this whole good-bye had a suspiciously fictional air about it, like the final scene of an opera?" and the 15 year old who replied, "Everything about our life here is like an opera." Then, at the outset of the second section, there was the author's apologia: "The synthesis produced by reading this novel—I allude to that ground where I allow the imagination of reader and writer to merge—must never be the simulation of any real ground, but should rather take place in a world where the appearance of reality is always accepted *as* appearance, with an authority all its own: I mean, as distinct from those novels that, with their verisimilitude, aspire to create a world of correspondence, always accessible as reality." Uh-oh, I thought, one of *those.* But I continued to read.

Donoso's tale is set sometime in the past, somewhere in the South American wilderness, at Marulanda, the opulent summer estate of the gold-rich Ventura family. When the adults and their vast retinue of servants depart for a day-long picnic, the 33 Ventura cousins, whose ages range from six to sixteen, suspect that their elders will never return. Releasing their mad uncle from his cell in the tower, the children unite, under his anarchic rule, with the nearby savages who work the Ventura mines. Though believing themselves to be away for only a day, the Venturas' absence inexplicably lasts a year. All allegorical hell breaks loose at Marulanda, as its chambers, labyrinths, and surrounding countryside dissolve and darken into a nightmare of violence, cannibalism, incest, and uncanny evil.

Jorge Luis Borges, the literary progenitor of Donoso, once said that he writes Spanish in an English manner. Norman Thomas di Giovanni, Borges's translator, explained that "since English made Borges and since he is giving Spanish an English cast, he fulfills himself in English, his work becomes more itself in English." I don't know if the same is true of Donoso (though, like Borges, he is fluent in English). I do know that the prose of this book, translated by David Pritchard with Suzanne Jill Levine, is magnificent. It's worth reading for the elegant brilliance of its syntax, metaphors, and vocabulary alone. But, in the end, *A*

House in the Country is grace without power, beauty without substance. Donoso wants not only to tell his tale, but also to simultaneously prevent us from believing it. He yearns to be both magician and shatterer of illusions, both Michelangelo and Laszlo Toth. If ever there was an illustration of pissing into the wind, this is it.

Borges also remarked, in an essay on Hawthorne, that "a single badly invented character can contaminate the others with unreality." Donoso has intentionally peopled a whole novel with characters he describes as "a-psychological, unlifelike, artificial." They are, he says, "emblems . . . who as such live entirely in an atmosphere of words." In fine modernist fettle, he relentlessly reminds us that his tale is "an artifice," and he interpolates his text to thwart any lingering suspension of disbelief. He informs us that a certain character "cannot die until the end of the story"; of another, he explains, "I not only used her as a deus ex machina to advance the action at that point, but I also introduced her with the idea of having her serve me later as a kind of vehicle for what I now propose to narrate." The effect is stultifying.

Like the old woman who spends weeks painstakingly embroidering an intricate sampler that expresses some hackneyed truism, Donoso has spent years crafting a novel that tells us fiction is made up. Does the magician need to announce that the lady in the box isn't really being sawed in half? In The Obscene Bird of Night, Sacred Families, and his other books, Donoso has shown himself to be a literary illusionist of the most masterful rank. "I couldn't resist the temptation," he writes here, "to change my key and employ in this present tale an especially exaggerated artificiality as a corollary to that unflinching ugliness" of the earlier books.

A creation of exaggerated artificiality, however, can satisfy only on an exaggeratedly artificial level. As literature, A House in the Country is really more an expression of academic art-consciousness than it is a novel. I doubt that anyone who has not spent the better part of his life at a succession of universities, as Donoso has, would even think of writing such a book. Early in his tale, Donoso shows us the stately Ventura library, with its rows and rows of fine-bound volumes. But when a secret spot in the woodwork was pressed, "all along the shelves panels of tightly ranged spines sprang open like drawers, revealing that inside there was not one page, not a single printed letter." A House in the Country reverberates with the empty echo of those trick books springing open. It is a grand intellectual feat, beautifully executed, but ultimately a barren and hollow one, moving neither the emotions nor the mind, raising only the eyebrows in passing.

As Henry James knew, it was the crack in the golden bowl, the flaw in its purity and perfection of form, that empowered it with mystery and meaning. José Donoso, trying to refute the flaw, the sublime lie, that is the basis of all fiction, has produced a literary uroboros, self-nullifying in its impotent and inert perfection. "I feel a twinge of insecurity," says Donoso near the end of A House in the Country. "I doubt the validity of all this, and of its beauty." Amen.

# 55

# Review of
*Renaissance and Reform*

Dame Frances Yates, the preeminent voice in Renaissance and Elizabethan studies, died in the fall of 1981, a few months after preparing the first volume of her *Collected Essays*. In her seventies she produced her two greatest works, *Astraea: The Imperial Theme in the Sixteenth Century* and, two years before her death, *The Occult Philosophy in the Elizabethan Age*.

Yates was a rare and wonderful sort of scholar, more concerned with knowledge than with vain exegetical displays. She knew that a single fact often outweighs a world of theories, and that a well-placed question can be more enlightening than a thousand rash answers. She was a historian of ideas. Her domain was the epoch that began in 1439, when, under the auspices of Cosimo de' Medici, Gemistus Pletho of Constantinople and Cardinal Bessarion of Nicaea revived the teachings of Plato and the Neoplatonists. This era, which the French later called the Renaissance, ended in the early 1600s, as the Inquisition overtook Italy and witch-hunts plunged England into darkness.

Yates cast new light on the big guns of her era: Spenser and Shakespeare, Copernicus and Galileo, Dürer and Michelangelo, Luther and Savonarola. Often this light is indirect, the result of illuminating more obscure, but no less intriguing, characters—Christian Cabalists and invokers of spirits, heresiarchs and translators of forbidden texts, mathematicians of the spheres and anatomists of melancholy. Their likes render the contents of *Renaissance and Reform* as provocative as its title is dull.

Giordano Bruno, the Hermetic philosopher burned at the stake in Rome in 1600, fascinated Yates. Besides writings about Bruno in her first volume of essays, she devoted a book to him in 1964 (*Giordano Bruno and the Hermetic Tradition*). Here she elegantly reveals how, in Padua in 1592, young Galileo most likely discovered and was influenced by Bruno's ideas. She also finds a connection between the execution of Bruno and the trial of Galileo, explaining how Bruno's use of Copernicanism as a hieroglyph of a magical reforming movement perhaps inspired the Inquisitors to perceive similar allusions in Galileo's strange new system of the universe.

In "Shakespeare and the Platonic Tradition," Yates begins with the startling observation that while more has been written about the Bard than about any other author, little attention has been given to his place in the history of thought. Setting out to determine Shakespeare's beliefs and their sources, she charts a course back through time, connecting him to Plato's *Timaeus*. Along the way, she meets Nicholas of Cusa, the 15th century German cardinal whose brilliant and perverse *De docta ignorantia* argued that true wisdom lay in "learned ignorance"—"the more profoundly we are learned in this ignorance, the more we shall approach to truth itself." In his words, she detects a foreshadowing of "Hamlet's whole state of mind." As to how Platonism reached Shakespeare, who was no Greek scholar, Yates comes again to Bruno, representative of "the latest phase of the Platonic tradition," who was writing in England while Shakespeare was a young man.

Other essays range wide within Dame Frances's domain of light and darkness. "Not a Machiavellian" examines the many ways in which *The Prince* and *The Discourses* have been misunderstood; and "The History of History" offers the most lucid definition I've ever read of the Machiavellian term *virtù:* "the active power in man which must inform a living society, and which can enable him to stand against the blind forces of Fortune." "Transformations of Dante's Ugolino" shows how the vision of Catholicism's supreme poet was revised to suit the purposes of Protestant anticlericals. "The Italian Academies" views the course of Renaissance learning through the four great academies in Florence, Rome, Naples, and Venice. The dissemination of that learning abroad is explored in "Italian Teachers in England."

Of what relevance, some might ask, is all this to the world today? Very little, I think, except, like all good history, to drive home the everlasting truth of Ecclesiastes—"there is no new thing under the sun." Our world is a different, less mysterious place than it was in the 16th century. Man has subdued nature. But as Yates remarks, he "has only rarely recovered the stance from which he was once able to paint like Leonardo and write like Shakespeare." And that stance was majesty in the face of mortality.

# 56

I had been doing a series for *Creem* called "Unsung Heroes of Rock 'n' Roll," in which I wrote about the forgotten rhythm-and-blues and country renegades whose music I loved, the rock-'n'-roll forbears whose music was better and more exciting than most of what passed for rock 'n' roll at the time. The first of these pieces was "Wynonie Harris: The Man Who Shook Down the Devil," which appeared in the summer of 1979. Harris was both the most sophisticated and the most ferocious of the postwar blues shouters. I remember shaking my head some years later when I discovered that, amid numerous footnotes, the annotator of the *Selected Letters* of Jack Kerouac failed to identify Harris in a 1950 letter to Neal Cassady that spoke of a "feeling for music" that favored the "the art-of-life Wynonie." This sort of thing always brings to mind the Charles Olson scholar who annotated the name Durante in Olson's "Post-West" as "Probably T. C. Durant and the Credit Mobilier scandal of the 1860s," instead of as Jimmy Durante.

It was in early 1983 that Michael Pietsch, a young editor at Scribner's, bought the notion of making a book that would comprise these *Creem* pieces and others written expressly for the book. *Unsung Heroes of Rock 'n' Roll,* published in 1984, was the beginning of a long friendship, as well as a long professional relationship, with Michael.

Neither of us knew how it happened, but the hardcover edition of *Unsung Heroes of Rock 'n' Roll* was printed on the best paper stock of any of my books.

# Excerpt from
## *Unsung Heroes of Rock 'n' Roll*

### *Esau Smith: The Hairy and the Smooth*

I first heard about him in the winter of 1982, from a half-assed south Jersey wise guy who used to come by a bar I occasionally worked at in Newark. The wise guy liked me because I had gotten tickets for his kids to see the Rolling Stones at Madison Square Garden. Since then, if it was a Thursday or a Friday (those were the days I usually worked there), and if he was on his way to or from the airport, and if he had time to kill, he would drop in, have two J&Bs, and leave a five-dollar tip. Though the tickets had cost me nothing but the price of a telephone call and the minor abasement of having to exchange hollow pleasantries with a record-company publicist, they ended up bringing me in more than two hundred dollars in five-dollar tips. Needless to say, he was my favorite customer.

He knew that I wrote ("Nicky the Book-Writer" was the droll sobriquet that he had bestowed on me) and that I had written a lot about rock 'n' roll. This, and those tickets, was why he told me what he did.

I did not believe a word of what he said, though I felt that he believed it, or, rather, that he did not disbelieve it. The more he told me, the more I grinned.

"Yeah, huh?" he concluded. "Well, not for nothing, but the guy's all right."

"Not in the head, it sounds," I said.

It was left at that for more than a year. I did not think again of what I had heard from my five-dollar wise-guy acquaintance about the character called Smitty who worked at his—it was partly his, anyway; I later found out that it had almost as many partners as customers—after-hours joint in Los Angeles. It was so patently incredible that it failed to titillate that gullible craving for contradictory evidence to the dull, known facts of life which we euphemistically call inquisitiveness. I had more important things to think about, such as why I was working twelve-hour shifts in a bar instead of leaving five-dollar tips to some other *citrullo* who was working twelve-hour shifts in a bar. Like the man said, life is funny. Soon it got funnier.

In the spring of 1983 I was sent to China by *Vanity Fair* magazine. On my way home, I stopped for a few days in Los Angeles. Sitting in a bar on Olympic

Boulevard one morning, I realized that I was only a few blocks from the after-hours joint that, back in Newark, I had so often been invited to visit. Maybe the five-dollar tipper himself would be there, I thought.

It was like every other after-hours joint I have ever been in, right down to the indoor-outdoor carpeting and the regulation ash-blonde dyke barmaid. There were three guys at the bar and four at the blackjack table. I took one look at the dealer. In a sudden, jarring instant, I knew that he was Smitty, and I knew—rather, I wanted to know—that his story was true. I put down five twenties and told him that I wanted ten-dollar chips.

"You can split pairs," he said. "Push goes to the house."

A couple of hours later we were sitting in Philippe's, eating lamb sandwiches and drinking beer. He told me that I had missed what's-his-face from Jersey by three days.

"He's some kind of guy, ain't he?" he grinned. "The joint is just a candy store. Him, a few other guys. I get a piece of the table, a small piece. He's got a broad out here or some shit. He hardly even looks at the joint's receipts when he comes by. He's good people, though, I'll tell you that. He's done good by me."

I agreed, told him about the Rolling Stones tickets and the fives.

"That's him."

As we eased, with our beer and our small talk, into the intimacy, however wary, of devious-cruising, chance-crossed kindred, I asked him straightforward if what our mutual acquaintance had told me about him was true.

He started slightly, looking as if to say, "He told you that?" Then he smiled sidewise. "You gonna write about it?"

"If somebody pays me."

"I like your attitude," he said. "But I wasn't made with a finger. You know what's-his-name. To me, that's as good a credential as you could have. That you're a writer, that doesn't mean anything to me. Don't get me wrong, I respect anybody who's self-employed. Hell, I like to read; I just don't have much time for it. You know who I like? I like Eric Ambler. You ever meet him?" I confessed that I had not. "He's probably dead by now," Smitty said. He drank some beer and looked away for a moment. Then he raised his left hand and turned it. "Anyway," he said, "if it is true, what does it matter?" I shrugged, and he smiled. We ordered two more lamb sandwiches and two more beers.

"Look at it this way," he said. "Some guy in yellow pants—I'm using this as an analogy; see, I read—he walks around shifting his belt like there's a gun in it, telling everybody that Jimmy Hoffa's buried under the track at the Meadowlands. Next thing you know, there's a thousand guys in yellow pants telling ten thousand guys in blue pants that Jimmy Hoffa's buried in the Meadowlands. It ain't long before the whole world—green pants, pink pants, the whole shooting match—thinks that Jimmy Hoffa's buried in the Meadowlands. Meanwhile, maybe he's working in a hardware store selling the shovels that nobody's buying to dig him up with. Do you follow me?"

My imagination dyed his graying clove-brown hair black, shaved off his moustache, restored to fullness the vestigial Southern accent that softly colored his speech.

"What I mean is, everybody believes that Jesse Garon Presley died at birth, but nobody's ever bothered to look up the death certificate."

I didn't nod, I didn't say anything. I just kept looking at him.

"As is usually the case, the truth is rather dull. There wasn't any dead child. There was just one mouth too many to be fed by some poor old sucker who couldn't saddle a Guernsey cow if he had four niggers holdin' it still for him. As far back as I can remember, I lived with my Aunt Reenie, in Belden, about ten miles from where I was born. I lucked out pretty good. Aunt Reenie was a good lady. She was my mother's cousin, a few years older than her. She's dead now close to twenty years.

"We were together a lot when we were little kids, especially in the summertime. I remember spending a lot of days playing near Chickasaw Village, which was about halfway between Tupelo and Belden. Me, Elvis, my mother, and Aunt Reenie. We got along. There didn't seem to be anything odd about the situation at all. If anything, I think I felt like I was better off. I ate better than Elvis, I knew that much.

"We were a lot alike. He was a little taller than me even then. He was a little slower, maybe, a little quieter. I used to clench my hand like this, like I was holding something in it. 'Come here,' I'd tell him, 'look what I got.' When he put his face real close to my hand—*wap* I'd smack him. What I never got over," he laughed in a bemused way, "was that he kept falling for it, over and over again." He paused. "Real interesting, huh?" To me it was, but I didn't say so. "It was Aunt Reenie who got us started in on the guitars, little old toy things she sent away for to Sears. We must've been ten then. It was Christmas, I know that much. We thought we were regular little Gene Autrys.

"It seems like I skipped as soon as I was old enough to raise a hard-on. I couldn't have been more than fourteen. Mom and Elvis and my father had moved up to Memphis right about then. I could have gone with them. I really think they wanted me to go with them. But . . ." He moved his shoulders.

"I was a crazy kid. I walked right out there onto Highway 15 like I owned it. It wasn't like I was running away, really. Aunt Reenie knew I was going. I didn't say I was going, and she didn't say she knew I was going; but it was understood. She had a Bible—she had two or three of them, but there was this one little old beat-up one that looked like it might've been autographed by Jesus Christ—that she kept a ten-dollar bill in. She took to leaving it on the wicker chair by the door, instead of on the mantel. This was her way of letting me know that she knew. I took them both, the bible and the ten.

"I ended up in Pascagoula. That's sort of the Pismo Beach of Mississippi. For a week I just sat out on the pier, eatin' vanilla cookies and smokin' cigarettes. At night I slept under it. Man, I thought I was it. The folding money started turning into silver, and I learned my first great lesson: a man can buy only so many vanilla cookies and Camels with a ten-dollar bill. I got a job as a delivery boy for a butcher. He was an old Irish guy named Davey Blue. I gave him a line of shit about how I was an orphan a long way from home. I think I took it from *Boys Town*. Aunt Reenie took me to see that one Thanksgiving or something when it came around, I guess so that I could see how well off I was. Anyway, Old Davey Blue had a heart of gold—hands like rusted, mussled-up anchors, but a heart of gold. He paid me two dollars a day, and he got me a little room in a boarding-house—I guess that's what you'd call it—that cost five dollars a week. It was a great set-up for a crazy kid that didn't want to do anything but eat cookies and smoke cigarettes on the end of a pier. I wrote a letter to Aunt Reenie, telling her that I was fine and for her not to worry. I didn't put a return address on it, though.

"I don't think I worked for Davey for more than a year. I lied about my age and got a job on the platforms. I guess, what with the Korean draft and all, they weren't being too choosey. So there I was, gone from ten to fifty dollars a week. And I was stashing most of it away, too, since my tastes still hadn't gotten too far beyond cigarettes and vanilla cookies—except for a certain girl that I ended up marrying, which I don't really want to go into here, except to say that she was the reason for my next move. I skipped on her and moved to Hattiesburg. That was in 1953, and I was a wise old man of eighteen.

"When I first hit Hattiesburg, I went to work on the platforms there, for Red Ball. That was one good thing about platform jobs in those days: if you had one in Miami, you could get one in Seattle. It was in Hattiesburg that I took up where I'd left off on the guitar, which, to tell the truth, wasn't all that far along, maybe the third page of *Alfred's Easy Guitar Lessons*. The foreman at the job had him a hole-in-the-wall bottle club out near the Okatoma turn-off, and we used to play there on weekend nights, me and this other kid who must have been stuck on page three of whatever the piano equivalent of *Alfred's* is. We'd do a lot of country stuff. Eddy Arnold, Lefty Frizzell, Hank Williams were real big then. People wanted to hear that stuff. We didn't only do country. Hell, we butchered just about every sort of music known to man, and a few that ain't. We had fun, and we made a few extra bucks.

"That's when I made my first record." He laughed and shook his head in good-natured delectation of what seemed to him to be a cherished, secret folly. "And what a record it was." Here he affected the voice of a deep-Southern radio pitchman: "'Bosom Divine' by Jesse Presley with Jo-Jo Fineaux and His Hatties-burg Hepcats." He laughed again; I with him. "Jo-Jo Fineaux was the kid that played piano with me at the club, and the Hattiesburg Hepcats were sons of the guy who put the record out. He owned a furniture store there in town. I think that record sold a good dozen copies, unless that old bastard with the furniture store made his own sons pay for theirs. I still got a few at the house. I'll bring one by the joint for you if you want.

"Like I said, I was making money. The trouble was, I was also learning how to spend it. I fell in with this guy that was on the arm at the club there. He did some small-time shylocking around town, and he had a cut of the numbers action, which was probably about two rolls of nickels a day. I fell in with him, taking numbers and shylocking for him down on the platforms. All the numbers action there—I guess it's still the same today—runs out of New Orleans, not out of Jackson like most people think. So, through this one guy I meet this other guy, blah-blah-blah, one thing leads to another, and I move to New Orleans. I took single action all around St. Louis Cathedral there. I worked straight salary. I could maybe have made more working percentage, but this way I didn't risk sharing any losses. A hundred dollars a week bought a lot of vanilla cookies thirty years ago, I'll tell you that much. I was like a pig in shit. I was still crazy, though. I remember I was drunk one night, and this broad at the bar—I didn't even know her—she was complaining that she had to go to New York to visit her sister and it was freezing in New York and she didn't have a coat, blah-blah-blah. I went out and bought her one, just like that." He paused. "Usually when I tell that story, I make it a mink, but it was just one of those ski-jacket things.

"It was right around then that I found out that Elvis was turning into tomorrow's news. I heard his record 'Milkcow Blues Boogie' on the radio. It was the third one he'd made. Jesus, I was excited. I hadn't talked to any of them, not even Aunt Reenie, in five years. But I really wanted to get in touch now, you know? I remember putting all those nickels in that pay phone, calling Aunt Reenie. She sounded a lot older, like those five years had been fifty, and she sounded like she was hearing from a ghost. 'Your daddy's been tellin' folks that'—and she couldn't finish. The old bastard had written me off! Elvis was starting to make it. People were asking questions, doing interviews and such. Somebody—it couldn't have been the old man; his wiles had quit somewhere round that first plus-sign in the second grade—somebody must have come up with this wonderful solution to the problem of the twin that wasn't around. Jesus, I felt like . . ." He sighed, and his exhalation was like an erasure of years.

"I gave Aunt Reenie two phone numbers, my number at the apartment and the number at the bar where I hung out. I told her to give them to Elvis or my mother, or to my old man if he wanted them. 'You still got that Bible?' she asked me. I told her that I did. 'Good boy,' she said, 'good boy.'

"Right after that, I got pinched taking the single action. I ended up doing three months for those guys down there. So I had no way of knowing if Elvis, or anybody, had called me back. The bartender at that place I hung out at was worthless, about as good with messages as he was with mixed drinks. I just didn't know. To this day . . ." He laid his fist without force upon the table. "And a few years later, at my mother's funeral, the way the old man tried to—ah, fuck it; the beer's talking now.

"Anyway, nobody called me once I was back out, that much I know, I figured, hell, what is this? I still had the foolish pride of a boy who'd been hit but not knocked down. I dropped my real name, came up with 'Esau Smith.' I had finally gotten to reading that Bible, and that's where I got the 'Esau' from. Look in Genesis and you'll see what I mean, or what I meant then. This character down there who ran a juke-box label had been after me to cut a record. I said I would under the condition that he put my new name on it. He finally agreed. That's how that second and final work of art came into being. I don't even know if I have any of those to give you. After that, I just sort of left the singing lie. I will tell you one thing, though. I always enjoyed Elvis's records, and I was always proud of him.

"One thing I knew for sure," his voice livened, "was that I wasn't cut out for doing more than a day's time. I talked to my friends. They put me down in some basement dive spinning a Big Six. Eventually I moved up to dealing. I was good at it. I was sharp and I was straight. They took me out of the basement and started me working at the fancy joint on Carrollton. I kept my nose clean and did well. I always dealt an honest game. Hell, in this racket you don't have to cheat. That push-goes-to-the-house shit breaks 'em all in the end.

"I stayed there until 1964, then I came out here. By then I was plain old Johnny Smith. I miss New Orleans once in a while. It's some kind of town, that's for sure. But it's quieter here. I have a wife, two kids. I ain't getting any younger." He took a last, slow swig, and he looked at his watch. "Then again, at least I'm still here."

I went back to see him the following morning. The same guys were sitting at the bar and at the blackjack table. An additional, younger patron had bestowed his presence upon the scene. He leaned over the bar, asking the barmaid if she liked raw oysters.

Smitty—or whatever it is that I should call him—bought me a drink. He alluded in no way to our conversation of the previous day. Nor, his eyes and manner insinuated, should I. Sure enough, he had brought the records for me. "Now, remember," he said lightly as he gave them to me, "if you listen to these things, it's just some silly-ass kid fucking around."

I smiled and thanked him.

"You gonna write me up?" he finally asked, in a clip.

"I don't know," I told him.

"Yeah, well, whatever."

A few days later, when I was back home, I put on one of the records, a 78 with a still-glossy blue label, onto the turntable. It lacked that certain salability without which few things in this world succeed. But it was, notwithstanding the Hattiesburg Hepcats, one of the finest things that I had ever heard, and it made me smile and it made me laugh.

> I dreamt last night of a bosom divine,
> A bosom so pristine, so pure,
> And from it bubbled whiskey like milk;
> I sucked till my poor jowls were sore.

If I never see him again, I'll never cease to wonder about him. Just as he, most likely, will never cease to wonder if that phone rang thirty years ago. The man, as usual, was right. Life is funny.

# 57

# God Is My Cosponsor

In his poem "Sunday Morning," Wallace Stevens described that particular time of the week as being "like wide water, without sound." This melancholy simile reveals Stevens to have been a man acutely aware of the vague and ethereal despair that enlaces the hours between the first dawn and the first noon of the week.

The Sunday-morning dumps are no mere poetical fancy. According to the Alcohol, Drug Abuse & Mental Health Administration (a cheery division of the U.S. Department of Health, Education & Welfare), the forty-eight-hour period in which Americans are most likely to commit suicide begins on Sunday morning. It cannot be said with any certainty that television plays a part in these self-killings; but it can be said with a great deal of certainty that Sunday-morning television is a singularly eerie, ashen, and forlorn thing.

Rise some Sunday, if you dare, before the sun, as I did rise not long ago. As dark night's death rattled the windowpanes behind me, I turned on my TV set. Something called "Modern Dentistry" was in full swing. Several minutes of root-canal passed slowly. I spat, then switched to an old and unfunny rerun of "I Dream of Jeannie." The faint, dull throbbing that I had begun to feel above one of my left molars was allayed by the familiar squeal of "Oh, master!" I dimly remembered that I had long ago wondered what it would be like to take Barbara Eden to bed. She was fifty years old now, I told myself. My couch creaked beneath me.

I turned to PBS, which was now starting its broadcast day. "Mister Rogers," in a blue zip-up sweater, turned to his goldfish and very slowly sang, "I'm learning to sing a sad song when I'm sad." It was more than a human heart could bear to witness. I hurriedly fled to ABC, where the International Lutheran Laymen's League reminded me that "This Is Life." Life ended and the Paulist Fathers took over. This week's "Insight" drama was called "God in the Dock." I watched as the Lord was brought before a black lady judge and tried for crimes against humanity—cancer, world hunger, and such. I thought I recognized God from somewhere, but I was not quite sure. By the time that the witnesses for the prosecution jumped Him and bloodied His nose, I realized that He was none other than Richard Beymer, whom I had last seen kneeling devotedly before Natalie Wood in *West Side Story.*

On another channel, I encountered Reverend Terry Cole Whittaker. Attired in a smart white suit and mauve blouse, her tinted blonde hair cut short, she pointed her finger at me and advised, "Remember who you are!" I silently vowed to do so, then switched to an adjacent station, where, on "Ever Increasing Faith," Pastor Frederick K. Price, in a plaid suit to end all plaid suits, scolded, "If you so sick you gotta whip on women, go find you some tramp to beat up on, not my daughters!" I nodded in abstracted agreement, and the good pastor asked me to send a "love gift" to Inglewood, California.

The sun was fully risen now, and the big guns of Sunday morning began to make their presence known. "We didn't plan this," said Oral Roberts as he dipped his fingers in oil and anointed his son Richard for the "*full* Holy Ghost ministry." Richard, wearing one of the largest diamond rings that I have ever seen, wept openly and embraced his wife, Lindsay. "This is one night that I've dreamed of," he blubbered.

I moved to CBS, glimpsing Bluto beating the living shit out of Popeye along the way. On "Face the Nation," a gentleman named Abdallah Bouhabib told me many things which I did not know, and which I have since forgotten, about his native Lebanon. U.S.M.C. General Paul X. Kelly sat next to him and said, "My glass is half full, not half empty." They agreed that America was not at war. Tell it to Olive Oyl, I thought as I turned to NBC.

On "First Estate," Dr. Russell Barber and Dr. John Heller discussed "shroud science." Dr. Barber held up a photo macrograph of a blood stain, then put it down. "If the spikes are driven in here," he announced, pointing to his inner wrist, "the body's weight can be supported." Not in the mood for shop-talk, I switched to ABC and "It's Your Business." I was just in time to hear an extremely grating voice shriek, "How do you *know* that? There's no empirical data to support that!" Marvin Kitman whined in retaliation. I returned to the more soothing voices of Golgotha.

At half past eleven, I saw David Brinkley doing strange things with his mouth on ABC. Walter Mondale stared vacantly, as if into an abyss. The last thing that I remember was Rex Humbard smiling that great big otherworldly smile of his and saying, "David was a success in his public life of killing giants, but he was a failure with his family." A commercial for *Dianetics* passed as in a dream; then noon came, and I was delivered.

What causes the Sunday-morning dumps? The pondering of this matter is perhaps better left to greater and more caring intellects than my own. What might be the cure for the Sunday-morning dumps? This much I know: it definitely is not TV. And I didn't lay a finger on that plaid pastor's daughter, I swear to Richard Beymer I didn't.

# 58

During the summer that *Unsung Heroes of Rock 'n' Roll* was published, I had finished the worst extended piece of shit I ever wrote.

I had agreed to provide the text for a book on Hall and Oates, a big pop act whose music I did not like. My agent had advised me against entering into this deal, as it reduced me to the status of "employee-for-hire" and deprived me of the rights to the text I was to write. But I needed money, as I had not filed an income tax return in five years and the government had caught my ass. Twenty thousand words didn't seem like such a big deal, and the twenty grand I was to be paid did look like a big deal. Daryl Hall and John Oates both lived in the neighborhood. Their manager, today the chief executive officer of Sony Music, was Tommy Mottola, whom I found to be a *cafone* and an even more despicable piece of shit than the "book" I was writing for him.

*Hall and Oates: Dangerous Dances,* was published, hastily, in September 1984, barely eight weeks or so after *Unsung Heroes of Rock 'n' Roll.* The title I gave it, *Dangerous Dances,* which ended up as the subtitle, was used by Hall and Oates as the name of their next tour.

I've tried to erase this work from my past, rarely acknowledging that it exists. It was, I feel, the last time that I wrote falsely, going through the motions like a cheap whore. The next little book that bore my name, written with Richard Meltzer and for nothing, was a wholly free and incendiary thing called *Frankie,* a work of fiction devised by us, five years earlier, when Richard was visiting New York and sleeping on my couch. *Frankie: Part 1* was published in January 1985, by Illuminati, who, before the project fell to abandonment, also published *Frankie: Part 2* exactly two years later.

# *Frankie: Part 1*

What you are about to read is ninety-eight percent fact. Because of the errant two percent, our editors tell us we must call it fiction, even though nonfiction out-sells the fake stuff twenty-five to one. But sales mean nothing to us compared to the semi-accurate reporting of a sordid tale that has lived in infamy for lo these almost many years. If, at times, our storytelling seems distorted, or even fantastic, don't assume automatically that you're in the no-man's land of the two percent. Consider, instead, how easy it is for the subconscious mind to erase certain unpleasant memories, to repress unwanted relics of paranoia past, to make a fairy tale out of history that will not make the dreamer wake, screaming, from a hard-earned sleep of peace

That few people care to recall the bizarre events of 1975-76 does not mean these events never happened. Face it; you were there: Frankie fucked your gal. He'd have fucked ours, too, if we'd had one. It is time, we most firmly believe, to replay the saga of the Frankie Years in their entirety; to tell it all, if possible, without rekindling alarm; in any case, to tell it.

If the writing is not always of the superbest qual you have encountered in your mouths or years before the printed page, remember that only one of us (Rosco) ever got his H.S. diploma (and did a semester—well, almost—at L.I.U.). But hiring a ghostwriter was not for us, and we quickly discovered that poetic li cense offers the working stiff a lot more leeway than a P.I. license, anyday. Hell, this literary game ain't half bad at all. *The Synonym Finder,* by J. I. Rodale and staff, has been a great help throughout.

If the dialogue ever seems too verbatim for your sophisticated bloodshot taste, let's just say we as shamuses used "any means necessary" to get the parties to put their memory caps on straight.

*Bud & Rosco Holiday*

## 1. Summer of @#%!

*Something was suspicious,*
*Her pudding was amiss:*
*The rumors they were vicious,*
*The taste of Frankie in her kiss.*

*You fucked Frankie,*
*Your yellow ribbon's turned to grey:*
*You fucked Frankie,*
*And now you're gonna pay.*[1]

*If your gal fucks you,*
*She'll fuck Frankie too.*
*She fucked Frankie,*
*And now you are blue.*[2]

*Admit it, gal, you spread your knees,*
*Admit it, bitch, you put your mouth where he pees.*
*There's nothing you can say, you dirty, rotten slut,*
*I've smelled your dirty laundry.*
*And I know Frankie's had your butt.*[3]

They called it the Summer of Love, 1975; Summer of Smut was a lot more like it.

Within a week of the monumental FCC decision to allow "shit," "piss," "fuck," "cunt," "damn," "ass," and "wienie" over the airwaves of America, the way-out world of pop music was deluged with songs about Frankie—Frankie fucking your gal, Frankie fucking your mom, Frankie fucking your sis, Frankie fucking your wife, Frankie fucking your . . . you get the picture. These songs were by and large, noisy and clangy as *heck*—Mantovani would surely have rolled over in his crypt. But beneath the savage lashings of the electric guitars, beneath the growling adenoidal vocals, beneath the frenzied, hopped-up boonga-boonga of the hard-rock drums, there was a cablegram from filthsville that even nonfans of these hits could not help but catch the tasteless fucking drift of.

The first of the lot was "You Fucked Frankie" by those popular TV entertainers Tony Orlando & Dawn, entering the "charts" on July 1 in the number nine position. On July 8, it made number one, and was joined in the Top Ten by "Frankie Fucked Your Gal" as recorded by oft-controversial folk-rock artist Arlo Guthrie, who took time off from his anti-Vietnam activities to join the Frankie bandwagon. (His dad, hard-ramblin' lefty Woodrow "Woody" Guthrie—a man of the old school just like Manto—would surely have rolled over in his worm pen too—had he not fortunately been cremated six years before.) A week later, inter-

---

[1]"You Fucked Frankie" by Tony Orlando and Dawn. Copyright © 1975 by Arthur Treacher's Fish 'n' Chips Music. Used by permission.
[2]"Frankie Fucked Your Gal" by Arlo Guthrie. Copyright © 1975 by Bound for Glory Music. Used by permission.
[3]"Frankie Fucked My Wife" by Peter Frampton. Copyright © 1975 by Benjamin Disraeli Tunes, Ltd. Used by permission.

national superstar Peter Frampton stole number one from Tony with his admittedly poignant "Frankie Fucked My Wife."

Before July came to a close, there were a good umpteen Frankie tunes—at least—in the national Top Forty: "Frankie Fucked Eleanor Rigby" by the Beatles, "Frankie and Annie Had a Baby" by that soulful Negro group the Midnighters, "Frankie Porked My Niece" by Ed Sanders of the once-banned Fugs, "Francesco Fucka My Baby" by Dean Martin (his most successful "side" in more than a decade), "Frankie Is a Punk Rocker" by the Ramones, "Have You Seen Your Mother, Baby (Lying Next to Frankie)?" by the ever-outrageous Rolling Stones, "Frankie's Pipeline" by Dick Dale and the Deltones, and close to many, many more.

Perhaps the biggest surprise of all—or maybe not so surprising, considering pop's proclivity for the so-called "answer song"—was "I Fucked Frankie" by the Singing Nun:

> *I fucked Frankie,*
> *But don't you dare call me a whore*
> *I fucked Frankie.*
> *And I'm goin back for more*[4]

And Sister Sourire was not alone among the gammers, as a trio of others scored with Frankie tunes as well: Marcie Blaine with "Frankie's Girl," Little Peggy March with "I Will Follow Frankie," and Marie Osmond with "I Screwed Frankie (Out of Wedlock)."

Who was this Frankie? What was the strange power he had over women? And more to the point, why was he dip-sticking every dame in captivity?

## 2. The Cold, Hard Facts of Life

On April 15, as all law-abiding Americans were paying Uncle (through the nose, we might add), the sleepy seaside community of Frankfurt, Germany, slept. A certain Hans Bruner, however, lay awake pining over his until-then loyal *Hausfrau's* infidelity of the night before. His eleven-year marriage-made-in-heaven turned to shit before his very *Augen*, he heads for his favorite watering hole, the Club Wurtzburger, in the Pflaumchen Strasse. There sits Heinrich von Eigenflugen, his friend.

"Ah, haben Sie einen Bleistift, mein guten Herr!"

"Not sehr gut, Heinrich. Meine Dame ist eine Schlampe."

"Eine Schlampe?"

"Eine filthy Hure."

---

[4]"I Fucked Frankie" by the Singing Nun. Copyright © 1975 by Miracle of Love Music. Used by permission.

"Eine Hure!"

"Sie ist der Schmutz!"

"Mein Gott!" Heinrich's lower lip drops in disbelief, coming to rest upon his foaming stein of Lowenbrau.

"Ja, es ist true. Sie hast ficken."

"Ficken! Meine Damen und Herren! Ficken who?"

"Ficken Franki."

"Franki?"

"Ja, *Franki*."

Krauts are like that. They take a long time getting to the elusive *point*. Kant called this "das Ding an sich." Kant could afford the luxury of eloquence—Frankie had never Ding'd *his* wife. But back to Hans and Heini. Slowly, with pain in his voice, Hans divulged the sordid details. How his wife had become a slut and a whore overnight. How, returning home after a hard day at the wurst factory, he had found her that evening Naked . . . drunk . . . wet! Massaging her privates with sticky fingers, uttering over and over that single name, those two gruesome syllables of horror: FRANKI, FRANKI, FRANKI!

He had hit her. Hit her good. (Krauts do such things. Remember?) The impact of the wallop shook alien semen from her innards. He saw it dribble down her leg—disgustingly. Yes, it had been awful. More awful than anything he had ever experienced.

Heinrich expressed sympathy. Little did he know that, across town, at this very moment, his beloved Hilda was straddling the maleness of this mysterious Frankie . . . four delirious orgasms already under her belt. In all their years of blissful marriage, Heinrich had only given her one—and that was with his tongue.

A new darkness was upon Deutschland. Soon it would be uber alles.

### 3. Statue of Lib Wets Pants

Many people have arrived on boats. For starters, there was Columbus. Then there was Valentino. The great Al Einstein. Opportunist scumbags such as Alexander Solszych . . . aw fuck, you know who we mean. They call it America the Melting Pot. But the Pot had never seen the likes of the man who set foot on her shore during the twilight hours of April 29, year of our Lord 1975. He had a stale strudel in his pocket, and he spoke not a word. The name on his passport was Constantine Constantinopolis. This was not his real name, nor was he Greek, nor was he here to open a souvlaki stand on the corner of Eighth Avenue and Fourteenth Street. He was here to fuck your gal.

He checked into the Holiday Inn on West 57th St. (bet. 8th & 9th), but the accommodations did not meet with his approval. It had something to do with the boeuf cordon bleu. After one night in this dump—during which he had left his dirty mark in no less than at least one chambermaid pudendum—he moved to the Plaza, where the beef was considerably better.

He remained in his room for a number of days, and came to know American television quite well. He especially enjoyed Mary Tyler Moore. Tolerating her wrinkles because her gams were "outasight," as American hipsters of the time were fond of saying, he made a note in his little leather book that he must some-day rip her marriage asunder with his mighty stem. He also liked *Journey to Adventure,* featuring amiable European Gunther Less, because it reminded him of all the places he'd been. Of the local New York shows, he was most taken with the ABC News, for it showcased the charms of a bubbly Negress (a terrible word you should *never* use) named Melba Tolliver.

*Must have that Melba tonight,* the gentleman thought upon viewing her shiny features for the third night in succession, *this chambermaid thing has gone far enough.* Finally acclimated to the city's brisk springtime air, he ventured forth, grabbing a cab to ABC's Sixth Avenue studios. A patient sort, he waited outside the revolving doors for a glimpse of the coffee-colored queen of reportage following the news's eleven p.m. installment. Close to half an hour went by. He waited and waited, and then—Melba.

"Melba, I presume." He spoke in perfect English, without a trace of accent.

"Hi, do I, uh, know you?"

"Only in your dreams, sister, only in your dreams."

She blushed. "Who *are* you?"

"Frankie's the name, lovin's the game. Would you care for a cocktail?"

They retreated to Ms. Tolliver's posh Upper East Side pad, where the man called Frankie proceeded to "have" the talented newsperson as no whiteboy had had her before. A close sin-counter of all three kinds was had by Frank, who pronged with gusto at each of milady's major holes d'amour before dawn had met the day—her "chocolate runway" in particular taking on new dimensions in smut-pun *double entendre.*

As the first ray of sunshine filtered through the art deco venetian blinds, Frankie rose to put on his argyle socks. Melba stirred. "Oh Frankie, you can't be leaving so soon. I could come at least another twelve or thirteen times before brunch . . . "

"Sorry, my darkish slut, I must be on my way." He zips his fly. "Hasta la vista, my coal-colored lady of cunt!"

"Oh Frankie, you say the *loveliest* things."

## 4. Broads Say the Darndest Things

ABC Nightly News, May 3, 6:08 p.m. (approx.)—After hemming and hawing her way through a story on the drowning death of an eight-month-old infant at the Brooklyn College Olympic-size pool, Melba Tolliver, "Greater New York's newscaster numero uno" in the opinion of the prestigious New York *Post,* took pause to get highly personal before an audience estimated at several million supper-time viewers. Shaken from their overcooked liver and mashed garbanzos, they heard the following: "Um, uh, babies are fine; in fact they're *great*. I hope to have one someday myself, and when I do the father will be Frankie. Yes, that's right, *Frankie*. Over the weekend an event occurred that has changed my life entirely. A man named Frankie invited me to sip a sloe gin fizz in a nearby candlelit bistro. Courtship is like that, but in this case no courting was necessary. Ladies, you know what I mean when I tell you his eyes made me an offer my heart could not refuse.

"Before the taxi ride to my apartment was over, Frankie had already removed my pantyhose in the crudest of fashions—actually, he just *ripped* them off me—and I made no effort to impede his progress. In the elevator—oh Jesus!—we engaged in what the French call 'soixante-neuf,' that's the one where you both . . . *you know*. Anyway, it was *incredible*. The rest of the night, his Johnson *would not quit*, and I took it in my . . . "

The gal who had twice received a regional Emmy as "female telereporter of the year" was not permitted to finish her sentence. A commercial for Qantas suddenly filled the screen, and the bimbo was dismissed without so much as a faretheewell. After the cute little koala had finished his sad tale of Aussie tourism gone amok, Roger Grimsby took the mike. A horny-as-heck colleague of M.T. who had long longed for her tannish goodies, Roger snidely groaned, "Look what women's lib has given us," but secretly he just wanted to throttle this Frankie but good. Imagine some sonofabitch from off the goddam streets copping the moisture he hadn't even managed a *sniff* of in all these years!

The next day, each of the three local rags covered the incident in its own inimitable fashion. In boldface caps the *News* declared, "MELBA MUCK MUZ-ZLED," while the *Post*'s headline read, "The Tolliver Case: First Amendment Infringement?" The *Times*, which lined the cat-boxes of only the uppercrustiest of homes, relegated it to page three: "Local News Figure Dismissed over Aired Comments." Those who could read, *read*. What they read, though, was mostly of Melba (who, under sedation, declined further comment)—her alleged paramour received no more mention than any Tom, Dick or Harry could've expected just from boogying one of the four million-plus galholes in N.Y.C. So much for our ever-inquisitive "fourth estate"!

But then came what we now know as Big Wednesday, a scant two days A.M. (after Melba), the day the shit really hit the media fan. In the morning edition of the *Times*, on page 27, an episode was reported of the sordid sort such a hifalutin' sheet wouldn't normally have printed on page hupteen thousand. But a bigwig was involved: Sol Urenstein, chief of sanitation for Co-op City up in the Bronx. Sol had been found dangling from the showerhead in the master bedroom crapper, the army belt about his throat straining to support his 268 pounds. According to the *Times*, the note pinned to his chest simply read, "She (vernacular for copulated with) Frankie." Police speculated that the she in question might very well be Urenstein's 29-year-old wife Bernice, who could not be reached for questioning.

Then, in the entertainment section of that afternoon's *Post*, an interview with actress Sally Field revealed the demise of her short-lived romance with popular leading man Burt Reynolds. Miss Field, in town on a shopping spree, was quoted as saying a "fabulous new beau" had entered her life. "I'm embarrassed to say I have no idea what his whole entire name is. I just know him as Frankie. But names aren't really important with a man who's such a *phenomenal lover.*" (Liberal tabs like the *Post* are fond of charming little euphemisms like that, leaving absolutely nothing to the reader's imagination while maintaining their status as a class operation.)

At that point, you'd have thought some enterprising Clark Kent or Lois Lane would've been right on top of things in the two-and-two department. But no, it was close to several hours before Mike McGovern did the addition for us over at the night desk of the *News*. Drunk as usual, he still had the wherewithal to peruse the competition for a paraphrasable item or two. He perused with curiosity the Sally item; he'd always wanted to bang that cutey himself. (Ah, the dreams dreamers dream!) Then, knocking over his half-empty fifth of Carstairs, he used the *Times* to mop up the mess. *Voila*—the crucial p. 27 lay there exposed in the rotgut damp.

If he'd been Plato or Aristotle, he'd have yelled, "Eureka!" Instead, he phoned up his drinking buddy Jimmy Breslin at O'Shaughnessy's Bar & Grill over in Queens and let the fatso in on the scoop of at least the week. Jimbo's Pulitzer alarm went off like a three-alarmer, but doubt filled his head almost as quick. With a history of dupehood going all the way back to '66, when Norman Mailer had actually conned him into service as his mayoral running mate on the "let's make New York City the 51st state" ticket, this goofus was finally beginning to notice the chuckles caused by his misplaced dumb-ass enthusiasm. "Ah, what the hey," he exclaimed, staggering to the back room to type out (one draft) a column entitled "Frankie Is Rankie: One Epidemic No Vaccine Can Stop."

"Up in Co-op City," he began, "where Bronxonians have valiantly sought escape from the torment of encroaching urban blight, the trashcans are especially full this morning, yesterday's eggshells and sardine tins festering under the feisty springtime sun. The man residents have come to revere as 'Daddy Garbage' will not be making his rounds today, or any other day. An out-of-towner known only as Mr. Frankie, a guy who has never attended an overcrowded junior high or viewed a hungry rat gnaw at the face of a dying junkie, has seen to that." He paused. *Yeah, the fuggin' Pulitzer,* he told himself, *sure as a bear shits in the woods.*

Maybe, Jim, just *maybe*—you do have a way with words and all. But right now, Mr. B., right this sec as you finger the shift key, your highly cherished Mrs. B. is being fingered as well. You guessed it . . . by Mr. Frankie. Ain't life funny!

## 5. A Nation of Cuckolds, A Nation of Sluts

News has always traveled fast. The so-called "electronic age" allowed it to travel even faster. But even the fastest electrons in America were scarcely able to keep up with the odious exploits of Frankie in the weeks that followed.

Still in New York, he fucked Greta Garbo, who promptly announced her long-awaited return to the silver screen ("I vant to be in porn"). Moving on to Chicago, he planted his heinous seed in the orifices of Gloria Daley, wife of Mayor Richard Daley, and six Northwestern coeds attending a performance by the Second City Revue. Next (if the consensus reconstruction of the alleged sequence is to be believed) he stopped briefly in Lincoln, Nebraska, to knock up Dick Cavett's mom. Outbreaks of Frankie were then reported in Tallahassee (a vacationing Bess Myerson), Nashville (country-western star Loretta Lynn), Atlanta (respected civil rights widow Coretta King), Butte, Montana (Carla Bley, on tour with her latest jazz "ensemble"), Phoenix (Arnold Palmer's better half Winnie, in town with her husband for the Andy Williams Desert Classic), Aspen (Andy's estranged squaw Claudine Longet, until then happily lovenesting it with skier Spider Sabich), Spokane (Dame Margot Fontaine, guest-hoofing with the Seattle Ballet), and of course Los Angeles, the fabled City of Sin (established starlets Yvette Mimieux, Anjanette Comer, and Lauren Bacall; TV weather gal Kelly Lang). Miraculously, the great state of Texas was totally bypassed (knock on wood, Longhorns!).

Dear Abby's opening tearjerker of May 27 was signed "Frankied": "My loving bride of 19 years has 'done it' with Frankie and is packing her bags. I know these are liberated times, and God knows we've both considered having affairs. But what about our seven children, ages 8 to 17?"

The poor sap should have left well enough alone. Miss Van Buren's reply, well-intentioned as it was, could only have rubbed salt in his wounds: "Dear Frankied: So your wife has gone and 'done it' with Frankie, big deal. I have recently been intimate with Frankie myself, and you don't see me abandoning the home fires, do you? Liberated, shmiberated, understanding is still the key. I suggest you let her date Frankie one night a week, for instance the night you play poker with the fellows. As to your children, perhaps you have a daughter or two already old enough to be 'broken in' by a stick man who really knows how, the one and only Frankie."

The reaction to all this hubbub was, in a word, *mixed.* Syndicated conservative William F. Buckley considered the whole thing no more than an update of the James Bond phenomenon of the sixties ("Like all irritating fads, it will pass"); pinko scribe Nat Hentoff called it a CIA plot ("What better way to undermine the meaningful breakthroughs in American socio-sexual behavior than to give headlines to gratuitous wife-plunking?"). Billy Graham called Frankie "Satan's most insidious earthly representative since Stalin"; his more relaxed cohort in godly matters, Garner Ted Armstrong, merely noted that "Biblical epochs have a habit of reasserting themselves in our time; if Lot could lay with *his* daughters, then why not Frankie with *ours?*" Dr. Joyce Brothers decried the tendency to mass hysteria, stating that Frankie was but "the latest occasion for American women to cry out their burning need for love and submission, although not necessarily in that order." But since Joyce, too, had "been with" Frank, her words were taken with a grain of NaCl. Black activist Imamu Amiri Baraka, meanwhile, called Frankie "the white man's last ditch effort to prove he's still got a podongo, y'know like it ain't atrofied (sic) from centuries of just passin' water and pushin' it up the missus' bonedry gazula three nights a month." Like we said, mixed.

Nor did the response of the guy and gal in the street towards things Frankie follow any party line tied strictly to their species of meat. "Macho" males gave their seal of approval to this all-time stud's masculine rampage, while others, sissies mostly, marked the man as bad PR for their gender. Some daring types dared to pose as Frankies themselves, with limited success, while the less daring condemned the "challenge of Frankie" as a bit much to emulate in this here day and age. Many rushed to shrinks with the dreaded word *impotence* on their lips, whilst towel-head shaman Maharishi Mahesh Yogi marketed the simple "mantra" *I am Frankie* as a guaranteed aid in the attainment of erection.

Members of mainstream women's groups protested their sex's wholesale refusal to demand something from Frankie in return ("How can so many among us give ourselves to this unrepentant *bachelor* for anything less than a magnum of Chanel #5—let alone a zircon on the appropriate finger?"). Hard-line feminists, on the other hand, were split into three major camps: those committed to each dame's inalienable right to spread 'em for whomever, be it Frankie or Joseph Zilch; those thoroughly disgusted with yet the latest overstatement in "the arrogance of wazoo"; those who had lain with Frankie. "Unaffiliated" females of all persuasions other than jasper waited in alleyways, hallways, doorways, and train depots . . . for Frank.

The changes inflicted by Frankie upon the very fabric of contemporary U.S. life could not be denied. Divorce rates were soaring, with lawyers handling Frankie-related cases (many manufactured, most, presumably, for real) having a field day. Alcohol abuse was steeply on the rise, as bars from coast to coast substituted "Frankie hours" for their customary happy hour. The law enforcement folks reported a sharp increase in incidents of wife abuse, as terminal monogamists galore, fearing a loss of hard-earned pelt, pummeled more than a few slumbermates for merely sighing Frankie's name. (Some accused pummelers were apparently named Frankie themselves, but paranoia occasionally makes second-guessers of us all. Even in the land of the free, the home of the brave.)

To make a long story almost not as long, the ultimate icing on this grimy, soiled cake was applied on June 16, when Johnny Carson, back from a three-week vacation in Bora Bora, tried out his very first Frankie joke: "You must've read the Bicentennial Committee is looking for something to place above the American flag during the Bicentennial . . . well how about Frankie? He's already been on top of everything else." As with all of Johnny's attempts at humor, it went over like a lead balloon. But Johnny's stamp had at last made the whole nightmare . . . official. The Frankie craze was, alas, here to stay.

## 6. Frankie Speaks

Few men worthy of the name can fail to remember exactly where they were on December 7, 1941, the moment they heard that the yellows had bombed Pearl Harbor, or on November 22, 1963, when the news rang out about J.F. Kennedy's brains getting spilled by a crackerjack assassin's murderous bullet. As dry runs for the recollective juices, these two dates were not half bad, you might even call them excellent. Excellent setups for the Big One, the one no man of penis is likely to ever forget: July 6, 1975. A day that, as Walter Cronkite so grandly put it, will long live on in infamy.

It seemed that every transistor in America was blaring Tony Orlando's "You Fucked Frankie." Melba Tolliver's successful suit against ABC, which had quickly led to the FCC's notorious Piss-Fuck-Cunt decision, had been hailed by her attorney, F. Lee Bailey, as "the most significant step in our time toward the full realization of the American ideal of free speech." But in light of the musical trend it had instantly spawned, many saw it as little more than the revolting first step in the willy-nilly legitimization of free filth. Nuclear family supporters *en masse* forbade their young ones from purchasing the new "Frankie sides"; others expressed their distaste in a more violent manner.

One Huspo, N.Y., widower was arrested and charged with the attempted murder-one of Big Apple "deejay" William B. Williams, whose response was almost stoical. "In a way, I'm not mad at the guy," the graying radio hepcat was quoted as saying. "I don't like these Frankie records any more than he does, and I certainly agree about the particular one he singled out, that Peter Frampton abomination about Frankie taking pleasures with his wife. The irony of it is the man's wife is safely dead and gone, but I can understand his twisted grief. But what am I to do? The boss gives me my playlist, and I do my job, just like I did my job back in the fifties when they told me to play that cradle robber Jerry Lee Lewis. The thing of it is, and I really mean this, we disk-jocks could probably have banded together and saved the world from the Rock-and-Roll Menace by '59 at the latest, but I'm sorry to say we missed our cue. Now this Frankie character, he's got to be the biggest evil since Yassir Arafat. But the music he's generated is only an unfortunate symptom—what can I say, it's my job to play it—while meanwhile men are fighting against men—and I've been an innocent near-victim of that—instead of joining together against Frankie, whoever the devil he is. In the meantime, if you want symptomatic relief, take an Excedrin. I really mean that."

The youth of America, however, took no Excedrin. Just as they had for the Mashed Potatoes and Heavy Metal, they wiggled their hips to the Frankie Beat.

Yes, it was 3:05 p.m. Eastern Daylight Time, July 6, when WNBC, New York City's hottest rock 'n' soul station, abruptly broke away from its ninth broadcast of the day of "You Fucked Frankie." A voice, tense with urgency, spoke the following words:

"This is a bulletin. We have just received word that Frankie has at last personally made his existence known. This is the Frankie who has been responsible for the current sexual spree that has wrought havoc throughout the country. The nature of Frankie's revelation is not yet clear, but informed sources assure us that this is not a hoax. We repeat: Frankie has spoken. We now return to our regular program."

Women across the vast metropolis clutched their stomachs with damp, concupiscent hands. Men swallowed hard. Newspersons rushed to the nearest phones.

Within minutes, there were similar bulletins throughout the land. Tens of millions sat glued to their dials. In towns without "all news" stations, panicky yokels were forced to endure the onslaught of one Frankie tune after another as men "just doing their job" fueled the palpitation with no letup or pity. Finally, at 4:30 EDT, came further details, more unsettling than could have been imagined.

It was revealed that, in the course of his Southeastern swing, Frankie had fornicated with Nora Ephron, wife of Carl Bernstein, celebrated reporter with the Washington *Post*. Although an esteemed journalist in her own right, Ms. Ephron deemed it unfitting to blow-by-blow the intimate details of their "sacred tryst." As she was later to tell Tom Snyder, "It was too beautiful a thing to consider turning into inky metaphors." Nora, however, did tell hubby of her experience—she felt they had that kind of marriage—and Bernstein, thinly veiling his informant wife's identity under the monicker "Deep Frankie," dutifully recorded his bride's disclosure. He later confessed that tears fell profusely upon the keyboard of his Smith-Corona as he began to peck out his first Deep Frankie report.

"Deep Frankie," wrote the broken Bernstein, "looked into the eyes of her sinful lover. One question overwhelmed her, and she begged him to answer it.

"'Who are you?' she asked, teetering at the brink of her eighth climax of the hour.

"He was silent for many moments. Then, as the lava began to gush from his organ into hers, polluting irrevocably what had once been good, had once been pure, had once cooked ginger duckling for her husband who had thought the world of her, he spoke.

"'I am Frankie. Frankie am I and always was. Frankie am I to ever be. I have lain with your mother, and her mother, and her mother before her, and all mothers and all of their tribe: wives and sisters and daughters. Before ever

Dante shared his measly manhood with Beatrice, I had had her, and her mother, and her mother before that. And Dante's mother as well, and his father's mother, and her mother, and all sisters and daughters and wives thereof. Before the Flood was I. Noah's mater familias had I, and all women then and evermore. I am Frankie. Now roll over, whore and wife of another. Roll over before I cleave thee in twain with my mighty stalk and staff.'

"As she rolled over in abject abeyance, Deep Frankie posed another breathy interrogative, seeking a loftier degree of clarity.

"'Why are you here, Frankie, in America, in 1975?'

"'I AM HERE TO FUCK YOUR MOM!'

"Deep Frankie swooned. Frankie pumped. There were no more questions, no more answers, only gutter expletives my reportorial ethos demands I delete. Frankie had spoken, and spoken he had."

By din-din of the 6th, every radio and TV call-letter in America had shouted those seven fearsome words, words which only weeks before they could safely have sanitized clean as a baby's butt: I . . . AM HERE . . . TO FUCK . . . YOUR MOM. By nightfall, the country was berserk with, to borrow the title of Erica Jong's subsequent bestseller, *Fear of Frankie.* Pandemonium erupted. There were 11,645 hospitalizations for "nervous breakdown." Women by the hundreds of thousands were locked from their homes by drunken, insanely jealous providers. Families huddled in churches, synagogues, ashrams, and in the many improvised "Frankie shelters" which sprouted throughout the major cities of our republic. There were no Frankie jokes anywhere. It was no longer a laughing matter.

And that's where we came in.

# 59

# Hillary Brooke's Legs

Miss Hillary taught me everything there was to know about sex. I was barely five years old at the time. The system of the world seemed to be a simple one. Bud smacked Lou. Mike the Cop smacked Lou. Mister Fields and Mister Bacciagalupe smacked Lou. Even Stinky smacked Lou. Life looked like a great proposition. I couldn't wait until I was big enough to begin smacking Lou. I started practicing on Joey Smigelsky, the little Polack who lived down the street. Then along came Miss Hillary, and the world was no longer so simple a place.

I think I might have heard her before I saw her. In any case, the first impression I remember seems to be aural rather than visual: the enchanting, enthralling cadence of her high heels click-clacking down the fateful hallway of the Fields boarding-house. The gratifying slapping sound of Lou's abasement faded from my consciousness. No longer did it hold for me the promise of life's fulfilment. Click-clack. I followed those heels.

I don't think I'd ever seen her before, though she had, as they say, been around. Later my sharpened eye would catch glimpses of her in *Sherlock Holmes Faces Death, Ministry of Fear, Big Town,* and other movies from the forties. (In fact, she had made her debut as one of the *New Faces of 1937.* This picture, which starred Milton Berle, is where Mel Brooks stole the idea for *The Producers.*) She had done a "Racket Squad" episode in February 1952. The following June, less than six months before moving into the apartment across the hall from Bud and Lou, she had appeared on "My Little Margie" as Roberta Townsend, the girlfriend of Margie's father, Vern. (Reflecting on this fiction several years later, I concluded its lesson to be that money could buy anything.) But I was aware of none of this. To me, the click and clack of those heels were like the wondrous first footsteps of Aphrodite in the wet sands of Cyprus. They signaled the miraculous arrival of a goddess whom no eyes before mine, except perhaps Bud Abbott's, had ever beheld.

"Now, boys," she intoned lightly, halting the rhythm of her steps, commanding attention throughout the kingdom of lust, confounding the Lou-smacking simplicity of life.

To look at her was to be given reason to live. She was tall, she was blonde, she was beautiful. The sea-born sway of her hips, undulating in counterpoint to the click-clack of her heels, was a symphony of all the wicked desires that had ridden the wind since time began; and her tits were as big as Joey Smigelski's head. Yes, I knew then and forevermore, she was it: the well-gartered inspirer of mortality's vain strivings. An image of divinity seeking desecration, she struck the deepest responsive chord that can be struck, a chord deeper even than greed.

Looking at her legs, I began to understand why Christ died. Long and shapely and smooth, veiled in the sheerest and tautest nylon, they were the alpha and the omega of sexuality. In the sublime, submissive inflection of her arching instep, in the exquisite curves of her seamed calf, in the ripe fulness of her thigh, where stocking, garter, and soft flesh formed their trinity of dangerous seduction—in all these magical things lay clues to the mystery of sex. They defined the power of femininity and summoned the power of masculinity that could overtake it. Many years later, looking up the stone skirts of the angels that Bernini had sculpted high within the cupola niches of the Vatican, examining those sixteenth-century marble limbs which gam connoisseurs held to be the models of leg-art perfection, I could not help but think, even as my mind's eye bestowed their seraphic feet with four-inch spike heels and sheathed their heavenly knees in DuPont taupe, that the great Bernini himself would have smashed these icons asunder in reverence had he been fortunate enough to gaze upon the legs of Miss Hillary.

Even within the frame of "The Abbott and Costello Show," Hillary exhibited a certain goddess-like transcendence of the mundane cares and desires that plagued her neighbors. Never did she work or worry about money. Perhaps her rent was taken care of by Vern Albright from the other show. Perhaps Mr. Fields was paid with monthly handfuls of her thigh-flesh, a currency far dearer than gold. The possibilities occupied my mind for many years to come.

Curiously, I began to see that this new, Hillary-centric universe also involved the abasement of Lou. It was true that Miss Hillary was the only person who was *nice* to Lou. She never abused him, and she even called him Louis. But, as I eventually realized, he was the only one who was denied access to her legs. Mike the Cop, Mr. Fields, Mr. Bacciagalupe, and especially Abbott—they were all playing Hide-the-Salsiccia with Miss Hillary. Slowly I apprehended the facts of life: he who is slapped wins Hillary's affection but never her fleshly favors. The sleazy glint in Bud's eyes postulated the inexorable truth that smacking Lou and hogtying Hillary with her own nylons were but the cast and draw of the same dealing hand. Without delay, I resumed practicing on Joey Smigelsky's head. In my mind as I walloped away, there was a lovely picture: Miss Hillary in her underwear, her trim ankles bound to the legs of the straight-backed chair in which she sat, purring "More, Bud, more," as Abbott sat peacefully by a window, smoking a cigarette and adjusting his boxer shorts, smiling to her, then turning once again to look out the window, down at the street. "Attaboy, Nicky," he hollered, "hit him again."

But the image I retained most clearly from those days was the courtroom scene in an episode of "The Abbott and Costello Show" entitled, for one reason or another, "Television." A drunk named John Rednose was suing Abbott and Costello. On the witness stand sat two of Hillary's girlfriends, Joan Shawlee and Veda Ann Borg, endlessly crossing and uncrossing their legs while chanting "He's positive, positive, positive." Overseeing the proceedings was Miss Hillary, resplendent in a black suit, matching beret, and white gloves. The judge beheld her legs as the sound of his gavel was overwhelmed by that more magisterial click-click; and high-heeled justice was done. This was not only one of the best leg shows of its day, but also one of the most succinct depictions of the judicial system ever enacted.

It all seems so long and so many legs ago. It was. Miss Hillary—which wasn't even her real name, I later discovered; it was something much homelier: Beatrice Peterson—is 68 years old now, living somewhere west of Paterson. Her day in the sun is ending, but the glory of her legs will—indeed, must—live on. Towards this end I lay the humble garland of these words upon her lap and reach out to smack my fellow man in thanks.

# 60

# Elmer Batters

Cruising beneath the Pacific aboard the submarine *Sunfish,* Elmer Albert Batters discovered that most of the men with whom he served cared more for Lady Liberty's legs than any other part of her. After World War II, when he began his career in pinup photography, his camera veered always seamward. He sold his photos to magazines such as *Humorama, Frolic,* and *Gala.* Then in 1956, he founded *Man's Favorite Pastime,* the first true leg-art magazine in the history of publishing.

"We couldn't find a distributor for it," Batters recalls. "I took an armful, started going down Beacon Street in Los Angeles. Every newsstand took it, and it sold out in no time. I was thrilled. But soon the bigger boys got wind of it and wanted in. I got out. After I left, *Man's Favorite Pastime* deteriorated into a bosom book." Undaunted, Elmer went on to publish *Sheer Delight* and *Black Silk Stockings.* "There were a lot of guys who preferred *Black Silk Stockings,* where the accent was on legs. We had a hit, but the backer started padding the bills. I got pushed out in 1959. Same old story."

In 1960 came *Tip Top* ("From the Tip of the Toes to the Top of the Hose"). On the basis of Elmer's photos, *Tip Top* was a grand success, and by 1965 it had inspired many imitators—*Naughty Nylons, The Nylon Jungle, Nylon Mood,* and more— all vying for a share of the market that just a few years before only Elmer had believed to exist. But the publisher of *Tip Top* wasn't satisfied. He wanted more— and he wanted Elmer to show more, too.

"I've never believed in the rough stuff," says Elmer. "Just legs. Raised skirts, lingerie, garters. That's as far as I ever wanted to go. But with this *Tip Top* guy I had to go the nudist-camp route. This I detested with a purple passion. There's nothing more disgustin' than to go to these nudist conventions where there's a thousand nudists standin' around wearin' nothin'!"

Eventually *Tip Top* was busted and Elmer found himself in court, after which, in 1966, he and *Tip Top* parted ways. In 1967, in the first issue of his new magazine *Thigh High* (not to be confused with *Nylon Double Take,* which he also started that year), Elmer announced the formation of his Royal Order of the Garter. "Leg lovers, unite! Now those of you who for years have admired the shapely stems of the femmes fatales can be assured of an organization devoted entirely to fans of the femur," Elmer proclaimed. Dollars filled his mailbox as leg men the world over rushed to join. He began producing little movies for sale to his members. In 1971 he published the first issue of *Leg Art,* available only to the esteemed Order. By the end of the decade enrollment had swelled to more than 20,000.

"Most members are pretty classy customers," Elmer says. "I get a lot of doctors and lawyers. Not long ago a group of high-ranking government officials from Japan came to meet me. They offered me enormous sums of money for rare issues of my early magazines, but I wouldn't part with them."

As with his customers, Elmer has never had any trouble attracting top-notch models. "At first I used to go to the nightclubs, like the El Rancho here in Hollywood," Elmer recalls. "I'd catch the strippers at closing time, and they'd let me shoot them in exchange for publicity glossies. But a lot of these strippers want more pictures than it's worth—a hundred, two hundred pictures. They'll break ya.

"Then I'd use some amateurs. When I'd take my car in for servicing, say, if there was a good-looking receptionist, I'd approach her. I was very successful that way. So many of 'em had an ego that, if they were approached right, they'd go along with it. I'd make it clear that there'd be no rough stuff, just leg art. Stockings, shoes on, shoes off, painted toenails.

"These days, most of the gals I use are very reliable. I pay 'em a hundred bucks a day. If the model's good, I can finish a shooting in about three hours. It's no fun to sit around and bullshit 'em. I shoot at my home here in San Pedro, and my wife is usually around. We keep it strictly legitimate. I don't sit around and fill 'em up with martinis."

When asked if his wife ever objects to any of this, Elmer is a little evasive. "Well, it's a living," he says. "Let's put it that way. She tolerates it."

Does lust ever intrude itself upon the daily duties of Elmer's business? "Oh, some of the gals used to ask me if I was, you know, *that way,* because I didn't make passes at 'em. This is just a business, I'd tell 'em. Besides, it's like we used to say in the navy, if a gal's an easy make, practically pushin your nose in it"—he lowered his tone to a dark whisper—"V.D."

Centered in San Pedro, Elmer's leg-art empire has now moved into videocassettes. Meanwhile, the classic leg art that he pioneered in the last 30 years has become remarkably sought after. Rare issues of *Black Silk Stockings,* which sold for 50 cents in 1958, now command prices of $50 and more. Last year a California collector paid $10,000 for a complete collection of early Batters, including prized first issues of *Tip Top* and *Leg Art.* Life indeed is brief, but hot garters are forever.

# 61

# Review of *Canned Meat*

After his New York debut last March, Hasil Adkins spent the Easter weekend at the Brooklyn home of his manager, Billy Miller. On the holy Sunday morning, Miller says, Adkins rose with a pressing desire to go out and buy "some leather hot pants with rivets." He was told that they would be hard to find, especially on Easter, and he ended up leaving town without them. Hot pants loom large in the worldview of Adkins. They seem, in fact, to be one of the very few phenomena of the past twenty years to have captured his attention. If there is an unsung, undying original out there, Adkins is it.

Adkins, who stays in shape by smoking cigarettes, has been making records, sporadically, for more than thirty years, mostly in his native West Virginia, and he sounds much the same today as when he recorded his first song, "I'm Happy," in 1956. It is ironic, and indicative, that his emergence from obscurity comes long after the fading of the so-called rockabilly revival, not to mention the real stuff, of which he was a first-generation, if anomalous, partisan.

While his influences are classic country, he admires Jimmy Rodgers, Hank Williams, Jerry Lee Lewis—he has made of those influences a music quite like no other. Adkins is a one-man band, with a voice that is part country and part nightmare alley, and his songs, which roll and howl through the shabbiest reaches of brilliance, dwell on those things, with or without rivets, that are timeless: love, decapitation, unclean sex, and at least one or two more.

Thanks to an act of great commercial imprudence, Adkins now can be heard on *Out to Hunch* (Norton, Box 646, Cooper Station, NYC 10003), which brings together 16 recordings from the late '50s and early '60s. A seven-inch Norton EP, *Haze's House Party*, features more recent material. As rat-shack bad as the sound quality of *Out to Hunch* and the EP sometimes is, the music shines stronger than much of what is to be heard, or overheard, these days. It is, old as it may be, music that the ear cannot date to any known time. It is what rockabilly might have been if Elvis and Jerry Lee had been Siamese twins separated at birth by Dr. Mabuse, or if Hank had lived to see the advent of 3-D and Andrea Dworkin.

As evinced by the material on *Out to Hunch,* Adkins's imagery is not always of the most accessible kind. There is, for instance, the girl, in "She Said," who "looked at me like a dyin' can of that commodity meat." But, most often, his feelings are straightforward: "I'm gonna put your head on my wall/And then you can't eat no more hot dogs," he sings in "No More Hot Dogs." This business of beheading is a dear theme, repeated, in a more deranged mode, in "We Got a Date" and "I Need Your Head" ("I got room on my wall . . . "). The EP features two of his current show stoppers, "Sex Crazy Baby" and "Do the Hot Pants with Me," along with—this is true—"She'll Be Comin' Round the Mountain." Hear, and know why the hat makes the man.

# 62

# How to Pick Up Girls
# in Albania

For some years now, certain bookstores in New York City have been selling, quite steadily, a paperback guide entitled *How to Pick Up Girls*. Symphony Press in nearby Tenafly, New Jersey, offers an entire line of mail-order books that are "exclusively devoted to helping you do better with girls." The Learning Annex, a trendy Manhattan night school for the postquiche generation, has even offered courses on how to meet members of the target sex.

Of course, all of the above are directed at the hopeless among us. Picking up girls in New York, a place where women so outnumber men that a relatively clean pair of socks constitutes the makings of a Romeo, offers not much more challenge than fishing in a barrel. After a while, the jaded philanderer finds himself venturing to distant places to test his skills. Finally, if he truly has the right stuff, he heeds the ultimate call to glory: Albania.

In the past, getting there was half the battle, as the Land of the Eagles forbade entry to American-born citizens, thus obliging seekers of the final conquest to acquire a false Italian passport and a convincing degree of fluency in that language. Now that Enver Hoxha, who ruled Albania with an iron hand from 1944 to 1985, has gone the way of all flesh, Albanian and otherwise, there is much talk that the most secretive nation in the world, under the younger and more liberal Ramiz Alia, may soon allow us Yankee scum to soil its shores. Whether one sets out tomorrow, the hard way, or awaits that forthcoming day of jubilation, he will do well to take the following tips to heart.

*Spare Tractor Parts.* The wise traveler will find room in his luggage for an old cogwheel or brake clutch, which possess wonderful aphrodisiacal qualities in the Land of the Eagles. Entire Albanian villages have been reduced to a state of groveling sexual enthrallment by means of a single transaxle.

*Meat.* The slenderest of lamb chops worn upon the lapel in the manner of a boutonniere is a love call that few Albanian gals can resist. More subtle, but effective, is the use of beef or pork drippings as cologne.

*Flattery.* This oldest trick in the book works as well in Albania as it does everywhere else—but with local variations. Tried and true lines include: "If King Zog had ever seen your face he would not have feared Mussolini." "What a lovely smock you're wearing." "The hair beneath your arms makes me hard," and the ever-popular "I would give a washing machine to lie atop you."

Of course, one should begin the ultimate adventure in the capital city of Tirana—more precisely in *the* place: the bar of the Dajti Hotel on the Boulevard of the Heroes of the Nation. It is here that Albania's "fast women" come to lay disgrace upon the graves of their families. One of them boasts an autographed photo of Rory Calhoun. (I have seen it.) The other is said to have had an orgasm.

Perhaps I'll see you there. I'll be the one with the kielbasa on my collar and the smirk of self-satisfied manhood upon my kisser.

# 63

I wanted to write a book about Michele Sindona, the infamous Sicilian financier who was believed to be the force at the heart of the world's evil. Publishers reacted at first with reluctance, feeling, they said, that it was too difficult an undertaking, that I would never pull it off. In the end, however, several of them came around, and I went with the highest bidder, Arbor House, who, in the fall of 1984, offered fifty grand.

Sindona was one of the most remarkable men, and the greatest mystery, I have ever encountered. As he was imprisoned throughout the time I knew him, I could only wonder at what he must have been like on the outside. The labyrinth of his tale took me to places I had suspected but never known to exist. The whole truth of that labyrinth was unknown, I believe, even to him; and, ultimately, much of what he did know of that truth died with him, when he either was poisoned or poisoned himself—no one still knows for sure—as the book neared completion.

In many ways, this was indeed an impossible undertaking, one which would have required many years and several million dollars to do right. And even then, I feel, the deadly light at the end of the labyrinth would merely have been glimpsed.

Though *Power on Earth* did well in Italy and Germany, and though it became something of an underground classic within the financial community and among scholars of the Mafia, it was not a success in America. It was published in the summer of 1986, at a time when its publisher was nearing the end of its own earthly days. But I don't think this much mattered. People prefer *The Godfather* and so-called investment-guru books to realities which are more complex and more difficult to grasp.

The British publication of *Power on Earth* was suppressed for legal reasons, and parts of the book were censored in America for legal reasons, too. But these parts, like much else that Sindona told me, would later, in *Trinities,* find their way into my writing under the guise of fiction.

# Excerpt from *Power on Earth*

## The Three Beasts

I had wanted to meet the Devil, and now here I was, toward dark, alone on a bench in a piny garden in a place called Voghera.

Where birds had swirled, lacing the dusk with song, there was now nothing; and there was no sound but that of the trees' sullen sway. The rosy flush and blue of the Lombardy sky were gone now, too. In the distance, the shadowy tide of nightfall rippled like a timeless haunting through the Oltrepo hills.

A lizard scudded up the statue of Garibaldi that stood nearby. It rested on the image's blackened shoulder, gazing upward, as if mesmerized by the waning moon. Little bats appeared, darting wildly amid the tall pines and round the statue; and the lizard vanished.

An old man approached. He sat on a bench across the path, and he began to pick solemnly through the lapful of dandelion greens he had gathered in his slow walk through this place. When his culling was done, he straightened his back and lifted his head, looking for a moment toward where the lizard had looked. Then he rose and was gone.

I was alone again. I let the night breeze take me. I watched the low-rolling clouds drift past the moon, veiling it; and I thought about what had brought me here.

Like most people outside Italy, I had first become aware of Michele Sindona more than a decade ago. He had taken over the Franklin National Bank in New York, and it fell. That was in the autumn of 1974. It was the largest bank failure in American history, and it was followed, days later across the sea, by the downfall of Sindona's Banca Privata Italiana. In the first week of the new year, his Geneva-based Banque de Financement was shut down. By then the Italian government had issued two warrants for his arrest on bank-fraud charges.

Only as Michele Sindona's empire crumbled was its vastness revealed. Through Fasco, A.G., his spectral Liechtenstein-based holding company, Sindona had controlled at least 5 banks and more than 125 corporations in 11 countries. His North American real-estate interests had included the Montreal Stock Exchange Building, Paramount Studios in Hollywood, and the symbol of the American public's loss of political innocence, the Watergate complex in Washington, D.C. His personal net worth was estimated to have exceeded $500 million.

The ruin of the man whom *Business Week* had called "Italy's most successful and feared financier," whom *Fortune* had exalted as "one of the world's most talented traders," stirred a storm that shook the ashlar of international finance. But that storm was only a prelude to the tempest that followed.

Sindona's clients and partners had been among the most important and respected institutions in the world: Continental Illinois, Gulf & Western, the Hambros Bank of London, the Banque de Paris et des Pays-Bas, Nestlé of Switzerland, and others. But it was his relationship with the least affluent of those clients and partners, the Istituto per le Opere di Religione—the so-called Vatican Bank—that proved to be the most sensational.

It was rumored that the Vatican, which had long done business with Sindona, had lost some $30 million when his empire fell. Roberto Calvi, a Milanese banker whom Sindona had taken under his wing, had been placed by his mentor to assume charge of the Vatican's finances. In 1977, Calvi's Banco Ambrosiano began to crumble, and the following year a massive investigation concluded that the Vatican had been involved with Sindona and Calvi in numerous questionable deals. Later, prison sentences would be given to two senior administrators of the Vatican Bank, and the Catholic Church would be immersed in a scandal from which neither penance nor lies could deliver it.

It was alleged also that the secrecy with which Sindona had always surrounded himself hid from sight his darkest partner of all: the Mafia. "Sindona rarely speaks for the public record," *Newsweek* had stated. "As a result, rumors abound. One moment he is allegedly the Pope's chief financial adviser; the next, he is supposedly the Mafia's No. 1 banker." By the end of 1978, he was presumed to be both those things. In the months and years to follow, the flames of his infamy—fed by the corpses of the victims of strange and violent deaths, by tales of conspiracies beyond the ken of paranoia—rose wildly higher toward heaven and burned more deeply toward hell.

In early 1979 the U.S. Justice Department indicted and charged Sindona with ninety-nine counts of fraud, perjury, and misappropriation of bank funds in the matter of the Franklin National Bank. Four months later, Giorgio Ambrosoli, the attorney appointed by the Italian government to handle the liquidation of Banca Privata and Sindona's other state-seized holdings, was murdered near his home in Milan by Mafia gunmen. Soon after that, in the heat of a New York August, Michele Sindona, whose trial was scheduled to begin in less than five weeks, vanished. He reappeared in Manhattan in October, with a bullet wound in his leg and a tale of being kidnapped. In March 1980, he was convicted of sixty-eight of the counts that he had been charged with. While awaiting sentencing at the Metropolitan Correctional Center (MCC) in New York, he took an overdose of drugs and slashed his wrist. But he survived, and a month later, a federal judge sentenced him to twenty-five years in prison.

In March 1981, after Sindona had begun to serve his time in America, a detachment of the Guardia di Finanza, investigating his case in Italy, raided the office of Licio Gelli, a known associate of Sindona's. A man of Neronic wealth and ways, Gelli was the grand master of a secret Masonic lodge known as Propaganda Due, or P-2. The raid led to a safe and a leather case marked "Fragile" and, within, a list of 962 supposed P-2 members. The list seemed to be nothing less than that of an underground, parallel state. It included the names of two current cabinet ministers, many members of the Italian secret-service and military hierarchy, diplomats, industrialists, police officials, bankers, and journalists, among them, the editor of Italy's most respected newspaper, the *Corriere della Sera*. Gelli, who had recently been seen at President Reagan's inauguration (the Republican Party of America was also found to be represented in the P-2 list), went into hiding, as the Italian government fell in the wake of the P-2 scandal. Gelli was later arrested in Geneva, while making a $50 million withdrawal from one of his Swiss accounts. He escaped from prison there and fled to safety. He is believed by many to be in Uruguay.

Roberto Calvi, Sindona's disciple and a revealed member of P-2, was arrested that same spring. He, too, disappeared; and in June 1982, his body was found hanging beneath Blackfriars Bridge in London.

While imprisoned in America, Sindona was charged in Italy with ordering the murder of Giorgio Ambrosoli, the state-appointed liquidator of his Italian empire. He was also indicted in Sicily, where he was accused of complicity in a $600-million-a-year heroin trade between Italy and America. In February 1984, as the government of Italy sought to extradite Sindona to stand trial for fraud and murder, Ambrosoli's killer, William Arico, was himself killed in what seemed to be a bizarre attempt to escape from a New York prison.

Sindona was rendered more and more as a dark and dangerous figure whose power within the Vatican and the spheres of international finance was equaled only by his power within the Mafia. From the presses of the United States, Great Britain, and Italy came sensational books about the entwined serpentine mysteries of the Vatican, Licio Gelli's P-2 lodge, and the death of Roberto Calvi. At the heart of these lurid mysteries was always Michele Sindona, who was no longer "the immaculate Italian banker" and "financial legend," as *Forbes* had described him before the fall, but rather "the Sicilian swindler who nearly bankrupted the Church" and "a powerful and respected member of the High Mafia." One book about him, an awkward blend of fact and gross fiction whose author (unbeknownst to the book's publisher and readers) was a convicted perjurer, was accepted by many at face value. By the spring of 1984, in another, more popular book, Sindona was even accused of having killed Pope John Paul I.

He had become the Antichrist, the Devil in chains, to whom the world turned to slake the cravings of its credulous paranoia, as if turning to the tree of the knowledge of good and evil itself. But none entered into him.

The mysteries enthralled me, as they enthralled many. I watched as his image shifted from flesh to fantasy, from the realm of notoriety to the realm of mythology; and I wondered at how, all the while, his own voice was unheard. And so one winter day, when the view of the world from where I stood was wearisome, I decided that I should meet the Devil.

I wrote a letter to him, federal prisoner Number 00450054, and I got a call from his American attorney, Robert Costello. He told me that Sindona had received my letter and was willing to see me, if I could arrange a meeting through Warden Dale Thomas of the MCC in downtown Manhattan, where Sindona was being held awaiting possible extradition (and where, only two weeks before, William Arico, Sindona's alleged confederate in murder, also facing extradition to Italy, had fallen from the prison roof to his death below). The warden acquiesced, and on a March morning, winter's last, MCC executive assistant Wayne Seifert led me to be frisked and to have my wrist stamped with the password of the day—the ink was invisible, but would glow beneath the black light of a farther checkpoint—then to the third floor, to the attorney conference room, a small and sunless chamber within a vaster plan of bleakness. There arrived at the door a tall, gaunt man in a prison-issue orange jumpsuit and sneakers. His gray hair was brushed straight back from his high forehead. His eyes, which were dark brown and lambent, seemed to hold what remained of his will; and what remained in those eyes was considerable. He extended his hand, then smiled.

"I am Sindona," he said.

During the hours of that first meeting, as wariness ebbed, he began to tell me the tale of his rise and fall. It was a tale that wound from small-town Sicily to the papal palace, from the gold-spun web of international banking to the Washington, D.C., corridors of power; a tale peopled by popes, presidents, prime ministers, shahs, and denizens of the political and financial night. As he spoke, his voice now and then rising, his hand now and then turning in emphatic *fioritura*, he rendered as children's romance all the speculation and calumny that had raged around him. It was, he said, innocence masquerading as worldliness, folly pretending to wisdom: the secondhand fantasies of those to whom neither he nor the others in his story were flesh and blood, but rather distant phantoms in a callow dream; those who, fancying themselves exposers of wickedness and crusaders for truth, wielded wooden swords against what were only reality's shadows; those who spoke of good and evil, but not of the dragons beyond those comfortable conceits. Their world was different from the world he knew. They understood little of the powers among which he had lived, and their tales of him were not his own.

To be sure, his was a darker and more terrifying tale. The Vatican scandal, the Mafia executions, the multimillion-dollar wheelings and dealings, the strange deaths and disappearances—these were only the whitecaps, the stormy surface of his tale. Revelations of greater evil lay beneath—revelations of international terrorism, political blackmail, money-laundering schemes beyond the grasp of any government agency, vendettas on the grandest, deadliest scale, and even secret nuclear-technology deals that have invested the most dangerous and unlikely hands with the power to destroy the world.

Of course, there was no way of knowing if his tale lay closer to the truth than the speculation and the calumny of those who never knew him. One thing was certain: The source of this tale, Sindona, alone knew the truth. And he had nothing left to lose.

There was something else. I remarked to him that it must have been an awful blow to have lost it all, to have gone from having nothing to having hundreds of millions of dollars to having nothing once again. His lips turned downward and he shrugged nonchalantly.

"If I were free tomorrow, I just start again. I make it all over," he said.

"Wouldn't it require a great deal of capital to get started?"

"Nothing," he said, his lips now turning upward, his eyes glimmering. "A thousand dollars. I go buy a Telex, a telephone connection. After that, no problem."

The possibility of laying open the system by which one of the world's wealthiest men acquired his fortune was, needless to say, no less intriguing than the arras-web of conspiracies, scandals, and mysteries that enwrapped him.

I visited him again the next morning. Toward the end of that long meeting, I handed him my pen and a sheet of ruled yellow paper, and he agreed to cooperate with me on a book. I looked at the signature that would later grow familiar—the *M* surging forward, the rest of the letters rising vertically as if to obstruct that initial assertive lunge—and I folded the paper and slipped it into my breast pocket.

Walking down to daylight, Wayne Seifert, the soft-spoken executive assistant who was soon to be raised to the rank of assistant warden, asked me what I thought of the MCC's most notorious resident. Like many Americans, he pronounced Sindona's first name as if it were a woman's, rendering the hard Italian *ch* as a *sh* sound. I told him that I was not yet sure, and I shrugged. I asked him what he thought of Sindona. "After a while, you just don't know," he said. "You stop trying to figure it all out."

Sindona's impending extradition became entangled in governmental procedures. Not long after I last saw him that spring at the MCC, he was transferred back to the federal penitentiary at Otisville, New York. We were in touch throughout the summer. Slowly, my desk began to fill with documents in two languages, and with the transcriptions of our talks. By summer's end, I had begun in earnest my search through the netherworld into which Sindona had invited me.

Suddenly, on September 24, a new extradition treaty between America and Italy became effective, and, on the following day, Sindona was flown without notice to Italy, where he was taken under heavy guard to Rebibbia prison, in Rome, and placed in the maximum-security cell that had been occupied by Mehmet Ali Agca, the mad Muslim who had shot Pope John Paul II in the spring of 1981. On the last day of September, a Sunday, two judicial instructors from Milan moved him north to the Casa Circondariale Femminile on the outskirts of Voghera, thirty-six miles south of Milan. There, the sole male inmate of a women's prison, he awaited his trial.

On the day on which he had arrived in Italy, I read in *The Wall Street Journal* of "the hope that Mr. Sindona might shed further light on some of the darker mysteries of Italian political and financial life in the past decade." But the bank-fraud trial, which finally began on December 3, brought forth little light indeed. He smiled at first through the iron bars of his courtroom cage. Then he ceased smiling, and eventually, as the trial progressed, he refused to appear in court at all. On the ides of March, 1985, he was sentenced to twelve years in prison. The prosecutor, Guido Viola, calling Sindona "one of the most dangerous criminals in judicial history," had asked for fifteen years.

All the while, I had been trying to get permission to meet with Sindona for more interviews. In his letters to me from the women's prison, Sindona told me that he was being denied all visitors and that only orders from the U.S. Department of Justice could sway the Italian authorities to grant an exception. Trudging through the tortuous bureaucracy of the Criminal Division, I found no one who was quite sure of exactly just what Sindona's present status was under the new extradition treaty. One gentleman, a Mr. White, professed an eager desire to be of help, and he assured me that he would personally attend to the matter during an official visit to Italy the following week. I never heard from him again. At last, I reached Murray Stein, the head of the Criminal Division's Office of International Affairs, and one of the authors of the recent extradition treaty. He told me that as long as Sindona was in Italy he was under the jurisdiction of that country alone.

"Every day he's there, a day is ticked off his sentence here," Stein said. "That's all. While he's there, he's theirs."

Meanwhile, one of my earlier inquiries to the Department of Justice had elicited a belated response from Mark M. Richard, whose letterhead identified him as a deputy assistant attorney general of the Criminal Division. "I suggest the following scenario," he wrote. "First, please contact the U.S. Consulate in Milan, and give the consular officer the name of an Italian official who can confirm that the authorization of the United States is required. . . . If such authorization is required, the State Department will contact the Department of Justice for our response, which in turn can then be communicated through official channels to the Ministry of Grace and Justice in Rome." He, too, assured me that, after all was said and done, the matter rested "solely with Italian authorities."

On April 16, a month after his sentencing, Sindona wrote to tell me that his lawyer Giampiero Azzali had obtained authorization for me from the Ministry of Grace and Justice in Rome, from the Magistrate of Surveillance of the Tribunal of Pavia, and from the director of the prison. But the Court of Assize in Milan, the remaining body whose permission I needed, was willing to grant us only two meetings of one hour each. Sindona said that the U.S. Justice Department had lied, that the Italian authorities would have yielded readily to instructions from Washington. Unless the Court of Assize could be made to bend, there was little hope of further interviews. And there was not much time: Sindona's next trial, for murder, was to begin in June. "They will keep me here, in isolation, for as long as they can," he told me.

A few weeks later, on a rainy day in early May, I called at the U.S. Consulate in Milan's Piazza della Repubblica. I explained my problem to one of the Italians who worked there. He regretted that it was not within his power to help me, and he brought me to the consular officer in charge, a Mrs. Patterson. I told her of my situation. "We," she said, "do not want to be involved." She said that Sindona—and there was aversion in her voice when she pronounced his name—did not happen to be an American citizen, and therefore was not a concern of the consulate. I reminded her that I was an American citizen. "Nevertheless," she said, her frigid manner waxing timorous round the edges, "we don't want to get involved." It was still raining when I left.

Above the entrance of the Palazzo di Giustizia (the Palace of Justice) in Milan, august words are set in stone:

*IURIS PRAECEPTA SUNT HAEC: HONESTE VIVERE*
*ALTERUM NON LAEDERE SUUM CUIQUE TRIBUERE*

"These," says the Latin in the rock, "are the precepts of law: to live honestly, to harm no one, and to give each his due." The author of those words was the third-century Roman jurist Ulpian. Their presence above the entrance to the Palace of Justice attests to the undying nobility of something—law as we know it—that was born in Italy long ago. But the fate of Ulpian, who gave those words to Rome and to the world, and who in time was slain in the imperial palace beneath the light of day, attests to other undying things, greater than justice and more deeply set in ancient rock than any words, which dwell in palaces such as this.

I walked up the steps, past the pillars beneath the Latin, and entered the vast babel that is the legacy of the oldest judiciary heritage in the world. The swarm of the wronged and the wrongdoing filled the halls and winding stairways, poured forth onto mezzanines, wandered apprehensively through mazy corridors, vanished into dim cul-de-sacs. The pandemonium of their confluent disorder was leavened by the grander swarm among them—the magistrates and lawyers, the clerks and sinecured myrmidons, the politicians and prosecutors who were the sacristans and thralls of the unseen, undying things, whose labyrinths these were. The entire phantasmagoria seemed to be presided over, orchestrated, by an uncanny sense of the inevitable. A man with the eyes of a corpse was led shackled through the halls by blue-suited ranks of carabinieri. The mingled swarms drew back, fixing their eyes on his; then chaos resumed.

I made my way eventually to the office of the Central Chancellery of the First Court of Assize, where I was told that I needed to submit, through that office, a formal petition to the president of the First Court of Assize. My petition—the chancellor suppressed a grin—would be processed, presented, considered, and answered in due course. Upon his desk were disorderly piles of what I presumed to be petitions in various states of due course. One of his assistants, who had been searching through a nearby file cabinet, turned just then and diffidently remarked that the president happened to be in his office this morning. Raising his eyebrows, the chancellor pushed forth his lower lip and nodded slowly to express the possibilities presented to me by this propitious happenstance.

The third-floor office of the president lay in the relative quietude beyond the swarming din of justice. The outer door was ajar, and I entered. The antechamber was empty; the secretary's desk was vacant. The door to the inner office was open. President Camillo Passerini, the man who would soon oversee the trial of Michele Sindona for murder, rose gracefully from his desk and looked at me inquiringly. He was a tall, silvering-haired man of natural, Augustan dignity, and his serene eyes were those of one who had looked long at, and beyond, the Latin in the rock. We sat, and he listened silently to the tale of my pursuit through the bureaucratic miasma of two republics. He steepled his fingers and looked away, toward the faint sound of the spring rain; then he looked to me. He nodded. The authorization I sought would be granted; the necessary papers would be ready in the morning.

And so, there I sat in the falling night in the little park in Voghera.

I was still uncertain. I knew by now that much of what the world believed about Sindona and the events surrounding him was not true, that it was the stuff of both fatuous misknowledge and of deliberate falsity; and, during the last fourteen months, I already had uncovered strong indications that past and ongoing governmental prosecutions of Sindona were often conducted more to suppress than to serve the truth. But I still had no way of knowing if Sindona's rendering of the truth was not just a different, more sophisticated, and more convincing lie. His tale, as he had so far shared it with me, was a powerful one, and the consistency and conviction with which he delivered its complexities were equally puissant. I recalled the words of one of his own favorite philosophers: "With all great deceivers there is a noteworthy occurrence to which they owe their power. In the actual act of deception," Nietzsche said, "they are overcome by belief in themselves."

The unknown truth lay between light and dark. In my solitary stay in little Voghera, I glimpsed something that brought me closer to it.

The founding stones of this place were cut from the rock—again, the ancient rock—and laid to rise in the names of saints upon a vanishing crossroads from the second century before Christ. Seeming neither to have thrived nor to have fallen since then, but only to have somberly replaced the stones as they crumbled with the passing of the ages, Voghera had retained something of a timeless cast.

History here was a dream, vague stains upon the stones. Spray-painted swastikas faded upon a bare and further-fading Communist Party bulletin board upon a decaying wall near the southern end of the main street, Via Emilia, which bore the name of a forgotten Roman consul, Marcus Aemilius Scaurus, of more than two thousand years ago. Nearby, in Viale Carlo Marx, a carousel stood motionless and deserted amid the gloom of trees. Posters announced the forthcoming thousandth anniversary of the death of a saint who died here on a May day in 986. More plentiful were the black-edged posters advertising funerals, bearing the names of the dead beneath images of the thorn-crowned Christ.

In the Piazza Duomo, the endless work of the stones was tended to. Tapping and chinking, two men in their sixties laid cobbles into the dirt where the stones of another day had been sundered free. They moved slowly, choosing each stone carefully from the heap behind them, wielding their mason's mallets with deliberation. Upon a scaffold set against the wall of the cathedral, another man daubed mortar between some stones that the centuries had unsettled.

Matrimonial banns were posted near the Duomo's entrance. They declared that the condition of each named husband-to-be was *"celibe,"* that the condition of his intended bride was *"nubile."* In the arcade across the piazza, there was a painted phallus, still clear beneath the evidence of much futile scrubbing.

An old movie poster flapped in the damp wind outside a tobacconist's door. Here and there, store windows were filled with the glimmering currency of the American moment—record albums, designer jeans, computer software. But these were fleeting things. It was the morbid effigy entombed behind a grille, the dead virgin beneath the altar of the Duomo chapel, that endured.

The knelling and the shadows in the streets were hers. And, on the May day I first encountered her, the sky, too, was hers: a looming, sunless, silent-raining thing of gray upon gray upon gray. The world is mine and I am hers, it whispered.

On another May day, the piazza was flooded with sunlight, and the key of the stone chinkings had passed from minor to major. There was a carnival of stalls, and all that the sea and the earth yielded seemed to have come somehow to this obscure place. There were golden quails and rubicund boars, bright-eyed swordfish and casks of salted cod, peppercorn-studded cheeses and the fruit of trees. The Duomo was filled with sprays of white flowers and cascading light through painted glass; the blue sky above, with gliding swallows and darting swifts. The world is ours and we are the breeze of day's, they sang.

But—dark, light—the world belonged to neither. Lady death and life's bright breeze cast their illusions over the surface of the earth; but it was the business of the stones that truly mattered, that remained constant. Empires rose and fell, and all the grand conceits of politics and philosophy with which men swathed their avarice and impotence were fading ciphers on a wall not built to last. Beneath that play of shadows were the forces that, like ancient stones, prevail.

My thoughts turned to one of my meetings with Sindona the year before. In the course of the hours, our talk had strayed somehow to Dante. *"Nel mezzo del cammin di nostra vita,"* Sindona began to recite from memory, *"mi ritrovai per una selva oscura, che la diritta via era smarrita."* It was the opening of the *Commedia,* which Sindona had never forgotten: "In the middle of the journey of our life, I came to myself in a dark wood where the straight way was lost." He waved his hand in a way that was both weary and angry. "This is the real Inferno," he said, and he seemed to mean not only the walls that surrounded him, but what lay beyond as well.

In that dark wood where he had wandered lost, Dante became aware of three terrifying beasts, which were the forces of the world's evil. Dante emerged from the dark wood, and at his journey's end saw the stars of paradise.

Michele Sindona, in his way, had come to a dark wood where three beasts—Church, State, and Mafia, the forces that prevail beneath the play of the shadows of the world—spilled the blood of their pitting. This was the heart of the tale.

In the morning, I would finally see him again, in the prison on the edge of town, and the tale of his strange journey would continue. But on this night, no stars of paradise, no stars of any kind, shone down.

As it happened, that morning, May 8, 1985, was Michele Sindona's sixty-fifth birthday. In younger years, he had foreseen many possible fates, but entering the autumn of his life as an inmate of a maximum-security women's prison was one he had overlooked.

Newspapers called this place a *"supercarcere,"* or "super-prison." Barely four years old, it was the first fully electronic penitentiary in all of Europe. Three television cameras in Sindona's cell oversaw his every move. A cadre of twelve guards, working in shifts of two, watched over him around the clock.

I was taken to the office of the director of the prison, Dr. Aldo Fabozzi; then to a grimmer, grayer place in the compound's far reaches. After passing through a Friskem metal detector, I was locked in a room that was divided by a screen from another, identical room. I sat at the narrow table on my side of the partition, and I waited until the door of the other room opened.

The orange jumpsuit, like the thousand-dollar tailored suits from Donini and Carraceni that had preceded it, was gone now. In his baggy brown corduroy pants, with the tail of his red sweater sticking out from under his brown sweater, with his worn leather eyeglass case protruding from his pocket, he might have been one of those old cavalieri who had not gone beyond the towns of their birth, whose wanderings from sun to shade, from shade to sun, were as familiar to those towns as the flight of birds above.

I saw immediately that he looked much better—healthier, calmer—than he had the last time I saw him. His brown eyes were bright, and though there had been reports in the Italian press that he was fasting from mortal fear, he had obviously gained some needed weight.

"The tortellini is good in this town," he said, patting his gut and smiling. There was an opening in the partition that allowed us to shake hands.

My first business was to have him sign an agreement stating that he would have no control over the book I was writing. As the eyes of a guard peered curiously at us through a small plate-glass window in the wall, this was done. The eyes vanished then, in time, returned again.

I told Sindona of the grace with which President Passerini had obliged me at the Palace of Justice in Milan.

Sindona nodded abstractedly. "He is not my enemy," he said. "I have no bad feelings for him. I don't think he has any for me. He only does against me what he must. Soon he must take part in the travesty of a trial, the outcome of which is preordained. The American lawyers tell me that I will be absolved, but they reason only in terms of the law and the facts, and do not take into account the political pressures that in Italy are decisive. I know otherwise, and I think the president of the court also knows otherwise."

His eyes, which had narrowed as he spoke, relaxed again, and he glanced at the pages of handwritten notes before me, displaying his uncanny and often disconcerting ability to read upside down anything that lay within arm's reach. It was, he had explained, a skill that had been his since childhood.

I asked, he answered, and slowly we drew closer to the woods beyond the shadows. As the hours passed, his spirits and the energy of his words were unflagging. Condemned to twenty-five years in prison in America, to twelve in Italy, and facing, at the age of sixty-five, yet another dooming, he was unvanquished; and the tale of his rise and ruin was as much marked by his savoring of its dark ironies as by the lingerings of bitterness. Toward the close of that first meeting in Voghera, I asked him what errant ray of hope sustained him. He looked at me and laughed softly, as if in wonderment that I did not already know.

"To die," he said.

# 64

Speaking of suppressed writing, *Frankie: Part 2* came out about five months later, in January 1987.

# Excerpt from
*Frankie: Part 2*

## If Girl Holes Could Talk

We went out and bought some beer and some gin that night, and we celebrated our first genu-wine assignment in a month of Sundays (and Mondays) (and Tues.). We nodded out about three in the morning, came to about ten-thirty. Hung the heck over, dusty sunlight streaming across our faces, it was hard to tell which was the bigger mess, us or our desk. If not for the fingerprint ink on Rosco's seersuckers, it would have been a tossup: both desk and Holidays were covered with beer cans, yellowed clippings, fingerprint powder, mini-reels of unwound recording tape, broken glass, and tit mags. No magnifying glasses, though. If you want magnifiers, go hire Sherlock Holmes.

The joint still stunk t' high heaven of the Lysol we'd splurged our expense advance on. A legitimate expense indeed—let's see Johnny Rutledge handle his malpractice chores with *eau de Holiday* up *his* nostrils!

"To work," Bud groaned, making him the official prime mover on day one of Operation Frankie (although Rosco, ever the eager beaver for credit due or un-, still maintains it was him who did the groaning).

"To work," Rosco (or Bud, as the case may be) concurred. (Hey Buddy, you got your memory up your ass or something?! I was first!) (Sez you, junior, sez you . . . )

Okay, sibling rivalries aside, to work is promptly where we went. As always, we started in the obvious place: the Manhattan White Pages. A smart dick knows to consult the Big Book at the beginning of every case.

"O.K.," Rosco talking, "let's see. Here's a Frankie & Jenny Beauty Salon, 2376 7th Avenoo. A Frankie of Florida, 131 West 33rd. A—Jesus fucking *Christ*, get this—FRANKI FOUNDATION WITHOUT THE E!"

Bud dials the number, 736–5518. It rings for many seconds. A male voice finally answers.

"Tell me, Mr. Whom It May Concern. Why do you want to fuck everybody's mom?" The male voice hangs up. We call him back, try again to pin him down, still no go. After about half an hour of this, we realize we may be barking up the wrong tree. It's to be expected this early in a case. Still, it might pay to try reaching him by mail . . .

"Let's try some sluts," offers Bud. "Look up some slut numbers."

"Good idea. *Yowsa,* here's a hot one named Cunto. Adrian Cunto, 210 West 64th Street. 586–5210."

We call her. She is not home. The filthy slut is probably out in some sleazy hotel with a syph dong in every aperture. Jeez. We make a note to keep after this Cunto dame.

Next we call a bunch of broads at random, all of 'em the kind that tries to keep it a secret. You know, the ones who just give an initial, like "I." Garcia or "M." Mizoguchi. They figure that way they'll avoid the random "obscene caller," but this time the laugh is on them. Of the nineteen calls we make, it seems every fourth or fifth has "known" Frankie. They admit it. Freely. Like there was nothing to be ashamed of. We don't even have to use our cover story on them, how we're selling subscriptions to *Frankie Illustrated* (which, of course, *n'existe pas*). But they won't talk *about* the sumbitch, not a fugging goddam word. All except for one "E." Wyrub, who, while cooperative, still fell short of giving us our first piece of concrete info: "Frankie's girls don't kiss and tell, but I will tell you his pene is *larger than life.*"

We were getting nowhere fast. We decide to relax a sec and chart a new course. First we'll define our terms. We call Renatus Hartogs, M.D., the eminent psychiatrist (you've read his column in *Cosmo,* right?), who is forever in our debt for a past favor involving (*a*) a twelve-year-old female "patient" (*b*) a gun that "accidentally" misfired (*c*) a nosy cop.

"Doc, give this some thought before you answer. What is a Frankie?"

"Ah! The ignoble and baffling *Frankus-universitatus.*" Amazing, these headshrinkers already had a word for it. "Yes, of course. There are so many explanations. The most popular of these, the one most doctors of the mind now agree upon, is that Frankie is nothing more, nothing less, than the archetypal symbol of the ithyphallus-as-badthing."

Thanks, Doc. Thanks a whole heaping helluva lot. Back to "go" without the two hundred clams.

Nothing left to do but put together the pieces, gathered from sources both pulp and cathode, that might give us a picture of Frankie's *modus operandi*. We go to the blackboard, splattered with sweet and sour sauce from a long-forgotten splurge on oriental cuisine, and scribble the hypothetical scenario:

1. Housewife at home alone, ironing the wash, TV droning away in the
   background, her seventeenths of an infant sucking on his/her rubber
   nip in its nearby pen. She is pleased, contented, perhaps even humming
   "Macarthur Park" (based on the average median record-in-common for
   the typical Frankied household).

2. Phone rings. It's Frankie. The psychological and biological causality is unclear, but she says, yes, do come over.
3. Frankie arrives, no dozen roses in hand (no buds have yet been found, according to media intelligence reports). Fucks her.
4. A note, declaring, "I have gone to Pascagoula to become a whore," is pinned to hubby's freshly laundered pillowcase. The baby's diaper has not been changed; it cries.

Hmm. We stood back and studied things step by step. There were too many holes (no pun intended)—too many hows, whys, and whuzzas. There was only one way to find out for sure if our synopsis was correct. We would have to become Frankies for a day. Look out, Cunto, here we come!

## 9. Frank Like Me

Hard-nosed dick work's one thing—contemporary dating's another. Pros that we were, we realized it had been many a moon since either of us had been horizontal with a real gal's steaming mush-pie. You couldn't really count the New Years "quickie" we'd had with Cherry, who spread her labiums for both of us down at vice squad HQ as a favor to our old pal Officer K—y. (A great mick, that K—y, and we're not about to blow the anonymity of so valuable a contact just this yet, tell-all book or no.)

We knew we'd better brush up on the do's and don'ts of 1975 ginch grope etiquette—like it or not. Frankie had to be a graduate *cum laude* of the academy of suave, and we'd have been a-holes deluxe to think we could get away with any less. Too many pseudo-Franks had already failed, and the stakes we were playing for dictated a complete run through of the finer points of seduction.

"Binaca oughta do just fine" was Bud's most on-the-money suggestion. "No need to burn your kisser with Listerine. Smooch her across the knucks when she gives you her hand, that's always good for some points. And remember, don't try any funny stuff till you've made her come at least once, no yanking out her pussy hairs or anything. They're all suckers for the Big O, and Frankie's got nothin' over the Holidays in that department. If it don't work for us, it ain't working for nobody."

### Bud's Report

When he's lying with a broad, a man stands alone. This was no time for the brother act, and a coin flip gave me first dibs on the directory. Knowing that rich marrieds are big on double listings, I perused the pages for a wealthy wedded socialite. Rothchild, Monica, wife (I was guessin') of Rothchild, Seymour, would do just fine. They named a wine after 'em, right? 440 E. 79th, how's that for a classy address? I told Rosco to go water the begonias so I could concentrate on my magnetism.

"Hello, Monica"—my very best Greg Peck immo—"this is Frankie."

*"Fra—??!"*

"Yes, toots, Frankie. How's about I come over and visit you in the sack this afternoon?"

"Why—uh—um—today's my mah jongg club—I—uh—*couldn't . . .* "

"Sorry, babes, Frankie takes no no's for an answer. I'll be at your vestibule at one-three-oh, on the button."

"No, please, my . . . I'm all out of disposable douche, I'll have to go to the store. Make it 1:45."

"See you then, sweetstuff, ta ta."

Shaved, showered, put on my freshest BVD's and the three-piece S. Klein's tweed I got special for Pa Holiday's funeral back in '69. Brushed my bridge-work twice just to be safe and took the 14th Street shuttle over to Lex, where I caught the express to 72nd, fancying the cab write-off I'd hit Rutledge with, come our first showdown at expensetown junction.

The dump on 79th wasn't quite the palace I'd had in mind, 26 floors of that light-colored fake looking nouveau-brick shit, and not even a senior-cit doorman to slip a fin to—one more fivespot from the Rutledge coffer into our own, a profitable day all around. She buzzed me up and greeted me at the elevator in one of those see-thru honeymoon specials down to her toenails (silver), the sheerest rayon acetate money couldn've bought. Before the mental note had even registered that this was sure as heck no natural blond, she was on me, yanking at my fly and slavering pink lipstick all over my Fruit-of-the-Looms. This was evidently one gal you didn't need to liquor up first . . .

After she'd goat-grunted her way to five (six?) lust-hump get-offs that reminded me mostly of a 1931 Mixmaster with a short circuit somewhere in the cord, I removed my spent pud from her heater, loosened my tie, and noticed the mammoth puddle of red-spotted squank-juice that had formed beneath her still-squirming buttocks as the air began to smell not unlike a tuna processing plant. Before I had time to scan the apartment for tell-tale signs of domestic bliss, she thrust her sopping monthlied love-clam towards my face. I almost retched. I knew it would've been Frankie-ish to just "go with the flow," but I wasn't about to risk mercury poisoning just for a job, not me.

"Frankie does not go down on the goulash, lady, I've given it up. Besides, I've gotta take a wee. Where's the commode?"

"Oh? Let me join you." Holy fuck, don't tell me the dame's hobby is watersports!

For my final compulsory poke at the swirling cesspool of her animal desires, I played it safe and stuffed my ears with handfuls of the slut's peroxide curls, almost muffling the goddam hubbub of her non-stop march to fulfillment.

Strange, but I was overtaken by a sudden flash of pity—for Frankie as much as myself. How'd the guy *do* it?

I feigned unconsciousness, but the ballbuster had other ideas. "Freddie?"

"Frankie."

"Well, whatever. I can't say it hasn't been fun. I may be a little kinky, but I think your spare tire and no chest hairs are really a turn-on. But Seymour'll be home from the office in ten minutes. You'll have to go now. But please do visit again real soon." Her unbobbed nose now supported hideous rhinestone specs—sheez, what a canine—so I quickly directed my peepers elsewhere, scrutinizing her Walter Keane big-eye print (framed) and 101 Strings LP collection.

As she rushed me to the door, it was fruitless to try and gather my shorts—one more disbursement for Rutledge. Somehow in the shuffle, however, I was able to rake up something far more important: a jar of S&W gherkins from the Fridge. There might be a clue there, there really might.

### Rosco's Report

Let Bud mock-Frankie a happily-married to his heart's content—no skin off *my* (circumcised) banana. It just made good sense for at least one of us to stick with a sure thing, so I scanned the list of random gals we'd called who'd already gone over the edge with the real Mr. F. Janet Svoboda, for inst, just around the corner at 532 Ave. of the Americas, had, just a few short hours before, acknowledged coition with the man we sought. She'd only heard Bud's voice, so this operation had to be one of the easiest I'd ever been a party to; kind of like shooting eels in a bucket.

"Ms. Svoboda?"

"Yes, who's this?"

"Frankie, my darling dearest love bunny. Are you by any chance available for a repeat performance by yours truly?"

"Hey, what *is* this? You don't sound a *bit* like Frankie." Shit, one detail I hadn't figured on. I'd have to improvise.

"You'll have to excuse me—cough, cough—I've got a cold."

"Oh Frankie, I'm *sorry*, are you feeling okay? Some nasty man called me before with the ugliest insinuations about our love. My lips were sealed—of course—but I just had to be sure it was *you*." Hmm, better lay it on thick . . .

"I swear on my Gogi Grant 78's, my one and only angel apple plumcake, 's *me*. Mind if I traipse to your digs and lie prone upon your Venus de Milo bod, arms included?"

"God, it *is* you"—hold the applause, just send the Oscar—"please hurry!"

But hurrying wasn't exactly the hottest idea. Older bro's advice about making sure she pops her cork seemed logical, so I beat off into my hanky, thick, steaming gobs of hot, white gism mingling with yesterday's snot. This guaranteed us a good half-hour of roll-around before my next load would spend itself in her ex-perienced cavity, more than enough time to send her to jollytown or my nick-name wasn't "Spunky."

Trou zipped up, a spiffy new *penus erectus* sprouted anew over fantasies of Georgina Spelvin, it dawned on me just in the nick: voice is cool, but facewise the eels're escaping through a hole in the pail. I rang her back with a real humdinger of an inspiration, telling her point-blank that my "thing" this week was chick's gotta wear a blindfold; if she wore it past her lip, it'd even keep the cold virus from entering through her oral opening (those four tough months of pre-med finally came in handy).

My every word was her command, and a chartreuse paisley scarf, from just be-low a shocking red mane all the way down to a jutting jetty of a jaw, greeted me fiercely as I arrived, huffing and puffing, at her fifth-story walkup flat. A plain white brazeer covered and supported a giganterrific stack, and her scanties looked like they just walked out of a zoo (off-zebra, kind of). Her gold stiletto heels from the racks of 14th Street's finest made me do some fast subtraction to compute her actual height—five foot two in stocking feet, give or take a cen-timeter.

"Oh, *Frankie*"—her yellow-green lips missed mine entirely, catching the dacron-polyester of my left shoulder in a passionate meeting of cloth—"it's so *good* to almost see you again!"

"Ditto, Jan, dumpling, let me—sneeze, sneeze—carry you to the bedstead, so we can immediately proceed to some serious whoopee." Fortunately, she was on the petite side (my athletic prowess having taken a temporary detour some-where around my 42nd birthday), and we made it to the mattress beside her 13-inch Sony (measured diagonally) without undue rupture to Sir Rosco's family jewels.

My skilled fingers had her Maidenform off in a jiff, and I beheld the most fantastic pair since Muriel Caponata back in '58, berry-like nips a-ripe for the picking. I pawed them right, daddy-o—her ribcage heaved, an effective and highly publicized sign of womanly delight—caught a healthy eyeful of her at-tractive spread, and went directly for the clit. Bowling three nights a week can give a man phenomenal digital control, and it wasn't long before her sighs told me it was *time*.

As today's gals are fond of such things, I allowed her to assist insertion of my fat, throbbing stiffy, and 35 seconds later—detection folk have an infallible "in-ner clock"—I shot my wad in her loose-fitting toybox. I knew I'd better act forth-with to sate this shapely number once and for all, so I journeyed south and gobbled her muff with vigorous aplomb. The taste was vaguely reminiscent of musty cheese, but my own sweet jizz enhanced the flavor and certainly made things bearable—gotta admit, I *liked* it. Scarfed her suet for what seemed like an eternity, until my mandibles finally went slack—that's all, folks.

"Let's take a breather—hack, wheeze—I could really use a drink."

"Ngh, rrh, ah . . . all I've got . . . unnh . . . I have a little Cinzano and some . . . Amaretto . . . help yourself."

I mixed the two, straight, in an unwashed plastic tumbler and thought, gee, I really oughta make this tomato shoot before she gets too suspicious. Luck was with me, as the booze and some strokes from my bowling hand yielded another workable boner before you could say *Jack Robinson* (the famous ballplayer). In her again, I did her right for a minute thirty-two, whereupon my jackhammer exploded in several distinct pulses of unwanted thrilling emission. Christamighty, better get to work with m' educated fingeroo . . .

Twenty minutes later, her girl-load finally gushed, slightly, and at last she was ripe for some preliminary interrogation. "Janet, my sweet patooty, when I was here last time, whenever that was, did I mention what hotel I was staying at? I forget, did I happen to tell you my sign or my annual income? Did I say anything about my favorite color, or colors, as the case may be? Also, I just started taking a growth drug—sniffle, snort—so I was wondering if I seemed taller or, y'know, *larger* to you."

"Whatsamatter, you got amnesia or something?" Her features appeared awfully tense under the paisley, despite her recent satisfaction.

"Nah, hey, I lose track, I'm such a busy man. And by the way, did I by any chance give you a snapshot of my likeness when last we made love?" I noticed the unretouched black & white of some grinning young jerkington high on the mantel. If the cat was Frankie, we'd be fat city in 48 hours. "I have a new one I think you might dig."

"Oh wow, I can finally replace my ex-husband Walter's graduation glossy that even his mother didn't want! Could you maybe autograph it for me?"

"Sure thing, precious—honk, hooter—I'll leave it by the doorjamb." I already had my threads back on, a stale pair of Ms. Svoboda's skivvies out of the hamper and into my pocket—Frankie's dried semen would give us his bloodtype. While in the rest room, I'd also scrawled SFF ("She Fucked Frankie"—which had by now replaced LAMF as the preferred ghetto graffiti) on the mirror, for reasons I'm not quite sure of myself.

"Oh fudge, don't tell me you're calling it quits so early. I still love you to pieces, even though neither your mouth nor organ could bring me completion. You have a miserable cold, it's *understandable*. You should see a doctor, get a B-12 shot or something. But please don't feel bad, I know next time you'll have me right up to my limit—58 per bed-down, 16 the first hour."

Holy mother of Mary—pardon my temporary feelings of "inadequacy"—maybe our pal Franklin really Had Something.

# 65

# Pentecostals in Heat

### Sex as A Last Rite

"It is good for a man not to touch a woman," St. Paul said. But, if men cannot be pure, "let them marry: for it is better to marry than to burn."

Jerry Lee Lewis, who knew those New Testament words well, found that the solution was not so simple. A bigamist at the age of 17 and later twice-wed to his teenage cousin, Jerry Lee had been marrying and burning, burning and marrying for most of his life.

He had been pumping piano and singing for even longer: pumping and singing and burning and marrying. In the summer of 1957, when he was 21, his recording of "Whole Lotta Shakin' Goin' On" brought him fortune and fame. That fortune and that fame seemed to be boundless. In December "Great Balls of Fire" rose high on the pop, country, r&b, and British charts, and it was believed that Jerry Lee was destined to seize the throne of Elvis, who soon would be shorn and shipped to Germany. But, that same December, Jerry Lee took as his third wife his cousin Myra Gale Brown, age 13. A few months later, at the start of a British tour, which was to give England its first shot of living rock 'n' roll, that marriage, hushed until then, was made into a public outrage by the slavering British press. After two shows, the tour was aborted—"BABY-SNATCHER QUITS," the London *Daily Herald* gloated—and Jerry Lee returned to America, which had seen him off in glory but which now, with prurient glee, threw stones of revilement and scorn. So it came to pass, in those distant days when impropriety was to popular idolatry a poison rather than a perfume, that Jerry Lee Lewis, less than a year after he had risen, fell.

He rose again a decade later—this time a country star—and, a decade after that, once again fell. There were no more big hits, country or otherwise. Fame became abject notoriety; his life, a tattered sideshow attraction. People no longer much followed his music. Instead, they followed his careening, downward rampage. It wasn't his records they heard on the radio; it was news of his shooting his bass player in the chest ("Look down the barrel of this," Jerry Lee had told him), of his being arrested outside Graceland for waving a pistol and drunkenly calling for Elvis, of the IRS seizing his property to satisfy liens exceeding his worth, of his lying near death in a Memphis hospital, his guts eaten away by whiskey and pills.

But always, throughout it all, he pumped and sang, burned and married. His cousin, "that bitch" Myra Gale, divorced him in 1971, claiming in her bill of complaint that she had been the victim of "every type of physical and mental abuse imaginable" and that her husband had threatened to "hire people to throw complainant in the river and to throw acid in her face."

Later that year, Jerry Lee married Jaren Gunn Pate, a Memphis divorcé pregnant with his child. They separated, reconciled, sued each other for divorce, reconciled, separated, sued again. In the spring of 1979, a few weeks after Jaren charged him with "cruel and inhuman treatment, adultery, habitual drunkenness, and habitual use of drugs," Jerry Lee was asked if he knew any more about women now than he had known two decades earlier? "Yeah. Pussy is pussy."

Awaiting her final settlement, Jaren testified that when she called Jerry Lee to discuss money, he told her not to worry, because "you are not going to be around very long anyway." Her final settlement never came—at least not the one she sought from the court. On June 8, 1982, she was found dead in a Memphis backyard swimming pool.

Almost a year later, on June 7, Jerry Lee married Shawn Michelle Stephens, a 25-year-old cocktail waitress from Garden City, Michigan. The marriage lasted 78 days. On August 24, Shawn's mother got a call from one of Jerry Lee's minions. "Shawn didn't wake up this morning," the caller said.

There was blood on Shawn's hand, in her hair, on her bra, on a lamp, on the carpet; bruises on her arms and hip. There appeared to be dried blood beneath her nails; and the ambulance man saw bright red claw-marks on the back of Jerry Lee's hand that morning. But the autopsy report, which made no mention of blood or bruises, attributed Shawn's death to an overdose of methadone, one of the sundry drugs kept in plenty at the Lewis mansion. Jerry Lee said that, yes, he and Shawn had bickered, but it was not serious. "I was in no mood to argue. All I wanted to do was watch *Twilight Zone*," he told the *Enquirer.*

The night after Shawn's body was found, her sister Denise telephoned Jerry Lee from Michigan.

"Your sister's dead," he slurred. "Your sister's dead, and she was a bad girl."

That same night of mourning, Jerry Lee made a call to a local bar in search of hypodermic needles. "Goddamn cops cleaned me out," he griped.

Shawn's remains were laid into the dirt in the Lewis family cemetery near Ferriday, Louisiana, where Jerry Lee was raised. It is the cemetery where his mother and his father lie, along with the brother he never knew, killed by a drunken driver when Jerry Lee was two. It is the cemetery where his two sons lie: Steve Allen, drowned at the age of three in Jerry Lee's Memphis swimming pool on Easter, 1962, and Jerry Lee Jr., killed on a Mississippi highway in the Jeep his father had given him in 1973 for his 19th birthday. (A third son, Ronnie Guy, born in 1955 of Jerry Lee's second wife, had been long ago forsaken as the bastard of her adultery.)

Eight months later, on April 24, 1984, Jerry Lee got married for the seventh time. He was pushing 49. His new bride, Kerrie McCarver, was 22. "JERRY LEE LEWIS' BRIDE REFUSES TO LIVE IN HOUSE OF DEATH" was the headline of the May 8 issue of Rupert Murdoch's *Star*. Jerry Lee's sister Frankie Jean was quoted as saying that Linda Gail, the youngest Lewis sibling, "told me she saw demons at the house." Frankie Jean told the *Star,* "There's something wrong there. I'm going to take a Catholic priest there—I believe God can do anything."

Jerry Lee perceived the satanic that year, too. As he saw it, Devon Gosnel, the U.S. attorney prosecuting him for federal tax evasion, was a "demon-possessed lady."

Then again, all his life, there had been demons. Always, everywhere, demons.

He had been raised up believing in God and the Devil, in salvation and damnation. God, he believed, had blessed him with a talent most rare. ("There's only been four of us," he would say, again and again. "Al Jolson, Jimmie Rodgers, Hank Williams, and Jerry Lee Lewis. That's your only four fuckin' stylists that ever lived.") But the Adversary, he believed, had claimed him along with that talent.

"Man, I got *the Devil* in me!" he had howled in the Sun studio that summer of his ascent, 1957, bemoaning the sinfulness of the music he was making.

That howling never ceased, but only grew more miserable with the passing of years. "I'm draggin' the audience to hell with me," he would say. "I'm a sinner, I know it. Soon I'm gonna have to reckon with the chillin' hands of death." Through drinking and drugs and graveyard darkness, he seemed intent on delivering himself to those chilling hands, but it was as if he bore the curse alluded to in Revelation: "And in those days shall men seek death, and shall not find it; and shall desire to die, and death shall flee from them." So, more and more, he made his hell on earth, and his music and his life, what was left of them, became a de profundis wailing—abandon and guilt, self-damning joy and lamentation—from the hellfire deep within him.

## A Curse on The Kennedys

Ask Jimmy Lee Swaggart, and he would tell you, too: Jerry Lee is damned.

They are cousins—born the same year, baptized into the same Assembly of God church, brought up together in Ferriday. They share a middle name in honor of the parish patriarch, their uncle Lee Calhoun, on whose piano they both learned to play. But one of them followed God. He spoke in tongues and preached the gospel. The other followed Satan. He pumped and sang, married and burned.

Jimmy Lee, too, was tempted to make the Devil's music, but he was strong. In that year of his cousin's ascent, Jimmy Lee was approached by a beast. "He had the body of a bear," Jimmy Lee recalled, "and the face of a man. The expression on his face was the grisliest I had ever seen. The beast was the picture of evil." Invoking the name of Jesus, Jimmy Lee vanquished it. On the first day of the next year, 1958, he became a full-time evangelist. "Glory! Praise the Lord!" he cried. "Jerry Lee can go to Sun Records in Memphis. I'm on my way to heaven."

As his cousin's name passed from fame to infamy, Jimmy Lee seemed to find that preaching about Jerry Lee was a good draw, and he continued to do so for many years to come. He, too, felt that Jerry Lee was dragging his audiences to hell. Just look at "Jerry Lee Lewis's mother," he exhorted in a 1969 sermon LP called *What Shall the End Be?* (Subtitle: "Is There Really a Curse on the Kennedy Family?" Answer: Yes). She was "lost, away from God, goin' to rock 'n' roll shows and drinkin' her *cock*tails, and she used to be saved and filled with the Holy Ghost."

While Jerry Lee fell and rose and fell again, Jimmy Lee rose and rose and rose. His gospel albums sold in the millions. (The second, *God Took Away My Yesterdays,* was made at Sun Records with the help of Jerry Lee and with Scotty Moore engineering.) It got to where he had to work out royalties with the Almighty.

"Now about these record albums," the Lord said to him.

"Father," he bargained, "would you take 90 per cent and let me have 10 per cent?"

Or so it is written in Swaggart's 1977 autobiography, *To Cross a River.*

In 1969, he began broadcasting his syndicated radio show, *The Camp Meeting Hour*—"I want you on the radio," the Lord had told him—and, in 1973, he made his move to television, again at the behest of the Lord. Eventually, he became the most popular evangelist on TV. His weekly show attracted more than a million households, and, by 1986, Jimmy Swaggart Ministries, based at his 270-acre headquarters in Baton Rouge, was bringing in $140 million a year.

As Jerry Lee descended further and further from grace to perdition, Jimmy Lee made televised pleas for the salvation of his soul, dedicated hymns to him, peered into the TV camera and cried out, "Why do you drink? Why do you take the pills? Why, Jerry, why?" And Jerry Lee, all the while, would attest to the truth of Jimmy Lee's words. "That man is a powerhouse for God," he would say. "Jerry Lee Lewis," on the other hand, he would say of himself, "is a *sinner,* lost and undone, without God *or* His Son."

"I made a promise for Jerry Lee," Swaggart says near the end of *To Cross a River.* "I will not be satisfied until I know he has entered the Kingdom of God."

A third cousin, Mickey Gilley, born in Ferriday the year after the other two, also found fame and fortune pumping piano and singing. Mickey, however, seemed to be obsessed neither by God nor by Satan, and, unlike his cousins, he never gave the impression that he was here as an advance-man for the Beast of Revelation. Mickey said that after reading Swaggart's autobiography, he called him up to congratulate him and to compliment him on its sincerity. "Thank you," his cousin told him. "I really haven't had a chance to read it myself yet."

(Swaggart and arch-rival Jim Bakker of the PTL shared a common coauthor, Robert Paul Lamb of Charlotte.)

But when Swaggart preaches, his sincerity is what raises him above the rest of the TV evangelists. He *believes* in the palpable everlasting flames of hell. Furthermore, he will tell you who's going there—Mother Teresa, the Kennedys, this uncle, that cousin—as no other mass-media preacher will. He sells the Holy Ghost in his sermons the way Jerry Lee sold it in his music: as something to fear and surrender to. To be sure, both of them—the self-sanctified and the self-damned—share the same terrifying eschatology, the same fulminous vision of good and evil embattled in darkness and light. The only difference is that they preach it from opposite shores of the river they call salvation: Lord and Lucifer unto themselves.

## Yodels from Hell

As last year neared its end—Swaggart's most prosperous year yet—Jerry Lee was checking himself into the Betty Ford Clinic in Palm Springs. It was, he said, a final resolute attempt to save himself. Then, little more than a day later, there came the news that he had fled the joint. As to where he had fled, it can be said with surety that the American recording industry did not much care. After 30 years in the business, he no longer even had a label. He was a ghost. He had once said that it troubled him to be called a legend, because he had always figured that to be a legend you had to be dead. Of course, he had been right; and he was a legend now for sure.

The world was ga-ga for Springsteen's box. Rock 'n' roll, or something like it, was now the official music of our debtor republic; and Bruce, the apotheosis of fruit-and-fiber soulfulness, was its Lee Iacocca Jr. "Born in the U.S.A." and Chrysler's "The Pride Is Back/Born in America" campaign were as one. Even President Reagan's sixth State of the Union Address, January 27 (the night before Jerry Lee's latest bride gave birth to Jerry Lee Lewis III), seemed to be inspired by the Boss. It was like a Springsteen concert, with Ron declaiming the political equivalent of "I wanna know if love is real" and his idolators swaying and cheering in mooncalf unison, red ties round all their necks instead of rags round their noggins.

Maybe the truth of the matter was that rock 'n' roll is impossible in an age of safe sex.

Then, through rain and snow and gloom of night, from Bremen, West Germany, there arrived a parcel of considerable weight. I opened it and beheld what was in it. Now *here* was a *box*. Soon, there came a second box, and then, in time, a third and final box. With each box covering a span of years—1963–68, 1969–72, and 1973–77—this collection from Richard Weize's Bear Family, called simply *Jerry Lee Lewis: The Killer*, comprises all that Jerry Lee recorded in his 14 years with Smash/Mercury, with the exceptions of *The Complete London Sessions* of

1973, available on two separate Bear Family albums, and the Memphis *Southern Roots* sessions of the same year, forthcoming. The boxes' 31 LPs contain close to 500 tracks, some hundred of which are released here for the first time, and all of them digitally reproduced from the original masters. Each box includes a book by Colin Escott, detailing the years covered, with a discography and a lot of pictures. Each box retails for more than a hundred dollars (available from Down Home Music, 10341 San Pavlo Avenue, El Cerrito, CA 94530). But this is not only the most ambitious, comprehensive, and expensive collection of its kind. If you like rock 'n' roll or country music—or, for that matter, drunken yodeling or the Holy Ghost or the Devil or whatever—it's also the best of its kind.

Jerry Lee devoured everything that came his way and transmuted it into something that was—just ask him—irrefutably his own. Others in his family spoke in Pentecostal tongues, but his was a musical glossolalia. Al Jolson's slick vocal audacities, Jimmie Rodgers's blue-yodeling, Freddie Slack's boogie-woogie, Hank Williams's stark gutbucket ululations, a myriad hymns and sinful blues—it all came together inside him where the Devil and the Ghost were, and it all came back out, in a storm.

One of the best instances of that storm is his performance at the Star-Club in Hamburg, Germany, in the spring of 1964. Whether or not these are the most remarkable live recordings in rock 'n' roll, as has been said, they are doubtless the most manic. To hear the band behind him trying to keep up with him as he jolts and rushes like a rat on fire, to hear them become more and more confused in the wake of his headlong frenzy, until finally, lost and flustered, the multifarious noise of their own bewilderment becomes a frazzled din as he bursts off alone toward what more resembles a Methedrine seizure than a song—to hear this is to understand the difference between rock 'n' roll and a Chrysler commercial. To hear him halt in the middle of it all to croon "Your Cheatin' Heart" to the screaming German crowd is to understand the difference between rock 'n' roll and Jerry Lee. Just as prodigious (and far better musically—he has his regular, American band with him) is his performance later that year in Birmingham, Alabama. Indicative of his contrariness, here, in Hank's home state, he doesn't sing "Your Cheatin' Heart," but instead premieres his version of "Hi-Heel Sneakers." Back in the studio in January 1965, he goes from a speeded-up rendition of the Midnighters' "Sexy Ways" (which somehow ends as "Whole Lotta Shakin' Goin' On") to the classic honky-tonk weeper "The Wild Side of Life," and from there to Big Joe Turner's "Flip, Flop and Fly."

He released his first all-country album that year, *Country Songs for City Folks,* but it was not until 1968 that he began to veer noticeably away from rock 'n' roll toward country—at least in his recordings. "Another Place, Another Time," the first of the long series of country hits that were Jerry Lee's resurrection, sounds as fine now as it did almost 20 years ago, a barroom lament in the classic tradition that knifed through the soft Nashville music of its day. The same is true of most of his other country hits; and his versions of "Born to Lose," "Cold, Cold

Heart," "There Stands the Glass," and "Waitin' for a Train," though not hits, are among the best recordings of his career.

During this time, the late '60s and early '70s, when he was in his thirties, his voice was at its peak. The youthful tenor of the Sun days was completely gone. But then, slowly, his voice began to show the ravages of 20 years of one-nighters and heavy drinking. "He sounds like Beelzebub," a friend said after talking with him one night back then. But that ravaged voice somehow suited him, for his music itself was beginning to sound like Beelzebub's basement tapes. More and more, as his singing came to embrace the less-exalted vocal arts of croaking, cackling, calling out one's own name, groaning, whistling and yodeling off-key, his pianoplaying grew evocative of that old upright that plays by itself in the haunted house. Except that Jerry Lee himself began to look like he could haunt houses for a living, this later phase of his music was quite nearly as captivating—though not nearly as salable—as what had come before, especially in the context of country music, where originality is measured by the cut of one's bluejeans. His suppressed 1975 version of Billy Swan's "I Can Help," with its mumbled taunting of Elvis, is a good example of the Beelzebub phase. The effect of his voice and piano playing, both shot to hell, was as creepy as it was funny. It was also why producers and record companies backed off.

Of all the music here that has not been heard before, the most intriguing and the best is the album of spirituals and preaching that Jerry Lee recorded at a Memphis church in December 1970, the month after Myra Gale sued him for divorce. Not only is it far better than his previous gospel album, *In Loving Memories* (which sold only 43,000 copies—the reason Mercury never released this one), it also affirms that Jerry Lee, as he had always claimed, could have been a first-class fire-and-brimstone pulpit man himself. As far as I know, it also includes the only recorded instance of his avowing "I'm goin' to heaven!" rather than to that more familiar place.

He jumped off that heaven-bound train a few months later. "Satan," he would say, "is the man that has power next to God . . . power more than Jesus. He tempted Him for 40 days and 40 nights," he would reflect aloud—"*and he nearly got 'im!*"

## The Big Vagina

"*Ubique daemon!*" Salvian the priest had cried a long, long time ago, and it still was true: The Devil is everywhere.

Tammy Faye Bakker saw him: "I put my hands out and said. 'In the name of Jesus, you have no power over me, Satan.' And it was like Satan was trying to kill me." Then Tammy Faye checked into the Betty Ford Clinic, not long after Jerry Lee slipped out, and she saw Satan no more.

Her husband, Jim Bakker, the head of the PTL empire, was himself no stranger to the Serpent. Questioned by the IRS about unaccounted revenues of

$14 million, his defense was that "the Devil got into the computer." He ended up beating the rap. But, this past March, when it became known that the Devil had gotten into his britches as well, Reverend Bakker did not get off so easy.

"HOTEL ORGY—FORCED INTO SEX WITH TWO EVANGELISTS," swooned the *New York Post,* its day made.

On December 5, 1980, the story went, Jessica Hahn, a 21-year-old Pentecostal church secretary, was lured from her New York home to Room 538 of the Sheraton Sand Key Hotel in Clearwater Beach, Florida. The man who brought her there was Bakker's PTL cohort and fellow evangelist John Wesley Fletcher, whom Jessica had known since she was 14, when she had baby-sat his son. Fletcher told her he and Bakker were doing a telethon in Clearwater, and they'd both like her in the audience.

In the hotel room, Fletcher gave her a glass of wine—drugged, she later claimed—and brought Reverend Bakker to her, then left them alone. "I didn't know women from New York were so beautiful," Bakker said, standing there, all five feet four inches of him, a WASP Froggy the Gremlin in a white bathing suit.

"Tammy is very big," he told Jessica. The look in his eyes conveyed the woe in his heart. Verily, spake those eyes, it is a terrible thing when a man's wienie and the asphodel of his wife's earthly beauty were as a lone plug nickel in a great collection basket, deep and wide. "She has made me feel very belittled. I don't know how I will come out of it. I don't feel like a man."

Then his Song of Songs began. He shed his terrycloth suit, baring his belittled loins, and he was naked before her; and he undid her brassiere, beholding her breasts, which were like two young roes that were twins, which fed among the lilies, heh heh heh.

"He started almost from the top of my head and didn't stop for what seemed like an hour and a half . . . he just did everything he could do to a woman . . . and he wouldn't stop. . . . He had to keep finding new things to do. I just couldn't stand him. I just wanted to pull out his hair."

Then Bakker was gone and Fletcher was back: "You're not just going to give it to Jim, you're going to give it to me, too." And the seeds of the two preachers were as one within her.

A few hours after her ordeal was over, Jessica turned on the TV. The flickering images of Bakker and Fletcher came to the screen.

"You had a good rest today," Fletcher was saying to Bakker. "Yeah, I need more rest like that," Bakker grinned. "The Lord really ministered to us today," Fletcher went on. "We need more ministry like that."

It was said that Reverend Bakker had been driven by jealousy, suspecting his beloved wife and coauthor (*How We Lost Weight and Kept It Off,* 1979) of fornicating with her producer, forgotten pop star Gary Paxton, who had not much been heard of since his "Monster Mash" faded from the charts 24 years before.

"Did Tammy ever put her hand on your organ while you were driving?" Bakker reportedly had asked him.

Paxton would not comment to the press. "I'll sue for slander" was all he said, then added: "My pastor said not to talk right now."

Meanwhile, Tammy Faye's philosophy gained currency: "I think every woman ought to wear eyelashes," she asserted. "Jim has very seldom seen me without makeup and hardly ever without eyelashes."

Bakker, joining his wife at the Betty Ford Clinic, maintained that he had been "wickedly manipulated" in a "diabolical plot" to take over his PTL ministry. He charged that the culprit of that plot was his fellow Assemblies of God minister Reverend Jimmy Lee Swaggart.

Swaggart, denying the accusation, denounced the Bakkers in his own inimitable way. They were, he declared, "a cancer that needed to be excised from the body of Christ." They had brought "terrible reproach to the Kingdom of God." He referred to Bakker's attorney, Norman Roy Grutman (who also represents Bob Guccione and Jerry Falwell), as a "porno lawyer."

And if there was one thing that Jimmy Lee hated, it was porno. In his 1985 tract *Pornography: America's Dark Stain,* he described publications that "offer advice to child molesters on how youngsters can most easily and safely be lured from playgrounds. Others discuss the joys of incest, and still others instruct fathers on how to clip locks on the labias of their little girls to 'keep them all for you.'" But, to Jimmy Lee, pornography encompassed far more than the wicked lore of labial locksmithing. Pornography was many things. It was "the chic California woman" in "a pair of *short* shorts, with several inches of derriere showing in the back and pulled up *very tight* in the front." Rock 'n' roll, too, was "nothing more than pornography set to music." And, surely, what went on in Room 538 of the Sheraton Sand Key Hotel was what Swaggart calls "pornography in the flesh."

"Satan is, of course, the fundamental author of all pornographic material." Thus, it was the Prince of Darkness himself, not Jimmy Lee, who was to blame for Jim Bakker's downfall.

On March 31, *The New York Times* concurred, sort of. On its front page that day, the results of a special Times/CBS News Poll were announced. Of those surveyed, "Forty-three percent said the devil was responsible" for the trouble of the Bakkers, "and 43 percent said he was not." It was added that "the margin for sampling error for this group was plus or minus four percentage points."

But, as Jimmy Lee and Jerry Lee surely knew, you couldn't render the Devil fit to print no matter how many decimal points you rattled and rolled.

## Cocksucker for Christ

By the time the third and final Jerry Lee box arrived from Germany, around Easter, Jim Bakker and his million-dollar racket were down the drain, all for a shot of sperm. They were yesterday's news. In late April, there were new accusations: Reverend Bakker had sung his Song of Songs not only to Jessica but to sundry whores as well, and he had—with or without makeup, it is not clear—lain with his fellow man, *contra naturam,* a cocksucker for Christ. Here in the U.S.A., where the pride was back, even our pharisees, even our Borgias were bland little men. Ronald Reagan—or Bruce Springsteen, one or the other—declared May 7 to be National Prayer Day and appointed as prayermaster Jerry Falwell, the smiling superstar Baptist now heading the PTL. Praise the Lord pass the lubricant, Endust to Endust, rebate to rebate. Selah, Selah.

But Jerry Lee, in the music and the madness in that box, was still kicking even if he was dead to the world, the world dead to him. And that kicking, I'm sure, will prevail after the Swaggarts and the Bakkers and the Falwells have faded and been forgotten. There is more of the Devil and of salvation—of the power of the eternal *idea* of those forces—implicit in that kicking than in all their crying unto heaven combined. And in this age of safe sex and safe rock 'n' roll, the fire in that power seems hotter than ever before.

It is hotter, certainly, than any fire in the soul or in the crotch of Reverend Bakker or Tammy Faye, the likes of whom threw stones that springtime long ago; and it is still hot enough, after all these years, to frighten and scorch them all—raving, demon-grappling Swaggart and fawn-eyed Falwell, too. They are the ones who have offered themselves to God, in public, like whores. But what God would want them? One that wears a moneybelt, false eyelashes, and does the monster mash? The Bible, in a verse such preachers rarely quote, damns priests who "teach for hire," prophets who "divine for money." Burnt offerings, not prayers or cash, were what the Lord told Moses to give. Jerry Lee's burnt offering—himself—may in the end get him a lot closer to heaven than either he or those on the other side of the river might imagine. Then again, heaven may turn out to be Room 538 of the Sheraton Sand Key Hotel. In the words of Isaiah: Who the fuck knows?

If there is something to be learned from all of this, other than that virgins should keep their "labias" locked in the company of evangelists, it is that Jerry Lee and the Devil have succeeded where Jerry Lee and his wives have failed, in making pretty music together, and that pretty music, at any price, is pretty music all the same. Whether love is real has nothing much to do with anything. It's whether the Snake is real that matters. That and royalties.

# 66

# The Short-Shorts of Satan

According to ancient holy teachings, Sammael, or Satan, had four brides. They were the demons of whoredom: Agrat bat Mahalath, Isheth Zenunim, Lilith, and Naamah. Maybe it was one of them that laid hold of the Reverend Jimmy Lee Swaggart and dragged him by his pecker to a sinful ruin on Highway 61.

Debra Ann Arlene Murphree was a 26-year-old woman who sucked cock for money. A lapsed Methodist and 10th-grade dropout from Patoka, Indiana, where, in 1982, she had left behind three children, Murphree had made her way to New Orleans, en route to nowhere, via Nashville, where she had learned her trade, and Tampa, where she had been busted for it.

God's man and the harlot: Their lives entwined in secret into a Cyprian knot, then came undone while the whole world watched; and, in the end, the holy man was fallen and the fallen woman was risen. Now, from the ashes, in a post-script to their parable, the one, in Baton Rouge, has struggled to return from the darkness. The other, in New York, has come shining forth, if only for a season's warm breeze, in the starlight of errant fame, the grandest whore of all. Let us turn to Revelations, chapter 23.

## To Golgotha in a Lincoln

Once upon a time in New Orleans, before the ban of 1917, prostitution thrived in the fabled red-light district of Storyville, on property owned by the Archdiocese of New Orleans, the Society of Jesus, and Tulane University. Prostitution still thrives, no longer licit, no longer fabled, on the outskirts of town, in the suburb of Metairie, along the gaudy, vicious stretch of Route 61 named Airline Highway. It was there, outside the Starlight Motel, that Debra Murphree was standing on a warm October day in 1986 when a tan Lincoln Town Car pulled over and its driver bade her to get in.

"All I want to do," he said, "is jack off awhile." He wore a red sweatband, a T-shirt, and baggy, gray jogging pants. A white handkerchief covered his crotch. He moved it, and she saw that his workout britches were torn open.

"He pulled his thing out and started playing with it," she would later recall. When he offered her $10, she demurred: "No way. I don't do anything for less than $20." After more prevaricating, he produced the desired $20. She did what he wanted, baring her breasts and vulva as he drove the side streets masturbating. When he was about to ejaculate, he slowed the car to a halt and slipped on a scumbag before bringing himself to release.

A few weeks later, the tan Lincoln was back. In the year to come, its driver and Murphree would meet about twice a month. Eventually, she took him to a room she kept at the Travel Inn Motel, 1131 Airline Highway.

"He wanted me to play with myself, pull my pants down. He'd say, 'It turns me on to see your pussy.'" He always brought lubricated Trojans in a blue pack. "If he knew I wasn't going to touch him, he wouldn't put a rubber on, he'd come in a handy. But if he wanted me to give him a blowjob, he'd say, 'Where is the rubber?' and put it on. Then he'd say. 'Just put your mouth as tight as you can. . . . I want it as tight as you can, like I'm fucking a virgin.'" He never tipped; "he was so cheap he would call and try to get me to get him off over the phone." He spoke little, and only of sex, and departed in somber haste as soon as his seed was spent. Their meetings usually lasted less than 15 minutes. As she put it. "He was cheap, but he was very quick."

She found him an attractive man of not uncommon desires. But soon she realized that he was not just another semen-spurting nobody with a Baptist mackerel for a wife.

"Do you know who you look like?" she asked him.

"Who?" he said.

"Jimmy Swaggart."

"A lot of people tell me that," he said.

Only once did he venture within her. "I want to put my dick in," he told her that day as she posed for him, face down, buttocks raised, on the bed. "He stuck it in and pumped a couple of times and pulled it out," Murphree remembered of that many-splendored moment.

"Oh, God," she heard him moan.

## Castration and Casual Dating

What Edward Gibbon referred to so felicitously as "the amputation of the sinful instrument" was seized upon early in the Christian era as a dandy way to combat the demons of lust. Those inspired by the praise of Jesus for men who "made themselves eunuchs for the kingdom of heaven's sake" were so numerous that the Council of Nicaea, in 325, was moved to shut out self-castrated men from the priesthood.

For Jimmy Swaggart, who so far has chosen prayer over the blade, there had always been demons. His life had been a war, ordained by him in the name of God, against them. As a boy in Ferriday, Louisiana, while his cousins Jerry Lee

Lewis and Mickey Gilley sought the fine forbidden scent of that thing against which the preacher at the little white Assembly of God Church on Texas Avenue so enticingly declaimed—that thing called sin—Jimmy Lee perceived it everywhere, like the ominous, dank breath of a beast, unseen and unknown, but forever near. In puberty, those younger cousins dreamed of Nellie Jackson's wondrous whorehouse in Natchez, just across the river. But Jimmy built himself an altar of logs amid the trees behind his home on Tyler Road, and he knelt there daily, praying to the whore-hating Holy Ghost to save him. For days at a time, he spoke in unknown tongues. In the eyes of all his kin, the boy was blessed. "Jimmy to us," Mickey Gilley would later say, "was like Jesus walking on the face of the earth again."

He preached his first sermon when he was eight, and, when he was nine, "God called me," he says. "He told me, 'You'll take my gospel to the world.'" He dropped out of high school, and, in 1952, when he was 17—the chosen have no time for casual dating—he wed Frances Anderson, a 15-year-old girl who, like him, spoke in tongues. They had a son, named Donnie, after the baby brother of Jimmy Lee who had perished in infancy.

Swaggart supported his family as a dragline swamper, and, on weekends, he preached. In 1957, he set out preaching full-time, roaming the countryside with wife, baby boy, and portable organ in a borrowed Chevrolet. The following year, Jerry Lee, who by then was the dark prince of rock 'n' roll, bought him a new Oldsmobile. In 1960, the year his mother died, Swaggart recorded the first of more than 40 gospel albums. They sold so well that the Lord wanted to talk royalties.

"Now about these record albums," the Almighty said.

"Father," he bargained, "would you take 90 per cent and let me have 10?"

Or so it is ghost-written in Swaggart's 1977 autobiography, *To Cross a River.* Later he would say, "Don't ever bargain with Jesus. He's a Jew."

By 1967, Swaggart was able to build a house in Baton Rouge. On January 1, 1969, he began his syndicated radio ministry, *The Camp Meeting Hour.* ("I want you on the radio," his garrulous God had told him in one of His increasingly frequent visitations.) That same year, he became the youngest evangelist to preach at the General Council of the Assemblies of God. In 1973, again at the behest of God, he made the big move to television. Ten years later, in 1983, he cut ribbon at his Jimmy Swaggart World Ministry headquarters, a 257-acre complex. The largest single construction project in Baton Rouge this decade, costing $1.25 billion, it became the home of the Jimmy Swaggart Bible College, with enrollment of more than 1000; the 7500-seat Family Worship Center; and the Zoe M. Vance Teleproduction Center, named for the Texas woman who bequeathed $8 million to Swaggart, in 1981.

At about 9:30 on the morning of July 1 1985, there was another heavenly call. "God showed me the harvest fields of the world," Swaggart claimed. "Told me that we were to telecast, put it in every country of the world where He would open the door." By 1987, employing more that 1500 workers with a payroll of $16 million, Swaggart was broadcasting in 143 nations, in 13 languages; and he was taking in upwards of $150 million a year. His private parsonage, which he described in humble terms, is in fact a manse of luxury, assessed at more than $1 million, on a 20-acre estate surrounded by a six-and-a-half foot wall topped here and there with razor-ribbon. The home of Swaggart's son, Donnie, and his wife, Debbie, is also part of the parsonage, separately valued at $726,000. Another house and 14 acres adjacent to the estate were purchased by the ministry for $750,000 as a home for Frances Swaggart's brother, Robert Anderson, on the payroll as a ministry vice-president.

## Sissies in Hell

Swaggart had risen, from nothing, to his power and his glory and his wealth by preaching a message that never changed. The Assemblies of God, of which he was a part, had its roots in the holiness revival that emerged within Methodism after the Civil War. Those roots could be traced ultimately to the Great Awakening evangelicalism of the early 18th century, to preachers such as Jonathan Edwards. Formally founded at the general convention of Pentecostal Saints and Churches of God in Christ, at Hot Springs, Arkansas, in 1914, the Assemblies of God doubled in size between 1928 and 1935, the year of Swaggart's birth, and stands today as the largest Pentecostal sect. Its fundamentalist tenets emphasize speaking in tongues, healing by faith, man's fallen nature, and redemption through repentance. Within the primitivism of the Assemblies of God, Swaggart was a primitivism unto himself.

"I believe there's a heaven! I believe the streets are made of gold! I believe the walls are made of jasper! I believe the gates are made of pearl!" he proclaimed. "I believe it's a real place because He said it was! *He can not lie!*"

Hell was just as real in all its terror, an eternal darkness of fire and brimstone and pain into which the damned were hurled screaming by the evil host of demons whose lord was the great Satan. Those demons rode the winds of this world, sowing sin everywhere.

It was in his cousins' music. "Any Christian who would allow any type of rock or country recording in his home is inviting the powers of darkness," he warned. "Any individual listening to it is entering into communion with a wickedness and evil spawned in hell."

It was in movies and on television. "*All* movies are wrong," he explained, and most television was "outright filth." It was, he said, "*impossible* for anyone, including a Spirit-filled Christian to look at this filth for virtually any time without becoming totally hooked."

It was in the way we dressed. "No Christian lady," he commanded, "should ever wear shorts," for her body was the temple of the Holy Ghost.

Yes, it was everywhere; but, most of all, it lurked between the legs. Homosexuals, said Swaggart, were "worthy of death." Pornography was an "onslaught from hell." Sex itself was an evil he called "pornography in the flesh."

"You can't dabble in sin," he declared; for "Satan is never satisfied until he utterly destroys those who succumb to his temptations."

Swaggart was relentless in his hellfire moralism. As Bakker, Falwell, Robertson, Schuller, and the rest peddled their lukewarm, smiling brands of have-a-nice-deism, he, dismissing them as "sissified preachers," would not mollify his fulminous vision of salvation and damnation. When, in March 1987, his fellow Assemblies of God minister Jim Bakker fell amid scandal, Swaggart damned him as "a cancer that needed to be excised from the body of Christ."

Refusing to dampen the fires of what he called his "old-fashioned, Holy Ghost, heaven-sent, Devil-chasin', sin-killing, true-blood, red-hot, blood-bought, God-given, Jesus-lovin'" theology, he became the biggest television evangelist in America, delivering in his transfixing way to devout millions the straight shots of guilt and fear and hope and joy they craved. The fury of his rapture swept them away and swayed them. He told them of the judgment day and the book of the seven seals, of the blood of the Lamb and the demons that rode the night, of many things wonderful and many things terrible. But he did not tell them about Debra Murphree's mouth, or about the Travel Inn Motel, where the hand that raised the Bible in wrath dripped with the trickling sperm of lust, where he who inveighed against the hot pants of perdition "liked to talk about how he'd like to see me in short-shorts, real tight."

## Down to the Damned

The man who ratted out Swaggart was Marvin Gorman, a brother of the cloth. Gorman, also an Assemblies of God preacher, had been the star of his own growing TV ministry, centered to the south, not far from the Travel Inn, in Metairie. Two years ago, he made the mistake of confessing a 1979 liaison with one of his flock to Brother Swaggart.

True, Christ had taught compassion, but, then again, He never had to deal with Arbitron ratings. Religion had become a rough racket since the days of the parables, and Swaggart lost no time betraying Gorman to the Assemblies of God executive presbytery, which, in the summer of 1986, duly defrocked him for flock-fucking. Since then, Gorman had filed for bankruptcy and moved his fallen ministry to a storefront.

His son, Randy, a Jefferson Parish deputy sheriff, sought to substantiate rumors of Swaggart's own salacious doings. Working with a detective, he humped his way through whoredom—no greater love knoweth any man than that of a faithful son—in hope of picking up the trail of Swaggart's pecker-tracks. He began paying Debra Murphree for sex not long after Swaggart himself did. On October 17, 1987, staking out the Travel Inn, Randy caught his prey, as Swaggart was photographed leaving Room 7 with Murphree.

The tires of Swaggart's Lincoln had been sabotaged to buy time for Marvin Gorman, who sped to the scene to find Swaggart hunkering in his jogger disguise at one of the flats. According to Gorman, he confronted Swaggart, who begged for the mercy he himself had never shown, swearing to confess to church officials. But no confession followed, and Gorman finally took his pictures and story to Assemblies of God elders. They summoned Swaggart to meet with them at the church's headquarters, in Springfield, Missouri. At that meeting, on February 18, 1988, he allegedly admitted to, among other things, a lifelong fascination with smut. Three days later, with no way out, he confessed publicly at his Sunday-morning service in Baton Rouge.

"I have sinned against you," he lamented, tears—unsissified, of course—cascading from his eyes; "and I beg your forgiveness." As to the nature of his sins, he revealed nothing.

Swaggart stepped down from the pulpit, complying with a lenient 12-week suspension imposed on him by the Louisiana District of the Assemblies of God, several of whose governing body, including its head official, also held positions at Swaggart's ministry. While the council in Springfield weighed his ultimate fate, he invoked the Devil as a scapegoat to deliver him from the ire of God in heaven and the closing of purse-strings in suckerdom.

"Satan was trying to destroy me with a terrible problem," he wrote to those on his mailing-list. "I have suffered humiliation and shame as possibly no human being on the face of the earth," and "I have bared my soul as perhaps no man has bared his soul before."

He turned 53 on March 15. Two weeks later, it was announced by Assemblies of God superintendent G. Raymond Carlson that his preaching credentials were being revoked for at least a year. The next day, Swaggart proclaimed he would defy the decree and return to his pulpit on May 22, the end of the three-month period the state office had imposed. On April 8, he was defrocked. By then, Debra Murphree had come to light. She had been interviewed for TV by WVUE, in New Orleans, and signed a deal with *Penthouse*.

"Put it on your MasterCard or Visa," Swaggart implored in a televised plea for money, on May 8, the foundations of his empire quaking from financial stress and disgrace. A few days before, Pat Robertson's Christian Broadcasting Network, itself suffering almost a 37 per cent ratings drop in the first quarter of this year, had canceled him. "It's not going to be easy for you to give," Swaggart said, "because Satan will stand at your hand to resist."

## Snakes

So arrived the day of Pentecost, white Sunday, May 22. More than 7000 converged at the Family Worship Center.

"Satan's doin' everything he can," remarked a maroon-blazered usher at the door, looking up at a black rain-storming sky.

"A girlfriend of mine took it so hard she wanted to commit suicide when this all first happened," a woman in her thirties told another as they walked together toward the building. "I had to minister to her for the longest time."

The masses made their way past the trophy cases ("Bible Quiz–1982 Nationals–4th Place"), down the long carmine-carpeted aisles, as the singing of the blue-and-white-robed choir filled the hall and lilted eerily from speakers above the restroom stalls and urinals.

> Tho' millions have come,
> There's still room for one,
> Yes, there's room at the cross for you . . .

Frances Swaggart, dressed in white, stood at the microphone and sobbed awhile. Then there stood Jimmy in a midnight-blue suit, white shirt, and yellow silk tie. He besought those in need of prayer "to come down . . . and the elders will anoint you with oil."

Laying his hands upon the head of a woman, he laughed maniacally. "Glory to God! *Bambadamos sai quanda rothshae keela bamado!*" he howled in tongues.

Offering buckets were passed around, and the sermon began. Swaggart told of two dreams he had about a year and a half ago. In those dreams, he said, he warred with two great serpents. Those dreams baffled him. But just a few weeks ago, God had explained them to him, saying, "Your struggle could never have defeated this enemy. But all I had to do was say, 'Satan, I rebuke thee.'"

Swaggart went on to speak of the blood of Christ that cleansed all from sin and guilt—"Don't look at the guilt! Look at the blood!"—preaching forgiveness with the frenzy with which he had long preached damnation. *"Humbalabala thun-ba d'rubashae!"* (When a black woman in the crowd threatened to upstage him with her own glossolalia, he summoned the tongue-police: "Help her stop for just a few minutes, please.") Jesus Christ—"and when you talk about Jesus Christ, you're not talkin' about a *sissy!*"—had atoned for us all. "Put the fire out in the brazen altar! It is no longer needed!" he cried.

Using a racing metaphor in his exegesis ("that's what it means in the Greek, honey") of Philippians 3, he seemed to come dangerously close to inadvertently recalling his whoring disguise when he offered "Your runnin'-suit doesn't look good" as an example of the sort of criticism that might distract the racer from "the prize of the high calling."

"So, I want to serve notice on the whole world out here: What's past is past! I'm not lookin' back! He that looketh back is not fit!" Furthermore, "I wanna serve notice on *demons* and *devils* and *hell*—the best is yet to come!"

He embraced a young cripple in the audience—"this is not a plant"—and spoke of a man named Robert—"I have no hands, no feet, and I'm blind," the man had told Frances—who recently donated $100.

"Guilt is not of God!" Swaggart concluded—an odd statement after a life of retailing the stuff; "I lay the guilt," he sobbed, "at the foot of the cross. I will never again look at it."

The rest of the world, however, seemed less willing to avert its eyes from the used scumbags of his laid-down guilt.

"Are you cured now?" asked Geraldo Rivera, who ambushed him that afternoon outside the Drusilla Seafood Restaurant.

"Most definitely. One million per cent."

"How did that happen?"

"A direct intervention from the Lord."

But at the evening service, the faithful numbered only hundreds.

"I have just gone back on television," he wrote a few days later in an Action-Gram to his flock, while the few stations still carrying him pressed to be paid. "I have passed through a time when Satan did everything within his power to destroy me, where the struggle against demonic spirits was so intense that at times I saw no way out." He had prevailed, he said; "But this terrible deficit remains."

Jimmy Swaggart, the anointed one, was going down slow.

## From Dildo to Donahue

On June 7, Debra Murphree, smiling and charming and dressed in a red knit miniskirt, sat before the crowd of reporters who had gathered at *Penthouse*. The issue with David Kennedy's pictures of her, posed the way Jimmy liked 'em, with and without dildo, had just come out. This was the start of a 10-city publicity tour.

Channel 5 News wanted to know about her future plans ("go back home, back to school, raise my children"). UPI Radio asked if she was worried about her 10-year-old daughter seeing the pictures ("yes"). NBC TV wanted motel-room details—"without being too graphic, of course, for television." Then it was off to do *Donahue*, where Phil led his own housewifely flock in praise of her. "Debra talks *jess like dis*," reported that guardian of the king's English, the *Daily News*.

Whether or not Jimmy Swaggart is, at this moment, holding the current *Penthouse* in one hand and his sinful instrument in the other is something we cannot know. He was a man who loosed imaginary devils on the world, and who, alone among men, in the end was destroyed by those phantoms. There is a sort of divine justice in that, as there is in the irony of his losing millions for something which he felt was priced too dearly at $20. "Whoremongers," it says in Revelations, "shall have their part in the lake which burneth with fire and brimstone." Swaggart rode to glory preaching of that lake; now he will go down to it, followed by the echo of his glory's epitaph: "He was cheap, but he was quick." Amen.

# 67

Before writing *Power on Earth,* I had begun work on a novel. With about a hundred pages in hand, Russell had set out to sell it and met with rejection after rejection. It was not a work of acceptable sensibilities or easily accessible morality, and no one knew quite how to pigeonhole it for the almighty sales force. Was it a crime novel or was it, God forbid, literature?

I remember discussing the fate of this unfinished novel with Russ in a Chinese restaurant in midtown around the time of the *Power on Earth* deal. He loved what there was of the novel.

"If we can't find a publisher, are you going to go on and finish it anyway?"

"Yeah," I told him. "But the asking-price then is going to be a hundred grand."

He looked at me, nonplussed. "Why?"

"Because I'm a prick."

We smiled, and the Chinese food tasted better.

Michael Pietsch was still at Scribner's. After publishing *Unsung Heroes of Rock 'n' Roll,* he had brought out a revised edition of *Country,* in early 1985. He, too, loved what there was of the novel, but Scribner's was against it. Michael left Scribner's and went to Harmony Books, a division of Crown, under the condition that he be allowed to publish my novel. We signed the deal for it in the summer of 1985.

*Cut Numbers* was published three years later, in the summer of 1988. It was for me as important a breakthrough as *Hellfire* had been six years before. As with *Hellfire* I had truly written for the first time, so with *Cut Numbers* I began to find the true voice of that darkness inside, a voice in which my reluctant trust would lead me eventually to light and to the rhythms of silence and wind.

# Excerpt from *Cut Numbers*

## 1

Clouds like gusted shadows of the dead moved past the Lenten moon, drifting west toward Jersey. Louie saw them.

The suitcase was heavy and unwieldy. As he came to Varick Street, he put it down. He rubbed the fingers and palm of his right hand with his left. He lighted a cigarette, lifted the case, and continued on his way. He walked slowly, not to lull the clanking of his load, but because night's end was for him the best part of the day. All was quiet except for the waking gray birds and the faint drone of scattered tunnel traffic. He felt strong and serene, unconquerable, if only for a breath or two, in the face of the coming day's inevitable attrition. Black became deepest blue, and the one star he saw vanished before him. He crossed Sixth Avenue. The church campanile came into sight. Deepest blue became day, and Louie entered the Street of Silence, where he was no longer alone.

A fading middle-aged woman stood near the curb, looking away as her leashed black animal released a long amber jet onto the tire of a parked Cutlass Ciera. Some yards away, from a building across the street, another woman emerged. She was younger, and her looks bespoke a greater devotion to the illusion of well-being. Her stretch pants and tent blouse were neatly ironed, and her hair was done in a silvered flip, similar to that worn by the model in the Alberto VO-5 placard in the window of Ralph's Mona Lisa Beauty Salon. She, too, had a dog, a small white poodle. The two women greeted each other like weary patrol partners on a doomed, senseless mission.

A nearby door creaked. The man called Il Capraio appeared. The women lowered their heads and silently walked away. Il Capraio looked after them. He saw Louie approaching, but he did not acknowledge him. Slowly, almost imperceptibly, he shook his head in what may have been an expression of annoyance, or perhaps disgust. He inhaled deeply, as if he had been burdened no less in the last moments than God had been throughout all time. Then he turned and disappeared behind the creaking door.

Louie passed by that door, not turning to look at it or at the adjoining black-curtained storefront, which peeling gold-leaf lettering alleged to be the Ziginette Society of Sciacca. A few yards farther, he opened the door of another curtained front and walked in.

It was dark. Al Martino's version of "Daddy's Little Girl" played distortedly on the jukebox. Four barstools were occupied by human figures in similar states of dissolution. Two of them were completely still, their heads down. Another leaned back, his arms folded across his stomach, staring at the glass of clear liquor before him. The fourth, the fancier of "Daddy's Little Girl," moved his head and emitted a sickly quavering sound in dire harmony with the jukebox.

Louie said nothing as he walked past their backs. He knew them all, and he was gratified that he was not among them this morning. Savoring his strength amid their weakness, he strode straight to the end of the bar. There, poised above a plastic coffee cup, veiled in a haze of cigarette smoke, was a face as cold and hard and untelling as a sarcophagal effigy worn down by time to barest relief. The nose on this face had been broken so often, so long ago, that it could hardly be discerned. The thin mouth beneath it was turned implacably downward, and the nacreous eyes above it were wholly occluded by thick bifocal lenses. Sparse strands of white hair, lifeless as painted lines, traversed the cast of the old man's skull. With his head slightly raised, staring toward the door in stony vigilance, he seemed always to be awaiting the arrival, or the return, of some terrible, inevitable thing.

"Good morning, Giacomo," Louie said. He put down the suitcase and looked into the old man's bifocals. Only then did the old man move his head.

"Is that good Louie or bad Louie?" he asked. He peered through his spectacles into Louie's eyes and saw that they were clear and calm. "It's good Louie," he said, smiling.

Louie lifted the suitcase and carried it a few steps to the small Formica-topped table that stood in the darkness between the jukebox and the toilet. The old man followed him, shuffling resolutely on the worn linoleum floor. Grimacing, he raised his left arm, which suffered less from arthritis than his right. He grasped the string that hung overhead, and a bare bulb flooded the area with harsh light. Two of the figures at the bar stirred, then were silent again. One of them lifted his glass and drank.

Louie opened the suitcase. Giacomo methodically removed its contents: four bottles of Dewar's, four bottles of Johnnie Walker Red, four bottles of Smirnoff, one bottle of Martell V.S.O.P., one bottle of Bacardi Dark, one bottle of Southern Comfort. He held each bottle to the light and examined its seal. He took the last bottle from the suitcase. It was opaque beige in color, and it had a fluted neck. He squinted at it, then sneered dismally at Louie. "Praline Liqueur? What the fuck am I supposed to do with this?"

"Are you kiddin'? The broads love it. It's like Kahlúa, Irish Cream, that sort of shit."

Giacomo looked away. "A hundred and fifty," he said.

Louie nodded, and the old man reached deeply into his pants pocket. He brought out a handful of folded money and held it close to his face, extracting three fifties. He gave the bills to Louie, then began moving the bottles, two at a time, to the shelves that were situated out of sight beneath the back of the bar. As he lowered the last bottle, the Praline Liqueur, he shook his head and coughed.

"You want coffee?"

Louie nodded, and the old man shuffled to the three-pot Silex gas range against the wall. He poured two cups and put a teaspoon of sugar and some milk in one of them. He carried them carefully to the end of the bar, placing the one with the sugar and milk in it in front of Louie, then he came around the bar, settled with some exertion onto his chair, lighted a cigarette, and resumed his posture of grim vigilance. The two of them sat in silence, drinking coffee and smoking. After a while, the old man turned and peered at the clock over his shoulder. It was a quarter to seven.

"The happiness boys," he said, gesturing with his chin toward the four figures at the bar. He took a handkerchief from his back pocket and removed his spectacles. Louie saw that there were drops of teary blood at the corners of the old man's colorless eyes. The old man wiped at them with his handkerchief, then eased his spectacles back on. "Shit-head there looks like he's ready for Perazzo," he said, indicating the slumped form nearest the door. "He can barely lift the fuckin' glass." The old man ground out his cigarette and sipped his coffee. "He wasn't drinkin' for the longest time. He came in here the morning of the Superbowl: 'Make it a short one, I got things to do.' Next morning, he's back, blown out of his socks. He's been burnin' with a low blue flame ever since. And this is, what, the first week of spring?"

"He's got money, then, huh?"

The old man increased his frown and shook his head. "A few bucks at first, but he's been runnin' a tab for weeks now. They're all on the muldoon, the four of 'em. If it wasn't for the young crowd, there'd be nothin' here lately."

"I figured the other asshole there'd be lyin' on the beach down there on that island he goes to."

"Ain't he a piece of work, though? He sticks up that fuckin' jukebox joint in Queens, then he sits around here playin' that 'Daddy's Little Girl' for a month. 'You're givin' it all back,' I told him. 'Nah,' he says, 'it's a different outfit.' How do you talk to somebody like that? 'Listen to the words,' he tells me. 'I used to sing it to my daughter.' You know his daughter? That pig that the sanitation guys used to hump?" The old man scratched his neck and put another cigarette in his mouth. "And get a load of Sleepin' Beauty over here. He's ready for a fuckin' room with a view on the East River."

"He owes me, that bastard," Louie said. "He's been dodgin' me for months."

"Points?"

"No. It was only a hundred, thirty cents on a dollar. He was supposed to pay off in five weeks at twenty-six a shot. He made two payments. Since then, *domani, domani.*"

The old man grinned. "Loan him another couple yards so he can pay his tab." Louie uttered a low guttural sound and grinned back at him.

The old man looked again at the clock, then he stood. "It is now post time," he announced. He strode firmly to the front of the room, drew back the window curtains, and raised the shade on the door. The bar filled with daylight. The old man leaned at the window, looking out. A young woman in a blue suit and white blouse walked briskly by, clutching her briefcase and averting her eyes from the window.

"Look at the ass on this one," Giacomo said, with something not unlike happiness in his voice. "Dressed for success. If only she knew." He nodded sternly, and there was nothing like happiness in his voice. "All these cute young girls with their big blue eyes, them and those boy-asses with the fancy haircuts, swaggerin' around like they're in one of them beer commercials on TV. They call these tenements co-ops. I swear, you could sell these kids shit on a stick if you came up with the right name for it. They'd buy the Brooklyn Bridge if you told 'em it was goin' condominium." The old man lighted another cigarette and blew smoke toward the window. "Someday, if they're lucky, they'll look up and see that co-op roof cavin' in and they'll realize they been carryin' thirty-year paper to live in some shit-hole that's been fallin' apart since Christ left Chicago, and they'll look in that mirror and see those gray hairs and all those new up-and-comers comin' up behind 'em; then they'll figure it out." He smoked and turned away. "Then again, who gives a fuck."

He slapped his hand down near where one man's head lay upon his folded arms. "Let's get this show on the road. Live people are comin' here soon." The head stirred. The old man moved down the bar, and one by one the other men were roused. They stretched, rubbed their faces, and nodded in miserable concession. They hailed Louie, seeing him now for the first time. The music lover reached inside his jacket and withdrew some crumpled dollars. He placed one of them on the bar, and he smoothed it with his hand.

"Quarters, Jocko. And another shot," he added, as if it were an afterthought.

"*Because you're daddy's little girl,*" Giacomo sang from the side of his mouth. His hand came down on the dollar, and he grinned to Louie.

As the voice of Al Martino rose amid the loud violins and surface noise, the front door opened, and there entered a small, smiling man in a tan twill cap and coat.

"Good morning, all you beautiful people," he said, his smile widening sardonically. He walked to the end of the bar, yelling "Sing it, you guinea bastard" as he passed the jukebox. He put a *Daily News* on the bar and rubbed his hands together. "In spring a young man's fancy turns to love. That's what they say."

Giacomo placed a spoon in a glass. He half-filled the glass with steaming coffee, then poured in Cutty Sark. He pushed the glass toward the small, smiling man.

"What was it?" the old man asked, after the little man had stirred and sipped.

"Nine-sixteen, Brooklyn. Three-eleven, New York."

"More cut numbers," Giacomo said. "What shit." He looked toward the window, receding into his dead vigilance.

The little man turned to Louie. "How's business, kid?"

"Business sucks," Louie said. "How's with you?"

The smile eased from the little man's face, and he breathed drearily. "I ain't had a hit in weeks," he said. He glanced at the jukebox, then at the music lover, then he drank. "This legal shit is killin' us. Everybody's playin' the fuckin' Lotto these days. Some days, the way things are goin', I think I'd be better off makin' the rounds with a shoeshine box." He finished his drink and pushed the empty glass forward, placing a ten-dollar bill beside it. With a fast flourish of his left hand, he indicated that he also wanted to buy coffee for Louie. Giacomo rose and filled the glass and pushed it back, then gave Louie a fresh cup of coffee. While he was up, he went to the switch beneath the counter. He flicked it twice and the volume of the jukebox, which now was playing "You Belong to Me" by Dean Martin, fell to a faint undertone. The music lover protested, but the old man just stared at him until he, too, quieted.

"Let's go to Martin's," the one nearest the door said.

"It ain't eight yet," the music lover said.

"Ah, fuck that joint," the third among them, the risen Sleeping Beauty, said. "Let's go to Brooklyn."

"Fuck Brooklyn," the fourth snarled. "You just wanna see that Irish cunt with the tits."

"I ain't goin' nowhere," the music lover said.

All of them except the music lover rose and gathered themselves to venture into society. As they did so, Louie also rose.

"Hey," he called.

The risen Sleeping Beauty turned. Louie beckoned him with his hand, then led him back to the Formica-topped table.

"What is this shit?" he whispered, looking into the other's downcast, reddened eyes.

"Things ain't been good."

"You're old enough to be my father and you're more stupid than I am. What is it with you?"

"Things, Louie, things." He drew slightly back as Louie moved closer.

"You make me look bad, you know that? I don't even really give a fuck about that. I don't. You know what I give a fuck about? I give a fuck about the fuckin' money. Seventy-eight dollars, I know, ain't nothin' to a bigshot like you. But to me seventy-eight dollars is seventy-eight dollars. And I want it. You hear me? I want it. That's it." Louie stared at him, seeing his breath grow deeper and his eyes become more and more like those of a child. "You shouldn't fuck your friends," Louie said at last, softly. The other nodded, and he muttered something. "Go on," Louie said, "try to straighten out. Do what you have to do, then come see me." He dismissed him with a sidewise toss of the head, then watched him join his two companions at the door.

"Always a pleasure." Giacomo waved to them as they left. He turned to Louie. "You're gettin' pretty good at that tough-guy shit, kid," he said, and grinned.

The small, smiling man took a long, final swallow, then smacked his lips. "Oh, well," he said, as he said every morning, "let me go. You want anything?"

The old man gave him two singles. "Four-oh-five, dollar straight, Brooklyn. Same thing, New York."

The smiling man held the dollars with one hand and scribbled with a short pencil onto a scrap of Yellow Freight System notepaper with the other.

Louie handed him a five: "One-eighty-seven for five, straight, Brooklyn."

The smiling man scribbled again, then put the money into the left pocket of his jacket, the pencil and paper into the right. He patted both pockets. "I'll see you people later," he said, then grinned and walked away. As he neared the door, it swung open. Three fat ladies huffed in, talking loudly and bringing with them the scent of Shalimar. "What was it?" one of them asked the little man in an urgent tone. He repeated the numbers: 916, Brooklyn; 311, New York. Winking toward the end of the bar, he hastened through the door.

"Three-eleven! My niece's birthday." The eldest of the women clicked her tongue. "I dreamt about her just the other night, too. Oh, well, what can you do."

Giacomo rose as the three women sat. He pressed three white plastic cups into three brown plastic holders and filled them.

"Hey, Jocko, gimme another fuckin' drink, huh?" the music lover called, pointing to his empty glass.

"Come on, watch your mouth. There's women here," the old man scolded. The fat ladies raised their eyebrows and moved their heads like bloated pigeons. The one who had dreamed of her niece primped her hair and clicked her tongue again. Giacomo placed the cups of coffee in front of them and collected the change that each of them had laid on the bar. He deposited the coins in the busted cash register, then tended to the music lover's drink.

"We gotta break it up after this one," he said. The music lover nodded, and the old man lowered his voice to a distinct whisper. "You oughta lay off this shit awhile, anyway. You're startin' to look like you could haunt houses for a livin'."

The old man poured himself another cup of coffee, then returned to the end of the bar, where he and Louie sat in silence and in smoke.

"I got sausage left over," one of the fat ladies announced, then nodded to herself. "I'll buy peppers."

"Green or red?" another said.

"You gotta be kiddin' me, red. Even the green are goin' through the ceiling." She sipped her coffee, then blew her nose.

The music lover muttered something. He finished his drink, raked his hand through his hair, and stood. He patted his belly and hoarsely bade good-bye.

"He was drunk, Jocko?" one of the women asked down the length of the bar. The old man shrugged.

"He was drunk," the oldest woman affirmed, pursing her lips and craning her neck knowingly. "You could tell by how he walked."

The fat ladies finished their coffee and inhaled tremulously.

"Good-bye, we'll see you tomorrow," one of them called. The others hoisted their waistbands and plucked through their blouses at the elastic cinctures of their brassieres. The door shut behind them, but the smell of Shalimar stayed.

"The old one, Mary, she still likes to fuck," Giacomo said. He began to laugh, but instead he coughed.

The room was silent then except for the sound of the old man's labored breath and the occasional ignitions of one or the other's cheap plastic lighter. Louie liked it like this: the quiet and the coffee and the somber, soundless figures passing beyond the pane as in a dream. He watched the sea of motes that swirled in the sudden sunbeam at the end of the bar, and he thought of Donna Lou and the wild golden downy curls that fell free at the nape of her neck, escaping his grasp like mercurial light whenever he gathered her waves among the fingers of his fist to draw her head gently back or toward him. He did not see the sunbeam disappearing, swallowed by the passing clouds of March, and he did not see the nearer darkness at the door.

He heard the old man mutter something in a mean voice. Then he saw the door open. It was Il Capraio.

Neither Louie nor the old man let his eyes waver toward him; they just listened to the sound of his steps. And he did not look at them as he advanced, but strode directly to them with his head cast slightly downward, as if watching the line of a distant horizon. Then he stood beside them.

He was a medium-size man of about seventy years, with a small gut and thinning gray hair that he brushed straight back. He wore a light-blue polyester suit, which his father had died in some years ago, and a shirt that was the color of the Praline Liqueur bottle. As always, he wore no jewelry except a wedding ring, turned around so that its large diamond was in his fist.

"Coffee, Frank?" the old man said. Il Capraio waved his right hand in the negative and scowled.

"Nice out today," he said colorlessly.

Louie and Giacomo concurred in kind. Il Capraio lowered his chin, then raised it. He addressed Louie: "You gonna be seeing your uncle?"

"Tomorrow, the day after," Louie said.

"Ask him whatever happened to Joe Brusher. You ask him that for me, all right? You remember, or maybe you wanna write it down, or what?"

"I got it."

Il Capraio nodded vaguely, then turned his eyes toward the line of another dim horizon. Louie and the old man listened to his receding footsteps and watched his back as he walked away and out into the wayward springtime breeze.

"I came, I saw, I conquered," the old man said. In his voice, there was more resignation than contempt.

Softly, drops of rain began to fall against the window, streaming down in windblown tendrils of wet refraction; and there was thunder. Louie lighted another cigarette and wondered.

## 2

Sitting at her drafting table, laying down pale blue bleed-lines on a fresh illustration board and nibbling with her teeth at the skin of her lips, Donna Louise Craven listened to the quiet young stranger in the cubbyhole across the way. He was talking on the telephone, saying "I love you, too." Donna glanced at him and smiled.

She waited until everyone around her had ambled out to lunch, then she lowered her T-square, wiped out her ruling pen, and looked at the telephone on the little wooden cabinet beside her. Uttering a throaty sound halfway between exasperation and abandon, she lifted the receiver and dialed. Her left hand closed tight on the arm of her chair as she listened to the ringing at the other end. Then Louie answered, and she raised her left hand to her throat.

"It's me," she said, smiling uneasily.

"And how are you, Donna Lou?" His voice sounded good to her.

"Oh, I miss you, Louie," she said, not really meaning to say it, starting to laugh and very nearly crying. "It's been awhile."

"Tell me about it. If the new issue of *Leg Art* doesn't come out soon, I'm gonna start contemplatin' the gay life."

She began to smile easily now. "That's one thing you never had trouble with, Louie, finding women."

## 17

Earlier that morning, on the other side of the river, Joe Brusher had stood at the drain-board of his kitchen sink squeezing the contents of a large can of Ronsonol lighter fluid into an empty Martell pint bottle.

Now, beneath the grassy ground where Louie sat, his maroon Buick hissed southward through the Brooklyn Battery Tunnel. He parked on Dwight Street, near Van Dyke, then walked to the old warehouses that faced the piers where Dwight Street ended. Joe Brusher disliked this part of South Brooklyn. He disliked its look and its smell and its people, and he always spat when he walked these streets.

He stopped at a narrow three-story building set between two other narrow three-story buildings. These three buildings were in practically identical states of dilapidation. Their windows, two on each floor, were either boarded up or broken. Brittle, flaking patches of dirty gray, the remnants of some long-ago paint job, clung here and there to their crumbling brick facades. But the middle building, the building where Joe Brusher stopped, was distinguished by a relatively new-looking steel door and jambs. Joe Brusher rapped hard on that door, hard enough and loud enough to scatter the gulls and pigeons that were the only visible life around.

A face came to the little wire-reinforced window set into the door. It was the face of a man who was in his forties, but it was a face that appeared much older than that. Its lymphatic pallor was that of a man who was a stranger to natural light and to peaceful sleep. His eyes, red and darkly shadowed, and squinting now through the smoke that rose from the cigar between his teeth, looked like open sores that would not heal.

The door opened halfway, and, around the cigar clenched in its teeth, that dire face spoke: "I'm on my way out here, Joe." It sounded like both an apology and a complaint.

"I ain't a customer, Billy, I'm a messenger."

"Another candygram from Staten Island?"

"Yeah, more or less."

The door opened wider, and Joe Brusher stepped into a small wood-paneled foyer lighted overhead by a bare pink bulb. The man locked the steel door behind them. Beyond the foyer, the entire floor was carpeted in red. The walls were painted pale pink. To the left was a horseshoe-shaped bar with gleaming cash registers set on either side of a well-stocked blue-mirrored partition. Along the opposite wall were three regulation blackjack tables with six seats set at each of them. From the center of the ceiling hung a large fake Tiffany chandelier. As warm as it was outside, the chill in this hollow place was unpleasant. It came not from air-conditioning, but from the foul humidity seeping through the dank sepulchral stone beneath the pink paint and musty red carpeting.

"So, how's business?" Joe Brusher asked offhandedly as he followed the man across the floor toward the open door of a poky room in the back.

"The guy that shapes up for me just left," the man grumbled over his shoulder. "He found three bucks and a ten-dollar chip on the floor. He's doin' better than me."

"Shit, Billy, you took enough of my money in this joint to keep your ass in silk for a hundred years."

The man said nothing; he just kept walking until he reached the little room in the back. In it, there was a desk of sorts—a piece of half-inch plywood anchored to the wall and supported underneath by lengths of two-by-four—on which there was a telephone, an ashtray, and a mess of papers. There was a swivel chair and a coatrack and a file-storage box made of corrugated cardboard and a billy club hanging from a nail behind the door.

The man sat in the swivel chair, relighted his cigar, and shook his head in what was intended to be a show of exhaustion. "So," he said, "whose stupid son-in-law wants to become a blackjack dealer now?"

Joe Brusher, standing there, smiled a little. He pointed to the telephone. "I think you ought to call out there," he said. "He wants me to bring out some papers. Some books, or some shit. I don't know. He'll tell you."

"Papers? What papers?" The man looked at the mess of papers on the desk, and he breathed hard. "What does he want?"

"Ah, Billy, you know me. I don't ask, I just do. Call him, he'll tell you what he wants. I don't like to get involved."

Joe Brusher reached casually into his jacket and took out his Martell bottle. He looked at his watch, then looked at the man, who looked at Joe's bottle, then looked at the phone.

"Want a drink?" Joe Brusher asked.

The man winced disgustedly at the bottle and waved his hand. "I'd shit blood for a week," he said.

Joe Brusher shrugged and uncapped the pint. The man began to dial. Joe Brusher stood the uncapped pint on top of the file-storage box. He took a cigarette from the pack in his pocket and he placed it in his mouth. Then he took a fresh book of matches from that same pocket, reaching across the desk for the ashtray.

Dialing the last digit, the man glanced up as Joe Brusher struck a match. Then he turned again toward the phone. In an instant, realizing that Joe Brusher did not smoke, his eyes shot around again and saw Brusher put the lighted match not to the cigarette in his mouth but to the ashtray in his hand; and he saw the ashtray flare as the open book of matches in it was ignited.

In that stilled moment of his confusion and dismay, the seated man moved the receiver from his ear, and his mouth opened in a trancelike way, then exploded in sound.

"What the fuck—"

"Catch!"

With a long underhand flourishing thrust of the bottle, Joe Brusher doused the man's face and front, and, simultaneously releasing his grip but not the impetus of his thrust, he let the bottle fly into the man's bolting lap. At the same time, into that lap from Joe Brusher's other hand went the ashtray's flaring flame.

The man was up and lunging toward him. His horribly contorted, howling face was little more than two feet from Brusher's eyes when it burst into blue incandescence.

The man's hands, which had grabbed for Joe Brusher's throat, now flailed furiously in the air, slapping and thrashing at himself as the lambent blue fire that played upon him began to ripple and to rise in fluttering tongues of yellowish flame. One hand soon also flared with glowing blue and ruffling gold.

The man waved it violently before him, as, with his other hand, he jabbed and pawed at the blinding burning of his eyelids, driving that wild burning deeper into the eyes beneath them with every frantic swipe.

Joe Brusher kicked the heavy swivel chair into the man's shin, jarring him backward in his desperate agony. The stench of scorched flesh and burned hair overtook the smell of the naphtha fumes. Convulsing and roaring before him on the floor, the burning man looked to Joe Brusher like a monstrous embryo aflame. The fire that danced now over every part of him could actually be heard—it was a flapping sound, like that of a wet flag in a low wind—and its heat billowed forth in waves. More and more smoke filled the room as the flames burned deeper, roasting the tallowy flesh beneath the skin; and the soot of the man's incinerated clothing flew through the air like mad black moths.

Joe Brusher took the billy club from behind the door and whacked the man's bared, blistering shoulder. It was like hitting a tightly packed bundle of smoldering papers—fiery cinders of charred skin swirled through the room. The man screamed hideously through black, swollen lips that bled from deep cracks. It was the loudest and most terrible scream that Joe Brusher had ever heard. He brought down the club again, across the skull this time, and the screaming ceased with a horrid bleat beneath the crunch of the blow. He dropped the club and backed away in disgust. Strips of blistering skin were crackling loose from the man's bashed head, and the flames were blowing them free like gruesome serpentine streamers. Embers were drifting and lighting throughout the room, kindling tiny blazes everywhere. There was fire in Joe Brusher's cuffs. He smacked it out with a hand that sweated and shook in equal measure.

He bent to retrieve the telephone receiver from the floor where it lay, quickly letting it go with a loud "Damn!" as the heated plastic seared his fingertips. He then raised the receiver by its cord and jimmied it back to its cradle. Taking from the desk the mess of papers, the edges of which were already curling with a slow fire, he looked about for a flame to further ignite them. With another "Damn!" he poked the papers into the fire that burned bright across the spasmodically heaving chest of the dying man. Then with that torch of paper he hurried the spread of the flames throughout that little room. The plywood desk, the cardboard storage boxes, even the phone were set ablaze. He tore off a piece of burning cardboard and carried it with him from the room, tossing it down to the red carpeting. With a frightful *whoosh,* the fire moved across the floor like a burning tide. Joe Brusher, caught off-guard by the velocity of this fuming chemical wildfire, staggered back, then ran.

He pulled hard at the locked door. In that moment, as thick, suffocating smoke began to fill the foyer like a deadly fog, a sudden and chilling dread wrenched his heart. In a flash no less sudden, he remembered entering this door. He saw the doomed man turn a key to lock it behind him, saw the doomed man remove that key and place it in his pocket; saw that doomed man now, burning and laughing, laughing and burning. That fitful, jerking heaving of his chest—it was laughter.

Then his hand was on the bolt-switch, and he was out of that place.

An hour and a half later, lying in a hot bath, he turned that hand slowly before his eyes and stared at it until it ceased to be his own.

On the following morning, in the sunny front parlor of a big house on Castleton Avenue in Staten Island, Joe Brusher extended that hand, and an older man in slippers and a robe put an envelope in it.

"Plant a tree in Israel," he said as he handed it to him.

Joe Brusher counted the money without removing it from the envelope. There were forty hundred-dollar bills and a check made out to him for three thousand dollars. In the lower left-hand corner of the check were written the words HOUSE PAINTING. He tucked the envelope into his jacket pocket with a trace of disappointment in his breath. He had been hoping for a little something extra.

"You did good," the man said, easing himself into an armchair. As he sat, his robe drooped open, exposing his boxer shorts—they seemed to match the wallpaper in this room—and pale spindly legs. "You see the *News* this morning?"

Joe Brusher shook his head in oblique distaste.

"'Gambling War in Brooklyn,'" the man mocked with a golden-toothed grin. "They bought it lock, stock, and barrel. The Jew lightnin', Joe, that's what made it look good. The paper said the cops called it a—what the fuck was it—a . . . "

*This guy's ready for a fuckin' E.E.G.,* Joe Brusher's inner voice mumbled as the man squinted gropingly toward the ceiling.

"'Detectives said the killing and arson were a new volley in the war to control illegal gambling in Brooklyn.' Yeah, that was it. That's what the paper said." The man scratched his chest through his undershirt. "So, Joe," he said, "tell me. How'd that little rat cunt-eater go when he went? How'd he check out?"

"You had to be there."

"But he suffered." It was a question expressed as a statement.

"Yeah," Joe Brusher said, not wanting to show his impatience or his disquietude. "He suffered." He thought of the previous morning and of the little something extra that he had not found in the envelope. "It wasn't too pretty there yesterday in that joint."

The man sensed the note of umbrage in Joe Brusher's voice. He nodded aloofly, disdainfully.

"You're getting dainty in your old age, Joe? You're a fucking floral arranger all of a sudden now?"

"Look, this was different." The words had an angry weight to them.

"*Different,*" the man said, sneering.

"Yeah, different. I coulda dropped that bastard in ten seconds. This was a major fuckin' production."

"It's what I wanted."

"It's what you wanted. So you got it."

"Watch it, Giusepp'."

Joe Brusher sat there, and he breathed deeply, and he told himself that September was now here and that its third Monday soon enough would come, and that then he would be free, forever, of cocksuckers such as this.

"You know, Joe"—the man's voice was subdued now, and his tone was almost avuncular—"it's like the philosopher says: Count your blessings."

Joe Brusher pursed his lips and nodded slowly as if in reflective cognizance of the wisdom not only of those words but of the man who uttered them as well. And the man perceived this to be good.

The morning sky was darkening. Driving back to Jersey across the Bayonne Bridge, Joe Brusher watched the first, misty drops of a late-summer rain splash and softly spatter on his windshield. He remembered a song called "September in the Rain." He had heard it long ago, a lifetime ago, drifting from a seaside bandshell through the starry rifts of a nighttime boardwalk under which he lay with his cock in the mouth of his best friend's little sister. He would have sung it now, but he couldn't remember the words.

# 68

# Exile on Twenty-first Street

It goes like this. I'm in my kid brother's car with him and his wife, coming home from a wake over in the old neighborhood in Jersey City. No one you know.

My brother asks me if Island is one of the dumb-ass companies that still sends me free records even though I haven't reviewed a record since Christ left Chicago. I don't know, I tell him. They all look the same. Well, if they do, he says, keep an eye out for the Keith Richards album; he wants it. All right, I tell him. We drive on in his shitbox through the slow river of dark night.

Island, it turns out, is not one of the dumb-ass companies that still sends me records. Fuck it.

A week later, Legs McNeil is sitting on my couch, grubbing my cigarettes. I haven't seen this guy in years. He is now happily divorced and an editor of *Spin*. Don't worry, I tell him, help yourself, I've got a carton in the other room. We talk about mashed potatoes and female body parts, then fall silent. He asks me if I want to write something about Keith Richards for *Spin*. All right, I tell him, get me a copy of the album.

But Legs discovers that the company doesn't want to let out any advance copies. They're afraid of a leak. A leak. What the fuck is this, a goddamn record album or a coded blueprint for biosensor circuitry?

They tell Legs I can hear the album if I go to 21st Street. I mean, I don't even want to hear the fucking thing. I heard "Happy" once, a long time ago, and that was enough. All I want is to glom a copy, slip it to my brother, then say some nice things about Keith, who deserves it. And where does 21st Street figure into this, anyway? I thought Island was on Fourth Street. Maybe the company isn't even Island, maybe my brother got it wrong. But, even so, what the fuck is on 21st Street? I wouldn't go to 21st Street even to hear somebody who could actually sing. I wouldn't go to 21st Street for a blowjob and a quart of Dewar's, even if they sent a limo. I mean, at least have the fucking class to come to me with the goddamn thing. Send a few armed Pinkertons to watch over me while I listen to it or whatever. But 21st Street?

I'm sure this is none of Keith's doing. We pissed in adjoining urinals once at a party 15 or 16 years ago at the Four Seasons and he seemed as nice a guy as ever you'd care to piss next to. (We had to leave early that night, Richard Meltzer and myself and our consorts, because Richard jumped into the fountain, and Atlantic Records, whose party it was, firmly held that improper decorum and rock 'n' roll simply did not mix.) But, even aside from that piss, Keith always seemed to be the sort of person who would never expect anybody to go to 21st Street for anything.

Which brings us to the album. I'm sure it's a very good record, even though the guy can't carry a tune in a fucking bucket; and everyone should go out and buy it now that it's been declassified. Keith, at the age of 44, has it all over Jagger. True, he looks these days like a disinterred corpse, but he's achieved in the midst of his decay a certain dignity. Jagger, on the other hand, beneath the thickening make-up of middle age, evokes in his silly quest for eternal youth nothing so much as a rock 'n' roll Joan Collins or Liberace. (Beware the watermelon diet, Mick, beware.) Does rock 'n' roll even enter into it at this point? I mean, is the rock 'n' roll of people in their golden Geritol years different from the jazz of Guy Lombardo or Lawrence Welk or a hundred other dead or dying geezers? Can there be such a thing as menopausal rock 'n' roll?

Keith Richards, at least, seems to have perceived the truth that the very notion of a middle-aged teen dream is an absurdity to all but the middle aged. He seems, in other words, to be learning what Dean Martin has long since known—that, in old Napoli, that's *amore*. Besides, anybody who doesn't like Bruce Springsteen, thinks George Michael should take a shave and get lost, and has never heard of Johnny Kemp has got to have something on the ball. God knows what the future holds for him. He's always had a unique voice, to put it mildly. Now that he's a good family man instead of a drunken junkie lowlife, maybe he can even team up with John Denver or Bobby Goldsboro if Mick doesn't come around. From heroin to Care Bears: the real story of rock 'n' roll.

The album [which is actually on Virgin] is called *Talk Is Cheap*. Twenty-first Street is still there. And my brother never got his fucking free record. Such is life.

# 69

# Review of
## *Killer: The Mercury Years*

I'm sitting there in Dennis Quaid's house, this white thing on La Sombra, last spring, a few months before that stiff *Great Balls of Fire* came and went. Though people tell me he's a prick, he seems like a nice guy. Maybe I'm a prick, too, that's why I can't tell; I don't know. But, anyway, now he goes to this piano he's got there, and I—all of us: some sort of secretary he's got, Rusty or Sandy or Smoky or some fucking adjective, and this other, younger bimbo who keeps looking at me, almost pouting, like, "Hey, you're supposed to know who I am. I'm famous." She does look vaguely familiar; maybe from one of those disposable-douche commercials, the one with the mother and daughter discussing douches out on the veranda?—we have to sit there as he goes through his Jerry Lee routine. I have to sit there, at least. The secretary can go in the kitchen and make calls and act busy; the other bimbo can go upstairs and emote privately, or flush herself with vinegar, or whatever; but I'm stuck. No calls, no vinegar, nothing. I'm a fucking guest in this white thing, and I've got no choice but to sit there and suffer the fate of entertainment. I'm probably supposed to express enthusiasm as well. I scratch my crotch vigorously—the traditional Albanian equivalent of polite appreciation. It only encourages him.

"There's only four stylists," Jerry Lee has said, again and again and again; "and that's Jerry Lee Lewis, Hank Williams, Al Jolson and Jimmie Rodgers. Rest of 'em are just *imitators.*"

The funny thing is, he's probably right. Quaid's imitation—this whole dumb movie, this reduction through play-acting of mythology to mediocrity—underscores the truth of Jerry Lee's vainglorious words. Most of the music in the air underscores it, too: this Muzak-on-the-elevator-to-middle-age that calls itself rock 'n' roll, as if it all wasn't over long before Elvis did the Clam, as if anything sponsored by Budweiser could have any life at all. But what underscores it best are the sound and fury of Jerry Lee Lewis himself.

When Jerry Lee left Sun Records and signed with Smash in September 1963, he was already a has-been, a wraith, at the age of 28. Risen to fame in 1957, fallen to infamy the following year—at a time when infamy did not sell—he was living out the self-fulfilled prophecy of his own damnation, the fate befalling those who, as he saw it, served Satan with their God-given gifts. It was that belief in the sinfulness of his own music, the sinfulness of himself, that set the music aflame with the frenzy of wickedness and the blackness of doom. Like his cousin Jimmy Lee Swaggart, he was a man for whom life had no meaning without the torments of hell.

Like the big 33-LP Bear Family Records set that documents the same years in full, the three volumes of PolyGram's *Killer: The Mercury Years* capture the essence and breadth of that Devil's music. Until the Bear Family set is made available on compact disc (so far, only the 1964 *Live at the Star Club* has been released on CD), this collection will serve the Devil well. This side of the Bear Family set, it brings together more wondrous rotgut country and feral rock 'n' roll than can be had anywhere else.

This is not the Jerry Lee Lewis of boyhood fame, the rock 'n' roll dark angel of the Sun years (chronicled by Bear Family on a 10-CD collection). It is the older Jerry Lee, roaming more wildly and grievously, seeking alternately to redeem himself and destroy himself, succeeding in both.

In the earliest of these recordings ("The Hole He Said He'd Dig for Me," from 1963; "Corrine, Corrina," "Mathilda" and "The Wild Side of Life," from 1965, stand out as the best), he still has the voice. By 1968—"Another Place, Another Time" and "What Made Milwaukee Famous," the country hits that resurrected him 10 years after his fall from grace—that voice has grown fuller and deeper, stronger and rougher: a perfect honky-tonk voice, imbuing the stuff with colors as rare as George Jones's or Lefty Frizzell's.

That voice is given its freest rein then. He transforms Merle Haggard's "Workin' Man Blues" into a thunderstorm anthem of drunkenness; claims "I Get the Blues When It Rains" and "Please Don't Talk About Me When I'm Gone" just as surely as Hank Williams had claimed "Lovesick Blues" from Tin Pan Alley 20 years before. Like the three corpses—Jolson, Rodgers and Williams—in whose company he places himself, Jerry Lee at his best brings together the murky tributaries of American music, black and white, secular and sacred, the ridiculous and the sublime, to create a brave, new and multifariously polluted delta of his own. Like them, he illuminates originality's heart of theft.

His brilliance at the piano follows a similar course, growing lusher and more severe in turns. By the time he recorded "Honky Tonk Wine," in the summer of 1973, the keyboard was no longer enough; he played the lid as well. This is the Jerry Lee Lewis with whom Thelonious Monk should have been placed in a studio, the Jerry Lee whom no amount of gross Nashville overproduction could turn to pap (and whom Nashville in the end therefore regurgitated).

Then, before long—"Haunted House" and "Born to Be a Loser" from the remarkable 1973 Memphis sessions; "The House of Blue Lights" and "I Can Help" from 1975; "Ivory Tears" from 1977—that voice becomes a distillation of grave-dirt, whiskey and lamb's blood: no longer just the Devil's music, but the Devil's voice as well. In many ways, these wails and growls from the abyss of the last days, these lamentations, are the most enduring of all.

A recent issue of the ever-enlightening *Globe* carried a story called "Why I Didn't Have Sex with Lisa Marie Presley." In it, Jerry Lee, looking in the accompanying photo like some student mortician's horrendous mistake, declares: "What worries me is that when I get to the Pearly Gates and they look at the things I've done in my life, what are they going to say? That's my number one worry."

This music reflects that wrenching eschatological concern, baring a soul torn by those eternal talons—heaven, hell and Lisa Marie Presley's brassiere—by which we rise or fall, conquer or are conquered.

# 70

# Miles Davis:
# The Hat Makes the Man

The word itself is deadening: *art*, a devalued dollar of a word, no longer backed by meaning, as drained of worth as the politician's *viability*, or the sportscaster's *awesome*. And yet we have no other, which only goes to show how little the stuff has served us. We've lost the dual sense of straightforward work and inspiration entwined in the Greek *techne* (lost to technology) and the Roman *ars*, and we've been left with something that has devolved into a euphemism for pretension, a silly syllable more suitable as a first name for a Linkletter or a Garfunkel than as a descriptive of creative power. Ours is an age in which phrases such as "the advertising arts" are uttered in earnest, in which pop singers speak of themselves as artists, in which the *poiesis* of Homer has been replaced by that of Jimmy Stewart. This was Andy Warhol's genius—to distill these twentieth-century sensibilities into an essence, to see the muses as the fast-food cashiers they were, to give us Art™ that went better with Coke. Like the old stuff, his art was honest. That great delusive folly of critics and scholars, the rubric of hidden meanings, like the eleven secret herbs and spices concealed in Colonel Sanders's fried chicken, served well as an advertising gimmick.

Of course, the gimmick is necessary. Art, like every other racket, needs it to survive. Like the spaghetti-joint owner who repackages his joint as a *ristorante*, the artist who wraps his wares in the pretensions of "his vision" wisely maximizes profits. It need not be anything new. Point-of-sale vision is a matter of style, and the usual sun-dried tomatoes and buffalo mozzarella should suffice.

But when style subsumes substance in art, when the designer-vision logo is given greater care than the thing itself, when the package becomes the product—in short, when art speaks its own name—that art is dead. Like dead flesh in freezer bins, it is often then in its most marketable state; but it has ceased to breathe, ceased to grow. The one thing it has over dead meat is that it keeps forever. We fill museums with the stuff and call it culture.

Rock 'n' roll, which once was junk—the best of it still is—now is regarded as art, collected and tended to by curators and archivists, taken seriously by those with a tendency to seriously take. We imbue with dignity that which in its purest spirit is anti-dignity, shriving ourselves like penitents of the intellect to redeem our souls from pleasure for its own sake. Rock 'n' roll, because its substance was as wild as its style, once was viewed as a threat to society. Now that it has been preened and cultivated—defanged, really—into a stylized pose of calculated but idle threat, society has given rock 'n' roll its imprimatur. Rock 'n' roll has become George Michael, so darlingly dangerous, shaving punctiliously to appear unshaven. In other words, art.

Long before rock 'n' roll fell victim to art, jazz met a similar fate. It was in the early 1930's that French aficionados such as Hugues Panassié and Charles Delaunay began taking seriously *le jazz hot*. Their Hot Club de France, formed in 1932, was the beginning of the cult of America that has since thrived in France, leading the world to a fuller intellectual understanding of all manner of things American, from the genius of Jerry Lewis to the existentialism of burlesque. Indeed, the cult movement that led to the likes of Denys Chevalier's *Métaphysique du Strip-tease,* in 1960, can be traced directly to the Paris publication, in 1934, of Panassié's *Le Jazz Hot.* But jazz refused to stay the same, refused to die. When bebop developed in the next decade, Panassié denounced it as a degeneration of *le vrai jazz.* Meanwhile, in its native land, bebop brought jazz the sort of intellectual attention it had gotten in France.

The bebop musicians were a new breed. There was an intensity about them as they performed, as if they cared not so much for entertaining others as for expressing themselves. The pose of the showman was replaced by that of the possessed and self-absorbed artist; the model of Duke Ellington's elegant professionalism, by Charlie Parker's tortured abandon. Of course, most musicians fell far shy of either Ellington's or Parker's brilliance. But by the summer of 1946, when Parker recorded his magnificent "Lover Man," jazz was as much about mystique as about music. Those musicians who cultivated that mystique, that aura of the serious artist, would define jazz and the concept of hip in the decades to come. Those who did not—Louis Jordan, Wynonie Harris, and others—no less creative, no less talented, would develop the fine, new music that eventually came to be called rock 'n' roll. (Jordan's hit "Choo Choo Ch'Boogie," from that same summer of 1946, is, in its way, as important as Parker's "Lover Man.")

Parker died young, in 1955, thus qualifying for admission to the tragic-genius pantheon of American mythology, right behind new inductee Hank Williams. By then, twenty-eight-year-old Miles Davis, who almost a decade before had replaced trumpeter Dizzy Gillespie in Parker's band, had eclipsed those mentors as the avatar of hip. His *Birth of the Cool,* recorded in 1949–50, was exactly that; and through the fifties, Davis was the watershed separating the hip from the square, the cool from the uncool.

More than any other jazz figure (one always had the impression that the oblique eccentricities of Thelonious Monk were natural), Davis seemed aware of the importance of packaging. Balancing substance and style expertly, he played hip to the hilt. He did not merely close his eyes to his audience as if transported by his art; he turned his back to them, a new essence of cool, as if they were not there. His music, the best and the worst of it, possessed the sound of brooding pensiveness, the sound of cool. Offstage, he wore that air of brooding pensiveness, that cool, like a stole: aloof, taciturn, unapproachable, vaguely angry, he brought new dimension to the gimmick of vision, implying ineffability through silence. Four books written about him failed to reveal much of what lay beneath the persona. Now we have his own book.

"For me, music and life are all about style," Davis says, striking a note of plain truth toward the end of *Miles: The Autobiography*, written in collaboration with Quincy Troupe. It is a statement that one would expect to find rather at the outset, where, instead one encounters the observation that, "Looking back, I don't remember much of my first years—I never liked to look back much anyway," a rather disheartening note on which to begin an autobiography. "Seems like," however, "I remember something about" a tornado: "that tornado left some of its violent creativity in me. . . . I do believe in mystery and the supernatural and a tornado sure enough is mysterious *and* supernatural." Sure enough, indeed.

The credo of style runs clear throughout. "I was buying myself some hip Brooks Brothers suits. I had myself a new horn," he recalls of his last days in St. Louis, tellingly placing the clothes before the trumpet. Arriving in New York ("in September 1944, not in 1945 like a lot of jive writers who write about me say"), Davis "saved up . . . and bought me a gray, big-shouldered suit." Later, riding high, the suits are Italian, custom-made: "I remember one night I was so clean that I was looking in the mirror admiring myself" before a performance; "I felt so good that I walked to the door and forgot my trumpet." In the late sixties, "I started wearing African dashikis and robes." There is a shop in London and "a guy there named Andy who in one night could make you the hippest pair of shoes you could imagine."

Beyond these sartorial superficialities, Davis seems to have served up shrewdly more the autobiography of the persona than the person. While describing his brother as a homosexual, Davis presents us with sexual memoirs that seem designed to dispel the rumors of his own homosexuality. As if believing that men strike women out of a sense of virile sovereignty rather than impotence, he boasts of beating his wives. "That was the first time I had hit her—though it wouldn't be the last," he says of one; "I just slapped the shit out of her," he says of another. He revels in the role of the pimp. "At one time, I had a whole stable of bitches out on the street for me," he claims. "I had other girls, too, that gave me money, a whole stable of them." From 1975 to 1980, his well-publicized period of self-exile, "I had a few rich white ladies who saw to it that I didn't want for money. . . . I had so many different women during this period that I lost track of most of them and don't even remember their names."

He seems intent as well on establishing his blackness. Though the man he considers his best friend, Gil Evans, was white, he sees the ogre of the "racist, white motherfucker" everywhere, especially in the recording industry. "Everyone knows that Chuck Berry started the shit, not Elvis," he says of rock 'n' roll, trying to illustrate the exploitation of blacks by whites. But Elvis came before Chuck Berry, and, in any case, both only took from those who came before. There is a forced blackness in lines such as "didn't want to hear no dumb shit off nobody" and "we didn't have to get no divorce," which strike as calculated to have us forget that Davis is the privileged, Juilliard-educated son of a successful dentist and candidate for the Illinois legislature. The arch "Later" with which he ends his account seems as ill-suiting as the jheri curls and parachute pants he now sports.

He is disdainful of the new avant-garde—Ornette Coleman, Don Cherry, and Eric Dolphy—whose 1962 *Free Jazz* marked the beginning of a new jazz-as-art era. He is disdainful, indeed, of anything new of which he is not at the center. He has much to say about the John Coltrane who played in Miles Davis's band; nothing to say about the Coltrane who reached his heights later with *Crescent* and *Meditations*. Wynton Marsalis is upbraided for "saying things—nasty, disrespectful things—about me." He dismisses the work of classical musicians, "especially if they're black," as "robot shit," but, in justifying his own recent work, explains that, "the drum machine is good because you can always take what it plays in one place and put it in another place because it always keeps the same tempo." Prince, we are told, "can be the new Duke Ellington of our time." (Could it be any coincidence that Prince also "said he wanted to do an entire album with me"? Davis dreams—his records for years have been an attempt in part to fulfill the dream—of a new music fusing high jazz and street-level R&B. It was a dream that didn't work for Archie Shepp, who tried it in 1970 on recordings such as "Stick 'Em Up." It is a dream that can never work, for, since their parting in the forties, the two musics have become oil and water. If and when it does work, modern R&B then will have passed from entropy to art.)

*Miles: The Autobiography* leaves one wondering what, if anything, lies beneath the butch posturings, the dashiki of black anger, the peevishness of an innovator growing old among the inevitable innovations of others. His fine old music stands on its own, apart from any of this. It always will. Let art and a good dry-cleaner have the rest.

# 71

# James Douglas Morrison, 1943–1971

Jersey City, June 1968. "Hello, I Love You." I remember not only where I was but also whom I was with when it came through the balmy early-summer air like the resurrection gust of Enyalios.

That's right: Enyalios. I knew the Doors, but I didn't then know of Enyalios. He was, I later found out, an ancient, forgotten god of destruction, a god whose name had lain hidden on clay tablets in Knossos from the second millennium B.C. until the turn of this century. The name had gone unuttered until the decipherment by Michael Ventris—just fifteen or so years before that summer of 1968—of the hermetic script, Mycenaean Linear B, that harbored it. Soon, just a few months after "Hello, I Love You," the publication of Charles Olson's *Maximus Poems IV, V, VI* would evoke the god as Enyalion, summoning the full force of the word power that seemed to tie the archaic Greek *Enyalios* of Linear B with the classical Greek *anileon* ("merciless"), the Latin *ad nihil* ("to" + "nothing") and *annihilare* ("to render unto nothingness"), and our own *annihilate*.

As I said, I didn't know any of this back then; and I didn't care, either. All I was concerned with on that June day—there were three of us—was ditching the guy and making the girl. I got lucky. But I really don't remember that part. What I remember is that gust of annihilation that in two minutes and fourteen seconds destroyed and delivered us from the utter bullshit that had been the sixties. We were free again, those of us who did not stink of patchouli, believe in the family of man, or eat macrobiotic gruel; those of us who found god—he dressed well—through smack, preferred our sex dirty, and supported our boys in Vietnam because it meant a surplus of left-behind pussy on the home front.

Of course, Morrison and the Doors had been instrumental to what was now being annihilated. The summer of 1967, the Summer of Love—was it *Time* magazine's phrase, was it Timothy Leary's, was there any difference, really?—had also been the summer of "Light My Fire." Jim Morrison became to rock 'n' roll the embodiment of every romantic pretension, from Rimbaud to shamanism, that its consumers, in those days of innocence, held so dear. It soon became apparent, however, that Jim Morrison, his figure ever darker and more estranged, wasn't only writing and singing rock 'n' roll songs but was also trying to vanquish his demons and curses by invoking new demons and curses. "I am the Lizard King. I can do anything," he had the strange, young nerve to say and believe.

"Light My Fire," the beckoning, the seduction, and "Hello, I Love You," the banishing—the only Doors songs to become number-one hits—were separated by a year. It happened that fast. The romanticism of "Light My Fire" had enthralled, but the death's-head within that flaming, Augustinian heart, that equation of love and the funeral pyre, went unheeded. Its singer was likened to Apollo and, as his excesses became legendary, to Dionysus—when in fact a more fitting, albeit equally callow, comparison might have been made, if not to obscure Enyalios himself, then to Apollyon, the Destroyer, the angel of the bottomless pit, "that old serpent" of Revelation 20:1. ("Ride the snake. He's old, and his skin is cold." Morrison, in "The End," would give those words the air of an elusive ancestral memory emerging from blackness to consciousness.)

"The Beatles' spiritual teacher speaks to the youth of the world on love and the untapped source of power that lies within," hawked the full-page advertisement in *Billboard* for the album by Maharishi Mahesh Yogi. That was in April 1968. The whole vast noisome toilet bowl of love, peace, and direct-marketing ahimsa was overflowing all over the fucking place. So, it was love they wanted. Love was all they needed. Well, that summer, Morrison delivered it, nasty and impersonal—"Hello, I love you, won't you tell me your name?"—like a cold hard blue-veined cock right up under the tie-dyed skirts of benighted sensitivity.

Morrison and the Doors, significantly, were absent at that great New Age Rotarian convocation in the sticks known as Woodstock. His and the band's success had waned steadily since "Hello, I Love You." It was over, in a way. Morrison had put the spirit of the sixties out of its misery. But he seemed unable to put himself out of his own misery.

What he wanted more than anything—more than fame, more than wealth, more than the wet genital submission that those things brought—was to be taken seriously as a poet. But he was too full of lingering youth, too unfinished to sense how little he knew about the job of turning a vision into meaningful words and rhythms. The Doors' most ambitious work was often their worst. Trying to make of rock 'n' roll something it could never, should never be, Morrison often seemed a pompous fool rather than the intrepid seer he fancied himself. With dark messianic urgency, in both his songs and his verse, he delivered images and ideas that sometimes were trite unto embarrassment. In *An American Prayer*, the little volume of poetry he published in 1970, he asked, affectedly forsaking any question mark, "Do you know we are ruled by TV." We may be surprised by the banality of those words, or by their arrogance, but we aren't surprised by the fact that a vanity press published them.

But Morrison's boyish failings efface neither the sporadic, gestating beauty of his vision and talent nor the frustratingly immense promise of what might have been. He and the Doors, in their four, fast years in the world's eye, made a music unlike any other, and that music was more often brilliant than not. "Roadhouse Blues," with its wonderful kiss-off to all epistemology ("I woke up this morning and got myself a beer/The future's uncertain, the end is always near"), especially in the immediacy of the concert version recorded during the 1969–1970 *Absolutely Live* tour, remains by itself a solid enough plinth for rock 'n' roll immortality to rest upon.

Had Morrison lived, that immense promise likely might have been fulfilled, and he likely might have got what he wanted. But he died at the age of twenty-seven—the same age at which, in 1913, Ezra Pound (who had also been a vanity-press poet) declared: "Most important poetry has been written by men over thirty."

It's difficult not to view as entwined serpents the obsessions at the heart of Morrison's vision and the shortcut he took to the grave. Those obsessions—common to all, but in him overriding—were sex and death; and, while he wore the uraeus of those obsessions well and always, he looked upon them as impenetrable enemies lying within. The wedding-in-song of love and the funeral pyre could be perceived as a comely lyrical conceit in the summer of 1967. But by the end, libido and death wish were one, inseparable.

There were lines in the poem "An American Prayer" that overwhelmed its failings and illuminated its black-diamond glintings and the magnitude of its promise. But in that illumination lay a dire shadowing. As if betrothing himself to death, Morrison, annihilation's fair boy, sees her as "pale & wanton thrillful." Toward the poem's close, he says, with an almost Miltonic metrical precision: "Death makes angels of us all/& gives us wings." In "Lament for the Death of my Cock," recorded on his final birthday, December 8, 1970—it seemed more a day of mourning than of celebration—Morrison declares: "Death and my cock are the world." Ultimately, libido itself succumbs: ". . . I sacrifice my cock on the altar of silence." And silence came.

For once looking—backward maybe, it now might seem—toward life, Morrison says with quiet resolution in "Lament": "Words got me the wound and will get me well." But a few months later, he was dead, and that was that. America loves the self-killed, the notches in lurid tragedy's gun; and Jim Morrison in death has been raised to the realm of the mythic through media grave robbers and their patrons. What he might have become is something that we can never know. What we can be assured of is that the glimmerings and bursts of that possibility, that promise, are enough to grant his legacy a place outside the junkyard of unrenowned obscurity where most rock 'n' roll and poetry alike come justly in the end to decompose.

If only he could have conquered that Lady Death who "makes angels of us all," if only he had hurled her into the dirt the way he fucked the sixties into the dirt, maybe he would still be around. But, then again—enough fancy talk, enough shuck-and-jive—it's like the man says: Better him than us. Shoot the shaman and pass the pastafazool.

# 72

# The Singer Madonna
# Arraigned by the Ghost of
# Pope Alexander VI

—You don't suck cock, is that true?

—That's true.

—Well, then, my dear, what good are you?

—I loosen the limbs and free the souls of the masses.

—You're thirty-three now, the age at which Christ died; is that true?

—That's true.

—Would you suck His cock?

—Yes.

—Even if He didn't buy your records? Even if He damned you as He spent Himself?

—Yes.

—So, you would render unto Christ what you deny Warren Beatty?

—Absolutely.

—You're thirty-three now, the age at which Ethel Merman recorded "Move It Over"; is that true?

—That's true.

—Do you see yourself following in her footsteps, clinging to a delusion of eternal youth while rotting shamelessly in public like so much over mascara'd carrion?

—My youth is not eternal.

—Your youth is behind you. Soon your child-bearing years shall be behind you as well. Having given yourself neither to maternity nor fellatio, you shall wither and be dust.

—I think you envy me my wealth and worldly glory.

—In my day I had more than you. And I did not have to prance about with a troupe of fag dancers to get it. I got mine the old-fashioned way: I seized it.

—But you went to hell for it. I'll go to heaven.

—Perhaps.

—Yes, perhaps.

—Ethel's there, you know, singing still: *There's no business like show business, there's no business I know* . . .

—Please!

—She and Dante. It never ends. On a good day you can hear them both: "I Gotta Be Me" and *terza rima*. You do have lovely skin.

—Thank you.

—My daughter had lovely skin.

—Did you fuck her?

—Only in the ass.

—That's another thing I don't do.

# 73

Lester Bangs, with whom I had drunk but whose writing I had never read, had died not long after *Hellfire* came out, in the spring of 1982. I remember him standing in my little apartment, holding *Hellfire* in his hands, looking down at it, saying "This is, like, a real book."

After he died, Bob Duncan, a neighbor in his building, told me that when he stuck his head into Lester's apartment to see Lester sprawled out dead on his couch, "What scared me was I had seen him look a lot worse." The next morning, Bob had headed out to buy beer, only to find the hall outside Lester's door blocked by a web of yellow police tape. "He's dead and he's still a pain in the ass," he said.

I don't remember hearing anything as fine as Duncan's lines at the Tribute to Lester Bangs that the Poetry Project held at St. Mark's, in the spring of 1992, to mark the tenth anniversary of Lester's death. My own contribution was a slightly rewritten version of a remembrance of Lester that I had originally published in the magazine *Chemical Imbalance* three and a half years before. What I read that night at St. Mark's was, again slightly rewritten, and annotated, subsequently privately printed in an edition of ten. It is the privately printed text that appears here.

# Lester

*Lester recorded an album in Austin, Texas, in December 1980. It was released the follow-ing September,[1] about seven months before he died. Somewhere along the line, he asked me to write the liner notes. This is what I gave him:*

Mr. L.C. Bangs, in a pair of sharkskin britches that once belonged to the Holy Ghost, walks down the length of the bar. He's carrying a little black bag, the kind they don't make anymore. He sets it down and reaches in, feels around: Johnny Ace's .38, Louis Prima's silver mouthpiece, Miss Audrey Williams's intra-uterine device wrought from the copper cuirass of love-slain Agamemnon. An Antibuse prescription bearing the last will and testament of Six-Cylinder Smith. Postcards from heaven. Decals from hell. Bumper stickers bearing the name of a future mayor of El Cajon. A faded Polaroid shot of She-Who-Sucks-in-a-Skirt-of-Snakes, taken two days before the operation.

He pulls something from the bag and smiles. The City of Dreadful Night smiles back. The three-card-monte dealers look up from their crates and call out their re-quests. One wants to hear the theme song from "The Brady Bunch," but nobody pays him any mind. He's sick, see.

*And there's a little story behind those liner notes that says something—about Lester, or me, or both of us; I don't know. What happened was, a few years before, in late 1976 or so, I had written liner notes for an album[2] by my buddy Delbert McClinton. They had ended up not being used; and they were still lying around. So I substituted Lester's name for Del-bert's, substituted Lester's hometown of El Cajon for Delbert's hometown of Fort Worth; and I gave them to Lester.*

*They suited him perfectly, he said; I really understood what he was all about.*

．　　．　　．

Lester and I met in early 1971, right after he had moved from California to Walled Lake, Michigan, to work for *Creem* magazine. I was hacking out a living as a paste-up man for the Lovable Underwear Company at 200 Madison Avenue, and I was writing on the side. He called me one night and asked me to write for *Creem*. By the time we encountered each another in the flesh, later that year at a party on Long Island for the Blue Öyster Cult, I was on the verge of quitting my job at the underwear company, which I did in January 1972.

Lester visited New York again in February and March of that year, and it was then that we began to get acquainted. We had a few things in common: Neither of us had college degrees to fall back on, and we were both drunks.

But, in more ways, we were oil and water. For the most part, we didn't like the same books, the same music, the same dope, or the same codependent cuties. My buddy Richard Meltzer and I spent a lot of time, it seemed, trying to shake the hayseeds out of Lester's head. One night, at a White Rose bar on Broadway, I picked Lester's pocket and then lent him his own money for cabfare.

One morning, the hayseeds were literal. He showed up at my door after waking up on a subway car not knowing where he had been all night, and there were strands of actual hay sticking out of his hair.

He drank brandy with red-wine chasers. There was a dinner party once at somebody's place on Jane Street. Lester arrived bearing a bottle of Ornical cough medicine. "This is the good stuff; you can only get this in Canada," he explained, as if he were one of those *cafones* praising the noble character and fine bouquet of some rare regional vintage.

On another night, he and Richard and I ended up getting drunk and sniffing lighter-fluid at Richard's place on Perry Street. There was a shoebox of antique postcards that someone had given Richard, and, in our drunken folly, we began inscribing them with cryptic messages and incomprehensible addresses, our fleeting whimsy being to gum up the local postal system on the following day. Suddenly, as Richard's and my dumb enthusiasm began to flag, it occurred to Lester that what we were doing was not merely having a bit of stupid intoxicated fun, but rather producing literature of no mean worth. "This is great stuff," he announced, his eyes widening in that rapt expression of lunatic epiphany that I would come to know so well. He went to Richard's IBM Selectric and began transcribing what we had scribbled. Richard and I could not decipher what we ourselves had scrawled just a while before, but the backs of those postcards made perfect sense to Lester. We looked on in bewilderment as he typed away, and listened likewise as he explained to us that he was going to sell the finished product to *Esquire,* and that we would split the loot three ways. As dawn approached and our yawning began to surpass our drinking, Lester finished his task and presented it to us, his coauthors. Consonants and vowels crowded the pages in scrambled configurations, like bugs escaping from a Linear-B Roach Motel. "Pretty good, huh?" he said.[3]

Such was Lester Conway Bangs in the thralldom of his most driving compulsion: the compulsion to write. He wrote more than anybody I have ever known. He could write endlessly, it seemed, on any given subject. The subject hardly mattered, really. The sound and fury of heavy metal, which he helped to put on the map, had its literary counterpart in his writing. "I can't understand poetry," he said to me one day as we were walking down Bleecker Street. It was sort of like, "My wife doesn't understand me." He wasn't talking about scansion, about the hard iambic and anapestic boiler-room of it; he was talking about the idea of it. "You either like it or you don't," I told him; "that's all there is to it." One of those poets I had never much read, William Wordsworth, said that the essence of poetry was "emotion recollected in tranquility." Maybe that was Lester's problem: There was no tranquility.

But if tranquility and poetry escaped him, sound and fury did not. He was always ranting and raving about something or other; and if he couldn't get a handle on Dante's vision of hell, he had no trouble at all with Ozzy Osbourne's. Just look at the waves and waves of all that wild, frothing stuff he wrote for *Creem* back through 1975. He could literally write a book in a few nights' time. Neither drunkenness nor narcosis hampered the compulsion to write. Rather, it intensified it. He would telephone in the middle of the night and read—to whomever he could reach; the identity of the victim did not much matter—one long manuscript or another that he had just completed; then, in the morning, he would remember neither having written it nor having made the call.

Lester's other great obsession was rock 'n' roll. I think he actually loved it. The most striking evidence of that obsessive love was not the reams he wrote about rock 'n' roll, not his band, Birdland, or the records he made,[4] but the way in which he privately held rock 'n' roll so dear. I remember one time—about the time of the postcards—when Lester spent the night at my place on Ninety-ninth Street and Riverside. (*Creem* or a record company usually provided him with hotel accommodations in New York, but he always preferred staying at somebody's apartment, since he couldn't stand to be alone.) I left him on the couch and went to bed. After a while, the sound of Little Richard roused me. I went into the living-room to tell Lester to turn it down, and I found that the noise wasn't coming from the speakers but from the earphones that Lester was wearing, volume turned to the maximum. And there lay Lester, sound asleep, snoring away in blessed peace.

Even more indicative was the night the apartment near his caught fire. (This was when he was living at his last worldly address, 542 Sixth Avenue, just north of Fourteenth Street here in New York, where he had moved after a falling-out with Barry Kramer at *Creem*, in the latter part of 1976.[5]) On that fiery night—I think it was the winter of 1980—when the firemen came through his window with their axes, warning him that the flames were near and that he should make a run for it, what among all his possessions did Lester choose to save along with himself? The Public Image Ltd. film-can album.

The obsessions with writing and music, of course, were only symptoms of a greater, deeper thing. Through writing, through music, Lester sought communication. He had questions and he wanted answers. Beneath all the new-wave bad-boy infamy, he was Paul Anka's "Lonely Boy," an innocent, a country bumpkin in the big city, an El Cajon wallflower transported by the miracle of Ornical and bourbon to stage-center at C.B.G.B. He was a romantic in the gravest, saddest, best, and most ridiculous sense of that worn-out word. He couldn't merely go to bed with a woman; he had to fall in love with her. He couldn't merely dislike something; he had to rail and rage against it. None of it was real, but, in the end, the phantoms of all that crazy love and anger, since they weren't his to command, conquered him.

The sad part of it was that he was beginning to wise up when the end came. After finally emerging late in 1981 from what seemed to be his last major toxic-psychotic go-round,[6] he was calmer and starting to see that amphetamine madness and drunken love were not staffs of life. Two of the more unnerving aspects of Lester's personality had always been that, one, he didn't like to eat, and, two, he never laughed at a joke. These, in anyone, are deathward ways. Toward the end, though, he was starting to smile, if not actually laugh, at the big joke at the heart of it all, and he was expressing an interest in eating. These may not sound like earth-shaking developments, but, then again, maybe you didn't know Lester.

There were intimations of mortality. He was sick of people sucking up to him to bask in his notoriety. "I'm just a big fish in a little pond," he said; and he was starting to see that this was just another hick town in a one-horse universe. He wanted to go to Mexico and write what he called "a real book."

The last time I saw him—there were a lot of phone calls after this—was on the night of February 10, 1982. He and I and a woman we knew went to eat at a Hindoo joint on Carmine Street. During dinner, we began talking about drinking. Lester was on the wagon. He began interrogating our companion, who was sipping a glass of wine, asking her how she could possibly be satisfied by that mere glass of wine.

"Don't you want oblivion?" he asked, in all sincerity and earnest.

A few weeks later, he found it. It was a Friday night, April 30. I was lying on a couch watching a bad movie. The phone rang. That was that: Lester Conway Bangs, 1948–1982. Like the man says: *Requiescat.*[7]

Lester Bangs, rock writer, is dead at 33.

After it was all over, I began wondering. It was, of course, the dope and the booze. But what else? "He died because he had a kind heart," somebody said. I laughed in her face. But I didn't laugh long. "The graveyard's full of nice guys." I had heard that phrase more than once, but I had never stopped to see through those hard words to the literal truth of them. And that, really, was what it all came down to: he was a nice guy.

## Notes

*Read at A Tribute to Lester Bangs, The Poetry Project, Church of St. Mark's in-the-Bowerie, May 15, 1992.*

1. Lester Bangs and the Delinquents. *Jook Savages on the Brazos* (Live Wire LW-3, 1981). Liner notes copyright © 1981, 1992 by Nick Tosches.

2. Delbert McClinton. *Love Rustler* (ABC AB-991, 1977).

3. Part of Lester's transcription of our postcards was published, not in *Esquire* but in the second issue of Richard Meltzer's short-lived magazine, *Ajax* (Summer 1972).

4. The Birdland EP (1977); *Jook Savages on the Brazos* (1981). Lester's 1980 version of the Velvet Underground's "Sister Ray" was released on a flexi-disc insert EP in *Throat Culture* No. 2 (1990).

5. By then, Richard Meltzer was living in Los Angeles and I had just moved to Nashville. I moved back to New York in April 1978.

6. Sometime before his birthday, December 14.

7. Friday, April 30, 1982, the eve of the Kentucky Derby, was a beautiful spring day. I had gone that afternoon with my buddies Frank Fortunato and Steve Kraus to see some sleazy picture called *Amin: the Rise and Fall*, after which we had walked downtown from Times Square to the Village. They went drinking, and I went home. I fell asleep on my couch at about eight that night, and I woke up around ten, with *The One and Only* on Channel 7. John Morthland called me at about half past ten and told me Lester was dead. For some reason, the full impact of Lester's death didn't hit me until the following Monday night, when sadness turned to dark anxiety. His remains were cremated, as he had said he wanted them to be, and there was a small wake of sorts on the Tuesday morning of May 4, at Redden's Funeral Home on Fourteenth Street. His ashes were late getting there from the crematorium in Jersey.

## Recommended Reading

Anderson, Roger. "Growing Up with Lester." *Throat Culture*, No. 2 (1990). Junior-high and high-school memories of Lester.

Bangs, Lester. "Bye Bye, Sidney, Be Good." *Throat Culture*, No. 2 (1990). Written in 1979; a rumination on death, inspired by the demise of Sid Vicious, interwoven with autobiographical loomings.

Bangs, Lester. *Psychotic Reactions and Carburetor Dung.* Edited by Greil Marcus (New York: Knopf, 1987).

DeRogatis, Jim. "Lester Bangs Remembered: The Final Interview." *Throat Culture*, No. 2 (1990). An interview with Lester done sixteen days before his death.

Meltzer, Richard. "Goodbye Porkpie Cravat." *17 Insects Can Die in Your Heart* (Los Angeles: Ouija Madness Press, 1982). Poem.

Meltzer, Richard. "Lester Bangs Recollected in Tranquility." *Throat Culture*, No. 2 (1990). The best piece on Lester yet written.

Meltzer, Richard, and Tosches, Nick. "Richard Meltzer and Nick Tosches Shoot the Shit." *Throat Culture*, No. 2 (1990).

Obituary (Bangs). *New York Times*, May 2, 1992.

Patoski, Joe Nick. "Joe Nick Remembers." *Throat Culture*, No. 2 (1990).

# 74

Weeks after the publication of *Cut Numbers,* I signed a deal with Doubleday to write a book about Dean Martin, who was the last living person who intrigued me enough to write a book about.

As it evolved, the book became more of a history of the Italian-American century as told through the figure of Dean Martin in the foreground. It was the hardest book, in terms of research, that I had written, for the worlds through which Dean Martin had moved, ever a stranger to those around him and at times even to himself, were as labyrinthine as, and spanned more cultures and time than, those through which Michele Sindona had moved. It was the first book I wrote using a computer, which helped, though I still typed as now, with only one finger, the index finger of my right hand.

*Dino* was published in the summer of 1992, as my father was dying. For years, he had busted my ass: "You keep dedicating these books to these broads. When are you gonna throw your old man a bone?" I dedicated *Dino* to him—it seemed the right one—and he lived to have the first copy, which came in time for Father's Day, not long before he died.

# Excerpt from *Dino*

It was like the guys from the other side used to say: *La vecchiaia è carogna.* They were right: Old age is carrion.

He was only fifty-four; he would turn fifty-five a month from this day. But he felt like an old man, like the carrion those old men spoke of in those days of shadow and sunlight; felt as if he had skulked and staggered and stridden through three lifetimes, been wrung and wracked and worn down by them. Sometimes those days of shadow and sunlight returned to him. They brought a calmness laced with chill, like nighttime pond-water in the woods of a dream; and the voices of the old men from those days came too, like haunted breezes rippling across that dream-pond. But more often, as time passed, nothing came, nothing returned to him, and the chill calm and the haunted breezes, silent and voiceless, seemed to emanate not so much from the remembered days, from the shadow and sunlight of memory, but from some farther place, beyond where the shadows deepened and the sunlight dwindled to blackness; from some forbidding but mesmerizing thing, some final dark seduction: dread, death's inkling, swathed in lullaby. He could feel it now, standing there alone with nothing inside him. He muttered the words aloud: *"La vecchiaia è carogna."*

He raised his eyes, squinted into the desert sky, which had no color and was only a vast empty glare. He saw them up there, big and black, flapping in dirge against the glare. He snorted a bleak, bitter ghost of a laugh.

It was May 7, 1972, and he was in a place called Chama, in northern New Mexico; slouched there, in the middle of nowhere, wearing a toy gun and dolled up like Giovanni Mack Brown; stuck there, in the middle of nowhere, fifty-something years old, playing cowboy with fucking Rock Hudson; stuck there, in the middle of nowhere, like a fucking *cafone*, wondering why, after more than twenty-one years of marriage, he was throwing away his wife for a twenty-four-year-old piece of ass whose lies he didn't even believe; wondering what the fuck he was doing there, for a lousy twenty-five grand a week when he had more millions than he could ever live to spend; wondering what the fuck he had been doing all these years.

Fuck the twenty-five grand a week. Fuck the cowboy hat and the cap pistol. Fuck all this shit. It was time to go home, wherever in hell that was.

He closed his eyes, feeling that dark seduction, that inkling, like the reverberation of a tolling in emptiness. The sunlight had never even been real. He had imagined it. The sky of the old days had been a sulfurous pall. The shadows had been real, the sunlight dreamt. He saw himself, half a century ago—a vanished breath ago, three lifetimes ago; it was all the same, improbable and without meaning—moving through them, the shadows and the sunlight. The toy gun and the cowboy hat had suited him well then. He was, after all, Tom Mix, *nevvero?* And this was, after all, *l'America.*

## II. Dreamland

The funhouse was a vast and wonderful place of imaginings and greed. One entered for a nickel, the twentieth part of a dollar. Even in this century, the painted face of the laughing man on the great western wall, faded and excoriated by the seasons of a century and more, could still be discerned: the slick black hair parted in the middle; the eyes wide and transfixed as if in the throes of an ecstasy more terrible in its emptiness and endlessness than agony; the thin-lipped, rollicking cancerous grin of metastatic delights.

> *"And the worst part of it, Amos, 's Sapphire thinks it's culture."*
> —KINGFISH STEVENS

Italians built the first opera house in America, with money raised among them by Lorenzo Da Ponte. In Europe, where he had been an acquaintance of the elderly Casanova, Da Ponte had written librettos for Mozart's *Le Nozze di Figaro, Don Giovanni,* and *Così Fan Tutte;* and in America he taught the poetry of Dante at Columbia University, where he held the school's first, nonpaying professorship of Italian literature. Like most of those who came to America from Italy before the last part of the nineteenth century, he was a northerner, a Venetian Jew who converted to Catholicism. His Italian Opera House, which opened in downtown New York in the autumn of 1833 with Rossini's *La Gazza Ladra,* was a great failure, and was abandoned after eight months and a loss of nearly $30,000. Da Ponte died broke in New York in the summer of 1838. That was the year Alexis de Tocqueville's *Democracy in America* first appeared in an American edition. "In aristocracies," Tocqueville observed, "a few great pictures are produced; in democratic countries, a vast number of insignificant ones. In the former, statues are raised of bronze; in the latter, they are modelled in plaster."

Henry James foresaw in 1886 a coming "reign of mediocrity." But the world that James portrayed with such brilliant elegance was already decaying around him. The reign of mediocrity, democracy's flowering, had come. America respected James; but respect is cheap, and she did not buy his books. She bought Mark Twain's. His sentiments lent eloquence to feelings that long had been held back in diffidence. It was Twain's mockery of the classical European store of culture in *The Innocents Abroad* that established him in 1869; established him not merely as a writer but also, among those not given to books, as an entertainer, a vindicator of the mob's cultural suffrage.

But it was neither Twain nor James who was the voice of the age, but rather Johnson—George Washington Johnson, the Whistling Coon, the ex-slave who became America's first recording star. For the first time, a common man achieved fame, a fame greater than Twain's, greater by far than James's, a fame won through the supremely democratic art of whistling. The centuries of quarrying rock and hammering gold for the glory of gods and men were ended. Carrara marble gave way to linoleum, granite to concrete and Sheetrock. All was transitory, nothing built to endure. Eternity ceded to the moment, as gold to plastic.

It was what democracy had wrought. As the fate of Lorenzo Da Ponte's opera house showed, it was not edification the child sovereign craved. It was entertainment. *Panem et circenses:* bread and circuses. These, Juvenal had decried at the turn of the second century, were all that his fellow Romans had come to care about. The mobs had forsaken the glory and beauty of Catullus and Virgil, Horace and Propertius; had let tragedy and comedy perish of neglect, giving over the theaters to crass pantomime and farce. Young, thriving America, with no past, no Virgil or Horace to detain her course, was by nature from the womb a land of bread and circuses.

The culture of the American gentry—that is, the culture of Europe which it appropriated for lack of its own—would never become the culture of America. The few had the wealth. But the mob had the numbers, the loudest voice. And, as ever, the cry of that voice was the same. In whatever language, it was for bread and circuses. It would be those who were most rightfully heir to the dead centuries' spirit, those who had fled here from Europe while Henry James and his like sailed there to bask, whose tastes would become those of the nation. They were the ones, *analfabeta,* unlettered, who built her; they, and their children, were the ones whose song she would sing, stealing at last the vulgar words and colors and chords from her own native winds.

America was a land of machines, and it was through machines, the miraculous handmaidens of mob culture, that the muses of illiteracy brought America her voice and vision during the years of the immigrants' waves. Centuries ago, movable type had given literacy to the common man. Now, through these wondrous newer machines, he would give it back.

On July 18, 1877, at his laboratory in Menlo Park, New Jersey, Thomas Alva Edison noted on a worksheet that he had discovered the basic mechanism that would enable him "to store up & reproduce automatically at any future time the human voice perfectly." He applied for a patent the following Christmas Eve, and he got it in February 1878. Five days later, the Edison Speaking Phonograph Company came into being. Victor introduced its Victrola in 1906, and within a few years, by the time the last of the Crocetti brothers arrived in America, there was a machine for nearly every home, from the ten-dollar Victor Junior with its horn of black-japanned steel to the opulent four-hundred-dollar Victrola XVI with its vernis-Martin finish, enclosed sound-box, and gold-plated tone-arm and trimmings.

The polyglot sound of it all, the Babel of the mob, merged in the breezes. In a town like Steubenville in 1917, the year Dino Crocetti was born, one could hear it: "O Sole Mio" by Caruso, still in the air since its release the year before, the most popular of the various recorded versions dating back to Francesco Daddi's in 1902; "When Irish Eyes Are Smiling" by John McCormack; "Jägerleben" by Karl Jörn; "The Darktown Strutters' Ball," the first recording by the Original Dixieland Jass Band; "I'se Gwine Back to Dixie" by Alma Gluck; and several versions of that wartime year's biggest hit, George M. Cohan's "Over There." (The world would have to wait until the following year for Caruso's multilingual version.)

This was the sound of America: Enrico Caruso and Alma Gluck gwine back to Dixieland by way of the Rhine to join Citizen McCormack 'neath the shamrock-spangled *bandiera* of the darktown Zion ball.

Drifting above it all on South Sixth Street in Steubenville, as other melodies prevailed above the Babel of other streets, there were "Marì, Marì" and "Mattinata," "Santa Lucia" and "Torna a Surriento." The last seemed to convey in the somber sweep of its melody and words the shadowing magic of those ancient breezes half-recalled.

> *Guarda il mare com'è bello!*
> *Spira tanto sentimento*
> *Come il tuo soave accento*
> *Che me, desto, fa sognar.*

Sixteen years after the patent of the phonograph, a man named Fred Ott sneezed in West Orange, New Jersey. Two days later Edison registered for copyright a forty-five-frame paper roll bearing the title *Edison Kinetoscope Record of a Sneeze, January 7, 1894.*

In April 1894, three months after Fred Ott's sneeze, the first kinetoscope parlor opened in what had been a shoe store at 1155 Broadway in New York City. There, entering beneath an illuminated dragon with electric eyeballs, one found two rows of five Edison machines lined along opposite walls. For two bits, an hour's wage, one could squint through the peepholes of either row, enjoying five separate shows lasting up to sixteen seconds each. Machines were shipped to Chicago, to Atlantic City. Soon the odd machines were everywhere, and soon enough came their greatest progeny—the moving picture.

Like the breath and shadows of ancient gods in older lands, sounds and pictures soon came to move through the air itself.

In 1922 the Radio Corporation of America began selling home radio-receivers, priced at about seventy-five dollars, and in 1924 Americans spent more than $350,000,000 on home radios.

America within the span of fifty years had set in motion the wondrous machinery of mob culture. The low had superseded the high. Tin Pan Alley had eclipsed Vienna. *The Temptation of St. Anthony* had been transformed from a fifteenth-century engraving by Schongauer to a moving picture with tits and everything. "Amos 'n' Andy" had easily wrested the airwaves from Rossini and Leoncavallo. Television was by nature from the electric womb such a child of the mob that many regarded it as civilization's end. Even the word repulsed T. S. Eliot, who in 1942 declared it "ugly" and its welding of Greek and Latin roots a mark of "ill-breeding." The thing itself, he would warn in 1950, was a "habitual form of entertainment." But Eliot, who, like Henry James before him, became a British subject, was an outsider to his own culture, just as those at its heart, the immigrants to his homeland years before, had been outsiders to their own, which he and other Americans claimed as theirs. In the country of his birth, they had danced to "I Wish I Could Shimmy Like My Sister Kate" while he, across the sea, wrote *The Waste Land*. Like his fellow Missourian Mark Twain, Eliot did not shy away from recording, but his records were nothing to dance to, and no jukebox ever played them. He plied his craft on radio as well, but neither an Amos nor an Andy was he.

It was not the free verse of *The Waste Land* that informed the mythology of the mob. A literature of freer prose already had risen to serve them, beginning with *Photoplay* in 1911. The reign of mediocrity—democracy—was flowering full. Henry James had been to the movies. Furthermore, he had liked them.

America alone among nations had conceived of her destiny as a dream. The American Dream, she called it. Now dreams as well as steel were her industry. Hard-girdered reality and flickering, lilting fantasy were the inhalation and exhalation of her being. It was her dreamland stars, not her statesmen or poets, through whom she found expression.

Dino Crocetti, an immigrant barber's son, born under a steel-gray sky, was to be one of those dreamland stars. He would do what no other of them could. Recordings, movies, radio, television: He would cast his presence over them all, a mob-culture Renaissance man. And he would come to know, as few ever would, how dirty the business of dreams could be.

# 75

# Oedipus Tex

We are gathered tonight at a place called Bosque Creek Ranch, a run-down, 350-acre spread about 50 miles south of Fort Worth, in the Emerald Hill country west of the Brazos. Our tents have been pitched among the oaks and pines, and we have followed a long torch-lit trail through the brush to a copse atop a lea, and here we sit, 70 or so of us, on bales of hay in a wide circle round a fire in a clearing amid the trees. Civilization, its majestic malls and golden arches, lies behind us. The call of the wild has brought us here; here, to become men. We have had our dinner of bison chili. Now, in the Sacred Grove, bathed in the eerie shadows of the dancing flames and moonlight, we scratch our balls and wait. The journey is about to begin.

Modern manhood. It, like Rogaine itself, took a long time to get here. It was in 1970, in Manhattan, that a small organization known as Men's Liberation, Inc., came into being. According to its founder and president, a guy named Zeigler, the group's central goal was that of "liberating ourselves from having to prove our masculinity 24 hours a day." Men should be free to show their sensitivity, to share their fears, anxieties, and pains; free to cry and express emotion without having their manliness impugned. Three years later, the middle-aged Minnesota poet Robert Bly published an essay called "I Came Out of the Mother Naked"—a strong admission for a Lutheran. In 1975 the essay served as the inspiration for Bly's first annual conference on the Great Mother. In the early eighties—by then he had divorced his first wife, Carol, and married a Jungian psychologist named Ruth Ray—Bly was holding mythopoetic seminars for small male gatherings. "I teach fairy tales," he explained. Realizing that he "had no fairy stories to teach men," Bly was drawn to the tale of Iron Hans, or Iron John.

As first set down by the brothers Grimm, the story tells of a king's son who frees the wild man that his father has locked in a cage. The wild man, Iron Hans, leads the boy into the woods and teaches him the secrets of manhood, after which the boy returns to marry his princess. As explicated by Bly, Iron John became a symbol of the need for men to free the inner Wild Man from the bondage of their fathers' psychological tyranny.

Meanwhile, the so-called men's movement was spreading. Its rising spirit could be witnessed in the weekly "About Men" feature that *The New York Times* began running in 1983. "And I began to cry," was the representative ending of one such weekly soul-sharing; another closed by reflecting "how hard it is to get out from under the shadow of a father who hasn't loved you." By 1988 groups such as the Austin Men's Center were blossoming here and there across the country. There was already a literature of sorts, but it was not until Bill Moyers's interview with Bly—broadcast by PBS as "A Gathering of Men" in January 1990—and the publication later that year of Bly's book *Iron John* that the movement—which Bly's ex-wife called "frightening"—truly found its voice. That voice commanded ten grand a performance by the time Bly quit the circuit in 1991.

Bly's book became an immense bestseller. Like Betty Friedan's *The Feminine Mystique*, it seemed to herald a new era. What had begun in obscurity 20 years before with Men's Liberation, Inc., now swept raging in the wind.

The age of the Wild Man was upon us. As great Achilles had once wept freely for fallen Patroclus, so modern man, shedding at last the fool's armor of machismo, was free once again to let flow the tears of his renewed sensitivity.

"Western man's connection with the Wild Man has been disturbed or interrupted for centuries now," wrote Bly in *Iron John*. "Most American men today do not have enough awakened or living warriors inside to defend their soul houses." The quest of modern man was to revive the warrior and reunite himself with the Wild Man from whom his father had estranged him. Scarred by dysfunctional fathering, he must bring himself to discover the wounds beneath those scars, must learn to feel and express the anger and grief of those wounds before he can grow to true spiritual manhood. It was this belief, propagated by Bly, that became the movement's underlying precept. "You cannot become a man," Bly declared, "until your own father dies." By that reckoning, Bly became a man at 61, when his alcoholic daddy finally croaked at the age of 87.

With *Iron John* the floodgates burst open. By 1992 the ogre of Daddy was everywhere. Doctors Marshall Hardy and John Hough confronted "the problem with patriarchy" in *Against the Wall: Men's Reality in a Codependent Culture*. In *Men Talk*, Dr. Alvin Baraff, "the founder of MenCenter," dealt with the "yearning for missed fathers." *Knights Without Armor*, by Aaron R. Kipnis, a specialist in "archetypal psychology and gender issues," discussed not only "the wounded male" but, more specifically, "the wounded penis." I for one was intrigued to read that "we discover our penises at a pretty early age. After all, there it is, just hanging out, right there within easy grasp." Kipnis even proposed a "new male manifesto": "Men are beautiful," he proclaimed. "We have the right to be wrong, irresponsible, unpredictable, silly . . . lazy, fat, bald." From John Lee, a founder of the Austin Men's Center, came *The Flying Boy: Healing the Wounded Man* and *At My Father's Wedding: Men Coming to Terms With Their Fathers and Each Other*. Lee brought to light such issues as "the lost father: our deepest wound" and "how the wound keeps men apart from each other and themselves." Sometimes, he wrote, a man "finds a woman who reminds him of his father [and] he loves her like the father he grew up with." Hmm.

Daddy, daddy, daddy. Wounds, wounds, wounds. Sigmund Freud, the crackpot granddaddy of them all, had coined the phrase "Oedipus complex" to describe every Tom, Dick, and Harry's subconscious desire to give his mom a shot in the shorts. Oedipus, however, had not only unknowingly porked his mom, but he had killed his father as well. In our search for manhood, it was that part of the myth that would illuminate the way for us, like the torchlights along the nighttime Texas trail that had led us to the Sacred Grove. "You cannot become a man," Bly had said, "until your own father dies."

John Lee, whose father, like Bly's, was an alky, took the idea further: Nothing short of spiritual patricide would do. "Each man," wrote Lee, "must find the manner that suits him to kill off the father who lives in his muscles, brain, soul, and dreams." Lee reflected that Sophocles, the ancient author of *Oedipus Rex,* "knew much about the father-son wound."

It was Lee who, along with Marvin Allen, founded the Austin Men's Center in 1988. Together they held the first Wild Man Gathering, at the Allen family's Bosque Creek Ranch. Today Lee presides in Austin as head of the Men's Center and publisher of *Man!,* a quarterly magazine devoted to "men's issues, relationships, and recovery." Allen, though still allied to the Men's Center, has also founded his own group, the Texas Men's Institute, and remains in charge of the Wild Man Gatherings.

Now, as I sit in the Sacred Grove, scratching my balls and awaiting the appearance of Brother Allen, I recall his friend John Lee's invocation at the outset of *At My Father's Wedding:* "Now join me as we go to the bottom of the well of our grief."

I knew long before coming here that I would be expected to bare my soul to my brothers in the course of our communal descent to the depths of that well. What dark and dire shame could I share? I wanted to do this right; I did not want to fake it. Preceding my departure for Texas, I pondered my dilemma, rummaging through my soul for a hint of human failing, weakness, or sin. Again and again I came up empty. Then finally, as the time for truth drew dangerously near, deliverance came. Seeking one evening to deposit an ounce or so of love within my cherished Louise, as a keepsake for her during my absence, I was rescued by taloned fate in all its horror—I couldn't get it up.

I had gone dick-dead on the very eve of my initiation into manhood. This was shame of no small order. "I thank God for my cock," Brother Lee had written. "I'm thankful that I'm a man and that I'm learning to listen to the wisdom of my penis." Now God and all wisdom had forsaken me. I would reveal myself as a worm among men. The bared souls of all could not but weep at the wretchedness of me. Yes, gentle reader, it is true. My cock was limp and lifeless, drained of all mythopoetry and power. A doctor had put me on Anafranil recently, and I tried to tell myself halfheartedly that this was the true cause of my tragedy. Yet I suspected that it was not, and I feared that my condition would prove chronic. And while it might add something to my weekend in the woods, impotence held meager allure for me beyond that paltry and fleeting reward. I remembered the words of Dr. Kipnis. *"Impotence* is an extremely loaded and sexist word," he had declared in *Knights Without Armor.* "This problem of unresponsiveness, which I now prefer to call *diminished erotic response,* is often the 'body's wisdom' in reaction to a lack of intimacy with a partner." Damn fucking right. That's what it was: diminished, fucking, erotic response. It was all Louise's fault, I told myself. She was wearing the wrong fucking hosiery, that's all. It was as simple as that. I was still telling myself these things when I arrived in Fort Worth a few days later.

So, all right, I had my fucking wound. Granted, it had nothing to do with my father. But I never wanted to kill him anyway. I liked him, loved him, all that shit. Matter of fact, he'd been listening to the wisdom of his prick longer than any of these guys.

But it takes more than wounds to become a man, and impotence alone would not be enough. There was something I still lacked. The instructions from the Texas Men's Institute were stern: *"Don't forget your drum!"*

And so there I was, with my friend Christina Patoski, driving all over Fort Worth looking for a drum. Finally, at Swords Music, I found one, a medium-sized Rhythm Band hand drum that set me back 18 bucks and change. Now I could relax—as well, that is, as might be expected of any impotent asshole preparing to descend to the bottom of the well of grief. I had my drum. As Christina and I strolled through the annual Main Street Arts Festival that evening, I felt prepared for the weekend to come. But we came to a crafts stall called Voyager's Dream and there, after hours of hunting for my sorry store-bought excuse for a drum, we saw all manner of exotic and manly drums on display—snakeskin drums from Nepal, goatskin drums from New Mexico, hides of unknown things stretched taut upon the hollowed trunks of trees.

"Ooh, you should get you one of these," Christina said.

"I've already got a drum."

"But yours is too utilitarian. Everybody's gonna have these cool, big old drums, and you'll be there with that dumb, dinky thing like some little old man would have."

She knew how to hurt a guy. There I was, tortured already by feelings of inadequacy due to my diminished erotic response. Now I was insecure about my drum as well. I had heard of penis envy but never drum envy. Yet on the following day, not long after arriving at Bosque Creek Ranch, I experienced it. From the trunks of cars and the beds of pickups came great, booming, tub-sized tribal war drums and waist-high rawhide barrel drums. Many of these were regulation Wild Man drums, I later discovered, from B. D. Drums in Washington ("owned, played, and endorsed by Robert Bly") or Taos Drums in New Mexico ("the heartbeat of the men's movement").

And what a crew it was that hauled those drums! We ranged in age from about 20 to over 60. One guy drove up in a car that bore MPATHY plates. Another arrived practically foaming at the mouth: "Even if I have to git down awn mah knees and make me a fake tombstone outta cardboard or somethin' and put her name on it—anything!—I got to git it outta mah system. I got to git down with that fake tombstone and scream it out: 'Mama, you *incested* me!'" Someone suggested that he had come to the wrong weekend: "Mother-son wounds is next month. This is father-son wounds." No matter; he was off on a different tangent: "Now, you take John Bradshaw. He's number one in the codependence-recovery field. . . ."

There was a father-and-son team. There were fat slobs with Hawaiian shirts and enough camping equipment for an expedition through northern Manitoba. There were meek, balding C.P.A. types, aging yuppies, and dead-eyed Son-of-Sam sorts. There was a Lakota Indian, an Air Force lifer, at least one physician, one lawyer, one professor; there were at least seven therapists.

"Men come to men's gatherings and men's groups not only to find their masculinity," Brother Lee tells us. "They are also in search of their feminine side, the princess within." More than a few, it seemed, would not have to search far. There was a young Tiresias, a doe-eyed boy who slithered lonely and silently and sadly among the trees. He looked like someone who had thrown in the towel about halfway through a sex change. There were Tweedledee and Tweedledum, a pair of forthright, unsmiling dainties who dressed alike, wore their hair cropped alike, traipsed around hand in hand, and shared the same tent. In fact, there are enough princesses in the movement to have merited the formation of Shaman's Circle, an organization that holds Gay Spirit Gatherings.

The ball-scratching has given way to drum-beating. At last our leader, Marvin Allen, appears, joining us with his own drum. He is a tall, graying man in his late forties with an easy, friendly grin. In real life he is a psychotherapist specializing in "adult children of dysfunctional families." His professional approach is eclectic—Gestalt, imago, psychodrama, even common sense—and he brings that approach to his Wild Man Gatherings.

Allen is a pretty sharp character, and much of what he says is on the money. He makes the point that men do not trust men, and that they fear one another. But then he goes on to say that in ancient cultures, this was not true. And that is where he leaves me. What of the internecine betrayals of dynastic Egypt, the murderous conspiracies of Hellas and Rome? No, all he can come up with are the Native Americans. But look where their trust in men got them. That is a point he does not address in the course of explaining why the Wild Man Gatherings embrace many of the rites and practices of the noble redskin. But Allen knows how to work a crowd, and his audience is a willing one, having shelled out $245 each and intent on getting something out of it.

Allen introduces us to his Texas Men's Institute partners, Allen Maurer and Dick Prosapio. The latter, a psychotherapist and Sioux scholar from New Mexico, goes by the name of Coyote and leads the Wild Man drumming. For a man in his late fifties, he is in great shape, and his pitch is an impressive one, neither overly romanticizing the redskin way of life nor overdoing the spiritual angle of ritual power. Maurer, on the other hand, is a bit too theatrical and, judging by his telling of the medieval Fisher King tale, would be well advised to go beyond Bly's allusions in *Iron John* and brush up on Frances Weston's *Quest of the Holy Grail.*

Homophobia, Marvin Allen tells us, has a deeper meaning than queers ascribe to it. It signifies any man's fear of other men. Most men, he says, are afraid of touching one another, lest their sense of masculinity be shaken or maligned. At this point I start to feel as if I am the only wop present in the Sacred Grove, except perhaps for Coyote Prosapio, who has gone Injun on his *paesan.* First the trust routine, now this. I remember my father paying me at the end of the first week I worked for him. I was a 14-year-old porter at his gin mill. "Ain't you gonna count it?" he asked me as I stuck the 20 bucks in my pocket. "Nah," I said, "you're my father. I trust you." He smiled. "Never trust nobody," he said, "not even your father." The cocksucker shortchanged me, too. It was a lesson I never forgot. But I grew up in an Italian home. We were always hugging and kissing. And we didn't give a fuck who saw us. After all, there was nobody else in the neighborhood but micks. So, we would learn to trust—no thanks, pal—and we would learn to hug—no problem—and we would feel anger and grief—side bet—and we would discover the Wild Man within. We are advised to utter the Indian exclamation "Ho!" to express enthusiasm, assent, encouragement, or empathy whenever a brother's words so move us. Would anyone like to say anything?

Tweedledee stands with his hands clasped before him as if in prayer. "I am a gay man," he enunciates in slow earnestness, apparently for the blind among us. "I have come here because I need to be accepted as a man by other men." There are scattered cries of "Ho!" A few drumbeats. "Thank you," says Tweedledee. Across the circle someone else stands. "Uh, I just want to say that, as I respect your space, so I want you to respect mine. And I don't know, what with AIDS and all, if I feel comfortable . . . "

The Italian Indian leads us in a round dance and song. After an invocation of our ancestors, we close around midnight with more drumming. This time around, the noise is thunderous. It and the wild-dancing fire are like a fulmination in the black breezy woods. Coyotes are howling in response by the time we're done. Our leader wishes us good night and tells us to be careful around the latrine pits: There are scorpions and black widows. There are also rattlesnakes, cottonmouths, fire ants, chiggers, ticks, mosquitoes, and nettles amid the bluebonnets. He doesn't have to tell us about the cowshit—we already know.

Back among our tents, a few of us try to build a bonfire of our own. With some kerosene from somebody's lantern, we finally succeed. Nature boys. The smart ones have brought lawn chairs.

Morning sun, morning dew. A strange sound: Somebody is listening to a self-help tape with a lot of soft, gurgling New Age music in the background. *"You now have no ego,"* the self-help voice drones soothingly. *"You are one with my will, serene, calm, at peace . . . "*

Breakfast is at 7:30, served outdoors behind the cabin where our leaders hang out. A bunch of us get there late and there's not much left. The Wild Man in me gloms the last of the eggs. Another guy surveys what's left. "Just what I always wanted for breakfast," he says, "peanut butter and beans." Then, heeding the call of the drums, off to the Sacred Grove we go.

Today is the day that we are to bare our souls, the day that we are to feel our rage and our grief. I've got my limp-dick spiel down pat in my mind. I'm sure it will be a showstopper. But somehow, on this sunny Saturday morning, something in me would rather wait to give my spiel under cover of the night. But what the fuck. No guts, no glory.

One obnoxious yuppie babbles about "quality time" and "double codependency." A few refugees from A.A. and N.A. do their routines: "I'm in A.A.," says one, "my ex-wife's in Al-Anon, and my daughter's in Alateen." There are terminal-recovery cases: self-described recovering addicts, recovering children of alcoholics, recovering codependents, recovering Baptists, recovering Catholics, recovering recoverers. One guy simply declares, "My son is a wimp. He's the same way I was. I'm trying to break the chain." And so it drifts, between honesty and absurdity. It's time to give them the dick, I figure.

But then, as others in the circle, one after another, slowly gather their courage to speak, I begin to see that the drolleries of my cock are as nothing in the sea of misery around me. The guy who was worried last night about AIDS now confesses that, after being abandoned by his father, he had been raped repeatedly as a young boy. Another man, whose parents kept him incarcerated in a box, recalls his earliest childhood memory: his father whimpering while his mother screams, "Let me tell you one thing about your father. He is nothing but a fucking queer! When we first got married, I had to go out with strangers just to be with a real man!" One guy remembers being raped by his father; remembers being forced to watch as his father cut the heads off of kittens; being forced by his father to stand for hours on a chair with a baling-wire noose round his neck strung to an overhead beam, hearing his father berate him and threaten to kick the chair out from under him. When the guy had grown, married, and had a daughter—he breaks down in tears when he tells this—the father returned like a nightmare and raped his little girl.

I feel like crying for some of these men. I can't understand why they literally did not kill their fathers. But then again, I don't know what it is like to really feel what they have felt.

We honor our "elders," those among us over 50. Then Marvin Allen instructs us to break the circle and go off, each of us alone, into the woods. "Pick up a branch or something," he tells us, "and when you're way off by yourself, draw a circle on the ground and invite your father into it. Tell him what you want to tell him. Do to him what you want to do to him. Let your rage pour out."

This, I figure, is a good time to take a shit. I duck into a clump of bushes where one of the latrines is located. After all, I have no rage toward my father, and I know the psychotherapeutic value of a good healthy shit. I'm sitting there watching a caterpillar crawl out of the coffee can that holds the toilet paper when all of a sudden I begin to hear it, one ungodly howl after another, near and far, from every direction.

"Fuck you! Fuck you! Fuck you!" hollers one, each expletive accompanied by a loud whacking sound.

"You suck!"

There are bloodcurdling wails, moans.

"Get the fuck outta my life!"

"I'm not your—"

What's that one?

"I'm not your—"

Sounds like it, but it can't be. I follow the sound until I'm sure. Yes. That *is* what he's screaming: "I'm not your bra, damn it. I'm not your bra!"

Many return to the grove flushed and sweating, or sniffling back tears. After some sharing, caring, and Ho-ing, we are asked to wander off again, this time in pairs of strangers. Each of us is to talk for five minutes, explaining why he feels uncomfortable opening up to the other. We are to look directly into each other's eyes the whole time. This is not quite as easy as it might sound.

Back at the grove after lunch—spaghetti *al piede*—we are directed to form a double circle, one group standing round the others, who remain seated on the bales. Those in the seated group are to close their eyes while the outside group slowly moves around, embracing the shoulders of each seated man and telling him what he himself would have liked to have known at the moment of his birth, a knowing that he would have liked to have grown up with. Then the circles are to reverse active and passive roles.

For many, this long exercise proves the most moving and most intense experience of the weekend. There are eruptions of happy sobbing as grown men are told in faceless whispering tones that they are not a mistake, or that they will always be loved, or protected, or accepted. It is a strangely effective process, both the give and the take of it. Seated with my eyes closed, I almost drift off into a sort of amniotic bliss, only to be jarred by: "Welcome to the worl', son. If you ever have problems, son, you jes' pitcher them problems as cinder blocks, and the Holy Ghost, well, he's gawn bash them ol' cinder blocks for ya, son."

As the sun starts to set, before we go down to our dinner of rabbit stew, Coyote tells us about the sweat lodge. It is, he says, one of seven rites of purification that were revealed long ago to the Sioux by an apparition known as White Buffalo Calf Woman. The sweat lodge, he says, is nothing like a sauna, nothing like a steam bath. Those of us who are claustrophobic or afraid of the dark or have any heart or lung problems should feel free to forgo the ritual.

Night has fallen by the time we strip to enter the lodge. In true redskin fashion, the lodge—or *lipi,* the spirit counterpart of *tipi,* or people-house—is a domed structure of branches covered with blankets. We crawl in, crowded close together in a cramped, tight circle, squatting, our knees pressed to our chests, around a pit in the center of the lodge. The pit is filled with molten rocks that have been glowing for hours on a blazing fire in a larger pit outside. Every once in a while, more incandescent rocks are shoveled into the lodge. It is pitch-black inside, and after a few minutes, breath is difficult to draw and the sweat begins to flow.

The first to leave in a panic are the claustrophobes, then those who fear the dark, and finally those who apparently subscribe to the old wives' tale that oxygen is somehow essential to well-being. But even then it is still cramped, and legs and backs begin to ache sharply. Coyote says his prayers, to the north and to the south, to the east and to the west, each direction signifying some attribute of the spirit, each prayer accompanied by the sprinkling onto the rocks of one substance or another—tobacco, desiccated leaves of this and that. After about 40 minutes—it seems like hours—I'm convinced that I've gone blind and am about to have a heart attack.

Just then the guy who was afraid of AIDS last night decides to have a vision, which he has to share with us. Great. Then Coyote says each of us has to make a vow aloud, followed by the ritual phrase "and for all my relations." By the time it gets round to me, I really do feel like I'm going under. I don't know what I'm saying, something vile, I don't know. "Hmm. Well, all right," Coyote says, begrudgingly tossing some goofer dust onto the rocks.

We stagger, panting, to the shower hose rigged to a tree across a little muddy stream. The water is ice cold. We were in there for more than an hour, it turns out. Purified is not the word. Later I would look up the sweat-lodge rite in a book called *Spiritual Wisdom of the Native Americans.* It shared a chapter with what was undoubtedly another joyful cleansing experience for the inner man: the Mayan enema ritual.

Sunday morning, after breakfast and "church"—a lone jaunt into the woods to commune silently with Big Mama—we wind down with a long sharing-and-caring session. The mood is lighter, looser. We all know each other's secrets now, and all we can do is bore one another or make one another laugh.

We are led to a different grove, farther off, one we haven't seen before. There are two arches made of branches, one perhaps 50 feet from the other. The nearer arch is hung with pine shoots and a cow's skull, the other with flowers. The area between them, we are told, is the "liminal zone." Each of us, to the slow, almost funereal beat of Coyote's big drum, is to enter through the first arch, which represents the death of our old self and the birth of the new, pass through the liminal zone, and emerge in manhood beyond the second arch.

Silly, yes, but a breeze as well, I tell myself. At this rate I'll be back in Fort Worth, swimming in the pool of the Worthington, by mid-afternoon. But little do I know my fellow man. For every guy ready to stride straight through this malarkey, there are a dozen who seem compelled to audition for the Living Theater in the liminal zone. One falls to his knees, forms a circle around himself with twigs, starts pounding the earth and screaming. "This is *my* space! No more fag-bashing! No more suicide! No more homophobia!" And on and on. Another, the Lakota guy, makes an interminable fucking speech. This starts a trend. Guys no longer are content merely to roll and thrash around and bark in the liminal zone. They engage in long, rambling discourses on their newfound manhood as well. Ho, already. But there's no end in sight. It goes on for fucking hours.

Then it hits me. The good part, the fun part, of this whole Wild Man business was the kid stuff—the beating on drums, the sleeping under the stars, the game-playing, the coyotes howling. It was not any renewal or discovery of manhood that made the weekend worthwhile. Rather, it was just the opposite: the release, the escape from manhood, if only for a breath. The manhood angle—this over-done bit with one-man shows in the liminal zone—was more tiresome than real-life manhood itself. And yet, having bought their tickets, many of the initiates seemed intent on creating a phantasm of the Wild Man that had been freed from within, intent on convincing themselves how much and how powerfully and how suddenly and incontrovertibly this weekend had changed their lives.

As each man passes through the second arch, an elder ties a kerchief around his neck, a polyester-and-cotton symbol of triumphant manhood. It is reminiscent somehow of the bravery bestowed on the cowardly lion by the wizard in another fairy tale.

So, in the end, we get what we pay for. Me, I got some color—and, oh yes, returned to the world better equipped to deal with the wounds of the penis. Heh heh heh.

# 76

# J. Edgar Hoover:
# The Burroughsian Nightmare

In the spring of 1958 *Black Mountain Review* published a story by a writer who called himself William Lee. It was the first glimpse of *The Naked Lunch,* a novel that would appear the following year under the author's real name, William Burroughs. That same spring, if we are to believe the account of Susan Rosenstiel, a select few gathered in a New York hotel suite to witness the somewhat grotesque sight of J. Edgar Hoover—Mary was the name he answered to—in a curly black wig, garter belt, lace stockings, and high heels—being serviced by a pair of teenage boys, one of whom wore rubber gloves. A year later, as Olympia Press was bringing out Burroughs' book in Paris, there was an encore of the scene in New York. This time, Hoover wore a red dress and feathered boa, and the boys wore leather.

Rosenstiel, whose memories enliven Anthony Summers' sleazy best-seller *Official and Confidential: The Secret Life of J. Edgar Hoover,* was married at the time to Lewis Rosenstiel, the Schenley Distilleries tycoon who was an associate of gangsters Frank Costello and Meyer Lansky, as well as of Hoover and lawyer Roy Cohn. Both her husband and Cohn, she says, shared the boys with Hoover on these occasions she claims to have witnessed.

Almost everyone in Burroughs' nightmare is an agent of one occult ministry or another, warring for control of body and mind in a wasteland plague-ridden by power addiction. For Burroughs, "Democracy is cancerous, and bureaus are its cancer." Burroughs describes Lee, his narrator/alter ego, as, "an agent"; and developing the character in the early '50s, he noted that Lee "looked like an FBI man."

By 1964, the year of the Warren Commission report's release, Lee, the central figure of Burroughs' ongoing fictions, had become Inspector J. Lee of the Nova Police. In *The Soft Machine, Nova Express,* and the rest, as in *Naked Lunch,* Burroughs presented a realm of twisted homosexuality, vast conspiracies, criminal underworlds, and dark authoritarian agencies—in other words, the same domain that we now associate with Hoover.

Though the contents of the Summers book are questionable (especially when compared to Curt Gentry's less sensational but more substantial biography), they are important in that they have set the cast of permanence to the image of a disgraced Hoover which revisionist history has long been sculpting. The official Hoover of 35 years ago now appears as unequivocally fictional as the Vigilante, the Gimp, Dr. Benway, the Heavy Metal Kid, and other shape-shifting characters of Burroughs' fiction. In fact, the G-man, J. Edgar Hoover of the Federal Bureau of Investigation, seems in today's light to be far more outlandish and sinister a figure than ever represented the forces of Burroughs' Nova Police. With his Mafia connections, endless doomsday files, leather boys in rubber gloves, and evil cabals, Hoover emerges as the Burroughsian nightmare come to life, a creature whose paroxysms of control and power-madness infected a rather real nation somewhere west of Interzone. Burroughs has always been fond of quoting the saying of Hassan i Sabbah—"Nothing is true, everything is permitted"—words that might well have been perverted to serve as the director's private credo.

Burroughs is a man of odd beliefs. In the fall of 1959, soon after he began employing his "cut-up" technique—scissoring his manuscript pages into strips, randomly rearranging them, and conjuring a new manuscript out of the retyped results—he came to believe that his cut-ups somehow revealed the subliminal prophecies of a deeper, more recondite consciousness. Later, his fold-in technique—in which "a page of text, my own or someone else's, is folded down the middle of and placed on another page" and "the composite text is then read across, half one text and half the other"—yielded, to his thinking, similar results.

Burroughs' earliest published work in this vein appeared in the book *Minutes to Go,* issued in March, 1960, and bearing a publication date of April, 1960. When we employ the fold-in method to two FBI memos from those same months Summers reproduces in his book, creasing page 270 back upon page 268, we have: "Noted on the top of Kennedy's element . . . Joe Fischetti . . . This photo included Senator Kid . . . hoodlums are financially several girls In the nude . . . It was secure . . . nomination for the president of pleasure cruiser . . . The thing Senator John F. Kennedy . . . the Senator would show such poon whereby . . . hoodlums will have openly displayed . . . Members were aware . . ." Through this fold-in, with several of the ellipses already supplied in Summers' text, a memo dealing with Kennedy's libertinism and another addressing his suspected ties to Chicago crime lord Joe Fischetti coalesce into a surreal account of Interzone machinations involving the spectral Senator Kid.

Cut up and folded in, two texts from the director himself, one a 1916 statement on crime and the other a 1941 letter to his beloved Clyde Tolson, are transmuted into the following Nova dispatch: "If this tremendous body of evil . . . the thoughts in my mind that I have for you could be welded into a unit of conquest . . . grossly insufficient to the feelings in my heart . . . Words are America . . . mere man-given symbols . . . would fall before it, not in a month, not in a day, but in a few hours . . . "

The cut-up, the fold-in and other related gimmicks have been parlayed by Burroughs, with an increasingly humorless pomposity, into one of the great literary rackets of the age. But could there be something to the dour old crackpot's claims after all? In them, and in the foreshadowing *Naked Lunch,* was Burroughs exhibiting some sort of uncanny prophetic vision? In content, if not in form, his conspiratorial "Nova Express" is not much more farfetched and incredible than the anti-conspiracy Warren report of the same year, and the world of Burroughs' fiction as a whole today seems less a paranoid wildfire and more an intuitive rendering of the then implausible but now accepted view of the director and his shadowy sphere.

Hoover hated writers. Files were maintained on Dashiell Hammett, Thomas Mann, Ernest Hemingway, Tennessee Williams, Truman Capote, and dozens of others. There was even a dossier on E.B. White, the author of *Charlotte's Web.* One can only imagine the bureau's file on Burroughs, whose *Naked Lunch,* when published here, in 1962, resulted in the nation's final legal battle between the First Amendment rights of a literary work and the forces of censorship so dear to Hoover's heart.

Nevertheless, Agent J. Lee/Burroughs and Director Mary/J Edgar were, in a sense, kindred. Both came from staid, respectable backgrounds. Both were homosexuals who were diagnosed as clinically paranoid. In 1939, Burroughs cut off part of his finger in a fit of lovesick dejection. That same year, in a moment of rare candor, Hoover expressed his fear of choosing a mate. If this partner "fails me, ceases to love me," he said, "it would ruin me. My mental status couldn't take it, and I would not be responsible for my actions."

Despite these sensitivities, Hoover was "a master con man, one of the greatest con men the country has ever produced," according to his aide William Sullivan. Burroughs, eighteen years the director's junior, certainly became something of a master con man himself, glibly and expertly cutting up and folding in his own persona to achieve a stature that perhaps exceeded both his straightforward linear skills and his well-worn sleights of hand.

Could it be that the younger man, a great believer in all sorts of hoodoo shuck and jive, was somehow in psychic empathy with the elder queen, himself a devoted disciple of Masonic mumbo-jumbo, a Knight of the Mystic Shrine who eventually attained the Ancient and Accepted Rite of 33rd Degree? ("Now this con involves Duty, Higher Duty and 32nd Degree Duty," Burroughs had written in an early draft of *Naked Lunch,* in a sequence involving a "manic FBI agent.") "All my writing comes from the psychic thing," Burroughs has said. "You sit down and a light turns on and you see a set or a character." Did he "see" Hoover's secret life and doings? These are questions that not even Susan Rosenstiel can answer.

In *The Seven Deadly Sins,* published a little over a year ago, Burroughs rails against "the Pride of viciously closed minds, Pride of power." In embodying that deadly sin and others, the gross, corrupt and garter-belted G-man who now creeps through our imaginations looms as the metastatic symbol of Burroughs' ultimate evil, whose "bureaus are its cancer." It is Burroughs, perhaps, who is the true chronicler, and Summers merely the late-coming mundane annotator of the novelist's audacious and inexplicable portrait. In the gray zones of reality, whose reports are more to be trusted, those of Madam Rosenstiel or those of Agent Lee?

The possibilities are enticing. Burroughs, of course, was too old to have been one of the rubber-gloved wild boys at Hoover's Plaza suite. But, then again, if we cut here and fold there, like so . . .

# 77

# Memories of Joe

Some people remember finding God or becoming aware of social injustice or the healing power of love. I remember discovering Joe Franklin.

I must have been six years old. P.S. 33 wasn't far from where I lived, and I used to walk home and back at lunchtime. It was during one of these midday school breaks that I discovered a strange show on Channel 7. It was called *Memory Lane*.

Looking back, I have no idea what I saw in that show. As I remember it, *Memory Lane* consisted mostly of old movie clips: the Keystone Kops, Fatty Arbuckle, and other antiquities that I did not find funny, then or now. I was into the good stuff: *Andy's Gang, The Abbott and Costello Show*. I knew the score, the name of the game. Through television, I already had a satisfactory protopathic sex life: there were the taut thighs of Sheena, queen of the jungle; the click and clack of Miss Hillary Brooke's high heels, a sublime symphony of all the wicked desires that had ridden the wind since time began, six years before. I was happening. Yet, day after day, I returned to *Memory Lane*.

It must have been the host: black-and-white male Caucasian of indeterminate ethnic origin, size, and age. His name was Joe. But what was it about him that mesmerized me, that lured me back again and again? Maybe it was his oddness. Aside from the guys with the big noses that made you laugh and the people who brought you your special combination number one, two, or three at the Canton Tea Garden, I was aware of only three races of manliwops, micks, and, as they preferred to be called back then, colored people. Joe did not seem to belong to any of them. In fact, he seemed to be more an erasure than a representation of type or personality, an identikit cipher of the nondescript. He had little hands, like a plastic doll's, and his forehead shone. I remember that.

I had seen Dracula rise from his coffin, I had seen the Wolfman howl, the Invisible Man unravel, the Mummy walk. But Joe and his baby hands and shining forehead were a weirdness unto themselves. Yet, I don't think it was the hands, the forehead alone. No. What it was, I now believe, was a sort of deep enchantment. Joe emanated from a different place, a place where time stood still, where there were no seasons and there were no meanings. I must have been drawn to his shoddy carnival of nihilism long before I understood it. And I suppose it proved ultimately unsettling, for I eventually stopped watching.

By the time puberty came and other enchantments beckoned—tobacco, dirty pictures, alcohol, drugs, and standing around spitting—I had forgotten all about Joe. Then one night, years later, sitting around sniffing Ronsonol and turning the television dial (for me, lighter fluid, which broke down images into buzzing fields of electric particles, was the ideal TV drug), I saw him: still living, still beaming, still shrinking, still talking with zero conviction about what he called, as if alluding to some dark Zoroastrian duality, "the *good* nostalgia."

Those were days gaudy with Day-Glo and noisome with patchouli. Men such as Maharishi Mahesh Yogi, Bubba Free John, and Baba Ram Dass were not without followers. But for me, there was Bubba Joe. I never went to Woodstock, I never marched. I never saw God, I never mourned the Kennedys. I didn't care about peace or love. I was into consciousness expansion, all right—the *good* consciousness expansion. Let others ask. Who am I? There were more important questions, and Bubba Joe confronted them: "Highway safety, pro or con?" ("We're being very controversial here.") Forget the Firesign Theater and all that balding-hippie jive. Joe was where the action was.

Joe's carnival brought out people other shows would not bring us: Frank Sinatra Jr., far more interesting *qua* specimen than Sinatra *pere* ("Next time," Joe would say, "bring pop by"); Georgie Jessel decomposing in public in his World War I uniform; guys who complained that "Tony Orlando stole my name"; Rocky Graziano; Bing Crosby dropping by for a chat on the way to the boneyard; ventriloquists who moved their mouths; people who seemed to exist only as fleeting fulfillment of Andy Warhol's line about everyone being famous for 15 minutes—a concept that originated, of course, not with Warhol but with Joe himself. "Come back," he told them all, "we'll do a whole hour next time." He claimed to have had Elvis on the show when Elvis was unknown. Maybe he did and nobody remembers; for, while many of Joe's guests have been remembered for many things, being his guest has rarely been one of them. Only the winners of his Miss Paint beauty-pageant extravaganzas (ballots available at all Martin Paint stores) seemed to be true Franklin-esque celebrities.

Joe was the avatar of postliterate, disposable American culture, the Lorenzo de' Medici of divine mediocrity. His show reduced all—not only guests and topics, but the world at large; every fake smile, pretension, and so-called meaningful dialogue—to its essence as filler, its essence as fodder for the cosmic joke. More than that, the show was fun. I've never seen more than a few minutes here and there of David Letterman, Jay Leno, Arsenio Hall, who-have-you. For me, they are the false smile from which Joe's shit-eating grin was a deliverance. One day in 1970 or '71, while working at the Lovable Underwear Company at 200 Madison, I called down to the deli for lunch, and my sandwich was delivered by a guy I recognized from Joe's show. His name was Judson Jerome, or Jerome Judson, or something like that, and he did spooky voices. He was as pleased to be recognized as I was to meet him, and he later brought me an autographed copy of an album of spooky voices that he had made. Hell, you could see all sorts of characters on Johnny Carson, but they weren't going to show up delivering your pastrami sandwich the next day. It gave me cause to believe that someday my Miss Paint might come.

Soon after I met the guy who did the spooky voices, I ended up running around with a broad who claimed that Joe had once propositioned her. Not that I believed her: She was maybe nineteen. Joe was, well, ageless.

But I played along anyway. "And you didn't fuck him?" I asked. I was aghast. An opportunity to share the miracle of love—the *good* sex—with the great man himself. She never looked at me the same again; nor I, her.

The origins of Joe, like those of the expanding universe, are clouded in mystery, and it takes some digging to unearth the facts. (You won't find this stuff in Drew Friedman's "The Incredible Shrinking Joe Franklin," or in the fine profile of Joe that appeared 22 years ago in *The New Yorker,* and Joe is conspicuously absent from standard television reference works.) Though sources list his birth date as "N.A." or 1929, he was born, in New York, on March 9, 1926, and was nineteen when he made his broadcasting debut, in 1945, as the host of a Sunday afternoon WNEW radio show called *Vaudeville Isn't Dead.* A subsequent WNEW show was *Joe Franklin's Record Shop.* By 1948, calling himself "The Young Man With the Old Records," he was hosting the *Antique Record Shop* (later called *Echoes of the Big Time*), on WMCA. By 1950, he had signed with WJZ, the forerunner of ABC. It was on WJZ-TV, in 1951, that *The Joe Franklin Show* was first televised: and, in 1953, ABC began regular broadcasts of his *Memory Lane.* By 1962, the great man was reduced to a 9 a.m. slot, and, on October 1 of that year, he left ABC and brought his show to WOR, which returned him to middays. It was in the mid-'60s that *Memory Lane* again became *The Joe Franklin Show.* By 1971, WOR had switched him to 9 a.m. with rebroadcasts at two in the morning. By the fall of 1981, he was flipped to 2 a.m., with rebroadcasts continuing at 6 a.m. The show moved from Times Square to Jersey the next year. Four years ago, the show was cut to a half-hour and moved to 1:30 a.m., with no rebroadcast. And now, after more than forty years, it ends.

T. S. Eliot—you remember him: the Georgie Jessel of free verse—called television an "ugly" and "habitual form of entertainment." But that was before Joe's reign. (Joyce Kilmer, pro or con? Come back, we'll do a whole hour.) At two a.m., Eastern Daylight Savings Time, August 7, 1993, television indeed became an ugly place. Could the Telepsychic or even Biond Fury himself envision what lies ahead: a city—a world—without the *good* TV? May Miss Paint have mercy on our souls.

# 78

# My Kind of Loving

What is it with you people who don't understand
   the senseless slaughter of animals?
What is it with you people
   who don't want to wear fur?
I want to fuck you in fur.
Kill me a Kennedy;
   that's my idea of foreplay.
Bring me his fucking pig-faced mick head
   on a silver platter—
No, better yet: Aynsley makes these plates,
   22-karat gold and blue Cobalt—
Fuck the silver; bring me his head on one of those.
Wear your diamond-seamed stockings,
   special shoes from Brazil.
I'll see you there.
I'll see you there.

# 79

In the fall of 1993 I was hired by *The New Yorker* to write a long profile of George Jones, who was perhaps the greatest living singer, and the greatest cipher, in country music.

The piece turned out longer, and better, than I had foreseen; and everyone from the assigning editor to the fact-checker loved it. In the end, however, it was felt that, while the piece would have been "perfect for the old *New Yorker*," it had no place in the vision of the magazine's new editor, Tina Brown.

A much-cut version of the piece was published in 1994 in *Texas Monthly*. The uncut version was published later that year in the *Journal of Country Music*, and in the summer of 1996 reprinted, with final amendments, in *The Country Reader: Twenty-five Years of the Journal of Country Music*. It is the latter text that appears here.

# George Jones:
# The Grand Tour

George Jones is sober, and he has been for a long time. "I ain't touched a drink in ten years," he announced to the packed crowd that had paid $40 a head to witness his hour-long performance at Tramps in New York City in November of 1992. Like his comment that he had not "been to the big city since '56," his announcement was not quite true. He had performed at Philharmonic Hall in the spring of 1972 and at the Bottom Line in the summer of 1980, and had accepted a Grammy at Radio City Music Hall in early 1981; and ten years ago, he had been drinking like there was no tomorrow. Still, this Manhattan appearance was a triumph of sorts. He was once again on top of the world. Six weeks before, he had been inducted into the Country Music Hall of Fame. His new MCA album, *Walls Can Fall*, was the best work he had done in years. And, though New York had always somewhat intimidated him, now, in his first show here since sobering up, he demonstrated to the cheering demographic crazy-quilt at Tramps that the powers of his unique voice, in a culture mad with neophilia and ephemeral sensation, seemed ever-compelling and everlasting.

Three weeks later, in his dressing-room suite at Bally's Casino Resort in Las Vegas, he strolled back and forth, chain-smoking Barclay cigarettes and imitating Ernest Tubb: "I'm walkin' the floor over you, . . . " he sang, mimicking the deep, gravelly delivery of Tubb's 1941 hit. Jones is sixty-one years old, short, and paunchy. The high-heeled cowboy boots he wears do not much enhance his size, and the robust midsection of his renewed health, combined with the facial characteristics that long ago inspired the nickname Possum, make him appear more possum-like than ever before. His hair in recent years has turned completely white. Fastidiously styled, with its overhanging forward-swerving eaves and impeccable scimitar sideburns, it is never tousled, always in place, like a sculpted pinnacle of incongruous permanence atop a distinctly mortal shell. Beneath his brown eyes, his cheeks are striated with deep fissures that are not so much the natural carvings of age but the ravages of mortification. When he grins, the furrows are less obvious; when his expression is blank or subtly scowled, as is more often the case, the furrows are like the scars of a recondite clawing.

Last night, he had worn a black glittery suit that had been made for him by Manuel of Nashville, the former protégé of and successor to Nudie Cohen of

North Hollywood, the tailor who had embroidered the musical notes on Hank Williams's lapels, designed Elvis's gold-lamé tuxedo, and taught a generation of country singers that lavender and orange were complementary colors. Tonight, as in New York, he wore crisp blue jeans and a Navaho-patterned Western shirt. He slapped his gut, that symbol of his return from the dead, smiled once, and his attitude changed suddenly from one of playfulness to one of tired resignation. "Let's get this over with," he said.

His band, the Jones Boys, had already taken the stage of the Celebrity Showroom. The six young men comprised a basic honky-tonk band: a steel guitarist, Tom Killen; a lead guitarist, Jerry Reid; a fiddler, Andy Burton; a piano player, Kent Godsen; a drummer, Bobby Birkhead; and a bass player, Ron Gaddis, who has been with Jones for almost twelve years and serves as the leader of the group. In instrumentation, the band differs only in its degree of skill and sophistication, and its casual, long-haired appearance, from the bands Jones sang with thirty-odd years ago. Back in those days, a good night's pay was $500–$600 a night, for three or four hours of music. These days, Jones gets anywhere from $20,000 to $50,000 a show. He plays a hundred to a hundred and twenty shows a year. The New York show was a rare exception: most shows last less than forty-five minutes. Last night, he was on and off within an hour. He had opened in New York with "No Show Jones," which he used to perform with Merle Haggard. "Tonight is the last night I'm ever going to do that stupid song," he had said onstage that night. Tonight, in Las Vegas, he opened with "No Show Jones," as usual. "We're gonna have a ball tonight," he declared, as he does every night. "We're gonna have a *good* time." As he did in New York, he warned that "We might be here till four in the morning." ("I'm such a hick that I believed him," said Michael Pietsch of Little, Brown after the Tramps show.) He did a total of seven songs, ending with his new single, "I Don't Need Your Rockin' Chair." Then—"Good night, everybody. Thank you!"—he was off in less than twenty-three minutes.

At a concession stand in the lobby area, there were GJ-monogrammed shot glasses ($3), No SHOW license plates ($3), GEORGE JONES embroidered caps ($12), ROCKIN' WITH THE POSSUM T-shirts ($15), and GEORGE JONES AND THE JONES BOYS satin tour jackets ($60). In the casino, George, his wife, Nancy, and I sat at a blackjack table, as we did last night, donating among us some several thousand dollars to Satan. Nancy drew two cards totaling twelve. "Should I hit it, honey?" she asked George from across the table. "I would," he said. Nancy drew a ten, and the dealer took her little pile of $50 chips. "It's only money," said George, pushing forward several red-and-black $100 chips and purple-and-black $500 chips. He was happy. He was finished with Las Vegas. Tomorrow his pilot, Don, would be flying him to Tennessee in their Lear jet. "I miss my girls," he said. He was talking about his cows.

It is no exaggeration to say that Jones is far more enamored of his cows than his career. Though he is the foremost of country music's living legends, he has not had a #1 hit since "I Always Get Lucky with You," in the summer of 1983. Since then, country music has become the domain of a new generation of rock-nurtured singers.

"They can play middle-of-the-road and pop and call it country all they want to, but I don't think they'll ever take the real thing out of people's hearts," Jones told me. "Nowadays it's strictly all fame and fortune and glory. In the old days, we did it because we loved to do it. It was a wonderful feeling, of course, knowing that you could make a living that way, doing something you loved to do, but it was never really about money. I think to be successful and stay successful a long period of time, you've got to love what you're doing."

Though he remains immensely popular in concert, and though his recent albums have sold hundreds of thousands of copies, Jones today has difficulty getting radio airplay. He is considered too old for the ever-younger image that country music projects. In early 1993, while Palomino Road, one of the new "bands with hair," was about to resurrect "Why, Baby, Why," his earliest hit, from 1955, his own current single, "I Don't Need Your Rockin' Chair," had not even broken into the Top Twenty of the country charts. Though Jones dismissed it as "this stupid thing," it was a good record, a nouveau-rockabilly celebration of old honky-tonk ways. Furthermore, its background chorus featured Garth Brooks, Travis Tritt, and many other of the biggest of country music's new generation of singers, nearly all of whom have named Jones as their idol, echoing the sentiment of Waylon Jennings that, "If we could all sound like we wanted to, we'd all sound like George Jones." As to the adulation he commands among the youngbloods, Jones is nonplussed. "That's the hard part to understand," he said. Maybe "they all pretty much like country music to start with, they just didn't get into it themselves." Nor does he understand why he is idolized by an increasing number of rock stars. "I was really shocked and surprised to hear all these rock stars make quotes about me." Likewise, he was "surprised a little, and happy" at the exuberant reception at Tramps.

The truth, to Jones, is simple. "Country music is something you love. It's a music you love. I don't know, for some reason, being a star or anything like that never did really enter my mind. If they hadn't paid me for singing, I would've still done it, long as I could've got enough to eat somewhere. It don't matter to me that much. I like to sing with my heart. I like to sing soul country songs. And that's the way it'll always be with me. And I've always stuck with that, and it's pretty much, I think, what's the answer for my success."

When I first met him, in Nashville, eighteen years ago, George Jones struck me as a prisoner, both in fact and in fancy. His life was falling apart, and, as he had taken increasingly to missing dates and vanishing without notice or trace, his career was crumbling as well. He was to perform a goodwill show later that day, April 20, 1976, at the Tennessee State Penitentiary, and, the day after next, was to be reunited in the recording studio with his ex-wife Tammy Wynette. To ensure that he stayed in town, his record company, Epic, and his manager, Shug Baggott, were keeping him under their guarded watch in the comfortably appointed basement of the Music Row building where Baggott maintained an office. But, beyond this droll subterranean captivity, his spirit seemed to be darkened by a greater, and indwelling, thralldom.

Back in March 1962, Jones had recorded a song called "Warm Red Wine." It was an old song, written by Cindy Walker and first recorded, in the spring of 1949, by Jones's Texas elder Bob Wills. But there was something about Jones's version, something about the pure, stark, sincerity with which he delivered the lament "I'm a prisoner of drink who will never escape," something about it that evoked horripilations of a rare and disquieting sort. It was more than a testimony to the power of Jones's singing; it seemed a personal testament as well.

In a few days, Jones would announce that he had won his battle against alcoholism. But it was not true; and seeing him that morning in his sunless lair, as he paced and sat and fidgeted and rose and paced, buoyant one moment, despondent and anxious the next, dressed in an immaculate athletic suit of sweatpants and sweatshirt, chain-smoking cigarettes and swigging Heineken from the bottle, as if the vestments of sobriety and cardiovascular well-being might abrogate the reality of the beer and the smoke, I could not help but think of the way he sang that song.

He was then, as he is today, arguably the greatest country singer alive. His was, and is, a voice capable of imbuing the commonplace sorrows and joys of the human universe with poignance and puissance, of crystallizing the simplicities of the mundane and the time-worn into subtle, complex new glintings, of discovering in and mining from the plain phrases, tired metaphors, graceless rhyme, and familiar melodies of songs a hidden, underlying honesty and depth, of transforming those songs from expressions of tailored emotion to vehicles of expressiveness itself. These are gifts that have been shared by Jimmie Rodgers, Hank Williams, Jerry Lee Lewis, and to lesser profundity a few other legendary country singers. But while Jones and his idol Hank Williams have both affected generations with a plaintive veracity of voice that has set them apart, Jones, unlike Williams, has further been gifted with a voice of remarkable range, natural elegance, and lucent tone. As Emmylou Harris has said, "When you hear George Jones sing, you are hearing a man who takes a song and makes it a work of art—always. He has a remarkable voice that flows out of him effortlessly, and quietly, but with an edge that comes from the stormy part of the heart." In that same understated edge, Jon Pareles of the *New York Times* has discerned "a universe of lonely torment." Gliding to high tenor, plunging to deep bass, the magisterial portamento and melisma of his onward-coursing baritone send off white-hot sparks and glissades of blue, investing his poison-love songs with a tragic *commedia-è-finita* gravity, inflaming his celebrations of honky-tonk abandon with the heat of careening, heartfelt delight, and turning songs such as "Warm Red Wine" into harrowing wails from the abyss.

Taciturn, inarticulate, withdrawn, brooding, and self-destructive by nature, George Jones has always seemed to express himself, and to assert and redeem himself, primarily through his singing; and the singing, in turn, has seemed to convey some sense of the power of catharsis it has held for him. In his best performances, the songs have served merely as skeleton keys to loose the vague, rhymeless shades of deeper and more mysterious feelings. Without a song, those feelings—all feeling, it seemed—remained hidden. He was a cipher: in song, a well of emotion and creativity; in life, an erasure of a personality evincing but the barest traces of sentience.

He seemed friendly, shy, and vacant. That he was, and for the last twenty years had been, the most successful singer in the business—second only in country-music history to Eddy Arnold, who had a ten-year lead on him—was something that seemed to be far less important to him than the bottle of beer in his hand. He was wholly unassuming and down-to-earth. One could readily believe the accounts of those who had known him for many years, that he had not changed much at all, that he had been impervious to fame and fortune.

I came away from that meeting liking him but feeling that I had been in the company of a man whose unequivocal soulfulness abided incongruously beneath an inert mind. Surely, I thought, this blankness must be an illusion, a deception, perhaps even of self, like the jogging suit. I was not alone. Others who met and worked with him shared similar feelings; and through the years, he, like Elvis, has evaded any in-depth interview, speaking only briefly to journalists and biographers, and then usually only to utter disjointed platitudes that did little more than convey his skewed and innocent sense of what a show-business personality ought to say. In the years after I met him, though lurid news of his deathward dissolution grew more widespread with his every downward lurch, the man who seemed to be self-destroying remained largely unrevealed and unknown.

George Jones is not given much to talk. He is a man of few words, whose passive silence many have found disarming. As his wife Nancy told a music-business executive who felt uneasy in Jones's presence, "George will make anybody nervous if you pay him any mind." There is a well-known story in Nashville of how Jones, yielding to pressure from his record company, once agreed to an interview, excused himself to go to the restroom a few minutes after the interview began, and was not seen for two weeks. Neither the two biographies of him, Bob Allen's *George Jones: The Saga of an American Singer* and Dolly Carlisle's *Ragged but Right: The Life & Times of George Jones,* both published in 1984, nor the many articles devoted to him offer much in the way of first-person revelation by Jones. In a 1981 *Village Voice* cover story, what little Jones had to say was made to suffice among descriptions such as how he "delicately set the glass of cold water on the white formica table in front of him, not too close but easily within reach." A 1992 cover story in the *New York Times Magazine* relied more on the words of Jones's record producers than on his own. When Elvis Costello conducted a brief chat with Jones for *Interview* magazine several months ago, it was done under the subterfuge of a casual telephone call. "Seemed like he was trying to *interview* me," Jones had said suspiciously after hanging up. Chapters of an authorized biography that were recently circulated among New York publishers by the William Morris Agency were regarded as too insubstantial by most of those who read them. Who was this guy, this seeming actuarial blip of a nonentity who belied his own apparent hollowness by singing as if his soul were on fire? What was it that made him the greatest country singer alive, and what was it that was driving him in a panic to his own waiting grave?

I thought about these things, still wanting to figure them out, when I began spending time with George Jones again recently. Passing time backstage, playing blackjack, or simply hanging out together, Jones was easygoing. But in trying to steer the conversation beyond small talk, he countered with a sort of disappointed resistance. Time and again, he promised me that we would sit down with a tape recorder. Christmas passed, the new year began, and still he proved elusive. I was sitting in a motel room in Brentwood, Tennessee, watching television, when Susan Levy of MCA Records and Nancy Jones worked out a plot by which we could snare George for that long-promised sit-down. On television, Sammy Kershaw, a country-music youngblood who wears a diamond stud in his left ear and idolizes George Jones, is promoting Pheroessence Star Clone, a perfume supposedly distilled from pheromones extracted from his sweat. Just dial 1–800–96-SAMMY. As it turns out, Jones is involved in the marketing of a far homelier product: George Jones Country Gold Dog Food. ("IF GEORGE SAYS IT'S GOOD . . . THEN IT'S GOOD BY GEORGE!") The stuff is made in Red Bay, Alabama, by Sunshine Mills, Inc., the producer of several other brands of basically identical dog food. Tomorrow Jones is to meet with Sunshine Mills executives. I will travel to Red Bay with Susan, who, once there, will feign being called back to Nashville on emergency business. This will leave no alternative but for me to make the 185-mile return trip aboard George's custom-made Liberty Coach bus.

The next day, at a company lunch, Jones is presented with a six-week-old Labrador retriever. Later we learn much concerning the various grades and price fluctuations of the rendered-pork-and-beef-fat mixture that arrives in Red Bay by the twenty-four-ton truckload at a rate of a 150 truckloads a year. We also learn the nature of "fish digest," one of the ingredients in George Jones Country Gold Ocean Fish Flavor Cat Food. (They are entrail pressings.) Throughout the day, which is one of intermittent rain and clouds, Jones does not remove his sunglasses. Outside the factory, standing in the drizzling rain, an unemployed carpenter named Billy waits in the hope of meeting Jones. "I want to shake that man's hand," he tells me. As we leave Red Bay at dusk, Jones at first is mad at his wife for her part in the plot. Then, after a fashion, he loosens up.

Long ago, I had encountered a prisoner of drink. Since then, he had been written off for dead, but had denied the doomsayers their satisfaction. I ex-

pected him to be somewhat changed; and he was, but not quite as I had antici-
pated. Now he struck me, oddly, as a prisoner of sobriety.

The east Texas town of Saratoga lies near Little Pine Island Bayou, in the heart
of the Big Thicket, a once-impenetrable 3.5-million-acre expanse of virgin pine,
cypress, and hardwood forest, meadowland, and backwater swamp that until
the mid-nineteenth century had been the hunting-ground of the Alabama-
Coushatta tribe, who are now relegated to a reservation in the Thicket's northern reaches. Located about thirty miles northwest of the port of Beaumont,
Saratoga was one of several Big Thicket sawmill settlements that grew into oil-
boom towns following the Lucas Gusher at the Spindletop Hill salt dome south
of Beaumont on January 10, 1901. Saratoga, like Spindletop, was a salt-dome
oilfield, and it was in Saratoga that the Mellon family's newly formed Gulf Oil
Corporation drilled its first producing well.

The population of Saratoga, which at the height of the oil boom numbered in
the thousands, has now dwindled to less than six hundred souls, though no one
has bothered to replace the sign at the town limits which proclaims its populace
to stand at a thousand. Those old-timers who remain agree that Saratoga has
been dying since the 1950s. First the wells went dry, and then, as boom-town
morality ceded ground to the Baptists, the bars were shut down and the town itself went dry. The Big Thicket itself has dwindled as well, down from its 3.5 million acres to less than 300,000, little more than 28 percent of which are
presently authorized for protection under the 1974 designation of the Big
Thicket as a national preserve. What is left of Saratoga lies at the edge of one of
the biggest parcels of protected preserve, the Lance Rosier Unit.

And what is left is not much. The broken stretch of Texas Farm Road 770
that serves as Saratoga's main thoroughfare passes a few rusted, lumbering oil
pumps, the tumbledown remains of an old fireworks stand, a Super Pak gro-
cery, whose dirty, broken plastic sign stands as Saratoga's most prominent and
modern feature; the First United Pentecostal Church, Dy's Toning Salon,
Brown's Gun Shop and Feed, and Don's Barber Shop. And, hidden back among
the trees, there is the privately run Big Thicket Museum. "Tourists from around
the Nation and the globe visit the Big Thicket Museum each year," says the little
leaflet, which describes the two-room museum as being located at the "biological crossroads of North America." Posted on a gate at the entrance to the road
leading to the Big Thicket Museum is a sign: SARATOGA, TEXAS. BIRTH-PLACE OF
GEORGE JONES.

The singer's father, George Washington Jones, the only child of a short-lived
and broken marriage, was born in Lufkin, two counties north of here, and
brought in his infancy by his mother, Mary Ferris Jones, to the Big Thicket
home of her parents. Before he was two, his mother remarried and left him behind to be raised by his maternal grandparents. In the mid-August heat of 1915,
twenty-year-old George Washington Jones married Clara Patterson, the nine-

teen-year-old daughter of a Big Thicket preacher known as Uncle Litt. Moving from one Big Thicket rent home to another, following work from logging-camp to sawmill to oilfield, George Washington Jones and his growing family settled finally in Saratoga, where, on September 12, 1931, in a small log-and-slapboard cabin, George Glenn Jones, the second son and last-born of George and Clara Jones's eight children, drew his first breath.

George's father was a drinking man. The death of his first-born child, seven-year-old Ethel, in early 1926, had driven him more deeply into drunkenness, and by the time his young namesake was born his reputation in Saratoga was that of a no-good drunkard who did not quite deserve the good and decent woman who was his wife. The drinking had caused a cold, deepening rift between him and his wife, who redirected much of her affection to her youngest child. "My mama," George would say, "loved me more than anybody ever did." It was Clara who raised George, like his elder brother and sisters, in the fold of her father's White Oak Baptist Church. It was there, beside her, that young George learned to sing. But it was George's father who gave him his first guitar, when he was eight.

"Little old Gene Autry guitar," George recalled, the better part of a century later, describing that guitar as if he could still see it: "Had a picture of a cowboy on a horse with a lariat, and Gene Autry's name. My Sunday-school teacher taught me the chords on it. I just fell in love with it, and I spent all my time with the guitar. It never warped. I carried it many times in the rain."

In 1938, about the time George got his guitar, his family also got their first radio. On Saturday nights, live from Nashville, there was the Grand Ole Opry, whose newest star, a thirty-four-year-old Tennessean named Roy Acuff, had joined the show's cast in February of that year, and who by the end of the year had enjoyed two immense hits, a mournful song of strange Pentecostal imagery called "The Great Speckled Bird" and "The Wabash Cannon Ball." George was mesmerized by Acuff's high, piney nasal style, and it became an indelible influence on his own singing.

"My daddy always got my sister and I to sing when I was a kid," George remembered. These were not pleasant performances for George or his sister Doris, who were roused from sleep by their father when he came home drunk in the middle of the night, alone or with his cronies, demanding entertainment and threatening violence if he did not get it. The resentment that George harbored for his father's drunken brutishness grew more intense with every command performance.

Huey P. Meaux, a Cajun born across the Sabine River, in Kaplan, Louisiana, in 1928, was raised in the town of Winnie, south of Beaumont. With a resumé that includes pop, R&B, and country hits as well as a federal-penitentiary stretch (and subsequent presidential pardon), Meaux, known as the Crazy Cajun and the father of swamp-rock, is one of the most colorful and irrepressible characters, and perhaps the most accomplished record producer, in Texas music. A friend of Jones since the late forties, Meaux told me that Saratoga, in the old days, "was a place you didn't go to unless you knew someone." The area had a reputation for lawlessness, violence, and hostility to outsiders. Towns such as Saratoga had given east Texas its notoriety as redneck country, as Klan country. "The Big T'ickets," Huey said, in that fine Cajun accent that still flavors his every word, "you just didn't go there."

Brown's Gun Shop is a cavernous warehouse. Feed sacks and farming tools line the walls, but the shadows in whose musty dimness they lie seem to be the real stock-in-trade. The worn floor-planks do not creak in any quaint sort of way, but rather seem to groan meanly at the intrusive affront of every step that dares to break the sepulchral silence of the place. Behind a sagging wooden counter, from other, gloomier shadows, emerged a middle-aged man as unwelcoming but otherwise as expressionless as the floor. His eyes were close together in their sockets and shone as dully as the dark steel barrels of the rifles gathering dust in their display racks. As he seemed to be the only sign of life in town on this bright Friday afternoon, I asked him, more or less, if he was the sole sentinel here at the biological crossroads of North America.

"Try Don," he said.

Indeed, the sign that hangs, swaying forlornly in the breeze, from a post at the entrance to Don's Barber Shop, advertising Family Kuts & Kurls in a sad, handlettered attempt at fully kappa'd, high-mall modernity, does little to prepare the visitor for the biological flurry within.

The young farmhand who sat in the shop's lone shearing-chair said with a grin that he had a George Jones cassette in the tape deck of his pick-up truck right this very moment.

Don let the comment pass. He was a balding man who appeared to be in his fifties, and as he worked his comb and scissors, his features, cast in aloof and faintly condescending detachment, possessed a vaguely sinister air.

"It's just to now to where he admits bein' from round here. We were just white trash, people thought. We had this reputation of hatin' and killin' niggers." He drew a bit of the young man's hair between his fingers and put the scissors to it. "Of course, it wasn't true."

"Yes it was," the young man grinned.

One of the old-timers sitting against the wall, a jovial heavyset man in his seventies, with white hair and a red face, uttered a sound that fell somewhere between a snort and a chuckle. "He'd set up by the drugstore and play his little old three-string git-tar."

"People round here now wouldn't think no more of George Jones than George Strait," said another, a gray-haired man in his late forties. "All the old-timers are gone now. My mother, who's dead ten years, went to school with him."

"His daddy was just a drunk, too," said Don, as if to dismiss Saratoga's most celebrated son as a common drunkard and nothing more. "He'd line 'em all up and whup 'em if they didn't sing."

Don remembered that his daddy was often visited by George's brother, Herman, whose boyhood habit it was to douse himself freely with the old man's hair tonic. One day, Don's father filled the hair-tonic jar with poke-salad oil, and the unwitting Herman barely knew the difference. "Wore it two, three weeks," said the barber with relish. "Stayed on there real good."

The white-haired man seemed to be transported by this talk of olden days. He looked through the window, peering wistfully across the street to a sign that stood among the weeds declaring the presence of the Saratoga First Assembly of God. "Used to be a beer joint right there," he said, as if trying within his mind to bring this place back to life.

Don piped up again. "They called him Greensleeves round here when he was a kid. See, he'd get dressed up in this white shirt when he went round singin' and playin' that git-tar of his for coins, and he had this way of wipin' his nose on his sleeve in between songs."

In 1941, the Jones family moved to Kountze, the Hardin County seat, some fifteen miles northwest of Saratoga. It was there that ten-year-old George began performing at the Saturday-night revival meetings of Sister Annie Stephens, the Sunday-school teacher who had taught George his first chords, and her husband, Brother Byrle. A year later, as wartime brought prosperity to the shipyards, the Jones family moved again, to Multimax Village, a government-subsidized housing-project in Beaumont, where George's father found work as a pipefitter at the Pennsylvania Shipyard. It was in Beaumont, during the war years, that George Jones, having reached the seventh grade, left school behind him.

And it was in Beaumont that young George became aware of a new sort of country music, something quite different from the old-timey string-band stuff that still represented the sound of the Grand Ole Opry. In Texas, as most everywhere else, the biggest hit of 1943–44 was "Pistol Packin' Mama." Written and recorded by a forty-one-year-old Texan named Al Dexter, "Pistol Packin' Mama" became the first country hit to be performed on "Your Hit Parade," radio's weekly presentation of America's most popular songs. (When the show's troupe performed Dexter's song, the word "beer" was censored from the lyrics.) In addition to being an immense country hit, the song, in the summer of 1943, crossed over to become a #1 hit on the *Billboard* pop charts, and, that autumn, crossed over to the "Harlem Hit Parade," *Billboard*'s early black-music chart. Following Dexter onto the pop charts was a cover version by Bing Crosby with the Andrews sisters. Lusty, capricious, raucous, and reflecting the sophisticated influence of western swing, "Pistol Packin' Mama" was the commercial apotheosis of honky-tonk, a burgeoning genre of country—and, at first, distinctly Texan—music that both celebrated the wild side of life and lamented its wages. Al Dexter himself had done much to set a precedent with his "Honky Tonk Blues" of 1936. By the time of "Pistol Packin' Mama," the dark side of honky-tonk was being explored in songs of fatalism such as "It Makes No Difference Now," written by Floyd Tillman and first recorded, in the fall of 1938, by Cliff Bruner's Texas Wanderers, and Ted Daffan's "Born to Lose," the other great honky-tonk hit of 1943–44, which was every bit as bleak and doomful as "Pistol Packin' Mama" was gay and upbeat. Tillman, Bruner, and Daffan had risen to prominence performing on radio station KTRH in Houston, whose broadcasts were heard clearly seventy miles away in Beaumont. These and other Texans—such as Jerry Irby, the Houston singer whose 1946 "Nails in My Coffin" was a danceable paean to alcoholic suicide, and Ernest Tubb, whose cover version of Irby's song became a nationwide country hit—defined the spirit and sound that overtook country music in the post-war years. But the greatest honky-tonk singer of them all, the greatest voice that George Jones had heard since Roy Acuff's, belonged to a twenty-three-year-old newcomer from Alabama.

It was in April of 1947 that George Jones heard Hank Williams for the first time. The record was "I Don't Care (If Tomorrow Never Comes)." It was followed in May by "Honky Tonkin'," and by midsummer, Hank Williams had his first hit, "Move It On Over," a raw-swinging piece of backwoods jitterbug jive that would stand as one of the seminal emanations of nascent rock & roll.

Hank Williams's music was a mixture of grave dirt, whiskey, and lamb's blood. Self-doomed and self-tormenting, Williams wrote and sang of a world where love danced endlessly with loss, sin with salvation, laughter with despair. It was for him quite natural to drift, as he did in a recording studio one day in April 1947, from "Move It On Over" to "I Saw the Light" to "Six More Miles to the Graveyard." For George Jones, there was something in his songs and the way he sang them that made a dark poem of all those things that he, George himself, did not yet, and in a way never would, understand: the drunken desperation of his father, the washed-in-the-blood Baptist howlings, and the powers of the heart that drove one man to whiskey, another to prayer, another to song, and another to all three. By this time, all the Jones children had set out on their own, save George, the youngest, who was left alone with his warring parents in a household of deepening misery. Jailed frequently for his drunkenness, George Washington Jones seemed no longer to be a man, let alone a father; and Clara, recoiling from his wretchedness ever further into herself, seemed to be drained of all love and life. To George, home had become a place where happiness never dwelled, and he stayed away as much as he could, wandering from one night to another among his scattered kin and returning time and again to Brother Byrle and Sister Annie. Hank Williams seemed to express something of the enormous confusion, desperation, and pervasive loneliness that George could feel but not grasp. He seemed, in a way, kindred.

"It was the songs," George would say; "the way he delivered 'em." He would search for a way to describe what he heard in them, but, in the end, "just a lot of heart and soul" was all that he could find.

By the summer of Hank Williams's ascent, fifteen-year-old George had teamed up with another teenage musician, Dalton Henderson, who had his own early-morning radio show on KTXJ in his hometown of Jasper, at the northern edge of the Big Thicket. George stayed nights with the Henderson family in Jasper, and it was on KTXJ, with Dalton, that George made his radio debut. He went on to bigger things in 1948, joining Eddie and Pearl, a husband-and-wife act that had something of a devoted following in Beaumont. When George's father lost his job at the shipyard and moved with Clara to nearby Vidor, Eddie and Pearl took him in to live at their trailer home. It was in the spring of 1949, while performing with Eddie and Pearl at radio station KRIC in Beaumont, that George met up with Hank Williams.

"He was appearing in town that night," George recalled. "He was a friend of the program director, Neville Powell; and Neville invited him by to do a song on our afternoon four o'clock show, you know, to promote his dance that night at, I believe it was, the Blue Jean Club, or the Old Corral. I believe it was the Old Corral. He was quite friendly. He came in, sat on the couch, and talked quite a bit with Pearl and all of us. I guess I was too scared to open my mouth; I just listened."

By the time he was eighteen, Jones, appearing alone and with other musicians, was a familiar figure in the Beaumont-area honky-tonks: the Teacup Inn on Sabine Pass Avenue, Lola and Shorty's down by the waterfront, Miller's Café on College Street, Glenn Vista on the old Houston Highway, Yvonne's out on the Port Arthur Highway, the Redtop Drive-In in Silsbee, the Gulf Inn down in Gilchrist, and a slew of other joints. He stood barely five foot seven. It was as big as he would ever get. His voice was something else: as big as the Texas sky, and growing.

It was during this period that Huey Meaux, who was barbering in Winnie and moonlighting as a drummer, came to know and perform with Jones, who, according to Huey, was "like any other kid. In them days, all you did was went to dancehalls and drank beer and fought all night, 'cause there was no other sports to do in them days. And that was the name of the game: who was the best fighter. If you didn't have a fight that night, the dance wasn't worth a shit. It's that way in them days. George was a pretty good fighter, but he was like me, got his ass whipped all the time. I knew him 'cause we'd hang around the joints and the places where music was at. Me and George, we always liked the joints. The *joint* joints, y'know, that would set maybe thirty people and had a little dance-floor maybe ten-by-ten, a jukebox blarin', that was it."

Though Jones would maintain that "it was probably in '56 or '57" that he began drinking, Dalton Henderson would remember him sneaking drinks when they were playing as kids in Jasper. "It would change his personality so much that it scared me," Henderson would say. And Huey clearly recalled of the old days in Beaumont that Jones "always liked his whiskey."

That liking was an ambivalent one. Jones hated whiskey for the grief it had wrought through his father. Huey recalled an incident at the Jones home in Vidor: "They had a frame house and them old-timey hedges, y'know. And George's daddy would stash his bottles in them hedges. I went out there one day with George, and George set fire to them hedges. Poured gas all the way down to the goddamn street, the highway, and set fire to that motherfucker. And when that sonofabitch went to burn, it went to blowin' up, brother, and the old man come runnin' out the goddamn house, man, and I'm gonna tell you somethin', he wanted to *kill* George." On the other hand, George was heading down that same lost highway.

It was at Playground Park, on the west side of Beaumont, that George had first met and performed with Eddie and Pearl; and it was at Playground Park that George met Dorothy Bonvillon, the daughter of a local banker. To those who knew him, it seemed that eighteen-year-old George rushed into marriage seeking all the security and happiness that family life had never provided him. He married Dorothy, in Port Arthur, on June 1, 1950. Ceding to the wishes of his Cajun father-in-law, George took a regular day-job as an apprentice house-painter with the Sargl Paint Company of Beaumont. Other jobs followed. He drove a 7-Up truck and worked as an ambulance attendant for the Williams Funeral Home. But George's heart was in the joints, and his marriage fell apart in less than a year. On June 23, 1951, Dorothy Jones, who was six months pregnant, filed for divorce, charging that her estranged husband was "a man of violent temper" and "addicted to the drinking of alcoholic beverages." She was awarded $35 a week in support, for the nonpayment of which, on August 24, George was held in contempt of court and spent five days in jail before his kin bailed him out. Barely a month later, thirteen days after his nineteenth birthday, he was jailed again for nonpayment. Dorothy gave birth to their child, a daughter named Susan, on October 28; and on November 16, George was brought to court again. Rather than face jail again, he decided to seek refuge in the armed forces. It was as a last resort that he joined the marines.

"I wasn't about to go in the Marine Corps. I tried everything else first. The air force put me on a waiting-list. The navy wouldn't have me, and I didn't like the army. When I went to the navy, they had a pretty strict test that I couldn't pass, but they said, 'You want to go in bad, don't you?' I said, 'Yes. I'd leave today.' They took me right next-door to the Marine Corps, and they swore me in. It was better than goin' back to jail."

He was shipped to California, where he completed his basic training at the San Diego Marine Corps Recruit Depot and was assigned to duty at the Moffett Field Naval Air Station in San Jose. On New Years Day, Hank Williams, age twenty-nine, was found dead in the backseat of a car en route to a show in Ohio. In April, Bill Haley's recording of "Crazy, Man, Crazy" swept through the air, giving America its first taste of white-man rock & roll. And in June, back home in Beaumont, Jack Starnes Jr., a local entrepreneur, and Harold W. Daily, the operator of a Houston juke-box-and-vending-machine outfit called Southeast Amusement, started a little record company named after an elision of their combined surnames: Starday. At the age of fifty-one, Daily was already known by the name of Pappy.

Starnes and his wife, Neva, had been running a joint called Neva's Dancehall out near their home on Voth Road since before the war. Through their honky-tonk, George had come to know them as well as their teenage son, Bill, who would later gain notoriety as a bank-robber before getting involved in the undertaking and music rackets. ("Very fast cat," Huey Meaux would say of Bill Starnes. "Too fast for the regular guys. He was about seventeen when he robbed the bank in Saratoga. Ran to Beaumont and threw the moneybags behind the jukebox in Neva's, yelled out to Jack, 'They're right behind me!'") For a year and a half, Starnes had managed Lefty Frizzell, a twenty-five-year-old singer from Corsicana, Texas, whose success, since the autumn of 1950, had rivaled that of Hank Williams. A boozer and a brawler, Frizzell, like Williams, was a honky-tonk singer. But his voice was as pure and pretty and melodic as Williams's was raw; and in it, Jones had found the last of his influences, an influence he had absorbed not only through Frizzell's Columbia recordings, but also in person, as Frizzell in 1951 had been a frequent performer at Neva's. By November 1953, when twenty-two-year-old George Jones returned to civilian life in Beaumont, Lefty Frizzell's star had already begun to fade, but the beauty of his voice had not.

Starday's first release, in June 1953, had been a novelty record by Mary Jo Chelette, an adolescent radio performer from Port Arthur who was managed by Neva Starnes. The company so far had enjoyed one hit, "You All Come," by Arlie Duff, a Big Thicket native who was known as "The Singing School Teacher" and was also managed by Neva Starnes. Released in July, Duff's record had appeared on the Houston territorial C&W charts in early October and by December had risen to the national country charts. The little company seemed to be growing: Don Pierce, a former owner and sales manager of 4-Star Records in California, had, for the sum of $333, joined Starday as a one-third partner, opened a Los Angeles office of Starday, and formed another company, Hollywood Records, which he ran as a black-music affiliate of Starday. The Duff record, Starday's first, fortuitous hit, was still on the national charts when, on the evening of January 19, 1954, Jones was summoned to the Starnes home to try his hand at making a record.

Gordon Baxter, a local singer and broadcaster who had begun his radio career, at KPAC in Port Arthur, in the summer of 1945, was also summoned that day to the house on Voth Road. The Starday recording studio was a room whose walls had been lined with cardboard egg-crating to enhance the acoustics. Fourteen-year-old Bill Starnes served as engineer, operating an old Magnacorder. (According to Gordon Baxter, the bank Bill later robbed was in the Thicket community of Sour Lake, and Bill "tried to make his getaway on the bus. They picked him up and the gym bag full of cash at the bus station.")

"I thought I was gonna be a hillbilly star, and so did George. I didn't know him at the time," Baxter recalled. "So, I went to Neva's. She had a few Magnacorders. I did my thing, and we played it back. I thought there was something wrong with the tape. 'It's dragging,' I said. 'No. That's how you sound.' I discovered then and there that I was tone-deaf, that I'd been gettin' away with it all those years. Then along comes this scrawny-ass kid and, damn, with his range and his volume, he sounded almost like an opera singer. I thought, 'Who is this kid?' Then I saw that his name was on the back of his belt: George Jones."

A few days later, there was an item in *Billboard*: "Starday Records has signed three new artists to recording contracts, with releases by George Jones, of Beaumont, Tex., and Gordon Baxter, assistant manager of KPAC, Port Arthur, Tex., scheduled to be released shortly." Released in February, George's first record was reviewed in *Billboard* in early March. "No Money in This Deal" was described as a "lively country novelty" with "a good catch phrase," while the flipside, "You're in My Heart," was perceived as too imitative of his hero: "Ditty, a country weeper, derives directly from the Hank Williams school." Nevertheless, "George Jones belts it out with fair effectiveness." More than forty years later, Jones himself would say that "No Money in This Deal" was, "Oh, just one of them stupid things you write at the time. Bunch of junk. It didn't seem like junk so much back in those days, but it would be junk today."

Beaumont was a wide-open town in the post-war years. Gambling, prostitution, and after-hours joints thrived. Hank Williams, a fervent collector of guns, was one of several honky-tonk singers who enjoyed a special relationship with the Beaumont Police Department. "Whenever he came to Beaumont," said Don Jacobs of the *Beaumont Enterprise*, "the cops would gather up all the Saturday-night specials they'd confiscated and sell them to Hank." Once, in town to do a police-benefit show, Hank took to shooting out the streetlights from the window of his suite at the King Edward Hotel. "They merely asked him to stop," recalled Ken Ritter, a music-business entrepreneur who became Beaumont's mayor in 1968. In the fifties, under the benison of Charlie Meyers, the Jefferson County Sheriff, and Jimmy Pocono, the mayor of Beaumont, the sway of the rackets remained unvanquished until 1961, when a senate investigating committee led by glory-hunting Congressman Tom James set Beaumont on its way to becoming what it is today: a town defined by sepulchral, dead-modern Methodist and Baptist church buildings, a downtown whose life has been lost to the malls and where the only thing open after sundown is a shabby McRory's on a deserted corner. In the days when George Jones was coming into his own, before it fell to decency, Beaumont was the honky-tonk heaven of the Golden Triangle, as Texans call that mating-ground of sin and salvation whose cornerstones of demarcation are Beaumont, Port Arthur, and Orange.

Beaumont, like Houston, had been a hotbed of western swing, the jazz-inflected music of the thirties and forties that had introduced both drums and the amplified steel-guitar to country music; and the honky-tonk bands that were heard thereabouts built upon that tradition of drums and amplified instruments. On occasion, George made music at the Gulf Inn in Gilchrist and elsewhere with old-timers such as Cliff Bruner, the western swing fiddler who had been one of the great pioneers of east-Texas honky-tonk. Floyd Tillman, the author of the honky-tonk classic "It Makes No Difference Now," was also one of Jones's early supporters, proclaiming one night from the stage of Yvonne's, "This guy's destined to be one of the greatest country singers in the world." But it was among musicians of his own age that he managed eventually to summon the power to free his own voice from the influences of Acuff, Williams, and Frizzell. In 1954, a new sort of sound was blossoming from the common soil of honky-tonk and other Southern music. They would call it rockabilly, and Elvis, who made his first records that summer, would be seen as its avatar. At the Ritz Club, a Beaumont after-hours joint where musicians congregated after work to drink and often play informally together until dawn, George and others breathed new life into the honky-tonk music that they had cut their teeth on; a new life that, through George and a few others, would keep country music alive and compelling through the rock & roll years to come. And, though he would never acknowledge it, the rockabilly impulse affected his sound as much as the lingering voices of Acuff, Williams, and Frizzell.

In early 1954, Starday teamed him with Sonny Burns. Not quite a year older than Jones, Burns was a hard-drinking singer from Nacogdoches who had begun recording for Starday in the fall of 1953 and in the spring of 1954 had a local hit with "A Place for Girls Like You." Like Jones, he was a honky-tonk singer, with somewhat more pronounced leanings toward rockabilly. It was a duet with Burns, "Wrong about You," that resulted in Jones's first appearance on the Houston charts; and the flipside of that record, "Play It Cool, Man, Play It Cool," recorded several months before Elvis's debut, bordered on pure rockabilly. The Burns-and-Jones duo became a familiar presence in Houston, performing at the Plantation Club, Bob's Tavern, the NCO Club at Fort Polk, the Magnolia Gardens east of town, and, most of all, a dive called Amma Dee's that was located on Canal Street, near Sonny's apartment. They became regulars as well on the KNUZ "Houston Jamboree," broadcast every Saturday night from City Auditorium (where, as an added attraction during the show of May 22, 1954, not long before "Wrong about You" hit the local charts, Sonny took the vows of his first, ill-fated marriage). In addition, George began working as a disk-jockey at KTRM in Beaumont, the station where twenty-four-year-old J.P. Richardson of Sabine Pass was developing the rockabilly radio persona that would bring him fame a few years later when he recorded "Chantilly Lace" as the Big Bopper.

Gordon Baxter, who served as the best man at Richardson's wedding, was by then also working at KTRM, and he recalled that it was at KTRM that Jones was nicknamed Possum. "One of the better DJs, Slim Watts, took to calling him George P. Willicker Picklepuss Possum Jones. For one thing, he cut his hair short, like a possum's belly. He had a possum's nose, and had stupid eyes, like a possum."

When asked what his KTRM show was like, Jones laughed openly. "Well," he said, "I can't remember what it was like too much, but it was, like, an hour show in the evening. I was playin' records. Had commercials in-between. The big old long reel-to-reel. I'd get nervous at first, when I first had the job; I'd get real nervous and break a lot of the tapes. That was the sad story back in those days, always breakin' tapes and havin' to splice and put 'em back together." Jones, Baxter said, "had to pull a mike shift to make a living." Jones agreed: "It was just a way to pick up a dollar."

Those were drunken days and drunken nights. Sonny, who would later feel that he was "the one who got George started drinkin' hard," was even more grave-bent in his ways than George. They sang drunk, for drunks. Even Jack Neil, the owner and manager of KTRM, was an alky. Every once in a while, old George Washington Jones himself would stagger reeking into the studio seeking to put the touch on his boy.

Once again, George felt himself drawn to the solace of family life that had eluded him. In late August 1954, in Houston, he met an eighteen-year-old carhop named Shirley Ann Corley, in town for the summer from the small Texas town of Center. On September 14, 1954, after a two-week courtship, he married her, in Houston, and together they set up home in Beaumont.

In the spring of 1955, when Elvis Presley covered Houston ground that was now long familiar to Sonny and George—the KNUZ "Jamboree," Magnolia Gardens, and so on—Jones met up with a childhood neighbor named Darrell Edwards. From the settlement of Depot Town, near Saratoga, Edwards, now in his mid-thirties, had been George's babysitter back in the Big Thicket. He was an aspiring poet and lyricist, and he gave George a copy of a song he had written, an uptempo god-damn-her-eyes honky-tonk ditty called "Why, Baby, Why." By this time, Jack Starnes had sold his interest in Starday to Pappy Daily and Don Pierce, and Starday had a new studio. From 1946 to 1951, Bill Quinn's Gold Star Records in Houston had issued records by a wide and exciting range of local talent, from Cajun fiddler Harry Choates to bluesman Lightnin' Hopkins. Now Pappy Daily had helped finance the reopening by Quinn of a bigger Gold Star Studio, which was to serve as the new Starday recording-center. It was to Quinn's new studio, on Brock Street, that Jones took "Why, Baby, Why." Pappy wanted to record the song as a duet by George and Sonny, but Sonny got drunk and failed to show up, so George did it alone. Upon its release that summer, it was the flipside of the record, "Seasons of My Heart," a song that Jones and Edwards had written together, that garnered attention, appearing on the Houston charts in late August. But "Why, Baby, Why" eventually overtook it, and, in late October, the month that saw the birth of Jones's second child and first son, Jeffrey Glenn, "Why, Baby, Why" broke into the national country charts.

"Why, Baby, Why" remained on the charts for more than four months, rising to the #4 position and allowing him to perform on the Louisiana Hayride. Broadcast by KWKH from the Municipal Auditorium in Shreveport, and carried by twenty-seven stations in four states, the Saturday-night Hayride was where Hank Williams had made his big-time debut and where Elvis Presley was now being featured. "I didn't get to know him that well," Jones recalled of Elvis in those days when they were both at fame's edge. "He stayed pretty much with his friends around him in the dressing-room. Nobody seemed to get around him much any length of time and talk to him." Except for the dressing-room friends, Jones, a loner even backstage, could have been speaking of himself.

Sonny Burns's popularity and record sales had until now overshadowed Jones's. But while "Why, Baby, Why" was rising on the national charts, Sonny's new record, "A Real Cool Cat," went nowhere. Burns lingered at Starday for another year, then faded. "He was a pretty nice guy," Jones would say many years later, adding, "He's a preacher now, in Lufkin. He's got religion." Setting off on his own, George gathered together four Beaumont musicians to serve as his band: guitarist Luther Nallie, who would go on to join the Sons of the Pioneers; his brother, Ray Nallie, on drums; steel guitarist Charlie Tucker; and fiddler Robert Shivers.

"We were with him, on and off, for several years," recalled Ray Nallie, who now runs Ray Nallie Motors in Kountze. "We all had jobs, and we'd work two, three nights a week. We worked all these little old beer-joints. Beaumont, Port Arthur, various places. Four hours a night. Eight, nine dollars a night. That wasn't low wages back then, but we were gonna quit him one night. This was at the 73 Club, in Winnie. We wanted $10 a night and he was only payin' us eight. So, he said, 'OK,' and we quit. And he got some coon-ass fiddle-player up there and played the job, man. So much for quittin'." George, he said, "was a good singer from the git-go. There's no one that can sing a song like George. He was just a little shit-headed at times, that's all."

In November 1955, Jones was sent on a tour of the Gulf Coast with Link Davis, Jerry Jericho, and other Starday acts. In December, out in the west-Texas town of Odessa, he opened for Johnny Cash, whose first record, on Sun, had just hit the national country charts. Three days after Christmas, the Sun-Starday troupe, which now also included the new-comer Carl Perkins, reached Texarkana, across the state. It was in the course of this tour that Jones sold the elements of a song called "Rock 'n' Roll Ruby" to Cash, who paid him $40 for it. As recorded by Cash's fellow Sun artist Warren Smith, "Rock 'n' Roll Ruby," Smith's debut, sold more than 70,000 copies. In April 1956, the same month that Smith's record went on sale, Starday released a double-sided hard-core rockabilly record by Jones, "Rock It" coupled with "How Come It," issued under the name of Thumper Jones.

"I don't guess I'm ever gonna live that down," Jones told me in 1976, before sobriety had in the least bit tempered the Jonesian flair for self-nullifying phraseology and shuffled-deck chronology. "I was actually gettin' started in the business about 1954 or so when all this rock & roll really started movin' in, and, of course, you know, you didn't have stations back then that played all that much country to start with. So, especially with rock & roll getting as strong as it was at that time, it seemed like country music was really a losin' battle except for the three or four major artists that had it made at the time, like Lefty Frizzell, Ernest Tubb, Roy Acuff, some of those people. So we decided to try one, sort of rockabilly-like. I was sort of ashamed to even do it at the time 'cause I was so country, so I just used a different name, went under the name of Thumper Jones." As for what he really felt about rock & roll (and here one encounters the true essence of Jonesian exposition): "I liked quite a bit of the things that came out then, because really you didn't have much else to like. You didn't have the radio stations playin' enough of the country music for you to really have a chance to listen to nothin' but country, so it was a lot of it forced upon us really." In 1993, he was more terse: "Hell," he said, "when you're starvin' to death, you'll try anything."

Jones had begun the year, 1956, with another hit, "What Am I Worth," which led to his debut on the Grand Ole Opry. The hits kept coming throughout the year, and, on August 25, he became a full-fledged member of the Opry, with his first long-play album following in October. That autumn, while Jones's alcoholic lament "Just One More" was on the charts, Pappy Daily negotiated a deal whereby Starday became an affiliate of Mercury Records, commencing January 1, 1957. "There was no such thing as production at Starday," Jones said, "We'd go in with the band, we'd go over the song, I'd look over and tell the steel player to take a break or kick it off, and I'd get the fiddle to play a turn-around in the middle. I'd just let them know if we were gonna tag it or not. We'd just go through it. We didn't take the pains of making several takes. Back then, over three or four takes, they'd say, 'My God, this is costing us money.' So we'd just get it down as good as we could. If we went a little flat or sharp in a place or two, they'd say, 'The public ain't gonna notice that, so put it out.' So we did, and it wasn't too successful, so I think maybe the public did notice it."

Beginning in 1957, when Starday moved its headquarters to the Nashville suburb of Madison, Tennessee, and George started recording in Nashville, those conditions were behind him. With each new recording, he sounded less and less like Hank Williams, more and more like George Glenn Jones. In the summer of 1958, when the Starday-Mercury affiliation dissolved, Pappy Daily sold out his interest in the company to Don Pierce and negotiated a new deal with Mercury for Jones and himself. That July, when Shirley Jones gave birth to a second son, George named him in Pappy's honor: Bryan Daily Jones. Pappy had taken over George's management from Bill Hall of Beaumont. As his manager, producer, publishing-partner, and friend, Pappy seemed to be the paternal presence that George had never truly known. Huey Meaux, who credits Daily with helping his own career as a producer get underway, said that George would have been lost without Pappy. "Oh, yes! He was George's career. He was George's daddy. He was George's everything. And George gave him a lot of goddamn hell, man. Gettin' drunk, gettin' in trouble, gettin' in fights. Pappy carried the big stick in Houston, and he was the only one that could sit down and talk to George. He was a very laid-back old gentleman, and he could talk to George in a way that George listened to him. Sometimes George would get mad at him, didn't want to work with him. But then he would go out there and would really fuck up. Pappy got George back together so many times it's unreal. He was the only guy in the world who could. Pappy had a heart made of gold, and he loved George's singin' above anything, but he also loved George kind of like a son. George was a son to him. I seen that closeness too many, many times, where if it had been me, I'd have kicked George right in the ass."

In September 1958, at Owen Bradley's basement recording studio in Nashville, George made the record that would take him to the top. Written by his buddy J. P. Richardson, "White Lightning" was fast, frivolous, and infectious, a song that George's singing redeemed and raised from the level of mere novelty. Richardson, whose recording of "Chantilly Lace" was currently high on both the pop and R&B charts, would not live to see the success of his song "White Lightning." On February 3, 1959, barely a month before Jones's record hit the country charts, the Big Bopper, age twenty-eight, went down in the same plane crash that killed Buddy Holly and Ritchie Valens. "White Lightning" remained on the country charts for nearly six months, rising to #1 in April and crossing over in May to the pop charts.

Years ago, George's parents had relocated to the outlying suburb of Vidor. "Serving Port Arthur, Beaumont, Orange, and bloody Vidor," is what Gordon Baxter, still a broadcaster in Beaumont, announces on the air when he gives the call letters of KOLE, which, off the air, he describes as "a little chickenshit station whose signal barely reaches the city limits." Bloody Vidor, as he puts it, is a town of perhaps 11,000 souls. Its one black resident, Vidor's first since the 1920s, lived under protective guard after moving there under a federal desegregation order in February 1993. During the sixties, there was a sign at the town limits: "NIGGER, DON'T LET THE SUN SET ON YOU IN VIDOR." Indeed, black visitors to the Golden Triangle are still warned against traveling to Vidor after dark, and though the town's Main Street, with its fast-food franchises and its one-story brick City Hall resembling a suburban doctor's office, today presents the bland, plastic, have-a-nice-day smile of mediocrity, it is a place not only where George Jones Country Gold Dog Food is on prominent display at Wood's Supermarket, but also where white-robed Klansmen burn crosses, hand out white-pride literature, and solicit funds to "Keep Vidor White." That bland, plastic, have-a-nice-day smile is the smile of the Klan. "Every Klansperson in Texas is invited," read one perky and politically correct rally-announcement, filed from Vidor, in the "News of the Greater Golden Triangle" section of the *Beaumont Enterprise* back in the feminist late seventies. And back in the late fifties, bloody Vidor was an

even far bloodier place. It was to that idyllic suburban cracker-land that George
Jones, flush with newfound prosperity, moved his family in 1959.

In early 1960, at home in Vidor, Jones wrote a song called "The Window Up
Above." Of all the songs he has written, it remains his favorite. "I wrote it in
about twenty minutes," he said. "I just came in off the road, about eight in the
morning. While breakfast was being fixed, I just sat down in the den and picked
up the guitar, and it was as simple as that. Sometimes it's hard to even figure
where the ideas come from." The idea, of a man's delusion of happy home-life
shattered by a single, providential glimpse of his wife's infidelity, was invested in
the song with the uncanny, dream-like quality of well-being subsumed by dread:

> *I've been living a new way*
> *Of life that I love so;*
> *But I can see the clouds are gathering*
> *And the storm will wreck our home.*

Though, as George said, it sometimes might be difficult to figure out where
ideas come from, "The Window Up Above" seemed to issue directly from a life-
long insecurity and ambivalence, a deep-rooted, heartfelt fear of the anguish
that lurked beneath the dream of hearth and home and happiness. Released in
the autumn of 1960, "The Window Up Above" remained on the country charts
for more than eight months. George even had Nudie of North Hollywood, the
celebrated tailor of egregiously gaudy Western wear, make him a stage-suit illus-
trative of the song, a chartreuse affair replete with teary faces peering from se-
quin-stitched windowframes. "The Window Up Above" marked what many
purists felt to be an egregious development in George's music itself: the use of
background voices to sweeten the effect of his own hard-edged honky-tonk delivery. Through the sixties and into the seventies, background voices and orchestral string sections were to become an increasing presence in country
music. Jones's voice, however, with its noble gravity, its capacity to wring from
every word its full color and power, and its instinctive poet's sense of rhythm,
usually was able to transcend the stultifying effects of the so-called "country-
politan" trend. Considering that Jones, for much of his career, has been a complaisant victim of minimal or bad production, insipid arrangements, and
frequently pedestrian or mawkish material, the surpassing power of that voice
as documented in such less-than-optimal recordings is all the more remarkable.

In the summer of 1962, "Tender Years," written by Darrell Edwards, became
Jones's biggest hit to date, remaining in the #1 position on the country charts
for seven weeks and crossing over to the pop charts. While the record was at its
height, Pappy Daily struck a lucrative deal for Jones and himself, as a producer
and artist-and-repertoire executive, with the newly formed country-music division of United Artists Records. Meanwhile, in Beaumont, Bill Hall and Jack
Clement, formerly a producer with Sun Records in Memphis and RCA in

Nashville, opened a recording studio, Gulf Coast Sound, downtown on Fourth Street, next to the King Edward Hotel. Visiting Gulf Coast one day, Jones became interested in an old tape-recorder that Hall and Clement had lying around gathering dust, while Hall was intent on selling him on a new song written by Dickie Lee Lipscomb and Steve Duffy, two young writers under contract to Hall-Clement Music. As Ray Nallie remembered it: "Bill was tryin' to get him to do this damn tune, 'She Thinks I Still Care.' But George wanted this old damn tape-recorder that didn't even work; it was just over there in a corner. Bill wouldn't even talk about it. He said, 'Listen to this damn tune, man.' And George listened to it, said, 'I don't like it, man. There's too many damn *just because*'s in it. I don't like the goddamn thing, don't wanna do it.' This went on for hours, seemed like, George wantin' to talk about the tape-recorder, which wasn't worth nothin', and Bill wantin' to talk about that 'just-because' song. Finally, Bill said, 'I tell you what I'll do. If you go 'head and record the goddamn song, I'll *give* you the fuckin' tape-recorder.' And that's how he did it."

Jones does not remember it that way. "No," he said, "I sorta flipped over the song when I heard it. I don't know where all those tales get started. There's a lot of hearsay." Jones recorded the song, for United Artists, in January 1962, and by mid-May it was a #1 country hit, a perfect country song of heartache and denial. Looking back, Jones would regard his United Artist years as perhaps his finest period. "We did a lot of the pure country then," he said. This was the time of several lackluster but commercially successful duets with Melba Montgomery, but it was also the time of his reconstituted-rockabilly hit "The Race Is On," and of less-known but magnificent performances such as "Warm Red Wine" and "Open Pit Mine," a chilling little tale of adultery and remorseless murder. It was midway through the United Artists years, the fall of 1963, that sixty-eight-year-old George Washington Jones was committed to the alcoholics' ward of the Rusk State Mental Hospital, north of Nacogdoches.

In January 1965, as "The Race Is On" was crossing over to the pop charts, Pappy Daily negotiated yet another and more lucrative deal for Jones and himself, with Musicor Records, a former United Artists subsidiary that had now been taken over by Art Talmadge, a friend of Pappy's from the Mercury days. The late sixties were a strange time for the singer. As the soul of America was set adrift in a Day-Glo cloud of patchouli-scented ahimsa and sensitivity, it seemed as if Jones, in his crewcut and his Nudie suits, strove, with the aid of an increasingly corny repertoire, to singlehandedly defend the citadel of Vidor, and all it stood for, against the encroaching horde of tie-dyed freethinkers. His role in the 1965 sixteen-millimeter redneck musical comedy *Forty Acre Feud* seemed a diametric response to *A Hard Day's Night;* and in the Summer of Love, as Jim Morrison's cry of "We want the world and we want it now" echoed through the land, George responded with a song called "Take the World but Give Me Jesus." At one point, late in 1967—by which time the singer had begun to let his trademark brushcut grow out a bit—he and Pappy Daily gave folk-rock their best shot with "Unwanted Babies," a garbled protest song written for Jones by Peanut Montgomery. Combining his middle name and his mother's maiden name, the record label bore the pseudonym of Glen Patterson. "We did a certain type of song that we thought might would sell at that time," George said, taken aback at the mention of it, "but it wasn't the type of song that I would've normally cut, and I just didn't want to use my real name." But perhaps his lowest moment was "The Poor Chinee," released in January 1968 and containing the unforgettable lyrics "Me likee bow-wow, very good chow-chow." (Perhaps a karmic connection to his future role as dog-food pitch-man.)

By then, Jones had built a new, bigger home, on Lakeview Road, in Vidor, where he had also, in the summer of 1966, opened an ill-fated and short-lived country-music park. In 1967, the year his father died, Jones committed himself briefly to a neurological hospital in the first of many attempts to seek treatment for alcoholism. His marriage, since 1964, had been coming apart. As his wife saw it, his drinking had caused the rift. Shortly after his release from the hospital, George began accusing Shirley of carrying on an affair with J. C. Arnold, a Vidor businessman and former friend of George's. She, in turn, accused him of having taken up with Melba Montgomery, with whom he still occasionally performed and recorded.

"I remember George goin' one night and shootin' his old lady's boyfriend in the ass," laughed Huey Meaux. Though all involved would later deny this alleged shotgun attack, it would remain a part of Golden Triangle legendry.

George and Shirley separated in the spring of 1968. Upon their divorce, George was ordered to surrender his share of their Vidor homestead and pay $1,000 a month in child support. Shirley later married J. C. Arnold, and George packed up, bade farewell to bloody Vidor, and moved to Nashville.

Two years before, while making a record with Melba Montgomery at Columbia Studio A in Nashville, George had met Tammy Wynette, a twenty-four-year-old former hairdresser from Mississippi who had recently moved to Nashville. By the spring of 1968, she was enjoying her fourth #1 hit, "D-I-V-O-R-C-E." One night not long after he moved to town, Jones interceded in an argument between Wynette and her second husband, the songwriter Don Chapel, who had introduced George to Tammy two years before. The couple had not been married long, nor would they be. George's drunken profession of love for her during the course of that angry night precipitated their break-up. The romance of George Jones and Tammy Wynette, the king and queen of country music, was like a Provençal love story in a land of Nudie-tailored troubadours. As if in public celebration of their romance, Tammy's recording of "Stand by Your Man" became a #1 hit that Thanksgiving week, and George soon responded with "I'll Share My World with You." By January 1969, George and Tammy were living together. With her as a singing partner, George rejoined the Grand Ole Opry, which he had left several years before, and together, consolidating their shows, they took to the road. In February, in Ringgold, Georgia, they married, and, in March, they moved to Lakeland, Florida. Together they appeared in *From Nashville with Music,* another cinematic prodigy in the tradition of *Forty Acre Feud.*

After fifteen years together, Jones had a bitter falling-out with Pappy Daily. "We were fairly close at one time," George would say in the way of explaining that sudden and long-mysterious breach. "Then the truth comes out. These people on the other end of the stick are in it for the money too. He was pitchin' me around to different labels and I kind of got tired of that. Made deals on the side for extra money for hisself, which I never found out till later. It was a good association the first few years, and then it kind of got a little more businesslike and they didn't live up to their part of the agreements." Jones began meeting with Tammy's producer, Billy Sherrill of Epic Records, and he made plans to sign with Epic as soon as his Musicor contract ran out, in the fall of 1971. George became a father again, in October 1970, when Tammy gave birth to a daughter they named Tamala Georgette. Once again, however, hearth and home were not enough, and it seemed that Huey Meaux was right, that George was lost without Pappy. Two weeks after the birth of his new daughter, Jones celebrated the opening of his second ill-starred entertainment park, Old Plantation Music Park, built on the forty-three-acre estate that surrounded their new home, a refurbished nineteenth-century mansion in the countryside outside of Lakeland. In the throes of the long and violent binge that followed, Jones was straitjacketed and committed to a padded cell at the Watson Clinic in Lakeland, where he was kept to detoxify for ten days and released with a prescription for Librium to quell his depressive anxieties. Six years later, he would tell Bob Allen, the author of the book *George Jones: The Saga of An American Singer,* that "a special doctor at the Watson Clinic had typed out three or four pages, in his words, describing this person that was me. He started off saying I was a shy person. I disliked violence but took a lot of abuse, just to keep from havin' problems." He had nothing against psychiatrists, he said, sipping from a glass of Jack Daniel's and 7-Up, "but I still think the best counselor in the world is yourself."

Joan Dew, then a journalist with *Country Music* magazine and the coauthor of Tammy Wynette's autobiography, *Stand by Your Man,* believed that Tammy was not only distraught by George's drinking but bored by the marriage as well. "I think she really got bored with him very quick down there," Dew told fellow country-music journalist Dolly Carlisle. "George is a little fuddy-duddy. He's like a little old lady. He's not exciting. He sits around and watches TV all day and goes fishing. George is only exciting onstage. He's not funny; he doesn't have a good sense of humor. He's smart but not intellectually witty. Apparently, he's a lousy lover. I haven't heard of an alcoholic who wasn't." Sex, Dew said, "was very, very important to Tammy. And I think by then she was bored."

In October 1971, Jones signed with Epic and began work with Billy Sherrill on an album called *Me and the First Lady.* Sherrill's production, influenced by

Phil Spector's "wall-of-sound" technique, was adept and sophisticated. Though the lush orchestral arrangements and saccharine background voices that were Sherrill's trademark were regarded by many as softening and diminishing the natural grandeur of Jones's voice, there can be no doubt that Sherrill's production helped keep the singer commercially alive at a time when country music was increasingly beset, and the old guard increasingly endangered, by the winds of a new era. Jones himself was ambivalent about the sound of his recordings. "I went along with the record company against my better judgment," he told me in the days when he was still working with Sherrill. "I didn't wanna do it, but I let them put strings on my sessions just out of curiosity, more or less, just to see what they might do. When you use strings and horns and all these things, you just don't have country music anymore. You abuse it. Billy Sherrill has always done what he thought would be best for me. He always has. And the sound he's given me is great. The strings, the big productions—Billy Sherrill thought this was the best thing. But we've talked about it, and were gonna get back to a more hard-core sound. I've got too much respect for country music to abuse it. I don't want eleven thousand violins and twenty trumpets on my records. If the song's there, that's all I need. That's all anybody needs. I like a good, solid honky-tonk song." His next album, *Alone Again,* released in October 1976, did indeed have a leaner and more visceral sound. But somehow, he would not begin to return fully in his recordings to that "more hard-core sound" for years to come; and in 1993, he repeated to me his intention of long ago: "I'm trying to get back to the pure country." It struck me then that, to him, "pure country" might be the unattainable goal that to some degree kept him moving onward.

The first George-and-Tammy duet, "Take Me," appeared on the country charts on Christmas Day. In 1972, the couple returned to live at Tammy's home on Old Hickory Lake in Nashville. Several months later, on the first day of April 1973, while George was off on another long binge, Tammy filed for divorce. They reconciled and purchased a luxurious new home on Tyne Boulevard in the Belle Meade section. Tammy's taste was as garish as George's, and they decorated their new home together. There was shag carpeting on the ceiling. In the spring of 1974, shortly after the death of his mother, George had the first of two immense #1 hits, "The Grand Tour," a song about a "lonely house that once was home sweet home." In the fall, there followed "The Door," an even bleaker song of marital dissolution and desertion, a song that invoked the memory of "the sound of my dear old mama crying." He was, at forty-three, at the height of his powers. That his own haunted childhood should now have led not to understanding or resolution but only to the plain, inevitable finality, and ultimate abandonment, of his parents' death seemed to deepen the haunted, and haunting, qualities of his own voice. On December 13, while "The Door" was rising toward the top of the charts, Tammy filed for legal separation; and a few weeks later, on January 8, 1975, she filed once again for divorce. George moved to Florence, Alabama, to be near his drinking buddy Peanut Montgomery and

Peanut's sister-in-law, Linda Welborn, with whom George had already taken up. By the time Tammy's divorce was granted, on March 14, Linda and George were living together, and George had begun his long, slow descent to the bottom. In June, his old friend Darrell Edwards, having fallen on hard times, traveled to Nashville in an attempt to see George. Failing to do so, he returned to Beaumont and blew out his brains. By then, according to many who saw him, George might soon enough be meeting up with Darrell after all.

That summer, Jones signed a management deal with one Alcy Benjamin Baggott Jr., a local hustler better known as Shug. Together, they reopened Shug's shut-down Nashville nightclub, renaming it Possum Holler. The nightclub became a center of, and Shug Baggott one of the key figures of, cocaine-dealing in Nashville. Before long, George, who had long indulged in amphetamine and sedatives, was addicted to cocaine as well as whiskey; and although in the spring of 1976 he made a pretense of overcoming his alcoholism and co-wrote with Peanut Montgomery a heartfelt song called "A Drunk Can't Be a Man," his addictions worsened. The news of Tammy Wynette's brief marriage that summer to realtor Michael Tomlin, and her subsequent marriage, the following summer, to songwriter George Richey, seemed to unhinge him. "I still love her, and that ain't gonna change," he told the writer Joan Dew, a friend of Tammy's. During a nine-month period in 1977–78, there would be fifteen break-ins at the Wynette home; once she would discover the words SLUT and PIG scrawled on her mirrors and television screen. On October 4, 1978, Wynette would be the victim of a yet-unsolved kidnapping. Abducted by a masked gunman from the parking-lot of the Green Hills Shopping Center, she would be taken to an isolated spot along Tennessee State Highway 31A in rural Giles County, beaten, nearly strangled with her own pantyhose, and finally thrown from the car, bruised, hysterical, and suffering a fractured jaw.

On the first of September 1977, with $36,000 in overdue child-support payments to Tammy outstanding, an order was issued for Jones's arrest. On the seventh—known by now as No-show Jones, he vanished and failed to appear at the Bottom Line in New York City for a show that had been anticipated as one of the media events of the season. On the thirteenth, the night after he turned forty-six, he shot at, and very nearly struck, Peanut Montgomery, who had recently quit drinking and found religion. "All right, you sonofabitch," Jones had hollered before firing his Smith & Wesson thirty-eight, "see if your God can save you now!" In October, pleading that he was "addicted to alcohol," the singer sought the mercy of the judge who had ordered his arrest for nonpayment. In December, citing more than $1 million in debts, he filed for bankruptcy in Nashville. Later that month, he was arrested in Alabama on charges of having "assaulted and beat" his ex-girlfriend Linda Welborn. In January 1978, after Shug Baggott was dismissed by him and filed his own bankruptcy petition, Jones was arrested again in Florence on charges, relating to the Montgomery shooting and its aftermath, of making harassing telephone calls and assault with a deadly weapon. "I realize that time's gettin' short," he told Bob Claypool of the *Houston Post.* "I don't have much time left to straighten up." By February, Jones was homeless, deranged, and destitute, living in the backseat of his car and barely able to digest the junk food on which he subsisted. The songwriter and singer Marshall Chapman recalled encountering Jones in an elevator at the Spence Manor hotel in Nashville. His weight was now down to ninety-seven pounds, and he held the front of his trousers bunched up in his fist to keep them raised. To Marshall, as he hurkled before her, trying dolefully to flirt, he seemed in his grisly deterioration to be no longer a man, or even human, but a creature not unlike the *ex-hominem* hedgehog of ineffable misery and penance described by Thomas Mann in *The Holy Sinner.*

His condition was such that it took him more than two years to complete *My Very Special Guests,* an album on which various other singers who idolized him, such as Willie Nelson, Linda Ronstadt, Elvis Costello, and Tammy, came to his vocal aid and support. Peanut Montgomery, who had dropped all charges against George, was still a sympathetic friend, and in December 1979, soon after the album was released, it was Montgomery who brought Jones to the Eliza Coffee Memorial Hospital in Florence. In mid-December, he was transferred to Hillcrest, a private psychiatric hospital in Birmingham that specializes in the treatment of drug and alcohol abuse. A month later, upon his release, the first thing he did was stop and pick up a six-pack. At the end of the month, after drinking beer and snorting cocaine, he held a press conference at Tammy Wynette's Franklin Road home, at which he proclaimed his newfound sobriety. "I read the Bible a lot while undergoing treatment," he said. "Now I can see all the way down the highway." Somehow, seven days later, he managed to record one of the great hits of his career. "He Stopped Loving Her Today," a song of a man whose pitiable, pining love is resolved only through his own death, became his first #1 hit in over five years.

"He Stopped Loving Her Today" revived his dying career. In October 1980, he swept the Country Music Association Awards; in January, he received a Grammy. But his resuscitated success did little to stay the course of his madness. Once again making a pretense of sobriety, in May 1981, he discussed his supposed rehabilitation with a writer from the *Washington Post,* but ended up saying, "You can't hide it, I'm going to have a drink. Hell, we're human." The singer Lorrie Morgan, who joined the Jones troupe in the early summer of 1981, recalled that "those were the no-show days, and it was very scary. The band would go on and stall for time, and the audience would get restless and start throwing stuff onstage, and sometimes George would show up and sometimes he wouldn't. If he didn't, nobody got paid." He was, she said, "a very hard person to get close to." In July, when Jones sought refuge from the world in the Golden Triangle, his relatives had him committed in Beaumont to Baptist Hospital, where his alcoholic father had died fourteen summers ago. By now, he had a new girlfriend, a thirty-three-year-old divorcée from Mansfield, Louisiana, named Nancy Sepulveda, whom he had met at a show in Syracuse, New York. On March 29, 1982, in Mississippi, they were arrested together on charges of cocaine possession. The next day, still in Mississippi, Jones lost control of his car and was hauled away by an ambulance to the Aberdeen-Monroe County Hospital. On the first of April, he was transferred to Hillcrest Psychiatric Hospital in Birmingham, where he remained for thirteen days. Upon his release, he once again proclaimed that he had straightened out his life, this time for good. "The world will see a big difference in me," he told a reporter from the Associated Press. A few weeks later, on May 25, he was arrested in a drunken rage near Franklin, Tennessee. Yet again he declared his sobriety. 'DRUNK' SINGER CYCLES OFF WITH GIRLFRIEND, TEQUILA, read the headline of a story in the *San Antonio News* of August 16, reporting an aborted show at which Jones had appeared late, announced to his audience that he was drunk, and had been roundly booed, and after which he left town "on a motorcycle, with his girlfriend and a bottle of tequila in a sidecar."

Nancy, who neither drank nor took drugs, found herself lost and confused in the vortex of George's self-destruction. When she had first met him, in 1981, he had not seemed all that far gone. "He was drinking," she said, "but he was fun to be around. We'd sit up all night talking. It wasn't love at first sight or anything like that. But I saw what a good person he was, deep down, and I couldn't help but caring for him. He needed somebody, something, so bad." But the whiskey by now had ingrained its poisonous control on every cell of the fifty-year-old singer's flesh and blood, and held his mind in the tidal sway of toxic psychosis. Still Nancy stuck by him, as none of the others had, neither threatening nor hectoring, condoning nor condemning. As Lorrie Morgan saw it, "Nancy really loved him. She was very devoted and dedicated to trying to help him. She withstood a lot of things that I never would have withstood. She really went through a living hell." On March 3, 1983, George married Nancy at the Woodville, Texas, home of his sister, Helen Scroggins. They set up home themselves in Woodville, and George, beaming with relative sobriety, went to work building a ninety-five-acre country-music park, Jones Country, in nearby Colmesneil. The park opened on the following Labor Day. He was still drinking only moderately and had taken to opening his shows with a self-mocking song called "No Show Jones," which he had recorded with Merle Haggard the year before.

When George had seen his own son Bryan strung out on cocaine earlier in the year, he had interpreted it as his own failing, or perhaps as divine retribution, and it filled him with self-revulsion. Nancy had been surprised to see that quitting cocaine had given George little trouble. The booze, however, was a different matter. His mind and his body still screamed for it, and when he started drinking heavily again, in the fall of 1983, it seemed as if his recent sobriety had been only one last deep breath before going under for good. Rampaging through Alabama, suffering from malnutrition and beset by madness, in early 1984, he ended up in a straitjacket at Hillcrest Psychiatric Hospital in Birmingham.

Physicians told Nancy that he was close to death, that any further drinking would be the end.

Released from the hospital in March 1984, thirty years to the month after *Billboard* had reviewed his first record, George Jones performed his first stone-cold-sober show. "It was terrible," Nancy said of that night in Birmingham. "We were alone in the bus, and he was like a scared puppy. 'I can't do it,' he said, 'I can't go on.' He was begging and breaking down and dying for a drink. And when he got out there on that stage, and after the first song, he looked out to me in the audience, and he seemed like such a poor, lost, wounded soul that I burst into tears." But he made it through that show, and he has not taken a drink since then. "All my life it seems like I've been running from something," he told a reporter from the United Press International in June. "If I knew what it was, maybe I could run in the right direction. But I always seem to end up going the other way."

Nancy, who is now George's manager as well as his wife and best friend, has almost singlehandedly set his career aright and kept it going. Not long ago, in the Chisos Mountains of southwestern Texas, I spoke to a twenty-four-year-old man from San Antonio named Mike Alvarez. A rodeo bull-rider, saddle-bronc-rider, and calf-roper who also worked as a trail-guide in the Chisos Basin of Big Bend National Park, Alvarez was an avowed follower and amateur singer of country music. He knew all the singing youngbloods—liked George Strait and Clint Black, disliked Billy Ray Cyrus—but when I mentioned the name of George Jones, the young cowboy seemed not to recognize it. Today Jones is attracting increasingly younger crowds to his shows, which long had been convocations of the middle-aged. Those in the industry see this turnaround as a result of Nancy's long and tireless promotional campaign on her husband's behalf. Serving as a catalyst, she has summoned the full support of record-company executives for an unusually passive artist, and tending to his affairs, she has helped him to clear up his debts and keep his business as well as his life in order. Since signing with MCA Records, in December 1990, George has achieved the stature due him as a living legend and American master; and by helping to keep the world at bay, Nancy has helped him stay alive amid the shadows of demons that still seem to darken his vision.

One gets the impression that, were it not for Nancy, George would not be performing today. He seems world-weary, more distanced from his own fame and idolators than ever before. From March of 1989 until recently, George and Nancy lived in a quiet, secluded area of Brentwood, Tennessee, in a home nestled among the mansions of Nashville bankers and brokers. In December 1993, they moved into a new home George built high on a hill amid the solitude of a hundred acres of prime, million-dollar farmland in Franklin. (George's forty-three-year-old daughter, Susan, lives nearby with her two children. George is estranged from his two sons and sees twenty-four-year-old Tamala infrequently. When I asked about his children, he fell silent, causing Nancy to revive the air with a laughing cry of "Next!") There George tends his prized herd of Santa

Gertrudis cattle. These cows, a large, chocolate-colored Texas crossbreed of Brahman and Shorthorn, seem to elicit a large part of George's worldly enthusiasm. He refers to them lovingly as "my girls," and, when he is not on the road, rises early every morning to tend to them and putter around his farmland, building little footbridges across his streams and squirrel-feeders for his trees, inspecting his holding-pen, barbecue pit, stocked ponds, and pear saplings. Like his routine of driving into Nashville every other day to have his hair trimmed and styled by Ray Gregory, his early-morning rounds at the farm have become one of the rituals of his life.

In Brentwood, I found neither many traces of the public career nor clues to the private man: a framed platinum album commemorating *I Am What I Am;* biographies of Connie Francis and Robert Graves on a sparse second-floor bookshelf; a closetful of neatly pressed, nearly identical blue jeans; a pair of large, ugly plaster "oriental" sculptures, the disposal of which Nancy has not yet been able to effect. Downstairs, in the basement, traces and clues become more visible. Above the door, a sign reads GEORGE'S DOGHOUSE. Within are boxes of old Nudie suits ("Looks like something Tammy Wynette would wear," says Nancy, extracting an especially tacky toreador-style jacket from a crumpled heap of sequined vestments), shelves of record albums, a coffin-like twenty-four-lamp tanning bed, and scattered memorabilia. On one wall, there is a painting of a dark-haired girl peering sadly through a window at a display of candy and sweets. George calls it "a picture from life's other side," after the title of a Hank Williams record. "Back in Texas, when he was trying to quit drinking, George used to sit by that picture all night," Nancy said. Beside the painting is a plaque bearing the words of the Alcoholics Anonymous prayer about changing what one can and accepting what one cannot.

"She's been a very big help in saving my life and career and just about everything," George said of Nancy, staring straight ahead into the rainy Alabama night. "They say when you get that low and in that shape, everybody needs some help, and if I hadn't got that help I probably wouldn't be here today."

We crossed the state line to Tennessee. The tape-recorder had been running for some time. It was the longest interview he had ever given. "Honey, are you awake?" he called out behind him through the darkened bus. "Can I have some ice water?" Beneath the mask of his sunglasses, his face lightened into a grin. "This man's talkin' me to death."

I asked him how it felt now, after nine years of temperance, to sing drinking-songs. The mention of alcohol seemed to disturb him. "I don't know why we're even discussing that," he said defensively. "I just think it was the environment that surrounded you back in those days. If I'd've never played in those places, I probably never would have started drinking."

"You think so, huh?"

"I would imagine. Being around it. Not so much stage fright, but being around people drunk all the time in the bars and the clubs and the taverns. Sort of being around it, you know, the environment. I'm fairly sure. It's just being around it all the time and other people doing it. Like the old saying, birds of a feather flock together." The last nine years, he said, have been "really like living in a different world. All the time you thought you were living, you really weren't." He said that he did not miss the other way. "No," he stated resolutely, "I don't want no more of that."

What was it that had finally brought him around? "Well, it was either quit or die. And I surely didn't want to die, so I made up my mind to quit." There had been no understanding, it seemed; nothing had been resolved. There had been only that plain, ultimate finality, death coiled and poised. He seemed no freer now than he had seemed long ago. In fact, he seemed more tense. The quality of clenched-teeth repression that has long been so powerfully effective in his singing seemed now to imbue his everyday speech as well. The demons had not been vanquished; unsuckled by liquor, they were merely subdued, less violent and more brooding wardens of the soul in a penal system wherein the only choice seems to lie between the death's row of abject drunkenness and the solitary confinement of dysthymic abstinence. In one cell or the other, it seems, he has always found refuge as well as attrition; and it has been from this big house of his own device that his profound voice has always risen in song.

But he was alive, and he felt physically better these days. "Oh, Lord, yeah," he said. Then he sighed. It was a sound lost somewhere between resignation and desolation; and in that same tone, staring straight ahead again into the rainy night, he repeated his affirmation, which no longer sounded at all like one of conviction, but rather simply of forbearance.

# 80

In November 1993, I was flown to London to get an award for *Dino*.

# My Overcoat,
# My Brains, and Me

From Sicily to the South China Sea, Hoboken to Hawaii to Hong Kong, I had, as the poster advised, seen the world. But I had never been to England. Odd for one whose stock-in-trade long has been the English tongue. Perhaps not so odd, though, for a New Yorker who had never ascended the innards of the Statue of Liberty until last year, when his seven-year-old niece visited from out of state.

But, no, this story doesn't start here. Not in irony, not in Sicily, not in Hong Kong, not in New York Harbour; not in London.

It starts here. In my head. What's left of it.

In writing my last two books—one non-fiction, the other fiction—I developed a strange new work habit. From the day I began each book to the day I finished it, I worked seven days a week, non-stop, week after week, month after month. In the past, writing books, for me, had been a lurching, sidewinding affair, periods of manic intensity interspersed with long breathers without so much as a book-wise thought. Now, however, it was as if I was afraid to stop once I began, afraid that if I did, I would never come back to it, or that the whole thing would somehow fall apart in my absence. So I sat and I worked, and when the work finally was done, I somehow fell apart in its absence. Fell apart. Less kind observers might say I became insane.

After the non-fiction book, I lost a girlfriend. By then, this had become a familiar pattern. With the birth of my first book, I had lost a wife. With the birth of subsequent books, girlfriends followed her into the Nick-less void of weeping, wailing and the gnashing of teeth. But this time around, with the novel, I lost a cashmere overcoat and half a tuxedo as well. A girlfriend can be replaced through charm. A coat takes money. Still, this is not a tale of loss. It is a tale of . . . Of what? Maybe in telling it, I shall discover a suitable noun.

A few weeks before finishing the novel, I had worn my tuxedo for the first time in nearly five years. On that long-ago previous occasion, in January 1989, I had been invited to the Grand Ballroom of the Waldorf Astoria, where Dion and the Rolling Stones were being inducted into that elusive and incorporeal Cleveland institution known as the Rock and Roll Hall of Fame. Then, last October, I returned in my tuxedo to the Grand Ballroom of the Waldorf. Instead of getting to see and hear Dion and the Rolling Stones and others perform, those gathered got to watch me and Gay Talese and others eat on that same stage. It was the first award I ever got that weighed more than a sheet of foolscap. The plaque, from the Columbus Citizens Foundation, was etched with the words, 1993 ITALIAN AMERICAN LITERARY ACHIEVEMENT AWARD FOR DISTINCTION IN LITERATURE. A homely sticker on the back advertised Sandy Steven Engravers, 4 West 47th Street ("Trophys Plaques Awards"). No hyphen on the front, no commas on the back. Very pre-Ciceronian. A military band played the Italian *inno nazionale;* an ageing bunch of greaseballs from Brooklyn invoked the golden age of dry-humping for postprandial slow dancing. David Dinkins, the avuncular black mayor of New York, evinced in his speech a greater knowledge of Italian-American writing than nervous, socket-eyed Rudolph Giuliani, who would win the mayoralty from him some weeks later, did in his. The food and wine were good, much better than the slop and swill provided by the Rock and Roll Hall of Fame. Gay Talese (best shirt studs: pearl; his father was a tailor) and I discussed Betty Page and Dean Martin. Had my no-fuck date not bitched about the traffic all the way uptown, it would have been a perfect night, the sort of night that Sandy Steven of West 47th Street might describe as gratifying memorable pleasant. But, compared to what awaited me precisely a month later, it was merely a warm-up. I was up for my first money prize, across the sea, in England. By October's end, I had finished the novel. A week later, tuxedo bagged and firmly in hand, I arrived in London. I was ready.

Of course, I knew I was a ringer. They would never, I figured, give the top prize to an American. Besides, my British publisher, Secker & Warburg, had just won the Booker Prize. They couldn't win this as well. But as one of the six short-listed finalists, I was guaranteed at least a thousand pounds. That, and the free trip, were enough for me. Little did I know then that the trip, far from being free, would end up costing me those thousand pounds and more.

A driver brings me in the rainy dark to the Franklin Hotel, a small establishment in Knightsbridge that is fabricated to look much older than it is. My room consists of a bed from which, with limbs outstretched, I can reassure myself of the presence of any or all of the four walls that surround me. I ask at the desk if I might be moved to a larger room. They are booked full, but they will see what they can do.

In New York, I had scrupulously counted out a journey's worth of vitamins, Prozac and Deseryl. Perhaps I will not go crazy this time, I had told myself. Perhaps I will be a *good* boy. I had been on Prozac and Deseryl for about a year. These antidepressants—fluoxetine hydrochloride (Prozac) and trazodone (Deseryl)—were supposed to transform my dysthemic, dysphoric brain to an Eden of sanguine tranquility and serene-flowing amines. As far as I could tell, this dope had no effect on me. It did, however, seem to have an effect on those around me. "You're more even-tempered, less black-mooded." It was simple enough. I went to the doctor once a month. He took my blood pressure, asked me how I felt, and shook me down for a hundred and seventy-five. Another hundred and twenty a month for the Prozac alone. In other words, I took the pills, I paid, and the people around me felt the effect. The things I do for love.

Prozac had been introduced to America amid a squall of controversy. A television programme about the new drug was titled *Prozac—Medication That Makes You Kill*. Would that there were truth in those words. But Prozac, I found, was nothing so much as a deceptive elixir of passivity and mediocrity. It made me complaisant, lustless and too prone to compromise. That the drug lately has become the most popular panacea in America bears out my view of it.

In a society predicated on and dedicated to mediocrity, the idea of a little black-and-green capsule that allows one to Have a Nice Day represents a miracle of sorts. In an age when sex has come to be equated with death in a way that bad French philosophers never foresaw, being a eunuch may be the new ideal.

As long as I was writing my book, none of this seemed to matter. Prozac helped to erase the concern for life itself from my consciousness, allowing me to concentrate fully on the imaginary existence at hand. The result was the best book I have ever written. And the darkest. Prozac, I discovered, was a superficial drug. It could never penetrate the delicate surface chemistry to the depths of the soul. Deep down, thank God, I was still a dirty rotten fuck.

But now the novel was done, and it was time to get back to life itself. The days of the complaisant bider were numbered and few. Somehow I know this even as I dutifully swallow my dope that first night and morning in London.

I have two full days to blow before the awards dinner, and most of the people I knew in London are now in America. On the eve of my departure, my friend Dick Blackburn had given me the number of "the most beautiful, most intelligent woman" he's ever known, in London on her way to India. I dial the number, speak briefly with some old codger with a hearing problem. Right, Dick. I have brought a list of books I'm searching for: the 1658 *Rare Verities* of JB Sinibaldus; Thomas Green's *The Art of Embalming* (1705); John Martin's *Gonosologium Novum* (1709); Horace McCoy's *No Pockets in a Shroud* (1937); the 1968 revised edition of *A Dictionary of Proper Names and Notable Matters in the Works of Dante;* and the Chapman (1618) and Cooke (1728) translations of Hesiod. All British books. What better place to seek them than London? I search. I come up empty. ("Not much call for that one," says the Bookseller to the Queen, through his nose, when asked for the Green.)

Dressing for dinner with Tim Hulse of Esquire and Minna Fry of Secker & Warburg, I regard the little orange pharmacist's sticker on the Prozac vial: the universal don't-drink symbol—a Martini glass crossed with a diagonal *verboten* bar—and the warning DO NOT DRINK ALCOHOLIC BEVERAGES WHEN TAKING THIS MEDICATION. Heh heh heh. So much for Prozac. At the St. Quentin's sister joint, the Grill in Yeoman's Row, we have oysters, steak and wine. And wine. Minna, it turns out, is leaving Secker soon and, like the most beautiful, most intelligent woman Dick Blackburn ever knew, is heading for India. The old pull of the

Ganges. Women who run with swamis. More wine. It hits me: if I can't have the most beautiful, intelligent woman Dick Blackburn has ever known, if I can't have *The Art of Embalming*, hmm, maybe I can have Minna Fry. Fuck India. I, downtown Newark's only begotten son, am Vedic enlightenment itself. I blink. There are now four of us. Another female. Maybe she has been there all along. I ask her if she believes in reincarnation. No, she says. Good, I tell her, good. She knows this club. We go there. We're the only patrons, have the barmaid all to ourselves. All we have to do is teach her how to make drinks. Dewar's, that's an easy one. First Minna fades, then Tim Hulse fades, then the one who doesn't believe in reincarnation. I meet the owners. They take me in the back. Cocaine? Don't mind if I do. It's been a long time. Back to the bar. Back to the back. The barmaid is learning. Back to the back. Back to the bar.

Somehow, God knows when, God knows how, I make it back to the hotel. When I wake, dressed from the waist up, I spend several minutes recalling my name. Starts with an N. That's good enough. Beside me on the bed is a crumpled paper sack. I open it and peer in. All the necessities of life, both physical and spiritual: four packs of cigarettes and one dozen spermicidally lubricated Durex Elite condoms, which, according to a sales receipt, also enclosed, I seem to have acquired at one Madesil Pharmacie. Ultimate Sensitivity. Ultimate Protection. Who could ask for more? I close my eyes. I will never drink again. I will go to India. Where the girls are. Ultimate sensitivity. This room is like a casket. That's nice. Ultimate protection. The telephone rings. Interviewers await me. I locate my britches, but not my brains.

Over lunch, the gent from the newspaper asks me if it's true that Madonna's bought the movie rights to my book.

"What's she like?" he asks.

My automatic pilot isn't functioning properly. God speaks to me directly: Fuck the food, drink the wine.

"A lovely girl."

I drink more wine as I talk. She gets lovelier with every sip.

"Who's going to play Dino?"

"I don't know. They don't tell me anything." Nobody tells me anything. A good reason to drink more.

Three interviews later, I am back on the Scotch, roaming in the dismal rain, looking for the joint with the back room. I don't find it, but I find the barmaid. Or someone like her. A barmaid. Magna Mater Spandex Medea.

"What's Madonna like?" she asks.

"Great legs. Like yours." Through my diplopic haze, I try to focus on hers. A quadruped. But a nice one. Unfortunately, she cannot lead me to *The Art of Embalming*.

Some men seek Christ in their darkness; others, the solace of hearth and home. I, the scissors and blade. But I never make it to the basement of Harrods, where, Minna assures me, I can get a good, old-fashioned shave and haircut.

And I never make it to the British Museum to see the Rosetta Stone. I am, I know, in a town of great cultural peerage. When was it that Caesar shook the Brits out of the trees, 54 BC, something like that? Two thousand years of civilization for the fossicking, and all I come up with are a few packs of smokes and a dozen scumbags. Evening falls, and it is showtime.

A tuxedo is not a neutral vestment. It bestows a sombre, dashing dignity on the clear-eyed and straight of gait, transforms the boozy into a caricature, a cartoon. I behold myself in the mirror: elegance in profile, *homo ebrius* head-on. Onwards, crabwise, to the awards.

"You don't really expect to win, do you?" grins Dan Franklin, the man responsible for the British publication of my book.

"I'm window-dressing," I laugh.

He has interrupted two simultaneous conversations I am engaged in with others at our table: one concerning Milton's *Areopagitica,* the other, less openvoiced, regarding the idiosyncrasies of Italian pornography. The more I drink, the more dazzling grows this arras-web of babble. Smut and Miltonic sophistry merge into a wholly new sphere of perception. *Donna leggiadra,* posed the way ya like 'em. This morning I could barely recall my name. Now, with great fluidity, I quote Latin from arcane seventeenth-century prose. The truth is incontrovertible. Liquor is the better part of enlightenment. My physician, Dr. Drinkmore, agrees with me in this matter.

I laugh a lot: the master of ceremonies is a funny man. I slip my prize money into my tuxedo pocket. (The engraved glass Mappin & Webb paperweight that came with it does not fit.) I dance the night away afterward, paperweight in hand. I fall in love. I go to the men's room. I come out. Love is gone. So be it. My paperweight comforts me.

Again, God knows when, God knows how, I make it back to the hotel, a fact I realize only upon waking to feel the now familiar walls. I shall never drink again, and this time I mean it. The master of ceremonies' punchlines, snatches of Miltonic sonnet and the blare of dance music rage within my addled midbrain. From here on in—stick that wine list up the Queen's ass—it's poached eggs, toast and tea. From here on in, I am one boring sonofabitch and out to prove it. Bring on the Rosetta Stone.

John Williams calls to invite me to a party. A party at a pub. I am scheduled to return to America tomorrow. Before I have an opportunity to compose the words to gracefully decline, the minor Mesopotamian god of evil to whom my soul is host sputters his eager acceptance. Before I know it, I am dancing again, dancing and drinking, drinking and dancing, somewhere on the outskirts of London.

What the fuck am I doing here? I wonder. The more I drink, the more I wonder, and the more I wonder, the more I drink. Maybe I should have stuck with the Prozac. No, absolutely not. Maybe I should have gone straightway from one book to the next. No, impossible. If only I had found *The Art of Embalming.* But I know myself. Though it is true that I have long ago given up on the possibility of permanent cohabitation with myself, I do exercise visiting rights. This has been one such visit, the writer and the degenerate. But soon the visit must end. An end dictated if not by sense, then at least by the self-preservation instinct of dehydrating electrolytes. He who quotes the forty-seventh fragment of Heraclitus—"Souls take pleasure in becoming moist"—bids adieu to he who quotes the forty-sixth: "A dry soul is wisest and best."

I sleep—let's call it that, anyway—through most of the next day. I gather up what is left of me. I have lost my cashmere overcoat, my cheque for a thousand pounds, and, most intriguingly of all, my tuxedo trousers. Cigarettes, scumbags and paperweight are all in order, a silent but telling testimony to the nature of my priorities. I look at the clock. Not much time to get to the airport. The taxi driver swears that he, and he alone, can get me there on time, on the condition that I do not smoke in his cab. I arrive at the check-in counter precisely three minutes after my plane leaves the runway. So much for the free ticket home. The next flight is tomorrow afternoon. I return to town, smoking profusely, in another cab; check into a hotel called the Chesterfield, on Charles Street. I spend the evening in the bar with a whispering proponent of the IRA. He seeks understanding. I seek deliverance.

Finally, I am airborne, asleep and subdued, skulking, trouserless, but with studded shirtfront and expertly knotted silk bowtie, through a designed by-Dewar's dreamscape. Not a bad idea, this, going to a different country to get drunk. Perhaps there's a travel agent that specializes in benders abroad. I think about my next book. I've got a title, but no opening line. It's a long flight, and I've seen the movie. The girl in the next seat isn't bad looking. She crosses her legs. Maybe just a little wine with dinner, suggests the Mesopotamian demon, an aperitif to get the appetite up.

But no. It is time to resume the mantle of my station, that of a taciturn middle-aged writer. Ah, to be young and drunk.

I began this little account, this little mercenary diary-note, with the promise, or at least the hope, of a fitting noun. Now I realize that our elusive substantive is gone with the overcoat, the cheque and the trousers. So be it. If only one reader comes forward to offer Chapman's Hesiod or an *Art of Embalming* or perhaps a *Rare Verities,* it shall all have been worthwhile. If not, I have my cigarettes, my scumbags.

It is time to return to the metaphor mines. But I, like all things good and bad, shall return. Unrepentant. Unredeemed. Untrousered.

# 81

From my notebook, January 1994.

Indo-European *ne* = the primeval grunt of negativity; negation; no.
—from which—
↓
*nek:* damage, destroy → Greek *nekros*
      & 
*nekut:* night → Greek *nux, nukhtos* →
      Latin *nox* → Italian *notturno;*
      Germanic *night.*
               DA       NE
               NE       DA

Indo-European *se* → Latic *sic;*
      Italian *si;* Germanic, *yes.*

Indo-European *leuk,* shining →
      Greek, *leuko* → Latin → *lux;*
      *Lucifer;* Germanic *light*
      (Sanskrit *loka:* open space, universe)
DA   NE
NE   DA
LEUK SE
SE    LEUK

leukoseneda     neleukseda
leukosedane
daneseleuk
Death is this night's light.
NE    NE     LEUK

in loka, in locus

# 82

After examining extant scraps of old journals, I can here date exactly the afternoon in question: Saturday, September 12, 1981, a muggy day that had begun with a walk through the San Gennaro feast on Mulberry Street.

# Nightmare Alley

It was thirteen or fourteen years ago, a Saturday or Sunday afternoon. I had no VCR, but I did have a beautiful girlfriend. I was pissed off at something or other, I went out for a walk. I came back. As I opened the door, I smelled reefer in the air, and I saw her lying there, drowsing on the couch in black underwear, black stockings, and black heels; and I heard it. Tyrone Power's voice, cool and dark, from amid the gray flickerings of the TV screen: *"I'm goin' right ahead the way I figured. The spook racket . . . I was made for it."*

In more moods than not, I think of it as my favorite movie. (I have watched it with every girlfriend since, though none has been quite so sophisticated in the dress-code department.) I first saw it, on television, as a kid. It was the first picture without monsters that I thought of as a monster picture. Years later, in the seventies, I found a paperback reissue of the 1946 novel, by William Lindsay Gresham. After epigraphs from T.S. Eliot and Petronius, the novel *Nightmare Alley* opens with the line, "Stan Carlisle stood back from the entrance of the canvas enclosure, under the blaze of a naked light bulb, and watched the geek." Little does he know he is beholding his own future.

And that is what the movie, like the novel, is about: one man's metamorphosis, his bizarre and fated descent to geekdom. But it is about much more as well: forbidden cons and unspeakable rackets, the horrors of greed and soullessness. To me, it is a film in a class by itself. Tyrone Power (who, if we are to believe *Hollywood Babylon,* had certain geek-like tendencies of his own) fought to star in it, against type and at high image-risk. Scripted by Jules Furthman, directed (at Power's request) by Edmund Goulding, imbued by cinematographer Lee Garmes, produced by—are you ready?—Georgie Jessel, *Nightmare Alley* was released by 20th Century Fox in 1947. It lost money (even though Power undertook a promotional tour for it in a DC-3 dubbed *The Geek*). But, its concocted last-minute happy ending notwithstanding, it stands today as one of the darkest, most psychologically chilling pictures ever made.

*Scarlet Street* ran a brief piece on the movie in its Spring 1992 issue. Another appeared in the October 1993 issue of *Firsts*. For facts, refer to them. But for infallible truth, pallie, hear me: this is one movie worth seeing again and again, one movie worth owning, one movie that is based on a borderline brilliant book and in some ways is even better than that book.

So, the girl in the black underwear is gone. But the last laugh will be on me, when *Nightmare Alley* arrives on video. I did eventually buy a VCR, and though I sit now alone on my couch, the spook racket, it comforts me.

# 83

I had signed the contract for my second novel, *Trinities,* in the summer of 1992, soon after the publication of *Dino.*

I had been paid fifteen grand for my first novel, *Cut Numbers.* The price for *Trinities* was a quarter of a million. It felt good to write as one wanted and to be paid a decent wage to do so.

# Excerpt from *Trinities*

## One

He stood there like the lesser part of his own shadow; stood there, as he did every night, on Second Avenue near the bodega at the southwest corner of 115th Street, a vaguely unsettling spectral presence in a fake-leather jacket. He was barely twenty-five years old, but all youth had been drained from him, and he had the sallow expressionless face of a corpse. Even the sparse scraggly hairs of his mustache were like those of postmortem growth.

In his left hand, he held a torn-open cellophane bag of Rolets barbecue-flavored fried pork rinds. Raking through it with the fingers of his right hand, he brought its remains to his mouth. He tossed the greasy bag to the pavement and with his fake-leather sleeve wiped the oil and crumbs from his mouth and mustache. He looked abstractedly at the back of the hand he had raised to his face. "*Mierda,*" he muttered. He was turning yellow again. He shook away the thought. No, he told himself, it was just the ugly light from the bodega. He looked up at the moon that rose in the darkening sky and saw that it too cast an ugly light.

"*El Jockey es vuelto,*" he muttered to those who passed: *los toxicómanos,* the wretched ones like himself, and the young roving ones that moved in loud gathering packs.

He had picked up too soon after rehab this time, he told himself. Tomorrow he would kick. If he chilled out now, he could do it on his own. No Thorazine, no detox, none of that shit. He still had some Trexan. He'd get him some methadone, some Librium. There was a meeting at Our Lady Queen of Angels. He'd be all right. *Mañana.* He cursed himself, but the curse was washed away by the gentle eddying tow within his veins of death's sweet tidal flow. He scratched through the fake leather at the sclerotic skin of his left arm and almost smiled as his eyes began to close.

"*El Jockey es vuelto, el Jockey es vuelto.*"

He had a taker, then another. It would be a good night, an early one.

Not far from where he stood, two men from Brooklyn sat at a table in the small dining-room of a tavern on the corner of First Avenue and 116th Street. The two men were in their mid-thirties. One, whom men knew as Willie Gloves, was overweight but not quite fat. His dark thinning hair, held stiffly in place by a glazed mist of styling spray, was already graying and receding at his temples. The other, Johnny Di Pietro by name, was lean and wiry, with his hair brushed back in chestnut-colored waves. The heavy man wore a long-sleeved floral rayon shirt and a gold bracelet; the other, a navy blue pullover and a black kid-mohair suit. They ate in easy silence, pouring occasionally from the bottle of wine that had been placed between them. Now and then, the lean man, who drank more sparingly and more slowly than the other, turned to look through the window at the shabby Chrysler that was parked outside.

Only two of the other seven tables were occupied. Beyond the latticed partition, men sat at the bar in hushed groups or alone in quiet drunkenness. Here, where the ominous Hispanic breezes of East Harlem did not enter, here, where the must and gloom of older and more ominous breezes lingered, even the jukebox seemed to whisper. At minimum volume, the crescendos of Jimmy Roselli's "Mala Femmina" drifted through the room like faint wisps of some distant angry sorrow. The two men from Brooklyn who sat eating with the bottle of wine between them had known this place since they were boys, and to them, the old man who ran the place and cooked the food had always seemed to be old. Now, with the passing of years, he had become more like a ghost than a man, and the joint itself, once bright with color, was now a somber chiaroscuro of brown and faded ocher hues, subtly ever darkening beneath a patina of nicotine and age. No, this was not so much a bar or a restaurant anymore, but a haunted sanctuary, and the old man was its sentinel, guarding something that was no longer there, preserving times and honoring ways that long ago had ceased to be except as a memory to him and the dwindling few, strangers now in their own streets, who continued to gather here.

But there was something about the squid in this joint that brought the two men from Brooklyn here again and again. It wasn't the sauce, thick and garlicky and wine-rich and good as it was. No. It was the squid itself. The old man's squid was not the bland white rubbery stuff that other joints served. He used only *calamaretti,* the smallest baby squid; and the flesh of their sacs and tentacles possessed a rare tenderness and a faint sweet taste of the sea. The *calamaretti* must be *freschissimi,* the old man never tired of explaining, using the Sicilian words *calamaricchi* and *frischissimi.* After two days of death, he said, their true succulence and flavor were lost. As a boy in Sciacca, he had learned to make squid from his uncle. He had learned to let the little ones die slowly on ice, for the cold, slow death relaxed their flesh and made them tender. He had learned to pull the tentacles from the sacs so the guts came out in one clean clot. Their tiny bulging eyes would still be clear and lucent as he cut above them. Their flesh was always sweetest in the spring, the old man said. And this was the spring.

Yes, there was something about the squid in this joint. It was the reason the two men from Brooklyn returned here Friday after Friday, year in and year out. And the fact that the old man served squid only on Friday was the sole reason that the sallow-faced figure in the fake-leather jacket had been allowed to live out the week.

The two men swabbed their bowls with crusts of bread and drank the last of their wine. One of them placed a fifty-dollar bill on the table, and, still unspeaking, they rose. From amid his hanging pots and pans, framed by the kitchen doorway, the old man raised one arm and waved it in a slow, slight arc. They returned the gesture, then made their way to the door, nodding their taciturn regards in passing to those at the bar who acknowledged their exit.

They walked to the shabby Chrysler, and the wiry man got behind the wheel. From the glove compartment, the other removed a Colt Woodsman .22-caliber pistol and a long, fat Gold Star silencer, and he married them. He rolled down the car window and extended his elbow from it, letting the weight of his arm rest in a natural position on the door. With his left arm across his midsection, he held the gun flush against the interior door panel, the snout of the silencer nuzzled near the crook of his armpit. The driver waited until the man with the gun was settled and still, and then he backed up to pull out. As he switched gears from neutral to reverse, a deep muffled clunking sound, like heavy objects thudding in a metal drum, issued from the underbelly of the car. Neither of them responded to it; they both looked straight ahead.

The car moved slowly west on 116th Street, then turned slowly south on Second Avenue.

"There he is," the driver said. "My new transmission."

The Chrysler came to a casual idling halt near where the young man stood. The young man peered at them for a moment, then approached the car.

He spoke softly in English to the one whose arm rested in the window: "The Jockey's back."

The elbow of the resting arm rose slightly, suddenly, and from beneath it there were three fast hollow pops of muted, rushing light. In the moment before he lurched backward and fell, the young man's eyes closed and his mouth opened, and he made a strange sort of sound. To the man in the floral shirt, he looked in that moment like a broad who was taking it up the ass and just starting to like it.

They were halfway across the George Washington Bridge before either of them spoke.

"Fuckin' spic looked like he was about ready to croak on his own," the gunman said. He lighted a cigarette. "You still got no idea what the fuck that was all about?"

The driver grimaced nonchalantly and shrugged. "Just some piece of shit sellin' dope to feed his own jones," he said. "Maybe he got too big for his Reeboks, stuck his chuchufritos where they don't belong. Who the fuck knows."

"Shit, he's the first fuckin' spic over the age of sixteen I seen sellin' dimes on the street since fuckin' God knows when. Besides, it must've been somethin' important, or they wouldn't have got us in on it."

The driver was silent, and then he spoke, and there was a grim resignation in his voice. "Nothin' we do is important," he said. "By now I got that much figured out."

The gunman looked out the window, and he nodded slowly, as if making a show of weighing the driver's words.

"Ah, you know your uncle's groomin' ya," he said.

"Yeah. To trim the weeds on his fuckin' grave. He's on his way out. They're just waitin'."

The driver drew a deep breath, and his eyes narrowed. He thought of all the nickel-and-diming he had been through in the last sixteen years. He knew more of this life than men twice his age. He had done most of what there was to do. He had run numbers and taken action, had handled jukebox routes and video slots. He had been a purse-man in two precincts, had handled the Teamsters' dirtiest paperwork in three different locals. He had turned stolen bonds and guns, booze and cars. He had dispatched legbreakers, overseen gambling operations, dealt everything from counterfeit fifties to swag Mass cards. He had seen the inner beast of this world laid out before him in gross vivisection. And still there had been no passage from the realm of nickels and dimes; no green light, not from his uncle, not from anyone.

They were in Jersey now, heading toward Bayonne: the long, slow way back to Brooklyn. The driver's mood lightened, and he glanced with a smile at the gunman. "What the fuck was that he said to you?"

"Who?"

"My new transmission. That island nigger back there."

"Oh. Him." The gunman uttered a sardonic guttural sound, a chuckle of casual derision. "'The Jockey's back.'"

The driver repeated the words: a quizzical mumble ending in a snort of low laughter. The gunman laughed then as well, in his own low way, and they drove on like that for a while, shaking their heads and grinning. The gunman sucked the last morsel of squid from between his teeth and spat it into the night.

## Nineteen

Black became deepest blue. Johnny gazed out into a cloud-vaulted cathedral of dawn. Stained-glass illuminations of gathering pale light coruscated through dark clouds in a synesthetic symphony, rose and gold, amethyst-violet and sapphire, pink and pearl. Slowly the clouds lightened to baroque billowings of agate gray, then wisps of byssus white. The cathedral evanesced in sighs of accrescent daybreak, and the plane soared low over the Alps. Johnny looked down. It was as if he were seeing from someplace west of heaven, from some colder, less known, and less blessed sphere of disembodiment, but one that shared celestial vantage all the same. Beneath him lay a hushed and haunting vista of snowy blue-shadowed valley slopes, lofty white mountain-brows, glacial crests that commanded the senses like majestic peregrine chords from the organ of creation.

The strange, beautiful world below enraptured and chilled him, breathed into him its immanent power as well as its loneliness. The golden light and pure blue sky of morning seemed somehow sacramental, marrying that power and that loneliness, assuring him that if he could carry the feeling of this moment with him, all would be well; that in moments such as this there was life. A deliverance, not from the fact of the common, foregone end in putrefaction that constituted man's only true brotherhood but from the fear of it, which governed and putrefied men's lives, laying waste to them with an anxious morbidity more devastating than death itself.

The strange cold beauty reminded him too of hell, the frozen region, the nethermost ring of Dante's ninth circle, where Lucifer rose like a mountain in icy crust from the frigid slopes at the heart of damnation, which in Dante's vision was the heart of the world. Dante's Lucifer had three faces, signifying his attempt to supplant the triune God: one face was vermilion; another, yellow; the third, the color of "those who come from where the Nile, descending, flows," that is, Ethiopia—nigger black. Those threes, those fucking threes. A terza rima of endless confluence. Dante had painstakingly set his *Commedia* in the year 1300, had begun it with an encounter with three beasts, had divided it into three parts, had divided his *Purgatorio* and *Paradiso* into thirty-three cantos each. Why had the years of Christ's life been numbered at thirty-three? Three times in the *Inferno,* Dante had invoked the Alps.

"*Le Alpi,*" said Louie Bones, coming awake with a yawn and a bestial stretch of his limbs, leaning across the vacant seat that separated him and Johnny, squinting into the morning. His sudden words, contorted by his waking yawn, were like a startling growl.

Soon Johnny could feel the descent in his ears. The bell tone seemed muffled, distant, as the sign blinked on overhead: FASTEN SEAT BELTS ALLACCIARE LE CINTURE. Then and now, the heart of the world remained the same. The wrathful and the sullen, tyrants and murderers. Sodomites and those violent unto God. Usurers and simonists. Hypocrites, thieves, and falsifiers. And, cursed beyond all, the traitors. ALLACCIARE LE CINTURE. LASCIATE OGNI SPERANZA, VOI CH'ENTRATE. Worse than the damned, however, were those consigned to the brink of hell, deemed unworthy to enter: *i vigliacchi,* the lukewarm, the neutral, the cowardly, those neither good nor evil, who lived with neither disgrace nor dignity. Well, Johnny would not be one of those.

The fifty-kilometer drive from Malpensa airport into Milan was the dearest cab ride that Johnny had ever taken. Louie, who had brought a sheaf of blue ten-thousand and russet fifty-thousand notes with him, peeled off two fifties, then three tens, *una lauta mancia* for which the driver thanked him profusely.

Louie and Johnny carried only one bag of luggage apiece. Both men believed in traveling light. Each had worn a suit and packed only three shirts and three changes of underwear. Better, they believed, to rely on laundry and dry-cleaning services, or to buy anew, than to be burdened. Still, rather than deprive the uniformed *facchina* of *una mancia,* they allowed them to bear the slight bags in from the street to the desk of the Hotel Principe di Savoia. Their two adjoining suites, overlooking the Giardini Pubblici, cost half a million lire each per night.

"There's a little dump on Via Fatebenefratelli, on the other side of the gardens, near Piazza Cavour," Louis said. "Like I say, it's nothing like this. But I'm a walker, and it's closer to things. Here, the Piazza della Repubblica—it's beautiful, don't get me wrong, but there's nothing here. That's where I'd stay if I had my druthers. No shit. The Hotel Cavour. Last time I stayed there, few years back, a fuckin' bomb went off right outside in the piazza. The papers blamed it on the boys, but I'm tellin' ya, there were guys from Sicily stayin' in that same hotel with me, and I know they weren't about to rattle any of their own bedsprings. That's the thing about bombs over here. Half the time, nobody knows who's doin' what. They even got a word for it now, the science of tryin' to figure out what's behind what. *Dietrologia,* they call it."

"Yeah?" Johnny said. "Sounds like they could take a few lessons from my uncle."

Louie snorted in agreement. "Anyway, here we are and here we gotta be. Somethin' like this, it's like fuckin' diplomacy, like a fuckin' summit meeting. We gotta put up a front, come on like we shit gold. That's business. Our Chink friend, he's doin' the same. He's right across the way here, at the Palace. So let's make the best of it. Which shouldn't be hard, since this joint *is* the best of it."

"We'll make the best of the best."

"Yeah, that's us. Best of the best." Louie peered out over the gardens. "Fuck it," he said. "R.P. Corp.'s pickin' up the tab anyway."

Since the day, not long ago, when Johnny had been appointed a general agent of his uncle's interest in R.P., he had wondered whose initials the shadowy corporation held. He had asked Bill Raymond, the lawyer at Novarca who handled what old Joe called paperwork. Raymond had explained that R.P. had been set up by hired lawyers as a bearer-share company in Holland. Protected by Dutch bank secrecy laws, the principals of R.P. were unknown even to those legal hirelings, who acted under unsigned instructions from Lupino, Novarca's phantom fiduciary company in Paraguay, itself a bearer-share company protected by secrecy laws. It was through fake consultancy contracts between Novarca and its untraceable bearer-share shelf companies that Joe and Tonio and Louie transformed dirty money into clean Novarca income. This, like the currency futures options racket that Novarca and its ghosts also employed, they had learned from some mysterious Sicilian before Raymond's time. But as to whose initials R.P. were, Raymond had not a clue, and it had slipped Johnny's mind to ask his uncle. Now he asked Louie, who smiled in a bemused way, as if the question brought to mind something pleasant, even wonderful, a serendipity long forgotten and unsavored.

"Ain't nobody's initials." Louie grinned. "R.P. is—Jesus, gimme a second here. Yeah. R.P. *Rapere pilam.* It's Cicero. 'Seize the ball and go with it.'" Louie spread his fingers as if his hands were grasping a large sphere. "The ball," he said. "The world. Seize the world. This guy we knew, this Sicilian guy, he used to say that."

Johnny thought of the lions of the Uoglobe symbol that Billy Sing had shown him.

The two men went out and walked south on Via Manin, along the western edge of the gardens, then crossed Piazza Cavour to Via Manzoni.

"Fuck New York," Louie said. "This is the greatest city in the world."

They came to an open ivy-covered gate set back from the street: number 12A. Johnny followed Louie through the courtyard that led to Ristorante Don Lisander. They entered an airy room with mint-green walls, arched white stucco ceiling, and fresh flowers. Vincenzo Raffa awaited them, sitting alone at a table for four with a bottle of Surgiva water. He was a handsome man in his middle forties with wavy hair of dirty blond and gray. At the sound of their footsteps on the tile floor, he looked up, and as they approached him he stood, showing himself to be the shortest of the three. He took Louie's hand in his own, smiling and nodding with slow, natural elegance, as if to say, Yes, it is good to see you once again. Louie introduced Johnny to him as *"un amicu nostru, un womo bravissimu, u niputi a Don Giuseppe."*

*"Lieto di conoscer La,"* Johnny said.

*"Per favore—dammi il 'tu,'"* said Vincenzo, asking Johnny to address him in the familiar second person rather than the formal third. In Milan, where Sicilian was often sneered at, Vincenzo spoke Italian, though his native tongue's predilection for avoiding *l*'s and turning *o*'s to *u*'s tended to betray his origin. Reflecting on Johnny's halting unease with the language, he said, "The pleasure is mine." His English was as ill-honed as Johnny's Italian, but he was less inhibited by lack of fluency than Johnny was.

Johnny was able to follow most of what the waiter told them. "What's *lanza*?" he asked Louie and Vincenzo.

"Mario's the only fuckin' Lanza I know," said Louie. "I thought maybe he said *manzo.* Beef."

"I was going to ask you," Vincenzo said.

It turned out to be turkey. "Everywhere else in this country, turkey is *tacchino*," said Vincenzo. "Here it is *lanza*. And they look down their snouts at *siciliano*. You figure it."

"What about *busecca*?" Johnny asked.

Both men sphinctered their lips and made sounds of throaty rapture, and Louie leaned toward Johnny and spoke in a low voice, as if he were discussing *la bisiniss'*. "It's this fuckin' soup," he said. "Tripe, eggs, and cheese. *Unh*," he added, as if striking a fuck-thrusting to the hilt.

They ordered their food, more water, and a bottle of Barbacarlo. They blew on spoonfuls of their *busecca* and brought the thick broth to their lips. Sounds of carnal delight rose from deep within them.

"*Sembra una pipa sotto la tavola,*" laughed the waiter in passing. Even Johnny understood that one: sounds like you guys are getting sucked off under the table.

"*Meglio di una pipa,*" Johnny answered, less uneasy now. "*Meglio.*" The waiter, Louie, and Vincenzo received his words with enthusiasm and laughter.

They did not speak of business until after the soup was eaten. It was Louie who spoke first.

"*Come sta Don Virgilio?*"

"*Bene. Tutto sommato, molto bene.*" Then Vincenzo reminded himself that Johnny was, as they said in Sicily, *u fardu*, an *italo-americano*. Though Louie too had been born in America, Vincenzo did not think of him as *u fardu*, but rather as some errant native seed borne away by the wind. Inside, he thought, Louie was Sicilian. Perhaps this younger stranger, this new *amicu*, would prove the same within. Knowing Louie, knowing Giuseppe and Tonio, he believed that proof would be forthcoming. "Yes," he said, "Don Virgilio is well. I was with him in April. The feast of San Giorgio. And we have been in touch."

The waiter brought small dishes of pasta in veal sauce. Louie and Vincenzo had poured their second glasses of wine, finishing the bottle. Johnny sipped sparingly on the one glass he would allow himself.

"His blessing in this makes me feel good," Louie said.

"Yes. Of course. But a blessing is often only as good as those whose heads it falls upon."

"How do you feel?"

"*Come un toro.*" Vincenzo grinned. "Like a bull. Like a blessed bull. And you?"

"For a long time, I felt a lot of things," Louie said. "Now I don't feel. It's time to do, not feel."

"And how about you, Johnny?"

"I feel like a season in hell is a small price to pay to get to the other side of this life."

"And what's on the other side?"

"The freedom to find out. Heaven."

"Well, then," Vincenzo said, raising his glass of wine, "here's to heaven." Louie and Johnny touched his glass with theirs, and the three of them drank.

"Now," Louie said, "let's get down to hell."

The waiter set down before Johnny a plate of stuffed anchovies and a dish of grilled vegetables.

"We go head-to-head tomorrow afternoon," Vincenzo said. "*Alle tre.* Three o'-clock. He wants to meet on Tao ground. I'll rendezvous with you beforehand. There's a bar on the corner of Via Giusti and Via Braccio da Montone. It's a block away from where we need to be. I'll meet you there at, let us say, a quarter to three."

"*E carcarazz'?*" And guns? Louie said, lapsing stealthfully into *baccàgghiu*.

"*Al bar,*" Vincenzo said, as if lackadaisically stating the obvious.

"Have you ever met this Ng Tai-hei?" Johnny asked.

Vincenzo shook his head. "But to the *cinesi* here, he is some kind of god. The way they speak of his presence here, it is as if Christ came down off the cross to walk among them."

"And how powerful," Johnny said, "is this Sole Rosso, this Tao?"

"Right now, their power is still dependent on our good will. But that is changing. Many still eat from our hands, but trouble has been growing. We look to New York and we see the future. Their strength, our weakness."

"Well, tell us," Louie said. "The ones who eat from your hands, what have they told you about Ng Tai-hei and his friends there, Asim Sau and Tuan Ching-kuo?"

"As I said, they view these men as gods. We had one highly placed rat, this Cho Sin-wo. He knew these men. He went to Hong King to see Ng Tai-hei just the other week. He himself never came back, but his tattooed hand arrived here in a package soon after."

"The head came to New York," Johnny said.

"Yes, I know. It reminds me of that *inno nazionale lesbico,* that lesbian national anthem"—he pronounced these English words as "lesspin nascio-nal ahn-tim"—"'I Fall to Pisses.'"

Johnny laughed. Louie had a blank look on his face.

"That Patsy Cline song," Johnny said.

"Oh," Louie said, still blank.

"So, from him, this Cho guy, what did you hear?" Johnny asked.

"You must remember this. Cho Sin-wo was not an intimate of these men. He was not"—Vincenzo's right hand spiraled heavenward—"he was not of their . . . *altezza*. And of course, there must have been bitter blood; otherwise he would not have come with us. But he did know them. He said they moved as one. They are not like three men who argue and fight among themselves, who harbor different notions and live in caution of betrayal by one another. Their heart is one, he said. They are like a beast with three faces. That is their power. He said they are men of great honor, but only among themselves. Nothing they say beyond themselves, either alone or together, can be taken for truth. Nothing they do can be taken at, how do you say, *valore apparente*. Again, these are one man's words. They sound good, but we must learn for ourselves."

"Well, shit," Louie said, "you could be describing us."

"Perhaps. But do we move as one? We have always been our own worst enemies. Our power has been torn apart from within so often that it is like so many broken twigs awaiting an outsider's match. Do we know of a beast with three faces?"

Johnny thought of his uncle, Tonio, and Louie sitting in that backyard less than forty-eight hours ago.

"It's just another fuckin' card game, like everything else in this world," he said. "They're out to fuck us. We're out to fuck them. What else is new?"

"The stakes," Vincenzo said. "The stakes are new."

"It never ceases to amaze me," Louie said. "Two enemies sitting down and lying to each other. That is how we do things. Not just us, I mean. The world. From the Roman Senate to the United Nations, this is how we do it."

"Maybe it's the only way there is. Maybe it works," said Vincenzo.

The waiter cleared their table, brought their salads.

"But we're not out to fuck them," Johnny said. "It's just business. A proposal of partnership."

"I don't know," Louie said. "Blowin' up half of Chinatown. Heads in the mail. Explodin' niggers. Plane crashes. Poison junk. Is that what these *Wall Street Journal* types mean by 'hostile takeover'? I don't know."

"They're meeting us," Johnny said. "That means something."

"Johnny's right," Vincenzo said. "We called, they came."

"Well, let the games begin," said Louie, signaling the waiter to bring coffee. When the espresso came, they toasted again, with their cups.

"To us," Vincenzo said. "*Buono fortuna.*"

"When we fight, we conquer," Johnny said.

"Ah," said Vincenzo, raising his brows. "*Come Confucio,* eh?"

"*Sì.*" Johnny grinned, surprised.

Louie paid the check, waving away Vincenzo's money. He gestured *nito* with his hand over the four fifty-thousand notes he had placed upon the check, indicating to the waiter that he expected no change. The waiter thanked him warmly, rushed off, and returned with three snifters and a bottle of Marc des Hospices de Beune, the stuff that grappa tried to be. But the men declined. "*La prossima volta,*" Louie told him: next time.

On Via Manzoni, in the afternoon sunlight, Vincenzo embraced both men. "*A domani,*" he said.

The meal and the siesta quietude of the city had a soporific effect on Johnny, but he did not want to sleep.

"You got the right idea," Louie said. "Stay awake, get a good night's sleep tonight, wake up fresh on Milano time. That's what I do. I don't believe in this jet-lag shit. It's like that fuckin' PMS with the broads. All in the fuckin' mind. Just another racket."

While Louie strolled among his favorite clothiers—Truzzi, on Corso Matteotti; Castellani, in Piazza Meda; the custom tailor Caraceni, on Via Fatebenefratelli, where he browsed among bolts of new cloth—Johnny set out on his own, directed by Louie in the general direction of Piazza del Duomo. The two had agreed to meet later at the Banca Masini in Piazza dei Mercanti, which Louie said lay close to the northwest corner of Piazza del Duomo.

Johnny emerged from the Galleria Vittorio Emanuele to the sight of the Duomo, rosy white and magnificent amid the tawdry arcades that surrounded the vast piazza like so many transported segments of Manhattan's Times or Union Square. As he made his way toward it, he was overwhelmed by the unimaginable labor manifest in its phantasmagoria of spires and the thousands of saints and scores of grotesque gargoyles that inhabited its façades. It was not so much beautiful as overpowering, as if in this one immense monument, men had tried to cram and crowd all the wonder of their visions and sweat of their brows. Its setting was sublime, a revelation of the soul's aspirations amid its truer actuality.

Inside, the cathedral seemed even more enormous. Stone pillars bigger than any Johnny had ever imagined seemed to stretch before him in endless rows, rising vertiginously toward the place where the lustrous stained-glass filterings of daylight dwindled and gave way to a world of shadows. He turned toward the rays of cool light drifting strongly through the colored windows. His eyes lingered on the stained-glass crest of the Visconti, which had become the symbol of this city: a great twisting serpent devouring a man.

Here and there as he walked, at altars nearby and in the far reaches, somber figures knelt in prayer or sat silently, cowled in the sepulchral twilight beyond where the soft rays and sighing candlelight reached. Johnny made his way slowly along the northern aisle, stuck a dollar bill into a box marked OFFERTE, lifted a taper, and lighted a candle. He knelt nearby, and he blessed himself. *Caro Dio,* he began silently, letting the Italian come slowly, to express as best he could his plain and simple prayer, for wisdom and strength—*dammi sapienza, dammi forza*—and his vow, both vague and strange: *fare buono.* He knew his Italian was not good, but he felt as if some genetic waterlock had been opened by his surroundings, allowing the subconscious memories of his ancestral tongue, the words and phrases and tones of his childhood's immersion, to rise and flow within him.

An old woman approached and stopped before the heavy bronze gate that separated a reliquary apse from the rest of the cathedral. She raised her hand to the sacred symbol on the gate and held it there as her mouth moved without sound. Then she removed her hand from the holy place and pressed it to her lips. Johnny watched her go on to another holy place along the wall of the cult of the dead, where she raised her hand anew. *Tutti vogliamo qualcosa,* Johnny said to himself: we all want something.

He made his way toward the main altar, looked awhile at Saint Carlo Borromeo, who lay, neither man nor ashes, in his casket of glass. He wanted to go beneath the ground, to the baptistry where Saint Ambrose had anointed Saint Augustine, but the baptistry was closed for the siesta. He thought of making his way to the cathedral roof, to the shadow of La Madonnina atop the dome, where, it was said, on a good day one could see the Alps. But he had already seen the Alps today.

Johnny found the Banca Masini, which lay amid dark, twisted streets nearby. Fixing the location in his mind, he wandered further. On Via Mazzini he paused to study the group of seedy young men that milled about outside the Bar Mercurio. Junkies, *tossicomani.* Then, although he had just eaten, the food in the window of Rosticceria Peck, on Via Cesare Cantù—tender young chickens and game fowl roasted and stuffed with sprays of rosemary and sage; bright grilled vegetables; a cornucopia of delicacies, raw, fried, and marinated—filled him with an ethereal craving, not quite hunger but a velleity. For weeks he had dwelled on death. Now, in the luxuriance of herbs that blossomed in earthy celebration from the assholes and gullets of those burnt-gold and chestnut birds, he saw life, a reason and a desire to live.

He found himself roaming the halls of the Biblioteca Ambrosiana, browsing among its treasures: Leonardo's *Codice Atlantico* in its crystal case, Raphael's sketches, Petrarch's copy of Virgil. In Room V, undescried amid the treasures, he came upon a small wood-and-glass chest. This dusty display, assembled by some forgotten curator at some forgotten time, contained curios that seemed to have been washed forth by the tide of some unsaid, unsayable truth: shards of human vanity, remnants of power and glory, broken by mortality and reduced to brittle, crumbling butterflies by time. There were three objects in the case. There was a waxen triptych, several hundred years old, that illustrated the states of blessedness, purgatorial biding, and damnation with a woman's face that was in turn serenely beautiful, disquieted, and gruesomely contorted. Beneath this triptych was a tawny ringlet, identified in Latin as a lock of Lucrezia Borgia's hair, snipped at the hour of her death, in 1519. To the left of it, simply labeled "*Guanti Portati da Napoleone a Waterloo 18.6.1815,*" was the pair of chamois gloves worn by Napoleon on the day the wind changed for him.

A few strands of brittle hair, a pair of gloves lingering long after the clutching hands that filled them turned to dust—*potere*'s lingering remains—beneath the portrait of that self-blessed, self-damned thing, the shade of every foolish grasping for eternity, every vain craving for power. To Johnny, it was all there, in that case.

*Salvia,* sage, he read, was recommended for soothing the grief of death. Its slow-wilting leaves were to be scattered on graves, along with that other sweet-perfumed herb of death, *rosmarinum,* used not only to adorn graves and places of mourning, but as a funerary balm with which to scent the dead. He thought of the birds in the *rosticceria* window.

Irony brought home the awareness of the truth that he had suppressed in the breezy blue light of this day, this day that had severed his umbilical moorings in Brooklyn, that had restored some faint sense of the illimitableness of his long-ago boyish musings. It was the eve of his descent. He was not here to feast. He was here to survive.

# 84

December 25, 1994

Dear Cubby:

Merry Christmas! Thanks for your letter of the other day. It meant, and means, a lot to me. I *am* doing well—better in any case. The trick, I think, is to never lose track of the beauty of this gift of life, to learn, or re-learn, to love and appreciate it. There once was a kid who lay on his back on the concrete pavement looking up at the sky in wonder. That was probably the only part of the kid worth saving, but he got lost, or discarded, along with the rest. That sense of wonder, or grace, is what I need to dig up and draw out again. I need to let in more light. And 1995 (why not?) looks like a good year for doing that. And I hope that the new year brings you all goodness, love to fill your heart and soul and loot to fill your pockets. You're a great man and a good man, and the world is better for having you in it. I hope to see or hear from you soon. For now, please don't hesitate to call if you need anything at all from my end.

# 85

# The Holy City

Dante did not write in the age of malls, but he would have recognized Las Vegas, in any age, for what it is: a religion, a disease, a nightmare, a paradise for the misbegotten.

It is a place where fat old ladies in wheelchairs, like wretched, disfigured supplicants at Lourdes, roll and heave in ghastly faith toward the cold, gleaming maws of slot machines. A place where Jerry Lewis maketh the heart merry with the guffaw of the abyss, where Barbra Streisand lendeth wings to the soul with the unctuous simulacrum of pay-as-you-go sincerity. A place where the Wagnerian evocation of Zarathustra brings forth Elvis in a girdled bodice and rhinestone cape. A place where Ken and Barbie can go to be bad, to samba beneath the artificial tree of unknowing. A place where every man can be Dino if he uses the right styling mousse and buys enough lobster fra diavolo for the seeing-eye bimbo in whose two he swaggers. A place where a theology of profoundest mediocrity makes of every Saul a Paul. A place where miracles do happen, along the line of Frank Sinatra's hair.

America alone among nations conceived of her destiny as a dream. The first temple of that American Dream, the heart of what, with a straight face, she calls her culture, was invented by Jewish immigrants and the sons of Jewish immigrants—Fox, Goldwyn, Loew, Zukor, and others—who founded the cheap dreamland of Hollywood firmly upon the principles and aesthetics they had learned from their shared background in the garment industry of New York.

And the *via sacra* of that dream led through the desert to Las Vegas. Like Hollywood, Vegas had been nothing. It was a forgotten Pueblo wasteland that the noble white man had not even passed through until 1829. In 1911, when it was incorporated as a city, its population was barely fifteen hundred. Gambling, outlawed in Nevada in 1915, was legalized again in 1931, when state legislation also eased divorce laws to increase state revenues. This made Nevada the only lawful game in America. But Vegas remained little more than a forsaken railroad-depot town. The gambling rooms, most of them located downtown in a two-block area around Freemont and Second streets, drew much of their profits from the paychecks of the workmen who were building the Boulder Dam southeast of town. It was another Jew from New York, Bugsy Siegel, who made Las Vegas a temple town of the American Dream.

In the summer of 1941, Siegel sent his henchman Little Moe Sedway to reconnoiter the Nevada territory. By then, the first of the fancy joints, the El Rancho Vegas, had opened in the desert outside town. Late in 1942, it would be joined by another. Built on the stretch of Highway 91 that came to be known as "the Strip," the Last Frontier, in addition to its casino, offered a showroom, a swimming pool, tennis courts, riding stables, and a hundred and seventy air-conditioned rooms with private baths.

The Last Frontier was nothing compared to the vision of Siegel's dream. In September 1945, a Vegas widow quitclaimed her failed dilapidated motel and thirty acres outside of town to Little Moe Sedway. The property was transferred indirectly to an entity named the Nevada Projects Corporation. In December 1945 ground was broken for Siegel's dream, the Zion he envisioned as the greatest gambling casino in the world. It was to be called the Flamingo.

The other major shareholder with Siegel, the true power behind him, was Meyer Lansky. Like Louis B. Mayer of Hollywood, Lansky had come from White Russia to the land of dreams, and now both were in the business of dreams, each in his own way. And there were other partners as well, such as Frank Costello. For the dream of America was not that of the Mogen David alone. Christ also had a wad to be reckoned with. Frank Capra, the Hollywood director whose work most reflected and influenced the mythos of the American dream, was from Palermo. He and Lucky Luciano, a habitual moviegoer, were born in Sicily in the same year, 1897. Luciano returned there as a deportee in 1946, the year of Capra's *It's a Wonderful Life,* the year of the Flamingo's grand opening.

The Flamingo, which opened the night after Christmas, 1946, was a bust. Siegel had drained the Nevada Project's shareholders of roughly six million dollars, and the casino in its first weeks took a beating for close to three quarters of a million. By late January, there was no choice but to shut it down. Siegel raised money to reopen in March, and by May the casino was showing a profit and Siegel felt sanguine. But his days had been numbered since the previous December, before he had ever opened the joint. There had been a meeting then of disgruntled shareholders, held behind Siegel's back, at the Hotel Nacional in Havana, where Frank Sinatra was performing as the Christmas attraction. They had all been there: Lansky, Costello, even the exiled Luciano, in from Italy. At that meeting, it had been decided that Bugsy had fucked them, and that Bugsy was wood.

In June, within twenty minutes of the carbine blasts that rendered Siegel so in Beverly Hills, Moe Sedway and two other men, Morris Rosen and Gus Greenbaum, representing Costello and Lansky, strode into the Flamingo, gathered the staff and announced that the joint was under new management. In the year that followed, the casino showed a profit of over four million dollars. Gus Greenbaum, in 1950, was officially proclaimed the first mayor of Paradise, the name of the valley through which the Strip runs.

And the Flamingo begat the many. The Thunderbird came in 1948, the Desert Inn in 1950. The Sands and the Sahara in 1952; the Riviera, the Dunes, and the Royal Nevada in 1955.

If Las Vegas can be said to have had a golden era, it began with the Flamingo and reached its zenith in 1960, when John F. Kennedy and the Rat Pack, symbols and spirit of a blithe, benighted day, together lighted the showroom of the Sands. By the end of that decade, the paradigm shifted. In 1969 Elvis, who had failed miserably in Vegas in 1956, effectively ascended to his kingship in that holy city of old-guard cool where Dino and Sinatra had reigned supreme for a decade and more. He had, in other words, become truly, majestically mediocre.

For that—malignant banality, the pestilent have-a-nice-day smile of devouring venality—is the spirit of Vegas, the spirit of the dream itself. Just as the schlock manufactured by the dream merchants of Hollywood came to be exalted, in this land of hoi polloi, as art, so the slick and sleek mediocrity of the Vegas showroom came to be embraced and emulated as cool.

In fact, the more popular a mecca it became, the less cool Vegas got. The theogony illustrates this. In the beginning were Dean and Jerry, who opened at the Flamingo in September 1949. Eden was new then, and the Flamingo still its jewel, the pleasure dome of the new prefab promised land: a land of chrome, not gold; of Armstrong linoleum, not Carrara marble; of heptalk, not epos or prophecy. There, married by God and state, anointed in the blood of Bugsy, *Unterwelt* and American dream lay down together in greed. Martin and Lewis were beloved of that dream, embracing and embraced by the spirit of a post-heroic, post-literate, cathode-culture America. And Dean, burdened even by the unnatural growth of Jerry, was as cool as it got: the idol not only of the suckers who bought the dream, but of the men who had built it as well. But as Vegas grew the pilgrims of its suckerdom became less elite. After Dean and Jerry came Louis Prima and Keely Smith. This was the Mosaic age of hep. Indeed, in 1955, when a full-page ad in *Variety* for the Sahara quoted Howard Hughes on Louis and Keely, his words seemed less uttered than carved in stone: "The more I see them, the more I enjoy them." Then came the Rat Pack, caricatures of hip selling themselves to the pseudo-hip. (Who were the hipper charlatans of that day: Frank, Dean, and Sammy, or Burroughs, Kerouac, and Ginsberg? It's a close call, but high-roll collars and mohair britches certainly have held up better than berets and bongos.) Then, returned from out-and-out unhip ignominy, came Elvis. And just as surely as Dean and Frank were usurped by him, so Elvis himself ceded to Wayne Newton.

With popularity came crass legitimacy too. In 1963, when Ed Reid and Ovid Demaris published *The Green Felt Jungle,* Vegas was still ruled by the great Judeo-Christian shadowland consortium that had raised it from the desert in the late forties. Today it is a corporate-run nightmare draped in the cotton candy of family values, a theme park where dead souls drift amid medication Muzak, believing, *knowing,* in their hearts that people who need people are the luckiest people in the world and that one should never, ever, double down on a ten when the dealer shows a face card.

But its sleazy soul remains the same. It represents the darker emanation of that other, older dreamland. Both sell the same delusion, the same narcotic. In fact, we can look at America as the sum, the garish metastatic necrosis, of that narcotic's effects. This at least serves to explain the collective sense of beauty we embrace as we follow Mandy Patinkin's siren song, or the brain-dead blare of rap, across the bridges of Madison County—or is it the information superhighway?—to the Astroturf shores of Lethe beyond. In the end, *It's a Wonderful Life*, or this season's computer-enhanced, bare-tit equivalent, and the flashing glow of the programmed slots are one in the same to he who peddles them. And it is the same sucker who falls for both rackets.

It may not be a wonderful life, but it's a wonderful nightmare. The best pieces in this book—scabrous, absurd, perceptive—illuminate that nightmare and offer a guide, a Baedeker to the bizarre, a Virgil in shades, not only to the holy city but to the off-the-rack soul that we, one nation under Frankie's toup, so strangely and so fatally share.

# 86

I wound up in the bughouse on the last day of January 1995. The following are scrawlings from what I wrote there.

"Ophis Ovum Opium Olé" was begun on January 14, 1995 and finished in March or April, when I was back on the street.

# Ophis Ovum Opium Olé

1/12/95, Laura
wore reptilian pantyhose,
8 yrs old, she said, 5
bucks the pair,
her hair up, all
chrysum and cornsilk,
we went to the Spanish
joint on 16th and ate
french fries, and
she said she wanted me to get her
some opium.

1/31/95, I lay
guarded, sedated, sick.
And now, here, end,
in rhythmus,
what began—I mean,
these poems, crus et tuber:
gam and spud—
in rhythmus,
23 winters,
untold legs, untold taters,
ago.

# 87

# There's a Woman Here, Baby

There's a woman here, baby,
looks just like Maggie,
another looks just like you.

# 88

# Who Holds in Her Belly the Power of Life

*2/17/95 pm*

Who holds in her belly the power of life
Who holds in her soul the secrets of night
Who rules with her eyes the sea and its might
Whose heart is the breeze, the sun and its light


*2/18/95 am*

Lord, I thank you for the gift and blessing of this day
and ask for the inspiration of strength, courage, and wisdom,
that I might open to and embrace through your guidance
what glimpses of serenity and happiness you offer.
May the gods without names redeem me
May this gift and this blessing and promise endure.

# 89

As the summer of 1995 neared its end, my mind went back to the summer of thirty years before: a summer that I had begun to see in new light.

# A Slab of Grease, a Bottle of Carbona, and Thou

When I was a boy, I had baseball cards. Now I've got these: little memorial prayer cards that they give out at wakes. Nobody trades these, nobody flips them. They're all the same. I've got a slew, from Perazzo and Nucciarone, Marshello and Introcaso, and they're all the same: the holy picture on the front, the name of the stiff and the hoodoo on the back.

Seasons and seasons of death: cancer wards and Coney Island bullets, alcohol and dope. The common end eats the lie of strength, the delusions of the will, casually, slovenly, like a bleak-colored bird eating stale, sodden bread. The darkness of one world becomes the darkness of another.

Like the wop in the toupe, I did it my way. I lived my life in darkness, and it was good. It served me well, that darkness.

But in the end darkness devours whom it serves. Those whose lives and sensibilities were bound with mine in the darkness that we shared are gone. They began croaking eleven years ago, and now they are all dead; their names are on those cards.

I was lucky. When the darkness of this world began to flow and rush into the darkness of the next, I made it out alive. But the seasons of death left me feeling not like a survivor, nothing so noble or romantic as that, but like something left behind, a remnant of my own black-iron past; left me feeling all alone in the dark, which, in a way, I always had been.

Homer alluded to Erebos as a place of nether darkness, a passage between earth and Hades. To Hesiod, Erebos was that and more: Darkness itself, the first of the gods to issue from Chaos. Hesiod was careful to divide this darkness from earthly darkness: "From Chaos came forth Erebos and black Night." In distinguishing the brother from the sister, the enigmatic dark of Erebos from the explicit dark of Night, Hesiod made of Erebos an immanence, a darkness not of the senses but of the soul.

> To dwell, to grope in Erebos;
> to be drained of marrow,
>     bereft;
> to lose

> the color and earthly pulse,
> the form of that sacred thing,
> mysterium tremendum,
> that was the beast of life itself,
> to go from sinew and strength
> to burrowing translucence,
> to know shame and know fear,
> to have the sea turn to sorrow, or
> worse, to shadow
> is to grasp the truth:
> that to betray one's nature
> is to be betrayed in turn.

I wrote these lines two winters ago, after a stay at St. Vincent's. The last of my friends from the old days, the black-iron days, was soon to take my place there, but he would not leave with his eyes open. The poem, the chill of darkness turning against me, was already coming, drifting down in stillness like the gray snow of that winter. Erebos was the gust that brought it home. As many times as I had read and returned to Hesiod, it had eluded me. That winter, I found it, grasped it; and my darkness, and my poem, found a name.

Once upon a time, I might have rendered all of the above in one glib paragraph. After all, isn't *glib* what this disposable-writing racket is really all about? But then there would have been nothing to glibly condense, for I would not have gone looking then, as I am now, through these words, for a way back to an errant ray of light elusively remembered, a way back to the ghosts of vanished breezes at a crossroads in the summer air of thirty years ago. If the way back winds through the eighth century B.C. and a bunch of latter-day stiffs, so be it; for that is the way. Be that as it may, however, let's get this show on the road here. I'll soon be writing my memoirs, *The History of My Dick;* this deep-roaming eloquence can wait until then. For now, enough of Homer and Hesiod; let the sea of rancid souvlaki grease that is their true legacy bear them away. Let's just say that I was one dark-hearted fuck. Let's just say my favorite song was "Sea of Love," and I thought it was about heroin. Let's just say I was a dark-hearted fuck for as long as I can remember, that most of my memory resides in shadow: shadow feelings and shadow deeds, shadow places and shadow faces. Pleasure, laughter, happiness: with the passing of time, memory adumbrated even these to shadow. But there is this one summer, the summer of 1965, that resplends with the light of the sun.

I was pushing sixteen. I had the world by the balls and I didn't know it. That's what my old man told me. He himself had once had the world by the balls and not known it. He and Willie Moretti had been going places together. Big places. Then Willie had taken two in the head, and that had been that. But that was, what, thirteen years before? I was sick of hearing it, already. I knew that somewhere in his vague, repeated lamentations of him and Willie and the balls of the world, there was supposed to be some sort of wisdom that was his patrimony to me, but I didn't want it, I didn't need it. I knew it all.

But he was right. I did have the world by the balls. Because the world then was one of illimitable possibility. This sense of illimitableness grew more seductive, more magically exhilarating as the spring sky deepened toward the rich blue of early summer, as the sky became a luxuriance of dreams, of delicate cirrus swirls like wisps of soul, mountainous cumulus drifts like billowings of eternity, each insinuating another world, another power, another bliss. To live beneath this sun and lucent blue, beneath the umbrous and radiant soft breath of those clouds, at a time when death did not exist and the breezes of life were still fresh on the skin; to feel that anything was possible and that the future was virgin and vast: this illusion, this truth, was about as close to having the world by the balls as I would ever again come for a long, long time.

I say that death did not exist. I mean that I felt that it did not exist for me. One of my earliest memories was of being waylaid by the grim reaper. I was five, walking alone in a storm-emptied street; he was hauling bundles of old newspaper in a rusted wagon. He drew a knife from among the bundles and put it to me. "Hey, kid," said the reaper, "wanna die?" I got away that day, and I had been getting away since. I had been shot at, stabbed, beaten, hit by a car, set afire by a Roman candle backfiring into my chest, knocked unconscious into a park lake and left for dead. But I was indestructible, blest. I had once jumped from a roof and seen only too late a spiked iron pole, taller than I, directly beneath me, like a waiting impaling spit. The pole went up my trouser leg, shot like cold hard ice past my crotch, came out between my waistband and my belly, barely grazed my ear. That said it all. When intramural race wars became a regular event every Friday after school at P.S. 24, I had not feared for my survival, even though I was on the minority, white team. Indestructible, blest. I could get away with anything.

I already had an arrest record on both sides of the Hudson. "You're on the blotter now!" my mother yelled. "This'll haunt you for the rest of your life!" Yeah, O.K., Ma, relax. Meanwhile, a squad car pulled up to take away my grandmother. She was from the other side, didn't know it was illegal to take numbers. God, she loved the numbers. She was *analfabeta,* and when I had been learning to read, every morning before I went to school and she went to work at the doll-eyeball factory in Newark, she had me consult her *smorfia,* her paperback dream-book, for her. "Look uppa dead baby inna dream-book," I remember her saying.

There were two kinds of men in the neighborhood. Those who worked and those who didn't. Those who didn't seemed generally to do better than those who did. They were sharp dressers with sharp cars, and their time was theirs. They were out there, in front of the joints, in front of the clubs, apricating and spitting, when the other guys were coming home half-loaded from work. I would be one of those that didn't work. Who wouldn't be?

And I didn't work that summer. My days as a barroom porter, mopping up piss and picking drunks' cigarette butts from urinals, were behind me. My time was mine. Soon I'd be old enough under law to quit school. I was already old enough to do everything else, and I spent a lot of time doing it.

I pursued the miracle of love. "Don't forget, you got a sister at home," my mother called down the block at my back as I went out at night. For a moment I took this to be a suggestion that I could get laid without going out.

I pursued oblivion. There was no problem getting booze from the old guy at Finn's Liquor Store on Ninth Street. We'd chip in for a bottle of gin, and one of us would go in to buy it, always careful to enter with a cigarette between his lips, the reason being that since the sale of cigarettes to minors was illegal, anyone smoking a cigarette, *ipso facto,* must therefore not be a minor. When there was no money for booze or dope, when we couldn't rob the money or the booze or the dope, we improvised. We sniffed a lot of glue, snorted a lot of Ronsonol and Carbona. When even that lay beyond our means, we smoked plastic, inserting the teeth of our cheap black combs into the ends of our cigarettes. It got to where our combs had few teeth.

What more could one ask of life? Truly the bounty of God's gift was like unto a comb whose teeth were beyond number and sweet in their toxicity.

And yet I wanted more. There was a stirring in me, a disquiet that neither the ambrosia of Carbona nor the splendor of Barbara Mason's legs could quell. Rock 'n' roll spoke to that stirring, that disquiet. But there wasn't much rock 'n' roll in the air. By this time, Elvis was dead and stuffed and singing "Do the Clam." The Beach Boys were big: surfer faggots. And the Beatles, with those silly little suits and silly little haircuts and silly little songs. I took one look at them and thought: these guys will never make it. But they were not only thriving, they were spawning, dropping Dave Clark Fives and Herman's Hermits from their egg sacs at every turn. Dion had faded, the Dovells had faded, the Shangri-Las were losing it, the Jaynetts had vanished. "Land of a Thousand Dances" by Cannibal and the Headhunters, "Game of Love" by Wayne Fontana and the Mindbenders, "Wooly Booly" by Sam the Sham and the Pharoahs, "Shotgun" by Junior Walker and the All-Stars, "Boy from New York City" by Newark's own Ad Libs: this is what rock 'n' roll, real rock 'n' roll, sounded like in the early months of 1965; and it was all but drowned out by this surfer-limey drivel. By May, Wayne Fontana was knocked out of Number One by—believe it: this is history; we are a sick fucking race—Herman's Hermits warbling "Mrs. Brown You've Got a Lovely Daughter." Who bought this shit? Who squandered their good American gin-and-glue buying power to consume this gurry? Then the Beatles took Number One, then the Beach Boys, and on and on. Rock 'n' roll was dead.

A few of the new limey bands had intrigued: the Kinks, the Zombies, the Yardbirds, the Rolling Stones. But by May of 1965, that intrigue had ebbed. Toward the middle of the month, however, at RCA Studios in Hollywood, the

Rolling Stones made the record that would redeem both rock 'n' roll and the season.

"(I Can't Get No) Satisfaction" seemed to come from nowhere: a burst of flame in the wasteland, like deliverance, in the last days of May.

It seemed to me an anthem, the only anthem to rouse me since the prepubescent appeal of the rockets' red glare and bombs bursting in air. Fuck Mrs. Brown's daughter. *This* was a record as stirring and belligerent with disquiet as the vague feelings in my blood. It hit the charts in early June. By early July it was Number One.

I once wrote of "Satisfaction," in the book *Stranded,* edited by Greil Marcus: "It was unlike anything else to be heard that summer of 1965. Lurid, loud, and concupiscent, it was at once a yell of impotence and indomitability. Its conspiratorial complaints sanctified our frustrations, and its vicious force promised deliverance. It gave us power over girl-creatures, and made of our insignificant, wastrel cocks spigots of wordless insolence—which, of course, we had always wanted them to be." Even though I might turn a phrase or two differently now, those lines, written so much closer in time than these to that song and that summer, still feel true, still feel right. But I know now that there was more. "Satisfaction" gave me faith. It gave me faith in rock 'n' roll. And while that is a profoundly stupid thing in which to have faith, it is better than nothing at all. But it also gave me faith in myself. Here was a song, a sound, that echoed things inside me that no other song or sound had done. And this song, this sound, had captivated the world: it dominated the charts throughout July, the biggest hit of the year. Those things inside me, maybe there was a power in them, maybe they could take me somewhere, as the rushing forward propulsion of this song, this sound, seemed to take me somewhere, as things inside the Rolling Stones had taken them somewhere, somewhere big, somewhere the price of Carbona didn't matter.

Yeah. Somewhere. I didn't know where. I had these uncles, my grandfather's brothers, from the other side. They didn't much bother with people. They sat in clouds of Parodi smoke, like ancient Ch'an masters from the wrong country, saying nothing, doing nothing. What was inside *them?* Where were *they?* Who were they? *What* were they? I began to wonder. My old man would beckon me away from others, would beckon me toward him and them. "Stay away from those guineas," he would say, "get over here with the *albanese,* where you belong." The noble Albanian connection. These guys were all born in southern Italy, but their distant ancestors, five hundred years ago, had come across the Adriatic from Albania. Half a millennium did not matter: the genetic memory of one sacred Albanian corpuscle in the veins was worth more than a gallon of wop blood. These were my elders, my role models. They and the guys with the sharp clothes. I was emulous of them: shiftings in twilight, spirits of the dead enlaced in smoke. I wanted to renounce my soul, like them, but my soul would not lie still.

The stirring, the disquiet, the newfound sense of blind propulsion, of forward-grasping impulse, that flowed through me this summer was everywhere: in those clouds, languorous and restless at once as they moved across the infinite blue that was past, present, and above all vast and virgin and boundless future; in the fine wild insurgence of "Satisfaction"; in the countless bated moments, the sun-drenched motes of illimitableness itself. Like the mesmerizing clouds with their evening breath of mother of pearl, their swells and plumes of fulgent gold and tenebrous rose, "Satisfaction" too seemed to breathe anew and darkly as dusk descended and the spell of night sighed its sultry coming, anew again and more darkly still in the owl-light, and anew yet again and darkest still in those hours when we roamed like little wolves, hours when the black night seemed to pant, hours lush and humid with silence and the scattered noise of danger and laughter and the clashings and couplings, the cursings and cooings, of glimpsed and unseen souls in desperate flux. Those nights of dark prowling seemed the best of times, times when anything might happen. But if anything did happen, it is lost to me now. Now it is the days I remember: the light.

It was in that light that I read *Last Exit to Brooklyn*. Selby's book was part of the miracle of that summer. I read it down at the Jersey shore. Asbury Park or some such dump beach place. It did not matter; all I knew was dumps. What mattered was that it was a dump where the scent and feel and sound of the sea merged with the sun and blue and buoyant cumulus driftings of the sky. Even then, as now, the breath of the sea was the only natural anesthesia, the only thing that could put me under, bring me something that felt like peace.

I had wanted to write for as long as I could remember. Many years later, I would come to understand this, would come to understand writing as an act of cowardice, an act born of fear: a way of fulfilling a need to communicate, to express and reveal oneself, obliquely, without ever having to face another, without ever coming out of hiding. And I was afraid. Though I made a great show of fearlessness, I was afraid of my own shadow, afraid of that soul that would not lie still; of everything, within me and without, which might lay bare the truth of me, whatever that might be. I thought I was alone in my inward cowering. I thought that by evoking and denouncing fear in others, I expelled and renounced my own. I did not know that fear was everywhere, in everyone.

So, being afraid to be who I was—whatever that might be, defined then, only and tenuously, by what undulated and whispered through me: the strange tidal undertow in my blood of those stone-faced old men in their clouds of smoke; the deliverance of a song; the theophany of summer sky and breezes, fleeting and more wistful with the passing and shortening of days, in a world of growing darkness—I wanted to write. And I read and I read. But nothing that I read had the power of that undertow or that theophany or that accruing darkness. Most of what I read was junk of one kind or another. *Requiem for a Schoolgirl* and *Naked Lunch* come to mind. I tried to read stuff such as *Moby Dick*

and the sonnets of Shakespeare, but it was lost on me. *Last Exit to Brooklyn* captured me, enthralled me, transported me as suddenly, as irrevocably as "Satisfaction," as the theophany of that summer sky, a theophany, a sky, seen
perhaps for the first time not through the eyes of lingering childhood, or perhaps for the last time through those eyes. Selby's book showed me that beauty
and power could be wrought from anything: from the weeds and broken glass
and broken concrete and broken souls that were what averted my eyes and my
feelings to the sky and the sea; it showed me that this power and this beauty
could be wrought without affectation or conceit. I felt this power and this
beauty without comprehending the majesty and mastery of rhythm and meter
and vision that lay beneath them, that produced them, that made *Last Exit to
Brooklyn* more a work of heroic poetry than of fiction. In time, as I came to understand these things, a concurrent understanding came to me as well. Selby's
work took on new meaning, illuminating for me the fact that if writing was indeed an act of cowardice, it could, as Selby showed, also be an act of courage of
the rarest and profoundest kind.

It was Selby's book that led me to believe that I could use what was within me
and around me to write. And it was Selby's use of biblical epigrams, to suggest
the ageless antiquity of any act or thought or condition, that led me to see that
there was indeed no new thing under the sun, that anything—*anything*—said today had been said better, more powerfully, and more beautifully, many ages ago.
I made my first unsure explorations toward the sources, the springs of the powers of expression that summer. I remember robbing *A Reading Course in Homeric
Greek,* two oversize textbook volumes, from some kid who was studying to be a
priest.

My primitive receptors groped for what was beyond their ken: a comprehen-
sion of the soul of poetry, its rhythms and its meters and the luminous properties beneath the surface of words. And there came that summer an emanation of
rhythm and meter and words in the service of vision—rhythm and meter so brutal and words so rough-hewn that, like those of *Last Exit,* their effect was in-
escapable, undeniable.

Bob Dylan, of course, had been around for a while. He was like Elvis in reverse: he started out doing the Clam, then he got good. His Clam, however, was
of a far more fraudulent nature than that of the fallen Elvis. Dylan, who was
Christian before Michael Jackson was white, was a fake who made fake folk music for fake folk. If there was anything worse than surfing, it was social conscience. The lonesome death of Hattie Carroll, the loveliness of Mrs. Brown's
daughter: I don't know which was worse. But Dylan, though continuing to hide
behind a fake name and fake persona, had begun to slough the desiccated skin
of false sensitivity. His last album, recorded in three days in January, released in
March, had been a farewell and a foreshadowing. But even its finest moments,
its bursts of subway-rhythmic imagery glimpsed while speeding through abandoned stations of forbidden thought, merely hinted at what was to cone.

Recorded in June, released in July, "Like a Rolling Stone" rose through the summer and by the first week of September blasted forth at Number Two, long and loud and hard and cruel, incongruous and marvelous, blessed and beastly, between the confectionery harmonies of the Beatles' "Help" and the Beach Boys' "California Girls."

By then the album containing "Like a Rolling Stone" was released as well. For me, *Highway 61 Revisited* fulfilled the promise of rock 'n' roll. It was not only great rock 'n' roll, it was a furtherance of rock 'n' roll. It was like nothing that had come before. No rock 'n' roll had ever been so forceful, so thunderous, so unrelenting, so intense, so driven and so driving, so ferocious of word and sound, so brazen in the magnitude of its electricity. The waves of its noise washed over me like waves of the sea, like sacrament. And in one of its songs, "From a Buick 6," I felt something like the power of poetry for the first time in my life.

Sure: there had been poetry of a sort in "Land of a Thousand Dances" and "Shotgun," in Dion and the Jaynetts, and I had felt it; and certainly there had been poetic power of the highest order in *Last Exit to Brooklyn*. But I had never perceived these things as poetry, and I had never perceived the power in what I did perceive as poetry, those printed lines of verse from whose numinous secrets my innocence and ignorance kept me. I felt that "From a Buick 6" was poetry—*I need a steam shovel, mama, to / keep away the dead / I need a dump truck, baby, to / un-load my head*—and I felt the power of it too, in the harsh rock-drill cadence of its mournful, strident blare. It was a detonating cap that blew me backwards into the void of that mystifying soul I had been thirsting to know, backwards through the wisdom of Charles Olson's law—*He who controls rhythm / controls*—to the sources of that wisdom and that control, and to the never-ending revelations of their secrets.

I still get a kick out of "Satisfaction." But its power for me has long since ebbed. That power was not innate, but imbued by the powers of the moment's breeze; not a power in essence but a power of time and place and callow stirrings. What remains, beyond idle enjoyment, is nostalgia, nothing more. But "From a Buick 6" remains a power, and I still regard it today as embodying and embracing the precepts common to all great poetry. In fact, I think it remains, with *Blonde on Blonde,* which followed it, the greatest, maybe the only true, example of rock 'n' roll as poetry, poetry as rock 'n' roll. It is surely Dylan at the height of his powers. (I'm amazed that anyone could regard another album as Dylan's best. Clinton Heylin, whose *Bob Dylan: The Recording Sessions* will be published later this year by St. Martin's, told me that his favorite Dylan album was *Blood on the Tracks,* an opinion that left me as impressed by the atrocity of his personal taste as by the superb workmanship of his study.) That Dylan uttered the brilliant Veltrine howl of *Highway 61 Revisited* when he was barely twenty-four is astounding, incredible, uncanny.

I remember how we got our copy, my buddy Phil and I. Many of our days that summer were spent in the environs of Hubert's Museum, a palace of nightmarish pleasures, a junkie-hustler-pinball-shooting-gallery-novelty arcade with an actual freak show in the basement, on Forty-second Street. (And the lowdown on Hubert's will definitely have to wait until *The History of My Dick*.) On one of those Times Square afternoons, when our endeavors had not panned out and our evil had borne no fruit, we ran into one of Phil's uncles, who was strolling down Broadway with a broad who was not his wife. "How's Aunt Rosie?" Phil asked him. It was a question that netted him a pound-note, more than enough for a copy of *Highway 61 Revisited* and two slabs of grease at the pizza joint on the corner: sustenance for flesh and soul alike.

Summer by then was almost through. The days grew shorter, the breezes cooler, the colors and drift of the clouds more melancholy in their opalescence. God only knew what lay ahead: it was beyond our dreams and nightmares both.

I did not stay in the light. My nature was erebotropic, and I wandered deeper into darkness, as even the illumination of that summer turned tenebrous inside me. I stayed in the dark for a lot of years. They shut down Hubert's Museum, but it remained open inside me. Only when I finally began to emerge in breath did the light of that summer return, only then—now, in the light of this summer—did I come to remember it, buried there in the dark, forgotten like desire and the sense, the lie and truth, of illimitableness itself.

"Satisfaction" and sunlight, *Last Exit to Brooklyn* and "From a Buick 6." A purloined Greek textbook and the ocean and a darkness in the veins. A slab of grease, a bottle of Carbona, and thou. As it is writ: memories, and destinies, are made of this.

# 90

A previously unpublished passage from a far-from-finished autobiography. How does one reveal in print the secret truth of one's life when lawyers disallow it?

# Excerpt from
# "Entering the Barrens"

Somebody sent me her obituary. It said she was a lover and patron of the arts. It didn't say she was a fucking pig.

It was about eight years ago. She and some other broad had some half-assed scheme for a movie deal involving one of my books. The other one, the good-looking one, the married one, lived in the neighborhood. I figured she was the one I'd end up fucking. But it was the pig, the lover and patron of the arts, who showed up alone for our second meeting.

"Well," she said, "are we going to have an affair?"

I was taken aback, insulted. Her words were an affront. I mean, she was a fucking dog.

"Maybe. If I get drunk enough," I told her.

"What do you drink?"

"Dewar's."

A few days later, a messenger showed up with a gift-wrapped fifth. The broad I was living with walked in just as I was throwing away the note that came with it.

She had a million-dollar joint with a swimming-pool out on the Long Island shore. She kept inviting me out there. Eventually, she took an apartment in the city too, a few blocks from me. She told me that she got down on her knees and scrubbed and scrubbed, telling herself that this would make her worthy of me. She told me about the artists in her life: some mo-mo rock star I remembered pissing on ten years before; some professional-mick writer on whom I would not deign to piss. I figured they were fucking her, and that made me smile inwardly.

Some years later I was drunk in a bar. She walked by with some sensitive-looking asshole in tow.

"Tonight's your night," I told her. The sensitive-looking asshole backed off, turned away. I actually would have fucked her, I was that drunk.

"Of all nights," she said. She explained that she was nursing the sensitive guy, whose marriage had just ended.

"You mean, you'd rather fuck him than me?" There was no end to the effrontery of this broad.

"No, no, no. I wouldn't fuck him," she bubbled. He turned farther away. "Look," she said, "I'll call you."

That was the last time I ever talked to her. When I saw the obituary, I wondered what she died from. It didn't say; it said only that she'd been ill. Maybe she did fuck the sensitive guy. Maybe she caught the AIDS and died. Lovers of the arts are like that. They can't tell the difference between a sensitive asshole and a guy who takes it up the ass. If there is a difference.

It was just a minor death, in a long season of many deaths. Those deaths would leave me friendless and fatherless, feeling like a lone survivor—no, worse, nothing so dramatic as that: a remnant, something left behind—of the black-iron days of my own past. Cancer wards and Coney Island bullets. The common end eats heroism, the common end eats nobility, casually and slovenly, as a bleak-colored bird, a cawing and scavenging thing, eats stale, sodden bread.

It was at one of these funerals that somebody reminded me that I had killed somebody on a summer night in Newark twenty years before. I had forgotten. Now I remembered.

# 91

I wrote two very different memorials to Dean Martin following his death on Christmas Day of 1995. One of them, published in the *New York Times,* was a piece of shit, or at least ended up being such by the time it reached print. The other, published in the *Village Voice* and reprinted here, was written simply and directly from the heart.

# Requiescat Dino

I spent Christmas quietly, pleasantly alone. Late in the afternoon, as it grew dark and I was preparing to go out, I turned on the radio. It was WCBS-AM, an all-news station, but what I heard was "That's Amore." I knew then that Dean Martin had died. I experienced an eerie and subdued wave of melancholy. I had never met the man, yet for many years—since long before I had thought of casting the shadow of his life through the pages of a book—I had felt an odd, abiding affinity with him, as of something in the blood, as with an old uncle to whom unsaid and unsayable ways, breezes of dark and light, bound me. I liked to know he was there, in this world, though I knew he long had been receding from it, and in this slow fade to black there likely was a cautionary lesson to be learned concerning those breezes and those ways. The little wave of melancholy brought with it chill, like the final stirring and vanishing of one of those familiar breezes from the world.

I had heard lately that he was in bad shape, but I had been hearing this for years. Every once in a while, someone would catch a glimpse of his solitary public decay in one of the three restaurants where in recent years he sat and drank and smoked and sometimes ate—Hamburger Hamlet, La Famiglia, and Da Vinci. The supermarket tabloids had been declaring him dead for years: "Frail Dean Martin Flees Hospital in Cancer Nightmare: Doctors Give Him Only Months to Live," announced the *Enquirer* in the fall of 1993. A few months later, it was "Beloved Dino Is Wasting Away." Then, in the spring of 1994, "Dean Martin: His Tragic Last Days." And yet the great man had lived on. He was quoted as saying he wanted "to die at La Famiglia with a Scotch in one hand and a cigarette in the other"; but he outlived La Famiglia and had to move on to Da Vinci for his J&B-and-sodas and his ashtray.

He was 78. I wanted him at least to hit 80, the age at which Buddha died. That is how I sometimes thought of him: the American Buddha. The idea of tragedy, of last tragic days, appeals and sells. But Jeannie, his wife of many years and in the end his closest friend, long had told me that somehow, in his seclusion and his silence, he was perfectly content.

A couple of months ago, I agreed to serve as the executive producer of a Dean Martin reissue for the Scamp subsidiary of Caroline Records. All I had to do was choose the recordings and write the notes. I was looking forward to him being alive when I wrote the notes, alive and in his 80th year when the album came out; looking forward to playing the Bodhidharma angle, saying that if Dino grew a beard and wrapped himself in saffron cloth, he would be considered a spiritual master in his silent wisdom and withdrawal from the world into contentment. And I would half believe what I would say.

It was, in a way, Dean's refusal to wear a robe of piety, his absolute and innate lack of pretension that has stood in the way of a wider recognition of and deeper respect for his work. Just listen, say, to his 1951 Capitol recording of "Torna a Surriento," or watch him in Billy Wilder's banned and overlooked *Kiss Me, Stupid,* from 1964. Of course, after a while, in his enlightenment, he stopped taking any of it seriously. Unlike Sinatra, he never adopted the air of *gravitas,* never bore himself with self-importance, or treated his work as if it were art. And that is why, in an age when pretense prevails over substance, every cough of Sinatra has been reverently preserved and packaged while Dean has been regarded with the insouciance with which he regarded the world. But Sinatra, for one, was aware of what lay beneath that insouciance, and his words upon Dean's death may be the most beguiling he has ever uttered: "He has been like the air I breathe."

While I was working on the long, strange book that came to be called *Dino: Living High in the Dirty Business of Dreams,* it was Jeannie who told me that I would learn nothing about Dean from Dean, that he had completely divorced himself from, had no interest in, his memories and his life. Still, I wanted to meet him and when the book was done and published, Jeannie set about arranging a rendezvous. At the last minute, Dean told her, "If I'm going to meet the guy I should at least show him the respect of reading his book first." Dean had read *Black Beauty* as a boy. Or so he claimed. Such was the extent of his reading. So that was that.

In the days following his passing I found that I wasn't alone in feeling that a breeze had died away. I ran into people who seemed to express something like sadness, something rarely heard in idle talk of a stranger's death. "Jesus," I heard more than once. "I was hoping he at least would've outlived that fucking Jerry Lewis"—a sentiment of sincerity if not quite of mourning and one of such seeming popularity that Hallmark might well consider its message for a mass-produced sympathy card. And me, meanwhile, with my poignant fucking breezes thinking out loud, "I hope those stupid sons of bitches at Dell know to reissue the paperback but quick."

Anyway, he was one of a kind, and he lived. A mystery maybe even unto himself: but he lived.

# 92

On the few occasions when Robert De Niro had spoken to the press through the years, his words and manner of speaking had always been mangled and edited to a false neatness and comprehensibility. In this piece, published in the March 1996 British edition of *Esquire,* I wanted to capture his true voice and his singular manner of trying to openly express what remains unarticulated inside him.

# De Niro

I remember him walking into a bar in the middle of the night 21 winters ago. By then Robert De Niro was known, but barely. *Mean Streets* had become something of a cult classic in the two years since its release, and *The Godfather Part II,* for which he would win an Academy Award as Best Supporting Actor, had just been released. But on this night, even if they could have recognized Robert De Niro, those in the bar could not recognize the man who had entered among them. An unknown lowlife amid a desolate scattering of others, he seemed to be one of those lost, lonely and disturbed souls borne away by the tide of that familiar urban insanity, the lurid or violent variations of whose common end was the stuff not only of Greenwich Village bars such as this but of the city's daily tabloids as well. He shifted, wired and wiry, and he paced, smiling with depraved enthusiasm as he announced—to himself, to no one, to whatever kindred souls might hear—that he had figured out how to make a bomb from a length of pipe. He said he drove a cab and could not sleep. Then he was gone. And some months later, unremembered and unrecognized as the deranged shade in that bar, there he was again, that lost taxi-driver, sounding and seeming quite the same, but up there bigger than life on a movie screen, confronting his image in a mirror and asking, *"You talkin' to me?"*

Now here we are, alone in a room with several chairs and something like mutual unease. We look around at the empty seats in shared indecision. I gesture to a broad table whose chairs are of the folding variety.

"This looks suitably uncomfortable," I say, and he nods as if that makes perfect sense.

The conservatively and casually well-dressed middle-aged man across from me emanates something more of gentility than of darkness or danger. He is rather subdued. The last thing he appears to be is an actor. He is too down-to-earth, too unaffected for that. Looking at him, it's hard to believe that he could convince anyone he was a killer—a cab-driver who could not sleep perhaps, but the most ordinary and benign of sleepless cab-drivers. And it is hard as well to picture him as the Cowardly Lion. Yet that is how it all began.

"I was around ten," he says. "I used to go to acting school on Saturday."

It was during that first year at the Dramatic Workshop that he played the Cowardly Lion in *The Wizard of Oz.* Once on the yellow brick road, he never looked back.

In New York, where his mystique seems to pervade the air, a sense of mythology has risen around him. His elusive presence, fabled more than witnessed, is as protean as it is on screen. People who have glimpsed him, or think they have glimpsed him or claim they have glimpsed him, or know someone who has encountered or claimed to have encountered him will tell you different things. They will tell you that he is very short, or that he is from the Lower East Side, or that he is a regular guy. But the truth is that he is none of these things; that when he was among them, people never really saw him, because it was never really him.

The facts of his youth are ordinary enough. He was born a few blocks from that childhood acting school, in Greenwich Village, on August 17, 1943. His parents parted, as amicably as parents can part, when he was two. The father whose name he bore, and whose physical characteristics he inherited, was a painter, and the actor remembers him moving in those days from one dank loft to another.

He remained close to his father, but it was his Irish mother, Virginia, herself an aspiring artist, who raised him. One account of his childhood describes him as "frail and pale", as "temperamentally shy and taciturn". I ask him to tell me in his own words what he was like as an adolescent.

"I don't know. I was OK." He ponders awhile. "That's a hard one. I can't . . ." He ponders some more. "I might have been introverted at times, but I interacted with other kids. I wasn't, like, I don't know"—his brown eyes glint slyly—"a writer. Some writers, they can't relate too well outside, they're not too communicative."

I ask the great communicator if the fact that his parents were both creative people made it somehow more natural, or easier, for him to pursue acting at such an early age.

"Yeah, they were helpful. They were supportive." He pauses, puts it another way. "They were not unsupportive."

It is clear that, in his youth, acting was the most important thing to him, as it has remained ever since. The impulse to act, that first timid roar from the Cowardly Lion, preceded puberty in its onset. He is not quite sure what record was playing the first time he danced. He grins happily, thinking about it, trying to remember, but in the end he can't. "Oh, God," he says, tentatively offering 'At the Hop' by Danny and the Juniors, which came out when he was fourteen. "Yeah." Then again maybe it was Bill Haley's 'Rock Around the Clock'. But then he clearly recalls more important memories. Not dancing, but studying: the Stanislavsky Method with Stella Adler at the Conservatory of Acting, when he was sixteen; at the Actors Studio, when he was eighteen.

Once on the yellow brick road, he never left it. For the past 42 years, acting has been De Niro's life, and in a sense more literal than figurative. He has not stopped. As we speak, his two most recent movies, *Casino* and *Heat*, released in rapid-fire succession, are playing simultaneously throughout America. He has completed work on another picture, *Sleepers,* and is presently working on yet another, *The Fan.* And that is the way it has been, as long as he has been able to have it that way, since his first job as an extra 35 years ago in something called *Trois chambres à Manhattan.*

He is open, honest and willing, if not quite eager, to talk. But when speaking of matters other than acting, he seems not so much guarded or hesitant as uncomfortable and unsure, as if straying too far from the known. Books, for instance.

"I have to read a lot more, because all I read is scripts now, stuff like that. There's a lot of stuff I should read." In his voice there is a hint of regret, but also a note of resignation, acceptance that this is the way it is, the way it has to be.

Even aspects of acting that exist outside, rather than within him, elicit a lukewarm response. When he recalls the movies that made an impression on him as a kid, he sounds like anyone reminiscing, just another middle-aged guy idly remembering when movies were movies: "*Rebel Without a Cause, East of Eden, On the Waterfront.* I liked—saw it the other day, Theodore Dreiser—*An American Tragedy, A Place in the Sun,* Montgomery Clift, Elizabeth Taylor. There was *Giant.*" And back then monster pictures were monster pictures. "There were some good ones. I liked *The Thing,* and *Invasion of the Body Snatchers.*"

Was it true, then, that he was not really a follower of, ahem, *le cinéma?*

"Well, there are a lot of movies I haven't seen. Like Marty Scorsese"—a grin, another sly glint—"knows every movie ever made since the beginning of time. So that's great. So I always ask Marty about this or that. I had to get an obscure film just the other day, I said to my assistant, 'Call Marty. I know he's got it.'"

He does not watch his own movies. "I look at the dailies," he says. "But watching 'em, no. I'll look at a rough cut with the director and tell him what I think. Then I might look at the final film with all the titles and music and everything done. And then I probably won't look at it for years to come."

Why can't he stop working? Is it a compulsion?

"No," he says without hesitation, then pauses, wavering a bit, as if he has never really thought about it and finds the thought somewhat troubling. "I hope not." Then he resumes composure, steadily reassuring himself as he speaks. "Eventually I won't work like this. I'll go into other things. But at the moment I've been working a lot."

What would he have done if acting hadn't panned out?

There is no answer to that question but a matter-of-fact blank: "I don't know what I would have done."

Was there a moment when he felt, when he knew, that he had made it?

"Well, I guess, when you do a big movie and you know you're gonna work again. Like *The Godfather II.* I figured, after that, I'll be OK. Because I'd done movies before that, but you never knew what was gonna happen."

Does he have any heroes any more?

"Offhand, I can't think of any." A plain and honest thought, but he seems to sense that it sounds terrible. "I'm not thinkin' it through," he amends. "I'm sure if I thought about certain people . . ." The tail of his voice curls away. He has balanced his cigar, which has gone out, at the edge of the table at which we sit, and he stares at it, dead.

But ask him about acting, the inward part of it, ask him about inventing a soul and submerging himself in it, and the floodgates burst. There is something wild and wonderful and primal in his grappling to communicate, to give verbal form to, what is essentially immanent and, for him, unutterable. The rare, sparse and padded published interviews with him through the years portray a man of calm, terse statements, puzzling simplicity and monosyllabic disinterest. The De Niro across from me, once the floodgates are breached, seems and sounds nothing like that man. The flood is anything but fluent, anything but lucent, and to be drawn into it is to become lost in it, along with him, again and again; but one is at least lost, and emerges with, the real Robert De Niro, a sense of him as he is and honestly sounds.

"Yeah," he begins prosaically enough, "you can do different parts." His words bring to mind the Dickens quote, "He do the Police in different voices," that Eliot originally placed at the head of *The Waste Land*. "You can play different parts where you become—I mean, you could imagine what the price would be you'd have to pay for playing a part, but you didn't actually—like you're someone who's on death row, you didn't have to murder somebody in order to . . ." And here he is lost. He concentrates, finds his way back. "You're not gonna go to the electric chair in order to experience the brink—I mean you can experience how it would be to be on death row and at the end of the day, actually, you're into the real thing."

I think of that picture *A Double Life*, the one with Ronald Coleman as an actor taken over by the role of Othello. I think of the attitude the ancient Romans had to acting, their feeling that it was wrong to surrender one's own personality and assume another's, that it offended against a sense of gravitas. Has he, De Niro, ever got lost among his characters?

"No. I have not. I don't know, maybe there are other actors, if they do, they went nuts, or they went off." He pauses, draws breath, and the floodgates burst again. "You can get into it in the sense where you feel inspired almost and you really know that you're in total control of what it is, and you know you're right on target, but it doesn't mean—like even a person committing some sort of act, whatever that is, or involved in a situation, it doesn't mean other thoughts don't go through their mind. The same thing with acting. Some of your best scenes are when you're, like, thinking about something else. Like I'm talking to you now and you're talking to me but I'm thinking about three other things and you're thinking about three other things. The same with someone who's committing some kind of an act. Good, bad, whatever it is. Or going through some sort of experience. They could be thinking at the same time about other things. But they're still going through that experience.

"It's like being in a dream, or nightmare, a nightmare that you believe totally when you're in it, when you're dreaming. It's the same thing. Sometimes in acting, you get to that point, you know you're really in that situation, you're not doing it any differently than you would be in life. Then, also, you have to think of the character and how they would react, the difference between you and the character . . . "

He seems lost again, suggests turning off the tape while he thinks. No need, I tell him. Together we examine the wondrous technology of the voice-activation feature on my new microcassette recorder. In time, slowly, he resumes. "When you're dreaming, you believe it, and you can get to a point where you're lucky enough to be"—intensely, oddly—"right . . ." He leaves the phrase hanging in air, as if the final word, "there", must remain unsaid to convey the unsayable sense of what he wants to say.

Does he ever find himself responding in real life not as himself but as one of his characters?

"If you're working on a character all day, at the end of the day, you can carry some of that over, in a residual kind of way. Or you've been hyper all day because you've been in a very emotional scene, that could carry over to a degree, but it's just residue, kind of like rippling, you know, ripple, ripple, ripple, till there's nothing."

I ask him if acting serves to exorcise his demons.

"Yeah, in a way it does. You can express certain things. You can play different parts, be different people. At least get a sense of what it is. Sometimes if you play a character, you put a mask on, whether it's literally a mask or not, which frees you in a sense to do something that's not you. It opens up a door. It's like when you're looking for a key to a character, you find something that enables you to do it in your way. It enables you to give up parts of yourself through something else instead of doing it directly.

"The whole trick about it is not to make it too much of a caricature. Because actors, a lot of times, they feel that they want to do more for a scene. Sometimes they do nothing, just stay there, and the presence alone is enough. And they feel: 'I've got to show some way that I'm this or I'm that.' And there's nothing, you don't have to do a thing."

Does one role stand out as hardest?

"They're all hard, in different ways. It's a diplomatic answer, but it's true. Movies are hard to make. Or acting in a play. I talk more movies because that's what I'm interested in. In a play, it's a tremendous amount of work and energy in another direction.

"They all have their own set of problems. Unique set of problems. Some are physically more hard. You know, obvious ones, *Raging Bull* or *The Deer Hunter.* I just did *Heat*. That was a lot of work—a lot of work, but in other ways. They're all different."

I want to get back to the demons. He seems in his pictures so at home with them, or they in him. Does he feel that people tend to regard him in terms of his most sociopathic roles?

"Probably some of them, yeah," he says offhandedly.

I remember, not long after *Raging Bull* came out, I was in an after-hours joint on Sullivan Street, and it seemed that, at the far end of the bar, all the young aspiring tough guys from the neighbourhood were making themselves over in the image of his Jake. I had witnessed other hoi-polloi makeovers inspired by other of his performances as well. How does it feel, I wonder, to influence the way people in the street walk and talk?

"Well, I don't know." But no, he does: "Yeah. Yeah. Yeah. Well, that's amazing. It's funny in a way. But . . ." He turns away, as if to comically hide; grins his berserk-executioner-on-the-town grin, his whole face beaming maniacally, his mouth happily scowling, an impossible marriage of the masks of tragedy and comedy that is the trademark mask of De Niro.

Does he ever miss anonymity?

"Well, I don't miss it because, I guess, I'm just very realistic about it. I had many years of anonymity. Even if it was 20 years ago, I still had many years of knowing what it is not to be recognized. But it's something you get used to."

Has he ever come very close to playing himself?

"Some things are closer to me, the way I behave, than others. And some things are closer to the way, could I say, that I think? *Midnight Run,* I liked. I had fun doing that. I mean, I wouldn't be the way that character is, but I could understand, I know the rhythms, he's from New York, and so on. We were having a tough time finding the other actor to play off. And then finally Chuck Grodin came and read, and Chuck really understood his character and therefore it helped me with mine. It's like two musicians, if they don't click off each other, it doesn't work right, ever. The rhythm is off. When you're lucky to play with somebody who gives you something, then it makes it easy. It's great when you can work with somebody that can help you. You help each other."

What other actors have given him something?

"Harvey Keitel. Joe Pesci. Chris Walken. There are others I can't think of offhand."

He tells how he first met Keitel, how he came to the role in which he began to hit his stride. The year was 1972. He had been getting feature roles in two-bit movies since 1963.

"I knew Harvey before, through the Actors Studio. And Marty I sort of knew when I was a kid. We had mutual friends, and I'd see him around. He'd done *Who's That Knocking at My Door?* with Harvey. I had done some other movies, and Marty wanted him for the part of Charlie in *Mean Streets,* and I thought, well, I don't know—sometimes as an actor you get this thing: I don't know if I can take that part because I've taken stronger supporting roles and now I'm talkin' a lesser part and blah blah; and I was saying that to myself. It's like takin' a position, you know, career-wise. But I really wanted to work with Marty, and I ran into Harvey in the street, and Harvey says, 'You know, you oughta do the part of Johnny Boy.' I said, 'Well, you know, I gotta tell ya, I feel that I should ask for your part. It's nothing against you, it's just that I feel careerwise, blah, blah.' I was honest with him. And not in a competitive way; I was just saying, you know, I don't know what to do."

His stunning performance as Johnny Boy in *Mean Streets* won him the role of the young Vito Corleone in Francis Ford Coppola's *The Godfather Part II,* which, in 1974, won him his first Academy Award. After that, as he says, he always knew he could find work.

Has he paid any mind to critics, then or now?

"Well, sometimes critics can be good—at least if they're good critics, if they're not attacking you for things that are out of your control, like your hair or your looks; I've heard some of them, pretty nasty, and that's unfortunate, and sometimes people like to read that stuff because they find it amusing in a sense, but it's not very nice and it has nothing to do with anything—but good critics you can learn from in the sense that they will be constructively critical and maybe say to you something that nobody else would say to you because they're afraid. So sometimes the only person you can really trust is a critic, 'cause they don't care."

The floodwaters seem to have dispersed. Tranquillity seeps in. We talk about this and that. He's making *The Fan* with Tony Scott. It's based on a novel that came out last year, about a guy who stalks a baseball star.

"And you're the stalker."

"More or less."

He says he's been carrying a few inchoate projects inside him. "Ultimately I've always wanted to write my own thing and do it. It just takes a certain type of commitment and focus and discipline that—I've just gotta do it."

What else is inside him? Religion maybe?

"Well, I believe in spirituality. I believe that there's something that goes on between people and forces that are not clearly understood, and some people, like psychics and so on, have some bead on it. I don't know how. Because I've been to psychics and they've told me things that have been very accurate, and friends of mine have gone to psychics in different parts of the world, they knew they were referring to me. I definitely feel there's something to that kind of stuff. It's all tied in somehow. I don't know how, but it works. There's something there."

"Yeah, well, talk about psychic. I've always somehow had the impression that you must have loved Abbott and Costello."

"Yeah," he beams, "I did. You're right. I always liked Abbott and Costello."

It is, you might say, a spiritual moment for both of us. I can see it now: *Abbott and Costello on Death Row.* Now, that's my kind of spirituality.

# 93

The unidentified woman in this exchange was the photographer Roberta Bayley, who still has great legs and denies them to me.

barely even remember that I had sex with them and I'm wondering if they member and whatever. . . .

ME: I coulda been one of those guys!

HER: I know. Well, you knew me back *then,* right? But you weren't interested ntil it was too late.

ME: So where does that leave us?

HER: I don't know. *(Laughs)* Did you learn anything?

ME: If I learned anything, I learned that my old ways—being an insensitive prick—served me better in many respects.

HER: Yeah, but to what end ultimately?

ME: Ultimately? To no end, except gratification on a certain level.

HER: Do you think part of the reason you were attracted to me is because you knew nothing would come of it?

ME: No.

HER: I find that's almost always a big attraction for men.

ME: No, that's never the case with me. Of course, once I have someone, I no longer want them.

HER: Right. Well, don't you think that's another factor?

ME: Oh, man, enough of this. I wouldn't even have you at this point.

HER: I'm just not your type.

ME: It's not so much you.

HER: It's my legs.

ME: Your legs are my type.

HER: And you've never even seen me in high heels.

ME: I think you're very selfish with your legs. I don't see how an involvement with your legs could lead to a sullying of your mind or emotions.

HER: This is where we part ways.

ME: And you think it's irremediable? Or do you think it might be resolved by counseling or further dialogue?

HER: Perhaps therapy. Psychotherapy.

# The Unfuckable

I'd known her for years, mainly as the friend of a girlfriend. Someday, I told myself whenever I saw or thought of her, someday. Eventually, one lonely season after the girlfriend had gone, I turned my eye to her—to her legs, to be precise. I took her out—an actual date, something I'd never done, then another, and another. I'd never pursued anything or anyone with such attention. But she, and her legs, were not forthcoming. I broached the subject: you, me, the many-splendored thing.

No dice. Failure. I knew gnawing within, and I knew mystification. As our relationship degenerated into friendship, the mystification lingered. Was I not, after all, God's gift to the target sex? What had gone wrong? Several years later, I wanted answers, and was driven to asking questions I'd never asked before. With naught but apprehension and a tape recorder between us, I sought only to know.

ME: You were the end of an era: the only one I wanted that I didn't get.

HER: Do you hold that against me?

ME: No. It passed.

HER: I didn't think you were courting me.

ME: Is that what you were looking for? You wanted to be *courted?*

HER: No. But—

ME: I did everything but beg. I tried everything.

HER: What are you talking about? You didn't even try to kiss me.

ME: I did kiss you, but you don't even remember. So give me some tips on this courtship racket, for the next time around. Where did I go wrong?

HER: You went wrong right at the beginning, when you left me waiting in that restaurant and you never showed up.

ME: That was a bad start?

HER: Bad is like much too mild a word.

ME: I think that you just wanted to remain wanted.

HER: Well, it's a good position to be in, cause you can't lose, right?

ME: But why the next guy and not me?

HER: What next guy?

ME: What do you mean—you think you've had it with sex?

HER: It's a question of chemistry. This to me is the fundamental difference

443

between men and women. I don't think men necessarily need sexual chemistry to be interested in sex.

ME: How often do you feel this chemistry?

HER: Lately? *(Laughs.)* Seldom.

ME: Why do you think this is?

HER: I don't know. I wish I knew. I'm guessing I'm just in a different place in my life. It's all so serious.

ME: Is it better this way? Is it worse?

HER: I can't say I'm bothered by it, but on the other hand, sometimes I'm curious about it. Then again, bizarrely enough, I could envision the rest of my life without having sex, just because the last few years have been pretty okay. Life is less complicated. Every once in a while I think, This is really strange. But it's not something that makes me feel like going to the doctor for hormone supplements to increase my sex drive. It's not on that level.

ME: You don't feel like you're missing out on anything? Like the sands of time are running out?

HER: I don't *feel* like I'm missing anything.

ME: I guess I missed the boat.

HER: By many years, Nick, so don't—

ME: Many years? *(Ponders)* When sexual desire comes to you, what form does it take?

HER: I don't know. . . .

ME: I mean, when you jerk off, what goes through your mind? Do you think of someone or something specific? What do you envision?

HER: What do I fantasize about when I *masturbate?*

ME: Yeah. It's gotta be something.

HER: No, no. It's just like a fantasy that's made up.

ME: Like a movie in your head?

HER: Yeah. Just some situation or something. But it's not like me and somebody, or anything like that. It's just some erotic ideas. It's not specific.

ME: Sounds sort of ethereal.

HER: No, it's just private. I'm not going to go into it. You say ethereal, but it's not like I'm thinking about angels. It's not a romance novel or something. It's probably something dirty, but it's nonspecific.

ME: Nonspecific dirty.

HER: Nonspecific in terms of me or someone I actually know.

ME: It's just you observing something?

HER: I don't know. I don't think about it.

ME: Okay. Back to you and me. Would my chances with you have been any better if you had been drunk?

HER: Well, everyone's chances with me are better when I'm drunk.

ME: And how about if I'd been a stranger?

HER: Yeah. And if you lived in a different city. I've usually chosen men I

---

didn't know and who preferably lived far away. When I think about marriage, it's to someone who's very rich and who rarely comes hom[e]

ME: But look at what we missed.

HER: I don't know. What have we missed?

ME: The chance to learn to hate each other.

HER: We don't need that.

ME: I guess what it comes down to is you represent a pair of legs tha[t] couldn't have. Aside from being a wonderful person, you have nice legs.

HER: Thank you.

ME: But you've got this problem: You can't free your mind from your [l]

HER: I can't do that, no.

ME: Wouldn't that represent a new and higher spiritual plane to aspire[ ]

HER: Why would I want to do that?

ME: To be nice.

HER: Nick, I'm—

ME: To be a pal.

HER: No, no, I don't think so.

ME: Is there some kind of waiting list for your legs or something?

HER: *(Laughs.)* If there is, it's a mystery to me.

ME: So in the end, who or what have I lost out to?

HER: No one. Ceramic tile. Kitchen remodeling—that's where my energy goes these days. My new floor is so cool.

ME: So you've invested your passion in a kitchen floor. Strange that you should find in a floor the qualities I lack.

HER: Did you really want us to have a sexual relationship?

ME: Yeah. To me, sex was always a good way to spend time.

HER: Right. But can you say that in the last five or six years you've had any casual sexual relationships? I haven't. I mean, you're the only person who even asked me out on a date, if that's what that was.

ME: Well, Jesus, you didn't show any appreciation.

HER: I most certainly did—I went!

ME: You went, but you didn't put out!

HER: That's not the equation, Nick.

ME: What *is* the equation?

HER: I wish I knew the answer, but I don't.

ME: You're supposed to be the Answer Lady. You're the one holdin' the deck.

HER: I'm no good at relationships.

ME: Let's forget about relationships. Let's get back to screw-and-run.

HER: I'm sure this is the last thing you want to hear, but if you actually like the person, why would you want to do that and then think you could still be that person's friend?

ME: Well, if no deep, neurotic personal attachment has developed—

HER: I don't know. Sometimes I see people now who I slept with once and I

# 94

*Esquire* asked a bunch of people to write about their favorite possession or thing. I had this big heavy ancient coin that for me possessed properties that were almost magical.

# The Coin

I've got this piece of cold, heavy metal. It's bronze, but it looks and feels like stone: dark, earthen brown, with a rich patina, deep, mossy green and azure. It's about two and a half inches across and weighs about half a pound. It fits comfortably in my palm but is too big to enclose in my fist.

It's one of the first, primitive Roman coins, an *aes grave,* cast about 230 B.C., between the Punic wars. Its raised obverse bears the double-faced head of Janus, the god of gods, who looks both to the past—the western land, the realm of the dead—and to the future, the eastern dawn. His gaze beneath the patina is still strong. On the reverse is a ship's prow, facing eastward. Two thousand years ago and more, this piece of bronze could buy a bottle of wine. Ten thousand of them could buy freedom for a slave.

Rome's first gold coin is almost as old. It's exceedingly beautiful, exceedingly rare, exceedingly valuable. But it's nothing in the hand, and the gold bears no patina, no glow of the millennium and more through which it has passed.

And that, to me, is what it's all about: the patina, the perspective of time. For me, this thing isn't so much a coin as a palpable emanation, embodiment and evocation, symbol and susurrus, of something inexpressive. The look of it, the heft and feel of it, are the look, heft, and feel of a shard of the eternal captured somehow, magically, in the metallurgy of vain mortality. I think of the countless unknown hands that held it in days of different gods. It's from a time before Christ or Caesar. It's as old as the words of Ecclesiastes—"The thing that hath been, it is that which shall be; and that which is done is that which shall be done: and there is no new thing under the sun"—words that this half pound of bronze so silently and eloquently expresses as well. And what's more, beyond that eloquence, wielded right, it can break a skull.

It sets me straight, this coin, when I look at it or think of it or hold it; and it means something, and it makes me feel good. So, sure, there's drowsing on deserted beaches. There's reading Dante or listening to "Sea of Love." There are certain breezes, certain blow jobs, a couple of restaurants in Milan. But they can wait. Right now, it's this piece of metal that looks and feels like stone, that fits comfortably in my palm but is too big to enclose in my fist.

# 95

# Why I Am Great

The title is Nietzsche's, the sentiment mine, and these few but eloquent words, written for naught, will not begin to explain it.

A few years ago, I wrote this book, *Dino*, that turned into a sort of Rorschach test for readers and reviewers; I've seen and heard it described as everything from prose poetry to pop biography, from a work of genius to a piece of vulgar pulp. Of this broad spectrum of responses, none surprised me more than that of *Real Crime Book Digest*, which cited it as one of the six best true-crime books of 1993.

When I met him in Chicago last fall, Jim Agnew, who runs this operation and who may be the only man on earth who thinks of me as a true-crime writer, asked me to knock off a few hundred words on myself as such. So—perhaps inexplicably—here I am.

Then again, let me try to see it from Jim's angle. Of the five nonfiction books I've written, two have dealt to some degree with true crime. The first of these was *Power on Earth*, about Michele Sindona, the infamous Sicilian financier who was believed to occupy the throne at the heart of the world's darkness, where the most secret and shadowy reaches of international finance, the Mafia, and the Vatican came together.

I had written a book called *Hellfire*, a sort of Old Testament biography of Jerry Lee Lewis, which had been received with some acclaim. Casting about for another biographical subject—it was what I had to do: no publisher would yet pay me enough to write what I wanted and, as much as I wanted to write *Hellfire*, as much as I loved and was proud of it, what I wanted to write next was fiction, which I had always wanted to write—I came to the conclusion that no one interested me.

Then one night I glimpsed his image amid the dead drone of the TV news, and I realized that Sindona was a man who intrigued me. I was told by many that he was unapproachable, by others that the governments of America and Italy were set on his silence. But I wrote to him at the federal prison in Otisville, New York, where he was then being held, and fortune was with me. He called me, told me he was willing to talk. Soon after, pending extradition to Italy, he was transferred to the Metropolitan Correctional Center in downtown Manhattan, and it was there that we met, in the cold March of 1984. Some months later, I followed him to Italy's highest-security prison in Voghera where, after a lengthy and convoluted journey through the maze of Italian governmental bureaucracy, I was finally allowed access to him. My long interviews with him, and the many letters and documents he sent me, served as the heart of the story. But the search to penetrate that heart led me to sources around the world: to judges and Vatican prelates, banking officials and politicians, lawmen and gangsters, federal archives and musty libraries.

My work on the book was nearing its end when Sindona sent me the last letter he was to write. "You know me well enough," he said from his cell in Voghera, "to know that I am not afraid to die." Two days later, on the morning of March 20, 1986—two years to the very day after I first met him—a dose of potassium cyanide ended his life. Even now it is not known if he killed himself or was murdered by those forces whose secrets he knew and to some degree had shared with me.

Sindona was the most remarkable and intriguing man I have ever known, and *Power on Earth* tells perhaps the most remarkable and intriguing story I have ever told. But that story is a profoundly complicated one, and people prefer simple fairy tales to the difficult truth. The book was not a great commercial success, but the education I gained in its writing was of the rarest and most valuable kind.

In the end I came to see *Power on Earth* as a grand failure—not in a commercial sense, but in a true sense. For it to have been all that it could have been, perhaps should have been, would have required another ten years' work and several millions of dollars with which to work.

*Power on Earth* dealt with the farthest reaches of evil—not as imagined, but as they are.

My next book, *Cut Numbers,* a novel, dealt with things closer to the street, things I had known and moved among my whole life through. After that novel, which garnered much acclaim but little gelt, greed compelled me to return one last time to nonfiction. Once again I looked around and once again I saw that there was no subject that interested me. Of course, I had long been proposing the idea of a book on Dean Martin, mostly as a way of shaking off bothersome publishers. It was true that Dino, avatar of anti-art mob culture, mystery unto himself, intrigued me immensely, but I also knew that no publisher was cool enough or wise enough to go for it in a big way. But Doubleday was, and Doubleday did.

*Dino: Living High in the Dirty Business of Dreams,* to me, is a history of the underbelly of American culture and of the Italian-American century, told with Dean Martin as the central figure, often in the foreground, sometimes in the background. It embodies my belief that the business of dreamland—American entertainment—is as dirty and as soul-destroying to its victims, its suckers, as the

# The Unfuckable

I'd known her for years, mainly as the friend of a girlfriend. Someday, I told myself whenever I saw or thought of her, someday. Eventually, one lonely season after the girlfriend had gone, I turned my eye to her—to her legs, to be precise. I took her out—an actual date, something I'd never done, then another, and another. I'd never pursued anything or anyone with such attention. But she, and her legs, were not forthcoming. I broached the subject: you, me, the many-splendored thing.

No dice. Failure. I knew gnawing within, and I knew mystification. As our relationship degenerated into friendship, the mystification lingered. Was I not, after all, God's gift to the target sex? What had gone wrong? Several years later, I wanted answers, and was driven to asking questions I'd never asked before. With naught but apprehension and a tape recorder between us, I sought only to know.

ME: You were the end of an era: the only one I wanted that I didn't get.

HER: Do you hold that against me?

ME: No. It passed.

HER: I didn't think you were courting me.

ME: Is that what you were looking for? You wanted to be *courted?*

HER: No. But—

ME: I did everything but beg. I tried everything.

HER: What are you talking about? You didn't even try to kiss me.

ME: I did kiss you, but you don't even remember. So give me some tips on this courtship racket, for the next time around. Where did I go wrong?

HER: You went wrong right at the beginning, when you left me waiting in that restaurant and you never showed up.

ME: That was a bad start?

HER: Bad is like much too mild a word.

ME: I think that you just wanted to remain wanted.

HER: Well, it's a good position to be in, cause you can't lose, right?

ME: But why the next guy and not me?

HER: What next guy?

ME: What do you mean—you think you've had it with sex?

HER: It's a question of chemistry. This to me is the fundamental difference between men and women. I don't think men necessarily need sexual chemistry to be interested in sex.

ME: How often do you feel this chemistry?

HER: Lately? *(Laughs.)* Seldom.

ME: Why do you think this is?

HER: I don't know. I wish I knew. I'm guessing I'm just in a different place in my life. It's all so serious.

ME: Is it better this way? Is it worse?

HER: I can't say I'm bothered by it, but on the other hand, sometimes I'm curious about it. Then again, bizarrely enough, I could envision the rest of my life without having sex, just because the last few years have been pretty okay. Life is less complicated. Every once in a while I think, This is really strange. But it's not something that makes me feel like going to the doctor for hormone supplements to increase my sex drive. It's not on that level.

ME: You don't feel like you're missing out on anything? Like the sands of time are running out?

HER: I don't *feel* like I'm missing anything.

ME: I guess I missed the boat.

HER: By many years, Nick, so don't—

ME: Many years? *(Ponders)* When sexual desire comes to you, what form does it take?

HER: I don't know. . . .

ME: I mean, when you jerk off, what goes through your mind? Do you think of someone or something specific? What do you envision?

HER: What do I fantasize about when I *masturbate?*

ME: Yeah. It's gotta be something.

HER: No, no. It's just like a fantasy that's made up.

ME: Like a movie in your head?

HER: Yeah. Just some situation or something. But it's not like me and somebody, or anything like that. It's just some erotic ideas. It's not specific.

ME: Sounds sort of ethereal.

HER: No, it's just private. I'm not going to go into it. You say ethereal, but it's not like I'm thinking about angels. It's not a romance novel or something. It's probably something dirty, but it's nonspecific.

ME: Nonspecific dirty.

HER: Nonspecific in terms of me or someone I actually know.

ME: It's just you observing something?

HER: I don't know. I don't think about it.

ME: Okay. Back to you and me. Would my chances with you have been any better if you had been drunk?

HER: Well, everyone's chances with me are better when I'm drunk.

ME: And how about if I'd been a stranger?

HER: Yeah. And if you lived in a different city. I've usually chosen men I didn't know and who preferably lived far away. When I think about the perfect marriage, it's to someone who's very rich and who rarely comes home.

ME: But look at what we missed.

HER: I don't know. What have we missed?

ME: The chance to learn to hate each other.

HER: We don't need that.

ME: I guess what it comes down to is you represent a pair of legs that I couldn't have. Aside from being a wonderful person, you have nice legs.

HER: Thank you.

ME: But you've got this problem: You can't free your mind from your legs.

HER: I can't do that, no.

ME: Wouldn't that represent a new and higher spiritual plane to aspire to?

HER: Why would I want to do that?

ME: To be nice.

HER: Nick, I'm—

ME: To be a pal.

HER: No, no, I don't think so.

ME: Is there some kind of waiting list for your legs or something?

HER: *(Laughs.)* If there is, it's a mystery to me.

ME: So in the end, who or what have I lost out to?

HER: No one. Ceramic tile. Kitchen remodeling—that's where my energy goes these days. My new floor is so cool.

ME: So you've invested your passion in a kitchen floor. Strange that you should find in a floor the qualities I lack.

HER: Did you really want us to have a sexual relationship?

ME: Yeah. To me, sex was always a good way to spend time.

HER: Right. But can you say that in the last five or six years you've had any casual sexual relationships? I haven't. I mean, you're the only person who even asked me out on a date, if that's what that was.

ME: Well, Jesus, you didn't show any appreciation.

HER: I most certainly did—I went!

ME: You went, but you didn't put out!

HER: That's not the equation, Nick.

ME: What *is* the equation?

HER: I wish I knew the answer, but I don't.

ME: You're supposed to be the Answer Lady. You're the one holdin' the deck.

HER: I'm no good at relationships.

ME: Let's forget about relationships. Let's get back to screw-and-run.

HER: I'm sure this is the last thing you want to hear, but if you actually like the person, why would you want to do that and then think you could still be that person's friend?

ME: Well, if no deep, neurotic personal attachment has developed—

HER: I don't know. Sometimes I see people now who I slept with once and I can barely even remember that I had sex with them and I'm wondering if they remember and whatever. . . .

ME: I coulda been one of those guys!

HER: I know. Well, you knew me back *then,* right? But you weren't interested until it was too late.

ME: So where does that leave us?

HER: I don't know. *(Laughs)* Did you learn anything?

ME: If I learned anything, I learned that my old ways—being an insensitive prick—served me better in many respects.

HER: Yeah, but to what end ultimately?

ME: Ultimately? To no end, except gratification on a certain level.

HER: Do you think part of the reason you were attracted to me is because you knew nothing would come of it?

ME: No.

HER: I find that's almost always a big attraction for men.

ME: No, that's never the case with me. Of course, once I have someone, I no longer want them.

HER: Right. Well, don't you think that's another factor?

ME: Oh, man, enough of this. I wouldn't even have you at this point.

HER: I'm just not your type.

ME: It's not so much you.

HER: It's my legs.

ME: Your legs are my type.

HER: And you've never even seen me in high heels.

ME: I think you're very selfish with your legs. I don't see how an involvement with your legs could lead to a sullying of your mind or emotions.

HER: This is where we part ways.

ME: And you think it's irremediable? Or do you think it might be resolved by counseling or further dialogue?

HER: Perhaps therapy. Psychotherapy.

# 94

*Esquire* asked a bunch of people to write about their favorite possession or thing. I had this big heavy ancient coin that for me possessed properties that were almost magical.

# The Coin

I've got this piece of cold, heavy metal. It's bronze, but it looks and feels like stone: dark, earthen brown, with a rich patina, deep, mossy green and azure. It's about two and a half inches across and weighs about half a pound. It fits comfortably in my palm but is too big to enclose in my fist.

It's one of the first, primitive Roman coins, an *aes grave,* cast about 230 B.C., between the Punic wars. Its raised obverse bears the double-faced head of Janus, the god of gods, who looks both to the past—the western land, the realm of the dead—and to the future, the eastern dawn. His gaze beneath the patina is still strong. On the reverse is a ship's prow, facing eastward. Two thousand years ago and more, this piece of bronze could buy a bottle of wine. Ten thousand of them could buy freedom for a slave.

Rome's first gold coin is almost as old. It's exceedingly beautiful, exceedingly rare, exceedingly valuable. But it's nothing in the hand, and the gold bears no patina, no glow of the millennium and more through which it has passed.

And that, to me, is what it's all about: the patina, the perspective of time. For me, this thing isn't so much a coin as a palpable emanation, embodiment and evocation, symbol and susurrus, of something inexpressive. The look of it, the heft and feel of it, are the look, heft, and feel of a shard of the eternal captured somehow, magically, in the metallurgy of vain mortality. I think of the countless unknown hands that held it in days of different gods. It's from a time before Christ or Caesar. It's as old as the words of Ecclesiastes—"The thing that hath been, it is that which shall be; and that which is done is that which shall be done: and there is no new thing under the sun"—words that this half pound of bronze so silently and eloquently expresses as well. And what's more, beyond that eloquence, wielded right, it can break a skull.

It sets me straight, this coin, when I look at it or think of it or hold it; and it means something, and it makes me feel good. So, sure, there's drowsing on deserted beaches. There's reading Dante or listening to "Sea of Love." There are certain breezes, certain blow jobs, a couple of restaurants in Milan. But they can wait. Right now, it's this piece of metal that looks and feels like stone, that fits comfortably in my palm but is too big to enclose in my fist.

# 95

# Why I Am Great

The title is Nietzsche's, the sentiment mine, and these few but eloquent words, written for naught, will not begin to explain it.

A few years ago, I wrote this book, *Dino,* that turned into a sort of Rorschach test for readers and reviewers; I've seen and heard it described as everything from prose poetry to pop biography, from a work of genius to a piece of vulgar pulp. Of this broad spectrum of responses, none surprised me more than that of *Real Crime Book Digest,* which cited it as one of the six best true-crime books of 1993.

When I met him in Chicago last fall, Jim Agnew, who runs this operation and who may be the only man on earth who thinks of me as a true-crime writer, asked me to knock off a few hundred words on myself as such. So—perhaps inexplicably—here I am.

Then again, let me try to see it from Jim's angle. Of the five nonfiction books I've written, two have dealt to some degree with true crime. The first of these was *Power on Earth,* about Michele Sindona, the infamous Sicilian financier who was believed to occupy the throne at the heart of the world's darkness, where the most secret and shadowy reaches of international finance, the Mafia, and the Vatican came together.

I had written a book called *Hellfire,* a sort of Old Testament biography of Jerry Lee Lewis, which had been received with some acclaim. Casting about for another biographical subject—it was what I had to do: no publisher would yet pay me enough to write what I wanted and, as much as I wanted to write *Hellfire,* as much as I loved and was proud of it, what I wanted to write next was fiction, which I had always wanted to write—I came to the conclusion that no one interested me.

Then one night I glimpsed his image amid the dead drone of the TV news, and I realized that Sindona was a man who intrigued me. I was told by many that he was unapproachable, by others that the governments of America and Italy were set on his silence. But I wrote to him at the federal prison in Otisville, New York, where he was then being held, and fortune was with me. He called me, told me he was willing to talk. Soon after, pending extradition to Italy, he was transferred to the Metropolitan Correctional Center in downtown Manhattan, and it was there that we met, in the cold March of 1984. Some months later, I followed him to Italy's highest-security prison in Voghera where, after a lengthy and convoluted journey through the maze of Italian governmental bureaucracy, I was finally allowed access to him. My long interviews with him, and the many letters and documents he sent me, served as the heart of the story. But the search to penetrate that heart led me to sources around the world: to judges and Vatican prelates, banking officials and politicians, lawmen and gangsters, federal archives and musty libraries.

My work on the book was nearing its end when Sindona sent me the last letter he was to write. "You know me well enough," he said from his cell in Voghera, "to know that I am not afraid to die." Two days later, on the morning of March 20, 1986—two years to the very day after I first met him—a dose of potassium cyanide ended his life. Even now it is not known if he killed himself or was murdered by those forces whose secrets he knew and to some degree had shared with me.

Sindona was the most remarkable and intriguing man I have ever known, and *Power on Earth* tells perhaps the most remarkable and intriguing story I have ever told. But that story is a profoundly complicated one, and people prefer simple fairy tales to the difficult truth. The book was not a great commercial success, but the education I gained in its writing was of the rarest and most valuable kind.

In the end I came to see *Power on Earth* as a grand failure—not in a commercial sense, but in a true sense. For it to have been all that it could have been, perhaps should have been, would have required another ten years' work and several millions of dollars with which to work.

*Power on Earth* dealt with the farthest reaches of evil—not as imagined, but as they are.

My next book, *Cut Numbers,* a novel, dealt with things closer to the street, things I had known and moved among my whole life through. After that novel, which garnered much acclaim but little gelt, greed compelled me to return one last time to nonfiction. Once again I looked around and once again I saw that there was no subject that interested me. Of course, I had long been proposing the idea of a book on Dean Martin, mostly as a way of shaking off bothersome publishers. It was true that Dino, avatar of anti-art mob culture, mystery unto himself, intrigued me immensely, but I also knew that no publisher was cool enough or wise enough to go for it in a big way. But Doubleday was, and Doubleday did.

*Dino: Living High in the Dirty Business of Dreams,* to me, is a history of the underbelly of American culture and of the Italian-American century, told with Dean Martin as the central figure, often in the foreground, sometimes in the background. It embodies my belief that the business of dreamland—American entertainment—is as dirty and as soul-destroying to its victims, its suckers, as the business of shadowland—American organized crime. Frank Capra and Lucky Luciana were born in Sicily in the same year and both men, each in his own way, grew rich in America through the business of dreams.

Again, as with the Sindona book, *Dino* took me to people and places I had not imagined it would.

People often ask me about how I find my sources and how I get them to open up to me. Simply put, it is a matter of knowing where to look; of knowing how to talk to people, and of knowing what you're talking about; of knowing wisdom from folly, lies from truth, and it is a matter of moving within many spheres. The guys at the club, the off-duty cop at the bar; scholars and cutthroats; poets and princes; mafiosi and priests—their spheres are often more symbiotic and similar than one might assume, and in this life it is best to be a worldly traveler and man for all seasons.

Maybe every writer who mucks about in the soul for his living can be said to be a true-crime writer of sorts. "For no man may lyve without cryme," as the fourteenth-century Gesta Romanorum so soundly put it. In that sense, the workings of the soul can be the greatest criminal mysteries of all. As to the lesser, but more immediate, mystery of why I have agreed to write this piece for free, I offer in the way of solution only that Jim Agnew is a nice guy, and that I, as my acquiescence attests, a far, far fucking nicer one.

# 96

# Sea of Love

It's likely that I heard this song when it was a hit in the summer of '59, but if I did, it made no impression. For the way I remember it from the moment I *really* heard it I was sure that "Sea of Love" was about heroin and the sweet, dark, tidal pull of oblivion; and in '59 when I was pushing ten, these things were not yet dear to my young heart.

I honestly never heard the song as anything else, least of all a simple, tender love song. Well, a love song maybe, but to Magna Mater Bubbonia herself, not to any *earthly* chick. It seemed too perfectly an invocation, a seduction, a surrender to that black sea. I even heard it as "Come with me *into* the sea," not "*to* the sea." And only in that black sea could the dream of love exist.

God, how I came to love that song. Here, within reach, I've got the original, by Phil Phillips (above), I've got it by Cookie and the Cupcakes, and by Katie Webster—two covers that followed the original out of Louisiana. I've got the big strings-of-smack orchestral version by the Honeydrippers, and John Fahey's instrumental haunting of it. There are others, but these are the ones I listen to, the ones that possess that sweet tidal pull.

But now I've come to perceive and accept "Sea of Love" for what it is—that simple, tender song I'd never heard it to be; the slow dance to end all slow dances, sure, but not with death. Now there are other evocations from other waves, other depths than those where the light of the moon and sun and stars don't reach. And that's cool, too. In life as in death, like religion or a decent pizza joint, "Sea of Love" delivers.

# 97

# Faraglione 9/16/96

From where we lie,
alone on the stones of this shore,
it is easy to see how the perfect circle of the sun descending
was a god to those who dwelled in the caves around us
easy to see from where we lie
that while theologies die, true gods do not

# 98

# If I Were Robert Stack

### If I Were Robert Stack

If I were Robert Stack,
there would be no unsolved mysteries.
If I were Robert Stack,
    I would walk in godly pride;
    would have pride of hair,
    would wear makeup and be damned
    proud of it.
If I were Robert Stack,
    I would know the score, and the score,
    it would know me,
and I would sleep without dreams,
    and my hands
    would tremble and my eyes
    would close when
    the well within me emptied
    of all but
    the terror of desire,
and I would get free suits,
    double-breasted one day,
    single-breasted the next.

### I, as Robert Stack, Knew My History

    I, as Robert Stack, knew my history,
    knew that Nitti died with bottle in
    hand
    down by the tracks—no white suit,
    no murphy from no window, as in that
    half-fruit playwright's dream.

I, as Robert Stack, through Desilu,
brought to you the truth,
in spirit and in substance.
I, as Robert Stack, knew my Milton,
brought pith on many a night to
the spine of dualism as you knew it.
I, as Robert Stack, dressed well,
did not overact and knelt before God.

## When I, as Robert Stack, Go in for the Operation

When I, as Robert Stack,
go in for the operation, I will know
the scent of alcohol on cotton, which
I have known before; but will know
the scent as well of my true soul,
of that mystery unsolved, indwelling,
beneath my hide.
And I will dress conservatively,
hem to patella and no whorish
neckline, and, as ever, will stand tall;
and the breasts beneath my Burberry
will know pride, and, though in my
autumn,
desire shall be mine to be fulfilled.
And I, as Robert Stack, will know
not only the feel of nylon
upon the varicosity of truth
but will know as well the pulse
of moon, of tide within the vessel of my
kind, and the armor of my sternness
will know softness, and I will smile
to behold the print of pale magenta
upon the teacup in my hands, held just so,
as I drink at last from life in freedom
and in full, in Lycra, and in pride.
And thus I go to Denver, with heartbeat
that is calm, knowing I do only as Jack
Palance would do, were he but half the
man, or half the woman, that I be. No, let
Jack sit in shame in blue kimono with

houseboy at his side. I am done with all
such doings, am done with all such lies.
And when I say that men, they are
such fools, I will know, mesdames, whereof
I speak, for I did walk among them.


### Knew I Then Azazel

Knew I then Azazel,
in years of desert roaming,
between *Untouchables* and
*Unsolved;* knew I then,
in silence and in solitude,
unemployment and uncertainty.
No free wardrobe had I then,
nor knew I hairdresser's comb.
And still I shed no tear
and left no bill unpaid,
and now stand tall as only one
who knew Azazel may.


## I, as Robert Stack, Address My God

Lord, though I mouth the words of others,
may the truth in my eyes belie them ever,
and thus may I, in first run or in rerun,
lead no man, or woman, astray.

Lord, may all know that in my mind
I wear a hat,
though none they see;
that in my mind I wear no trousers,
though well creased and cuffed they see.

Lord, may they know these things,
and know then as well, all viewers
of the Lifetime Network, Television for
Women:
no wife, no daughter, is safe from me.

Lord, in thy mercy, forgive me.

## What I, as Robert Stack, Would Eat

Pork and eggs.

## What Bob Stack Et

Pork and eggs.

## January 13, 1997

I, as Robert Stack, who was born
seventy-eight years ago on this day,
lay aside Matthew Arnold's musings on age
and shut the light: *humanus sum*.

What Hesiod knew of neuroscience
we have yet to relearn.
To rend the tawdry man-made fabric of the
intellect,
to cut the throat of fear and ask of our gods
nothing
but power enough to kneel and conquer—
such are the ends, such the cures,
such the only freedom from plague and from dark
that ever we shall know.

Knowing this, I, as Robert Stack, upon this
night,
shut both book and light, and eyes as well.

# 99

July 4, 1997

Dear Stéphane:

Thanks for the good things and letter. You sound good, and that makes me feel good.

Today is a big American so-called holiday. Really, it has always been nothing more than a traditional excuse to blow up the streets and light up the skies with fireworks; and this has been the whole fun of it since I was a little boy. This has always been against the law. But this time—for the first year in history—it is actually impossible to buy fireworks. I spent two days scouring the usual Chinatown and Little Italy sources, and both the Asians and the Italians have been shut down by the police. I feel that this is a turning-point—New York, A.D. 1997—the final suppression of independence, on this so-called Independence Day. There is not the sound of a single explosion in the city air. I returned from my fruitless searches in the streets of my youth feeling like a stranger in my own neighborhood—changed so much even since the writing of *Trinities*—not so much a neighborhood as a suburb, infested by day-tripping law-abiding yuppie scum, of this city which seems to me to be more and more a great and hideous Disney mall. It is very depressing indeed, this death of the underworld and of shadowland and of local character and of old ways. Concurrently, the last of the old neighborhood *padrini* is standing trial with the full forces of the federal government against him. If he is convicted, this neighborhood is as good as dead. It makes me yearn for the past, and leaves me with a sort of motherless, homeless melancholy.

But fuck it. It is a big world—big enough so that no one gets to know it all, anyway—and I have the gift of breath and all the wisdom that the breezes of this world contain. Besides, I have pork roasting in the oven, and I have cigarettes, and I have a dark poem running through my blood.

I think you are right about that girl wanting to open herself to you because you refused to fuck her. Fucking her mind—entering it, I mean—offers greater and stranger fruit.

As for your coming to town this month, I hope I am here for your visit. There is a chance I may go to Cuba next week, but I do not know. Be sure to call me, and if I am around, we will get together.

For now, my friend, keep doing what you're doing. I got as much out of our meeting and talks as you did, and I know that we will know one another for a long, long time.

*NICK*

# 100

August 13, 1997

Dear Jim:

Have just returned, night before last, from a month of fucking round the hemisphere, from Cuba to Bora Bora: many hammocks, many lizards. Came back to find that the big beautiful old tree on the corner of Bedford and Commerce, with which I've had what is probably the longest-lived love affair—hey, man, let's go all out: *re-lationship*—of my life, is now gone, destroyed by a fucking garbage truck. My corner looks naked, desolate; and I'm convinced that this is a sign from God, the final sign, that I am now a stranger in my own neighborhood, indeed that this neighborhood, what used to be this neighborhood, no longer exists, and that it is long past time for me to move on.

On the esoterica front, I have been searching for an R&B record that Sonny Liston supposedly made in the late sixties. Let me know if it passes your way.

I'll be leaving town again soon, but I don't yet know exactly when. For now, buddy, all best.

Later,

*NICK*

# 101

August 18, 1997

Dear Stéphane:

Thanks for your great letter from Quebec, the magazine, and the CD, which is playing as I write this. (I still haven't seen this *Lost Highway* picture—haven't seen much of anything—but the other day I did see this new *L.A. Confidential*, which is all right until it turns into a fucking "moral tale.")

I've been back now about a week: Cuba, Mexico, California, Bora Bora—a month of lizards and hammocks, from the cheap, primitive, and wild (Cayo Largo, south of Cuba, accessible only by recycled, falling-apart windowless World War II surplus Russian transport prop planes) to the exorbitant, pseudo-primitive, and tame (Bora Bora, via Air France L'Espace 180 to Tahiti). Hammocks, lizards, and, I suspect and hope, the first lines of detail on the face of an embryonic new novel.

What you say about the poseurs of L.A. is on the money, my friend. To me, it is and has always been a grim and vacuous, fraudulent and vile place: the distillation of all that is wrong, the philosophers stone that turns flesh to plastic and soul to arid air. Every time I return from there, I tell myself, well, that's it for this lifetime, never again; and yet, for one reason or another, I end up there again.

I am really, truly sorry we missed one another, but I have the feeling we will see one another soon, either New York or Paris, or somewhere in Europe.

I fell in love this summer—last thing on my mind, last thing I expected; but I did. Beautiful, serenely smiling, twenty-eight-year-old with a soul like a white fucking bird from a summertime in another age, lighted here on my lap via Babylon or a dream. Anyway, she's off now, back to school down South, where she's belatedly getting a master's degree, and I miss her (which is something I never do, because I'm usually relieved, feel freed when they're gone). Life is fucking strange. As if you didn't already know. That knowledge is part of the master's degree that we share.

Your spread on me in the magazine looks great, reads great; and I thank you. Yeah, please be sure to send me more copies, for friends more fluent than I.

Anyway, my friend, I hope this finds you grinning your grin and borne away by the tide of that "big change" you feel happening. Let's let the winds take us both: there's nothing to hold onto but abandon.

I think of you often and well, and I hope to hear from you soon. For now, as always, all best.

*NICK*

# 102

August 23, 1997

Dear Sweetness, Dear Light,

Here's our bench, in falling daylight, and in solitary starlight.

Also—God, they seem now to be so a part of that bench and that solitary starlight and that blessed thing that blossoms from our shared breath—those words I told you about: the closest, in their mystery and their clarity, to pure and perfect wisdom I have ever found. To think of them, the pure and perfect articulation, in word and in rhythm, of that pure and perfect wisdom, lying buried and unknown in a desert wasteland throughout the ages: the pure and perfect parable of the truth they illuminate and address.

May you and me bare and let loose that thing within, and taste the dew of that wisdom, and embrace it, that happiness, and be borne away by it, and have what is there for all, but which most leave buried and unknown, from cradle to grave, in the wasteland of fear through which they drift.

The magic and miracle of a few Coptic words found crumbling in the middle of nowhere. A bench on Sixth near the corner of Bleecker. A star above: the same star that shone down on those lost words, and on whoever was their vessel, and that shines down still, on that bench, and on us, and on the magic and miracle of certain breezes, within and without, that bear the serene and thrilling beauty of that ancient wisdom, that bear the ethereal and wild seeds of every immense moment of the immense gift of life which for this breath is ours. May we open ourselves to every moment, and to that immense gift, finding it on that bench beneath that star, on every bench, beneath every star, for that is where it is: everywhere, awaiting us to open ourselves to it.

It's now some hours later, getting late. Again, I won't read what I've written, but know that when I write to you like this—like I've never written to another—words flow from me the way feelings flow silently through me when we are close; words that seem to try to express something of those feelings, words that yearn for you, that seem to try to summon, to invoke you, that closeness and, strangely that silence whose wondrous expressiveness lies beyond that of these or any words.

What a caption this has turned out to be for an aim-and-shoot shot of an empty, beat-up bench, an aim-and-shoot shot of a holy place, an aim-and-shoot shot of a breeze and a breath and a wordless poem whose sound is a sigh.

*Love,*
*Nick*

# 103

August 25, 1997

Dear Cubby,

I don't know how you feel, but you sound fucking great. Yeah, they shot Lincoln, and the guy who did it didn't make out too well, either. That menopause line cracked me up, and, for me, a good laugh, however fleeting, is these days the hardest drug to score.

As in every letter I've ever got from you, you are a well of strength and inspiration. May every breath fill you with the blessing that it is. Me, I let that blessing pass without gratitude all too often, getting bent out of shape by things at which those turtles and cockroaches you mention never even grant a glance. The more I can give myself to that light within and without, let's call it God, the more, I believe, I will cease to give a fuck about that which is apart, beneath, and antithetical to Him and to the main event.

I am truly happy, my friend, that you're up for this compact-disc thing, and am excited about the stuff you mention that you've written to be read aloud. I will call or write soon with the details, i.e., the exact date of the session, which will almost definitely be in the latter part of September. I think it is now just a matter of Harold, the producer, choosing and booking time at the right—read, I figure: good and cheap—studio in L.A.

So I look forward to talking to you and seeing you soon. For now, as ever, all good things.

*Nick*

# 104

## *Spud Crazy*

### *Screenplay*

BLACK. SILENCE.
WORDS scroll slowly:

> Papa, the Incas called it, pale
> sacred tuber, gift of gods
> who dwelt above.
> The Spaniards brought it east,
> across the sea, where other gods
> dwelt above.
> The chronicles give us the name:
> Gonzalo Jiménez de Quesada;
> the chronicles give us the year:
> Anno Domini 1531.

As the WORDS scroll, a small, soft patina emerges from the BLACK, lower right. Slowly we see that this dim shimmering of light is the black-nylon-stockinged lower LEG of a woman. The camera closes on her ankle, slowly follows the rising curve of her calf, the bend of her knee, her thigh, moving ever closer, into the texture of the nylon itself.

> Nylon, E.I. du Pont de Nemours
> & Co. called it.
> After ten years of toil,
> they announced its creation to the
> world,
> in 1938; and on May 15, 1940—a
> Wednesday—the first nylon
> stockings, like the breath of
> the spud-giving gods,
> caused the earth to tremble.

The slow-rising and closing ECU moves from the black denier of the stocking-top to the flesh of the woman's thigh, magnifying soft hair and the topography of skin. Passing over this ghostly terrain, we vanish momentarily into a pore, emerge, and slowly see that the terrain is somehow different. As the camera pulls slightly away, we see that the ghostly terrain of the woman's skin has become that of a potato's skin. The POTATO revolves very slowly, like a misshapen globe on its axis, a world unto itself in blackness. The camera closes into an eye of the potato, until all is BLACK.

> Such is the sum of history,
> such are the holy years.

The camera pulls back from the BLACK hole, emerges from the bore of a GUN-barrel: a .38-caliber revolver in a pale HAND amid shadow.

Sudden CUT to subway roaring, screeching loud into deserted, sinister station. We look down on subway car's sole passenger: dark-haired GUY. From over his shoulder, we see him turn to look through the subway window. On the platform, there now stands a WOMAN, gazing at him through the window.

GUY's POV: close up of WOMAN's face. Her eyes close slightly, her lips slowly part in strange, trance-like sensuality. Her mouth opens wider, and we glimpse the moisture of her tongue.

We hear the GUY's HEARTBEAT. Louder.

WOMAN's eyes are now back in her head. Only their whites show. Her face convulses almost imperceptively. Orgasm? Seizure? Death?

The HEARTBEAT grows louder, faster.

From her open mouth, a large writhing SNAKE bursts forth into the GUY's POV. Its horrible HISS overwhelms the HEARTBEAT and the sudden renewed screech and roar of the subway.

Sudden CUT: the HISS of the snake becomes the HISS of French fries frying in a metal basket in a large greasy fryer of bubbling, sputtering oil.

INT. DINER KITCHEN. Noisy. Sleazy. We follow the French fries as they are turned out and served. The WAITER is vaguely ominous, with the broad, stone-like features of an old Peruvian Indian.

CUT to a plate of fries being set down with a bottle of ketchup at a table of three young NURSES.

Close-up of NURSE speaking animatedly, wide-eyed and giddy:

> NURSE
>
> . . . this big fat black woman, and she's just sitting there, hours and hours, she's just sitting there, and nobody's paying her any mind—doctors, orderlies, nobody—it's like they think she's there waiting for somebody she brought in or something, and finally the shift boss goes over to her and says—

INT. HOSPITAL EMERGENCY ROOM. Close-up of grey-haired DOCTOR in horn-rimmed glasses, white shirt, tie, and white hospital jacket.

> DOCTOR
>
> What can we do for you?

INT. DINER. Close-up of young NURSE.

> NURSE
>
> And she says—

INT. HOSPITAL. Close-up of heavyset inexpressive BLACK WOMAN.

> BLACK WOMAN
>
> I got a plant growin' out my cookie.

INT. DINER. Reaction of two young NURSES: giddy, aghast, but still immersed in swabbing their French fries through ketchup, devouring them.

The vaguely ominous WAITER peers toward them.

INT. HOSPITAL. Close-up of DOCTOR. In the lenses of his eyeglasses, we see the dual reflection of a tangle of sprouting tendrils protruding from what must be the darkness between the fat legs of the BLACK WOMAN.

INT. DINER. Fast close-ups: French fries entering NURSES' mouths; WAITER's menacing eyes.

INT. HOSPITAL. Close-up of forceps holding dank potato with its tangle of sprouting tendrils.

INT. DINER. Fast close-ups: French fries entering NURSES' mouths; WAITER's menacing eyes.

INT. HOSPITAL. Close-up of forceps placing potato in enamel tray.

INT. DOCTOR'S OFFICE. DOCTOR sits at his desk, gazing through window at hard rain and darkness. Thunder. Lightning. He turns away, faces the presence whose shadow falls across the desk. He looks disturbed, mystified, grave.

> DOCTOR
> That's the third one this week.

BLACK. Crack of thunder, lightning.

WORDS on BLACK, each line punctuated by BLACK:

> She wore diamond-seamed stockings,

> BLACK.

> twenty-five grand the pair.

> BLACK.

> She made fried, she made mashed,

> BLACK.

> she made baked and pancakes, too.

> BLACK.

> Maureen was her name.

CUT to .38-caliber REVOLVER in pale HAND amid shadow. The camera enters the bore of the gun-barrel; moves through blackness; emerges from the darkness of the vestibulum of a VAGINA, glimpsed only for an instant.

CUT to close-up of WOMAN's face. It is the woman from the haunted subway platform. She may be dead. Tongue-like, the reinforced-nylon toe of a stocking slips subtly from between her lips.

Romantic male VOICE-OVER as the length of the STOCKING is drawn slowly, bizarrely, ethereally from between her still lips.

                              MAN'S VOICE
              She had a stocking
              in her mouth the night
              I met her
              & removed it slowly
              inch by inch
              damp & rustling
              from her mouth
              softly softly
              basely purring

EXT. Seedy, foreboding TENEMENT on Lower East Side.

TWILIGHT. Close-up of WHORE's FINGER, its long nail painted dark, on DOOR-BUZZER.

CUT to .38-caliber REVOLVER in pale HAND amid shadow as BUZZER loudly buzzes. Camera pulls away and slowly we see INT. Seedy APARTMENT and the GUY whose hand it is. He is handsome but unwell, both unsettled and unsettling: wiry, pale, neuresthenic, unshaven, with troubled, sleepless eyes. He stands, stashes gun in drawer, beholds himself in dirty mirror. BUZZER loudly buzzes.

CUT to EXT. Close-up of WHORE looking over her shoulder, somewhat apprehensive, somewhat impatient. She is about twenty, a very beat twenty. Entrance BUZZER sounds, loud but sickly, and she heaves the door open.

INT. GUY'S APARTMENT. As heavy, high-heeled footsteps on the stairs grow nearer and louder, camera pans faded dirty walls—old books on dusty shelves—and closes on inside door as footsteps come to a halt outside it.

                              GUY
              It's open.

WHORE enters, looks at him, looks around.

                              WHORE
              Half now, half later, okay?

WHORE's hand takes folded hundred-dollar bill from GUY's pale hand.

WHORE

I gotta use the phone, okay?

GUY nods toward old black rotary telephone.

Close-up of WHORE's finger—that long, painted nail—dialing.

GUY watches her. His POV: Her legs, the curve of her thighs and ass in her skirt.

Close-up of WHORE's mouth speaking into telephone.

WHORE

Yeah, it's me. Everything's okay.

Her POV: Circular inset at center of rotary dial, through the dirty plastic of which a telephone number printed on yellowed paper is barely visible.

WHORE

Three-seven-two, four-four-nine-five.

She hangs up, looks at her watch. GUY gestures to wooden chair facing him, three feet or so across from where he sits. WHORE sits. GUY says nothing. The SILENCE between them grows nerve-racking. WHORE draws a deep breath, uneasy but somewhat bemused.

WHORE

What is it, baby?

GUY seems unable to express himself.

WHORE

Tell me.

GUY

I miss my mother.

WHORE

Okay, baby.

WHORE's hand moves idly to her breast. Abstractedly, as if by rote, she begins to unbutton the top button of her blouse.

GUY shakes his head, dismissively.

                    GUY

No, no, no.

WHORE is nonplussed, taken aback by the tone of his voice. Something like a smile, a faraway and fatal look, comes upon the GUY's face.

                    GUY

Are you hip to Cybele?

EXT. Dark blind ALLEY. Close on far end. A large, bulging burlap sack is set amid filth. Printed on it: U.S. NO. 1 IDAHO POTATOES NET WT. 100 LBS. The bulges and protuberances of its load do not seem to be those of potatoes. Close on blood seeping from corner of sack into a gathering pool. Camera ascends to wall of graffiti above sack. Spray-painted is the classical Greek for Cybele: Κὔβέλη. Camera ascends to night sky above alley. Sparse stars in blackness.

FLASH of windswept Phrygian landscape (modern Turkey) in spring light: meadow, almond trees, temple ruins.

Wake of flash leaves nothing but the soft spring light.

Romantic male VOICE-OVER as the light dims to darkness, until once again sparse stars appear in blackness.

                    VOICE
      I, with a knife to the throat of Cybele,
      lie beneath the sky of spring,
      awaiting night and the sapphire light of
      stars
      whose birth was her, my mother's, own.
      Her eyes are unafraid,
      as I feared they would be;

      and the tide of her breath,
      which was once my own,
      within the April of her breast
      and the April of her neck,
      governs more than does my hand
      the stillness of the blade;

      and her blood is my blood, and the blade
      is the blade of that which is

between us, alone, and in the end
governed
neither by hand nor by breath
but only by what the sapphire light
of this, her evening has ordained.

INT. APARTMENT. The GUY is now standing over the sitting WHORE, his hips level with her eyes. She looks up at him, apprehensively.

CUT to GUY from behind.

> GUY
> C'm'ere. Look.

From behind, we see GUY unzipper his trousers to WHORE.

> WHORE (aghast)
> Oh, my God.

FLASH of something indistinct, grotesque, like scar tissue, or a growth (but it could be an aspect of that same Phrygian landscape in ECU).

> GUY
> She never finished. She never finished.

He reaches out to stroke her face. His pale hand shuts out the light, and all is dark.

EXT. Seedy ITALIAN RESTAURANT. Night. Rain.

INT. Seedy ITALIAN RESTAURANT. The GUY sits alone at a table. He looks bad. The place is empty but for another LONE PATRON, a COUPLE at one table, a PARTY OF THREE at another. There is something unbearably sepulchral to the tableau. The GUY raises a glass of Scotch and water to his mouth, and we see his hand shake. A short old grey-haired Sicilian waiter dismally approaches.

> GUY
> What does the ossobuco come with?

> WAITER
> Risotto. Polenta. Whatever you want.

> GUY
> How about potatoes. Can I get potatoes with that?

> WAITER (shrugs)

Whatever you want.

> GUY

Potatoes. I'll have the ossobuco with potatoes. Mashed potatoes. Can I get mashed potatoes?

> WAITER (shrugs)

Whatever you want.

WAITER turns to shuffle away.

> GUY

Wait a minute. Just gimme mashed potatoes. Just gimme a big bowl of mashed potatoes.

He drains his drink, puts down the empty glass.

> GUY (cont.)

And another one of these.

WAITER stands over him. His death-mask expression takes on a suggestion of vague concern, a look that is almost paternal.

> WAITER

You look-a like a nice-a boy. I hate to see it. I got a son, he's-a your age.

WAITER shakes his head sadly. Then he sighs with grim resignation, looks away.

> WAITER (cont.)

Why don't you just go down the street, eh?

> GUY (bewildered)

Down the street?

WAITER looks at GUY as if the GUY is being a wise-ass, just his chin, gestures harshly "down the street," and addresses him sternly, as if washing his hands of him.

> WAITER

*Down the street.*

EXT. Night. Rain.

INT. Dark, sleazy, smoky JOINT. A bar, tables. A small, shabby stage. Cadaverous male CLIENTELE, some sharply attired and evil-looking, others nondescript and skulking. The BAND is barely visible as shadowy figures in a far corner.

From darkness, a cheesy nightclub drum-roll; microphone distortion; a male voice—unctuous, stagy, carny, but possessed nonetheless of a strangely poetic power.

> MASTER OF CEREMONIES
> Somewhere, in a dream that's
> half-forgotten,
> Seventeen blondes, three
> redheads, and a
> brunette, in heels
> And hose, posed
> the way ya like 'em,

As the unseen M.C. delivers his lines, the camera pans the CLIENTELE: some enthusiastic, leering knowingly at the M.C.'s words; others impatient, dismissive; some drunkenly laughing, talking, coughing; others distracted, intense, sociopathic. The GUY looks about him, transfixed, unwell.

> MASTER OF CEREMONIES (cont.)
> Stoop to reap
> mature, tawny-skinned
> Beauties from the rocky
> soil of Maine;
> Somewhere in a dream that's
> half-forgotten.

From the CLIENTELE: whistling, applause, groans, jeers, calls of "Fuck you," "Get a job," and "Stick it up yer ass." One of the sharply-attired men: "You call that a fuckin' poem?"

Close-up of GUY's face.

FLASH of Phrygian landscape.

FLASH of blood dripping from potato sack in alley.

FLASH of GUY's pale hand reaching out to touch WHORE's face.

FLASH of WOMAN in underwear and stockings, bound to chair in vaulted subterranean dark, ankles tied with rope, wrists tied unseen behind back of chair,
gagged with potato in mouth, eyes of weary terror; box marked GENUINE
IDAHO at her feet, overflowing with potatoes; the SHADOWY FIGURE of a
man dressed in a fine dark suit holds a gun to her head.

INT. JOINT. The voice of the M.C. resumes over lingering crowd noise.

> MASTER OF CEREMONIES
> What more luxuriant
> rustle than
> Spud in hose?
>
> Thinking this, I
> slipt it in—

Again, as the unseen M.C. delivers his lines, the camera pans the CLIENTELE:
some enthusiastic, leering knowingly at the M.C.'s words; others impatient, dismissive; some drunkenly laughing, talking, coughing; others distracted, intense,
sociopathic. The GUY looks about, transfixed, unwell.

> MASTER OF CEREMONIES (cont.)
> O, Idaho! O, Denier!
> Put stockings on your
> Legs & Arms
> Put something in yr
> Mouth

Again from the CLIENTELE: whistling, applause, groans, jeers.

> MASTER OF CEREMONIES
> All right, you sick fucks, enough of your shit for one night. Are
> you ready for some spud action?

CLIENTELE: enthusiastic cheers, whistling, applause, scattered drunken chanting that sounds eerily ritualistic.

> MASTER OF CEREMONIES (cont.)
> Are you ready for some gams?

CLIENTELE: intensified enthusiastic cheers, whistling, applause, scattered
drunken chanting that sounds eerily ritualistic. The GUY looks about, transfixed, unwell.

MASTER OF CEREMONIES (cont.)
You sound like you're ready, fellas, and you're in the right place. But first let's hear it for the one and only, our own—
*Larry!*

CLIENTELE: groans, jeers, applause, execration, as LARRY takes the stage. He is a tall, thin, sickly man with long scraggly hair. He wears a long threadbare robe. Above his left hip, there is a large protuberance beneath the robe.

LARRY
Please feel free to move more closely to the stage

Be neither ashamed for my sake nor afraid for your own to look on me, for beneath this mortal shell lie heart and soul just like your own

I refuse to live on charity or secluded from society, and I receive no money for my appearance here

My sole income is derived from the sale of these miniature Bibles, which though barely larger than a matchbox contain every word of Old and New

A quarter, four bits, a dollar bill, let the wise man's words guide your giving: here but for the grace of God go you.

I have seven perfectly formed brothers and sisters

In fact unlike the others with whom I share this stage I was not born to life this way

Until the age of seven the sun did smile down upon me as upon all others

That was the age when I entered this very room beneath the crossroads of the world

It was my dear father who took me here, for edification, enlightenment, amusement, those same eternal enticements that bring you yourselves to stand before me on this day

We saw the doe's trained fleas and the elephant-skinned lady, Karl the Frog-boy, the man from World War Three, John Dillinger's death-mask, the Lord's Prayer on the head of a pin, and more.

Now, to your left, you'll see a shuttered door to a room now sealed

That door long ago stood open and by it stood a sign: A FEAST FOR THE EYES, two bits

I could not imagine what awaited within, but my dear father knew only too well: "It's not for us, pal, it's not for us"

Some days later I returned again, alone, in sinful stealth
with my two bits
      And my eyes, yes, upon her they did feast: she who had no
name and who walked with her face behind her
      Thenceforth lust like a succubus grew within me, then blos-
somed forth from me

LARRY unties his robe. He is naked but for a long strip of cloth wound about
his waist and groin like a Hindu loincloth. An end of this cloth is draped to
cover the large protuberance above his hip. He lifts this covering, and the camera pans the CLIENTELE: groans of revulsion, some familiar, some shocked;
wincing, morbid fascination; cruel laughter, whistling.

LARRY (cont.)
The hideous stillborn twin you now see hanging from my
side—look at it long, look at it hard: this is the true face of
personal growth
      Seven times I—we—married her, she upon whom my eyes
did feast, she who had no name
      It was to feed the stillborn twin.

      That's it, miss, step right up, don't be afraid
      Touch it if you will, some nerves near our shared veins still
live.

CLIENTELE: groans, jeers, applause, execration as stage darkens, joint darkens.

MASTER OF CEREMONIES (cont.)
Let's hear it for Larry. Come on, you fucks. Have a heart. Have
something. Come on. *Humani nil a me alienum,* hey, fellas?

Cowbell sounds loudly through microphone.

MASTER OF CEREMONIES (cont.)
It's that time, gents, it's that time.

CLIENTELE exchange knowing glances.

MASTER OF CEREMONIES (cont.)
Put a stocking on your dick and smear it with mashed potatoes; then ring that chowtime bell.

Again cowbell sounds loudly through microphone. Noise of CLIENTELE.

> MASTER OF CEREMONIES (cont.)
> She got ever'thing on her legs that a gent likes to see on a
> purty gal's legs. She got fingerling, she got russet, she got
> Idaho, she got Maine. She got it all. The one, the only—*Diane!*

CLIENTELE goes wild with lecherous enthusiasm as drummer in shadows begins a tawdry strip-tease beat.

Soft spotlight on stage, bare but for a caneback chair and a microphone upon it, its cord snaking offstage into darkness.

> MASTER OF CEREMONIES (cont.)
> Don't forget to use yer hankies, gents. Lenny's your mop-man,
> and he sure would appreciate that.

DIANE stands center-stage, her back to the audience, the chair between her and the wall, its seat facing the wall. She is the woman from the haunted subway platform. She wears a black brassiere, a black silk scarf, long black satin gloves, and a black half-slip. Under the slip, she wears black panties. Beneath her black panties, she wears a black garterbelt and sheer black stockings. Beneath her stockings she wears sheer beige pantyhose, and beneath her sheer beige pantyhose, she wears ultra-sheer nude pantyhose. Over her pantyhosed, stockinged feet are opaque black knee-high stockings and, over them, lace-trimmed white anklets. She wears black high heels.

She leans slightly, her arms outstretched, hands on the curved caneback of the chair. She undulates seductively, slowly turns to face the CLIENTELE, who fall into an expectant, depraved hush. She takes the microphone in her hand, turns the chair round, sits on it, and crosses her legs. She rubs her legs softly together, holding the microphone to them. The sound of their rustling nylon scroop fills the hush. She stands, removes her slip, rubs the slip to herself, casts it to the floor. She raises the microphone to her lips.

> DIANE
> The Hosiery & the Spud—these are the ikons
> Drop the ancient tater into the 12-denier stocking—Touch
> Okeanos (nylon & spud)
>
> Gift of Iao
> fingers of Gaea;
> stocking/spud
> & leg

She sits, lays the microphone at her feet. The camera moves between her and the CLIENTELE as she slowly, seductively removes her shoes, anklets, and knee-high stockings, caressing each item, drawing it up her body, kissing it, her eyes closing as if in unspeakable prayer. We see that some of the CLIENTELE are obviously masturbating, while others seem to be deep in unspeakable prayer of their own, and a few seem to be immersed in both. There is much perspiring, much sucking on cigarettes and on drinks.

DIANE unhooks her garters, removes her garterbelt, casts it down. She stands, undulates; and as she does so, her stockings wilt down her thighs and calves. The camera continues to move between her and the ever more intense CLIENTELE as she pulls off the stockings then slowly peels down the beige pantyhose.

She kicks her shoes and discarded hosiery into the audience. SLOW MOTION of hosiery—diaphanous, fluttering, falling in dark smoky space; ravenous grasping hands in air of CLIENTELE.

From her bra, DIANE pulls out a small gleaming POTATO-PEELER, brandishes it somewhat playfully, somewhat menacingly toward the CLIENTELE. She clutches the crotch of her pantyhose with her free hand, puts the tip of the PEELER to it. ECUs of CLIENTELE's eyes; ECU of PEELER to crotch; ECU of DIANE's eyes.

FLASH of Phrygian landscape.

FLASH ECUs of CLIENTELE's eyes.

FLASH of blood dripping from potato sack in alley.

FLASH ECU of PEELER to crotch.

FLASH of GUY's pale hand reaching out to touch WHORE's face.

FLASH ECU of DIANE's eyes.

FLASH of WHORE, in underwear and stockings, bound to chair in vaulted subterranean dark, ankles tied with rope, wrists tied unseen behind back of chair, gagged with potato in mouth, eyes of weary terror; box marked GENUINE IDAHO at her feet, overflowing with potatoes; SHADOWY FIGURE dressed in fine suit holds gun to her head.

Violent RENDING sound.

FLASH of GUNFIRE.

INT. RECTORY. Close-up of CHRIST's face on crucifix on wall. Close-up of GUY's face. He looks worse than ever.

> GUY
>
> I need to talk to somebody.

PRIEST, at his desk, fingers steepled before him, regards the GUY. He nods, slowly, meaningfully. He continues to nod, slowly, and his expression and manner subtly take on a portentous, even scornful, air.

> PRIEST
>
> Everybody needs to talk.

> GUY
>
> It's just that I—

> PRIEST
>
> Everybody needs to talk. Well, I tell you something, pallie: sometimes I need to talk, too.

PRIEST stands, leaps acrobatically onto desk, looks down portentously, scornfully at GUY. His eyes grow distant, as if seeing not only one man but all mankind.

> PRIEST
>
> GENTS, Attenzione!

CUT with CHURCH-ORGAN BLAST to FLASH, like an icon aglow with holy radiance, of French fries arranged to seem at the point of overspilling, McDonald's-advertisement-style, from a black-satin high heel.

CUT to CLOSE UP of PRIEST's demented, scowling face.

In choreographed dance steps, the PRIEST kicks Bible, papers, paraphernalia from desk as he vociferates. His gestures, movements, and stentorian tones are a blend of Elmer Gantry, Professor Harold Hill of *The Music Man,* and a madness not unlike demonic possession.

> PRIEST (cont.)
>
> What would you rather do with your
> tongue?

Would you rather lick a woman's flesh
or talk to her?
Or are you one of those,
further doomed,
lost and undone,
torn between the two;
one who would do both,
or would rather the one,
whichever,
but settles, or would settle,
for the other?
Tell me: which are you?
Psychiatry,
psychology,
therapy,
psychopharmacology—

As PRIEST continues to vociferate and dance, we see, intercut:

Close-up of GUY's tormented, frightened eyes.

Close-up of CHRIST's painted eyes on crucifix.

Close-up of PRIEST's angry, demented eyes.

Close-up of GUY's tormented, frightened eyes.

Close-up of CHRIST's painted eyes on crucifix. Camera pans down the crucifix.
The loincloth about the waist and groin covers a large protuberance above the
hip, like that of Larry.

FLASH of Larry lifting the covering from his hip.

FLASH of GUY's pale hand reaching out to touch WHORE's face.

PRIEST (cont. v.o.)
You don't need them; just come to me,
And tell me:
which are you?
And I'll tell you
all about yourself,
parse your soul,
cauterize the hole,

    set you right,
    set you free.
    And the best part is, I charge only
    fifty bucks a pop;
    Seventy-five for the bald
    or broken of heart.
    So tell me—cash on the barrelhead, pal—
    which are you?

The camera zooms into the blackness of the priest's cassock, emerges from the bore of the GUN-barrel: the .38-caliber revolver in the GUY's pale hand amid shadow.

Sudden CUT to subway roaring, screeching loud into deserted, sinister station. We look down on subway car's sole passenger: our dark-haired GUY.

DEAD SILENCE, SLOW MOTION: from over his shoulder, we see him turn to look through the subway window. On the platform, there now stands a WOMAN, gazing at him through the window.

GUY's POV: close-up of WOMAN's face.

WORDS on BLACK:

    She touches it & dreams of Olmec eye

WOMAN's eyes close slightly, her lips slowly part in strange, trance-like sensuality.

WORDS on BLACK:

    the lips parted slightly wet

CUT to WOMAN's mouth opening wider. We glimpse the moisture of her tongue. We enter the BLACK of her mouth.

Sudden renewed screech and roar of the subway.

FLASH of large writhing SNAKE bursting forth from WOMAN's open mouth.

FLASH of GUY's pale hand reaching out to touch WHORE's face.

FLASH of WHORE, in underwear and stockings, bound to chair in vaulted sub-terranean dark, ankles tied with rope, wrists tied unseen behind back of chair, gagged with potato in mouth, eyes of weary terror; box marked GENUINE IDAHO at her feet, overflowing with potatoes; SHADOWY FIGURE dressed in fine suit holds gun to her head.

FLASH of GUNFIRE.

FLASH of blood dripping from potato sack in alley.

INT. RECTORY. The crucifix is gone. The PRIEST is alone, at his desk, his chair turned round, his back to us. In slow revolution, his face is revealed. His eyes are opaque white, unseeing. Within this whiteness is the windswept Phrygian landscape

> PRIEST (v.o.)
>
> Looking at you,
> it comes over me—
> volo stuprare,
> volo futuare.
>
> I need yr legs,
> I need yr hose
>
> Come: let me worship
> at the reinforced
> crotch of yr Hanes
> off-black pantyhose.
>
> Culmination midst
> the nylon,
> Gnosis twixt yr gams.

GUY's pale hand reaches, in SLOW MOTION, out to touch WHORE's face, which fades to WHITE. Emerging simultaneously from WHITE is the profile of the face of DEMETER in stone (as from the marble relief, Eleusis, c. 450 B.C. now in the National Museum, Athens).

On soundtrack: "Rotundellus" (Galicia: Cantiga 105), as recorded, on *La Lira d'Espéria*, by Jordi Savall (*vièle ténor*) and Pedro Estevan (percussion).

Camera closes in. As detail disperses and fades, as the momentum of the "Rotundellus" gathers, there emerges amid grainy WHITE the distant grainy image of a WILD MARE running free, moving subtly from still to slow motion to full and turbulent speed.

VOICE OVER

And thus when Demeter in Arcadia,
as Erinys, the Angry One, avenger and fury,
having taken the form of a mare, was mounted
in violence by the stallion Poseidon,
bearing then Arion the damned
and the daughter, she of secret name,
it was because of her flanks
and her withers.

Clunis sancta.
Femur sacrum.
Sura beata.

And the haunches of the goddess are thine—
femora diducere—
and the flanks of the goddess are thine.

As the poem ends and the "Rotundellus" comes to its climax, the camera closes in on the racing image of the mare, enters it, until all is flurrying darkness.

ECU of PEELER to crotch. Violent RENDING.

EXT. NIGHT SKY. Sparse stars in blackness. Camera descends to dark blind ALLEY.

GUY emerges from ALLEY. He walks away, down deserted, rain-wet street, his back to us. We hear his footsteps as he moves ever farther, vanishing from sight.

WHORE, in underwear and stockings, bound to chair in vaulted subterranean dark, ankles tied with rope, wrists tied unseen behind back of chair, gagged with potato in mouth, eyes of weary terror; box marked GENUINE IDAHO at her feet, overflowing with potatoes; SHADOWY FIGURE dressed in fine suit holds gun to her head.

The WHORE strains and squirms in her bondage. The SHADOWY FIGURE moves closer, his gun to her head. He fires: GUNSHOT. All disperses to white amid the loud blinding glare of the gunfire.

From WHITE emerges:

INT. HOSPITAL ROOM. Close-up of drip-bags, fluid moving through I.V. tubes inserted into GUY's wrists. GUY is semiconscious, strapped to bed. On the wall above his head is a crucifix.

INT. JOINT. Raucous noise. Amid CLIENTELE, the GUY sits smoking, drinking, I.V. tree beside him, tubes in his wrists.

Noise fades to SILENCE. SLOW MOTION: DIANE unhooks her garters, removes her garterbelt, casts it down. She stands, undulates; and as she does so,
her stockings wilt down her thighs and calves. The camera continues to move
between her and the ever more intense CLIENTELE—including now: GUY,
smoking, drinking, I.V. tubes inserted into his wrists; PRIEST, his eyes opaque
white, unseeing; grey-haired DOCTOR in horn-rimmed glasses, white shirt, tie;
WAITER with the broad, stone-like features of an old Peruvian Indian—as she
pulls off the stockings then slowly peels down her beige pantyhose. From her
bra, she pulls out a small gleaming POTATO-PEELER, brandishes it somewhat
playfully, somewhat menacingly toward the CLIENTELE.

FLASH of windswept Phrygian landscape.

FLASH of GUY's pale hand reaching out to touch WHORE's face.

FLASH of GUNFIRE.

INT. HOSPITAL ROOM. The GUY's breath is heavy, and as his eyes slowly
close, we descend with him into darkness. From the sound of his breath come
words, as in a slow stream of ebbing, fevered consciousness. From the darkness,
in ECU, emerges the gleaming nib of a fountain pen. The camera pulls back,
follows the SLOW-MOTION downward tumbling of the pen through dark
space.

GUY (v.o.)

1/12/95, Laura
wore reptilian pantyhose,
8 yrs old, she said, 5
bucks the pair,
her hair up, all
chrysum and cornsilk,
we went to the Spanish
joint on 16th and ate
french fries, and
she said she wanted me to get her
some opium.

BREATH: dire, unconscious, maybe dying. The SLOW-MOTION downward tumbling of the pen through dark space continues, ever more slowly, ever more fatally.

> GUY (cont. v.o.)

1/31/95, I lay
guarded, sedated, sick.
And now, here, end,
in rhythmus,
what began—I mean,
these poems, crus et tuber:
gam and spud—
in rhythmus,
23 winters,
untold legs, untold taters,
ago.

INT. GUY'S APARTMENT. Old black rotary telephone. Close-up of WHORE's finger—that long, painted nail—dialing. Slowly coming into view, beyond her, in the bedroom: the figure of the GUY on his disheveled bed. He is partly, messily covered—most of his face, most of one arm, his breast and midsection, one leg down to his foot—by a dirty white sheet. BLOOD seeps through the sheet where it covers his groin.

Close-up of WHORE's mouth speaking into telephone.

> WHORE

I'm done.

Sudden BLACK and loud opening DRUMBEAT of "Mashed Potato Time" by Dee Dee Sharp. The song plays as the credits roll.

# 105

The lyrics for "The Things I Got" were written in late 1996 or early 1997, and set to music and recorded by Homer Henderson in the spring and summer of 1998. The final verse, appended as an afterthought, was omitted from the song as Homer sang it.

# The Things I Got

*Bought me a Dustbuster, baby*
*Don't need your ass no more;*
*Yes, bought me a Dustbuster, baby,*
*I keep it right by the door.*

*And dig it, babe:*
*I have had passed down to me*
*Big Joe's little silver case;*
*I'm right as right can be.*

*Find me a gal with triple-crown withers,*
*Flash that thing right in her eyes;*
*Blind her with the light,*
*Tell her my new lies.*

*You know it worked for Big Joe,*
*You know it's gonna work for me;*
*Twixt Dustbuster and that little silver case,*
*You know I shall be free.*

*Steak for breakfast,*
*Gal-meat on a rainy day,*
*Keep my Dustbuster charged up, baby,*
*When I go out to play.*

*May be a brunette or a redhead,*
*She may be short or she may be tall;*
*It's just like those pantyhose you wear—*
*Whoa, one size fits all.*

*Yeah, I got that thing in my pocket,*
*Dustbuster on my wall;*
*Baby, I don't need your love,*
*Just got the cravin', that's all.*

*Got a gimmick for my dick, babe,*
*Got a gimmick for my arm,*
*Don't wanna hear nothin' about nothin',*
*Gonna do some big-time harm.*

*Give me a dick-suckin' angel*
*Wears endangered-species shoes.*
*Open up that little silver case—*
*You know I just can't lose.*

*Got me a Dustbuster,*
*Don't need you no more;*
*Ain't no end to what it can do,*
*It's got attachments galore.*

# 106

The lyrics for "Ash Wednesday" were written after "The Things I Got," probably during the Lenten season of 1997.

# Ash Wednesday

*Got my ashes on my forehead,*
*Got my dick in my hand,*
*Gonna sit right here*
*Get straight with the Man.*

*Stelazine in my veins,*
*Murder in my soul;*
*I wanna kill you, little pal, 'deed I do,*
*But I got no energy to dig no hole.*

*They gave me a gun with no bullets, a dog with no teeth,*
*Told me, "No drinking on the job now, boy,*
*Just set right there till daylight, guard the gate";*
*Stuck it out to payday, couldn't buy a date.*

*I been to the cave of the Great Mother,*
*I been to Newark too,*
*Ain't nobody gonna fuck with me,*
*'Cause I know the secret that Saint Thomas knew.*

# 107

Graydon Carter, the editor in chief of *Vanity Fair*, called this long, hard story "a masterpiece. The best thing I will ever have published, in fact."

# The Devil and
# Sidney Korshak

This is the story of a boy, a dream, a law degree, and a gun. It has no beginning and no end, but opens in the American desert on an October day in 1961, with a car emerging as a shimmer in the sun. In the car is Sidney Korshak.

It happens to be the feast day of Saint Teresa, who tasted the great love of God with an open mouth, and Dion's "Runaround Sue" is rising fast on the charts. This serendipity serves as an orchestral stirring as distinct as any I might devise for this tale, which reveals itself only in luminous flashes. Imagine a tale never meant to be told. Imagine a shimmering web of complexities dissolving ultimately into darkness.

Hollywood was largely the invention of Eastern European Jewish immigrants and their sons. Twentieth-century organized crime in America was a primarily Jewish-Italian coalition that shared the sensibilities but lacked the ethnic purity of the true Sicilian Mafia. In America, *Unterwelt* and Mafia were one, and it was in organized crime that the myth of the great American melting pot became reality. Organized crime in America was democracy in action.

Louis B. Mayer and Meyer Lansky both came from White Russia to the land of dreams, and both were pioneers in the business of the new land, each in his own way. Harry Cohn and Mickey Cohen were born to Russian Jews in New York, and both went young to California. One became the fearsome head of Columbia Pictures, the other the fearsome renegade of Hollywood crime.

Though Hollywood was far more segregated than organized crime, not everyone in the movie racket was a Jew. Frank Capra, the director whose work most reflected and influenced the romance of the American Dream, was from Palermo. He and Lucky Luciano, a habitual moviegoer, were born in Sicily in the same year, 1897. One peddled escape through flickering fable, the other through dope and booze and broads.

It was the Eastern European diaspora in America, and the embrace of Jew and Italian, that brought about the marriage of shadowland and dreamland, first in Hollywood, then, as Howard M. Sachar writes in *A History of the Jews in America,* in that "new and even more garish pleasure-capital in the nearby Nevada desert" developed by "still another confraternity of Jews."

Sidney Korshak, the guy in the car that is the shimmer with which we began, was a son of that diaspora, and of that embrace. He spent most of his life at the shifting crossroads of shadowland and dreamland. He may have been the crossroads of it all.

Luciano was deported from America in 1946, the year of Capra's *It's a Wonderful Life,* the year of the opening in Las Vegas of Ben Siegel's Flamingo, a lone fluorescent cactus blossom on a desolate stretch of Highway 91 known as the Strip.

Kay Kyser was in the air. The bandleader's "Ole Buttermilk Sky" was No. 1 as Bugsy readied the Flamingo that December. Lew Wasserman, who had started out with Kyser, was a big deal in Hollywood now.

So was Korshak. But he remembered that ole buttermilk sky.

By '61 the Strip had grown into the dreamed-of mecca of worldly delights, fast money and fast women, so alluringly revealed to the masses the previous year in the classic Rat Pack movie *Ocean's Eleven.* Beneath the Technicolor fantasy lay truth, forbidden and forbidding. Every joint had its bloodstained secrets, its hidden cabals of sub-rosa ownership and looting. Korshak knew them all.

"We stand today on the edge of a new frontier," John F. Kennedy had said accepting his party's nomination in 1960. The smile of that first made-for-TV president hung over this promised land, where the New Frontier was no vapid metaphor but an already decaying carpet joint. Soon that hollow jack-o'-lantern of a smile would be blown to hell, and Korshak would know something about that too.

His car moves fast on the three-lane northbound blacktop of the divided highway. Across the road, to the left, the Hacienda, the Strip's southernmost joint, can barely be glimpsed. The bigger places loom ahead. To Korshak, the growth of this place is so familiar that he has long since ceased looking at it, long since ceased regarding it as anything more than limited testimony to the subtleties of his own dexterity. For him it is merely there now and seems especially flat in daylight, when the demons sleep.

At night there are few whom the city cannot bring to awe. At dusk the big jagged petals of the Tropicana's monstrous tulip-shaped fountain light the sky with neon flashes of rose and aqua. The giant misbegotten fiberglass sultan astride the Dunes glows with arms akimbo. The reborn Flamingo, the Sands, the Desert Inn, come magically alive with lightning winks, serpentine undulations of pastel light. The ungodly expanse of neon, incandescent bulbs, Plexiglas, and sheet metal that is the façade of the Stardust, more than 200 feet across, will, as if by *fiat lux* of some Demiurge-in-Shades, become nothing less than its own dazzling, lurid galaxy. Beyond, the neon shrikes of the Thunderbird stir beneath the moon, and, south of the city limits, the Sahara tower looms ablaze. But Korshak is no longer enthralled.

His car pulls smoothly into the *porte cochère* of the Riviera, halting in the canopied shade. Built Miami-style with Miami money, the hotel is the first Strip high-rise, nine stories of coral-colored concrete that went up six years before, in 1955, the year that James R. Hoffa, vice president of the International Brotherhood of Teamsters, consolidated scores of small pension funds in 22 states into the Central States, Southeast and Southwest Areas Pension Fund. Under Hoffa, who is now the president of the Teamsters, the Fund has become the Mob's chest of gold in Vegas, with assets reckoned at a billion.

The Riviera, with its fleur-de-lis papered walls and Fontainebleau stylings, is packed with swarms of Hoffa's men, conspicuous amid the swagger of Ban-Lon and slender iridescent ties, of kid mohair and sharkskin cut in the beltless, narrow-lapelled look of cool known as "Continental." Hoffa's men are a subduing presence in drab suits, button-downs, go-to-church haircuts. Not the usual Teamster crowd—they are attorneys gathered for the 10th annual meeting of the Teamster lawyers conference. Few party girls mingle. Hoffa, 180 pounds of muscle packed into less than five and a half feet, frowns beneath his crew cut at those who are entrapped by the snares of lust. He has been known to stalk out of a joint at the drumroll of a striptease and is now convinced that the government is using women to fleece his men of the union's secrets.

Today, Hoffa occupies the Presidential Suite, the Riviera's best. But indicted the week before for the alleged abuse of Teamster funds, he is not happy. Though he has stated publicly that the indictment will not concern the conference, there is a certain ominous gravity in the air.

The Riviera, promoted as "*FUN* around the clock!," maintains its ambience of festivity—Juliet Prowse in the Versailles Room; the Vagabonds, the Personalities, the Tunesters in the Starlight Room. Yet the soul of Hoffa seeps through.

Everyone knows him. He has been on the covers of *Time* and *Newsweek* twice. His nemesis, Robert Kennedy, the punk attorney general, has described his power as second only to that of the president of the United States.

Practically no one, on the other hand, knows Korshak, who strides forth into the air-conditioned lobby of the Riviera on this hot autumn day. He is a tall man in his early 50s. The faces of some gain character with age, but his has not. Somewhat handsome in youth, he is big-eared and jowly now: a near-featureless head of wan clay. His ample snout, rather than distinguishing its unremarkable environs, seems simply the midden of further plainness.

He dresses well, in the manner of one who believes that in the big race it is ultimately the conservative who scores. The off-the-rack blues and blacks of the Teamster lawyers, these are not his taste: the fabric, weave, and texture of his socks are finer than those of the suits in which they'll bury these guys. He is beyond cool, distinguished, self-assured, but—like his name, an ethnic blur—essentially nondescript. Sidney Korshak sounds no high notes.

Nothing about the man is obvious. Yet within moments of his unexpected arrival, Hoffa is moved hurriedly to humbler quarters, and Korshak rises—with escorts—to the Presidential Suite. Hoffa, who understands the dynamics of it all, complies. Hoffa, who keeps a battery of 150 legal experts, including Edward Bennett Williams, is well aware that the man who has claimed his quarters is a lawyer of a different kind.

To Hoffa, there was nothing nondescript about Korshak, whose aura was his, his alone. With Korshak, Hoffa well knew, the flesh played second to the fable, fantasy, and formidable fact of the man.

As it was in Vegas, so it was in Hollywood. Dominick Dunne, who moved west in 1957, remembers first encountering Sidney Korshak several years later at the home of Paul Ziffren, the entertainment lawyer and former assistant U.S. attorney who was once considered to be the most important force in the California Democratic Party. The Ziffrens, Dunne told me, "had this fantastic beach house, and they used to give these Sunday night parties, and this one was, I think, being given for the writer Romain Gary, who was the French consul in L.A., and his wife, Jean Seberg—the actress, you know, who later had that terrible death." (She committed suicide after years of F.B.I. harassment and the failure of her career.) "Sidney was there, and I remember Natalie Wood was there. I mean, it was a jazzy Sunday-night group."

Dunne, who enjoyed taking social snapshots, was well known for bringing his Rollei camera to parties. "Not knowing that the man was never photographed," Dunne casually snapped a picture of Korshak that night from across the room. "I could hear this collective gasp. I didn't know what I had done, and then someone said, 'Don't take a picture of Sidney!'

"He was a presence in a room," Dunne said. There were those whisperings about him. "Vegas. . . . Mafia. It always seemed kind of unreal to me. It just sort of added to the glamour of it. . . . There's always that wonderful feeling of"—and here Dunne himself whispered—"knowing someone in the underworld. Especially in Hollywood.

"For some reason, which I never understood, he was always nice to me." Dunne found himself invited to the Korshak home, at 10624 Chalon Road, in Bel Air, where Sidney and his wife, Bernice, usually called Bee, hosted an exclusive party every Christmas Eve. The Korshaks lived in luxury fabulous even by Bel Air standards. Chagalls and Renoirs adorned their walls. Their wine cellar was considered one of the finest in Los Angeles. But the compound was also a stronghold with a secret walk-in vault and a sophisticated and elaborate security system.

"That was the first house I ever went to in my life where there was a guard with a gun at the door," Dunne said. "It gave me the creeps, if you want to know the truth. . . . I went to visit Phyllis McGuire once in Las Vegas—incredible woman. A guy with a machine gun answered her door. But it was at Sidney's that I saw that first."

Dunne said that Sidney and Bee Korshak had "a terrific marriage. I mean, who knows? It had the look of a terrific marriage." A friend of Bee's saw a union that was not so terrific. Sidney, said the friend, was "just a bastard" who asked his mistresses to family parties. The friend interpreted this as proof that Korshak was not "owned by the Mob." A perceptive and informed observation, but one that also brings up the possibility that Korshak, as many suspected, was not among the owned, but the owners—a man above the rules of decorum.

In the land of dreams, Sidney Korshak was a shadow among shadows, a wisp of smoke curling around the brighter lights. What the Eisners, Ovitzes, and Geffens are to all that glitters now, Sidney Korshak was to all that was dark. His legend beguiled the legendary. His was the hidden mystery at the heart of the furnace of illusion and delusion. To some, he was evil incarnate; to others, the nicest guy in the world.

He was a lawyer, yes, a serpent of the bar, and in many respects he may be regarded as an exemplar of the species at its most evolved, but that is too convenient a label by which to define or dismiss him, for his domain lay beyond the imaginings of most members of his profession. But how vast and forbidding was his domain? In truth, then, just who, or what, was Sidney Korshak?

When he died, on January 20, 1996, at his home in Beverly Hills, the truth remained largely unknown. SIDNEY KORSHAK, 88, DIES; FABLED FIXER FOR THE CHICAGO MOB. Thus the headline of his *New York Times* obituary. And thus the *Times* of Los Angeles: SIDNEY KORSHAK, ALLEGED MAFIA LIAISON TO HOLLYWOOD, DIES AT 88. As far as underworld figures go, as far as Hollywood potentates go, even as far as lawyers go, the name of Sidney Korshak meant little to the masses. But in the inner sanctums of the underworld, Hollywood, and the law, among those whose celebrated eyes and ears the masses know and revere, the name meant much. It invoked the myth and mystery of the man believed to have represented Mafia law west of Chicago, the man believed to have controlled the inner workings of Hollywood, Las Vegas, and God only knows what else.

Bill Roemer considered Korshak to have been nothing less than "the most important contact that the Mob had to legitimate business, labor, Hollywood, and Las Vegas." Roemer was 24, a college boxing champion and Marine who joined the F.B.I., which under J. Edgar Hoover officially denied the existence of organized crime in America. In the fall of 1957, when the New York state police busted a conclave of 70 Mob leaders who had converged for a national conference at the country home of the Sicilian-born president of the Canada Dry Bottling Company, the ensuing headlines rendered Hoover's position untenable. Thirteen days later, a directive from Hoover declared war against the gangsters. Bill Roemer, assigned to organized-crime investigations in Chicago, planted the first bug in F.B.I. history—in Celano's Custom Tailors, at 620 North Michigan Avenue, the downtown headquarters of the Chicago Mob.

Roemer, who did not smoke, died of lung cancer last June, never revealing to friends that the end was near. When I reached him at his home in Tucson, he explained that he had the strength to talk only in the mornings, but he wanted to help me. In several conversations, he told me kindly and lucidly what he knew of Sidney Korshak.

Roemer remembered the exact date the bug was planted: July 29, 1959. "Jimmy Celano had a private office in which he had a bar and a sofa and a desk and a couple of easy chairs and a safe and so forth. This was the meeting place, mornings and afternoons, of the Chicago Mob."

The device that Roemer and his men installed "was an old World War II–vintage microphone. Today they have microphones the size of your fingernail that don't have to be wired. This one was the size of a pineapple, and it was hard to conceal. We put it behind the radiator, then had to wire it out of the building to a place where we could monitor, five miles away, at our office." (The thought of five miles of covert wire gave me pause. A source explained, "We used the telephone lines. In other words, we wired it down to the mainframe, and the telephone company cooperated.")

I asked Roemer if he had been scared going in. "Yeah. There was anxiety. We heard and we suspected there was a guard inside with a shotgun, and if he heard us he had every right, legally, to shoot us as we came in."

The pineapple, nicknamed Little Al, worked for nearly six years, including the summer of 1965. Through it, the voices of Chicago's shadowland potentates—Tony Accardo, Gus Alex, Murray Humphreys, Sam Giancana—helped to reveal for Roemer and the F.B.I. the inner workings of their familial enterprises, a world at whose center lurked the presence of Sidney Korshak.

But Korshak's voice was not among those heard. "I think he was smart enough to know that sooner or later Celano's was going to be identified as the Mob headquarters," Roemer said. "I don't think he wanted to be seen there, and I don't think he wanted them seen at his law office at 134 North LaSalle. I think they met surreptitiously."

There were, however, veiled references to Korshak, as well as equally cryptic telephone messages left at his office by callers from Celano's. Roemer mentioned a code name, Mr. Lincoln, but was unsure as to whether it referred to Korshak or one of the callers—a man named Murray Humphreys. Known as the Camel, more often as the Hump, this British-born hood, who died in 1965, was regarded as an elder statesman of the Chicago Mob's ruling elite. "I remember him [Humphreys] calling Korshak's office and asking for Mr. Lincoln. Or no—excuse me—he told Korshak's secretary that it was Mr. Lincoln who was calling."

There was an F.B.I. control file kept on Korshak: No. 92–789. The prefix, 92, Roemer explained, designated racketeering; the number 789 was an identifying number assigned sequentially. "In other words, after we established the Chicago program in 1957, Korshak was the 789th file that we opened under that program. Sam Giancana, for instance, was 92–349."

But "to my knowledge," Roemer said, "we never went out and conducted any real investigation on Korshak." The reason was that "we just never investigated lawyers in those days." The bureau, of course, was itself made up predominantly of lawyers.

Korshak was already bigger than Chicago by the time Little Al was installed. Though he kept a place at 2970 Lake Shore Drive and his office at 134 North LaSalle Street, by 1959 he also maintained residences in Las Vegas, at the Essex House hotel in New York, and in Los Angeles, where there was a permanent suite at the Beverly Hills Hotel. There was also a summer home in Paris and a villa at the Ocotillo Lodge in Palm Springs. A house in Van Nuys, California, was held in the name of his wife. The Bel Air home became his in the spring of 1960.

In 1958, Bill Roemer was sent by the Senate rackets committee to serve a subpoena on the Chicago gangster Gus Alex, an associate of Korshak's then in hiding. On July 14, 1958, Roemer called on Korshak, whom he found to be "a refined, finesse-type guy" who "dressed very, very well" and "had himself under control." Korshak patiently told Roemer that, although he knew Gussie, it was only because their wives were friends. Roemer suggested that, if this were true, perhaps he should be talking to Korshak's wife, Bernice.

"You leave my wife out of this," Korshak said.

Roemer calmly told him that if Mr. Alex could be found in the next few days, there would be no need to bother Bernice.

When nothing happened, Roemer telephoned Korshak: "Well, Mr. Roemer," the lawyer began, "I guess you will have to talk to Bernice then. I'll tell you where you can reach her this evening. She will be at the Mocambo on Sunset Boulevard in Los Angeles having dinner with Peter Lawford and his wife."

As Roemer knew, Lawford's wife was Patricia Kennedy, one of Jack and Bobby Kennedy's sisters. Jack was a member of the rackets committee, Bobby was its chief counsel.

Roemer called the bureau in Washington and told his supervisor where and with whom Bernice Korshak could be found that evening.

"Are you kidding, Roemer? They wouldn't touch that with a 10-foot pole."

Although Korshak moved secretly in the world of shadows, he moved openly in the world of dreams. He was "probably the most important man socially out here," gushed Hollywood columnist Joyce Haber. "If you're not invited to his Christmas party, it's a disaster."

His magic proved as potent in Los Angeles as in Chicago. Producer Robert Evans was a regular at Korshak's parties. Nick Dunne said that "Bob wasn't such an asshole in those days." He "was hot stuff, and Sidney adored him, absolutely adored him."

When Charles Bluhdorn, the Austrian immigrant who transformed a small Michigan autobumper business into Gulf & Western, took over Paramount Pictures in 1966 and brought in Evans to run it for him, both were outsiders, mavericks. As a woman who wishes to be identified only as a "Beverly Hills socialite and wife of a retired movie mogul" told me, Bluhdorn "bought Paramount to get laid. It was that simple." Bluhdorn and Evans hit it big in 1970 with a piece of schmaltz called *Love Story*. By then Bluhdorn was involved with the infamous Sicilian financier Michele Sindona, who would die in prison under mysterious circumstances. (Bluhdorn's own death, during an international flight in 1983, would be regarded by many as mysterious as well.) Korshak was no stranger to Bluhdorn. Evans brought them together in the days before *Love Story*.

Without Korshak, *The Godfather*, the crowning glory of the Bluhdorn-Evans reign at Paramount, would not have been what it was. Neither Francis Coppola, the film's director, nor its star, Marlon Brando, could envision the picture without Al Pacino as Michael Corleone. But Pacino was bound by contract to do another movie at MGM, whose top brass refused to release him. Coincidentally, problems threatened the construction of the MGM Grand Hotel in Las Vegas. Korshak agreed to intercede on behalf of Paramount. Within 20 minutes, Pacino was free and MGM looked forward to a brighter tomorrow. Evans has described Korshak as "my *consigliere*," as "my godfather."

Indeed, it has long been believed that the character of the *consigliere* played by Robert Duvall in *The Godfather*—the lawyer who had that horse's head put in the producer's bed—was based on Korshak.

I asked Mario Puzo, who wrote the original novel, about this. He said that when he wrote *The Godfather*, "I had never heard of Sidney Korshak." Like so much else in the novel and the movie, it was a fanciful and romantic figment that the imagination of America accepted as fact. "The word 'godfather' had never been used in a Mafia sense," Puzo said. But after the book and the movie, "they even started calling themselves godfathers." Puzo laughed his friendly laugh. "It's a fairy tale."

The author did, however, eventually come to know who Korshak was. "It was obvious," he said, "that he was the lawyer for the guys in Chicago."

In the fairy tale, things are simple, clear, and vivid: the horse's bloody head is placed beneath the silken sheet without waking the producer. We do not question this—and that is that. In the real and far more incredible world of Sidney Korshak and his associates, things are more complex. Every move, every moment, is a nexus of further intricacies, each ultimately unraveling—infinitely, it seems—into darkness.

Korshak strides across the lobby of the Riviera on a hot autumn day and Jimmy Hoffa steps silently aside. Korshak picks up a telephone years later and *The Godfather*'s problems are solved. Simple enough, until one wonders how and why.

The Riviera was clandestinely controlled by a consortium. Moe Dalitz represented the Cleveland-based, predominantly Italian Mayfield Road Gang and its predominantly Jewish counterpart, the Cleveland Syndicate. (Dalitz, who once listed his religion as "preferably Jewish," was a founding member of the latter.) Meyer Lansky spoke for himself and his New York associates. The guys from Chicago spoke for themselves and their friends at home. The union of this triumvirate, not only at the Riviera but also at the Stardust and Desert Inn, was established on January 5, 1961, when Dalitz met in Chicago with two of that town's criminal lords, Tony Accardo and Sam Giancana.

Before hitting Cleveland, Dalitz—born in Boston on Christmas Eve 1899—had been a member of Detroit's Purple Gang. It was in Detroit that he came to know a young German-Irish kid named Jimmy Hoffa, who had moved there from Indiana with his widowed mother in 1925. Hoffa became president of Detroit Local 299, and in 1936 married a Polish girl. But despite his later puritanical leanings, Hoffa had a mistress named Sylvia Pagano. She brought him together with Dalitz, who gave him his first payoff. He was introduced by Paul "Red" Dorfman, a former Al Capone associate, to the guys in Chicago who eventually helped him gain the presidency of the Teamsters. The Teamster pension fund headquartered in Chicago was by the time of Hoffa's rise "managed" by Dorfman. Lucrative contracts for the union's insurance went to an agency set up by the Dorfman family, an agency in which Sidney Korshak was a key stockholder.

The hundreds of millions lent by the Fund to Vegas casinos and other Mob enterprises were arranged largely by Korshak, who collected a generous fee for every deal made. When Korshak entered the Riviera that day, it was not just as one of the forces who ruled it. He was also a representative of those who ruled Hoffa and the Fund. In a manner of speaking, he owned not only the joint, he owned Hoffa too.

As for the call that straightened out both MGM and *The Godfather:* Korshak's friend Kirk Kerkorian, the former used-car salesman who had taken over MGM, has been involved in Vegas since the days of Bugsy Siegel. The land on which Kerkorian erected the MGM Grand was purchased from Moe Dalitz. When Kerkorian sold his Vegas interests, it would be to the Hilton organization, whose executive vice president of the casino-hotel division had ties to Lansky, Dalitz, and Red Dorfman's stepson, Allen. The Hilton was one of the many corporations from which Korshak drew consultancy retainers.

The financing and building of the Grand involved a complicated real-estate and film-leasing deal between Kerkorian of MGM, Bluhdorn of Gulf & Western, and Lew Wasserman, by now the head of MCA. The deal would be mediated, in the fall of 1973, by their mutual friend Sidney Korshak. Wasserman's rise had brought him in contact with the underworlds of both Cleveland and Chicago; MCA's ascendance in Hollywood in the late 30s was simultaneous with the Chicago Mob's infiltration, through union control, of the movie business, and with Sidney Korshak's own move to the Coast. Wasserman was perhaps the most powerful and revered figure in Hollywood, and Sidney Korshak was perhaps his closest friend.

In the life of Sidney Korshak, these are mere moments, which offer a glimpse into the specter, shadow, and power of him. They are illuminating glimmers on a gossamer web of remarkable complexities, a pattern of associations which dissolve ultimately into darkness. From Gulf & Western to Hilton and Hyatt, Max Factor to Schenley, the Los Angeles Dodgers to the San Diego Chargers, Diners' Club to the Madison Square Garden Corporation, Korshak represented more than a hundred corporate clients, whose affairs he sometimes spun inextricably and often imperceptibly with those of clients who dwelled in less public venues. One thing is clear: all roads lead back to the city of Chicago, where the web had originated.

Harry Korshak—a Jewish immigrant from Kiev, Russia—came to the West Side of Chicago late in the last century. There he married Rebecca Lashkovitz, also an immigrant, from Odessa. They had three sons. The eldest, Theodore, born in 1903, would not be publicly acknowledged in later years by his younger brothers, Sidney and Marshall. Ted's first known arrest, for disorderly conduct, came in 1925. Under his rightful name and various aliases—Fred Korshak, Phillip Korshak, Phil Cohen, the list goes on—his rap sheet, mostly for narcotics violations, stretched over the next 30 years. Most of these run-ins ended with discharges. In January 1950, following a narcotics bust by a lieutenant of the Illinois state attorney's office, he was sentenced to a year in the House of Correction. The last mention of him, in a Chicago Crime Commission memorandum of September 1955, states that Ted Korshak was believed to be living, off and on, at the Park Shore Hotel, 1765 East 55th Street. He was "alleged to be a narcotic addict and somewhat of a confidence man. When necessary, he got his daily bread from either his two brothers or his mother." Ted died in Chicago in September 1971.

Sidney Roy Korshak was born on June 6, 1907. He attended Marshall High School, where he enjoyed something of a reputation as a basketball player, and the University of Wisconsin where, like Bill Roemer at Notre Dame, he was a collegiate boxing champion. He graduated in 1930 from the law school of DePaul University in Chicago and followed in the footsteps of his Uncle Max, who had served as assistant corporation counsel for Chicago from 1911 to 1915. Sidney's own career as a city lawyer, however, did not last long.

Our first public glimpse of Sidney Korshak, in May of 1931, is in a report of his arrest, with his brother Ted, following an early-morning brawl at a nightclub called the Show Boat, at Clark and Lake Streets in the Loop. According to one report, "Police who searched the brothers later at the detective bureau said they found a gun in Sidney's pocket." Booked on charges of carrying a concealed weapon and disorderly conduct, he was released, pending arraignment, on a bond of $2,400. Ted, previously scheduled to appear in felony court two days later on a charge of larceny, was released without bond. At Sidney's arraignment, charges were dropped.

The earliest documentation of Korshak's private practice appeared soon after his arrest: in two hand-written court reports, from September and October 1931, S. R. Korshak is listed as the defense counsel at the bench trial of a pair of young hoods charged in the matter of a stolen Chrysler. Korshak lost the case.

The Hollywood columnist James Bacon worked for the Associated Press in Chicago in the 1940s. During this era a crusading judge had started the practice of using vagrancy arrests to harass wealthy gangsters. "That's when I first became aware of Korshak," Bacon said. "They would arrest these guys on vagrancy. They might have 20 grand on them, but they would be arrested for vagrancy. Sidney was always the lawyer down there defending them. I remember there was one guy, Sam 'Golf Bag' Hunt, who always carried a machine gun in a golf bag instead of a violin case."

Bacon, who would also know Korshak in his golden days in Los Angeles, said he was "very charming and soft-spoken," a "very pleasant" man, "a very likable guy." He certainly did not *seem* like a Mob figure. "If you'd known him, you'd have liked him." Bacon told me. "He was that kind of guy."

James Bacon figures that it was Jake "Greasy Thumb" Guzik who brought Korshak into the fold of the Mob. This echoes what Bill Roemer told me, that it was Guzik "who developed Korshak." Guzik, Roemer said, was "the original leader of the connection guys. We called them the corruption squad. They called themselves the connection guys." They were the ties between those in the shadows and those in the light.

Guzik's deadly protégé, Gussie Alex, would later assume his mentor's role as the Mob's connection man. Alex, born in 1916 and now imprisoned, has been described as "the political fixer and power behind First Ward politicians" and as a "ruthless, vicious killer" whom Chicago police acknowledged as "one of the wiliest and slickest crooks" in the city.

In 1956, when Guzik died, Alex—according to Roemer—"took over the responsibility for Korshak in the Mob." Roemer said that after Humphreys died in 1965 Alex became the top connection guy "right into the 90s, until he was convicted and went away to prison." (Alex, now 80, a man with a long history of mental breakdowns, is scheduled to be released in the spring of 2006.)

When Alex applied to rent an apartment on exclusive Lake Shore Drive, in 1957, he submitted a letter from Korshak, who recommended Alex as a man of "excellent financial responsibility" who he was sure would be an "excellent tenant."

A confidential report found in the files of the Chicago Crime Commission states that "documents relating to Marshall Korshak [the third Korshak brother] and Gus Alex were first discovered by John McShane of the Senate Rackets Committee and that Bob Kennedy was fully briefed on the contents." However, "it had been Kennedy's policy throughout the hearings to shy away from matters concerning possible political corruption."

Jerry Gladden, the chief investigator for the Chicago Crime Commission, had been a sergeant in the intelligence unit of the Chicago police department. Shortly before his retirement last fall, he told me that Bobby Kennedy's policy was Chicago's policy. "We didn't look at any political guys if we wanted to stay in the unit."

In Guzik's era, Gladden said, "everybody made money and nobody went to jail. In those days, it cost Guzik a hundred dollars to walk through the Loop. He made no bones about it. There were certain cops who used to walk the Loop. Michigan Avenue, Main Street, looking for him. . . . Bondsmen, to pay back favors, had parties once a month, and they had all the girls there, and the booze and what have you, and their favorite judges and lawyers and policemen would be at these things. Everything was for sale. They were selling murders for 10 grand."

Korshak's parties in these years were much remembered. A former Chicago judge has been quoted as saying, "Sidney always had contact with high-class girls. Not your fifty-dollar girl, but girls costing two hundred and fifty dollars or more."

Capone was 21 when he arrived in Chicago from Brooklyn in early 1921, brought to town by his boyhood idol, Johnny Torrio, a former Brooklyn gang leader who had been imported in 1909 by Big Jim Colosimo, the profligate vice lord of the South Side badlands. Colosimo's partner in crime was his wife, a slovenly madam named Victoria Moresco. According to Richard Lindberg, the author of *Chicago by Gaslight,* Jake Guzik and his brother Harry were already working for Colosimo as pimps and brothel keepers by 1910, the year that the lavish Colosimo's Café opened on South Wabash.

Colosimo was murdered in the spring of 1920 at the age of 43, following his divorce from Victoria and remarriage to one of his café singers.

Torrio took control of Chicago through 1925, when, following an attempt on his life and a stretch in jail, he "retired" to New York, where he became the éminence grise, elder statesman, and adviser to a group of younger men that included Frank Costello, Lucky Luciano, and Meyer Lansky. Capone held Chicago from 1925 to 1931, when he was indicted, tried, and imprisoned for income-tax evasion. Through those years, Jake Guzik was his closest ally.

Short and pudgy with sunken, bulging eyes, Guzik was violent neither in word nor in deed. Irving Cutler, the author of *The Jews of Chicago,* told me of Guzik's storming into the office of the *Jewish Daily Forward* one day, raising hell about a piece implying that he was a gangster. The editor asked why Guzik was angry with the *Forward* when the *Chicago Tribune* printed far worse about him far more often. "Because my mother reads *your* paper," he bellowed. Later, in 1928, when his mother died, Guzik, pulling up in a black limousine to the Orthodox synagogue at 30th and Wabash, paid the rabbi $500 to ensure that her soul would not be swindled out of a full 30 days of *Kaddish.*

Joe Kraus of the Chicago Jewish Historical Society believes that it was Guzik who brought in Sidney Korshak. But he also refers to the Korshak family's political connections: Sidney's uncle Max M. Korshak, whom Sidney used as a reference in his application for membership in the Chicago Bar Association, was a master in chancery of circuit court, and a cousin, Don Korshak, was an assistant state's attorney. In a city where crime and politics were so inextricably entwined, it may have been through family that young Sidney entered the shadows. Perhaps the decisive connection was that of neighborhood, that of Magen David.

By the time of Capone's reign, Guzik lived comfortably in a respectable suburb. But he had grown up, according to Richard Lindberg, "in a Jewish neighborhood right along Roosevelt Road, just a little bit west of Maxwell Street. This encompasses an area of Chicago called Douglas Park. It was an extension of the original ghetto on Maxwell Street that was inhabited by a number of Eastern European Jews coming over in the 1880's and the 1890's."

This part of the West Side, known both as Douglas Park and Lawndale, was also where the Korshak family settled and lived. Evidence suggests that Sidney's father and Uncle Max were in Chicago in the 1880s, and Max, born in 1884, may have been an American by birth. In any case, they were there before Guzik and were roughly Guzik's age. They may have started out in the original Maxwell Street ghetto, and, as they prospered—Harry in the construction business, Max as a lawyer—moved to better quarters. The Korshak home, where Sidney and his brothers grew up, was at 3112 Douglas Park Boulevard, in a preferred part of the neighborhood.

Cicero, Capone's headquarters, lay just west of Lawndale, and it has been rumored that, as a student, the young Sidney Korshak worked occasionally as Capone's chauffeur. But it is unlikely that the two ever met. Capone was sentenced to 11 years on October 24, 1931, five days after Korshak's first known clients were sentenced. Though Frank Nitti became the figurehead of the Chicago Mob when Capone went away, the true powers were Tony Accardo, Paul Ricca, Capone's cousin Charlie Fischetti, and Guzik. These were the men who controlled Chicago for the next 20 years, and Sidney Korshak knew and worked with them all.

In those days, Korshak cut quite a figure. Tall and lean, he had deep hazel-brown eyes and black hair, groomed straight back in a lone full wave. Except for the telltale reminders of work beneath his eyes, he looked more a society play-boy than an immigrant's young attorney son.

It was with a splash of glamour that Chicago at large came to know him. Following New York's precedent, breach-of-promise suits involving broken betrothals were outlawed in Illinois in June of 1935. On the morning of June 29, a rush of seven such suits were filed before the ban went into effect. One was brought by the stage and film starlet Dorothy Appleby against the Chicago furniture heir Sidney M. Spiegel Jr.

Appleby, 29, was described in a *New York Review* profile of 1930 as "one of our most prominent flappers." In 1925 she had appeared to be married to Teddy Weinstein, a Broadway character who also went by the name of Teddy Hayes and who told people that he was Jack Dempsey's trainer. He revealed their marriage as a sham during his courtship of Ruby Keeler (before her marriage to Al Jolson). In 1931, in what the New York *Daily Mirror* called "a romantic tantrum," Appleby married Morgan Galloway, a Kentuckian. A week later, she attempted suicide in the lake in Central Park.

Three years after their 1932 divorce, she met Spiegel, who she said won her heart in a whirlwind Hollywood courtship. In her Chicago suit against him, which she entered fresh from a Maine drunken-driving bust, she sought a quarter of a million, claiming that he had promised to marry her aboard the *[Iaccute]le de France*. The suit was filed for her by Philip R. Davis, for whose law firm, at 188 West Randolph Street, Sidney Korshak then worked.

The suit, handled by Korshak, was settled out of court in September. Spiegel's attorney maintained that the would-be bride netted under a grand, but the coverage that came with it was priceless for the actress. Korshak also parlayed that publicity into local celebrity.

DOROTHY TO WED HER LAWYER, proclaimed a Chicago headline of September 19, 1935. The story that followed mentioned what was likely Korshak's first trip to Los Angeles: "Korshak was on his way home yesterday with Miss Appleby's promise after visiting her in Hollywood." Beneath a photo of Korshak, dapper and somewhat louche, was the italicized phrase *Wins Client's Hand*. It was reported that "Miss Appleby, playing in Jean Harlow's new picture, confirmed the engagement."

The Harlow movie, *Riffraff,* was not notable. But the year of Korshak's visit to Hollywood was. Harlow was the lover of Abner "Longie" Zwillman, an East Coast gangster tied to both Moe Dalitz and the Chicago outfit. In Hollywood, the man who kept an eye on her for Zwillman was Johnny Rosselli, a Capone man before he joined forces with Jack Dragna, L.A.'s pre-eminent criminal presence.

When the International Alliance of Theatrical Stage Employees (IATSE) struck for better wages and conditions in 1933, the studio bosses called Rosselli in as "labor negotiator," a role for which Sidney Korshak's prowess was to become legendary. The alliance's president, George Browne, had been one of the Chicago Mob's second-rate local leaders. His assistant, Willie Bioff, was a pimp, thug, and shakedown man controlled by Capone's heirs.

At a 1934 Chicago meeting (Browne and Bioff were not invited), Rosselli explained the profit structure of the movie industry, and a plan was laid for a

wholesale extortion operation of the major studios through IATSE. Rosselli
would operate as the puppet master of Browne and Bioff. With a new strike,
against Paramount theaters, in the fall of 1935, IATSE dealt its first blow. Soon
union members were hit as well—with a 2 percent levy on all pay, a shakedown
that IATSE's rulers designated as strike insurance. Within six months, the
blackmailing was refined: the major studios would each contribute 50 grand a
year to IATSE in return for labor peace.

Korshak's engagement to Appleby was still in the news in Chicago as 1935
neared its end. "I am going to spend Christmas at Palm Springs, Cal., and New
Year's Day in Mexico with Miss Appleby," said the lawyer. According to one report, he added that Mexico would be a "good place for a wedding ceremony."

In the summer of 1938, when the Chicago *Daily Times* reported that an argument "about $150" had developed into a fistfight between Korshak and a bailiff
outside police headquarters on South State Street, the attorney was described as
"reportedly" still "engaged to movie actress Dorothy Appleby." After that, there
is no further mention of her in the life of Sidney Korshak.

The youngest Korshak brother, Marshall, born in 1910, had pursued a political career after graduation from John Marshall Law School in Chicago. His offices would include alderman and state senator (1950–62). "Marshall was an
important legislator and politician," Bill Roemer told me, "and, of course, we
always felt that he was put in there because he was the younger brother of Sidney."

Marshall was a rising figure in the city's Democratic machine when, in February 1939, Sidney himself had a brief flirtation with political office, as a candidate in the 48th Ward. Tom Courtney, his endorser, was a state's attorney whose
reign on the West Side was maintained in close cahoots with Guzik and other
underworld figures.

In December of 1939, Korshak formed a partnership with Harry A. Ash, a former Cook County inheritance-tax attorney and a former assistant attorney general of Illinois. Their offices were located at 100 North LaSalle, which was also
the address of the First Ward Democratic headquarters, the front for the Mob's
connection guys—Guzik, Humphreys, Alex and the political figureheads in their
grasp.

Back in California, Bioff and Browne were headed for trouble. The locals had
lost their autonomy, and union members who dared to protest ended up out of
work and often beaten up. A Los Angeles attorney, Carey McWilliams, stirred an
assembly committee of the California legislature to investigate IATSE. Two days
before public hearings opened, in November 1937, Bioff paid a $5,000 "re-
tainer" to one Colonel William Neblett, who was associated in the practice of
law with William Mosley Jones, speaker of the California assembly. The investigation that ensued was a charade: halfhearted, short-lived, and inconclusive.
Chicago's stranglehold on Hollywood seemed invincible.

In 1938, however, a formal complaint against IATSE was filed with the National Labor Relations Board on behalf of the Motion Picture Technicians Committee.

The government was building its case.

Late in 1939, as Korshak and Ash opened their LaSalle Street practice, Bioff was extradited from Los Angeles to Chicago to face an outstanding 1922 pandering rap. Upon his return to Chicago, several men arrived at his room at the Bismarck Hotel, on Randolph Street, across from City Hall and around the corner from Korshak's office. Among them was Charles "Cherry Nose" Gioe, a 35-year-old cohort of Tony Accardo, who had been involved in the original IATSE-takeover plans. Bespectacled, with a deep-dimpled chin, a receding hairline, and a not unpleasant grin, Gioe introduced Bioff to another relatively young man with a not unpleasant grin.

"Willie," he said, "meet Sidney Korshak. He is our man. I want you to pay attention to Korshak. When he tells you something, he knows what he's talking about. Any message he might deliver to you is a message from us."

Bioff was remanded to the Bridewell prison to serve out the pandering sentence. Korshak visited him there in 1940. But the young attorney had problems of his own. George Scalise, a former pimp whom the Chicago outfit, in cahoots with New York, had placed as a shill union president, was under grand-jury investigation for looting the 70,000-member Building Service Employees International through fraudulent accounts set up by his order. Found among subpoenaed union records were canceled checks made out to Korshak. Called to criminal court to testify before the grand jury on May 13, 1940, Korshak said that he had been paid $8,750 by the union in March: $3,750 for drawing up new bylaws, and five grand for surrendering a contract that retained him at $15,000 a year to act as counsel for the union.

Though the press made no note of it, the state's attorney questioning Korshak was Tom Courtney, the West Side power broker who had sponsored him in his political candidacy the year before. As he left the grand-jury room, Korshak told reporters that he had never met and did not know Scalise.

Willie Bioff, upon his release, returned to California. On May 23, 1941, a federal grand jury indicted him and Browne on charges of conspiracy, extortion, and racketeering. The trial of Bioff and Browne opened in federal district court in New York in October of 1941. Brought to the stand, the executives of the major studios explained elaborate methods of padded expense accounts and bogus vouchers used to conceal payoffs. Bioff laughed out loud in court as a Warner Bros accountant testified that one such remittance was entered as entertainment for the picture *Gold Diggers of 1937*.

Throughout the trial Bioff did exactly as Korshak had advised him. He admitted openly that he had personally collected more than a million dollars from movie officials, but he denied that it was extortion money.

In November, when the verdict was delivered, after less than two hours of deliberation, Browne and Bioff were both found guilty of all charges and sentenced to 10 years in federal prison.

Two years later, government investigators in New York uncovered evidence of the greater conspiracy that had operated behind Bioff and Browne. Confronted with this evidence, Bioff, who had previously followed Korshak's counsel and taken the rap for the Mob, decided to tell something of the truth.

In March 1943, grand-jury indictments for violations of federal racketeering statutes were returned against Frank Nitti, Paul Ricca, Johnny Rosselli, Cherry Nose Gioe, and several others. One of them, Nick Circella, alias Nick Dean, had fled when he had originally been indicted with Bioff and Browne. After being apprehended, he had pleaded guilty but refused to talk, and was sentenced in 1942 to eight years.

Rightly perceived by the Chicago outfit as a weak link, Circella had already begun to cooperate with the prosecution. In February, his girlfriend, Estelle Carey, was visited by friends of the innocent. She was gagged and tied to a chair: gasoline was poured over her, an ice pick was plunged into her vagina, a match was lit, and she was left to die aflame.

Frank Nitti's reaction to the indictments came six hours after they were handed down. Waving a 32-caliber pistol as he staggered along the Illinois Central Railroad tracks, he raised the gun to the side of his brown fedora and blew himself to hell.

Harlow's watchdog, Johnny Rosselli, sensing the coming storm, had enlisted in the wartime army. His regiment was destined for Normandy, but the grand jury got to Rosselli first. He became the last witness to be called before the grand jury, yet remained a stand-up guy. When the indictments came down, a separate charge of perjury was announced against him. Arraigned in uniform, he was moved from the Waldorf-Astoria to the Tombs.

The trial got under way on October 5, 1943. Willie Bioff, the government's star witness, was asked about IATSE's alleged five-year plan to take over 20 percent of Hollywood's profits and a long-term plan to gain a 50 percent interest in the studios themselves.

"If we'd lasted that long, we would have," Bioff answered wistfully.

His character was brought into question, and he admitted that he had once organized the kosher butchers of Chicago to prevent price-cutting, which kept the poor from getting meat.

"Too much meat is bad for poor people," he rejoined. "Anyway, Jewish people are subject to high blood pressure and diabetes."

By way of self-explanation, he reflected, "I was just an uncouth person, a low-type sort of man. People of my caliber don't do nice things."

Then, in Chicago, the headlines hit: CHICAGO LAWYER "OUR MAN," SAYS BIOFF AT MOVIE TRIAL, declared the *Sun;* BIOFF NAMES SID KORSHAK AS MOB AID, declared the *Herald-American.*

At the time, Korshak was out of town, serving in the army as a military instructor at Camp Lee, Virginia. In Los Angeles in 1941—the year he counseled Bioff at the Ambassador Hotel—he had met a former model, dancer, and ice-skater named Bernice Stewart. In August 1943, when Korshak was on leave, they had been married at the Ambassador Hotel in Manhattan by a city magistrate. Upon his discharge, his address would no longer be that of his mother, 5050 Sheridan Road. He and Bernice would move into the Seneca, at 200 East Chestnut Street, a 16-story luxury property owned by the Mob financier Alex Louis Greenberg, who would be slain in 1956, two years after a confidential source advised the F.B.I. that Korshak was a hidden owner with Greenberg of the Seneca.

The verdict for Rosselli and his friends came down a few days after Christmas of 1943, and in April of 1944 they were sent to the federal penitentiary in Atlanta. Their 10-year terms were cut to a third, thanks to Korshak, who brought about their parole, in August 1947, with a letter written for him by the Illinois state superintendent of crime prevention, his former partner Harry Ash. The parole was a scandal, resulting in a congressional-committee investigation and the resignation of Ash. It was also a work of wizardry, resulting in the everlasting awe and esteem of the underworld for Sidney R. Korshak, attorney-at-law.

Bioff and Browne were released from prison early, too, freed by an appreciative government late in 1944, soon after Rosselli and the others had begun serving their time. Assuming a false identity, Bioff lived for a decade in Phoenix, where he became a friend and adviser of Senator Barry Goldwater, who knew him only by his assumed name of William Nelson. It was under the name of Nelson that Bioff, with the boldness of a fool, took a job in 1955 as an entertainment consultant for the Riviera. In November of that year, back home in Phoenix, he turned the ignition key in his pickup truck and was blown asunder.

Throughout the 30s and 40s, whatever notoriety befell Sidney Korshak was local, confined to a Chicago public that seemed to either shrug forbearingly or smile understandingly. Except for *Variety*, the national media had ignored Bioff's testimony about him. All that changed with a feature story in the September 30, 1950, *Collier's*. "The Capone Gang Muscles into Big-Time Politics," by Lester Velie, was point-blank: "Legal advisor to some of the mob is Sidney Korshak." In addition to his underworld connections, Velie exposed Korshak's ties to political leaders such as Jacob Arvey, the chairman of the Cook County Democratic Party.

Visiting Korshak at his plush offices on North LaSalle, Velie had noted frequent telephone calls from intriguing characters, including Jake Arvey's connection man, Artie Elrod; Joe Grabiner, identified as Chicago's biggest layoff bookie; and Tom Courtney's cohort police captain Tubbo Gilbert, described as "the richest policeman in the world."

At a luncheon interview with another source, Velie mentioned these callers. "The next day an amazing change came over Korshak's office. Suddenly, over the switchboard, all callers lost their identity and became Mr. Black, Mr. White, Mr. Green. Callers in person also took security measures." Velie tried to interview Jake Guzik, whom he found in the company of Gus Alex.

"I don't give no interviews," Guzik said.

"How do you make a living?" the reporter asked.

"I play the horses."

Soon after the *Collier's* article appeared, investigators for Senator Estes Kefauver's organized-crime committee arrived in Chicago. Among those interrogated was the paroled Cherry Nose Gioe, who was Korshak's neighbor at the exclusive Seneca.

Korshak himself was subpoenaed by the Kefauver committee on September 1, 1950. Curiously, however, he was never called as a witness. Curiously again, on October 26 he ostensibly took it upon himself to come forward, telling reporters, in the words of the *Tribune,* that he "appeared voluntarily before the investigators to clarify allegations which appeared in a recent article," and that he "told George S. Robinson, committee investigator, that Velie's magazine story was a 'series of diabolical lies' and that Velie was a 'journalistic faker and unmitigated liar.'"

It is curious yet again that no record or transcript of Korshak's meeting with the Kefauver committee exists among the voluminous documents relating to its Chicago investigations. This may have been because, as he claimed, he "appeared voluntarily" and thus, by conditional agreement, his words were to be treated as wholly off the record. Then again, it may be true, as has been asserted, that the real purpose of Korshak's meeting was blackmail. As reported many years later by Seymour Hersh of *The New York Times,* "One trusted Korshak friend and business associate recalled in an interview that shortly after the committee's visit Mr. Korshak had shown him infrared photographs of Senator Kefauver in an obviously compromising position with a young woman." According to Hersh's source, "A woman had been supplied by the Chicago underworld and a camera had been planted in the Senator's room at the Drake Hotel to photograph her with Mr. Kefauver."

Korshak's words to the reporters that autumn day were, in effect, his farewell to them. For the rest of his life, he shunned all publicity, and for more than a quarter of a century his name and image all but vanished from public awareness. He became not only the most potent but also the most invisible of powers.

Los Angeles, where nothing was real, was a good place to pretend to be an illusion. When Korshak was mentioned in an Associated Press dispatch from Hollywood in the summer of 1952, it was as an innocent. The item reported the ejection of the actor Gary Merrill from an affair at the Mocambo. Merrill, the husband of Bette Davis, had disrupted a speech by Danny Thomas with drunken heckling. The party had been given by Harry Karl, the wealthy head of a chain of shoe stores, in honor of a visiting Democratic national committee-man from Illinois, Korshak's old friend Jacob Arvey, who had just triumphantly put across his protégé, Adlai Stevenson, at the Democratic National Convention. Present with Karl, his wife—Marie "the Body" McDonald—and the Arveys were Sidney and Bee Korshak.

The *Chicago Tribune* was given pause. An editorial remarked:

> Attorney Korshak's status as joint guest of honor with Col. Arvey is interesting. . . . The friendship between Korshak and the man who made Stevenson governor and had more to do than any other man with making him the Democratic nominee for President is worth a moment's reflection. Senator Kefauver paid a chilly little social call on Stevenson last week. We wonder if he referred to the friend of Stevenson's friend whom he had met professionally. And we wonder about Stevenson's boast in his Governor's day oration that he was happy to be a captive of the city bosses.
>
> Arvey is a city boss. How much of a piece of Stevenson does he own, and, by extension, how much of a piece of the candidate does Korshak own? And, if they have a piece, how much of that piece can the mobs call theirs?

Gradually more strands of the web are visible; every moment a nexus. Harry Karl, the shoe king, would divorce Marie McDonald. Some said that upon the death of Harry Cohn, the former head of Columbia Pictures, Korshak brought Karl together with the widow, Joan. They were married in the Korshaks' Chicago apartment, at 2970 Lake Shore Drive, on September 1, 1959. A few weeks later, in Los Angeles, Joan filed for divorce from Karl.

It is believed that Cohn, who left Joan an estate of $4 million, had been fronting for underworld Chicago investors at Columbia. The story goes that when his estate went into probate, Korshak connived the marriage of Cohn's widow as a scheme through which the true investors in Columbia could regain title to their holdings without disclosure in public records.

Several months later, on June 4, 1960, Korshak acquired his Bel Air home, at 10624 Chalon Road. The grantor-grantee records of Los Angeles County show that the property was granted to Korshak by deed from Karl's Shoe Stores, Limited. Karl was also a husband of Debbie Reynolds, whom Korshak helped to make a wealthy woman, reportedly negotiating a million-dollar deal for her Las Vegas debut. (A 1963 F.B.I. dispatch, grasping for details of the activities of the ever more elusive Korshak, reports that he was "present at the opening performance of the Debbie Reynolds show at the Riviera Hotel in Las Vegas, Nevada, in January, 1963.")

The veteran director George Sidney's wife, Corinne, grew up in Brentwood as the daughter of a prominent criminal-trial attorney, Carl S. Kegley. "When I was a little girl," she told me, "my sister and I had these little identical pleated red skirts and red Dutch hats. My father took us to see the Kefauver committee

hearings. We watched them question this man, Frank Costello, from the Copacabana supposedly. And I thought, Why are they being so mean to this man?
Mean. Asking mean questions, being mean and rude."

It was a childhood memory that evanesced. Corinne grew up, studied journalism at the University of California at Berkeley, became a model with 29 na-
tional-magazine cover credits, was the first full-face *Playboy* cover girl, in May
1958, became an actress in film and television, and ended up as a Vegas show-
girl. In 1968 she married Jack Entratter, a former front man of Frank Costello's,
the man whom she had seen interrogated. Entratter, at that time the president
of the Dunes, for many years had run the Sands, the headquarters of the Rat
Pack during the golden years of Vegas. The marriage soon ended in divorce, but
the couple remarried in 1969. "I spent most of my time in the powder room,"
she told me. "Sometimes I tell people that's why I'm still alive." In Vegas, "I had
bodyguards around me at all times. I never went for a walk with the dog that I
didn't have two guys either watching or following me."

It was in Vegas, before her marriage, that Corinne had met Korshak. "I think
it was the Gourmet Room, about '67, '68. It was an era, if you can imagine,
when, in Vegas, we dressed up. Beads, real jewelry. There wasn't a woman sitting
there without a 10-carat diamond or a suite. We all looked the same. We all had
the same hairdresser. We all had the same jewels. We all had the same collections
of Impressionist paintings. We wore sable and chinchilla. We dressed to go to
dinner in Vegas."

For Corinne, there was no Korshak aura. "Sidney was a suit, as they say. That
was my impression." Korshak's wife, she said, "wanted to be Cyd Charisse. Cyd
told me that."

As Corinne speaks, her three poodles yap incessantly. There is no great
wooden-door in the Sidney home heavy or thick enough to baffle the frenzy of
their high-pitched, piercing yelps. As they cry out for death at my hands, theirs
become the prominent voices on my tape.

"He was deified by himself and hated by others." Irv Kupcinet, the best-known
newspaperman in Chicago, was a close friend and ally of Sidney Korshak's. It
was in Kupcinet's *Sun-Times* "Kup's Column" that the Korshak-engineered
takeover of RKO from Howard Hughes was revealed in September 1952. When
*The Wall Street Journal* reported the takeover the following month, it described
Korshak as "a sort of catalytic agent" who "is excluded from the group which
purchased Hughes' stock."

This group included Ralph Stolkin, the Chicago businessman who built
an empire "upon the foundation of a yokel gambling device—the punch-
board." Stolkin's father-in-law, Abe Koolish, who had been indicted in 1948
for running a mail-order-insurance racket, and Ray Ryan, an oilman who had
been a business associate of Frank Costello's, were also included. Arnold
Grant, like Korshak, was not a purchaser of record but was named the new,

$2,000-a-week chairman of RKO. He had been a member of the Hollywood law firm of Bautzer, Grant, Youngman and Silbert. Greg Bautzer of the firm was also a Korshak associate. Bautzer was the lawyer who had worked for Bugsy Siegel and Meyer Lansky, setting up the corporation from which the Flamingo was born. He was an attorney who never tired of telling his tale of deflowering Lana Turner. ("I didn't enjoy it at all" was Turner's less told side of the story.)

Korshak was retained—or, perhaps more precisely, retained himself—as RKO's labor-relations consultant. It was a role he did not long keep, for when the government and press began looking into their backgrounds, he and Koolish resigned.

The screenwriter Edward Anhalt remembers a night in Dave's Blue Room in 1946. Bugsy Siegel was there. Ray Ryan was there. The producer Cubby Broccoli, later known as a close friend of Korshak's, was there. Some years later, Tony Curtis wanted to do a movie about Bugsy. "Tony just loved Ben Siegel," Anhalt said. "So we went to Howard Koch, and Paramount decided that I would do the script and Tony would be Ben Siegel. In the process, someone told me to call Korshak, who had represented Ben Siegel.

"So I had lunch with him a couple of times, and we talked about Siegel's murder. He said, 'You know all that bullshit about Ben being killed because he spent too much money? Absolute fiction.'" He was killed, according to what Korshak told Anhalt, because he was beating up on Virginia Hill, and her first lover, "the guy from Detroit," in Anhalt's words, "the guy from the Purple Gang," who was very fond of her, "was very offended by it." "He warned Siegel, and Siegel paid no attention to the warning, and they whacked him." The guy from Detroit would seem to have been Moe Dalitz.

Korshak, Anhalt said, "was very mellow," with none of the airs of a gangster. In this respect he reminded Anhalt of Frank Costello, whom Anhalt also met: "Neither did Costello have any image like that. If you didn't know who he was, you'd think he was a pants manufacturer or something."

Irv Kupcinet, whose first column appeared in 1943, told me last summer over lunch in Chicago that he knew Korshak for "about 50 years." As a friend, the attorney was a man "who could turn more tricks with a telephone call than anyone I knew." Professionally, "he was not beyond using his labor negotiations to strike up deals. He could call off a strike with a phone call, which he did any number of times. He was very close to Jimmy Hoffa, and Hoffa respected him." After the Mob moved in on the Teamsters, Kupcinet says, "Sidney was very important in getting loans through Jimmy Hoffa."

When Hoffa disappeared, there was speculation, Kupcinet told me, that "Sidney had lost his main man. But it didn't turn out that way. He still had plenty of clout with the people that succeeded Hoffa."

F. C. Duke Zeller, the author of the recent *Devil's Pact: Inside the World of the Teamsters Union,* told me that Korshak continued to work closely with Frank Fitzsimmons, who took over the Teamsters in 1971, while Hoffa was imprisoned. Zeller, who worked for 14 years as a government liaison and personal adviser to four Teamster presidents, told me that "virtually every Teamster leader on the West Coast, in the Western Conference, answered to Sidney Korshak."

I asked Kupcinet about Hoffa's disappearance. "Hoffa," he said, "made one of the few mistakes of his life when he got into that car and sat in the front seat. Ordinarily, Jimmy Hoffa would never sit in the front seat. He would never sit in the front seat. And they put the thing around his neck and strangled him and knocked him off. A lot of people who knew Hoffa couldn't imagine why he did that." Kupcinet said that it was "hinted that it was his adopted son," Chuckie O'Brien, who set him up, a charge also made by the late Teamster president Jackie Presser in the book *Mobbed Up,* written by James Neff. In Duke Zeller's book, O'Brien reiterates his long-standing denial.

Presser, believed to have been a government rat, told Zeller in 1986 that Chicago wanted him killed, and that Korshak was "a key player." There was more. Presser, Zeller told me, "always felt that Korshak was dealing with the White House and had some sort of revolving-door status there. Jackie was both jealous of it and feared it."

George Sidney had told me that Korshak once remarked to him that "the secret of my success is I never go to trial." He was a lawyer who stayed out of courtrooms. As far as Irv Kupcinet knows, "the only time he ever appeared in court was on my behalf, when I was arrested out there for drunk driving." It was back in 1958, and Kupcinet was acquitted.

Korshak was "a man who was more investigated by more authorities than any person I ever heard of: the F.B.I., the Secret Service, the local police in various communities. Never once was he ever indicted or charged with anything."

Korshak was "a very dear friend" who would "do anything in the world for you." But Kupcinet conceded there was also a dark side: "He could be very tough on some members of the Mob who would get in his way and interfere with him. He knew and had the backing of [Chicago crime boss] Tony Accardo. Tony Accardo loved him: he depended on him." Korshak, Kupcinet said, "was considered to be a fair-haired boy in the organization with the blessings of Tony Accardo."

According to an F.B.I. informant, it was also through Korshak and Jake Arvey that Accardo and Gus Alex, by 1961, were able to acquire large blocks of stock in the Hilton hotel chain. Korshak was involved not only with Hilton but also with the Hyatt chain, having arranged a Teamster loan for Hyatt. He was close to the Pritzker family, who owned Hyatt, and to the Hiltons as well. Today, Korshak's son Harry is married to the sister of Trish Hilton, the widow of Nicky Hilton.

Besides Lew Wasserman and Paul Ziffren, one of Korshak's closest friends, Kupcinet said, was Frank Sinatra. "Frank and Sid were very close friends. Very close friends. I know Frank leaned on him for a lot of political and legal advice." In 1976, when Sinatra married Barbara Marx, Bee Korshak was the matron of honor. It was a wedding that Ronald Reagan interrupted his presidential campaign to attend.

Reagan's involvement with the triad of Korshak, Wasserman, and Ziffren was an important one. A former client and longtime associate of Lew Wasserman's, Reagan had been supported by Korshak in 1970. And though he was a leading Democrat, Paul Ziffren was to become, in 1979, a law partner of William French Smith, the personal attorney of Reagan, who would later be named attorney general. One of Reagan's first acts as president would be to call for cuts in the Justice Department budget, cuts which the F.B.I. warned would mean "no new undercover operations" against the Mob, Korshak, the forces of Chicago, or associates (such as Moe Dalitz) of Reagan's "best friend," Senator Paul Laxalt.

Kupcinet said, "All the boys were close to Sid." As for his involvement with the Mob, "There's nothing wrong with that. Some of our best lawyers—Clarence Darrow, Edward Bennett Williams—represented the underworld. They're entitled to the best law money can buy," Kupcinet said with a grin.

I had heard that Korshak's friend Paul Ziffren was a notorious womanizer as well. "Paul," I was told, "had a lot of girlfriends around town who might sing for you." Another source told me that he knew from Joe Bonanno's mistress, a former prostitute who serviced Ziffren often, that the great Democrat led a secret life of diapered sexual infantilism.

I asked Kupcinet about the women in Korshak's life.

"He didn't fool around with women."

"He didn't? Yeah, he did."

"A few."

"Stella Stevens, somebody told me."

"Stella Stevens. Very close to Stella."

"And come on."

"Jill St. John."

"Then he liked the girls."

The actress Jill St. John, who declined comment for this article, was involved with Korshak in business too. In 1968 the Chicago millionaire Delbert Coleman, a friend and client of Korshak's and the chairman of a Beverly Hills conglomerate called Parvin-Dohrmann, bought 300,000 shares of Parvin-Dohrmann for $35 a share. St. John bought in for a thousand shares. In the months that followed, the value of the stock, manipulated on the market by Coleman and Korshak, increased by 300 percent. Korshak, who, of course, had been appointed labor counsel of Parvin-Dohrmann, negotiated the company's

$15 million purchase, with the proceeds of the artificially inflated stock, of the Stardust Hotel and Casino. (Years earlier, the Accardo and Dalitz factions had vied for control of the hotel and Korshak had acted as mediator.)

Korshak's fee for arranging the Stardust purchase by Parvin-Dohrmann from the Mob—which, it was likely, would never truly lose it—was half a million, paid in secret. It was Parvin-Dohrmann's failure to disclose this payment to its shareholders that resulted in the Securities and Exchange Commission's suspending trading in Parvin-Dohrmann and ultimately entering judgments of permanent injunction and disgorgement of profits against Korshak, St. John, and others. Korshak arranged for Edward Bennett Williams to represent St. John at the hearings. For his half-million-dollar fee, Coleman later said, Korshak simply made an introduction over the telephone.

In 1972 the Internal Revenue Service charged Korshak with fraud for declaring a $10,000 gift to St. John as legal fees to her attorney. The charge was one of many that the I.R.S. brought against him after a long and determined investigation. Korshak, the agency reckoned, owed $924,000. There may have been those who thought he was getting off easy, but Korshak fought the I.R.S. for two years. Together he and Paul Ziffren, a former Internal Revenue Service counsel, must have proved formidable, for, on the eye of a scheduled Tax Court trial, the I.R.S. settled with Korshak for 20 cents on the dollar, and all fraud charges were dropped.

The great bonds of Sidney Korshak's later life had been forged in Chicago in the 30s. Twenty-three-year-old Lew Wasserman had arrived in town from Cleveland at the end of 1936 to work for the Music Corporation of America (MCA), an agency that had been founded in Chicago by Jules Stein, an Indiana-born graduate of the medical school of the University of Chicago. Stein and his partner, Billy Goodheart, started out promoting bands in the clubs of Capone's South Side. MCA found its first big act, Guy Lombardo, in 1928, and by the mid-30s had Harry James, Tommy Dorsey, and Artie Shaw.

"Lew's last job in Cleveland," said Dennis McDougal, who is working on a biography of Wasserman, "was as acting general manager of the Mayfair Casino, which was basically a very high-class, high-roller Mob casino. The hidden owners were Moe Dalitz and his partners, the Silent Syndicate who founded the Desert Inn and went on to become the hidden owners of the Riviera and then ultimately La Costa." Wasserman's rise at MCA in Chicago was meteoric. Within a year he went "from just another shipping clerk," said McDougal, "to what he later described as the national director of publicity."

MCA, according to McDougal, was involved with the Chicago Mob "up to their eyeballs," working closely not only with Chez Paree, the outfit's premier club, but also with Ralph Capone's places on the South Side. As Irv Kupcinet told me, "When you worked in nightclubs in that era, you had to know the underworld, because they dominated the field, and if you wanted to work, you had to be with them."

Joe Glaser was a fight promoter and fight fixer for the Capone Mob. His family owned several Chicago nightclubs, including the Sunset Café, which he managed. Louis Armstrong, who in 1935 aligned himself with Glaser (who would be the performer's manager for the rest of his life), played there in 1927. Armstrong later moved to New York, returning to Chicago in 1931 to play the Show Boat, the same year and joint in which Sidney and Ted Korshak had been arrested for brawling.

Glaser worked briefly as an MCA agent in the early 30s, and when he later incorporated his own agency, the Associated Booking Corporation, in 1940, it was with a loan from Jules Stein. According to Dan Moldea, the author of *Dark Victory: Ronald Reagan, MCA, and the Mob*, it was Glaser who introduced Stein to Korshak. It seems likely that it was Stein who then introduced Wasserman to Korshak.

Paul Ziffren, an Iowa boy, attended law school at Northwestern University in Chicago and became a member of the Illinois bar in 1938, beginning his practice in Chicago, where he became a partner in the firm of Gottlieb & Schwartz in 1942.

Ziffren moved to Los Angeles in 1946, becoming a partner in Swartz, Tannenbaum & Ziffren, then, with his brother, establishing his own firm, Ziffren & Ziffren, in 1950. By 1950 Ziffren and his friends were all in L.A. as were guys like Rosselli. Wasserman moved to the new West Coast office of MCA in 1939. Joe Glaser eventually moved west as well, establishing the Beverly Hills office of Associated Booking three blocks from that of MCA.

Korshak controlled Associated Booking, however invisibly. Though he was the most legendary lawyer in Hollywood, he never opened a law office in Los Angeles or bothered with a license to practice in the state of California.

"It was casting, in a sense," George Sidney told me, of the days he ran Columbia for Harry Cohn, the days when they would call in Korshak to take care of things. "You would cast an actor, you would cast a lawyer."

Frank Rothman, the venerable Los Angeles attorney and former head of MGM, was a friend of Korshak's for more than 30 years. "He was not an admitted California lawyer," Rothman said, "and he referred a considerable amount of legal business to me." Rothman found Korshak to have a stern exterior but to be "very warm, very gracious, very thoughtful. You had to know Sidney to see all these great qualities." He was "a meticulous dresser. He was a gentleman, an absolute gentleman. You never heard any profanity out of Sidney. You didn't hear any forceful statements out of him. He was never threatening or anything of that kind. He was just a real elegant man."

Sidney Korshak and Lew Wasserman, Rothman said, "were two of a kind, but Sidney negotiated more as the lawyer and Lew negotiated as the party to the negotiations. The way it would work was, if Lew didn't get it done, Sidney would get called in." Korshak "would always have lawyers with him. He was always very careful not to practice law in California. That's why I was in the picture. I was the lawyer."

Korshak, Rothman said, "was at the Bistro almost every day." He owned a piece of it and was known to conduct much of his business there, at a corner table equipped with two telephones. When he operated out of an office at all in Los Angeles, it was at Associated Booking. While Glaser handled a roster of black acts that, besides Armstrong, included at times Billie Holiday and Charlie Parker, Korshak cultivated his own small circle of entertainers: Tony Martin, whom he knew from Chicago, and Tony's wife, Cyd Charisse; Dinah Shore; Debbie Reynolds; and Jill St. John.

Tony Martin, older than Lew Wasserman but as open and radiant as a flower in the sun, speaks fondly of Korshak. "I first met him in 1933 in Chicago at the World's Fair, and we buddied around," he told me. "I was a singer, he was a lawyer, that's the way it was." Martin, at the time, was traveling with Tom Gerun's orchestra. Korshak "recommended me to play the Chez Paree when I was out on my own and already in movies." He remembered Korshak and their lifelong friendship fondly. "He loved good food, and he used to take me to these wonderful restaurants in Chicago, the fun places. And then he moved out here, and my friends were his." He mentioned several names, among them Harry Karl, the late shoe king, and David Janssen, the late actor. "Most all the gang is gone now."

I asked Martin if Korshak was a fun-loving guy.

"Oh, yes. He was at the ball games all the time. We had a box together. He was a Dodger fan, so was I. We used to go to all the ball games at night."

It was Korshak whom Walter O'Malley, the Dodgers' president, had called in to prevent an opening-day strike by Teamsters parking-lot attendants at the new Dodger Stadium in 1962. Korshak not only prevented the strike but had the parking concession awarded by O'Malley to a new outfit, Affiliated Parking, connected with a different Teamsters local. The 1962 Nevada charter of Affiliated Parking showed Korshak to be an owner of record. In 1960, Korshak had been similarly called in to resolve labor difficulties that threatened the start of the Santa Anita racing season.

Was there ever an air of danger about him?

"Oh, no, no, my goodness, no. He was like a little baby. He always tried to help people. I'll say that, he always tried to help people. He'd help anybody. He loved his family. His two sons were his treasures."

Martin never saw him "be a heavy in any way, never. Of course, I don't know his business. Whatever he did, he must have been successful, that's all I know. I found him to be a gentleman all the time. His language was perfect. He was not a drinking man, and he didn't smoke. He was a robust, tall good dresser. He loved to get his clothes at Pucci's in Chicago. In fact, he bought me my first good suit from Pucci's."

Soon after Chicago gained control of the Riviera, Gaming Control Board records showed Tony Martin as a licensee with a 2 percent share of the Riviera listed in his name.

The trio of Korshak, Wasserman, and Ziffren were a portrait of refinement, elegance, and respectability. Together, they were the triumvirate of absolute power in Hollywood. When they moved in concert, there was not a candidate that could not be elected or ruined, not a problem that could not be caused or solved, not a deal that could not be made or killed.

Today they are all dead except for Wasserman, who is now in his 85th year and has declined my request for an interview regarding Sidney Korshak. He has also declined to speak with Dennis McDougal, his biographer. I asked Dan Moldea if Wasserman responded to *Dark Victory*.

"Yeah. God. I was told by a person who was at a meeting with him—a good, credible guy, a fringe Mob guy in L.A.—that Wasserman slammed his fist down on the table and said, 'I want Moldea destroyed.' He didn't want me killed or anything like that. He just wanted me *destroyed*. And I'm still here."

Silence on the subject of Sidney Korshak among those who knew him is pervasive. Tony Martin assured me that speaking to Sidney's son Stuart would "be no problem." Stuart, Martin told me, "went to Yale, you know, and studied law. He's a nice boy, a real fine boy." Unfortunately, a message left for him at Korshak, Kracoff, Kong & Sugano, his law firm, remained unanswered, as did a letter I sent to Korshak's widow, Bernice.

Korshak's other son, Harry, produced a couple pictures for Paramount during the Bluhdorn-Evans years—*Hit!* and *Shelia Levine Is Dead and Living in New York*—and one, *Gable and Lombard*, for Wasserman's Universal. I heard that he had since devoted himself to painting and was living in London. The producer Sid Beckerman, a great guy to those who know him, a tough-guy legend to those who tell tales of him, said that he remembered meeting Harry at Paramount. Harry, he said, was "also a lawyer, although he's never practiced law." Beckerman recalled him as "a nice kid."

Reached in London, Harry Korshak did indeed seem like a nice man. But there was nothing he wished to say.

"I really have no interest in contributing anything," he said, in a manner that seemed not cold but sadly sincere. "I'm terribly sorry," he said.

Dani Janssen, the widow of David Janssen, said, "Sidney was my late husband's surrogate father practically. Very, very, very close. I'm so close to Bee that I wouldn't do anything without her authorizing it. I can't, in other words. I hope you understand the position I'm in."

Dani is a charming woman, and we continued to talk awhile. She asked me why I was writing about Sidney Korshak.

"They asked me to." It was the simple truth. The thought had never occurred to me. Later, after eight months' digging, I would wish it had never occurred to them either.

"Ah, that's a good answer."

Like Tony Martin, she had only the fondest memories of Korshak. "He was such a great, human friend," she told me. "Without Sidney I may not have lived through the losing of David. He was extraordinary—that's all I can say."

Then she told me what I knew, and what I was coming to know better every day. "Actually," she said, "Sidney was an enigma."

Enigma. The Englishing of a Latin rendering of a Greek word, ultimately from *ainos*, Ionic and poetical, for "fable."

So where does the fable of Sidney Korshak end? Where does the truth begin? Where—between the "little baby" who "always tried to help people" and the man who was "the most important contact that the Mob had to legitimate business, labor, Hollywood, and Las Vegas"—does the real Sidney Korshak lurk? Or are they one and the same, a Janus of good and evil?

During our mutual musing one evening, Joe Kraus of the Chicago Jewish Historical Society wondered aloud if the mystery could ever be solved.

"One thing you can be sure of," I said, "is that he was brilliant. He was invaluable." All his life, I said, all around him, they went down in their own blood. Gioe was murdered by his own in 1954. Bioff was blown up in 1955. Alex Greenberg was hit in 1956. Gus Greenbaum, the manager of the Riviera, was murdered in his bed, his throat cut from ear to ear, in 1958. Giancana in June of 1975, Hoffa in July. Even Rosselli, what was left of him, his legs and torso sawed apart, found in an oil drum floating in Dumbfoundling Bay in the summer of '76. Ray Ryan, blown to hell in 1977. Dorfman, slain in 1983.

Sidney Korshak, who moved among these men, who knew the secrets that they knew—not only the secrets of the forbidden anatomies of Vegas and Hollywood, of politics and the Mob, but also the vaster secrets, of the fates of the Kennedys and such, that Giancana knew and Hoffa knew and Rosselli knew— and more, the secrets of the fates of those men themselves. Sidney Korshak, who lived unseen in the unseen heart of the beast, and who at the same time "entertained beautifully in Bel Air." Sidney Korshak escaped—no, prevailed, prospered, in blessed fortune—without so much as a scratch.

The relative anonymity and subdued respectability that Korshak had cultivated since 1950 was jeopardized in the summer of 1976 when a four-part front-page series by Seymour Hersh and Jeff Gerth appeared in *The New York Times*. Though, like the forces of the government for so many years, the series could not conclusively indict him on anything, it did have its effect. Korshak, escaping the glare, entered Michael Reese Hospital in Chicago, where he remained for the duration of the series, "suffering," it was reported, "from diverticulitis"—in this case, a linguistically interesting ailment, it and "diversion" sharing the same root.

Nat Hentoff, writing in *The Village Voice,* came to the defense of Korshak, "a citizen whom the government has not been able to nail and so now is delighted to try in the press. Sy Hersh is protected by the First Amendment. Even a Sidney Korshak should be protected by some of the others."

Jeff Gerth told me that, in the researching of the story, there appeared to be a leak from the accounting department of the *Times* back to Chicago, where his movements seemed to be closely monitored through the paper trail of his expense reports. And perhaps it is no more than mere coincidence, but all the documentation gathered by Hersh and Gerth was subsequently lost during a transfer from one *Times* office to another.

In a 1978 report, California state attorney general Evelle Younger included Korshak in a well-publicized list of organized-crime figures with ties to California. In the spring of 1979, during a statewide racetrack strike, Korshak was asked to step down as a labor negotiator, "only because of the press of his other business." That summer, the Justice Department began an investigation of the Riviera, reportedly focusing on Korshak.

In 1980, when columnists wrote about Korshak's attendance at Frank Sinatra's birthday party, it was later reported that Korshak's name was not supposed to have appeared on the version of the guest list supplied to the media by Sinatra's public-relations retainers.

Soon, Korshak appeared no longer to exist, except by implication and in rumor. Like Leverkühn in Mann's *Doctor Faustus,* he seemed merely to fade away to stillness.

In 1981, Jimmy "the Weasel" Fratianno ratted him out while testifying before a pension-fraud committee in Washington, telling that a Chicago crime boss had once warned him to keep away from Korshak lest his ties to the Mob be revealed.

In 1982 the New Jersey Casino Control Commission denied Playboy Enterprises a casino license after raising questions about Korshak's involvement with the company. In 1985 the same commission rejected the Hilton corporation's application primarily because Hilton had kept Korshak on the payroll for 13 years. Nobody at Hilton seemed to know what, if anything, Korshak had done for them in those 13 years. During the commission's inquiry, the counsel for Hilton asked Korshak to supply his files concerning his work for Hilton.

"Sue me," Korshak told him.

He moved from Bel Air to Beverly Hills, to 808 North Hillcrest Road. It was flatter there, and he wanted to go for walks. One day in 1994, Dave Robb of *The Hollywood Reporter* waited outside his house with a camera. When Korshak emerged, Robb followed him to a mailbox, where old Sidney stopped to mail a letter. "I walked up to him and took a couple of pictures. I said, 'Are you Sid Korshak?' And he said, 'Yes.' And I'm sure he thought I was the hit that he'd been waiting for for 50 years. I said. 'I'd like to take a few pictures of you.' He stood there very nice, and I took some pictures."

When Dominick Dunne saw him last, he was no longer walking. "Years had passed, and I had become a different person. My life changed. My daughter was murdered, and I started this new career writing, and a whole new life opened up to me, and I became known and successful. So I went back, and I was at a party at Chasen's in a private room. All the great old-timers were out for this party, all in wonderful glittering dresses, and Billy Wilder and George Burns and that whole era of the 90-year-olds. I was back in Hollywood. The waiter comes over to me and says, 'Mr. Dunne, Mr. Korshak would like to see you.' It was the first I realized he was there. And he was over in the corner, and he was in a wheelchair, like this"—head down, off to the side, stricken—"and I said, 'Sidney, I'm just so thrilled you remembered me,' and I took his hand, and he said to me, I'll never forget, he said, 'I just wanted to tell ya I'm really proud of what you've done with your life. I read everything you write.' Well, I mean, it was nice. It was fuckin' *nice*, and I wanted to hug him."

Marshall Korshak died in Chicago on January 19, 1996. The next day, at his home in Beverly Hills, Sidney Korshak's heart went dead.

The funeral service was private, its whereabouts unknown to the media. It was at Hillside Memorial Park. Besides Bee and the kids and Stuart's wife and daughter, there were about 150 others. Among them were Barbara Sinatra, Robert Evans, Dani Janssen, Niki Bautzer, Tony Martin and Cyd Charisse, Angie Dickinson, Suzanne Pleshette, Rona Barrett, and Sidney's longtime physician and friend, Rex Kennamer.

By midsummer some of the women around Bee were indulging in gossip, al- most certainly unfounded, about Sidney Korshak's having left his wife with noth- ing. Even in Beverly Hills terms, it seemed inconceivable that Korshak had not left behind wealth untold. A search of Los Angeles County public records revealed that there was no probate, no visible assets except for the Beverly Hills home, which was part of a family trust. It sounded strangely familiar: Frank Costello's widow, Meyer Lansky's widow. They, too, it was said, had been left with nothing. Then, toward year's end, Bee took some work as an interior decorator. One project was the Sinatra home on Foothill. Around this time she anonymously auctioned off some jewelry through Christie's in New York. In February of 1997, reached for comment, Bee said simply that everything had been left in the family trust. Yes, she said, she had redone the Sinatra home, but this was nothing new: she had worked as a designer for 25 years, and had done all the Sinatra homes since Frank's marriage to Barbara. And, yes, she had in fact anonymously auctioned her jewelry, but not everything, only pieces she no longer wore.

And, so, Sidney Korshak. Good or evil. All-powerful or legal automaton con- trolled by others. The few whom death has not silenced—Lew Wasserman in his tower of ivory, Gussie Alex in his cell, a gentleman in Florida whose peace I would not disturb by naming—have silenced themselves, and, besides, I'm sure, know merely parts of a story that only Korshak himself could have told.

A dark breeze in Chicago becomes an evening chill in L.A., a shimmering in the desert becomes a hearse beneath the winter sky, and the uroboros of a tale with no beginning and no end, a tale never meant to be told. Time rolls on: other breezes, other chills, other shimmerings, other hearses.

The only true secrets are those that remain hidden. The only true mysteries, those that can never be solved.

# 108

From my unfinished book on Emmett Miller, the mysterious blackface Georgia cracker jazz singer. My perennial obsession with Miller predates, and is apparent in, *Country*, twenty-odd years ago.

Like Dean Martin in *Dino*, Miller here is the figure in the foreground of a much larger and even more shadowy picture: the picture of a dying and largely undocumented culture, and of its myriad breezes enlaced in the winds of time.

# Excerpt from
## *Where Dead Voices Gather*

The fascination that black folk culture, real and imagined, held for whites ran deep in the homeland of Emmett Miller's youth. Joel Chandler Harris (1848–1908), from small-town Georgia, worked at a number of Southern newspapers, including the Macon *Telegraph,* before joining the staff of the Atlanta *Constitution* in 1876. His Uncle Remus stories, which began to appear in the summer of 1879, depicted a rich and relatively authentic world of black dialect, folklore, and humor that in many ways represented a marked contrast, and in some ways was a literary parallel, to the ersatz black folksiness, quaint dialect, and burlesque of the minstrel shows. That is to say that the character of Uncle Remus was essentially, like the idyllic vision of minstrelsy, a figment of white fantasy—Harris saw Remus as having "nothing but pleasant memories of the discipline of slavery"—but the tales and fables of Brer Rabbit that Harris told through Remus were the genuine stuff of black storytellers long before Harris. In 1883 Harris wrote to *The Critic* to say that, contrary to the stereotypes of minstrelsy, he had never seen a slave play a banjo. "I have heard them make sweet music with the quills—panpipes; I have heard them play passibly on the fiddle; . . . I have heard them blow a trumpet with surprising skill; but I have never seen a banjo." Harris left the *Constitution* in 1900 and started his own *Uncle Remus's Magazine* in 1906. He was the author of two novels and several volumes of short stories, but it was the Uncle Remus tales that brought him fame. For Ezra Pound, born in 1885, the phonetic wordplay of Harris's dialect was both an early source of inspiration and a life-long source of fascination. It was from the Uncle Remus stories that Pound in the 1920's drew the nickname Possum for T.S. Eliot, the nicknames Tar Baby and Brer Rabbit for himself.

If Macon can be said to have had a place in publishing, the journalist and author Harry Stillwell Edwards (1855–1938) and his publisher, the J.W. Burke Company, must be said to stand at the center of that place. Among Edwards's many books was *Eneas Africanus* (1919), the slim epistolary tale of "an old family Negro" who becomes separated from his owner in 1864 and finally finds his way back to his Georgia home after an eight-year journey through seven states, sheltered by kindly white folks along his winding way. He returns with a group of blacks in tow, presenting them to his master: "I done brought you a whole bunch o' new Yallerhama, Burningham Niggers, Marse George! Some folks tell me dey is free, but I know dey b'long ter Marse George." The tale of this "vanishing type" is "dear to the hearts of the Southerners, young and old," says Edwards in his little preface. "Is the story true? Everybody says it is." So popular was *Eneas Africanus* that in 1920 the Macon publishing company of J.W. Burke offered it simultaneously in five editions, ranging in price from fifty cents for the paperback to two and a half dollars for the illustrated ooze-leather edition.

In Edwards's tale, the owner of Eneas is a man named Tommey. Is it mere coincidence that the errant slave in William Faulkner's *Go Down, Moses* bears the name of Tomey's Turl?

In this autumn of 1928, had a citizen found his way to the right Manhattan speakeasy, he might have encountered not only Emmett Miller but William Faulkner as well. It was in New York in October of this year that Faulkner, sojourning from Mississippi, completed *The Sound and the Fury.* Faulkner, it is said, was once thrown out of a speakeasy for singing "I Can't Give You Anything but Love"; and this was the season of that song: Cliff Edwards's big hit record of it was in the air, and there was another by Seger Ellis.

I like to think of the two of them meeting, the singer with the trick voice and the singing author of *The Sound and the Fury,* lost in the after-hours haze, two visionary sons of a dying South.

# 109

# Night Train

The corpse was rolled over and laid facedown on the metal. It was then that the coroner saw them: copper-colored whipping welts so faint and ancient that they might have been those of a driven slave.

To say that Charles Liston was indeed a slave would be to render cheap metaphor of the man. And yet, Liston—the most formidable, the most unconquerable of heavyweights—had been enslaved by forces as brute as the lash: enslaved, conquered, and killed.

Born with dead-man's eyes, he passed from the hell where his scars were inflicted, through an underworld of streaming sweat and neon, to that anonymous slab. There on that black winter night, the myth of Liston—which, for 27 years, has lain like a viper coiled deep in our heads—began.

I remember the figure of Sonny Liston from my boyhood: those narrow-lapelled sharkskin suits, that left hook, the scowl. It strikes me as odd, looking back, that a black man could have held such allure for a white kid like me. It may have had to do with the fact that Sonny—as he had, surprisingly, come to be known—was as feared by blacks as by whites. He was pure outlaw, so far from safety that no one could reach him. His badness made race a trivial concern.

Maybe that is why, in this debased age, when gangster affectations have become middle-class commodities, Liston is rousing punks once more. "This bitch talks a game harder than Sonny Liston hits," growls the *noir*-jazz-rap poet-singer Toledo in "Downtown," and in "Triumph" Wu-Tang Clan invokes the champ's unholy name like a spirit from a vanished time. Just as the forbidding reality of him transcended color, so has his current, unexpected renaissance: Holy Hand Grenade, three white boys from Philly, have a song named after him on their debut album. A piece of effete fiction in *The New Yorker* bears the title "Sonny Liston Was a Friend of Mine."

He was no friend of mine. But as the years passed and I learned more about the fights, and saw more boxers hit, I realized that there was no other like Liston. There never had been. There never would be. And the more I observed, the more I sensed that his secret history would reveal one of the great Mob stories, a hard-luck tale that segued into a murder mystery whose solution seemed as lost as whatever those dead-man's eyes took in before they closed for good.

A guy who knew Sonny once said, "I think he died the day he was born." But no one knows when that was. His life began and ended in a blur. Only the men who killed him knew the date of his death: his corpse had been waiting a while by the time it was found. And nobody knew exactly when or where he was born.

He was among the youngest of a brood of 25 who knew a common father but different mothers. That father was a tenant cotton farmer named Tobey Liston, and the mother who bore Charles was Helen Baskin, who had another son, E. B. Ward, from a previous union. Tobey and Helen had moved to Arkansas together, from Mississippi, in 1916, when he was 50 and she was 16.

After the world came to know him as Sonny, Liston would often say that he had been born in Pine Bluff, Arkansas. He would also tell you that he was born in Little Rock, and on one legal document, he stated his birthplace as Memphis, Tennessee.

His mother would say that her son claimed Pine Bluff because "his manager told him to give a big town," and Pine Bluff was bigger than Forrest City, where, according to her, he was brought into this world. "He was never in Pine Bluff," she would say, "and I never been there, either."

Helen remembered the house where he was born as a cypress-board shack. "It had no ceiling. I had to put cardboard on the walls to try to keep the wind out." He was given the name Charles L. Liston, not by her or by his father, but by the "old woman who delivered him." If the "L" stood for anything, she never told, or no one recalled. He was, Helen said, the 9th of the 10 children she bore Tobey. "I noticed his big hands when the mid-lady brought him to me," Helen said.

The truth seems to be that Charles L. Liston was born some 17 miles northeast of Forrest City, in St. Francis County, in the rural community of Sand Slough, a part of the 1,800-acre Morledge Plantation, where Tobey worked the fields and where Helen was known as Big Hela.

As to his date of birth, at least half a dozen have been set forth. Liston himself—who in 1950 gave his age as 22, and in 1953 gave it as 21—finally settled on May 8, 1932, saying that anybody who doubted it "is callin' my momma a liar." After her son chose this date, his mother insisted on another—January 8, 1932. This day, she said, had been duly recorded in an old family Bible, but the Bible, she added, had been lost somewhere along the way. At times, she gave her version as January 18. "I know he was born in January," she said. "It was cold in January."

In Arkansas, countless bodies of water left by the shifting courses of rivers and streams have borne the name of Horseshoe Lake. The Listons' shack was situated on one, and Sonny loved to swim, and to ride his mule, Ada. The son of George Morledge, who owned the plantation where Tobey sharecropped his 50 acres, remembered Charles as "overgrown, never too bright, and pretty much of a loner."

Writing in 1963—some months after Liston became the heavyweight champion of the world, some months before the March on Washington, which led to the Civil Rights Act of 1964—a local reporter observed, "The average eastern-Arkansas Negro is still virtually a slave, and was even worse off during the Depression days."

Charles Liston was a child of those Depression days in eastern Arkansas, the son of a slight man whose scowl was as cold and cruel as any boss man's. To Tobey, born a year after the Civil War ended and the 13th Amendment abolished slavery, the passel of children he bred were beastlings of burden. If they were big enough to go to the table, Helen remembered him saying, they were big enough to go to the fields.

She recalled a couple of vanished one-room country schools where Charles "went a little bit, whenever his daddy would let him." But the boy never learned to read or write, and by the time he was eight, Tobey had him laboring full-time. "All I ever got from my old man," Sonny would say, "was a beating."

That was about all he would ever say of his childhood, but his words spoke of wounds beneath his copper-colored welts, memories that left him as hurtful as he was hurt, as deadly as he was deadened. The soul beneath his layers of scar tissue was to others hidden and unknowable.

Sonny, his mother said, "was a good, obedient boy" who "never give me any trouble, never." He was "big and strong."

Helen left the plantation and her family during World War II, when assembly lines beckoned with the dollars of wartime prosperity. She found a job at a St. Louis shoe factory. In time, Charles fled Arkansas as well. Gathering wild pecans and selling them to buy a one-way bus ticket, he went to St. Louis in search of his mother. He arrived in the dead of night. Some cops found him, lost and wandering, and took him to a café. Somebody there knew where Helen lived, and the cops got him there.

"I say, 'Sonny, why you come here?' And he say, 'Mama, I got tired of that cotton patch.'"

That is the way she would tell it. But nobody, including her, knew him as Sonny back then. That name did not come until later, after other cops delivered him to another place.

He claimed that he tried to go to school in St. Louis, but said the kids in the elementary class shamed him, laughed at him, because he was so much bigger than they were. He was like a grown man from the backwoods set among them to learn to read and write. His mother swore that he held jobs, at a poultry-packing plant, at an icehouse. But the earliest documentary evidence of the existence of Charles Liston shows no sign of school, no sign of dead chickens.

By the winter of 1949, Liston had fallen in with another, younger Arkansas native, Willie Jordan, who lived on North 10th Street, not far from 1006 O'Fallon Street, where Liston and his mother lived. A third cohort, whom they knew only as James, also hung with them.

The St. Louis police first became aware of them on the fifth night after Christmas of 1949, when a young clerk, Anthony Bommarito, reported that he had been robbed by three black men on Biddle Street, in the Mississippi waterfront area where the downtown black and Italian neighborhoods merged. The Description of Persons Wanted, on the second page of Complaint No. 94710, lists the offenders, beginning with "#1 Negro" and reducing the others to just numbers and ditto marks.

Three evenings later, on January 2, 1950, Antonio Tocco, a 59-year-old Italian immigrant, had just closed his vegetable store on North Seventh Street when, according to the police report, "three Negro men threw dirt in his face, and then beat him and dragged him into the alley where they knocked him down and kicked him." The take was nine dollars in ones.

On the evening of January 13, an 18-year-old white dockhand was approached by "three negroes" while walking near his home on North Eighth. "The #1 Negro struck him in the mouth knocking him to the street," whereupon "all three negroes held him down" and robbed him. The take: six dollars in folding money, a buck fifty in change.

Later that night, at a joint on O'Fallon, down the street from his mother's place, Liston, the "#1 Negro," was drinking with his cohorts and a Louisiana man named Sterling Belt. According to Liston's subsequent statement, Willie Jordan suggested that they could pull down some easy money by robbing the night attendant at the Wedge Filling Station at O'Fallon and North Broadway. Belt, who had a 1948 Mercury sedan, agreed to drive.

Arriving round midnight, the three men looked through the rear window of the station and found the attendant alone. A drunken soldier in uniform walked haplessly their way. From behind, Liston took him with a right-arm stranglehold. Jordan went through his pockets. They found one nickel, which they took, then sent him on.

Liston, Jordan, and James then entered the station. Jordan told the attendant that he wanted a can of gas. When the man turned to get it, Liston took him from behind while James went through his pockets and Jordan removed the money changer from his belt. They ran to the waiting Mercury and drove to Ninth and O'Fallon, where they divided the money: about 10 bucks each for Liston, Jordan, and James; 3 bucks for Belt. Liston bought whiskey, and they drove in the early-morning blackness across the river to East St. Louis, Illinois.

The next night, Liston met Jordan and Belt again at the bar on O'Fallon. Belt had a gun this time, and according to police reports, Jordan suggested looking for "a likable place of business to hold up." Driving west on Market Street, they came upon the Unique Cafe, where the counterman was alone. Again, Belt stayed in the car. Liston took the gun, shoved it into his own pocket, and entered the diner with Jordan. When Liston pulled the gun, Jordan grabbed it, pointed it toward the counterman, and announced, "This is a holdup." They came away with $23 in paper money, $14 in coins. This time, Belt's cut was doubled to six bucks.

The cop who collared Liston was 24-year-old Patrolman David Herleth of the Fourth District. "Now, here's about four, five, six jobs," he told me, looking back, "and the guy"—he was talking about Liston—"wore the same clothes all the time. Dumb street kid. Yellow-and-black checked shirt. He got the name of the Yellow Shirt Bandit."

Herleth caught Liston on the cold, rainy night of the Market Street robbery. It was sometime after one o'clock on the morning of January 15, and the policeman was staked out close to the bar on O'Fallon. "I don't remember whether a car stopped or what, but he come runnin' over from this rib station towards his house. I put a .38 on him, said, 'Whoa, hold it,' all that good stuff, 'hands against the wall.' Shook him down. No weapon, but he had rolls of nickels in the hammer pocket of his overalls—he was wearing bib-type overalls and this yellow shirt."

Police reports of January 15 and 16 recount Liston's responses to questioning. "I won't go into how they talked to him," Herleth said, but in the course of his confession, Liston ratted out his accomplices.

Headlined MAN CAUGHT 25 MINUTES AFTER $37 CAFE HOLDUP and describing him as "a bandit," a small item in the *St. Louis Globe-Democrat* of January 16 gave "Charles Liston, 22, Negro," his first notice in the press.

Pleading guilty on all counts to multiple charges of robbery and larceny, Liston was sentenced in May to five years at the Missouri State Penitentiary in Jefferson City. Upon entering prison, on June 12, he stated his place of residence to be Lynn, Arkansas; his age, 20.

"I'm not sure how he happened to get into so much trouble," Helen Liston would say. "You know, it's sometimes the company you keep which run your luck into a bad string. He was just a country boy. He didn't know to do nothing." She simply could not understand. He had, after all, taken religion down home. "I heard him confess. I used to tell him he had to cultivate his religion. He said he would."

By the time her son got out of the joint, Helen was gone again, off to Gary, Indiana. She and Charles were never to see much of each other from then on. And by the time he got out of prison, Charles was a boxer named Sonny.

Although many have taken credit for it, no one knows who in prison gave Liston the nickname of Sonny. But the man who first put gloves on his fists was the Reverend Edward B. Schlattmann.

"The Catholic chaplain," Schlattmann explained to me, "was also director of athletics. No extra pay, of course." Retired and in his 89th year when we spoke last summer, Father Schlattmann clearly recalled Liston's arrival at the Missouri State Penitentiary in the summer of 1950.

"He was a big, husky guy and always getting in fights with other men." Like other inmates with the tendency to brawl, the new arrival was put into the main-yard ring by Father Schlattmann. "After four weeks of fighting, nobody in the penitentiary would get into the ring with Sonny."

When Schlattmann was transferred, his place was taken by Father Alois Stevens, who had been chaplain at Algoa, an intermediate reformatory nearby. The Reverend Jack McGuire, then an assistant at the Jefferson City parish, remembered Stevens mentioning Sonny: "He told me that there was this great big monstrous convict. . . . They had to put two men in the ring with him at the same time."

Stevens told McGuire that he thought Liston "could have a very successful career as a pro boxer, but they couldn't get him paroled, because he couldn't even sign his name," and they would never be able to line up a job for him.

Father McGuire had gone to the seminary "a little late." Though he was only 28, he had been a sports-writer for the St. Louis *Star-Times*. He knew Bob Burnes, the sports editor of the *Globe-Democrat*. Burnes called Monroe "Munsey" Harrison, a former boxer who had become a coach and trainer. Harrison went to Jeff City in February 1951, taking another trainer, William "Tony" Anderson, and Thurman Wilson, St. Louis's best heavyweight.

Sonny's trainer was a fellow inmate, Sam Eveland, a young 1950 Golden Gloves champ. Eveland remembered Harrison and Anderson as "short, heavyset black people. Good people." And he remembered Liston fighting Wilson, who is said to have gone two rounds, then called it quits with the words "I don't want no more of him."

"A good kid," Eveland said when asked what Sonny was like back then. "Yeah, he was an animal, all right. He was still a kid, though. He had a good heart."

Tough-faced Sam showed me an old Christmas card from Sonny, the three-cent stamp on its envelope post-marked Philadelphia, December 8, 1961. He also dragged out a note from around that time: Sonny had learned to write his name longhand, and he wanted Sam to have his first autograph. "Poor Sonny," Sam said. "Poor kid."

On the night of February 22, 1951, Harrison rushed into Burnes's office. "He was breathless," Burnes wrote. "You finally found me a live one," Harrison told him.

It was Burnes's hope that Munsey Harrison would become Liston's manager. But Harrison knew that he could not do it alone. Though respected as a trainer—he was Joe Louis's favorite sparring partner and taught Archie Moore his great "turtle defense"—he worked as a school custodian to make ends meet. He knew that he lacked the capital to manage properly a fighter of Liston's astounding potential.

So he turned to Frank W. Mitchell, heir to the *St. Louis Argus,* the oldest of the weeklies serving the local black community. No stranger to boxing, Mitchell already maintained a stable of several fighters.

With Father Stevens and Bob Burnes, Harrison and Mitchell campaigned for Liston's release. Meeting with the parole-board officer, Mitchell promised that Sonny would have a job and proper training as a boxer.

Liston was paroled to Mitchell and Harrison on Halloween 1952. After Mitchell got him a job as a laborer and a room at the Pine Street Y.M.C.A., Liston's training began. And something else began when he heard his song. The next March, tenor saxophonist Jimmy Forrest, a 32-year-old son of St. Louis, broke the R&B charts wide open with a brooding siren's tune, a wordless evocation—slow and wild at once—of vague and dangerous beauty. It was called "Night Train," and Sonny Liston would play it again and again, at every workout. It became the soundtrack of his every blow and heartbeat, until the very end. He had always been on that night train, had been born to it. And now, though released to the dream of a golden new morning, he was about to enter its darkest tunnel.

They wanted to get Sonny into the Golden Gloves. There was no age restriction, but legal proof of age, any age, was required. In Arkansas in those days, an affidavit from an older family member sufficed to establish a record of birth. And so it was, in January 1953, that Sonny Liston came to be born on May 8, 1932, and so it was that Liston, who had been 22 in January of 1950 and 20 in June of 1950, turned 20 once again in the spring of 1952.

Sonny had not yet achieved much refinement of style. He did not finesse his opponents; he simply obliterated them, usually without using his right fist. "He had absolutely no right hand at all at this time," recalled Jim Lubbock, a *Globe-Democrat* reporter. "But he had a left like a pile driver."

That February, Liston swept the competition in the open and novice heavyweight division of the *Globe's* 18th annual Golden Gloves tournament. Then, joining other local winners in Chicago, he took the Midwest Golden Gloves heavyweight title from Olympic champion Ed Sanders. At the national matches, in March, Liston became the Golden Gloves heavyweight champion of America. In June, wiping out Herman Schreibauer of West Germany in less than a round, Liston became the International Golden Gloves champion as well. By then his right fist was less idle. It was a single blow of that right that felled Schreibauer.

In four months, Liston had risen to the top of the amateur standings, and few believed that there was a man whom he could not take down. GLOVES KING LISTON READY TO TURN PRO, declared the *St. Louis Post-Dispatch* after the Schreibauer fight.

Liston's contract with Harrison and Mitchell granted them half his purses in exchange for all his expenses. The managers discovered, however, that it was difficult to find willing opponents, and when they did, winnings were small. The first fight they lined up was against Don Smith, a newcomer out of Louisville who had won his two previous matches with impressive early-round knockouts. The Liston-Smith fight—held in St. Louis on September 2, 1953—ended in a knockout by Liston with the first punch of the first round. By the spring of 1954, Liston had fought four fights, all in St. Louis, all victories. His first out-of-town fight, on June 29, 1954, was a televised match in Detroit against John Summerlin, a veteran from Michigan who had lost only once in his 22-fight career. Liston entered the ring at the Motor City Arena an underdog, and walked out a winner. Six weeks later, in a rematch at the same ring, Liston won again.

When Liston lost in September to Marty Marshall, a lesser Michigan heavyweight, it was to be the only loss during his climb to glory—the story circulated that Liston, never having seen anyone he knocked down get back up, was so bewildered when Marshall rose from a first-round knockdown that Marshall caught him unawares with a punch that dislocated his jaw. The truth is that the punch that fractured Liston's jaw came three rounds later. Liston, busted jaw and all, lost only by a close decision after the full eight rounds. He went on to fight Marshall again, twice in the next 18 months, and he beat him on both occasions.

By the time Liston was fighting out of town, Mitchell was his sole manager. "I was committed to paying $35 a week for Sonny's support," Harrison would explain, "and my wife got sick and I just couldn't afford it. I had to turn my share of the contract over to Mitchell." Harrison spoke these words at a time when Liston was the heavyweight champion of the world and he himself was still a school custodian. "Let's face it," he added, "a poor, colored trainer just don't ever wind up with 50 percent of a heavyweight champion's contract."

When Harrison died, Bob Burnes, eulogizing him, told a different tale. "There came a time," Burnes would write, "when Monroe Harrison came into the office on a Tuesday afternoon." Harrison's demeanor "surprised me because I knew that Sonny had won the night before in Chicago, but that's all I knew."

"They took Sonny," Harrison said, according to Burnes.

"Who did?"

"Two guys touched me on the shoulder during the sixth round," Burnes claimed Harrison told him. "They said, 'We're taking Sonny,' and I said, 'When?' and they said, 'Right now.'"

"That was the beginning," Burnes would write, "of the takeover of Sonny Liston by the mob."

But Liston never fought in Chicago on a Monday night. He never fought there at all until 1958, after his association with Harrison had ended. Burnes's tale would be accepted. But Liston's takeover had begun long before.

Frank Mitchell—pillar of the black community—was, in his management of Liston, a front man for the interests of one John J. Vitale.

In the days of which we speak, professional boxing was largely the domain of the International Boxing Club, formed in 1949 by James Dougan Norris, a

Chicago sportsman who—with his father and a partner, Arthur Wirtz—owned the Chicago Stadium, the Detroit Olympia, the St. Louis Arena, and stock in Madison Square Garden. Although Norris bankrolled the I.B.C. and was its president, the corporation was masterminded by Truman K. Gibson Jr., a Chicago attorney whose involvement in boxing came through his friend heavyweight champion Joe Louis.

Born in 1914 on an Alabama cotton plantation and raised in Detroit, Louis had been the first black champion since Jack Johnson lost to Jess Willard in 1915. Successfully defending his title a record 25 times in an unprecedented reign from 1937 to 1949, Louis (described by one writer as a fighter with "murder in his heart and thunderbolts in his gloves") was perhaps the only hero that Sonny Liston ever had.

Gibson, a black southerner, attended the University of Chicago and was admitted to the Illinois bar in 1935 and to the bar of the state supreme court in 1939. He met Louis during World War II when, as an aide to Secretary of War Henry Stimson, he arranged the fighter's tour of army bases in Europe and North Africa.

After the war, Joe Louis—who had served in the armed forces for four of his years as champion and who had donated the purses of his 1942 title defenses to the Army and Navy Relief Funds—was called upon for back taxes. He turned to Truman Gibson, who set up Joe Louis Enterprises, Inc., to help the exploited champ.

In 1949, Gibson cut the deal which—through Louis's resignation as champion—created the I.B.C. The pact involved Norris and Wirtz's purchasing, from Louis Enterprises, the contracts of the four contenders for the title. This ultimately gave the I.B.C. exclusive promotional rights to the heavyweight championship.

Once in control of the heavyweight title, the I.B.C. set out to place under contract the leading contenders in every principal division. The I.B.C. of Illinois grew into a network: the I.B.C. of New York, the I.B.C. of Missouri, etc. Norris and Wirtz gained control of the Madison Square Garden Corporation. Exclusive television contracts were negotiated with NBC and CBS. Gibson, Norris, and Wirtz—the I.B.C.'s board of directors—would later tell the Senate Subcommittee on Antitrust and Monopoly, "During the period 1950 to 1959, practically all of the championships in the major weight categories were staged by one or the other of our organizations."

Yet there were problems, including the resistance of managers and boycotts by the Boxing Guild. Some believed that the I.B.C. would fade. Those doubts were silenced by a man whom old-timers recognized as the sovereign of the sport: Mr. Gray.

Or, more poetically, The Gray. He had more names than God: Frank Martin, Frank Tucker, The Man Down South, That Party, That Man, Our Cousin, Our

Friend, The Uncle, The Ambassador, and—back in a less polite era—Frankie the Wop and Dago Frank. Though his real name was often believed to be Frank Carbo, he was actually Paul John Carbo, born on Manhattan's Lower East Side in 1904.

Carbo was well mannered and well dressed. Most photographs show him smiling warmly, even when being taken into custody. He was, as they say, a gentleman among gentlemen, and—in a phrase less often turned—a killer among killers. His criminal record has been traced back to 1915, when he was 11. In 1928 he caught a murder rap and was sent to Sing Sing. Three years later, on parole, he was charged with the Atlantic City killing of millionaire bootlegger Mickey Duffy.

His next homicide arrest came in 1936 for the murders of two Mob bootleggers in New Jersey.

In 1940, Carbo and others, including Bugsy Siegel and Louis "Lepke" Buchalter, the head of Murder, Inc., were indicted for the 1939 Hollywood killing of Harry "Big Greenie" Greenberg, a Lepke defector. A turncoat ratted out Carbo, and a witness said she had seen him running down the street puffing a cigar after the shots. But all charges were dismissed.

By 1935, Carbo had become the licensed manager of middleweight champion Babe Risko and other boxers. By 1940, at the time of the Greenberg indictment, he was referred to as "a New York and Seattle fight promoter." By 1942, when the charges were dropped, he was "Frank Carbo, former fight promoter." After retiring from the daylight of the boxing world, Carbo became the leviathan of its night side. He had helped many men—and killed others. Most managers, promoters, and fighters were in his debt or feared him. There were few who did not court his favor.

James Norris knew Carbo casually. Both were gamblers who lived the lush life, and—as Truman Gibson told me—"Jim was enamored of all the Mob guys." Norris himself recalled how Carbo became the vital catalyst in the I.B.C.'s success. Encountering Norris one day, Carbo asked how his venture was going.

"Oh, no good," Norris said. "If it isn't the managers, it's a lack of talent or some other problems nobody could anticipate."

These words, Norris later said, were designed to elicit help. "As I recall, he grumbled and said he had problems of his own. I asked him if there was anyone that he knew we could use that might be helpful."

"No," Carbo told him.

Soon after, however, James Norris and the I.B.C. solidified their relationship with Carbo by placing Viola Masters, Carbo's future wife, on the payroll. She performed no known function but received $40,000 over three years. Further considerations ensured a marriage of the interests of the I.B.C. and those of Frank Carbo, a secret partnership in which both parties would prosper.

"And was that policy that you finally decided on," the Senate investigating committee would later ask Gibson, "to cooperate with these underworld elements?"

"No, not to cooperate, but to live with them."

Carbo's lieutenant was Frank Palermo, a man everybody knew as Blinky.

"Do you know a Frank Palermo?" Sonny Liston would one day be asked by one of the investigating committees.

"No," he would say. "I never heard of Frank Palermo."

The inquisitor pressed him, again and again.

"You mean Blinky," Sonny said. "Yeah, I know Blinky. Everybody knows him."

Palermo, who lived in Philadelphia, was a licensed manager through whom Carbo shared in the direct control of many fighters, such as Billy Fox. Betting on Fox in his 1947 fight against the favorite, Jake LaMotta, Carbo made one of his greatest scores. No one but Carbo, Blinky, Jake, and the bagman knew that LaMotta had agreed to throw the fight to Fox in exchange for a shot at the middleweight title.

Fixed fights were actually rare. Truman Gibson says that of perhaps a thousand fights promoted by the I.B.C. he knew of only a few that were fixed.

In a world of guys who have been around, Truman Gibson has been around longer than any of them. Now in his 80s and still robust, sharp, and practicing law, Gibson hasn't lost the gleam in his eyes. Sitting in a Chinese restaurant in the On Leong section of Chicago, he told me about the fixes he knew about. The biggest was Archie Moore's dive in his 1955 New York title bout with Rocky Marciano. It was Marciano's last fight, and the fix ensured that he would retire undefeated. Afterward, Truman Gibson went with Moore's manager, Jack Kearns, to see his fighter in San Diego. "Archie was happy and took us to his offices, beautifully appointed. Then he said, 'I want you to meet my partners.' Brought two guys in, and Kearns looked over and said, 'You dirty son of a bitch.' The minute he saw those guys he knew what had happened."

The gleam brightened when Gibson told me of a second fix, involving a fighter named Red Top Davis. "The lamb was killing the butcher in this case," Gibson said. "Frank Carbo was the victim because the guy he was betting on took a dive. They wanted to throw Red Top in the Hudson River; they did everything to him."

Besides Palermo, there were others through whom Carbo controlled fighters such as Virgil Akins, 1958 welterweight champion, who came up in St. Louis with Sonny Liston.

Akins was managed jointly by Eddie Yawitz of St. Louis and Bernie Glickman of Chicago. Yawitz was a rich pharmacist; a bookmaker operated from his drugstore. Glickman, founder of the Kool Vent Awning Company, met Tony Accardo, Mob boss of the Windy City, when he installed awnings at Accardo's River Forest home. In 1951, Accardo gave him the opportunity to manage a few up-and-coming fighters.

In 1953, Glickman was introduced to Carbo and Palermo. Within a year he was handling fights and money for them. In time, the two Frankies gave him a piece of Virgil Akins, delivered to him by John Vitale, the St. Louis gentleman whom Frank Mitchell fronted for during his years as Sonny Liston's manager of record.

When Mitchell died in 1970, obituaries spoke of a publisher whose paper, the *Argus,* had "won recognition for its reporting and interpretation of racial problems." They spoke of a man "active in police-community relations work." They did not speak of his hidden criminal record, which included 18 arrests for gambling, seducing others into wrongdoing, and counterfeiting.

From the government transcript of Mitchell's 1960 testimony before the Senate Subcommittee on Antitrust and Monopoly:

> "Did you at one time manage a heavyweight contender named Charles 'Sonny' Liston?"
>
> "I take the Fifth Amendment."
>
> "Were you the on-the-record manager of Liston from 1952 until 1958?"
>
> "I decline to answer."
>
> "During the period . . . is it a fact that John Vitale was the undercover manager of boxer Sonny Liston?"
>
> "I decline to answer."
>
> "You are directed to answer."
>
> "I take the Fifth Amendment."
>
> "During the period from 1952 until 1958, did you give this man, John Vitale, the proceeds from Liston's purses?"
>
> "I decline to answer that question."
>
> "In March of 1958, did you go to Chicago with John Vitale and meet with a man known as Frank 'Blinky' Palermo?"
>
> "I take the Fifth Amendment."

John Joseph Vitale headed what there was of the St. Louis Mob. Born in 1909 in the city's Sicilian section, Vitale headed Anthony Novelty, a jukebox, pinball, and vending-machine business operated by his lieutenants. His record of more than 20 arrests stretched back to 1927, including two busts for murder.

St. Louis was never a Mob stronghold, more an outpost of Chicago, and in the old Missouri city Vitale's power was equaled—if not surpassed—by that of the so-called Syrian Mob, the criminal segment of the city's large Middle Eastern population.

"Is it a fact, Mr. Vitale, that from 1952 until 1958, Frank Mitchell acted as a front man for you in the management of Sonny Liston?"

"I stand on the fifth amendment."

"Do you know the present No. 1 heavyweight contender, Charles 'Sonny' Liston?"

"I decline to answer on the grounds that I may tend to incriminate myself."

"You are directed to answer the question."

"Fifth amendment."

"Is it a fact that in 1958 you divided up Sonny Liston with Frank Palermo and Frank Carbo and he is presently managed undercover by you, Frank Palermo, and Frankie Carbo?"

"I decline to answer on the grounds I may tend to incriminate myself."

"Would you care, on the basis of your general knowledge of boxing, to give the subcommittee some of your own thoughts as to how to eliminate underworld racketeering and monopoly in the field of boxing?"

"I take the fifth amendment." Pause. "What a question."

Vitale shared control of St. Louis's organized labor with the Syrians. In 1952, not long before Liston was released from the Missouri State Penitentiary in Jefferson City, Vitale began feuding with Joe Gribler, the head of Local 110, the most important of the city's labor unions, and with Gribler's aide, George Meyers.

Meyers was shot in the head that spring, Gribler that summer. A Vitale ally—a South Side Syrian gambler named Raymond Sarkis—was appointed to head the union. On the night of the slaying, Gribler was seen getting into Vitale's car. Vitale was arrested on suspicion of murder, but never tried.

When Sonny Liston was paroled in the fall of 1952, his jobs were all Local 110 jobs. Larry Gazall and Terry Lynch were kids working at the Union Electric plant in South County. The boys had gotten their jobs through Ray Massud, a Lebanese union boss who was related to Sarkis. Like Liston, they were hod carriers who unloaded firebricks. With them on the job was Ray Massud's son, John. "He probably weighed about 300 pounds," Lynch recalled. "Him and Sonny used to have a contest of hitting each other. John would get him at the end of the boxcar and run at Sonny and hit him as hard as he could and wouldn't even budge him. Sonny would have John about a foot away from his shoulder, hit him, and just knock him on his ass."

Lynch and Gazall remember Sonny fondly. "He was a real nice guy," Gazall said, and his pal agreed: "He was quiet . . . like he was embarrassed about his being uneducated and things like that."

Claude E. Lyles Jr. also worked with Sonny, and his memories are similar. "He didn't want to talk to anybody," Lyles said. "Whenever he went over to eat, he would sit by himself. He didn't want anybody to sit with him."

Recalling his time with Sonny Liston at Union Electric, Terry Lynch brought up something rather specific and perhaps important. "Some days, he wouldn't be there." The belief was that Liston had a side job, that he moonlighted as "a kind of chauffeur, quasi-bodyguard." For Ray Sarkis.

Sam Eveland, the inmate who had been Sonny's trainer in prison in Jefferson City, recalled walking toward a joint called Preacher's within six or seven months after Sonny got out of prison. "I seen him driving a Cadillac," Eveland told me. "He had a big black Cadillac and he was eating a hot dog. I brought him in—it's an all-white tavern—and I said, 'This is gonna be your next heavy-weight champ of the world.'" The rumor, said Eveland, was that "Vitale had got ahold of him" and "gave him a job being a strongman."

Liston would say that it was Vitale who introduced him to Sarkis.

William Anderson, a retired police officer, remembered the old days well, days when he trained and fought on the St. Louis Golden Gloves team with Sonny. "Well, Sonny to me, I mean, I see him different than most people. People saw him as a thug, a hooligan . . . always beating people up. But I saw him a little different. He was a tough, no-nonsense guy, but we had a lot of fun together."

Anderson also knew Vitale. "J.V.," he called him. He said that "J.V. was really involved deeply with boxing. He had his hand in just about everything."

It has been said that Sonny worked as a leg-breaker for the union, and Anderson believes this to be true. "He was kind of a heavy man for the union," he said, "him and a man named Big Barney Baker."

I remembered Truman Gibson, that gleam in his eye, saying of Sonny, "Barney Baker was his guy."

Robert Bernard Baker. He liked to tell a story about how he had fought on the U.S. boxing team at the 1936 Olympic Games in Berlin, how he had stood in the ring before Hitler with a Star of David emblazoned on his trunks.

Big Barney Baker. Born in New York in 1911, he had spent the 30s on the West Side waterfront of Manhattan. The 40s found him in Florida, working for Jake and Meyer Lansky at their newly opened Colonial Inn, and then in Washington, D.C. There, in 1950, he was elected president of Local 730.

Barney Baker had gone to the Lanskys as a wanted man, sought in a New York murder case. And when the heat followed him to Florida, he headed west to Las Vegas, where he took a room at the Flamingo, which was not yet officially opened, as Bugsy Siegel, whom he had met in Florida, had not quite finished building it.

He was big, well over 300 pounds, at least thrice wed, and, according to one union official, "very gregarious." Though Baker was known as a labor organizer, and as "a feared enforcer" and "special-assignment expert," Truman Gibson sees him as one of the great mystery figures of our time. "He was ubiquitous," Truman said. "Always appearing on the scene. In Detroit, in Washington, in Las Vegas." The files of the Warren Commission show that Jack Ruby called him during the weeks preceding the assassination of John Kennedy.

Said Gibson, "Baker was—all of this was—*is* related to Sonny because he is the guy that controlled Sonny's destiny. Never in front."

From his position at Local 730 in Washington, Baker rose in the Teamsters to serve both Harold Gibbons and Jimmy Hoffa, and he was—according to Gibson—very close to Paul Dorfman, the power behind the Teamsters. It was Gibbons who sent Baker to St. Louis in 1952 to straighten out some trouble at a taxicab company owned by Vitale's associate Joe Costello.

William Anderson recalled that Liston did some work for Costello. Sonny and Barney, Anderson said, "were musclemen for the union. And Barney was a great fight fan."

Liston, interrogated by Senator Estes Kefauver, in 1960:

"Do you know John Vitale?"

"Yes, I know him."

"Do you know a person named Barney Baker?"

"Yes, I met him."

"By the way, what does Mr. Baker do for a living?"

"I couldn't say. I'm not—I don't know."

"What does Mr. Vitale do for a living?"

"I wouldn't know either."

"How did you come to meet this fellow Barney Baker?"

"I have a very short memory."

"Do you believe that people like this ought to remain in the sport of boxing, Mr. Liston?"

"Well, I couldn't pass judgment on no one. I haven't been perfect myself."

"Since you left St. Louis in 1958, have you met Mr. Baker?"

"Yes, sir."

"Where did you meet him?"

"Chicago."

Chicago. Sonny couldn't get there fast enough. By 1956, St. Louis had become his hell. He was the only real contender who ever came out of that town. But, instead of being treated like a hero, he was despised.

Liston's rap sheet from 1953, when he got out of prison, to 1958, when he got out of St. Louis, shows 14 arrests.

In my journey through the chthonic regions of Sonny Liston's St. Louis, Lieutenant Colonel James J. Hackett, who recently retired after 42 years on the force, was my Virgil. He spoke straight and gave me history that can be found in no book, led me to people and places that only few knew about. When we met, he was counting down time to his retirement. I began to feel that the mystery of

Liston had rekindled his street detective's sense of excitement, and I am thankful.

I asked Hackett to study Liston's rap sheet and, if he could, analyze it as if its subject were without name or identity. He scrutinized it carefully for a few minutes.

"Most of these are just sausage pinches," he said matter-of-factly.

I hesitated a moment, then asked what a sausage pinch was.

"A sausage pinch. You pick the guy up, put him on the steel for 20 hours, feed him a bologna sandwich, send him home."

Twenty hours on the steel: no way out without a lawyer bringing habeas corpus. Liston would remember those nights on the steel.

Under questioning by the Senate subcommittee, he was asked if he recalled a certain arrest during which he stated that he had been introduced to Ray Sarkis by John Vitale.

"No; I don't. The way it is there—I mean I may have said anything because they just kept grabbing me, picking me up, holding me overnight. If nobody come down to make a squawk to get me out, they keep me; then they finally let me go. Next day, back in. So what am I supposed to do? I said what they wanted me to say, because who wanted to sleep on that cold steel all that night?"

Sausage pinches. Nights on the steel. I asked Truman Gibson if he thought Sonny was a victim of police harassment.

Truman thought a moment. "Well," he said, "some people invite harassment."

The more Liston drank, the more he got in trouble. And Sonny drank a lot. "Canadian Club," Sam Eveland said. Truman Gibson named the same brand. "By the bottle," he added. "He loved the 1843 bourbon," William Anderson said. Lowell Powell, a black cop who befriended Sonny, said, "He'd drink anything. He would drink white lightning."

This went against natural law. Boozers made bad boxers. "The fighters in those days, they didn't drink," Gibson said, but Sonny "was a heavy drinker. He might have been an alcoholic." He seems to have had a sense of shame about his drinking, a shame that compelled him to hide it from priests and certain others. Booze was his mistress, his one true lover. And, in time, his devourer.

On Sonny's rap sheet, Hackett saw one entry which he designated as more than a sausage pinch. It occurred on May 5, 1956. There are a lot of tales about that night. According to the story accepted by police and the press, Patrolman Thomas Mellow, aged 41, was making his rounds when he saw a taxi parked in the alley beside Liston's home, at 4454 St. Louis Avenue. The car's parking lights were on, and Mellow asked aloud whose cab it was. A man on the porch, Willie Patterson, said it was his.

Mellow told him he could get a ticket and suggested that he move the cab. "Then," as Mellow told it, "Liston came down, 'You can't give him no ticket,' he said, real tough-like. 'The hell I can't,' I said. I took out my ticket book, flashlight, to get the city sticker number off the cab. Liston came over and gave me a bear hug from the front, lifted me clear off the ground."

In the alley, the three men struggled, and Liston took Mellow's service revolver. Patterson said, "Shoot the white son of a bitch." Liston put the gun to Mellow's head. Mellow hollered, "Don't shoot me." Liston then struck the cop over the left eye "with either the gun or his fist. It took seven stitches. My left leg was broken in the knee from the fall or somebody stomping me."

Liston "appeared to be drinking; the fellows that arrested him had a little trouble."

According to Liston: "I called a cab to come pick me up. I saw the cab pull up into the alleyway, and I hurried out of the house. Meanwhile, a cop came up and told the cabbie he was going to give him a ticket. I said, 'How come you going to give this cab a ticket? He's just doing his business.' Then the cop turns to me and says, 'You're a smart nigger,' and when I say 'I'm not smart,' he reaches for his gun and tries to take it out of his holster, but I take it away from him. Later the cop said I was drunk. Now how could a drunk handle a sober cop trained to make arrests and to pull his gun? I never drink any hard liquor anyway."

It was likely that neither man told the truth. But as one veteran of the force summed it up for me, "This Mellow was no prize."

In the end, Liston pleaded guilty and was sentenced, in January 1957, to nine months in the city workhouse.

According to the papers, a woman on the porch of the Liston home was said to have heard Mellow cry out, "Don't hurt me." She was identified as Geraldine Chambers, who was in fact Sonny's girlfriend. On August 28, four days after Sonny was paroled from the workhouse following a seven-month incarceration, he and Geraldine applied for a license, and on September 3, 1957, they were married by the Reverend G. L. Hayden.

Cops such as William Anderson and Lowell Powell had been Sonny's friends. "I was a policeman and he was something of a thug," Powell recalled, but nonetheless their dealings were amicable. In the big picture, however, there was no love lost between Sonny and the cops. The assault on Mellow exacerbated the situation. "At that time," Powell said, "the policemen were the real bosses around St. Louis, and fighting a policeman was unheard of, really. We'd call them 'nixie fighters.'"

Captain John Dougherty was a man with a penchant for running people out of town. He had got rid of Barney Baker. As Dean Shendal—a former owner of Caesars Palace, who specialized in sticking up bookmakers as a kid in St. Louis—remembers it, there was nothing like the ire that Liston brought out in Dougherty. "Five coppers tried to lock Sonny. This ain't no bullshit story. They broke hickory nightsticks over his head. They couldn't get his hands cuffed. He was a monster."

The tale has been told that Dougherty literally took Liston to the tracks at the outskirts of town, stuck a gun to his head, and told him to leave. Sonny's story, though less melodramatic, amounts to pretty much the same thing: "Well, the captain, Captain Dougherty, told me to my face, if I wanted to stay alive, to leave St. Louis." Dougherty's words were: "If you don't, they'll find you in an alley."

Sonny Liston fought only one fight in 1956, none in 1957. In January 1958 he left St. Louis for his first professional match in Chicago: a second-round knock-out of Bill Hunter. John Vitale delivered Sonny, as he had delivered other St. Louis fighters, to the fold of the Chicago Mob through Bernie Glickman, who was to be Frank Mitchell's new partner in the management of Liston. Glickman, whose welterweight Virgil Akins was on the verge of becoming champion, saw in Liston the greatest possibility he had ever known.

But Carbo and Blinky soon came to feel that Sonny was too big for Chicago. Sam Giancana, who had taken over from Accardo the previous year, returned from a meeting in Philadelphia and called Glickman.

"He meets my father at the Armory Lounge," Bernie's son, Joel, told me. "They're having dinner, just the two of them, and he tells my father that he had to give up Liston." Glickman was to receive a buyout price of 50 grand.

Liston's next fight took him to Chicago as well.

"Well," as he would tell it, "I went up to fight this fight and Frank Mitchell told me when I left St. Louis that it would be a man by the name of 'Pep' Barone to come up with the contract and for you to sign it and he will get you East, where you can get sparring partners and more fights, a better trainer."

The five-year contract with Joseph "Pep" Barone entitled Barone to 50 percent of Liston's income. An unwritten clause, the only clause that mattered, would deliver most of that percentage to Carbo and Blinky; a piece would go to Barone himself, and lesser pieces to Giancana in Chicago, as well as Vitale and Mitchell in St. Louis.

The contract was signed on March 11, the night of the fight: a fourth-round knockout of Ben Wise at the Midwest Athletic Club. Sonny returned to St. Louis to fight Bert Whitehurst on April 3. It was another win for Liston.

After that, Sonny left St. Louis for good and moved to Philadelphia, where Blinky awaited him. His next Chicago fight, a third-round knockout of Julio Mederos, was his first nationally televised match, part of the I.B.C.'s Wednesday-night program on CBS. On August 6, in another televised I.B.C. fight in Chicago, he knocked out Wayne Bethea in the first.

There was no stopping Liston. By the end of 1961, his professional record, marred only by his sole, narrow-decision loss to Marshall, consisted of 33 wins,

23 of which were knockouts. Only one man stood between him and the heavy-weight championship of the world. Still, Liston was in a bad place.

Ben Bentley, the I.B.C. matchmaker, publicist, and ringside announcer, was Liston's first promoter in Chicago. Blinky was a man whom Bentley considered to be "a good friend," and Blinky was one of the few men who seemed truly to care for Liston. During the period when Bentley was close to Liston and traveled with him constantly, Blinky would call frequently, instructing Bentley always to call him back collect from a pay phone at such and such a number.

Recalled Bentley, "He'd wanna know how did he do in training, how is he do-ing in training, does he see this guy, does he see that guy, who's his sparring partners, is he behaving himself, is he runnin' around?" When they were to-gether, Blinky would put his arm around Bentley and say, "Tell me, has he been drinking?"

Blinky seemed to be one of the few men whom Liston trusted. He was the sort of tough guy that Sonny had always wanted to be.

But then Blinky and Carbo disappeared. A 1959 federal racketeering trial in Los Angeles, involving the extortion of welterweight champion Don Jordan, ended in the conviction of both men. In 1961, Carbo was sentenced to 25 years, Blinky to 15. For Sonny, there was no one left to turn to.

Floyd Patterson was the heavyweight champion, and he did not want to fight Sonny. The National Association for the Advancement of Colored People was against the idea of a Patterson-Liston fight. Its president, Percy Sutton, came right out and said it: Patterson "represents us better than Liston ever could or would." Liston was seen, by black as well as white, as the Bad Nigger.

"That bum Patterson don't want to fight me," Liston complained on April 10, 1961, in one of the letters he "wrote" through the hand of another.

On April 19, Liston announced that he was buying back his contract from Pep Barone, whose role as a front man for Blinky and Carbo had been widely publicized by the Kefauver hearings. On April 25, Liston signed a new contract, with George Katz, a Philadelphia manager who was as white, straight, and worthless as they came.

His former manager, Barone, had not been licensed to manage in the state where he operated. Now, soon after his cleansing, Sonny lost his license to box in the state where he lived. On May 17, he was arrested for disorderly conduct and resisting arrest, charges later changed to loitering. A sausage pinch, as the guys in St. Louis said.

On June 14, in the dark before dawn, 29-year-old Dolores Ellis was driving through Fairmount Park in the Philadelphia suburb of Lansdowne. Two men in another vehicle came abreast of her car, directed a spotlight toward her, an-nounced that they were police, and motioned her to stop. One of the men or-dered her out of her car, and she complied. A park guard happened by, and the two men sped away. The guard, in pursuit, fired a warning shot and caught them after a half-mile chase.

There, sitting calmly behind the wheel, was Sonny Liston.

His new manager came to his defense: "Sonny is a fun-loving person who likes to play pranks."

On July 14, Liston was suspended indefinitely by the Pennsylvania Athletic Commission. He spent the next months in Denver with Father Edward Murphy, a Jesuit priest he had met in 1960. The press made much of Sonny's "rehabilitation."

Finally, after many hours of complicated negotiations and much bargaining, Liston's shot at the title was scheduled. He trained for his bout with Patterson with a new version of "Night Train," by James Brown's Famous Flames: same night, same train, but with a rhythm like a nasty automatic's instead of Jimmy Forrest's big bad long revolver.

"Never before have I had such a feeling against any fighter," Sonny announced three weeks before the fight, which came on the night of September 25, 1962, at Comiskey Park in Chicago, where Joe Louis had won the title back in '37.

In boxing, nothing is better for business than a fight between a black man and a white: such is humanity shorn of hypocrisy. Short of that, nothing is better than a fight between good and evil. "If Liston should be lucky enough to win," said Patterson, "I hope you'll accept him the way you accepted me. You know, there's a little bit of good in everybody." And Liston, beholding Patterson, had said simply: "I'll kill him." There in Comiskey Park, on that chill, gray night, there was such a fight, perhaps the most dramatic of them all, and barely had breath been drawn by the more than 18,000 gathered there, and by the half a million gathered before the closed-circuit screens of America, when an astounded silence overtook them, and then a loud and roaring anger. The match lasted 126 seconds, and ended with Patterson on his back, looking up, stunned, at the new heavyweight champion of the world.

James Baldwin wrote of leaving the fight in a state of sadness, of going "off to a bar, to mourn the death of boxing; and to have a drink, with love, for Floyd."

Two weeks later, back in Philly, Liston was busted again in Fairmount Park. According to the officer who pulled him over for driving suspiciously, "He became very nasty, and he said that I was prejudiced because he was colored." When Liston stepped from his Cadillac, "he staggered and swayed."

On November 30, Sonny and Geraldine left Philadelphia and moved to Chicago.

Ben Bentley served briefly as Liston's publicity director. He recalled the spring of 1963, when columnist Drew Pearson invited him to bring Sonny as a guest of honor to a Washington banquet for the Big Brothers of America. An audience with President Kennedy could not be arranged; Attorney General Robert Kennedy was, at the time, engaged in a crusade against the element which had produced not only the new heavyweight champion of the world but his own family's fortune. Liston was invited, however, to meet with the vice president. In Lyndon Johnson's office, amid various decorative objects and mementos, there was "an alligator or something," Bentley recalled, "made out of leather or something."

"I know where that comes from," Sonny said. "That's what we made in prison."

After a few minutes with Johnson, Sonny grew restless, leaned toward Bentley, and whispered, "Let's blow this bum off."

Sonny was in a foul mood that day, and he started drinking. When they arrived back in Chicago that night, Sonny went off. About two or three in the morning, Ben got a call. The caller was a black ex-cop who sometimes served as Sonny's driver and bodyguard.

Sonny had just raped the bodyguard's wife.

The crime—Liston's first known rape—never made the papers. Matt Rodriguez, the superintendent of police in Chicago, is one of the few who ever knew of it. Some years later, the bodyguard told Rodriguez that there had been a "settlement."

That spring of 1963, Sonny and Geraldine left Chicago and moved to Denver.

On July 22, at the Las Vegas Convention Center, Sonny fought Patterson one more time. Again, the fight lasted less than a round. Now there was nobody left to fight except a 22-year-old kid from Louisville named Cassius Marcellus Clay Jr.—a child of the light who seemed all that Liston was not: a good, clean, middle-class boy who, instead of bringing shame to America, had brought her a gold medal from the 1960 Rome Olympics.

During my time in St. Louis, Jim Hackett had been studying the film of the Liston-Clay fight. He was transfixed by the fleeting glimpse of a figure in Liston's corner, a man who seemed strangely familiar to him. "This guy had a straw hat on," he said. Then it hit him. The fellow had been a cop years ago in St. Louis, and Hackett was certain that if he could be found he could unlock a door that no one had ever succeeded in opening.

Hackett put the word out. With the help of his friend William Anderson, the man in the straw hat was found. Hackett called him; Anderson phoned, too, and also paid a visit to his home. The mysterious ex-cop was, however, not forthcoming, despite our many attempts. Then one morning I dialed and he picked up.

"Wasn't no straw hat," he said. "Was a little old stingy-brim, porkpie."

He decided to talk, but didn't want "all that quotation-mark shit." He told me that he had known Sonny in the old days and that, in 1963, when he retired from the force, Liston had hired him as a bodyguard and right-hand man.

Though Sonny and Geraldine were childless, Geraldine had a daughter, Bernice, from a previous union. Sonny, though no one knew it, had fathered a daughter of his own not long after leaving prison. Following their move to Denver, he asked his new right-hand man to take him to her.

"He hadn't seen her in life," the ex-cop said, "but he knew who the mother was." My new acquaintance found Sonny's daughter and accompanied the boxer and Geraldine when they went to meet her. "Boy, you could tell she was Sonny's daughter. She looked like he spit her out.

"So, we were sitting at the dinner table, and she had done some things that he didn't like. She had taken some money off him or something, and he said, 'Here's this police detective, and he's gonna get you.' I said, 'No, baby, I'm not gonna bother you.' So he didn't know how to admonish me. He said, 'You know, you're not nothing, you just nothing,' and blah-blah-blah.

"The J&B was talking. I introduced him to J&B, and he drank it all the time he was champion. So I said, 'Well, I'm sorry you feel that way.' He said, 'You know, I'm tired of you,' and this, that. . . . I thought about all the guys that he had hit, you know . . . and I said, 'Well, Geraldine, I'm talking with Sonny, and we're doing some arguing, and I'm no match for Sonny in a fight. I know that he's the heavyweight champion of the world. . . .' I could see Sonny had balled his fists up. 'All I want you to do is stand out of my way and let me out of here.'

"The next day, he was crying, telling me he was sorry and all that. I said, 'What you wanted was to pop me. . . . But if you hit me in the jaw, it's not gonna be like that. There won't be no apologizing . . . because if you miss and you don't knock me out, I'm gonna have to kill you.' So we made up and we got even closer."

"When the J&B started working," said my friend with the hat, "that's when his personality changed. When that whiskey took over, he was Mr. Hyde."

As far as is known, Sonny's sexual assaults were confined to the period of his championship reign. One incident involved a motel chambermaid, remembered the man in the porkpie hat. "The girl's crying and everything and getting ready to call the police. She said, 'I'm gonna call my husband.' I said, 'You tell your husband, but don't get the police right now.' I talked with the husband, and I got about two or three thousand dollars in 10s and 20s and 50s and laid 'em on the table. I said, 'She said he did, and he said he didn't. I'm not trying to buy him out of it, but money beats nothing.' That guy picked up that money and didn't look back."

I asked my informative acquaintance about the most famous fight, that stingy-brim night in Miami Beach, February 25, 1964, that momentous occasion when Liston was vanquished by Cassius Clay.

It was barely three months after the Kennedy assassination and the Liston-Clay title fight was the first blood revelry that a post-hysteric America allowed herself. The crowd that gathered at Miami's Convention Hall and all the other crowds—the bread-and-circuses populace—that gathered in the closed-circuit showrooms and theaters throughout America were there not so much to see a contest, for no contest was foreseen. An Associated Press poll of 32 boxing experts revealed that all but 2 predicted that Liston would win by a knockout. This sense of the inevitable evinced itself in the lackluster gate at Convention Hall, where only about half of the 16,000 tickets, priced from $20 to $250, were sold. What crowd there was seemed part of a masque in a season of psychic plague.

The air of festive anticipation was an unsettling one. The scent of dear perfume and fancy cologne mixed with that of cheap aftershave, smoke, and sweat. The oversize head of tough-guy manqué Norman Mailer was no longer alone in blocking the view at ringside. Beside him sat fellow tough guy Truman Capote and Gloria Guinness of *Harper's Bazaar.*

Clay's pulse had raced to 120 during the weigh-in, and the adrenaline of fear seemed still within him as he entered the ring. That fight-or-flee rush drove him forward and into Liston with a frenzy, and he took the first round. Sonny began to grind him down in the second, but his blows were delivered with none of the awesome power that in the past had felled man after man. In the third, Clay opened a cut under Sonny's eye, drawing forth what Sonny had given no other man since the days of those whippings. In the fourth, Sonny connected repeatedly, but again, his blows seemed oddly restrained, and Clay came in again to bruise Sonny's fearsome face.

At the end of round four, Clay came to his corner screaming surrender. "I can't see," he wailed to his trainer, Angelo Dundee. "Cut off my gloves. Call off the fight." At the sound of the bell, Dundee pushed Clay to his feet.

In the fifth, Clay, who claimed difficulty seeing, had no difficulty in dodging Sonny's punches, which seemed at times designed not so much to hit Clay as to punctuate the air of his blind bob-and-weave. Clay reached out his left arm and rested his gloved fist against Sonny's nose, as if to keep the beast at bay. Though Sonny's reach was greater, he never struck or swatted that arm away.

At the end of the round, Clay's vision returned, and Barney Felix, the referee, who was about to stop the fight and award a technical-knockout victory to Liston, allowed the match to continue. After six rounds, the fight was even on points. The bell sounded to signal the start of the seventh round, and Liston just sat there, refusing to come forth and talking of a numbness that ran from his left shoulder down to his forearm.

When Liston failed to come out of his corner in the seventh round, the man in the porkpie hat knew what others did not know.

"I had bet what we called a lot of money on Sonny," the man began. "Three or four thousand. Then I said, 'Sonny, I'm gonna put more money on you.'"

"He said, 'Don't put any more on me, man. Two heavyweights out there, you can't ever tell. . . . You've got enough bet.' That's as far as he would go with me.

"So, later on, after he lost the fight, I said, 'Sonny, why would you let me lose my last penny on a fight? . . . You could've at least pulled my coat.'

"He said, 'With your big mouth, we'd both be wearing concrete suits.'"

Bernie Glickman from Chicago was around that night. His son, Joel, said, "Right before the fight, my father called me up. He knew I liked to gamble and he knew I loved Liston. He said, 'Don't bet. There's something wrong. I don't know what it is.' I'll never forget that. I didn't listen."

A Chicago bookmaker remembered it all. "The biggest key to it was the odds. The fight was five-and-a-half-to-one, and by fight time it was down to about two-to-one. One guy, he called me from Vegas, he wanted to bet five grand on Clay. He was looking for four- or five-to-one, but I'd already heard they were down to three-to-one. So I said I'd give him three-to-one. But for a fight to have dropped down like that. And if you knew anything, there was no way Clay could hurt Liston."

I always thought it was a dive, had never believed the story about Liston's quitting because of a bad left shoulder. This was a man who had gone four rounds with a broken jaw and with no title at stake.

But no one I knew could figure the payoff angle. Then, one night in Chicago, a wise adviser told me to look to the East. To Mecca.

Liston had his crew in Miami: Pep Barone; his new managers, the Nilon brothers; Sam Margolis, an old partner of Blinky's; Joe Louis; Irving "Ash" Resnick, a Vegas hustler he had met while training for the second Patterson fight.

Among Clay's crew was Malcolm X. The two had met in 1962, and though Clay's interest in Islam had already blossomed by then, it was Malcolm who cultivated and, in Miami, completed Clay's conversion. Malcolm had fallen from grace with the leaders of the Nation of Islam in Chicago. He was afraid of violence. He saw Clay as a way to reinstate himself, and offered to deliver the fighter to the faith. He would bring him to the Savior's Day convention on the day after the big fight. The Chicago leaders believed Liston would win. But the idea of a Black Muslim champion held great power for them.

"They were rough people," Truman Gibson mused when I broached the subject.

Clay was the first great fighter in boxing's post-Carbo age. He had, so to speak, been born to freedom and was virgin meat as far as the Mob was concerned. Soon, when his contract with the Louisville Group expired, he signed with a Muslim manager.

A tithe for Islam surely would not be too much to ask of a man as blessed as Clay. And from that tithe Sonny might draw a portion. Clay had a big future. To Sonny, a man who felt rather than knew his age, a cut of that future might not have seemed a bad deal.

Soon after the fight, the victor proclaimed his conversion and announced his new name: Muhammad Ali. His jubilation was real. Knowing nothing of what Sonny knew, he had no reason to disbelieve that he was the greatest.

"White people wanted Liston to . . . kill poor little Clay," said the Honorable Elijah Muhammad, ruler of the Nation of Islam, on Savior's Day. "But Allah and myself said no. This assured his victory."

There are many stories of the immense losses Ash Resnick incurred in Miami by betting on his friend. There are whispers of suitcases of cash sent by Ash to New York, where other, less ostentatious bets were made.

The suspicions and trouble stirred by the Miami fight were such that no state with a reputation for boxing would sanction the rematch, and it was held before a sparse crowd at a schoolboy hockey arena in Lewiston, Maine. One thing is certain: in that May 1965 rematch—it was Liston-Ali then—Liston lay down in the first, revealing less acting ability than in the *Love American Style* episode in which he later appeared. "I had overtrained," Liston would say. But that fight was not merely a fix; it was a flaunted fix, foolishly attributed by interested observers to physical intimidation by Muslims reportedly gathered to seek revenge for the recent assassination of Malcolm X (who, as history would reveal, had in fact been murdered by members of his own faith).

In Denver, a month after losing the title, Sonny started getting into police trouble again. In March 1966, he moved to a home in Las Vegas purchased from financier Kirk Kerkorian. The house, at 2058 Ottawa Drive, in the exclusive area of Paradise Township, was less than a mile from where his buddy Joe Louis lived, at 3333 Seminole Circle, in a house bought from Johnny Carson.

During 1966–67, Liston fought abroad exclusively. "This fighting is for the bird," reads a letter of January 1967. In May of 1967, the Listons returned from Sweden with a three-year-old boy, Danielle, whom they said they had adopted.

"I'm my own manager now," Liston declared in the summer of 1967, a few breaths before musing, "All I need is a manager. Somebody with a nice, clean record." That fall it was rumored that Sammy Davis Jr. would take the job.

Interrupted by an arrest—for drunken driving, in February 1969—Sonny fought 10 fights between March 1968 and September 1969. He won them all, nine by knockouts. In December 1969, at Kirk Kerkorian's new International Hotel in Vegas, three-to-one underdog Leotis Martin knocked him out in the ninth.

There would be one more fight, with Chuck Wepner, on June 29, 1970. At the weigh-in and press conference a few days before that Jersey City fight, a reporter asked Liston if he would request a license to fight in New York, which had always been denied him.

"I'm on my way down," he snarled. "The hell with New York."

Wepner recalled that it was a surly motherfucker who looked down impassively at Wepner's hand when he extended it for a pre-fight shake before the press.

The fight ended in a win for Liston only when Wepner, one of the great warhorses of boxing, could no longer see.

Three men had flown from Las Vegas with Sonny to the Wepner fight: Johnny Tocco, Davey Pearl, and Lem Banker. Tocco—who died in 1997—had been Sonny's trainer in St. Louis and, at the time of the Wepner fight, was back with Liston again. Pearl, a legendary referee, performed duties usually taken care of by a manager. Banker was a Liston buddy, recently described by *The New York Times* as "perhaps one of the most successful gamblers in Las Vegas."

Pearl, who is now 80, took early-morning runs with Sonny. Some days, Liston wasn't home when Davey arrived. According to another friend, Gene Kilroy, Liston was, as often as not, shooting craps at Joe Louis's, where the fighters gambled on the bedroom floor. Joe, according to another close source, was a craps degenerate. Truman Gibson, Joe's old friend, claimed that America's most beloved boxer had also become a junkie. Gibson remembered Louis as so strung out that he was hearing voices from an air conditioner. Louis was hospitalized for a breakdown in 1970.

Banker—now 70—said that, sometime after the Wepner fight, a Las Vegas sheriff told him, "I know you're friendly with Sonny. Tell him he's hanging around the wrong people on the West Side. We're gonna bust these guys."

Charles Broadus, known as Doc, recalled running around with Sonny. "We drank together," and chased women. "We had fun. We'd run together day and night. We enjoyed what we was doing, and that was that." As far as Broadus knew, Sonny never messed with dope.

He did mess with girls. "Hey," Dean Shendal said. "Ever see him in the dressing room? Holy Christ, he could scare a horse." But no one who knew Liston believed that he was on dope. However, according to the man in the porkpie hat, he was selling it.

He had received a long letter from Sonny. "I guess everyone was upset over the fight," it said, in reference to the Miami mess, but it was good "to know I still have Friend. I know Friend ar much better then money." The letter ended, "I hope to see you when I get some money. I had not for got you."

On his way to visit his brother in Los Angeles, the man in the porkpie hat stopped in Vegas. It was maybe two weeks before Christmas 1970. "I came looking for Sonny and he wasn't at home, so I talked with Geraldine for a while. She said, 'Sonny has gotten unruly.' I said, 'Isn't he coming home for dinner?' She said, 'No, he doesn't trust me on food and things; he gets his little Kentucky Frieds and things, and you can catch him over there at the Hilton Hotel. You go to the casino, and if he's not there, you just stand there five minutes and he'll come through.'"

The Hilton—it was actually still the International—was only minutes from the Listons'. "I was there, I'd say, five minutes before he touched me on the shoulder. So we spent the evening together. We had both just ordered new Cadillacs. I had got mine, he was waiting for his. He wanted me to stay, but I had to go. He drove me to the airport." He did not seem unruly. "He was in a very friendly mood."

Another person who saw a lot of Sonny in those days was Ash Resnick, one of the owners of Caesars Palace. In 1974 he would be convicted of tax evasion for failing to report more than $300,000 skimmed from Caesars. (The decision was later overturned.) The same year, eight sticks of dynamite were found under Resnick's car. According to Dean Shendal, who had been his partner in Caesars, Ash put them there himself; they were "nothing but Texas saw-dust." Two years later, he was shot at, or so it seemed. Ash was, as comedian Shecky Greene put it, "a Damon Runyon character" who "could be very loyal and very good and then turn around and do something that you couldn't believe." Everybody loved Ash. But, as Lem Banker said, "nobody trusted him."

Though Resnick was often considered to have been Mobbed-down, those who knew him saw this as a self-perpetuated myth. His real connection, according to Shecky Greene, was "a New York man called Abe Margolis in the jewelry business. Every time he needed money or something, he'd get it from Abe. I think Abe is even the one who gave him money to go into Caesars."

Ash and Sonny were very, very tight, but no one could figure why. "Ash had him hypnotized," Dean said. "I don't know how."

Lem Banker saw Sonny a day or two before Christmas, when Sonny and Geraldine came by to visit. On the day after the holiday, Geraldine left town to visit her mother in St. Louis. She returned home at about half past eight on the night of January 5, 1971, to the smell of death.

Sonny Liston lay back in his underwear on the upholstered bench at the foot of his velvet-covered bed, his feet on the floor, his shoes and socks beside them. According to the report from the Clark County coroner's office, "Decedent was in a bloated condition and gas was escaping from his nose. Blood appeared to have come from the nose and it appeared that blood had soaked and dried in the bedspread at the decedent's head. Decedent's fingers appeared dehydrated."

According to the sheriff's office, a quarter-ounce of heroin was found in the kitchen. There was marijuana in the pocket of Liston's trousers. There was a glass of vodka on a nightstand, and on a dresser a .38 in a holster and a wooden cross. The television was on. On the basement bar lay Sonny's hat and the December 28 *Las Vegas Sun*. Papers from the 29th lay stacked on the porch.

Curiously, though news of Liston's death was published throughout the country on January 6, no mention of it was made in the *Las Vegas Sun* until January 7. A day later, the *Sun* ran a small piece under the heading NARCO AGENT LAST PERSON KNOWN TO HAVE SEEN SONNY LISTON ALIVE. According to the *Sun*, an unnamed undercover narcotics agent had visited Liston at home on December 30. The alleged sources of this information were "sheriff's detectives" who "refused to divulge the nature or reason" for the visit, "but did say Liston was in apparently good health."

Puncture marks were reportedly found on Liston's arms, and initially the cause of death was attributed to a drug overdose. After much controversy and further study, however, the death was reattributed to natural causes: lung congestion brought on by poor oxygen and nutrient blood supply to the heart muscles.

Some accepted this. Some believed that Sonny did indeed die on dope. But most of Liston's close friends cited his phobia of needles, a trait which had been evident as recently as the previous November, when he had been hospitalized. Chuck Wepner, who had fought Liston six months before, told me that Liston definitely didn't box like a junkie.

Many of Liston's pals say that he was murdered. "A friend of mine called me, said, 'Man, they found Sonny dead,'" one recalled. "I said, 'I'll be damned, they got to him.'" On the Strip, in joints in Chicago and St. Louis and New York, you hear many things: That Sonny was involved in a big dope deal. Or a shylocking operation. All sorts of things. It is necessary to remember that killing Sonny would have been no mean feat. The moment his killers started toward him, as somebody said, "that woulda been all she wrote." The consensus is that they put something in his drink, then gave him a hotshot. Dope, shylocking. Whatever it was, it came down to money.

Lem Banker, who is convinced that Sonny was murdered, spoke of an ex-cop imprisoned in Carson City who claimed that Ash Resnick offered him a contract to kill Sonny. The story is that Ash and Sonny had a big falling out. Over money. Banker doesn't believe the story. "Ash didn't have Sonny killed," he said. "Ash did a lot of things, but he wasn't a murderer."

Just as someone in Chicago had told me to look to the East, someone in St. Louis told me to look to the calendar.

You see, the answer—if there is one—may lie in the timing. If a deal with the Muslims had indeed been made whereby Liston was to receive in secret a percentage of all of Ali's future earnings, that deal would not have been worth much. Since early 1967, Ali had been inactive. There were no earnings. But in late 1970, a deal was brokered for an unheard-of $5 million fight with Joe Frazier.

By the time that fight was fought a few months later, Sonny lay beneath the Las Vegas dirt of the Garden of Peace at Paradise Memorial Gardens. A bronze plaque bears his name and the words A MAN.

The mystery of a death serves only to distract us comfortably from the mysteries inside ourselves. Ultimately, the true cause of Sonny's death was the mystery in him.

"He's dead, that's all," as Davey Pearl said. As another man said, he was born that way.

# 110

May 1, 1998

Dear Privileged Intimate:

The artist formerly known as Nick has disembodied. Those seeking communion have the following options:

· Electronic ███████████████
· Facsimile: ████████████

Those desiring his image and voice may find these at www.exitwounds.com.

Those wishing to make considerable financial offerings may seek his agent, Mr. Russell Galen, the president of the Scovil Chichak Galen Literary Agency, Inc., 381 Park Avenue South, Suite 1020, New York, NY 10016. Mr. Galen may be reached by telephone at (212) 679-8686, extension 302; by electronic mail at Rgalen@aol.com; and by facsimile transmission at (212) 679-6710.

The artist formerly known as Nick hopes to see you again on September 21, 2021, at the grand opening of his 1321 Club. Membership in this private club is by formal invitation only.

This information will not be repeated.

Πάντα ῥει

# 111

# Hymn for Charlie

Running in worn-out shoes into cars for insurance money, stealing moonlight that falls through the branches of trees. Defrost your heart, baby, crowbar them knees. Jesus comes on Sunday in a big old car: whitewall tires, suicide clutch, and the smell of gasoline. But out here, it's a long way from Sunday: notes sweet and strangled and crying for life, or another drink, or more of that moonlight, through amps that got none. Things out here that Memphis never seen: wildflowers on fire with the Lord's gasoline. Blood running out of one vein, Holy Ghost pumping something new in the other wrist. Feel that hand start fluttering, making sounds on them strings like this. Defrost your heart, baby, blow a kiss this lonesome way.

Theft of moonlight: 99 years. White car coming, baby, have no fear. Put away that liquor, lay down those pills: he twice born will be twice killed.

# 112

To: Russell Galen
Subject: ████████

Dear Russ:

Thanks for your e-mail regarding the new ██████████ bullshit.

I should like this lawyer, or whatever the fuck he is, to be advised that he should go fuck himself and his mother. If his mother is dead, he should dig her up, then fuck her.

I should like ████████████ to be advised that the aforementioned lawyer, or whatever the fuck he is, has killed the deal and the understanding between ██████ and myself.

Regarding the specific item, i.e., the $10,000 up front for the option coming out of ██████'s pocket, the price, thanks to the intervention of this lawyer, or whatever the fuck he is, is now $20,000. Furthermore, this $20,000 is to be paid in full before June 15, or there will be no deal at all: nothing for little ██████ to peddle, no movie for little ██████ to play producer.

We have here entered the realm of no compromise: $20,000 in my fucking pocket by next Monday, or that's that.

Please convey all this to Sally Wilcox at CAA.

I'll look forward to talking with you soon, buddy. For now, as ever, all best.

*Sincerely,*
*Nick*

# 113

# Please Be Quiet—Please

Raymond Carver's collected poems arrived as I was engaged in annotating an anthology of my work spanning the last thirty years. Introducing an early poem of mine, I deliberated on parenthetically inserting the modifier "bad" before the noun "poem." Thus this book, entitled *All of Us* (Alfred A. Knopf, $27.50) arrived just in time, telling me that, while honesty is noble and perspective valuable, there is really no need to show my hand. Much of this collection of Carver's so-called poetry is, indeed, more than parenthetically bad. Yet it is presented, by a somewhat reputable publisher, replete with formal textual back-matter, as poetry pure and simple.

To me, Raymond Carver's words of writerly prose are like so many blades of dry, brittle weed in dead air: weeds sprouting from the cracks in the thick concrete of a stifling middle-class morality and an insufferable middle-class manner. He wrote as if the writing were an end and not a means as well; and he wrote badly in that his technical proficiency, instead of articulating what was within him, was merely the well-laid surface of the concrete that separated feeling from expression.

Poetry demands a greater technical proficiency than prose. Rather than being merely the funny-looking arrangement of lines on a page by which most recognize it, poetry—the real thing—cannot be made without a good working knowledge of rhythm, the colors of words, and, especially—when they are to be forsaken—the metrics of the ages of which a poem is merely an echo. One cannot make new meter without being steeped in the old. As T. S. Eliot said, "There is no escape from metre; there is only mastery," and free verse "is only possible for a poet who has worked tirelessly with rigid forms and different systems of metric."

Too much of Carver's "poetry" is not poetry. As if unaware and incapable of the essential powers of rhythm, Carver wrote verse that was too often little more than that mere funny-looking arrangement of lines on a page. But not even rhythm could have resurrected some of these lines from the dead, for they are of the most mundane and prosaic kind. I here open the volume at random. Beneath the good title "Mesopotamia" lie these dreary lines:

> Waking before sunrise, in a house not my own,
> I hear a radio playing in the kitchen

A few pages later, beneath the bad title "The Possible":

> I spent years, on and off, in academe.

This plain statement—and that is all it is; the lines go downhill from there—is telling. It illuminates the nature of what is wrong not only with these words that Carver placed oddly on the page but those words, too, that he placed in proper prose form. He was, ultimately, a writer of academe: too cerebral for his own good and possessed of a solipsism that led him to think that waking to the sound of a radio was an experience worth expressing. As such, academe has embraced him, and it will doubtless embrace this collection.

There are moments when Carver approaches something like poetry, as in "Spring, 480 BC" and a few others here. But for each of those moments, there are a multitude that present themselves with opening lines such as "You soda crackers! I remember when I arrived here in the rain."

In fact, one need not waste time reading Carver's verse, as the appended index of first lines says it all. Again at random:

> Hanging around the house each day,  39
> Happy to have these fish,  121
> He arose early, the morning tinged with excitement,  260
> He began the poem at the kitchen table,  200

To regard this stuff as poetry is to buy into and further the lie that poetry is the desiccated and self-absorbed preciosity that today commonly bears its name. This book is, for the most part, nothing more than some mediocre, boring shit written by a guy too boring to be bad. (Don't worry, this can't hurt his feelings, he's dead.) The problem, in the end, is not that this is not poetry. The problem is that it is not much of anything else, either.

I was paid, albeit quite modestly, to linger amid these lines. I suggest that others await a similar circumstance.

# 114

These poems, written over the years 1992–97, form part of the collection *Chaldea.*

## Hymn to Paean, Physician of the Gods

This is the season of the nine sorrows,
when the gods turn away from souls
and leave them for the beaks of the scavengers,
Erebos-birds, and worse.

In this season, all remembrance turns to dust,
a resonance, a dying chord, occult and unspeakable,
in the immense empty chill of a tideless hour.

In this season, sorrow caverns me like an illness;
in this season, only prayer can heal, and I wait,
incanting, biding, over the corpse of magic.

In this season, I as always refuse to die,
for I am born to eat the flesh of scavengers,
am born to watch over the corpse, to protect it
from the desecration of medicine and thought,
till it doth rise, like a glory, within me,
and the nine sorrows return to the earth,
freeing my kind to receive the season of manumission,
to lie on our backs beneath Dyaus Pitar
and the soaring things that drink and sing its gold.

In that season shall strength return
with its old caress and purse of moments,
its hungers and its light.

## All of Gust and Sigh

May what has been given us,
        this tidal sigh of breath,
give life in turn
        to what lies in us,
unimagined, holy,
        and waiting to be born.

## Old Nick's Song of Songs

Some guys go for the bra-zeer region,
Some guys, they like the Greek,
Some gents prefer the delta of Venus;
To each man his meat.
Me, I'm sort of a blow-job guy,
I never stick it in below.

## May the Gods without Names Redeem Me

I pray to a memory
I kneel before a weathered stele
I invoke the stars of an ancient blessing
I utter the names of phantoms
I carry within me the soul of the savioress
I know the way to the sea
I open tombs
I seek the air
I know the colors of breath

## Ptolemy II

Behold me,
            Ptolemy,
who once was capable of love
            but now am not.

Know that on the eve of the celebration of your birth,
            when I slew and severed into many
            our son,
I did unto him else besides,
            and blest him too;
and the gods smiled down, as they do now, upon me,
            Ptolemy,
who once did love,
            but now do not.

## Dante in Ravenna

From where he stood, he could see it:
the ocean's edge:
the slate-colored sea and the breaking wintry froth
that was the color of the moon

She had dreamt it all—the glimpse
in the narrow street, the parting, and the star that
three times shone; but she had not dreamt this.
Always she had said the souls of the dead
were drawn away by tides; and so he had come here
to wait.

Day came in the east, and the slate-colored water
went golden with swallowed starlight from beneath;
and he stood there, meeting the sun of his fortieth year.
And in that breath that bore no power and drew no light,
in that dead Lenten moment, that susurrus,
that copse of ended evening
        at the edge of the woods of raging sadness,
        the edge of the woods of raving madness,
it came and seized the source of breath itself, and all within,
        deliverer, redeemer, inspirer,
        demoness of eleven names and more;
        divider of destinies and days;
        beloved.

## Contrapasso

Without breeze
and having forsaken all wisdom
and knowing no poem
or human soul
can save me,
I lay myself down
and await whatever god
bears mercy and power in measure.

Eternal stranger, bear me.
Eternal stranger, rise.
Eternal stranger, bear me.
Eternal stranger, rise.
I give myself to you
who gather the pieces of me.

## From the Dream-book of Artemidorus

I walked with the coward Christ into the desert beyond
    defiance.

He spoke of the properties of certain stones,
not as one expounding might, but as one summoning,
        uneasily, unsurely
        what once had been held clear in mind
        and close to heart, but long had been let go.
Green basalt, lapis, syenite:
        these are the stones whose natures
        can be made to govern
        the winds that deliver
        one to good and one to bad,
        one to darkness, one to light.
Red jasper, haematite,
        the daimon-stones: therein seek
        the dividers of destinies in their wrath.
Carnelian, schist: as breeze to soul,
        one to the other.
And on, until his words were done.
I turned away and took him.

## Invocation

Let's see a show of hands.
I want to know. Who among us—
        man, woman, or beast—
Jerks off standing up.
I want to know: who's strong, who's tough.
I want to go back to Homeric days.

Let's see a show of hands.
I want to know. Who among us—
        man, woman, or beast—
Lives by a code.
Be it of good or evil, it matters not.
But I want to know: who's strong, who's tough.
I want to go back to Homeric days.

## What the Coptic Guy Said

Louie remembered what the Coptic guy said:
*If you bring forth what is within you,*
*what you bring forth will save you.*
*If you do not bring forth what is within you,*
*what you do not bring forth will destroy you.*

# 115

From *Scratch,* a novel I have been writing since 1994, and which I believe to be the best thing I have until now written.

# Excerpt from *Scratch*

## 3

Jabbo descended to the town. He took a swig, rounded a sloping bend that curved through a cleft between two rocky knolls. The boughs of the trees that grew vertically from the banks of that cleft formed a bower over the road, a tangled vaulted arch that shut out the sun. As he entered into those bowered shadows, the town vanished; it was no more, and for a moment he thought it may or may not ever have been; and he took another swig. And then he emerged, and there it was, beneath him.

He slowed down, lowered the window, drank the silence and the weft of the birds through it; the smell of black upturned earth and clover and the sweet lucent air and blossoming trees. He did not know birds by their sounds, and he did not know trees. Pigeons, yes, their gross guttural cooing he knew. And gulls. And oaks, they were the ones with the acorns; and the one the Chinks in Chinatown called tree-of-heaven, ailanthus, that bitter weed-tree of his life, of the crevices and the gratings and the alleyways that used to be. But beyond that, no. And that made it all the more something of wonder, this weft of the birds and the soft shimmering of the branches in the breeze beneath the sun like a radiant golden planchet in the endless cerulean sky. He finished the last of the liquor, threw the bottle from the car, hearing it shatter against stone, adding his signature to the rhapsody of the stillness and the birdsong and the shimmering.

A small spotted beetle lighted on his forearm. He shook it violently away. That was the trouble with nature. It was always crawling all over you.

He would be able to get himself a pint up ahead. There had to be a liquor store. There had to be.

And gas. He was running low. He looked at his watch. He'd been driving for close to five hours. How far was he from New York? he wondered. Far enough, he figured, far enough.

Fuck the pint. He'd get a fifth. He'd get a fifth and maybe spend the night. Think things over, figure out where he was going from here.

> The live ones or the dead ones,
> The tied-down-on-the-bed ones;
> I dig girls,
> Whoa-oh, baby, yeah, I dig you.

Oh, yeah, baby, I dig you. I dig you. I sure dig you. Oh, yeah, baby, I sure dig you.

He wished Sam was with him. Or somebody like her. He could start his life all over for real then, like he wanted to. They could be alone together, like in that storybook picture from when he was a kid.

He lighted a cigarette, blew smoke. He told himself he would quit drinking. He would get the fifth, and after that was done, he would quit. He could do it. On his own. He'd done it before. On his own. The drinking only made things worse. It no longer worked like it used to. It used to bring him oblivion, and that oblivion was sweeter than a mother, sweeter than any broad. It was like church to him. It vanquished the demons. It delivered him from misery and destroyed the world, within him and without him; the world and all time. But then it changed, and he grew as miserable in oblivion as in wretched dry existence. And the demons were no longer vanquished by it; they thrived on it, grew more powerful and fearsome, as if that oblivion was succor to them now instead of him, sustaining and strengthening them as it sapped and debilitated him; as if even it, so cherished by him, had abandoned him like all cherished things. And yet he remained chained to it, as its pleasures became agonies, as it caused him to fall and to crawl and to vomit the blood and the lining of his stomach, as it gave the demons form and voice; as it delivered him to one intensive-care unit after another, then summoning him to rise, slip the catheters from his wrists, and drink again. And he did not want to end up back in the hospital. He could not end up back in the hospital. Not now. It was as simple as that: he couldn't, for he no longer existed.

Helen drew the curtains against the daylight and knelt forward into the bed. She shut her eyes, feeling nothing but the deep drumming labor of her heart within the weakness of her body. It was a weakness not of weariness or illness, though she was indeed weary and was indeed ill. It was the weakness of a body coming apart, of the withering of muscle and the brittling of bone, the wasting away of tendons and ligaments that held them together. It was the weakness of a malnutrition and an atrophy that had seeped from spirit to substance, the coming apart of a body forsaken by the mind as the mind had been forsaken by the soul.

The town was real, but it was like the town in the train set at the department store at Christmas; not a hamlet, bigger than that, with a broad main avenue and a sort of square with a big bank building with a big dome roof, and church spires off in the distance, but, yes, there were old wooden houses with old wooden trim—not cottages, or maybe they were, what the hell did he know; cottages didn't have to be made of stone and thatched roof, they could be just quaint little houses, couldn't they? And though most of these old wooden houses were big, some of them were, yes, quaint and little, and some of them, many of them, especially near to the main avenue, set back from the shaded streets that intersected it, weren't old and wooden, but old and made of stone, not brick but stone—and there were trees and winding paths, trees and trees and trees, as if, big domed bank building and spires and all, the place was as much woodland as town, and it was, yes, overwhelmingly it seemed to be, you could feel it, quiet and without time, like in a dream without fear. You could hear the people no more than the birds, it seemed, and even the cars and the pick-up trucks seemed to move and to huff in a hushed and easy way. And there was that stuff, it was everywhere, all green and rust-colored, amid the hillocks and trees and rocks where the road leading to town became the big broad avenue of the town; that stuff, like in the train set, what did they call it? Lichen, that was it, they called it lichen; it came in little spongy clumps and you could glue it by the tracks or the depot or wherever you wanted. Only this wasn't spongy clumps and it wasn't glued down, it was real; and he must have seen this stuff, this real stuff, God only knew how many times before in how many places, but he had never thought of it as such before. As lichen, that is, or as anything. And there was no train in sight, but, yes, entering town, there were tracks that crossed the road, old rotted wood ties and rails sunk deep in the blacktop.

Jabbo pulled into the gas station beyond the big bank building, where the broad avenue, becoming once again a road, leading out of town, across a bridge, instead of into it, dwindled to a row of old brick warehouses and mills and over-grown lots and the sound and smell of sawing and sawdust, the sawing too, like the cars and the pick-ups, somehow muted.

"Howdy," the grease monkey said.

"Howdy," Jabbo said. He got out of the car, stretched, breathed away the lingering sensation of motion, breathed in the feel of this place, quiet and without time, like in a dream without fear. He looked around himself, smiled through the sickly electric haze of the booze in his blood and brain. For a moment the air settled the nausea in his guts and was like balm on that deeper illness, quelling his consciousness, sweet and soothing to the open wound inside him. For a moment he forgot about that cell, forgot about Harry, forgot that the dead matter between his legs was dead or even there, forgot that he did not exist. For a moment.

The grease monkey smiled to him. He smiled to the grease monkey. He glanced at the grease monkey's crotch, as a faggot might do. He was doing that more and more lately, glancing at the crotches of men, at those who still possessed the power that had left him.

"Where can I get a bottle around here?" Jabbo asked, knowing full well that he could find a bottle on his own, granted that there was one to be found, granted that this was not a dry county, but wanting to ask, enjoying the asking, the novelty of it, the unaccustomed nonchalant friendliness of it. This grease monkey here, lost in this quiet without time, born into it likely, he didn't know about that cell or about Harry or about any of it. To him, hell, Jabbo was just a man like him. A little older than him, maybe, and therefore due that much more respect, but a just a man like him all the same. And this is what neighborly strangers did in places such as this, Jabbo told himself: they engaged in the gentlemanly art of conversation.

Jabbo peered into shadowy clutter of the open office adjoining the garage. What an easy fucking joint this would be to rob.

"McGill's," the grease monkey said. He gestured with a toss of his head in the direction whence Jabbo had come. "Right off the square, just past the hardware."

"What about a place to stay?"

"Hotel here, guy who has it, he's just waitin' to die, place is fallin' apart, only folks he gets, folks waitin' to do die too, old folks, got nowhere to go, they go there. Them and a few, what you call, these here history buffs, come through once in a while. Somebody stayed there once, somebody who shot somebody or some such thing. They'd rather set there, look at that overhead fan, than be out the motel by the college with the rest of 'em, I guess. That's your nearest place, really, the motel, out toward the college, thirty, thirty-five miles out aways, turn off on Route 21 up here aways. Other than that, you got a few of these inns and such, these bed-and-breakfast deals, this quaint sorta thing, over here aways. This time o' year, off-season, not a bad deal. Clean, quiet, you like that sorta thing." He gestured again with another, vaguer toss of his head. He told Jabbo that there were three inns, and he gave him directions to the best of them.

Jabbo stood there, enjoyed the rich smell of the gasoline, the soft squeak of the squeegee as the grease monkey cleaned the windshield.

An inn. Jabbo had never stayed at an inn. He was going to go down the Jersey shore that time, to that inn there, with Dorothy, but he ended up getting pinched, and they never went. And he knew that guy that had that place upstate there, what's-his-name there from the joint on Hester Street; he'd been invited but he'd never gone.

Jabbo paid the grease monkey, tipped him a fin, for there, Jabbo told himself, but for the grace of God went he, and because a fin in a fucking place like this was a fucking fin; it bought respect and gratitude and deference, as it should, and was not taken lightly or for granted.

"Why, thank you, sir," the grease monkey said, "thank you very much."

Hell, a deuce would have played just as well. Come to think of it, this guy was likely doing better than that fucking bank, sticking up everybody in town, milking a fortune out of every transmission and every muffler with this garage of his. He should've given this guy shit, that's what he should've given him, he should've given him shit. Fuck this guy. Fuck this guy and his dick that worked. The smile drained from Jabbo's face. He got in the car, shut the door, and pulled out hard over gravel and weeds.

He got him his fifth, and a carton of smokes, and he found him the inn.

It was set back in sunlight amid gloom, among spruce and pine and tall red cedar that filled the air with scent; and the spandrels and turned posts, the balusters and rails of the wooden porch were smoky blue and white, the colors of the little berry cones, like juniper, that dappled the green of those tall red cedars, and all around the mossy stonework base of that porch, blooming from the thick bushy tangle of dark heart-shaped leaves that surrounded it, there was more blue and white, clusters of violets blossoming in the first breath of spring. The face of the inn, all that Jabbo could see of it, uncoursed mortared rock of deep brown hues, was lush with clinging vine like tendrils of a verdant embrace that perhaps had been upon a time demure and playful but now had grown rapacious and deadly and seemed about to subsume the place, to swallow it and silence it and quench its light in the damp leafy cloak and clutch of its sovereignty. The windows, trimmed in what once must have been that same smoky blue and white but long since faded to grey, were like eyes looking out from beneath that embrace, eyes of sad calm no longer telling or beholding; and only one, alone and gabled, higher than some of the spruce and the cedar but not than the pine, peered out above the reach of the tendrils.

Jabbo told the lady that he wanted that room, the one up there by itself with that lone gable window. There seemed to be no one else around, just him and just her. She was older than Jabbo, maybe in her late forties, and she moved as if she had been here all her life, here in this very place, amid the scent of the spruce and the pine and the cedar, amid the sunlight and the gloom and the creep of the vine, hearing nothing but the birds in the air of that scent. She was nice. Jabbo liked her. The way she smiled. Her tits too. They were nice. Being alone with her, here, in this place, like this, felt good.

All he brought in with him was the fifth in a paper sack and the carton of smokes, and she looked at those things and at him in a funny sort of way. And then she smiled. It all seemed so natural. Everything about her seemed natural. Her smile was as natural as the funny sort of way she had looked at him and his fifth in its paper sack and his carton of smokes. It did not occur to Jabbo that she could smell the liquor on his breath too, and the smoke, that she looked upon him as liquor and smoke, a creature of those things, arrived oddly before her bearing his sustenance and nothing else.

"How long will you be staying with us?" she asked him, and as she did she seemed taken by the whimsical notion of this being a fanciful question to ask of one who might at any moment combust spontaneously, go up in a puff of stale smoke and alcohol fumes. This made her smile, and looking at him made her smile some more. There was something about this stranger, something behind that pallid skin and bloodshot, bleary eyes.

"I don't know. A day or two."

"And how would you like to pay?"

"Cash." He withdrew a few hundred-dollar bills from his left pocket, held them in his hand.

"That's not necessary," she said. "You can pay when you leave."

She was nice, all right. Her tits too. They were nice, all right. He liked her. She was sweet, all quiet and easy and all alone in the breeze and scent and stillness of these parts; all alone and waiting, waiting for something, a man, a man like him. So sweet, so quiet, so easy she would be when she caressed him, healing him, saving him, up in that room. And when he was whole again, when he was a man again, he would devour her, fuck her mouth and her ass and her cunt until she was possessed and there was nothing in this world but him and them as the vines and the earth swallowed this place, devoured it, dark and damp, as he devoured her, and it would not matter, none of it, the end of the world and the end of this place, and she will never have known that he had not been whole, that he had not been a man, only that he had been the end that she had awaited all this time in the breeze and the quiet and the faint sad scent like juniper.

They were alone, now, in the stillness of this moment, in the bated uncreaking breath of this place in the middle of nowhere. He could take her now, get the gun from the glove compartment and take her now, take her upstairs and tie her to the bedposts and gag her and blindfold her so that she could not look upon him. He could do that, and he could drink some, then be gone.

"Here to fish?" she said. She said this to every man who arrived without a woman, said this to all of them, did not care, was not really interested; it was just something she said.

"Pole's in the trunk," he said. That might not be a bad idea: sober up, dry out, lay back, do some fishing, think things over. He could get him a rod and reel at that hardware back there. You put the sinker on the line, the bait on the hook, and you waited. Nice and peaceful, you waited. It could not be that hard to get the hook out of the fish's mouth; he could figure it out easy enough, with no one there to watch and judge and mock him and see him as a man who could not do what a child could do, and after that it would not matter who was there to watch him, because he would have no trouble getting that hook out, he would be like a man doing manly things, and if anybody looked at him funny or said something about how he fished, he would tell them that this was the way we did it when we were kids, we were city kids and we did not know, and they would respect that, looking upon him as a tough guy from the city—no, better, as a tough kid who had grown into a seasoned and sensitive man, as one both street-smart and wise, having led a full life, fuller than theirs, and having come here to pause and to reflect and let them bask in his wisdom and his worldliness, and they would not know that he had never fished, which was a manly thing that men must do, and was scared to take the hook out of the mouth, which was a manly thing that men must do, that he was scared to gouge himself or get bit. They could grill the fish outdoors, him and her. Grill them over the sweet-smelling kindling from the trees. She would clean them and bone them, smile to him as the sun went down, smile as someone falling deeply in love, and the sun going down would be like the end of the world, and she would let him do anything to her, want him to do anything to her, and by then, by that time, he will have been whole, she will have healed and cured him and surrendered herself to him as she had surrendered herself to nothing but the stillness and the breeze and the loneliness and the longing that were the mornings and the evenings of her life before there was him. And the fish would crackle in the kindling smoke, like when men cooked trout at a campfire in the movie, alone in the wilderness, alone with themselves and strong, only he would be stronger for he had her, and he would be the only man, uncompared to any other, the only man in her world, in their world, the world of this dream that was theirs, that was safe and secure from the world of fears and lies that he had left behind, for that world could never enter through her, for she protected him from it, and where there had been many lies, there would now be only one, the lie of this moment, the lie of this dream, which would be made true by her belief, be made to feel like truth anyway, and that would be good enough, would be more than he had ever known; and it would smell so good, and it would taste so good, better than anything he'd ever tasted before, for he'd never tasted anything like that before, never eaten fish that was fresher than what you could buy in a store or a restaurant, never eaten fish that was cooked over sweet-smelling kindling gathered from the sun-warmed damp close around of pristine piney ground; never done these things, though he must not tell her so, for to her he brought worldliness and manliness and the knowledge of the experience of all things that lay beyond her; and he would wash it down with cool spring water, for he did not drink, and clear water was what a clear mind craved, was the nectar of clarity and peacefulness and strength; and he did not need liquor to lie down beside her, because they were as one, and his lungs in that bed no longer choked from the must of old demons; and they would not speak, there would just be the sounds of the crickets and the birds in the last rays of light through the shivering trees, and they would shiver too later beneath the quilt, and he would sleep without dreams, and morning would bless them and it would all still be real.

"Do you like trout?" he asked her, slipping the bills back in his pocket. Shit, he thought, she would ask him to sign the register, fill out some sort of card, and he had forgotten the name on his license. But she did not ask him to sign any register, did not ask him to fill out any card, nothing.

All she did was look at him funny again. She did not understand why anyone would travel any distance to come to a body of still and placid water that no one in these parts even called a lake. They called it a pond. And to her that pond was not a place of romance or reverie, but a murky pool of melancholy purlings, a brooding-place, a breeding-place, whether in sunlight or evening's stained-glass shadows, of all those dismal and elusive hauntings that brought down a soul in sadness, as if to the baleful and devastating emptiness, the nothingness of place and time and spirit, that lurked beneath that stillness and placidity.

"You come here to fish trout?" No, she did not understand why men, like fools with no souls to be brought down, came here to fish the simple sunless slimy creatures of that brooding; she did not understand. But she knew that this man was not one of them.

"I could smell it in the pan now," he said, grinning, as a man should grin, seeing her in the sunset, feeling the breath of her against him. But you did not use a pan with a grill, or did you? But the men, alone in the wilderness, they used a pan. And hickory wood. It must be hickory wood they used. That was the only wood whose smell he knew of, though he did not know the smell itself. That and pine, of course. But it was not just pine he smelled outside here. There was something sweeter, gentler, stranger. Maybe that was hickory. Yes, hickory-smoked trout. He had seen that once, in a store or on a menu. But it wasn't the same on a menu, it wasn't real, like here; it was a racket, it was bullshit, all bullshit. Like what's-his-name's joint there. That cocksucker. But he got him, all right, he really got him that night. Got sick of his fucking shit and gave it to him. *How come you call this a 'talian rest'rant?* Should've broke that fucking wine bottle across his fucking Genoese face. He should have. You hold it in, it's no good. You hold things in, they eat away at you.

Yeah, nice tits for an old bag. Bite off her nipples and use them for bait. Maybe that's what Andy and Opie used. Aunt Bee, she had big ones. Yeah, Monday nights, remember? Eight, nine years old. That stone skipping across the surface of that lake, and that whistling. Found that folded instruction sheet from the tampon package in the street. Good stuff. Showed it around. Left it spread out on the teacher's desk, heh heh heh.

Hickory-smoked tit-meat, heh heh heh. Maybe invite her up for a drink. Romance. That's what these broads want: romance. Tit-meat sizzling in the pan. Mmm, just like mom made. Heh heh heh.

She placed the key in his open hand, and he slowly ascended the stairs, the carton of smokes under his arm and the paper-wrapped neck of the fifth in his fist. He thought of the way she smiled, the way she put the key in his hand. She was looking for it, all right. Oh, she wanted it, all right, that bitch; she wanted it.

Beneath the high slant of broad rafters and roof beams, the walls were a light airy blue. But the floorboards and furnishings were all of dark wood, a shared darkness of hue that seemed to have been arrived at through common age and atmosphere rather than by common origin or design. A large ornate armoire, a crude small table and two armchairs by the whispering sheer curtains of the lone gable window, the carved posts, head board, and foot board of the bed, a night-table on which rested an old black rotary telephone and an amber glass ashtray atop a crocheted doily: the varied grains, the heartwoods and sapwoods of these things, their stains and finishings, were all now as from one wood, seeped and shrouded in dim cloistered time. And it was this dark wood, this shadow-wood, that cast its spell over the light breeziness of blue walls and high ceilings, that gave the room its somber air.

Jabbo stripped to his skivvies and lighted a smoke. He poured liquor into a glass from the bathroom and he sat by the lone gable window and drank it. He laid the dead fingers of one hand upon his crotch, thinking of her, downstairs, breathing and moving about beneath him as she pictured him, thought of him with his hand upon his crotch, above her, alone with her in this place. With the dead fingers of his other hand he smoked and drank. In time, the hand upon his crotch grew still, dead fingers on dead flesh; and only the other hand stirred, as he smoked and he drank and he gazed from the open gable window, seeing nothing but the sky turning grey above the spruce and the cedar and the pines, hearing nothing but the pressure of his blood and a faint dire shrillness in his ears.

He drank down the better part of the fifth. The sun going down through the trees was a dull ebbing glare, colorless and diffuse, in the grey of the sky. He stared into it, through the muscae that swarmed his vision like bright shifting translucent insects, that were to his seeing as the faint dire shrillness was to his hearing; stared into it, letting the dull ebbing glare infuse his mind, until the throbbing in his brain and in the sky were one, colorless and diffuse, a fading empty bleat. He raised himself up, staggered slowly to his jacket, which lay on the bed; groped through its pockets, withdrew a little plastic straw and a small foil-wrapped bundle. He stood there awhile, as if lost, swaying slightly in static ataxia. He staggered to the toilet, fumbled at the opening of his shorts, and drew out his cock. His flesh was clammy and unpleasant to his touch, but the air upon it felt good. Nothing came. He flexed the muscles of his abdomen, feeling a dull pain in his side and seeing his sickly cock twitch as he strained, until at last he pissed, his urine splashing from him in spurts, then streaming long and hard, dark and burning. Reaching out and steadying himself against the wall with the fist that clenched the straw and foil-wrapped bundle, he leaned forward over the toilet and retched. Nothing came. He had not eaten in three days, had taken in only booze and smoke; but nothing came, not even of the booze, nothing of its bitter black silt, its saburra of clotted poisons and poisoned blood. With the back of his clenching hand, he wiped the watery drool of spittle from his mouth, the watery tricklings from his bloodshot eyes. Breathing heavily, he staggered back to the window. He poured another drink and lighted a cigarette. He drank and he smoked. He opened the foil-wrapped bundle, which held five glassine packets of heroin. He smoothed the aluminum foil upon the table with his hand, then emptied three of the packets along the center crease of the foil, forming a ridge of crystalline white powder. He placed the straw between his lips, raised the foil toward him, leaned over it, ran the flame of his lighter beneath it, sucked through the straw at the smoke that rose from the smoldering dope, again and again, until all that was left of that crystalline white powder ridge was a thin tracing tarry stain. Then he drank some more, and he closed his eyes, and when he opened them, the dull ebbing glare was gone and the owl-light of the grey sky was dwindling, and the branches of the spruce and the cedar and the pines could be heard more than seen, shadows stirring amid shadows in the rising chill of moonless night. He did the last two dimes and emptied what remained of the bottle into the glass, filling it nearly to the brim. He lighted a cigarette and sat there, trembling in the chill, staring at the liquor in the glass, at the owl-light glimmering in the night-darkened amber. The slits of his dead eyes narrowed in the mask of his dead face. Then the owl-light vanished, from the amber in the glass, from the slits of his eyes, from the pallor of his flesh, which shuddered now like that of a newborn bird fallen frail and naked to the ground. He did not drink much more, but made sure to leave the glass nearly full, that it would be there should he need it, that the knowledge of its being there would comfort him, that he would not be left alone in fear and pain to perish without even the dregs of his sanctuary.

In the cold sweat and fever of his endless night, Jabbo, limbless in his damnation, slithered through dank undergrowth and black slime. Floundering in the terror of his new form, flailing phantom legs and arms, suffocating with the agony of summoning all strength and force and power to stir and impel appendages that no longer were there, growing ever weaker and more paralyzed with the exhaustion of that impotent summoning strain, until the strength and force and power themselves no longer were there, not even within him, and all that remained within him was the silent scream of unendurable helplessness and unendurable horror and unendurable fear, and only the paroxysms of that horror and that fear compelled him forward in the asphyxiating cocoon of his new and horrible form, forward into the dank undergrowth and black slime of eternity, an eternity that was both infinite and constricting, all-swallowing and all-smothering. Each paroxysm drove him not only forward but downward, as gravity and his panic conspired to draw him ever more deeply beneath the sucking surface of the slime, toward where other things slithered, greater than him and more unspeakable and more unthinkable and more horrible than himself, slithered not in spasms of impotence and fear but in the slow massive undulations of creatures immeasurable in their whole.

With an explosion of blood pressure and pulse, he woke with a gasp, only to find that he was a serpent dreaming as serpents do. He was cool, like the mossy rock on which he lay. He slid from beneath the shade of broad leaves. The sunlight felt good. He drew warm air deep into his lungs. There was no sound. He moved through the grass fluidly and silently, wondering where the sounds of the world had gone. He began to suspect that he still lay asleep on cool rock beneath the shade of broad leaves, lulled by the vibrations of the earth through the smooth scales of his belly. Then, in the silent meadow before him, he came upon the scarf-skin of his kind: a still ghost, pale and tawny, dewy with the traces of the stranger who had shed it. He crept slowly to it, slipped forward the pink fork of his tongue to taste the dewy beads like tears. Then he felt a faint sound in the silence: the gliding presence, not far off, of the one whose slough it was. He wove toward it through the glade, feeling that its own movement had ceased, that it awaited him. Still there was no sound in the world but the sound of him and of the stranger. Then its eyes, the black and the emerald of that awaiting, were upon him. His heart quivered, obscuring the subtle vibrations of the earth, and the cloaca of his sex stirred beneath him against damp dead leaves. The stranger raised its head, opened its soft cloud-colored mouth to him. Suddenly his fate, their fate, saddened him. His heart slowed, and the vibrations of the earth reverberated through that sadness, penetrating it, deepening it, echoing it with the waves of silent sadness of the world itself. He wished to wake from this dream, to slink from beneath the shade into the sunshine and breathe the warm air and feel the sounds of lush life around him and the exhilaration of the tangled thicket roots against his scales as he wandered with a full belly to the water to drink, to be rid of this dream with its strange sudden sadness, its pleasance turned to dread. But the sense of sadness at his fate grew deeper, for he seemed now to recall that he, asleep or awake, had not been born to this world in the form now reflected to him in those black and emerald eyes; that he, the consciousness and pulsing organs in this coiled sheath, had been born long ago into another flesh, had fallen from that to this graceless state. And so too it was with the stranger, from whose soft cloud-colored mouth now came a whimper, a lone high note of mourning from some undreamt, unknown, and frightening place within. And the whimper, that lone high note, became a cry, and drew from him, wrenched from him, sucked from some like undreamt, unknown, and frightening place within himself, a cry of his own, which resounded in violent tremor through the length of him; and their cries became one, grew deafening and shrill, and the vortex of it turned the world to a scream, the hill on which they lay and the trees all around and the valley and town below, and it bore them away, that scream, in a storm of shrieking blackness, and he could not wake, not from beneath the shade of broad leaves, or from beneath eternity, or from beneath the dead weight of himself; he could not wake.

With an explosion of blood pressure and pulse, he woke with a gasp, only to find that he had already drunk the last of the whiskey. He had no more, no pills, no nothing. He cursed himself and the world. His body quaked and he was too weak to stand. He fell again upon the bed, groaning not as one in pain, which he was, but as one doomed to the clutch of demons. He felt himself unable to breathe, sure to die, the hours passing in endless moments of agony and of terror. Open or shut, his eyes saw the same: shifting horrors of the beckoning dead, the *danse macabre* of a mind torn open by the cawing beaks and talons of forbidden planes. He did not want to die so far from home. But where was home?

He tried to make a lullaby unto himself of the moaning of his pain and fear: a wounded and pathetic sound, more a threnody than cradling-song, the wailing of a motherless child over the dying son of himself. But he would not die, he told himself. It would not be like those other times, when mind and body came full apart. He was not that bad this time. He would not have a seizure and he would not die. He had not drunk that much that long. It had been but barely a week, and he had only quit eating a few days ago. Still, without pills, you never could tell. The pills, they saved you from the seizures. Sure, even with them you could die. He had seen men die like that, even on Ativan, even on Dilantin. Right under the nurses' eyes, they'd up and died. You never could tell. Dope was one thing, juice was another. Kicking the shit was a bitch, but it couldn't do you in. Only booze withdrawal could do that, only booze withdrawal could kill you dead. But he was not going to die. Pills or no pills, he was not going to die. It was the horrors, that's all. The horrors was all he had. As long as he knew that, he was all right. His body had not shut down. He just had the fear, that's all. Couldn't nothing kill Jabbo. Nothing. He would be all right.

His hands went numb, his feet and legs convulsed with painful crippling cramps, and he could not draw breath. The irregular pounding of his heart filled him with hysteria. Every dilation and contraction seemed to be his last: the arsis of every stillness in his breast seemed so frighteningly not a lull but an end, death itself, that he gasped, panicking, for the next beat, which in turn seemed to bring the blast of thrombosis and occlusion; and on and on, worse and worse, as his chest tightened and his lungs seemed to collapse beneath the pressure of that tightening, taking in less and less air the harder and more wildly he gasped, and the vessels in his brain seemed about to burst in the blinding ache of his skull; and he lay there, gagging and gasping as if in apoplexy, unable to move his legs in their excruciating paralysis, feeling paralysis creep across his face as well, his body trembling, his tongue bloated and twitching like a lizard trying to leap down his throat; and he saw himself stiffening in death in this bed and in this room, or lame and drooling and slurring in a wheelchair, his mind gone, or worse, his mind still there, the weeds of all that was within him brooding sad and wild behind eyes that could not stir in a face that could not speak and a body that could not move, or lying there, his lifeless legs being stretched, day after day, in the therapy room of some prison ward, the end of the line; and he was wild with the idea, insane with the grieving of it, that he had delivered himself there, to that death, or that chair, or that ward, by delivering himself here, to this heart attack, this stroke, of his own free will and one bottle too many; and he cursed himself and cried for himself, and he whimpered like the snake in that dream, or was it a dream; and from the well of his pain, he begged God to save him, as he had begged before, so many times, only to spit in God's face once the saving was done, only this time, please, God, this time it would be different, please, God, it would not be the same. *Our Father who art in heaven.* He wanted to suck the tit of that statue. But he must not think that. *Hallowed be thy name.* It was not him thinking that. No, it came from somewhere else. God would understand. Even Christ, he was tempted; even Christ had bad thoughts. God understood this. That time he had baptized Rosario's kid. *Rinunziate a satana?* the priest had asked him. *Rinunzio,* Jabbo had said. And that statue, it was still there. He renounced Satan, but all he saw was that statue, looking at it as he had looked at it when he was a kid, thinking of all the tits he had sucked since then, but it had all begun with her, with that statue.

His heartbeat, like the punishing anger of God, took away his breath and immersed him anew in fear. *Thy kingdom come.* What came next? Thy daily bread. No, my daily bread, our daily bread. No, thy will. Thy will. *Thy will be done, on earth as it is in heaven.* You couldn't see the nipple, just plaster tits in plaster folds of cloth. But that look on her face. That look on her face. Cold plaster, blue paint. Cool against his mouth it would be, like the feel on his fingers, his forehead, of holy water from the marble font. *Give us this day our daily bread,* right, that was it, *and forgive us our trespasses as we forgive those who trespass against us.* If he could suck on tit, he would be all right, he would not die. It would ease him, and he would be all right. God must want him to think this. It was a good thought. Or maybe God was the devil. Maybe God was Satan. Maybe God would not come for Jabbo. Maybe only Satan came. Maybe there was no God. He had never really believed in Him anyway. It was all right to think that, because it was true, and God could not bear a liar. That broad downstairs, she had nice ones. Jabbo would suck them, and she would stroke his head and make sweet sounds and love him and it would be all right. This forlorn notion seemed to be so surely his dying thought, the pang of final longing, lost and undone, that he renewed his prayer and his begging unto God, believing neither in prayer nor in God, but praying and begging all the same, until his prayers and his begging grew more desperate, and he reached out in his prostration, grasping wildly beyond the God of his knowing, beseeching blindly, that gods without names might redeem him. He lighted a cigarette with tremulous hands, and he lay there smoking, feeling the smoke penetrate deeply into his lungs, filling them, expanding them, as the night air alone had failed to do, and he waited, for death or for whatever errant ray of mercy might alight upon him; and the crippling spasms in his feet and limbs eased, and his heart eased and his brain eased, and he knew that he would be all right. And when that cigarette was done, he lighted another, and he thanked God, and he lay there smoking, thinking about those seizures that came, took you unawares, just when you thought all danger had passed, hours or even days after you'd taken that last drink, hours or even days after you'd begun to feel all right, telling himself not to think of such things, telling himself to just lie there, smoke and suffer, and be thankful to God. He thought of that time he almost died, lost in the nightmare of delirium tremens, lying there in his own blood, unable to stand, able barely to crawl; if that broad down the hall, that half-nigger broad he'd been trying to fuck, had not seen the door open and called out to him and got him to St. Vincent's, he would have been dead; he almost died there, in St. Vincent's, as it was. He owed that broad his life, though he cursed her when he got the bill. He had gone through hell that time, lost in a nightmare that was real as day. But there would be no delirium tremens this time; it was not that bad. Or maybe he was beyond delirium now; maybe the deeper hell into which he had descended after emerging from the hell of that delirium had left something like scar tissue in his mind, leaving it dead to other nightmares as scar tissue was dead to pain while keeping alive the awful memory of what had put it there.

Through the lone gable window came the wisp of dawn's blush, dulced by the sound of birds deep in the trees, a soft and delicate chirping like droplets of musical dew. To Jabbo, the gentle illumination of faraway light and the motes of song within it were sweet as dope, and he lay there calming as the magic of that dope, God's own dope, washed over him, nuzzling him, caressing him, forgiving him. His eyes fell shut, and he slept, and he did not die.

He remained in that room, as light came and light went, for nearly two days. The first time the woman knocked on the door, he told her to go away. He thought of asking her for pills. Every broad had pills. Valium, Librium, something. But he did not; he just told her to go away. When she knocked again, that evening, he accepted the fried chicken, mashed potatoes, and peas she offered him. He had no stomach for food, and he did not want it. Smoke and water were enough. But he took it. The first bite brought bitter juices to his mouth, and pain to his throat as he swallowed it, and sickness to his guts when it went down. But it went down, and it stayed down. And the coffee, which was warm by the time he got to it, tasted good and felt good inside him. When the woman came back to take the tray, he hoped that she might stay. His mind was still not right, and the illness and weakness in his body made him feel like a sick child, and somehow he thought she might stay. If not to suck his cock, then just to comfort him, like a mother, or a sister of mercy, or as one lonely soul drawn to another. But all she did was ask him if he was feeling any better and whether he'd be staying on. She did not even sit. She just stood a moment at the foot of his bed, barely looking down at him. She asked him if he wanted more coffee, and he said yes. When she left, he thought how, if his dick still worked, he could stroke it to a good stiff hard-on while she was down there getting that coffee, and when she came back up, she would see it there, angled up all big and hard under the sheets, and he would lie there, his eyelids down, making believe he was more out of it than he really was, pretending not to be aware of that cock pitched up like a tent pole under those sheets, pretending not to be able to see her looking at it; and then, maybe, she would be different, she would say something, something playful but something dirty, and he would say something back, something all enfeebled and pitiful but horny and seductive too; or maybe there would be no words, maybe her hand would come forward in silence, be on it, stroking it through the sheets, then that hand would work its way under those sheets, and he would feel it, all soft and nice and cool on the hard hot shaft of it, and just as she had it all cooled down like her hand but harder and harder yet, she would bend down and plunge that coolness into the wet heat of her mouth, and she would clench her fingers tight around the root of it, moving them up and down, up and down, as she sucked, and he would explode into her mouth as she sucked harder and clenched tighter and moved her hand faster and faster; and then she would loosen up on him, gently, like a mother, or a sister of mercy, or one lonely soul drawn to another, and she would wipe it on her face and kiss it and lick it clean. And, thinking this, his dick did stir somewhat, and he took it in his hand beneath the sheets and closed his eyes and thought of these things, begging God once again, not for life but for his tissue to fill with blood, and, who knows, it might have happened, but she was already coming back up, he could hear her on the stairs, and whatever there was of it, it shrank in his hand, and that was it. She just put down the coffee and said goodnight and that was that. So he got up, still shaky. He sat by that lone gable window and was lost for a moment in the silence of the stars and the scented night sky. He had him a smoke and he drank his coffee and cursed.

Beyond the woods, the undertaker's wife took her tea to the window and looked out at the darkness of the big red oak amid the shadows where the woods began, the darkness and the shadows of the lone view from this house she had never liked, the lone view that allowed her to forget, or at least to ignore, that she lived in a house whose business was death; and she told herself that if she found the right doctor, maybe he could help her.

Above the trembling black silhouette of the trees, the waning, paschal moon rose in its eastward sigh.

Eos, Eostre, Easter. Estrum, estrus, estrogen.

The warm tea in her belly brought back the forgotten strange dream of last night. In this dream she was not dead but lay waking in a meadow beneath the clouds. In the gourd of her belly, something slithered. She remembered now, at the window with her tea, the tale that had scared her so in her youth, a tale that had been forgotten with the passing of years, as the dream of last night had been forgotten with the passing of moments. In that tale, a girl sunning herself naked by the pond one summer afternoon had drifted off to sleep, and while she slept, a water snake, one of the little live-born ones, wandering newborn from his brood, had entered her. Now, at the window with her tea, she mused that this childhood tale must have entered her in her sleep, just as the snake had entered the girl in the tale. She tried to remember how the tale ended, but she could not. She tried to remember how the dream ended, but she could not.

Nor, looking into the night, could she remember the names of the nine heavens: only the first, the low-lying heaven of the moon, and the eighth, the heaven of fixed stars, the seed bed and resting place of souls; and not what lay between and beyond. But there, before her, in the glitterings, the soul-sparklings, of that eighth heaven, were forgotten tales not of youth alone but of the youth of the race, stirrings, slitherings, exquisite and awful, in the girlish gut of ancient, ageless dreams.

Big Bear, Little Bear. She-bear and her baby boy, come to hunt her, come to kill her dead.

Her eyes drifted through the seven stars of the Big Dipper, the seven stars of the Little Dipper: blue-white diamonds in the black of the sky. Stella Maris, the North Star, the Star of the Sea, dazzled brightest among them. Her daddy long ago had guided her wide eyes unto that star. Her daddy long ago had taught her with a whispered rhyme to cast her wish upon that star. Where was his? Was it right there before her, alone and brilliant and shining upon her, or lost and unseen, one hydrogen ember amid the myriad of some distant unknown cluster aswirl in the black of infinity? As many souls as there were stars. So Plato said. Each soul to a star, destined and allotted from the soul-brew of the universe by He who was the maker of the gods and all things. And mounting each soul on its star, as on a chariot, He revealed and instilled in all of them the nature of the universe and the laws of their destiny. And anyone, upon his incarnation, who lived virtuously for his appointed time, mastering his passions and his fears, would return home to his native star and dwell in bliss. And anyone who failed would be changed into a woman at his second birth. And if that soul still did not refrain from wrong, its mortal shell would be reduced to that of some animal suitable to its particular kind of wrongdoing.

And maybe Plato was not such a fool. Maybe Plato was right. Maybe this was why there were more women than men, and more lower creatures than men and women together. All those cold and vacant stars, all those wandering homeless souls. Some stars did seem to glow more warmly than others, regardless of their distance, regardless of their size.

Her hand lingered between her breasts, distractedly, gently, barely touching the crossed folds of her robe, as if fondling the imaginary dangling pearls of a necklace that was not there, lost not in thought but in the colors of thought.

And what was the color of fear, and what was the color of sadness? What was the color of hate, what was the color of love? The soul had three parts but many colors. Yes. Three parts. Everybody remembered Gaul, but Helen remembered the soul. The soul was divided into three parts. In the cask of the skull lay reason. Between midriff and neck, the emotions; in the belly, the desires, the hungers, the wants.

The sky beyond the stars was black: the sum of all colors, the absence of all colors in a world without light.

Her hand curved softly downward, across her belly, to the flank of her right side: the liver, the seat of fear and of calm alike, organ of the soul's divination and dreams, the source of the power of prophecy, which came only when reason was vanquished, in sleep or the madness of disease.

And where was hers, her own native star, in which her soul was nurtured and to which it would return? And what was the wickedness that had brought her back with a womb inside her to suffer anew?

For a moment it was as if the stillness of the stars entered her. Then the heavy creaking of her husband ascending the stairs drained the night sky of its spell.

# 116

What follows is to be the first line of a novel called *In the Hand of Dante,* a novel that takes place both in the present and in the early years of the fourteenth century.

# Excerpt from
## *In the Hand of Dante*

Louie pulled off his bra and threw it down upon the coffin.

# Bibliographical Appendix

*A chronicle of bibliographic data and*
*debris relative to the foregoing*

The pieces of this collection have been arranged, as far as the author's memory and the available facts have allowed, in the order of their origin—that is according to the chronology of their writing rather than of their publication. In most cases, these chronologies, that of writing and that of publication, are one; but in not a few cases, they are not. Thus, in this bibliographical chronicle, an entry bearing a later publication date may be encountered before an entry bearing an earlier publication date. This indicates that the former was written, but not published, before the latter. As for the cited dates of publication themselves, it should be borne in mind that popular periodicals are almost always postdated. Referred to as "cover dates," these dates extend variously into the future rather than reflect the actual time of publication: for example, a monthly magazine issued in August will be cover-dated as September or October, while weekly and biweekly periodicals will often bear dates, respectively, of one or two weeks into the future.

Conversely, renegade underground publications as well as the most esteemed of scholarly or literary quarterlies are often issued long after the date they bear, usually because of financial or production difficulties. (For example, the exalted journal *Dante Studies* is now running so behind schedule that the latest volume bears a date four years past.) Though not as extreme as this example, renegade underground periodicals also often reach publication long after their planned and designated cover dates. Thus, such a publication dated Spring or as Summer of a certain year may actually not have seen the light of publication until the autumn of that year or the winter of the following year.

In either case—that of popular periodicals bearing cover dates out of time in one way, that of underground or literary periodicals bearing cover dates out of time in the other way—such are the skewed dates upon which library science, cataloguing, bibliography, and therefore to no small degree literary history itself are based. Again, the sequence of the bibliographic chronicle that follows, corresponding directly to the sequence of the pieces of this collection, has been arranged, as far as the author's memory and the available facts have allowed, to reflect the chronological reality of publication as well as of origin.

Excerpts from books have been placed at their times of publication, as their origins, evolutions, and writing spanned years and thus elude any alternate accuracy of proper dating, other than that offered in the explications of the introductory passages preceding these excerpts in the body of the book itself.

Many of the works cited in the following chronicle are the stuff of the bookshelves and microform files of libraries. Some are lost amid the strewn arcana of a publishing otherworld. At which library might one's search for a complete series of *Teenage Wasteland Gazzete [sic]* or *Chemical Imbalance* not be in vain? Perhaps, however, their day of archival scholarship nears, as may be indicated by the current acquisitions and activities of the Underground Press Collection at the Special Collections branch of the University of Chicago library and other institutions.

The poem "Still / Life," written about 1969 and—*mea culpa*—bearing this puerile title, was destroyed about three years later. The fragments of it, as published here, unearthed from memory over a period of years, were first published, in slightly different form, as "In the Hospital," in *Chaldea* (New York: Cuz Editions, 1999).

Review of *Paranoid* (Black Sabbath). *Rolling Stone*, April 15, 1971; reprinted in *The Rolling Stone Record Review, Vol. II* (New York: Pocket Books, 1974).

Review of *Good Taste Is Timeless* (Holy Modal Rounders). *Rolling Stone*, June 10, 1971.

Review of *Joseph and the Amazing Technicolor Dreamcoat* (The Joseph Consortium). *Rolling Stone*, June 24, 1971; reprinted in *The Rolling Stone Record Review, Vol. II* (New York: Pocket Books, 1974).

"Absolutely Dead!" *Fusion*, September 17, 1971.

"Leuk." *Rolling Stone*, September 16, 1971.

"The Heartbeats Never Did Benefits." *Fusion*, October 15, 1971.

"God-Crazed Hippies Reap Boffo B.O." *Creem*, November 1971.

"Be Bop A Lula." First published as "Gene Vincent/Death," *Phonograph Record Magazine*, December 1971.

"The Box." *Creem*, February 1972.

"The 24 Hr Sound of Country Gospel and the Dark." Previously unpublished.

"Beyond Euclid: Pool!" *Teenage Wasteland Gazzete*, Spring 1972.

"The Real Avant-Garde." *Fusion*, July 1972.

Review of *Gately's Cafe* (Michael Gately). *Fusion*, 1972.

"Muddy Waters Rarely Eats Fish." *Oui*, January 1973. With Richard Blum and others.

"Eye: Disease." *Raunchy Rock*, Vol. 4, No. 1 (January 1973).

Review of *The Mollusks of Tartura*, an imaginary album attributed to Sandy Pearlman. *Rock*, April 23, 1973.

"Sex and Booze." *Sunshine*, No. 14 (Spring 1973).

"Valerie." *Raunchy Rock*, Vol. 4, Nos. 9–10 (September-October 1973).

"Screamin' Jay Hawkins and the Monster." *Creem*, August 1973; reprinted in *Unsung Heroes of Rock 'n' Roll* (1984).

"Patti Smith." First published, as "Penthouse Interview: Patti Smith," *Penthouse*, April 1976.

"Country." Record reviews. *Gig*, February 1977.

Excerpt from *Country* (Briarcliff Manor, NY: Stein and Day, 1977). Most recent English-language edition: Da Capo Press, 1996.

"When Literary Lights Turn on the TV." The *New York Times* (December 25, 1977). The author's original title, if there was one, is lost to him.

Letter (March 8, 1978). Previously unpublished.

"Patti Smith: Straight, No Chaser." *Creem*, September 1978.

"God Created Dean Martin in His Own Image, Then Stood Back." *Waxpaper*, No. 32 (October 1978); reprinted as a review of the album *Once in a While* (Dean Martin), *Creem*, March 1979.

"Jim Morrison: The Late Late Show." *Rolling Stone*, January 25, 1979; reprinted in *Contemporary Literary Criticism*, Vol. 17 (1981).

"Blondie Plucks Her Legs." *Creem*, June 1979; reprinted in *New Musical Express*.

Review of *Always Know* (Thelonious Monk). *Rolling Stone*, August 9, 1979.

"The Gospel According to Jerry Lee." *Country Music*, October 1979.

Journal entry (November 14, 1979). Previously unpublished.

"A Christmas Carol." First published as "Sleazy Greetings and a Happy Nuke Year," *Penthouse*, December 1979. The author's original title is here restored.

"The Sea's Endless, Awful Rhythm & Me without Even a Dirty Picture." Prologue to *Stranded*, ed. Greil Marcus (New York: Alfred A. Knopf, 1979).

"The Sweet Thighs of Mother Mary." Written about 1979/80; first published and recorded in 1998: *Nick & Homer* (New York: Chaldea CD-101, 1998); issued also as a 45-rpm single (Dallas: Honey HON-110A, 1998); and presented also through the Internet site www.exitwounds.com.

"Pizza Man." Written about 1979/80; first published and recorded in 1998: *Nick & Homer* (New York: Chaldea CD-101, 1998); presented also through the Internet site www.exitwounds.com; and issued also, in an alternate-take version, as a 45-rpm single (Dallas: Honey HON-110B, 1998).

"Lust Among the Adverbs." *Penthouse*, February 1980.

Letter (November 1, 1980). Previously unpublished.

"Purity." First published as "The Adolf Hitler Fast Food Franchise," *Penthouse*, March 1981. The author's original title is here restored.

"Pizza Man." *Genesis*, November 1981.

"The Butt and I." From *Rear View* (New York: Delilah Books, 1981).

"Pleasant Brits and 180-Degree Spins." *Country Music*, September 1981.

Excerpt from *Hellfire* (New York: Delacorte Press, 1982). Most recent English-language edition: Grove Press, 1998.

"Felicity Opens Wide." First published as "Heavy Competition," *Oui*, April 1982. The author's original title is here restored.

Journal entries (1982). Previously unpublished.

"Good Book Made Better." *Penthouse*, September 1982.

"Lust in the Balcony." *Forum*, October 1982.

Review of *A Child's Adventure* (Marianne Faithfull). *Vanity Fair*, June 1983.

Review of *The Maximus Poems* (Charles Olson). *The Village Voice*, December 6, 1983.

"Elvis in Death." First published as "The Death of Elvis," *Goldmine*, No. 92 (January 1984), but written for *American Dreams*, edited by Maurice Kennel (Zürich: U. Bär Verlag, 1984), in which it appeared as "Der Tote Elvis"; reprinted as "The Death of Elvis Presley" in *Elvis: Just for You*, edited by Trey Foerster (Iola, Wisconsin: Krause Publications, 1987); reprinted in *The Elvis Reader*, edited by Kevin Quain (New York: St. Martin's Press, 1992).

"Maybe It Was My Big Mouth—Carly Simon: Free, White, and Pushing Forty." *Creem*, January 1984.

Review of *A Choice of Enemies* (George V. Higgins). *The Village Voice*, January 31, 1984.

Review of *The Garden of Priapus* (Amy Richlin). *The Village Voice Literary Supplement*, February 1984.

Review of *A House in the Country* (Josè Donoso). *The Village Voice*, March 27, 1984.

Review of *Renaissance and Reform* (Frances A. Yates). *The Village Voice*, May 22, 1984.

Excerpt from *Unsung Heroes of Rock 'n' Roll* (New York: Charles Scribner's Sons, 1984). Most recent English-language edition: Da Capo Press, 1999.

"God Is My Cosponsor." *Penthouse*, November 1984.

*Frankie: Part 1*. Richard Meltzer, coauthor. (Los Angeles: Illuminati, 1985).

"Hillary Brooke's Legs." *Kicks*, No. 4 (June 1985).

"Elmer Batters." First published, as "Legs Forever," *New Look*, August 1985. The certainty of the author's original title is lost to him.

Review of *Canned Meat* (Hasil Adkins). *The Village Voice*, July 1, 1986.

"How to Pick Up Girls in Albania." *New Look*, August 1986.

Excerpt from *Power on Earth*. (New York: Arbor House, 1986).

Excerpt from *Frankie: Part 2*. Richard Meltzer, coauthor. (Los Angeles: Illuminati, 1987)

"Pentecostals in Heat." *The Village Voice*, May 12, 1987.

"The Short-Shorts of Satan." *The Village Voice*, June 21, 1988.

Excerpt from *Cut Numbers* (New York: Harmony, 1988).

"Exile on Twenty-first Street." *Spin*, November 1988.

Review of *Killer: The Mercury Years* (Jerry Lee Lewis). *Spin*, March 1990.

"Miles Davis: The Hat Makes the Man." Previously unpublished.

"James Douglas Morrison, 1943–1971." Forward to *Mr. Mojo Risin': Jim Morrison, the Last Holy Fool* by David Dalton (New York: St. Martin's Press, 1991).

"The Singer Madonna Arraigned by the Ghost of Pope Alexander VI." *Throat Culture*, No. 3 (March 1992).

"Lester." Liner notes for the CD reissue of the 1981 Live Wire LP *Jook Savages on the Brazos* by Lester Bangs and the Delinquents (Hamburg: Moll 6, 1995). Previously published in somewhat different form, as "Lester," in *Chemical Imbalance*, No. 8 (December 1988), and, as a privately printed volume, *Lester* (New York: Dreamland, 1992).

Excerpt from *Dino* (New York: Doubleday, 1992). Most recent English-language edition: Delta, 1999.

"Oedipus Tex." *Penthouse*, December 1992.

"J. Edgar Hoover: The Burroughsian Nightmare." *Newsday*, March 28, 1993.

"Memories of Joe." *The Village Voice*, August 17, 1993.

"My Kind of Loving." Written in the midnineties. First published in *Open City*, No. 4 (Spring 1996); reprinted in *Chaldea* (New York: Cuz Editions, 1999). Also recorded twice: for the spoken-word anthology *Relationships from Hell* (New York: Big Deal 90104-2, 1994); and for *Blue Eyes and Exit Wounds*, the author's spoken-word collaboration with Hubert Selby, Jr. (New York: Pay or Die CD 753, 1998). The European edition of this collaboration (Paris: Escape / W.O.M. CD 6773, 1999) includes the publication of this poem and the CD's other works in booklet form.

"George Jones: The Grand Tour." *The Journal of Country Music*, Vol. 16, No. 3 (1994); reprinted in *The Country Reader: Twenty-Five Years of the Journal of Country Music*, edited by Paul Kingsbury (Nashville & London: The Country Music Foundation Press & Vanderbilt University Press, 1996).

"My Overcoat, My Brains, and Me." *Esquire* (British edition), April 1994.

Notebook entry (January 1994). Previously unpublished.

"*Nightmare Alley*." First published, under "Video Hit List," *Videoscope*, Vol. 2, No. 10 (July 15–September 15, 1994).

Excerpt from *Trinities* (New York: Doubleday, 1994). Most recent English-language edition: St. Martin's, 1995.

Letter (December 25, 1994). Previously unpublished.

"The Holy City." Introduction to *Literary Las Vegas: The Best Writing about America's Most Fabulous City*, edited by Mike Tronnes (New York: Henry Holt, 1995).

"Ophis Ovum Opium Olé" (1995). Published in *Chaldea* (New York: Cuz Editions, 1999).

"There's a Woman Here, Baby" (1995). Previously unpublished.

"Who Holds in Her Belly the Power of Life" (1995). Previously unpublished.

"A Slab of Grease, a Bottle of Carbona, and Thou" (Summer 1995). Previously unpublished.

Excerpt from "Entering the Barrens" (1995). Previously unpublished.

"Requiescat Dino." *The Village Voice*, January 9, 1996.

"De Niro." First published as "Bobby's Back," *Esquire* (British edition), March 1996. The certainty of the author's original title is lost to him.

"The Unfuckable." First published as "Spurn, Baby, Spurn," *Details*, May 1996. The author's original title, with Samuel Beckett still in mind, is here restored.

"The Coin." First published as "Time Traveler," *Esquire*, June 1996. The author's original title, if there was one, is lost to him.

"Why I Am Great." *Real Crime Book Digest*, Vol. 4, No. 1 (Summer 1996).

"Sea of Love." *Details*, July 1996.

"Faraglione 9/16/96." *Chaldea* (New York: Cuz Editions, 1999).

"If I Were Robert Stack." First published in *Smokes Like a Fish*, No. 2 (December 1996); subsequently the central poem of a cycle published in *Gentlemen's Quarterly*, August 1997; reprinted in *Chaldea* (New York: Cuz Editions, 1999).

Letter (July 4, 1997). Previously unpublished.

Letter (August 13, 1997). Previously unpublished.

Letter (August 18, 1997). Previously unpublished.

Letter (August 23, 1997). Previously unpublished.

Letter (August 25, 1997). Previously unpublished.

*Spud Crazy*. Unproduced and previously unpublished screenplay.

"The Things I Got." First published and recorded in 1998: *Nick & Homer* (New York: Chaldea CD-101, 1998).

"Ash Wednesday." Previously unpublished. Recorded by Homer Henderson but as yet unreleased.

"The Devil and Sidney Korshak." First published, as "The Man Who Kept the Secrets," *Vanity Fair*, April 1997. The author's original title is here restored.

Excerpt from *Where Dead Voices Gather*. (Excerpt from "unfinished book on Emmett Miller.") This book, now finished, has evolved into a wide-roaming work entitled *Where Dead Voices Gather*, to be published, by Little, Brown, in 2001.

"Night Train." First published, as "The Outlaw Champ," *Vanity Fair*, February 1998. The author's original title is here restored. This story was the origin of the book, published in England, under the author's preferred title, as *Night Train* (London: Hamish Hamilton, 2000) and in the United States—ironically, in the light of *Vanity Fair*'s change of the original title of the Korshak piece—as *The Devil and Sonny Liston* (New York: Little, Brown, 2000).

"Dear Privileged Intimate." May 1, 1998. Mailed extensively in the late spring of 1998. Later published in *Open City*, No. 7 (Winter 1999), with the Greek of Heraclitus garbled in the process.

"Hymn for Charlie." Published as the introductory poem in the booklet of the Charlie Feathers CD set, *Get with It: Essential Recordings* (Nashville: Revenant 209, 1998).

E-mail (1998). Previously unpublished.

"Please Be Quiet—Please." *Bookforum*, Fall 1998. This little essay centering on Raymond Carver's *All of Us: The Collected Poems*, was written without title.

From *Chaldea* (New York: Cuz Editions, 1999). Several of the poems here selected from this collection—which spans the years 1969 to 1998—were previously published elsewhere: "Old Nick's Song of Songs," *Smokes Like a Fish*, No. 3 (October 1998); "May the Gods without Names Redeem Me," *Long Shot*, Vol. 21 (January 1999); "Dante in Ravenna," *12-Gauge Review Online* (www.12gauge.com), No. 9 (1999); "What the Coptic Guy Said," *Long Shot*, Vol. 21 (January 1999). Additionally, "May the Gods without Names Redeem Me," "Ptolemy II," "Dante in Ravenna," "Contrapasso" (completed at 3:45 A.M., November 3, 1994), "From the Dream-book of Artemidorus," and "What the Coptic Guy Said" were included among the recordings of *Blue Eyes and Exit Wounds*, the author's spoken-word collaboration with Hubert Selby, Jr. (New York: Pay or Die CD 753, 1998). The European edition of this collaboration includes the publication of these poems in booklet form (Paris: Escape / W.O.M. CD 6773, 1999). Many of these poems are further presented in electronic print and/or audio form through the Internet site www.exitwounds.com. The recording of "What the Coptic Guy Said" was also released as part of *Rage: CD Anniversaire 5 Ans, Volume #2* (Paris: Rage CD Supplement Gratuit Rage No. 37, 1998).

Excerpt from *Scratch*. Previously published, in somewhat different form, as "I Dig Girls," in the collection *Chaldea*. Also recorded under that name, again in somewhat yet different form, as part of *Blue Eyes and Exit Wounds*, the author's spoken-word collaboration with Hubert Selby, Jr. (New York: Pay or Die CD 753, 1998). The European edition of this collaboration includes the publication of this variant excerpt in booklet form (Paris: Escape / W.O.M. CD 6773, 1999).

Excerpt from *In the Hand of Dante*. This is the opening line of a book that takes place simultaneously in the early fourteenth and early twenty-first centuries. It will be published, by Little, Brown, early in the holy year of 2003.